Cover design, photos and artwork by Kevin Panozzo

kpanozzo@gmail.com

www.kpanozzo.com

Copyright © 2011 Kevin Panozzo

ISBN: 0615552285
ISBN-13: 9780615552286

KEVIN PANOZZO

Tête Pressée

To my family
And the whole Nice crew
With endless thanks and love

"As ever, he is surpriz'd by the fierceness of their bodies, their inability to hold back, the purity of the not-yet-dishonest,— 'twould take a harder case than Mason not to struggle with Tears of Sentiment."

- Revd Wicks Cherrycoke

Contents

1   A Burden of self-indictment

In which Calvin convicts
himself doubly of murder.

Stanley Arbuckle detested tisane. Arniche Van Brüsel, however, the star-crossed industrialist from Senegal via Willebroek, Belgium, and lead protagonist in Arbuckle's latest literary opus, *Dog Days in Dakar* (validation of which was cut drastically short by way of deportation), drank nothing but. And so Calvin sat with Arbuckle in the kitchen of the *maison de maître* just down the street from the Nice opera house and drank tisane, the latter making dour faces with each forced gulp. Meanwhile, in the same kitchen, Nadine put forth her best Florence Nightingale as Gem happily regaled her with the colourful musings of his ill-interpreted dreams, his latest victory over the wolves, his latest defence of the innocent lambs.

The weekend was intended to be one of relaxation, recovery and reflection—a weekend that might allow Calvin to square himself and establish a certain mental footing, that he might step firmly in some decent new direction. But Gem couldn't help himself. Or maybe, thought Calvin, he just didn't give a damn. Hell if they weren't so close to being on that twelve-o-seven to Imperia, and from Imperia, a short bus ride to Laigueglia.

Just then, as though it weren't all quite bad enough, Calvin was touched by a tremendous aching for one Klarysa Pavlichenko. Rather thoroughly dominated and more than a little disgusted, Calvin stood and made for the door.

"Where you off to, mate?" asked Gem, as Nadine applied a final ointment to several of his lacerations.

"Bar des Oiseaux."

"Bah! Not that shite bar."

"The very one, in fact."

"Wait two minutes. We'll go to the Whales."

"I'm going to the Oiseaux."

"But I've been barred from the Oiseaux! You know that, Calvin!"

Calvin paused at the front door and turned to face Gem from across the room. "Yes, Gem," he said. "I do." And then he left.

Calvin installed himself at a table in the cramped space of the Bar des Oiseaux, dejected, misshapen, twisted around a pint of non-descript lager, provoked by determined demons and broad-reaching inquisitions. Having slipped under for a moment, he was presently jarred to by a tubbing baritone: "Ho-ho-ho!"

Ridiculed, thought Calvin, regaining his wits, in his own low-rent dream state. How would Gem have interpreted this—as the fiendish embodiment of some nebulous social ill to be cured by a medicinal course of fists, boots, razor-lined palm fronds? Only too surely.

The voice returned. "Calvin, have you passed out in your beer?"

The Butcher! Another harmless black nightmare, thought Calvin, made pale under the harsh light of certain realities.

"Why, we've not yet reached midnight," the Butcher noted.

The Butcher, one of the weaker links in the crew's collective chain, wrote semi-erotic shorts for an obscure high-end travel magazine that catered to a wealthy swing-curious British set. While most writers are at their best addressing subjects with which they have first-hand experience (à la Stanley Arbuckle), the Butcher did quite well for himself despite his inexperience, for although he was celibate, his was an involuntary celibacy. In his favour lay a long-fanged rodent of lust, which burrowed deep into his guts and gnawed feverishly away in the endless tracts of his intestines. His eyes twisted in his balding dome and dissolved like sugar in the presence of any young Niçoise, alluring and liquid as they tend to be. The Butcher was his own worst enemy. That he was aware of the fact was one of his few endearing qualities.

"What of it, Butcher?" replied Calvin, pressing the heels of his hands to his brow. "Is the approach of midnight not my new greatest fear? What will midnight bring but another day of bracing against the fallout of one new storm or another, this one dropping black boots and bombs, that one raining sharpened knives, the other promoting who knows what—Russian slugs, Balkan entanglement, stone duck heads from atop black canes kissing ruddily against the temples of the blackmailed? Don't you know well enough to leave a sleeping dog lie? Why, the gongs of midnight compose the death knell I specifically wish to avoid."

"Ho-ho-ho! Sleeping, were you? Just now? You're joking."

The Butcher boasted a rich Liverpudlian baritone. How a stark district like Everton raised a beast as buttery and fat-livered as the Butcher is an anthropological and culinary mystery, both. The Butcher was soft and cultured, like a Camembert. He was thoughtfully perfumed. He was pure sweet butter. Lyon envied Nice her claim to such a creamy wellspring as the Butcher. Les Marseillais would have happily traded a rail-car of olive oil for a few pats of Butcher haunch in which to sauté their garlic. A Périgourdin would have given fifty geese *gavage forcé* and tromboned of neck for a block of the Butcher's fine *foie gras*. Hansel of fairytale fame would have been relegated to the dog dish had the old witch seen the Butcher mincing about the forest. And mince he did, the *grand délice*, feet barely touching the ground whether static or in motion, a mark *dans les rues gourmands* of Vieux Nice. A wee glimpse of the Butcher set the Niçois to licking lips and passing shirtsleeves over the corners of their salivating mouths. As is every tentative doe, the Butcher was conscious of the appetising effect of his mass and manner on his predators and as such, he harboured a tenacious mistrust of all things French. To bid him *bonjour* elicited little more than a narrowing of the eyes and a suspicious chuckle. Calvin was a fan of the Butcher and was frightened for him. The Butcher stood less of a chance than the rest of the crew, all members of which fully expected to eventually find him devoured, reduced to a sorry scattering of thin bones and fancy shoelaces in a grimy back alley, picked clean by tooth and nail of the less attached Niçois youth. Calvin, however, feared a much worse fate for him—self-death.

On that September evening, the Butcher was accompanied by Edward. Eddie. Safety in numbers, though two geese do not a gaggle make. Eddie positioned himself at the Butcher's eight o'clock, in the broken flying-V formation of those with limited numbers. Eddie was a less likable version of the Butcher. One did not feel sorry for Eddie the way one felt sorry for the Butcher. Not even the Butcher could develop much of a tolerance for him. But he had money, did Eddie. A lot of it. And he spent a good deal of it on champagne, which, on occasion, made him worth suffering.

Eddie wore an expensive camelhair overcoat that was enormous, ill-fitting, too small. Underneath it he wore a starched white button-front shirt and pleated chinos. In the mild crown months, Eddie would trade his full-length chinos for those that quit at the knees; the camelhair coat remained. He was a graduate of England's prestigious Rugby School and with all due respect – for he did try in his own cumbersome, tasteless way – a less impressive bloke one could not find.

The Butcher extended a hand and Calvin shook it. Butcher's hands were fine, like bone china, pinkish-blue and translucent.

"You all right?" asked the Butcher in rich Liverpudlian.

Still groggy, Calvin responded, "Sure. They don't hurt anymore at least. They'll turn all manner of ghoulish colours when your nose gets smashed. Hell, Butcher, how can a fellow from Everton not know that?"

The Butcher, however, who had decidedly little interest in another fellow's wellbeing, was not enquiring about Calvin's blackened eyes, or the fact that he had passed out at the bar. He was only extending a verbal greeting to go along with the handshake. Calvin realised his gaffe and tried to recover. "You all right?" he returned. But it was too late. The Butcher snorted, embarrassed for them both.

The Butcher's fingers were slender rum-soaked ladyfingers extending out from a dainty scoop of tiramisu. Withdrawing one's hand after shaking the Butcher's triggered a childish instinct to lick clean the sticky-delicious residue of rum, sugar and mascarpone.

"You know Eddie," stated the Butcher as a matter of course. "Were you really asleep just then?" he asked despite himself, immediately wishing he could rescind the question.

While the Butcher may have been mildly concerned, no amount of concern had ever forced his tongue—it was the curiosity talking. To be sure, no bloke was more fearful of having to help out his fellow man than was the Butcher, and he would never enquire after a fellow's wellbeing were he not such a nosy bastard.

"It seems that way," replied Calvin. "I may've drunk too much, though I suppose there's a chance that adorable waitress slipped me something."

Eddie wanted for nothing more than to be loved by someone, anyone, and the poor beast had absolutely no idea how to bring it to pass. He took a shot at impressing Calvin. "That waitress?" he asked. "She's called May. She's from Suriname. But trust me, mate, you don't want any of *that*. She's too easy. Now, if fresh fish is what you're after, I'll take you to Monaco. Let me tell you about the time—"

"Hell, Butcher," Calvin interrupted. "I don't know if I can walk."

The interruption was designed to keep Eddie from recounting, yet again, the story of his one big night in Monaco, during which he and a mate from Rugby School shared a washed-up starlet after she had been dumped by her abusive Monagosque. In the wake of the dumping, she had tried unsuccessfully to drown herself, first with booze, then the sea, and finally decided to give herself over to the first pair of Italian leather loafers she might find slapping wealthily along in front of the moonlit Grimaldi Forum. The lucky loafers were, of course, Eddie's—the poor unfortunate dame.

"Honestly," begged Calvin. "Be a pal and help me back to my flat."

The Butcher stared, newly embarrassed and with mounting concern—the embarrassment for Calvin, the concern for himself. "But you live just around the corner," he said. "You're joking."

"You fellows always know when I'm joking, don't you," said Calvin with new disgust for the crew. "It matters not what I may say to you lot, it's all a big joke. What if I were to tell you, dear Butcher, that I could use a weekend in Italy – Laigueglia, for example – like we used to do, with a view to," Calvin paused to kill his beer, "with a view to unwinding a bit, massaging the healing process, so on and so forth. I mean right now. Let's go. What would you say?"

Traditionally, the Butcher fell silent with drink, while Calvin grew loquacious. Such facts might lead one to guess them complementary drinking partners. They were not. Driven to fits of frustration by the Butcher's slippery lack of engagement and commitment – and the Butcher was, by all means, distant and noncommittal – Calvin would often attempt to trap him in a prolonged stare of smouldering animosity, which typically caused the Butcher to melt with embarrassment, chuckle in disgust and despise Calvin for exposing some of the shortcomings for which he needed no help from Calvin or anyone else in recognising and lamenting. The two lads were like brothers, and brothers will, from time to time, behave cruelly towards one another, even during the best of times. And this was not the best of times. Far from it.

The Butcher looked at Eddie, then back to Calvin, who had not expected an answer. After brief deliberation, the Butcher said, "Well, I'd probably reflect on what a daft idea it was, considering it's almost midnight and we're all *shit*faced."

The Butcher surprised himself by that line. He liked it a hell of a lot.

"And then," he continued, "as I was contemplating the shocking de*gree* of stupidity on display, you'd be staring at me exactly the way you are now, like *I'm* the horse's arse."

The Butcher! Calvin glared at the man who, upon facing such challenges, had habitually and with sweet little resistance, given himself over to the gears of depression and embarrassment, and who on this occasion did absolutely nothing of the sort. On the contrary, and perhaps for the first time in his life, the Butcher glared right back at Calvin.

"And then," he finished, "sure; I'd look at you, full of contempt and say, 'You're joking!'"

Any fellow privy to the details of their shared years would be helpless to fend off a smile upon witnessing the Butcher's assertive riposte. Calvin and the Butcher each fought his own widening smile until laughter burst suddenly from them in unison.

"By god, Butcher!" Calvin exclaimed. "Lord only knows what hell has gotten into you, but for crissake, cage and feed it!"

Eddie was visibly pleased by the ludicrous exchange—finally, two horse's arses to deflect some of the unflattering attention he couldn't help but draw to himself. "May, please…" he said, catching the waitress by the arm as she passed. "A bottle of champagne please, love. Three glasses."

May nodded and bestowed a South American smile so warm and genuine it made a fellow want to be a better, braver man.

Said Calvin, "That's awfully good of you, Edward. Now sit, fellows, sit."

They squeezed two more chairs around the small table. The Butcher aimed a satisfied nod at Calvin, the type shared between two fly-by-nights who somehow managed to salvage a mutually beneficial deal.

"Hell, Butcher," burst Calvin anew, with gladness. Spurred by a recent memory, he asked, "You still hounding those two Moroccan kittens, you?"

"Ho-ho-ho!" the Butcher boomed.

"*Ping*-pong!" cried Calvin, shaking his head fondly. "Hell, who could've known?"

The three-piece ensemble balanced on the tiny stage was really heating up. Several lamps placed throughout the bar made warm halos of muted persimmon. Every now and again, a flash of orange would run a short distance and jump from the bell of the trumpeter's brass horn. May arrived with the champagne. They shared the same essence, she and the bottle—both gorgeously shaped, both glistening in the gathered humidity, both making grown men lick lips like children lost in lemonade dreams. Three tall flutes were placed before them and each was provided with a sparkling charge of golden wine.

"Ta, love," said Eddie, handing over enough blue-hued notes to pay the bottle and make a generous tip.

"*Ta*," mocked the Butcher, winking at Calvin. "Gritty. Rough around the edges, our Edward."

"You can go to hell, Steven," said Eddie, as a matter of fact. "Di*rect*ly."

"Now, Edward," Calvin piled on.

"You can join him, Calvin. Honestly, the gratitude of you lot. A fellow isn't treated this way in Monaco—not when he's just bought champagne."

"It's true," Calvin admitted. "You deserve better drinking mates."

"You're not wrong," Eddie agreed.

"But we're what you've got, so quit whingeing and drink up."

The three raised their glasses, clinked them unceremoniously and drank.

"Oh, that's good," said Eddie, looking into his raised glass, admiring it, eventually confiding in it. "The gratitude of these two."

"Out on the piss to-night, lads?" asked Calvin, marginally restored of spirit.

Replied Eddie, "Does a Toby jug hold water?"

"I should think the right one just might."

And with that, a union of three exiled misfits was confirmed, courtesy of a bottle of good booze, a bop-jazz ensemble, the smile of a beautiful southern woman and the common hope of making it through another night alone, together on the blue coast.

When they had drunk the bottle dry, Calvin stood, bid them adieu and left.

Having reached his building, he dragged himself up the four flights of stairs, exhausted, his shoes slurping a progressively heavier slide-step, up and across each tiny hurdle. Finally reaching the fourth-floor landing, he slid his key into the armoured door, snapped open the locks, threw open the door and fell headlong into a deep dark purple well...

"Kid. Hey, Kid!" *he say to me, grabbing on my foot and shaking it good.* "Wake up! Going to burn a Rizla on your forehead!"

"Quit, Pug," he says. *"Stop foolin."*

He got two fists shoved into his playground pockets, rocking back and forth on toes like they got lightning in 'em. He a devil in dusty canvas.

"Get up, you slag. Tell me who did it. I can help you out, mate. We've got to set it straight wiv the wolves."

"Not tonight, Pug. Not tonight," he says.

"Give us a necktie, then, mate. I'll handle 'em on me own like."

"I'm not feeling so good."

"Aren't you, now," I say.

I pull two fists of glassy marbles from me pockets and let them rain to the ground. They bounce and bounce ever-higher off the tile floor and explode in great firework blooms over the old town.

"Look!" he cries after them from his sickbed, swiping his hands down over the front of his trousers, as a lad does to ready himself. *"Look there, now, the fourth of July! I'll be dog gone if it ain't!"*

I crane and heave a high-octane laugh and spin cartwheels out the window and off the rooftop. I thought it might provide the boy wiv a laugh like, but he only clouds over and clutches at his stomach.

"Don't go!" he cries.

"OK, OK. No more fooling about." *Pug, he come back.* "Now, stop your whingeing, mate."

"Who you calling a mate. Sit down, Pug," I tell him. *"Lay down on that couch and don't go nowhere."*

"There's only a chair here."

He can't understand.

"Don't worry, Kid. I'm here. I'm sitting."

"You left first, don't forget. You always leaving. You left first, Pug." He didn't appreciate that. Always easier to leave than to be left.

"It happens when a lad grows up like," I tell him.

"How come you acting so strange, saying this and that about a ladge and a mate. You a sure enough ladge! Look here, a big one, too. How old are you, you big old ladge?"

"Not so old. Firty-free is all," I say. The number tickles him so. He's curled into a ball, there on the bed, laughing and laughing.

"You almost a hundred! How old am I am, you old ladge?" he asks through his laughter.

"I would say you must be," *Pug wrench his jaw like a mechanic,* "oh, you must be about eight-years-old, I'd say."

"That's pretty old. Not as old as you, though, Pug."

He snorted with laughter and got me to laughing a bit, as well.

"Pug," I echoed, wondering after all the years. "I haven't heard that name in years."

"How come?"

"Those days are long gone, mate. You're going to see. You grow up and people call you by your Christian name, don't they."

"Everybody call you Gemini now?"

"It's me Christian name, isn't it. One day, everyone is going to call you Calvin."

I worry about the lad. *Pug sit in the chair and sip hot tea from a white china cup. The cup twinkle like a star in the outer space of his dark workman body. Pug, he a working man now, like his pops. Always been a working man.* I'm concerned for the boy. He's too sensitive. He remembers too much.

"It's a pretty cup. I like to see you holding nice things, Pug. Where'd you get it at? It look good in your hand. Where'd you get it at?" Sparks flash in his eyes when he blink. He look sad.

"Go easy, mate. Go easy. Take your time, lad."

"Who you calling a ladge? You sicker than me as crazy as you talking. Whatchoo mean days long gone? Stop fooling, now." Thoughts occur to him, histories occur to him. *"Stay with me, now, Pug. See here, ain't I sick. Ain't I sick. Take my hand. You got to stay with me now, Pug. You got to follow me."*

"A lad can't go back to where he's never been."

"Back where?" he asked, confused. *"You talking crazy. Whatchoo mean a ladge can't go back where he never been? We best friends, Pug. You got to follow. You got to stay with me."*

"Shhh, shhh. It's OK, Kid."

I forget the boy is only eight-years-old like. I hadn't even left for England for anovva couple years. He doesn't know noffing about all that. Doesn't know noffing about Old Blighty.

"It's OK. I'm sorry, Kid. Go easy."

He doesn't know about California yet. Doesn't know about death, doesn't know about anyfing, really. Eight-years-old; only fing he knows about is Garfield. And playing ball and getting in trouble and making his mum cry. And he knows about Nicki. I don't fink it wise at the moment to tell him he's not in Garfield. I'll stay wiv him. I'll go back like, at least where I can, at least where history allows.

"Don't worry, Kid," I tell him. "I'll stay with you. I'll follow you back where I can."

I drop anovva fistful of glass peeries onto the tile floor. They bounce once, twice and shoot up into the sky, exploding in a hailstorm of red, white, and blue rhinestones over the French Riviera.

"*My Nicki,*" he say. He slipping us back to Garfield *Sweet young thing. She love me, boy. Ain't we going out to California and get married soon as I can drive. Going to buy us a house and a lemon tree and she going to make us lemon pies. It make her smile when I talk about those lemon pies she going to make. Pug, he scratch his head like a mechanic.*

I try to pull him back. "Mate, mate, what do you fink about this?" I say. *A white butterfly flop wet from his tea cup, shake its wings hard and then flutter up and away. It explode in candy sparks high above... I don't...*

"*Where are we, Pug?*"

He doesn't know noffing about France, noffing about the sea. He doesn't know the names. He only knows about Garfield and the pavement and the salty tears *Thick and slow inside watch cogs and wheels catch for a moment and then slip and slip.*

He slipping us back. He don't know about death. But Nicki's ma and pop, they know. He slipping us back to Garfield. Listen how he talk about a wedding and lemon pies *Pug, he hang his head and rub a scar on his hand.*

Seem something fast and funny always happen on the playground and then I got to go to the principal office again.

"*Pug!*"

"Quit your worrying, boy. Look how I'm staying with you. Look how I follow where I can."

Always boys in the principal office, big ones, small ones, mostly skinny ones, somebody ma always upset, crying and giving her boy a earful.

"Your ma calling you, Kid."

"*Where she at?*"

"She in the kitchen."

"*Go on, Ma. I'm sick. I'm in bed. What is it?*"

"Tell me, boy, what did I do wrong?" his ma yell from the kitchen. "What did I do to have my son end up like this?"

She want to know. She want to learn what she did wrong.
"*She ain't crying, Pug.*"
"She is too crying."
"*No she ain't!*"

Calvin woke the next morning under a burden of self-indictment. It came as no surprise to have woken with grave remembrances of the fallen lad near Garfield Park, but there were also the motley visions of Victoria's death, and he hadn't dreamt of her. In Calvin's head and heart, there was a thread beyond the untimely grip of death that bound the two tragic events, though he hadn't until that very miserable early morning convicted himself doubly of murder. The conviction was ludicrous, but so fired the pre-dawn synapses of his taxed and addled mind.

He woke facing the cold stone wall that met the long edge of the bed, with his arm flush against it, his hand palming it, his face just inches off its surface, the warmth of his breath turned back towards his lips, as though Victoria were still lying in the protective bend of his battered body. Having slipped back under, just below the surface of the shallowest, most delicate end of the dream world he thought: How cold my baby is this morning. Hope she's not coming down with something.

Though in truth, Victoria had always *been* down with something. His last conscious remembrances of her had come to him seven months prior, when an old man on a sunny balcony advised Calvin to marry; though the old man was an intentional *célibataire* and the integrity of his advice jeopardised by the curious lengths to which he went to net drinking companions. Spring had arrived, Calvin was in love and a postcard from Gem appeared in the post-box. With the postcard held instinctively close to his chest, Calvin looked over one shoulder and then the next, just to be safe. (Hot southern cities come with siestas. Gem, who never tired and never had need or want for downtime, disagreed with siestas and spent them, largely, stoking the crew's collective flame. One never knew when Gem's words – even those scratched in his wangled illegible hand onto the back of a picture postcard – might require those in his company to raise fists or bottles or flee a scene. It is nearly impossible to run in slippers and flip-flops, which is why Calvin wore laced sneakers whenever knocking about town with Gem and the lads.)

The postcard, sent from Napoli, where Gem spent winters overseeing the annual maintenance of a yacht, was benign. He had written to inform Calvin that he had quit his flat in Nice and was in need of a new one. Gem was constantly in need. He had needs, many needs. As soon as he satisfied one, another presented itself. His life revolved around satisfying his needs, a fact that seemed as archaic as it was elemental. Gem was not a thrill-seeker, yet there was something to the frenetic pace and vivacity of his life that gave one the impression that he lived life on the edge. Whatever it is that makes a lazy man perfectly unbelievable and unable to convince another of anything at all, there was something to Gem, something to his energy and commitment that made him terribly convincing. As such, one rarely begged for the reason behind his need. One merely enlisted himself to help further the cause, even when doing so brought prospects of bumps and bruises and worse. Gem's needs were quite simply inevitable.

The following day, a scintillating day in March, Calvin arranged to see a flat overlooking the port and Mont Boron. The proprietor, gaunt as a switch and wearing faded blue coveralls, was a spindly old Toulousain, a semi-retired tile-man who was perpetually between jobs. He leaned himself languidly out the window, while Calvin was shown about the flat by an estate agent who was keen on keeping Calvin far away from the barmy old bloke. She was a stuffy old bird, the agent, with a puckered beak and wings pinned to her sides.

"*Par ici*! *Par ici*!" she insisted. "Don't mind that old fool!"

They disappeared down a short hallway and came instantly upon a small bedroom and a bath, both perfectly stuffed with all manner of personal effects. They returned to the salon to find the old man on the balcony with two café chairs. Between the chairs was a metal ice bucket, dimpled and winking in the late-morning sun, and a new bottle of *pastis*. The agent berated the old fellow in a screeching torrent of colourful French, in reply to which, the old man smiled deafly and waved Calvin over towards the liquid picnic. Waddling, huffing and cursing, it appeared the agent might jump straight from the balcony and chance a flightless death, leaving a flock of burnt feathers to flutter down among the yachts and dinghies.

The flat was unfit to be rented. The ad in the *Nice Matin* was but a ruse to attract those with whom the old proprietor might share a drink. The flat was tiny, situated on the fifth floor of five in an ancient building without an elevator and, therefore, of potential interest only to young single dwellers who, by the fact of their youth, were still active in their giving and taking. The old man was kept alive by his interaction with those who came to view the flat. The agent, his sister, did not approve.

At the bidding of the old man, Calvin cracked the seal and tilted the bottle, in turn, over one glass and then another. The *pastis* swirled in amber clouds about the melting ice. Calvin and the old man nodded, touched glasses and drank. The sun shone brightly, high and hot above the balcony, above the long line of trimmed palms below. The water in the port, capped on three sides by Italian balconies and pink and ochre, twinkled dark and light between the bright white boats at dock.

The old man reminded Calvin of Mario, the concierge at the Pensao Miroslav in Lisbon, where Calvin and Victoria spent a summer month in the hills, among Portuguese smiles and streetcars, eating fish soup and drinking *vino verde*. With Mario, it was always *si*. Everything *si*. Sad and long and drawn out *si-i-i* when the answers were obvious. All things were possible with Mario. No request was too burdensome. At every turn in the life of the average fellow, all he hears is *no*. To all inquiries, all requests, good dreams and bad, he invariably receives a well-rounded *no*. With Mario, however, all things were possible.

"Mario, might I pay on Friday instead of to-day?"

"*Si-i-i*."

"Mario, might I possibly trouble you to see this letter to the post?"

"*Si-i-i*."

"And might I bring you a cold beer or two for your troubles?"

"*Si-i-i*."

Good old Mario. Worked and weary, though never without a smile—a genuine smile! Beautiful in its selflessness and ragged sadness, a smile and manner no rich man could affect.

On the balcony above the Nice port, the old Toulousain asked of Calvin, "*Es-tu marié, mon gar?*"

"No, sir," said Calvin. "I'm not married."

"Well, you *ought* to be. It is not good for a man to be so free. He becomes destructive and decadent if he is not forced to practice restraint."

At the old man's behest, Calvin poured more *pastis* and began recounting remembrances of Sarrià, an outlying Catalan village that came to be annexed during the expansion of Barcelona and was then forgotten all over again. On the *carrer principal* in Sarrià was a bar owned by a man who Calvin had once called *Papá*, a man he thought might become his father-in-law. The bar had a long zinc counter that ran nearly the length of its interior, like those found in the cobbled hills of Lisbon. Stainless steel refrigerators with glass display windows modelled puddings and other *postres*. Two old espresso machines of Italian make lined the back wall and a big smoke-stained clock hung above them. A steady reluctance shone in the eyes of the locals, the barmen and the labourers. They were proud, indigestible and slow to trust. They passed from generation to generation the genetics for patience and resistance, and waited for the day when expansion and evolution will have finally run its course. Sugar-topped pastries lay sparkling under a shining glass-top extension that rose up and rounded back towards the deep edge of the bar. Walls, the colour of *crema Catalana*, were coated in ancient paint and stained by tobacco smoke. Early-evening bartenders, solemn in their white button shirts, polished glassware in silence, their faces dulled by the wild persistence of time. On occasion, they would whir with professional animation, slicing great blocks of *manchego* and *jamon* and long batons of *fuet*. They knew to pace themselves for the eventuality of endlessness. On Friday and Saturday nights, however, the bar came alive. Calvin sat on his favourite stool at the end of the bar, closest to the great picture window that gave onto the street, where he watched and dreamed and guessed after the life stories of passersby. On weekend evenings, the barmen came spinning to life in a manner one thought impossible during the week. They proved as graceful as dancing figurines, the kind Calvin imagined turning at the top of the hour in all of the great plazas of Switzerland during winter holidays; twirling and bending, wielding long knives, handling plates and glasses as though the evening were festively choreographed on rods and hinges. Calvin loved those festive evenings and carried his memories of them to Tuesday night sittings, when the bar had regained its impersonal sobriety.

One December evening, with the cold night air sparkling and still, a young girl, not more than a few years Calvin's senior, stepped into the bar from off the holiday main street. She had fine features,

Aztec-black hair and the miracle eyes of Raul Gonzalez. She wore a red mohair coat with a pleated puff collar and carried a short stack of packages finely wrapped in white foil paper and tied with red ribbon. Calvin was seated at the bar, not quite twenty-six-years old at the time, injured and beautiful, with wild dancing eyes of thinly pooled green, the whites of which were still pristine with youth. A Lennonesque mane, which benefitted from a slightly tighter wave and a deeper autumn stain, fell thick and not unfeminine about his angular features. Calvin was a dark, pensive figure, incapable of believing someone might find him beautiful, or even just handsome. If she had noticed him at all, she gave no indication. She set her packages on the barstool between her and Calvin and remained standing, ordered a *caña* and an espresso and poked through her coin purse for the correct change. The bartender placed before her a small glass and one smaller yet, the latter centred on a ceramic *soucoupe*. The nicks and dings in the bar top caught the glow of the strung Christmas bulbs and reflected a silver universe of unnamed constellations. She finished the beer in three deft swigs, knocked back the coffee in a single go and left with her packages before the last copper coin came to rest. Calvin watched the dizzying dance of that last coin. At the door, she stopped and turned, looked directly at Calvin and fairly shouted, "*Hasta luego!*"

Startled and unprepared for recognition of any kind, he mouthed a silent, "*Hasta luego.*" At the very moment he did so, from within the kitchen a fatherly voice bid lovingly and with great volubility, "*Hasta luego, mi querida niña!*"

That, as Calvin explained, was the first time he had set eyes on Victoria, and the memory of that night, recounted solely to entertain the kind old Toulousain, was the last time he consciously thought of her before that morning, when after the torturous dream of the fallen lad near Garfield Park, he lay in bed, stretched miserably along the cold stone wall and lamented his failures.

Among the bankrupt senses that were once so rich with Victoria's presence, only Calvin's sense of smell managed to occasionally confirm his memories of her time alongside him—the soft scent of her Spanish skin, a pale fading butterfly flapping ever-weaker in the armoire at the far back of his room. How he had tried to preserve her memory by planting at the bottom of the armoire a selection of the abandoned clothing from her abandoned life. Memories of Avinguda Diagonal in Barcelona, where they shared a bench in the light of a slanting autumn sun that made middle-length shadows that never came to hide under a fellow's shoes the way they did during the high summer months. There they would eat *bocadillos*, drink wine, talk and marvel the plane trees on the broad avenue with their mottled skin, their graceful disease, fatigued from the relentless summer; church bells in the distance marking the time with soft iron clangs, cardiganed professors sailing model schooners tethered by leashes on the shallow sea of a ceramic fountain in Spanish blue patched here and there with dead leaves of dark umber, speaking in scholarly tones on the science of sailing, of ship-building, of ballasts—the importance of staying upright. And where university girls, like Victoria once was, with thick shining hair and cheeks made pink by morning's cool kisses roll past on black bicycles, the kind one watched among the moss and damp of the canals ringing central Amsterdam, gliding past in silence and fog, along cobble and brick and over tram lines and under the lean-to houses of charcoal and light, corroborating their stoic silence, and over the cushion of damp, in umber alleyways, the sidewalks that rise and fall for bridges and green water, loose brick clacking under sole and tire, encouraging false notions of invincibility—for those girls, too, God bless them, are vulnerable. The young, like Victoria, fluent on their black winter bicycles with their white winter heads, and long dark-knit coats and knee-high boots, tight and black, rolling too purposefully for leisure; too leisurely, too endlessly to make believe there's an appointment somewhere to be kept.

But Victoria kept her appointments. Every damned one of them, of which there were precisely four on the busy morning of the day she died—one to dispute a statement of account with one domestic service provider or another; one with a seamstress to reattach the top button of a blouse she hated, but wore nonetheless; one with Calvin to ask if he would always love her, regardless of her damages (a question he met with the sourness of self-pity, as well as a short, impromptu list of detailed conditions); the last with a crumbling bridge over a shallow river near Valladolid, a river that Calvin had never known and had since come to rename the Styx. Victoria, ever more his poetry than his girl, not only for her artistry and beauty, but for her lack of obviousness and sturdy substance, her lack of proper handles, most of all, of course, her death.

Years later, once in a great while, in the blink of a butterfly wing, one stray molecule of her aromatic essence would catch and arrest him, and the heavy hammer of *saudade*, evading its mystical catch, would come swinging down on heavenly hinges to deliver its blow to skull and brittle bone; shattering, scattering the lad violently into a million bittersweet shards. Try as he did, however, to not disturb it in its fragile flutter, the butterfly, so soon whisper-weak, was inevitably swept away by the broom of wild rushing seasons, Klarysa's brief occupation there in his bedroom, the bully bouquet of medical wraps and salves—all the prevailing odours of life's victories and defeats that, thankfully, deny a lad in his ill-advised efforts to trap ghosts in a wooden box.

But hell, the butterfly was long dead, and with it died Calvin's ability to torture himself with memories of lost opportunities and her tragic fate. The last handful of years had in fact passed famously, with all the verve and excitement expected of a healthy, vigorous boy harvesting in the prime of his life, twinkling, like crystalline sugar under bright lights. What on earth then, wondered Calvin, staring up at the flaking ceiling, had turned the tide and caused the summer to bear its teeth so viciously?

"Damn right I'm crying! Look how many tears you can draw from your mother."

She crying all right and she watching Kid for answers. He only eight-years-old and he know the answer. Might be the only answer he do know, but she don't know and she won't believe him anyhow. The answer is that she ain't done nothing wrong and how crazy everybody get over a fight in a schoolyard. He only eight and he got lots of time to learn to be a good kid. His pops the only one who seem to understand. His ma say how come you end up like this, always in trouble. But he only eight-years-old.

Ma and Pop come to school and get me out of trouble from the principal.

"Something's got to be done about that boy of yours, James. What's wrong with that boy, anyhow? Why won't he learn?"

Laika exits a pet store in Venice, California, with wet defiant eyes. She's holding a birdcage with two birds in it, two lime-green parakeets. She finds a space for the cage among all her belongings in the back of an old station wagon and dries her eyes with the end of her shirt sleeve. Today is the end.

They come all the way to school. Get out the car and walk they way up the sidewalk to the school. I watch them in my head and I get sick. It make me sick to watch Principal Dobey sitting at his desk. He got a shirt on and a tie. I watch his skin and his head almost bald and I feel so sick I want to run away. He smell nasty like a old man with a old shirt. He don't like me anyhow and I don't like him. Teeth all cricket and brown and he smell like a old man. Sometimes I get so sick I start to cry. Ma and Pop come in and I'm so thankful and ready for trouble, ready for a whooping, just get me the hell out from that office, away from the smell of that man who make me sick. Ma beg him and she cry and that make me the sickest of all. Make me so sick I want to scream and hit somebody and fight. It make Pop sick too but not like me. I'm too afraid to look at him cause all this my fault, but finally I look at him angry enough to run away right now. I want to scream look how Ma behave, Pop! Pop don't say much. He look around at everybody, sick like me. He got one hand in his coat pocket and I hear his car keys. He crushing them like gravel he so sick. His boy and Ma bringing him strife. Principal Dobey, he smell like bacon and perfume and sweat and Pop losing pay coming here to this school. Principal Dobey got skinny arms and a belly that hang over his belt and his hands, they white and weak. That's what make Pop so sick and me too. Dobey lean back in his chair and lace his hands on his belly and he tell Pop crazy things and then he say, "Yes, Mr. Stony, Yes. Calvin is going to be a fine boy just as soon as he—"

"Beg your pardon, sir?" *Pop say. He say it hard and I start to cry from being so proud of him and so ashame he got to come get me out the principal office and get sick like me.*

"Sir, sir, he is a fine boy. A fine boy, sir. Please don't think for a second that I... It's just that he—"

Ma jump up with her wet eyes. "I try Dr. Dobey! Oh, how I try. I'm always telling James—"

"That's enough, Irma." *Pop say it low and final like somebody drop a iron shot-put on the gymnasium floor. Everybody understand enough been said.*

"Stand up, son. Come here. Did you apologize to..."

Kid watch Nicki when she walk *People in the street don't know. Running, running, I can't keep my hands off sparkling things. Got to remember.*

"Look at me when I'm talking to you, son. I say did you apologize to Principal Dobey?"

"Yes, Pop." *Past the chain-link fences where brothers throw dice, skin glisten soft. Theys flowers.*

"Did you mean it?"

"Yes, Pop." *Can't keep my hands off sparkling things.*

"Oh, yes, Mr. Stony, I think the boy—"

"Good day, sir."

A good-looking boy with prep-school eyes invites Katie to spend a weekend on a Colorado mountain top. His mother is going to have a birthday and she wants to meet this girl he's always talking about.

Katie is nervous with excitement. She says yes, sure, she would love to go. Katie ain't never been to a ski resort. Today is just the beginning.

Walking out the principal office it feel sunny and light like Saturday morning even though I'm going to get a whooping after school. In the secretary office, boys sit side-by-side like scared pups. They next, boy. Pop hold the door open for somebody parents. Pop nod sick at the man and the man nod sick back. I know what they saying with them nods:

"These boys of ours."

"Goddamn right these boys of ours!"

"Still…"

"I know, I know."

In the hallway, Ma tell me to get to class and stay out of trouble. I hate when Ma come to school. She always crying about things this and that, she always make me feel ashame.

Pop look at me and he say, "You see what you do to your mother? She only wants what's best for you. You're a good kid, son. Best start acting like it."

"I will, Pop."

Dez, he unzip a old duffle bag in the back of a dusty old brick building in Garfield. He sit on a rickety army cot and put the duffle next to him. He take out a wind-up clock and two pictures, but he don't know where to put them. He turn around like a boy who can't find his ma. He drag up a heavy cardboard box and put the clock and pictures on it. He get sad for he got to find new homes for old things in a dirty old warehouse. He put some shirts and pants and socks and drawers in a old filing cabinet. Dez, he got to stay sober.

I watch them walk away. Pop throw his arm over Ma shoulders. He say something in her ear and she smack him hard on his ass. Pop throw back his head and laugh real loud. That great laugh from Pop shake and rattle the lockers.

"What you going to do, Pug, when Nicki and me move to California?"

"Go easy, Kid," I say to him easy as moonlight. "Go easy. See if I ain't following you."

Bird, he close his eyes and try to get inside the music. He sit on a long brown couch in the backroom of a record store. He got a pen and paper and his fingers move full of grace on the pen like it got red-brass valves. He got to get inside the music. He feel the horns. He always feel the horns. He try hard for he want to describe it to people in magazines, but he can't lick it. That paper stare at him with loud blank looks. He can't lick it.

"Oh, God, no! Oh, God, no!" *somebody ma cry out.*

Pug turn into a grove of weeping willow trees surrounding a dark lake. His fingers, they crying whips. They bend low and tickle the earth.

Got to pay attention.

2   Klarysa Pavlichenko

In which Calvin delivers a valise
and falls in love on a pine bluff
over Cap d'Ail.

Some eight months earlier, on a sunny February morning, just weeks before he had sat on the balcony above the Nice port with the old Toulousain, Calvin left the flat en route to the Café de Turin at Place Garibaldi. In Nice, *Le Château* refers to a jutting landmass atop which sits the ruins of an old Roman castle. The port is situated to the east of the chateau and Vieux Nice, the old town, is situated to the west. As such, the Vieux lies bathed in cool shadows until the morning sun overcomes the chateau. The Café de Turin sits just north of the chateau and so its sweeping terrace is awash in sunlight from the moment the great star awakens in the Mediterranean sky. The waiters, in their black and white formal wear, shuck oysters and arrange crab, langouste, prawn, urchin, and sundry fresh catch over beds of wet seaweed. Garibaldi and two majestic lions claim the centre of the *place*, their trio of gazes follow Rue de la Republic east towards the Italian border.

On that morning, all signs pointed to another sparkling winter day in the Southeast corner of the Republic. Calvin ambled along Avenue Jean Jaurès with a weather-beaten valise in hand. Up ahead, he heard the familiar yapping of an Australian terrier fringed with platinum blue hair. Monique sat at a table for two on the terrace of the Café de Turin. Across from her was the clammy terrier, its front paws planted resolutely on the white tablecloth, its short hind quarters tamping anxiously upon the wicker chair pulled close to the table's edge. The dog was called Khali, after a supposedly famous composer or director of cinema, Calvin couldn't remember which. What it was barking at God only knew.

Calvin and Monique greeted each other warmly, coming together somewhere between sitting and standing, offering the traditional cheek-to-cheek *bisous*. Until recently, Calvin and Monique had spit venom at one another, had extended the tips of their personal differences with the aim of drawing blood. Having put forth considerable effort and learnt to accept their respective differences, however, they were able to greet one another with graciousness. During the brushing of cheeks, Calvin noted a stain of raw oysters on her breath.

"What is it," she demanded suspiciously of his smile.

"Nothing, dear girl," he replied, studying the bouncing blue-fringed terrier. "Simply in rare spirits this morning."

Oyster breath has a way of levelling a playing field. Such tiny victories aided Calvin in his attempts to cope with Monique's vainglory.

"Thank you for the valise," she said, eyeing it with distaste. "A more bruised and dust-covered one evidently eluded you."

"Most blokes in need of a valise—"

"The ones I had to offer him," she interrupted, flipping Khali a pink *crevette*, which the dog snatched cleanly in mid-flight, "are apparently too feminine for his taste. He *is*," she purred, "rather masculine."

"When do we get to meet your new beau?"

"Like all things, in time."

"Why doesn't he buy his own valise?"

But Monique had fatigued of the topic and Khali was now barking its fool head off. None of the clientele seemed to mind—the French worship the canine. Only the girl seated alone at an adjacent table wrinkled her nose – a decidedly adorable button of a nose – in disapproval. Monique had allowed the dog's incessant paws to tamp a brown halo on what was otherwise pristine white linen. Funny, the seemingly inherent tendencies, thought Calvin, of high-rent individuals for low-rent behaviour. One of the crew had coloured the dog's hair with a blue felt-tip marker towards the end of a maddening month of dog-sitting, while Monique was away on tour—a decidedly low-rent act, to be sure, but then, unlike Monique, none of the crew had ever put themselves forward as high-rent individuals.

Monique had little in common with the crew, in general, or Calvin, specifically. She was a Sorbonne-trained cellist from Oxford. She was opinionated and certain that the one right answer to any question or dilemma was there for the taking, if only one were provided with a sprawling rent-free penthouse in which to focus and contemplate. She was suspicious of those around her; although, in light of mankind's track record, she eyed the future with solid-gold expectations. By contrast, Calvin was a sulphur-infused knockabout from the American Midwest. He was compromising and certain that to any one question or dilemma there were a million right answers, or quite possibly none at all. He was a bright lad, but one who had stumbled upon his intelligence later than most, and quite by accident. Owing to a fine memory, he scored good marks at all levels of the public education afforded him (first by the state, later by his struggling parents and the broth of his own labours), though he was thoroughly convinced that he hadn't generated a single remarkable thought until some time after his twenty-sixth birthday. He trusted those around him; although, in light of mankind's track record, he eyed the future with grave concern.

Khali continued to bark. In an attempt to soothe the miserable creature, Calvin made to caress its blue head, but it snapped at him like an angry turtle.

"Be nice," admonished Monique, the reprimand aimed squarely at Calvin.

"What the devil is he going on about, anyway?"

"He's vexed because I won't give him an oyster. I know they're his favourite," she seemed to plead with the dog, "but he's on a regime. Khali, *arrête*!" With an objectionable face, she flipped the dog a black-spiked urchin the size of child's fist. "He may eat all the urchin he wants, however. I find them offensive."

Having eaten nothing that morning, Calvin salivated. "They are an acquired taste," he said, eyeing the dog with malice and envy.

"I do not believe in acquiring a taste for foul foods," said Monique. "There are more than enough delicacies in the world that taste exquisite from the first bite."

Khali deftly brought the urchin down to his chair, where he proceeded to attack it with all the skill and dexterity of a sea otter. Calvin watched, anxiously awaiting the moment Khali would take a long black needle to the snout, but it was not to be. To his great disappointment, the fat little tramp sucked clean the pasty under-filling and sat poised for the next offering. It sat haughtily in its café chair like a crown prince, with urchin paste spackled to its chin and whiskers, its black-bean eyes unblinking and shining brightly with flawless stupidity.

Calvin disliked the image of any dog begging at the table for food. It was as much a mockery to the inherent strength and ability of the canine as it was to the command shown by Man in his domestication of the able beast. Victoria had owned a magnificent male Doberman. Calvin loved it dearly. It knew better than to beg for food when Calvin was present and it resented him the denial, despite the fact that Calvin kept the beast better fed than he did himself. The dog was enormous, well-mannered and as intimidating as a black wolf. At any social gathering where food was served, the beast would square up before the weakest of the guests (faultless in its selection) and beg with pathetic eyes for the whole goddamned plate, or whatever meagre scraps of gristle or garbage might fall to the floor. Calvin would have preferred to lock the dog in another room for the duration of the meal, but Victoria wouldn't hear of it, and despite Calvin's stern appeals against scrapping off to the dog, the chosen guest would invariably let fall a strip of fat out of fear or annoyance when Calvin wasn't looking. In the end, neither guest nor dog was satisfied, and they rankled Calvin equally—the dog for begging and the guest for conceding. Had the guest whacked the dog good on the snout, or had the dog devoured the man and steak in one go, Calvin would have cheered the victor. How much better to see an animal abide its true nature and seize what it might with tooth and nail. Or likewise, see which of his guests would fight back with chain or whip or steak knife. Now that, thought Calvin, would be something to see! Have a dog be a dog or else make it into something else and call it by another name.

Calvin bid farewell and headed off around Place Garibaldi, past the antique merchants and up the backside of the chateau. The back passage to the chateau was peaceful. The trees formed a plush green canopy through which the sunlight refracted and flittered. At the first bend, the canopy broke and one was afforded a clear, elevated view over Vieux Nice and the northern quarters. In the distance, beyond the port, the *moyenne corniche* rimmed its way around the arid hills of pine and palm that extended to Monaco and beyond.

Calvin stood at the edge of the chateau nearest the port and watched down over the scrub and succulents that clung with determined roots and knuckles to sheer rock, rock that broke sharply away and plunged into an easy turquoise sea that breathed and sighed and from time to time foamed white at its stony edges. The sky was thin and cerulean. He stood contentedly with his hands shoved into his pockets. High above the port, the air was crisp. Watching out over the sea before a blinding sun, he filled his lungs with the clean winter air and felt very much alive.

He bubbled with sudden laughter at the recollection of Khali seated at the Café de Turin, tucking into the urchin. Almost instantly his contempt for the mutt transformed into something of admiration. Unlike the dog, Calvin was self-conscious. He cared too much how his ways and actions were perceived. And what had he gained for the good behaviour born of his concern? Why, he hadn't even taken a crust of bread that morning, while the fiendish canine was feasting on fresh seafood! One had to hand it to Khali, admitted Calvin; the little grunt had clearly established a first-rate mode of survival. The damned thing was a model of resourcefulness. Hell, bacteria and pestilence might learn a thing or two from the crafty mutt. There were times when Calvin wondered if he hadn't inadvertently given in to a domestication of self, and yet no one was caressing him on silky bedding or feeding him fancy meals on any given morning.

"Bah!" he burst excitedly. "Spring is on its way, and with it a fresh go of things, new strategies, new beginnings." Then, lowering his voice to a murmur, he optimistically declared, "The war is not over my mangy whiskered adversary. I am ready for the fight! I will regain the teeth of my poor ancestors and we will fight it out on all fours, if that's what it comes to!"

"My word!" someone gasped behind him.

Calvin turned and came face-to-face with the girl who had been seated alone at the Café de Turin, the one with the button-nose. "Had I the slightest notion you might be plotting war," she notified him with a kittenish frown, "I would have *surely* stayed far away."

The girl's voice was buoyant with youth, though she wielded her words with a dextrous flair. There was a viscosity to her accent, which announced that she was not a native English speaker. Her words were born somewhere in the back of the mouth, not at the teeth as with English, or in the throat as with French. Still, her grammar would prove perfect and her vocabulary extensive. She was called Klarysa Pavlichenko. She was from Odessa, Ukraine, and she put stars in Calvin's eyes.

"Never fear," said Calvin, playing up to the provocative twinkle in her eye. "It will quite likely remain a civilised campaign. And if it all goes horribly awry, I'll see to it that you're the first evacuated. But just *what*, exactly, Klarysa from Odessa, did you make of that mutt seated at the table adjacent you, the one devouring shellfish like some make of clamorous sea-monster?"

"Its blue mane was intriguing," she replied without hesitation. "The rest of the act was tedious, excessive and deserving of rebuke in the form of a swift slap."

As one might simply describe the Taj Mahal as a wonder, one might so describe Klarysa as pretty and be done with it. And though no audience will have been deceived by such modest descriptions, even the least curious mind would demand something more substantial for the price of admission. *Alors*, Klarysa was fresh. She was finely tuned and balanced, at once exotic and domestic. There was a terrific innocence about her that was nevertheless accompanied by the ready arsenal of cunning and wits privy to all battle-tested survivors. Even in her more excitable moments, there was a constancy of restraint to her manner, her line, her form, her cosmopolitan rhythm. Her physical features cooperated as do those of most fellows, though parts of her seemed to have won certain individual liberties. Her hair, for example, varied not only in style, but in hue, ranging in colour from rosewood to mahogany to bistre depending on her mood, the weather and the time of day. Asleep in bed, the waves of her hair might overflow the edge of her pillow in currents of garnet and gold. When anger and impatience forced her hand, she might pull it back into a severe spout of shining onyx. The same could be said of her eyes, which shone with the amber fire of red topaz on sweltering beach days, reflected a dark and mysterious glint on rainy winter midnights, and on overcast Saturday afternoons in autumn, appeared layered with the same shifting browns on which lovers tread in November-wet forests. She mostly dressed in the manner of other European girls her age, but altered the lines and deployed various tailoring techniques in appropriating an air of finesse beyond the collection of her years, which amounted to a scant twenty-four, so that while she fit without flaw into any uniform gathering, she was invariably the first noticed upon closer inspection. She was an inherently efficient girl, despite giving no stock to any concepts of economy, traditional or otherwise. Her tack towards anything was almost always the quickest and most direct. She was graceful. She followed literally and figuratively in the footsteps of cats, and though she was petite, no one would say she was small.

Klarysa asked if Calvin wouldn't care to join her for a picnic. A couple of hours later, they were talking and laughing and commenting on the temperamental shades of blue that tended to colour a winter sea, on a blanket spread over a grassy bluff near Cap d'Ail. Klarysa lay flat and extended herself to full length—a length, thought Calvin, which would fit all too nicely across the back bench seat of an old Ford Galaxy. She made a pillow of her suede Pumas and watched the sky as they talked of triumphs and tragedies and the trifles between. Once or twice she extended an arm towards him with two of her slender fingers signalling victory. In response, Calvin tempted between the legs of the V with a lit cigarette; then watched as it yawned shut and brought the cigarette to her lips. He watched the light dance on those red-candied lips when she puckered for a drag, and watched sun-sparks flicker at the teeth when she giggled at one of his jokes. At some of his better jokes, she would roll on her side in ticklish laughter and take his hand or wrist or ankle, as though for air. And Calvin did what any fellow would do—he told more jokes.

The picnic was simple but elegant – fresh breads, cheeses, tapenade, *fougasse*, *foie gras* and wine – and though she was most often subdued in a crowd, Klarysa was not afraid of dramatics. "Isn't it *gorg*eous?" she asked, marvelling a wedge of aged *cantal*. She seemed to take surprisingly little for granted. The truth is, she harboured a vast wishing well of sentimentality that could be accessed by the flipping of any old copper coin. Several of her anecdotes suggested an ardent appreciation for fiscal responsibility, though one had the impression it was more of a general philosophy than any commitment to practical application, for she professed very little personal wealth, even less need of it, and no desire whatsoever to raise the grade of her flat financial trajectory. And yet she was the youngest in a family that had once known lofty status—status privy to a class of people that are known to whinge and moan when deprived of their luxuries and conveniences. But while Klarysa was known to neither whinge nor moan, it must be said, for example, that she did prefer rather strongly to have her way, and did not care a hell of a lot for the word *no*.

Calvin and Klarysa ate and drank and talked and talked, and it seemed they might never run short of topics to discuss—rich foods and wine tend to sedate all but those who are falling in love. Klarysa recounted the details of her life in Odessa. There was a time when the Pavlichenko name was well known and the family well connected. Calvin knew embarrassingly little about the former union of Soviet republics, its peoples and its cultures, and was ashamed of the fact. For crissake, he thought critically, a fellow should know *some*thing about the countries his home nation had, throughout his life, relentlessly demonised. (It occurred to him that there was a whole lexicon of buzzwords – in which *Soviet* and *Communism* were but two entries – designed and promoted to trigger conditioned responses of fear and hatred in American minds.) Unable to offer something more substantial, Calvin mentioned that he lived for a short while in a room of an old chateau in the hills of Antibes that was built as a residence for the Davidoff family. Klarysa took a drag from her cigarette and said upon exhaling, "Tobacco magnates lead fine lives, I suppose, but one need not defend one's honour as a vintner."

"I'm sorry," said Calvin with a smile. "I don't follow."

"You know—the horrendous histories of plantations and what not. When a final product requires decidedly more labour than art, more muscle than wits... What I mean to say is that organised labour from almost any perspective tends to make a nasty animal of Man."

"But how... I mean, what does that—"

"Sorry, sometimes I forget we've only just met," she said demurely, putting her hand on his. "You see, my family were vintners. We owned a wine estate in Odessa—a champagne estate, to be fair."

"Is that right?" said Calvin, impressed.

"Bah, it was a long time ago. At any rate, wineries smell nicer than... tobacco curing houses or however they may be called—or so I imagine."

"I see. That explains why you spend time in France," he ventured.

She withdrew her hand. Eyeing him, she challenged somewhat coolly, with a tight intelligent smile, "Does it, then?"

"I don't know," he replied, retracting slightly. "I would imagine you feel an affinity for France, what with its rich history of agricultural…"

Klarysa turned her face to the sea and composed her lips into a smile. Her eyes, however, reflected no humour.

"No?" Calvin prompted. "The cradle of champagne…? Nothing?"

"My grandfather was murdered, Calvin," she said flatly.

"Oh. Oh my. I'm… I'm terribly sorry…" he said, clumsy in his empathy, fumbling in the dark for correlation.

"What does that have to do with anything?" she spared him the burden of asking. "Hell, *I* don't know. I really don't."

She squinted at the sun, which had begun its quick winter descent.

"He was found dead between the rows of vines in his own vineyard," she continued. "Oh, I have nothing against the French. I really don't," she seemed to say to the sun, or to the gods responsible for its creation. "I don't." Then turning back to Calvin and his inquisitive gaze: "I don't."

But in a way, she did.

The Pavlichenko wine estate was referred to throughout the Ukraine by patrons and detractors alike as The House of Omega. The family leveraged creativity and innovation and at times controversy to overcome steep odds and flourish in the ever-precarious wine industry of the Russian Empire and the Soviet Union. Klarysa's grandfather was a visionary whose untimely death marked the fall of the estate. Emotional damages and criminal advice led the heirs of the ruined estate to sell the land for kopeks on the ruble and the family soon found itself living hand-to-mouth in four cramped rooms under one roof, the same crumbling roof under which Klarysa was born. The only vestiges of the prosperity and *haute-couture* that had for decades been associated with the House of Omega and the Pavlichenko name were found in a tattered album of faded photos and her grandmother's faded recollections.

As a child, Klarysa was gifted, determined and bored frequently to tears. And so, as do many precocious children who lack positive outlets through which to channel their brassy energetic currents, she misbehaved and found trouble. Three days before her fourteenth birthday, with the house silenced by sleep, she slipped away and ran off to Kiev, where she put her faith in a seemingly sweet old granny who successfully lured home the hungry child with the promise of *perohy* and raspberry *kissel*. They passed through a little gate and a tender garden and into a modest cottage, where the grandson boxed Klarysa several times on the noggin and relieved her of a threadbare and nearly jangle-free coin purse. The grandson proceeded to berate his grandmother for netting such skimpy perch and threw Klarysa back into the raging river of the big-city. Having been rendered penniless and tattered, which in truth rather succinctly described her life condition, Klarysa stowed away on an Odessa-bound train, hiding in the loo of the penultimate railcar for the full duration of the seemingly endless journey. At the terminus, she slid open the door to find a conductor awaiting her exit. When she produced neither ticket nor fare, he apprehended her, grabbing her brusquely by the wrist, and yanked her toward an office of reckoning. With her free hand, young Klarysa reached into her handbag, extracted a penknife and with a rehearsed flick of the wrist, made its tip disappear in the conductor's upper thigh. She vowed to be more astute the next time she ran away from home, which was one year removed, on the eve of her fifteenth birthday—the prospects of a bankrupt birthday had a way of inciting brash action from the pert lass.

A girl of her youth – especially one shouldering the burden of such comely good-looks – learnt a hell of a lot on the road and in the streets, or else she was swallowed whole trying. Klarysa was encouraged by the confirmation of her quick wits, resourcefulness and toughness, though she was equally discouraged to learn that her chosen path would force her to rely to such a heavy extent on an ability to out-fox and out-run and find sleep among the down and out in unmentionable dosshouses, despite cold and hunger and the clammy discomfort of tear-streaked cheeks.

The single rudder that kept her from being blown adrift was the memory she had constructed of her grandfather, from fable, fact and photo. With his memory as her strength, she defined a goal for herself, one which, if accomplished, would revive the family name and restore her grandfather's legacy. It was a long shot, but by maintaining her focus and pushing forward, she was able to drive her way through a brutal chop and come to plane on relatively placid waters. And though the struggle never did harden her heart or embitter her soul, it did lend her personage a tempered edge of autonomy and an appreciable flame of sovereignty, which, for all its undeniable merit, might occasionally flare up and singe the hairs of even the not-so-delicate or nonchalant.

Klarysa had written off school at an early age. Unable to see the point of it, she fared poorly. She found traditional schooling, based predominantly on memorisation and recall, to be a waste of time, when one could be out in the world accomplishing things. One morning, at the age of twelve, she called her family to attention and asserted (in English, no less) that, "One need only speak well and act quickly to get by in a sufficiently fashionable manner." She added that, "It is of little import *what* one actually says or *how* one actually acts," and concluded by citing that she, "Hadn't, to date, been proven wrong."

Her family didn't understand a word she said. They only grew suspicious and worried. An older brother showed his appreciation for the dissertation by socking her good in the arm, and then in the other. Her mother, who was prone to fits of neurosis, rang the parish priest the following day, just to be safe.

Klarysa could be mystifying at times, but overall, she was a jovial and effervescent girl. And despite her savvy, there was an endearing flightiness about her, which may have been an affectation, one could never tell. Perhaps her insouciance was a happy result of having learnt at an early age that she could achieve virtually anything she set out to achieve, with little or no assistance.

"What," asked Calvin, "brought you to Western Europe?"

Without deliberation she replied, "Ease and opportunity." It was a plain and simple truth.

"Oh, look!" she said suddenly, having spotted a wee brown lizard. She hopped to her feet and tip-toed softly to where it lay sunning itself on a rock warmed by the sun. There she squatted down on her haunches and quickly gathering her long hair, brought it around in front of her with instinctive knowledge that trimness and tidiness aid inspection. "I can see him breathe," she said. "How quick his little lungs. The sun on his skin makes rainbows."

"Rainbows," Calvin echoed quietly, in awe, as he watched her.

He thought of his youth in Garfield, all the grey negations, the littered puddles made heavy with filtered metals when rain fell about the southern rims of the Great Lakes. The reflected array of colours that Klarysa attributed to rainbows, Calvin associated with the oily sheen of pollutants on stagnant water—yet *she* was the one who grew up on a diet of dry black bread and millet in a cramped home that reeked of primer oil and the human grease of too many people in too small a space.

Calvin was overcome by a wave of gratitude. He looked about, took a deep breath and studied the details of the day in hopes of committing them to memory. Though it was only February, the warmth of the sun and the absence of wind allowed them to shed their jackets—determined children have been known to induce spring simply be refusing winter its demands. Towering pines, with their lack of lower branches, resembled paint brushes loaded thick with forest green and stabbed into rocky flats from which they stretched high for a blue canvas. Seagulls looped high beyond the edge where the land fell away, steep and jagged, into the sea; rising and falling, those coastal scavengers, those silver ravens of the sea, wailing drunkenly, riotous in their grotesque merriment. Calvin sensed a young bud flowering inside him. It was wet and spring-green and petalled with hope. Watching Klarysa, he thought he might scoop her up and carry her off to wherever her whims dictated; scoop her up in his arms and hold her, protect her from all harm. The happy thought was married to an urge to laugh, to run, to flap wings with the gulls and mock their ridiculous ecstatic cries.

The day began its retirement. The sun had become a late-winter peach sinking slowly beyond the horizon, gaining intensity with its departure. Klarysa sat up to watch and wrapped her arms tightly about her knees. Calvin did likewise. A breeze snaked its way through the pines and licked their bare limbs, bringing to attention a fine white fuzz on Klarysa's forearms. The sun danced a brilliant show before them and cast cold hard shadows aft. With a cupped hand, Klarysa shielded her eyes and looked over at Calvin, in silence, her cheeks featured in deep rose, her button nose squinting with her shining eyes. He leaned into her slightly, as though he might kiss her, but just then a chilling breeze blew past, causing a great shiver to rattle its way through him. She was about to say something, was perhaps going to encourage him to take certain liberties, but she suddenly squinted hard, her bright smile bursting wide, and with clenched teeth, shrugged her shoulders and, in fact, the entire sum of her person, to fend off a shiver of her own.

Finally, she whispered, "Would you like to go to the cinema to-night?"

"I would," he said, emulating her softness.

The sun seemed to struggle against its own impending death. Summoning all its fire, it flung sideways a fistful of sparkling diamonds, a billion in count; sent them scattering across the sea, like skipping stones that eventually catch the surface and sink. Though these did not sink, but rather remained floating and shimmering in a luminous net of blinding light. Inevitably, the shining star soon slipped into the darkening sea and all of the sparkling diamonds dissolved into nothing.

Calvin and Klarysa spent the next five days tripping blissfully through the discovery of one another, in warm cafés and in the shadowed alleyways where, pressed body-to-body against humid vine-covered heights, heads and hair and hands smashed sacrificial flowers between flesh and stone; steam rising, sweaty in winter wool, pinned hungrily under the dripping eaves and archways of the musty winter quarter, body and hair and hips. She took him in, took him down and down and down until he drew back and pulled her into the rip tide of his body, his grip, the vine-like tendrils that wrapped about her waist, her back, her neck, until she moaned.

And then she hopped a plane and flew home, back to the burgeoning Latin buzz of Barcelona. Naturally, Calvin was surprised to learn that Klarysa lived in Barcelona, though not only because of his former ties to the city. That night, cosy in bed and just off the edge of deep sleep, he thought dreamily of her, of Barcelona and of redemption. He wondered if the arid Catalan climate was capable of accommodating such a verdant vessel. Her mouth must surely suffer, the wet-bruised pink, the white summer peach minus an indelicate bite, the endless cherry wound with glistening nectar-rimmed edges. He slipped joyfully off the edge and free-fell towards dreamy unconsciousness. In his final hazy moments, rapidly leaking the logic of wakefulness, he resolved to send her boxes of moisturising lotions and lip balms and crate after crate of fresh aloe.

They shredded shoulders and biceps deep amber, the sun make stars on they skin, high-tops squeeching, stopping, starting, back-door cutting on cement. A young whelp with chin lifted above the horizon, looking down an adolescent nose. A camera snap.

"Mama won't let me leave Garfield."

Smooth palms, long black children fight fast and beautiful around a orange ball, gazelles bent at the waist, ready to trigger springs, jungle sweat, slap inner-city skin, long diagonal bounce pass break the press, push the rock, lob to Sugarbear on a high-flying oop, a wide-winged brown bullet from a gun.

This ain't California! "This is Garfield."

Sugarbear long and lean kiss two fingers and wag them at Charlene, the most beautiful girl in the world. Charlene drink lemonade with Tammy. Nicki squeeze my hand, she kiss me on my neck. You see what Sugar done! Take him, Sugarbear! Take him, brother!

I watch Nicki when she walk. Got to pay attention. Got to remember. People in the street don't know. Running, running up Roosevelt and slow down past Roosevelt High, past the chain-link fences where brothers throw dice, curbs and brick and old gas station, Two J's, sun hanging up off the street above brick warehouses and the river and the old iron bridges.

Nicki, she light in her step, braids and ponytails. Can't keep my hands off sparkling things, a finger glide slowly from her neck, past her shoulder, down her arm, she glisten soft in July hands, make a humid silk of her skin, rich color where the sun kisses and bends away. Nicki smile at me. She squeeze my hand.

Damn right I'm crying, boy. How many tears you can draw!

"Shhh," *Nicki say.* "It's OK, baby."

Want to sit in the clouds at the top of the world and make flowers with her, but they know about death. Theys death on my hands. Nicki squeeze my hand, she kiss me on my neck. Theys flowers.

How many tears you can draw from one woman!

How I keep slipping. "Theys flowers, Nicki, and..."

"Shhh," *she say.* "It's OK, baby. Look at me. I'm here now. It's OK."

See what you do to your mother. *My chest beating hot and deep. A broken gear catch and hold and then slip and pound hard against its housing. Tears pumping up in my eyes.*

"Is it OK for you?"

"Of course it is, Kid," *Nicki say.* "It's heaven."

You're a good kid, son. Best start acting like it.

A red hibiscus flower fall from the sky and land on the curb.

"Oh, God, no! Oh, God, no!" *somebody ma cry out.*

I watch Nicki. I'm afraid not to watch, afraid she might disappear. Thirteen-years-old and I can't keep my hands off things that sparkle. Her nose, her lips, her cheeks and her lips again, all flowers, more and more flowers. Sun lick up yellow flames on tangerine-flake fender, green sparkle from a long potassium tongue, beat fire hydrant force reds, shoot white-blue water on steaming oil-stained street, white letters on black rubber wrap silver rims, hum hot under disco-gold Chevy Nova, liquid gold, burnt chrome, steel blue like a blowtorch. She let me watch, Nicki let me touch her flowers. Her cheek, her lips, the corners of her mouth, her shoulders. She give me her flowers.

"What did I do wrong, boy," *she ask me*, "to have my son end up like this?"

"*Please don't cry, Ma. I'm real sorry.*"

"Too much talk of flowers from that mouth of yours. All the while throwing fists in every direction. Flowers in one breath, cuss words the next. You're going to have to grow up one day, before it's too late. Flowers and fists! Who can believe a boy like that? You can't believe yourself."

In the daytime I believe just fine. When I'm with Nicki, I believe just fine. A young whelp with chin lifted above the horizon, looking down an adolescent nose. A camera snap.

"And in the night?" *Ma say.* "Talk to me about the nighttime, boy!"

I can't seem to answer. My chin lift, my eyes turn black. I shut it out. Canary and blood-red paint on plate glass window, revolution posters, street-soldier silhouette in the crosshairs of a rifle scope, Blue Note and Verve, brass horns and black vinyl, Bird's long cool burgundy Cadillac with crisp white ragtop, listen to my nine-millimeter go bang!

"Talk to me about the nighttime, boy!"

"*It's daylight out, Ma.*"

"You're dreaming again! Stop fooling yourself, boy. You're sick again, aren't you?"

I can't find an answer. I shut it out. Bird look up from behind the counter, easy brown muscles peak and dip below a white tank undershirt. Gin and tonic with ice and bright green lime in a tall glass that bead wet. He smile wide like a great cat. So smooth his laughter, soft, soft, purring like a long, low cat. Sssssss, black cat.

3   On courting princesses

In which Sandoval calls out a
princess and Calvin flaunts his
riches.

The month of May ushered in the region's famed coastal
weather and ripened the fruit of Calvin's hopes for a honeyed future
with Klarysa. The inebriating qualities of late spring and young love
forced his hand when, upon hearing the buzz of the *parlophone*, he
looked down from the balcony and spotted Sandoval's massive
curly-topped cranium bobbing impatiently in the alleyway. Instead
of waiting quietly for him to bugger off, Calvin answered the call,
though not without having a stitch of fun at Sandoval's expense.

It was unnecessary of Calvin to visually identify Sandoval from
the balcony, as Sandoval was the only imbecile on earth who leaned
on a buzzer for a good minute. It was a standard non-verbal
proclamation of his annoyance at the inhabitant's virtually
inescapable failure to answer the call within two or three seconds.
Sandoval was meticulous and demanding and had a magnificent
attention span. He was also lousy with impatience and proud of the
fact. He was enamoured with the line *You got to want it*, and was
convinced that any man who practiced patience simply didn't want it
badly enough.

Calvin waited at the *parlophone* for another half-minute to let
Sandoval stew in his boots. Finally, he answered. "Hello?" said
Calvin questioningly, as though he weren't entirely certain the
buzzer had sounded.

"Hallo, *you* in there!" flew from Sandoval's cavernous gob. "What the hell took you so long to answer the—"

Calvin toggled the switch to make the line crackle.

"Can you *hear* me?" Sandoval barked. "I say! Can you hear me?"

Absolutely nothing annoyed him as did having to repeat himself.

"Who's there!" Calvin demanded, feigning annoyance of his own.

"It's *San*doval!"

"Sandoval, is that you?"

"Sweet Christ *yes* it's me!"

"Must be a short in the line. Repeat, Sandoval, repeat!"

Sweat sizzled on his brow. "I *said*," he began, but then paused to see if he might fool the crackling line. It worked. "I said you'll never get anywhere with that *loose* attitude of yours! For crissake, Calvin, take control of your life!"

"I'm working on it," said Calvin. "Have a little patience."

"Sure! As if *I'm* going to stand by and wait for *you* to…"

But Calvin had rung off.

Sandoval's family had moved from Puerto Rico to Brooklyn, New York, when Sandoval was just a big fat baby. Having arrived in the US with little more than a will to succeed, the family made good on its crap-shot at the American Dream. Sandoval was the first in his family to attend university and he made the most of the opportunity. He was smarter than most, worked harder than all and rather effortlessly eschewed the troubles and temptations that face so many of America's young inner-city minorities. His accomplishments were the result of his own enterprise and hard work. In turn, he had no sympathy whatsoever for any fellow who hadn't the wherewithal to pull himself up and out of the gutter. So too, he was envenomed by the mere whisper of the next wave of immigrants benefitting in any small way from his hard-fought gains, and lobbied passionately to have the full perimeter of the lower forty-eight sealed off once and for all time with concrete ramparts and razor wire. His voice boomed with military combativeness and intolerance. *You have to have confidence* was one of the inane pep-rally lines he was known to roar, as though confidence were a simple matter of choice, a mere flower for the picking and one which the world's low and grovelling lot chose to indolently dismiss.

His enthusiastic rhetoric notwithstanding, Sandoval was one of the most frightened and cantankerous fellows Calvin had ever known. He kept three guns stashed throughout his Brooklyn home and recounted with disconnected zeal all the advantages to each ingenious hiding place. Why, should a spirited band of miscreants burrow beneath the city streets and force entry through the impregnable concrete foundation of his Brooklyn basement – which would undoubtedly occur, he insisted; it was only a matter of time, the borough was going to hell – oh, the welcome it would receive upon entry. (Upon first hearing of Sandoval's guns, Calvin reflected upon the day some years back, when, in response to a sudden pinch of vulnerability, he marched off with defensive vigour and purchased an expensive suit and tie combination, which he wore proudly and securely home from the tailor's and not once again thereafter.)

Sandoval had succeeded in admirable fashion and was stout in his conviction that anyone who wanted it badly enough could have it. In all his blessed days and nights, not once did he consider that he may just have been the most talented, hardest working, flat out luckiest jerk on the face of the earth.

Calvin and Sandoval went and paid a call to Zachary Tiller. Tiller led a sentimental starry-eyed existence above the *Marché aux Fleurs*. He was a regular fellow from an unknown town in Kansas or Oklahoma, a town that had lost favour with the spectacular imminent end of the twentieth century. Once a land rich with zinc and lead, the town had been mechanically raped, chemically poisoned, rendered a worthless and murderous wasteland and finally returned to the Native American tribe from which the government had originally stolen it. Tiller was a gracious, generous pushover whose greatest weakness was romance. He spent his days in love with the idea of being in love. The achilles of the affair was women, and the fact that one of them would inevitably get in the way and muck up the works. Occasionally a demure young woman would wilt under the weight of his dedicated poetry, his moon-lit prose and sugar-glazed couplets, and at the stroke of a sultry midnight, cuddling at the edge of the sea, with its wavelets licking the shore and the snuggled collection of their twenty toes all in a row, Tiller would coo Pablo Neruda's *Clenched Soul* in a smooth tenor: "'Why will the whole of love come on me suddenly when I am sad and feel you are far away?'"

But she would interrupt him, a-burst with fatal emotion, "Enough! Here I am! I love you, Zachary. I always have and I always will!"

To which he would cry, "Hold on a god-blamed second. I'm not done yet! 'The book fell that always closed at twilight and my blue sweater—'"

"But Zachary, take me now!"

"Blast you, Marie! What the devil has gotten into you?"

The expansive, full-throttled love, the kind that wanted to entangle itself in the limbs and mental webbings of living breathing bodies, was not the kind of love for Zachary Tiller. He preferred his love in the form of a concise, petrified nut with no chance of cracking. He wanted his love to be static and immobile, preferably in theoretical or literary form. Anything ruddy and kinetic – wet lips, probing tongues, hungry hands – scared the hell out of him. He cultivated a liquid love culture in the bottom of a glass from which he would never drink. He would slosh it about with dedication and study the viscous legs than ran suggestively down the sides of the glass, but never would he bring the beaker to his lips. At the edge of any affair, Tiller would turn into an anxiety-riddled beast. He would poison the arrangement before it could flourish, break it off and then run away, weepy and lovesick, to face alone what was at once his newest affliction and oldest panacea. It was not difficult to like Tiller. He was sweet and lost. His voice reached one softly, as though his words had been run through a filter of freshly gathered hydrangea petals. His greatest quality was his complete lack of cynicism, though now and again he would say something so annoyingly innocent that one fantasised of doing him the great service of slapping the gullibility clean from his sticky gob.

Having collected Tiller, the three made off in search of cold beer and a warm terrace. Despite Sandoval's protests, they took a table on the terrace of the Bar de la Degustation, overlooking the fountain in the Place du Palais de Justice. Sandoval detested the cut of life that congregated on the steps of the Palais de Justice and in the alleyway leading away towards Place Rossetti and Les Deux Frères. Sandoval had speculated on the future of Nice, purchasing several properties in the old town, and anything that vaguely threatened his net worth set his nerves on edge.

"Someone around here had better start cleaning up these streets, before the whole goddamned town is infested. Tourists don't want to see all this," he warned, moving his hand generally about in the air. "And without a healthy tourist industry, you watch what happens to your property values."

"When you say *your*—" began Calvin.

"I mean *mine*," he growled, ever-unappreciative that Calvin's inability to crack the housing market translated to a lack of concern for the future present value of Sandoval's financial holdings.

"You see a fellow with a tattoo, Sandoval," said Tiller mildly, "and you want him locked up."

Sandoval shrugged. "I'm not the only one. Gem would agree with me."

"No he wouldn't," said Calvin.

"It's funny how much my frustrations ruffle you two, but neither of you have anything to say about Gem when he runs about town cleaning up the alleyways."

"You and Gem are both from the streets," noted Calvin, "but that's where the commonalities end. Gem loves the streets; you hate them. Gem pokes his fists at a very specific bloke or two when he feels – rightly or wrongly, you're free to decide – the fellow has it coming to him. You, on the other hand, connive and lobby and write checks and, when you're at your best, take down countless innocents who haven't the wherewithal to dodge the line of fire.

"I play by the rules," said Sandoval unbendingly. "I follow the laws."

"Bah, you write the rules; you make the laws."

"Someone has to. There are very few true victims in life, Calvin."

The sparring continued through the clinking of glasses, the bids of good health and the swilling of beer, and when the topic had finally been run into the ground without concurrence or resolution, they let it fall.

"How is it going with Klarysa, anyway?" asked Sandoval with the look of disdain he reserved for any financially poor fellow who nevertheless appeared to be at ease.

"Grand," said Calvin. "I'm going to see her next week."

"In Barcelona? How good of you. She's been here to see you enough times."

"True. It's not as though I haven't offered to do the travelling, mind you. She said it's better for her to come here."

"Better?" asked Tiller. "How come?"

Calvin shrugged.

"I'll tell you why," Sandoval offered. "Because princesses get on very well in France."

"*Prin*cess? What do you mean by calling her a princess?"

"Don't get wet, Calvin, it's just an observation."

"A poor one. The family is bankrupt."

"*Bank*rupt?" said Sandoval incredulously. "Not a chance. Bankrupt girls don't dress like that. Don't walk like that, either. Doesn't she work?"

"She studies. She's a student."

"A *stu*dent? A student of what?"

"Hell, I don't know," said Calvin. "International relations."

Sandoval looked away with narrowed eyes, recalling a leftover rogan josh that had gotten pushed to the back of the frigo and that would soon go off if not eaten. He repeated pensively, "*Bank*rupt. Huh."

"What now," Calvin reluctantly demanded.

"Nothing. I was just trying to decide if you had the moxie, the pluck to make it with a bankrupt princess. No, *you* stop it, Calvin—she's a princess all right. And I decided you just might have a chance with her… *if* she weren't so good-looking. But she is. So no, you're sunk."

Sandoval recounted the story of a former flame called Vanessa, whose family hailed from Lafayette, Louisiana, once knew great wealth and status and boasted the effortless tracing of family lines back to early-nineteenth-century French royalty. Vanessa was embittered not by the decimation of the family bank account, but by the loss of status and, moreover, recognition. She tirelessly sought out those who might corroborate her class and uniqueness, and found more than a few, owing largely to her perky breasts, shapely legs and bushy-tailed derriere—trophies not confined to any dusty or venerable trophy case. Not many suitors, however, qualified. She approved of almost no one; not even the wealthy. In fact, the only lot she disapproved of more than the poor and the monolingual were the *nouveaux-riches* (a label that adhered itself to a preposterous majority of America's rich), whose vulgar comportment betrayed an ignorance as to the proper carriage of old money, true wealth.

Tiller hypothesised left-handedly on Calvin's behalf, "Hanging one's hat on Calvin's hook is bound to bring few opportunities for advancement – be they social or financial – and yet Klarysa seems to go for him just fine."

"Why, thank you, Zachary."

"I have considered that, Till," admitted Sandoval with a raised eyebrow. "It is all very perplexing."

"Why, Sandoval, does the prospect of true love have no bearing in your world?"

"Listen, Till, you keep your heals dug into any relationship for more than two weeks and then you can speak on the matter. Look, Calvin, I'm only concerned for your wellbeing. I'd hate to see you run over by this dame. She's a challenge, that one. It's obvious."

"What woman isn't challenging, Sandoval?" said Calvin.

"Sure, but you're lazy."

"We have different pursuits, you and me. That doesn't make me lazy."

"I mean to say you're a dreamer and an idealist when it comes to relationships. You can't handle the grind, Calvin. You don't believe in relationships that come with thorns and require work. And if you want the truth from someone who knows, you don't have the finances to court a princess."

"What load of rubbish!" chimed Tiller. "The only thing that matters to you, Sandoval, is finances."

Sandoval held a long shrug of prideful concurrence.

Calvin wanted to respond, wanted to deny Sandoval his claims, but too many wheels were turning at once. None of Sandoval's observances were blatantly false, but they were historical observances voiced long after Calvin had consciously resolved to approach his new relationship with patience, acceptance and thoughtfulness. Calvin was determined to better himself and Sandoval had no confidence that he might succeed.

Calvin, however, found Sandoval's notions of Klarysa to be a bit more troubling. There was indeed something about her, the tiniest mercurial something that might divert one's attention from the task at hand for just a wee instance, just long enough to cause one to knick the thumbnail with the chopping knife instead of the carrots on the cutting board. Nothing ominous, but something—a challenging something, as Sandoval had noted. Calvin had likewise acknowledged a slightly firmer grip on the handlebars in easing the early stages of his relationship with Klarysa in the right direction. There was nothing questionable or taxing in his efforts, nothing laborious. Quite simply, and for the first time in his life with such wakeful consciousness, he had committed himself to the work and had given himself over to the grind that was common to all intimate relationships. He was happy to commit, so desperately did he long to succeed in his relationship with Klarysa. He was eager to do his best, eager to invest every ounce of the patience and attention currently in reserve from having shamefully economised such currencies when with Victoria.

Sandoval's self-satisfaction brought Tiller to blush. "You never dream of stepping out and taking a chance, Sandoval," he said. "I ad*mire* Calvin. It's true he's a glutton for punishment and makes rash decisions. True, too, that he'll readily cut off his nose to spite his face and will flay himself open on any given Wednesday morning just to make sure he's still bleeding red. And there's that idea of his of pain as a ready reminder of one's humanity and fragility—"

Calvin interrupted, "Get to the compliment, for crissake."

"Right. The point is: Calvin takes chances. He lives life, Sandoval! You would never dream of taking the risks he takes."

"Risks? That's not risk-taking!" Sandoval objected. "You, Tiller, have apparently been fooled by all the smoke and whistles," he railed, as though Calvin weren't present. "You seem to think a real train is coming through. But there's no train; Calvin is all smoke and whistle. When the going gets tough, when the resistance becomes too great, he bows out, retreats or rolls the dice – what you consider taking a risk – and sets himself back two paces. Then he'll regain the two paces at some later date, call it a profit and celebrate like he's won an award. But it's all just relative gains. There's nothing *real* about his successes. Chart his progress over the course of any given day and he appears to be a successful little ragamuffin. Why, at any hour of the day he can be found lounging in the sun somewhere singing the praises of monks or celebrating the advent of the croissant. Chart his progress over a ten year period, though, and the line is dead flat."

Finally poking his dire face at Calvin, who was slouching so low in his chair it seemed he might slide out of it, Sandoval continued, "You're not actually gaining any ground the way you live. It's all just a lot of wasted motion without going anywhere. For crissake, Calvin, how many hours, how many *days* have you spent throwing stones into that goddamned sea? You're not *gett*ing anywhere. Don't you see you're just paddling upstream and staying in the same place?"

"I thought we were talking about Klarysa," replied Calvin, deadpan.

Any conversation with Sandoval might start off pleasantly in Timbuktu, but he had an uncanny knack for twisting it into an argument and bringing it back home to rest on the deficiencies and missteps of whomever it was he was speaking with. Calvin had always wished he were able to let such disapproval wash over him without burning. He inched up slightly higher in his seat and reached for his beer. Tiller took up the argument on his behalf.

Calvin pursued the life he felt best suited him – which some would argue is quite an accomplishment in itself – though he was fairly tormented by his lack of eloquence in articulating a defence of self against detractors, such as Sandoval.

The waiter at Degustation was an ancient fellow. Calvin watched him admiringly as he made his way towards them with another round. He set the beer on the table and Calvin paid the round. The old man thanked him, flashed a wink and a smile and moved off to the next table. Calvin never took his eyes from the old fellow, watching him as he went, recognising that he felt for the old waiter something akin to the feelings of admiration reserved by children for their greatest heroes. In their truest and most unrecognised sense, such feelings do not flower from any longing for fame or fortune, but from a longing to know the warm glow of assurance and security that tends to emanate with blinding radiance from one's heroes.

Calvin suddenly saw the old man as the personification of his defence of himself and his present path. The crafty old *Niçois* in the autumn of his life, still fit and trim and quick of mind, still engaged in life, integrated and relevant, zipping about with energy, laughing with the young and the old and slinging about beers on a sunny terrace. This man was the personification of Calvin's argument. And that was what Sandoval would never come to understand: it wasn't that the folks who followed a different philosophy than his were lazy, or even that they were opposed to a padded a bank account. It was that most of them were not willing to live the life of heavy sacrifice required to pad a bank account. It was often a matter of choice, a matter of values, and Sandoval expected his American values to hold rank throughout the world.

Newly inspired, Calvin fired back, "What's wrong with maintaining ground, paddling upstream, as you say? Do you not see the beauty in the stroke and motion? Why, can't a fellow just make motions for the sake of making motions, for the sake of working out the head and heart? Where, exactly, are all you over-achievers racing off to, anyway?"

"Retirement. That's where. *Early* retirement!"

Sandoval wasn't quite so facile a beast as that, but there was honesty in his response.

"Re*tire*ment, you say. If that's the case, then I must be your role model."

"Like hell you are."

"No? I retired before the age of thirty."

"Pah!" Sandoval spat. "You still scurry about like a rat from job to job."

"Perhaps," admitted Calvin. "But a well-fed rat."

Calvin's main source of income was gutting and cleaning fish brought into port by small charter boats—fish for folks in foreign lands who preferred theirs beheaded and skinned before making it to the plate. Occasionally he tended bar at velvety affairs on the yachts in Cannes and Antibes, lent a hand to the gardening staff at the estate of a famous Swiss *chocolatier* on Cap d'Antibes, looked after a friend's magazine kiosk near the Galleries Lafayette when the friend was sick or away on holiday, and for several weeks during the summer helped Madame Andretta set up vegetable stalls before sunrise at the market on Cours Saleya. For his efforts he earned fair wages, ate a seal's catch of fresh fish and seafood, vegetables to last the winter, sustained a golden tan, danced 'til dawn and drank perhaps a bit more than is healthy.

"I'll give you this much," patronised Sandoval, "you manage a great tan and you eat well."

"Which alone makes me a hell of a lot better Puerto Rican than you are."

"The honour is all yours. The problem is you're broke. Which, incidentally, helps you in your pursuit as champion of Third World—"

"Broke? Impossible! I'm a millionaire. It's true I haven't the damnedest notion where all the money is, but I must be a millionaire. How else could I afford this millionaire lifestyle? Sea and sun all day, fresh seafood and veg and good wines every night, croissants and coffee on sunny French Riviera terraces every morning, friends on every corner, security benefits of the Fifth Republic, exotic weekends and holidays. Look around you, you big dope—we've got everything a fellow could ever want and most of it is all but free! Hell, while you slave away in your glass and aluminium box, I'm living out your golden retirement, with all the good juice still in my bones no less! How the hell you can waste the best part of your young, healthy days and nights, so that you might sequester yourself away in some sprawling mansion with rooms you'll never set foot in, when you're old and irrelevant, is beyond me."

It was all a bit over the top, but Calvin had submitted to Sandoval's condescension and disapproval for years. He was in love, was on a good and frothy roll and was going for broke; to hell if he should make a fool of himself. Sandoval had opened his mouth to protest, but Calvin halted him.

"What a sad and angry bull you are, Sandoval! Try laughing a little for crissake. No bank balance or title is going to fill your heart with joy. By god, you're dead before you've even reached retirement! Re*tire*ment. Ha! Then you're really going to cut loose, is that it? You've missed the whole point of life, which is to actually *live* a bit of it. You're already dead and buried, you! We are who we are, Sandoval. If you're not laughing to-day, you're not going to magically start laughing in your retirement. Dreaming of a grand future is fine, but not at the expense of one's youth."

Sandoval, having listened to every word of Calvin's rant, was as moved as a slain elephant. "You think your princess will buy all that rot?"

4   A return to forever

In which Calvin stares down
ghosts and laments the condition
of his boots.

The crescent moon hung an easy lopsided grin, not so high
above the decadence describing the port of Antibes. Women danced
barefoot on teak decking while their men, who had addressed the
yacht just hours prior, combed and composed, now wrestled in great
orgy and fell akimbo into the sea, where a good many of them, in
chain reaction, offered up a medley of five-course dinners to the
nocturnal water-beasts of the Mediterranean. Galas on Nightmare
Nolan's yacht were boozy, high-watt affairs.

Calvin, having worked the bar that night, was accused by one of
the guests (pretty and leggy, she, but cold and insecure and anchored
by unseasonal restraint) of having ushered too many an upstanding
gentleman to the brink of alcohol poisoning and drowning and,
worse yet, high-society embarrassment. This, she accused, as the
husband cannon-balled the foredeck Jacuzzi wearing naught but a
black bow-tie and a lace garter belt too great in circumference to be
that of his wife. It is true that Calvin had never slopped together
drinks at such a rabid pace or with such slapdash accuracy. It went
against everything he held in the way of veneration for the barman's
craft and it pained him, but that raving bourgeois lot had long
overshot the point of discerning a Sazerac from a Slippery Nipple. It
mattered not what he sloshed up onto the bar top, they took to it with
an apocalyptic bent, dumping drink after drink down their gullets, as

though each man had seated within him not a tissue-lined stomach, but a galvanised spittoon. Naturally, someone would have to pay the price. By the small hours, the contours of elegance and grace had given way to the weighty shapelessness of gross indulgence and feral instinct. It was a free-for-all.

When the last of the guests had gone home or gone down to bed below deck, Calvin trudged down the gangway and on to the quay with thoughts of home and bed and with a gorilla fatigue pounding heavily upon his shoulders. He hadn't gone far, when he heard the wail of a lone wolf ripping through the cool morning stillness, echoing hauntingly off the ramparts. Aroused by whatever genetic vestiges of the beast remain within domesticated Man to acknowledge the call of the wild, Calvin turned to doff his cap in a show of respect. It was only then that he recalled the fact that there were no wolves on the Cote d'Azur. On a slim stretch of golden beach given to by an archway built into the thick stone ramparts, Calvin spied a sad black Labrador retriever, howling, bawling, suffering a criminal's ration of verbal and physical abuse from its down-and-out and drunken owner. Good lord, thought Calvin. Welcome to the slaughterhouse, old boy.

Over the course of the night, Calvin had received several interesting employment proposals. As an agreeable and appreciative lad with a natural flair for mixing a good drink, he was highly eligible on the Cote d'Azur and many of the guests at the yacht parties expressed desires to do him a good turn, to give him work or rent him a flat at discount or otherwise be his saviour. He had come to learn, however, that no job secured during such soirées could be counted on. On one occasion, Calvin presented himself at a villa on the Monday morning following a proper Saturday night affair only to be informed by the unexcitable staff that his would-be employer had been committed to hospital for a good stomach pumping. Likewise, there were chairmen, board members and presidents with whom he had spent nights locked arm-in-arm, yowling burlesque tunes, recounting racy jokes and agreeing to the terms of potentially lucrative deals, only to show up the following day at the villa, the pier or the restaurant to find his champion with no recollection of the preceding night, unable to recognise Calvin from Mohammed, and accusing him of solicitation, all the while threatening to exercise a direct line with the commissariat.

Among other engagements secured for the week, Calvin arranged to help Nightmare Nolan process a skiff of Dorade Royale. To clarify, lest one wrongly jump to the conclusion that yacht proprietors scrape fish guts in their spare time, Nightmare Nolan was no yacht proprietor. To be sure, yacht proprietors are not so named, not even in jest. Nightmare was a deckhand, plain and simple, and nightmarish in terms of mischief. *Nightmare Nolan's yacht*, then, should be understood to mean the yacht on which Nightmare worked.

After scaling and gutting a skiff of fish, a fellow carries the odour with him for the following day or two and wakes in the night with fish scales biting his ankles. The pay, however, which includes a bucket of fresh fish, if one is working for the right monger, was decent. Calvin would wash off at the end of the day by taking long deep strokes to the bottom of the sea. He would dive in off the white break wall that protected the Nice port, where the sea floor falls quickly away and the water turns sapphire; hold his breath and dive deeper, deeper until his ears popped and the water turned cold and refreshing—a depth that was adequate for cleansing, apologising, praying, accepting. And then charging quickly to the surface for air, where a silk-blue sky hung patiently, waiting to wrap his wet baptised head. And sometimes he would realise he still smelt of fish, but so too that it was OK.

On the eve of any holiday, Calvin preferred to usher in the holiday spirit with a dinner at a decent restaurant and a cocktail or two at one of the finer hotel bars. On the eve of his trip to Barcelona, he looked in at the Rive Bleue, found the bar sufficiently lively and took a table near to where a skilled pianist occupied himself with uninspiring jazz standards and lounge numbers.

Just as Calvin was served a drink, however, the pianist changed course, sliding deftly into a moving rendition of Chic Corea's *Where Have I Known You Before*, and from there, directly into the epic *Song to the Pharaoh Kings*. As the last notes died on the piano wires, Calvin applauded and cheered, "Chick Corea! Hot damn!"

The pianist was a slender gentleman on the approach towards middle-age, a man of notable refinement. He nodded modestly at Calvin, picked a wineglass from the piano top with lithe fingers and sipped what looked to be a Cahors. With the wineglass still in hand, he eyed the keys rather pensively and tickled a short succession of minor chords. Finally, he rose from his bench and traversed the short stretch of marble to Calvin's table. Extending a hand to Calvin, he smiled kindly and enquired, "Your name is Jack, no?"

Calvin gripped the man's hand. It was shrew-brown and softer than suede. He looked into the man's eyes and sensed himself tripping uncomfortably down a lost *paseo* of forgotten ghosts and blurred remembrances. "Afraid not," he replied. "Name's Calvin."

"Hmm."

The pianist eyed him quizzically, as though a long-trusted map had steered him in the wrong direction. Then, instantly forgiving the map, he said good-naturedly, "Beg pardon; you look like someone."

"Jack?" Calvin shot curtly.

"Right. Jack. Funny how that happens." And with the slightest bow, he headed back towards the black baby grand.

Calvin, still grasping uneasily at the vague straws of familiarity, surprised himself by calling after the fellow, "It is a clever ruse, that."

"I'm sorry?"

"Bah, we *don't* know each other. That's all." It was an attempt to convince himself as much as the pianist.

"Fine, fine," said the pianist, nodding gentlemanly consent.

"Regardless of your playlist, I mean."

The man stopped and turned once again to face Calvin, though he had shelved his former air of acquiescence. "Excuse me?" he challenged. "Playlist?" A light plum stain tinted his fine Iberian features. "When was it you last heard Chick Corea follow Mel Tormé? I assure you I do my best to craft my sets to the perceived tastes and sensibilities of the crowd, which is ever in flux."

"Why, you don't mean to say the Chick Corea number was intended for me."

"Of course."

"But how did you know—"

"Call it a gift."

"Well then," began Calvin somewhat suspiciously, "my apologies. You hit the mark."

Calvin adored Chick Corea, not only for his compositions and performances, but for his foundation of the jazz fusion group Return to Forever.

"But why that number?" Calvin pressed.

"*Pharaoh Kings?*"

"No—*Where Have I Known You Before*. What are you insinuating? Admit it, neither of us knows Jack."

The pianist bestowed upon Calvin the smile of a patient professor for a talented but underachieving student. "I would bet," he said with a playful wink, "we both know quite a bit."

Calvin, who had long quit American idiomatic expressions – they only confused in Nice – had failed to recognise his own pun, and so he heard in the pianist's reply, not a playful response, but an allusion to a mutually held secret.

"Good evening," bade the pianist, retreating to the piano, leaving in his wake a subtle scent of dark chocolate and sandalwood.

Easing himself onto the bench, he took a draught of wine and began to play anew, skilfully addressing a few more Chic Corea numbers from the same album. The cleanliness of his solo renditions left the onus of fusion to the listener. One familiar with the original versions could not help but mentally reintroduce Di Meola's guitar and Stanley Clark's double bass, and in doing so, catalyse a return to former days, places, memories inspired by youth, young love and musical genius. Calvin, now under the influence of the complex time signature and singular rhythmic pattern (not to mention the ruby dose of bourbon and port) returned to a Spanish corridor that was sad-patterned with gorgeous nostalgia, sanguine stained and bittersweet and now too, thanks to Klarysa's presence in Calvin's life, newly *florecido* with rose moss, spring-green and spotted with carnival-coloured blooms. For Calvin, the return to forever was largely a return to Barcelona—much more than a city, an evidently recurring theme of cracked and gilded timelessness, of endless lives and loves, of new beginnings and old ends.

At next break, Calvin waved the pianist over to his table.

"Have a seat?" he suggested.

The pianist sat, easy as a diplomat.

"I believe," said Calvin, "I've cracked your code."

Had he a gat, he may well have brandished it just then.

"You've peculiar mannerisms," admitted the pianist.

"I tend to speak with my mouth, not jazz compositions. *Where Have I Known You Before*? You play better than you communicate. But what if I had not recognised that number? Would you have eventually come out and asked me? The jig, sir, as they say, is up."

"The *jig*?" begged the pianist.

Calvin winced at the confused idiom. "Look, Harlan," he said directly, but there came no reaction from the pianist. "You *are* Harlan, right?"

"Harlan?" begged the pianist with some confusion.

It was a ridiculous attempt, Calvin admitted to himself. He knew, after all, that the pianist was not Harlon, his former arch-nemesis, the Spaniard who had stolen Victoria's heart—if one could ever own another's heart that it might one day be stolen.

"No. My name is Hector—"

"*De donde eres*, Hector?"

"Spain. Castelldefels. *Sabes*—"

"*Si*. Catalunya. Southwest of Barcelona."

"Right. Are you familiar with—"

"Barcelona? Yes. Castelldefels? No."

"Do you always eat the ends of others'…" he paused for the interruption, but Calvin had fatigued and given up. "Nothing. That's better."

"Bah, have a drink," said Calvin. "My apologies; I was following a line."

"What sort of line?"

A tuxedoed waiter appeared at Hector's shoulder without having been signalled. It was not Hector's first time in a classy bar. He knew all the angles.

"The kind I often follow and typically regret," replied Calvin. "The crooked and broken variety. I blame curiosity."

"I don't believe it is fair to blame curiosity for a basket of unfavourable results," said Hector.

The Spaniard pulled a biro from his jacket and wrote on a cocktail napkin. He folded the napkin and holding it between his index and middle fingers raised it as though looking to have a ticket stub validated. The waiter, still docked at his shoulder, took the napkin and disappeared.

"Curiosity is static," continued Hector, stowing his biro. "As static as Garibaldi's frozen lions," he said, in reference to the statue in the centre of Place Garibaldi, "iron bolted to their stone pedestal and staring back for all eternity towards the homeland of the proud Carbonari."

"Fine. Have it your way—curiosity is inert and the success or failure of any man is a burden born strictly in the gut of his own actions. Still," Calvin concluded, "I will ever contend that life is simpler for the less curious."

"But I never said that curiosity is inert. I said it is static. A rock is inert. You will agree that there is great difference between a rock and a sleeping lion, though neither may move. As for the simplicity of life of the less curious, by *simpler*, do you mean to say less difficult or less complex?"

"I mean to say life attacks the less curious with a limited set of household blades. What's the difference, anyway? Complexity implies difficulty."

"What's the difference?" echoed Hector with reproof. "Have you no appreciation for the power and beauty of your own language? So many words to choose from. If only you had the curiosity for it."

"Listen, curiosity is not my problem. These bones could benefit from a little less curiosity. My problem is that my tongue tends to conspire against me. The trouble I might have avoided over the years if it weren't for this wayward gob."

"Precisely. Clearly, you need to pay closer mind to your words. Look, there is always a difference, a difference between any two words, emotions or intentions. Life is neither static nor inert. Realities are in constant flux, changing with every passing second, thereby making every second valuable."

Hector shot a disapproving eye at the waiter behind the bar and with an index finger tapped thrice on the face of his watch. The waiter returned a seasick smile and shot through a swinging door with a porthole.

"At any rate," he continued, "do not blame curiosity for the troubles you may encounter. Life is a matter of style and strategy, a matter of presentation. It is the way in which we manifest our curiosities – *how* we wake the sleeping lion, if you will – that dictates a taming of the beast or an arena-style mauling. Perhaps what you want to say is that curiosity holds no relevance for those who put forth no effort to remember or revisit their memories. For what is the point of forcing the flower of one's curiosities if there is no desire to remember its colour and scent? Listen, if one asks of propagating the breed, the answer is procreation. If one asks of self-preservation, however – a topic much closer to the heart of modern man, for he is a wildly egotistical and insecure beast – the answer is remembrance. By keeping alive the past, through remembrance, Man hopes to extend the window of his own existence, that he might stitch his loop in the grand fabric of time. There is no legacy without memory. Do you want to be remembered, Calvin?"

"Hell, I don't know. I've never thought about it. Legacies aren't typically assigned to fellows like me."

"Well, I believe you, even though dreamers are the consummate rememberers."

"What," said Calvin, "gives you the idea that I'm a dreamer?"

Hector didn't deign to answer; he only smiled.

"Fine," Calvin conceded. "But I remember as a means of…" he searched for adequate words. "My memories are rich and bold. Hell if I haven't a whole raving gallery of them and I rather cherish most of them, in part because I know they are the only treasures I'll ever possess."

"Very nice," said Hector, with sincerity. "Anyway, as memories have increasingly become a currency of the ego – a postulation, sure, but supported by the fact that every generation has assigned greater value to the notion of legacy than the generation to have preceded it – the act of remembering, which is, in its truest form, selfless, has largely undergone a mutation."

"How so? Think we could get another drink around here?"

"Why, no entity is ever remembered, per se, as much as the lingering vestiges of an entity are *used* by the living in the same manner that supplemental dietary vitamins and spiritual wadding are used: to correct deficiencies and fill voids—deficits born of a fear of mortality and non-existence, poverties that seem to grow with the passing of each generation."

"I don't know. Here we are, two strangers remembering Chick Corea and Return to Forever."

"Sure, but how does Chick benefit from our remembrances? How does Van Gogh, who died a miserable paint-eating wretch, benefit from the genius status granted him to-day? If a thing does not know it is being remembered, then any homage is homage only to the living, by the living, and for the living. We pay homage only to appease our own egos, and the perceived need to pay homage extends directly from our own desires to be remembered and admired."

"What discourse! But what is it you truly lament—curiosity as a mistaken scapegoat, or the failure of the living to selflessly remember?"

"My boy, you will find that I lament neither. On the contrary, my curiosity cannot be contained and regardless of the manifestations of my curiosities, be they miracles or atrocities, the memorial grout of my name will only ever be used to fill spiritual cracks in the psychic walls of my survivors. We die and we die quickly, and how the living choose to play with the trinkets and trifles left in the vaporous wakes of our departure is irrelevant."

The waiter, having finally returned, set a glass of red wine and a Ruby Manhattan on the table. As far as Calvin could tell, neither had been ordered. The waiter handed Hector a cocktail napkin that was origamically folded into a rudimentary thistle, or a crown. Hector shook his head before unfolding it, and again when he finished reading it. "No, no," he denied the waiter. "*Dites-lui que nous avons eu un accord.*" The waiter nodded humidly and left.

"Do you like to gamble, Calvin?"

The two touched glasses and drank.

Calvin waggled a nonpartisan shoulder in response to the question. "Not really. I enjoy the occasional wager if I have a hand in the outcome. I find the role of invested spectator to be perfectly agonising."

"But a bet is a bet…"

"Someone told me that there is always a difference," said Calvin, one brow agreeably arched with leveraged wisdom.

Delight squeezed in next to Hector and put a hand on his richly clothed knee.

"One approaches any fix," Calvin elucidated, "with secret knowledge as to how he has personally fared in similar situations. Then he can long or short himself, so to speak. Such a fellow has inside information."

"It is true that one should never bet on a man who won't bet on himself, and there is equal authority in the converse, *if* the subject has a sufficiently sober character, of course."

Encouraged by the pleasant exchange, Calvin added, "I may even give odds if I like the angles." Self-consciousness forced him to disclaim, "Though I never said it's been a terribly lucrative tack."

"You know," said Hector, watching his own hand tamp an unlit cigarette on the wooden arm of the chair, beyond the edge of the velour upholstering that offered the elbow a cushioned respite, "confidence is paramount in my line of work."

"Can't afford clammy palms when you're tickling the ivory, now can you."

"I am a good deal more concerned with clammy palms before customs officials."

Hector gave his wine glass an aerating whirl and watched the legs streak down into a blood-red pool. The easy murmur of the barroom and the still blue sea, which had until that point hummed softly in Calvin's ears, was popped by the spiky lyric of the words *customs officials*.

"Why, you've stopped eating the ends of my sentences," said Hector with a gamely smile.

"My apologies for that. I was rather taken aback. I thought I smelt a conspiracy. You remind me of someone I've not seen in many years, an enemy, if you will."

Funny, thought Calvin, how the word *enemy* seemed archaic, innocent in a way, almost comical.

"Oh," said Hector. "How unfortunate."

"If it's any consolation, I no longer wish him an imminent and excruciating death."

"Don't tell me," he said, leaning in to flit the backs of two fingertips against the shin of Calvin's trousers, "the dashing rogue stole your girl, ha-ha."

Calvin turned cold. "Does any other crime," he replied, "warrant the *enemy* tag? You're wrong about the dashing part, though." Then, assuming the damp smirk of cracked custard, Calvin shot back, "So, you play jazz numbers for customs officials, then."

Just then, a small swarthy-skinned gentleman in a fine lightweight coat approached, becoming the third point of an equilateral triangle. Hector excused himself, stood and allowed himself to be led away by the man in the fine coat.

"Customs official?" wondered Calvin when they were out of earshot. "Bah!"

Left alone, Calvin lost himself in idle thought. He stared with self-consciousness at his boots and thought for the first time in years that the notion of a new pair was not a terrible one. Despite a scrubbing shower at the beach after his swim in the sea, he could still feel the phantom fish scales in his socks. His final thought before Hector's return: How much better the job would be if the fish came dead on arrival. Calvin might poke a back-alley punk in the nose and watch him blow blood bubbles, but clubbing a fish to death was barbaric.

Hector returned and reclaimed his armchair, as one of the waiters wheeled silently past with a dolly stacked five high with fire-branded oak cases of something worthy of packing in fire-branded oak cases. Hector nodded amiably as the waiter passed, then snatched up his wine glass with a flourish and proceeded to seek out the impurities and perfections within. He snapped to as though he'd only just remembered Calvin sitting there. "I'm back," he said cheerfully.

"*Bienvenue*. I take it you're a distributor, then—of sorts."

"Of sorts. I dabble in wine and cigarettes, primarily. And I play piano, but you already know that. What line of business are you in?"

"Me? Why, I dabble in fish, primarily."

Hector drew from his a cigarette. "Fish?" he confirmed with held breath. He exhaled only when Calvin nodded in affirmation and his disappointment was carried away towards the biscuit ceiling on rising strata of steel-blue smoke. They both watched in silence as he tapped out the ashen end of the expiring cigarette in the bottom of the *cendrier*. Hector looked up at Calvin with sudden optimism, certain that he had just discovered the secret silver lining of Calvin's profession. "Dead or alive?" he shot with a wink.

"The fish? Dead. They arrive at the port just fine, but of course we kill them at once."

"Oh, I see," said Hector, with new disappointment. "For eating, actually."

"Yap," said Calvin, throwing back the warm lining of his glass. "For eating. Hook and reel, downriggers and what not. The occasional gaffe, rubber mallet, filet knifes, that whole lot."

"I see. Dead fish. For eating. It's far more lucrative, you know, to trade in living things. Take birds, for example. Can't get enough of them in Barcelona. Typically you're talking ten-peseta parakeets, but there's a hell of a market for the big beauties, the ones with no business this side of the equator. In every building, wire cages dangling in the Catalan sky from empty terraces. Folks have better things to do, it seems, than sit and look at their caged birds. Good that you don't traffic live stuff. It's a horrible racket."

"See here, I don't traffic anything, dead or alive."

"Of course not."

The spectre of conspiracy descended once again around Calvin, though, for all the drink and engaging banter, its presence was accompanied by the scent of benign charm.

Said Calvin softly and with a wry smile, as though baiting a competitor, "Where have I known you before?"

"Ha-ha. Yes. Do you play? The piano is free."

"I don't, thank you. Besides, I must be shoving off shortly."

"There are fish somewhere, I suppose," Hector toyed, "awaiting the queer mercy of your mallet and blade."

"I've bags to pack, actually. I do more than bludgeon sea creatures, you see. I'm off to Barcelona to-morrow," he finished, wondering if he would still smell of Dorade Royale upon arrival.

"Wonderful," said Hector. "How do you travel?"

"By rail. Second class. Correspondence at Portbou."

"How about that, I head off in the very direction to-morrow morning."

"Funny. That should surprise me," said Calvin. "And yet it doesn't in the least. I should marvel the coincidence, and yet the ever-festive bells of coincidence lay in perfect silence."

Responding with equal gamesmanship, Hector said, "I hope you have reserved your seats. You will find we are not the only two en route to Barcelona to-morrow. Of course, reservations are unnecessary when one makes the journey by private auto." He paused to take a draught of wine before cutting to the obvious proposition. "It also bears mentioning that an auto cuts the travel time in half. And good company is a premium regardless of the means of transportation."

"I appreciate the compliment as much as I do the offer."

"Both are fair, no doubt."

"All the same," assured Calvin, "I've already purchased tickets and, well, a chauffeured trip to Spain… Why, it sounds expensive."

Hector, perhaps encouraged by Calvin's easy repose before such an abrupt offer from a perfect stranger, signalled for another round and introduced himself in greater detail.

Hector was a self-taught pianist who grew up playing limited-chord religious arrangements for the congregational choir at a catholic church in Castelldefels. Childhood blossomed for young Hector in the manner it did for most lads who endured under the abominable Franco regime—stunted and without expansion or inspiration, like a tender rosebud confined to a windowless cinderblock oven. Siding, then, with church, in lieu of anything decent in the way of state, he took advantage of an available upright piano and made a second home and make-shift practice studio of a vacant room in the church presbytery. It was there that the head cleric eventually forced Hector into positions that lead frightened children to make horrifying compromises.

Having given up on politics and religion, he turned to his one and only beloved mother, who lashed him both with words and kitchen implements and demanded that anyone – her own child included – who would dare accuse her one and only beloved brother of child abuse and incest was bedevilled and in dire need of the psychiatric and spiritual help that only the church could provide— help, she roared, that Hector would be forced to seek elsewhere were he not to repent and own up to his fantastic lies.

Finally, some few years later, having quit the church, the state and the household, he joined a black-haired, black-eyed band based in Barcelona – one categorically bankrupt of both money and talent – and armed himself with a songbook that would cause the eyes of Franco, priests and parents alike to bulge in horror and disgust. Like many boys who become disenfranchised before puberty runs its full course, Hector committed himself to a style of music and a style of life that pointed dark fingers at the church, the government and all other sets of society that boasted authority, legitimate or otherwise.

He dreamt of wild subversive UK nights, where the music was edgy and the kids were jet-black and white and fighting with furious colour. There, in the streets and bars and clubs that throbbed with electric distortion, he began speaking English with all the bob-headed birds dancing in his head as he slept away his days in the yard of a decommissioned power plant in the Poblenou barrio of Barcelona. He penned long and lyrical letters to his brother back home in Castelldefels, detailing a magical place in his dreams called the United Kingdom. Hector called it punk; his family called it a ticket – *ida solo* – straight to damnation.

In his early twenties, the first of several botched suicide attempts by his brother sparked a filial flame within him, which he had previously been perfectly content to leave extinguished. A fellow, figured Hector, would need two free hands to make an honest attempt at a move to England, and so, with one hand struggling to lug the torch for his morbidly melodramatic brother, Hector finally aborted his dream of a life in the UK.

Hector recounted the details of an unforgettable evening that had taken place perhaps a decade prior, an evening spent with his brother and his brother's then girlfriend, the latest in a long line of young girls to have been promised his undying and undivided dedication. It was to be a dinner for three at his brother's flat, a dinner to which, by way of hand-written invitations on home-pressed paper of cotton pulp and wild flowers, the importance of punctuality was painfully impressed. The girlfriend, perhaps properly conditioned, arrived neither early nor late, not by a second. She was right on time, right on cue, as it were. Hector arrived one minute past the defined hour, an unnoticeable offence in all situations, save for those in which the host, on a excruciatingly morbid bent, cannot hold his breath for more than sixty seconds. Upon entry, Hector found the girlfriend teetering atop a step-ladder, hacking savagely away with a long blade at a thick white cordon, jerking at the end of which was Hector's brother, as a pot of soup reached a brisk boil on the stove and several blocks of *Queso Manchego* looked on, aghast. With all appetites sufficiently ruined by the enticed encroachment of death, the three sat in silence at the kitchen table and drained two bottles of the carefully aged vintage port that Hector's brother had bought by the caseloads for such special occasions. With his neck ravaged and raw and his body half an inch taller for the suspension, Hector's brother glowed happily, watching the light of the setting Spanish sun dive through the windows and lay obediently on the tiled floor, at his feet, in neatly folded tangerine squares, as the girlfriend picked and twisted the top button of a blouse she hated, but wore nonetheless.

In a show of gratitude on the heels of the successful rescue mission, his brother and the girlfriend invited Hector, who at that time was living with his sister in Southwest France, to visit them at the asylum for the psychologically troubled to which they had self-admitted themselves (the brother for the latest suicide event, the girlfriend because she could neither sleep nor wake without his daily doses of pain and chaos). It was a placid little clinic on terraced grounds in Opio, France, at the beginning of the foothills of the Southern Alps. Citing common sense, Hector's mother told him to stay away. Up until that point, however, common sense told him that governments should not murder its own people en masse; that priests, while they might *men*tally molest the congregation, should never *phy*sically molest the congregation; and that mothers should side with their victimised children over their alcoholic and paedophilic brothers. Common sense, thought Hector, be-damned.

On the eve of his departure for Opio, the depraved uncle-priest asked Hector for one more favour—strictly platonic this time, said the uncle, swear to God. Nearly two decades had passed since his hideous propositions in the church presbytery and so Hector begrudgingly complied. On the following morning, the uncle loaded Hector's auto with twenty cartons of cigarettes purchased from a local vendor, and with a wink and a smack on the derriere, said a quick prayer and charged Hector with the task of bringing back as many bottles of decent *Chateauneuf-du-Pape* as he could, through any means, legal or otherwise, amen. Apparently, the congregation embraced Gallic notions as to the earthy, gamy flavours and tannic finish of Christ's blood, although a good Bourgogne could just as nicely wash down Christ's body.

Hector passed a number of pleasant afternoons at the clinic, where his brother, infatuated as he was with Van Gogh's dedication to anguish, sat in the sun with easel and canvas among centuries-old olive trees and lush grape vines and both painted and ate paint. Following the stay in Opio, Hector passed several relaxing and wallet-terrorising days in St. Tropez. Finally, feeling as invigorated as he had felt in years, he set off for Spain. On the *route nationale* (which he preferred to the faster, toll-dotted *autoroute*) that ambled away west from Nimes, tree-lined and golden, the car refused to continue for lack of petrol. Gravity and good luck pulled the vehicle downhill and into a nearby petrol station. With no money to speak of, Hector traded a case of rosé, which he had purchased from a winery in Carnoules, for a tank of low-octane petrol. He got as far as Perpignan, where he was once again forced to barter for petrol. Learning quickly and applying a thicker layer of salesman grease, he scored another tank, this time for only four bottles of what the station manager agreed upon tasting to be a rosé that was both powerful and elegant and offered a generously lasting aftertaste.

Whereas the average fellow would have been elated over having settled such an unorthodox transaction, Hector leaned against the side of his car with a pensive cloud pinned to his brow. He realised that he would have managed a better deal on the petrol in France had he bartered what remained of his Spanish cigarettes. Should he need more petrol once crossing the border into Spain, that would be the time to unveil the good French wine. The trick was to buy locally for less and trade in foreign markets where such goods could not be found or where they were otherwise taxed as imports. He chalked it up to experience and pressed on.

Disenfranchised and historically abused, but so too, savvy and generous and eager to shed a cynical skin that never hugged him quite right in the first place, Hector was pleasantly surprised by the tickling economics of such prospective dealings. As he pointed his car towards the Barcelona outskirts, which began to show in the distance like a collection of grey stained teeth jutting skyward from a parched and neglected mouth, he dreamed of the possibilities. Before long, he quit the organisation for which he was disappointingly employed in France, and so began the left-handed career of one Hector Romero.

All transactions were cashless—only loons and loyalists, he would contend, concerned themselves with exchange rates and commissions. In turn, he funded his life not with legal tender, but with wine and cigarettes, Suisse chocolates, Russian caviar, truffles from the Piemonte and other region-specific delicacies. A few times each year, he might flap about Flanders for *dentelle de* Bruge, rare comics from Brussels and beer from the famed Trappiste brewery in Westvleteren. He might likewise detour through the smaller Dutch towns, where locally tolerated wares might squirrel themselves away in several of his automobile's many false fittings.

He knew little need for money, for he was never far removed from a stash of contraband that was only slightly less liquid than cash, and with which he bartered for beer, beef and any conceivable service, including minor surgery. On the first of each month, for example, he would deliver a case of good Bordeaux and a *ballotin* of Pierre Marcolini truffles to the *portera* of his building, an iron-willed woman who effortlessly prevented the otherwise shattered calm of invading guests, functionaries and administrative envoys.

"When you truly desire something," Hector professed, tying the ribbon of his story, and that of his offer to Calvin, together in a bow of conclusion, "financial hurdles are the least of your concerns. As for your train ticket, I could not promise you more than seventy centimes on the franc, but there is a market."

"You mean to say," began Calvin with an air of admiration, "that there is a secondary market for second-class train tickets?"

Replied Hector, while caressing the fat and well-mannered bulldog that had materialised at his side, and which upon inspection, was no bulldog at all, but rather a short and stubby column of crated cognac and calvados stacked two-high, "There is always a market."

Calvin played along cautiously. The idea of arriving in Barcelona in half the time had its appeal, but he was not completely comfortable with the idea of owing favours to such an unknown character, despite the fellow's charm and pleasing demeanour. Calvin countered, "Look here, I'll split the cost of the trip with you."

"No, no. I find the passing of money, when neither party is a merchant or *caissier*, to be graceless enterprise."

"How about we split the cost of the trip," repeated Calvin, driving a puckish bargain.

"How about *I* pay *you* to come along," said Hector, giving the negotiation a sudden turn.

"Ha!" burst Calvin smilingly, enlivened by the spirited exchange. His admiration for the charismatic Spaniard was growing, despite himself. "Clearly," he played, "truths are halved and confidences veiled when two *inconnus* launch a bidding war, each to his own detriment."

"Strangers? Here I thought the bourbon and wine had conducted us at least into the territory of acquaintances."

"What's the catch?"

"There is no catch. I don't want your money. That's all. I don't like the feel of money; not in my hand or in my wallet. Why, I have a mind—"

"*Mon*ey. Pah," Calvin interrupted. "I give a damn about money."

"And yet you just cited concern over the expense of a chauffeured trip."

"Mainstream Western economists will have you believe that the cost of any deal is adequately addressed by measuring its effect on the wallet alone. They take no time to consider, for example, psychological costs. The price of the gun, the bullet and the burial don't begin to address the true cost of pulling the trigger. Now, what's the catch?"

Hector smiled, and then stated with disarming candour, "On the off chance we are stopped at the border, no amount of clever chatter will keep you from being charged as a co-conspirator."

Having caught Calvin's interest through engaging conversation, he now sought to appeal to the waggish and sportive subdivisions of Calvin's character. "Such risk – low as is it – and any resulting mental fatigue," he concluded, "should be considered your price of passage."

"In such a fix, I would simply explain that I was offered a ride, and plead ignorance as to the contents of the truck's hold."

"Voila. You've thought it all through. Easy," agreed Hector. "Even easier than you think, for you've vastly overestimated the scale of my business. Trucks are conspicuous, require paperwork and beg to be searched. I drive a Citroën, a *deux chevaux*."

"A passenger car," said Calvin, feigning nonchalance. "How inefficient."

"Inefficient? But what is efficiency to a man of my age? Tedium is all. What need have I..." Hector interrupted himself, as though having perceived the need to readdress certain fundamentals. "Lest you forget, the Mediterranean basin is home to ancient cultures, peoples who have never assigned great value to efficiency. They have not yet learnt to strangle themselves with the ropes of false urgency and progress. Efficiency holds relevance only for star-seekers. My pursuits do not include fame or fortune, but rather inconspicuous, sustainable gains. That is the key to long-term success. Many find your countrymen to be a manic, short-sighted lot." His shrug told Calvin to pay it no mind. "I don't know. I rather admire your freshness. But we are too old a people to be so freckled and boyish. There was a time when we, too, were infatuated and shot for the moon. We have come, however, to prefer a return to forever. At any rate, the drive from Nice to Barcelona is a dream. I've run it a thousand times and hope to do so another thousand times or more. I am familiar with every beauty mark, every blemish, every bend in the road."

"The fact remains," said Calvin, "I don't care to gamble if I haven't any say in the outcome. I reckon I'd feel vulnerable in your *deux chevaux*. What's in it for you, anyway?"

"It is true that I am most at peace when following the winding roads of this diverse continent. Though on occasion, loneliness will force its unwelcomed way into the passenger seat. Your company would be a refreshing diversion."

"What do you make of my concerns?"

"As I mentioned, that is the price of passage." For a brief count, Hector picked over Calvin with studious eyes. "Are those the boots you'll be wearing to Barcelona?" he asked.

Calvin looked down at them, and then back at Hector. "Sure," he said. "I guess so. Why?"

Hector brushed away the question. "Let me also say that if you wish – perfectly up to you, of course – I might offer you the opportunity to earn a little extra money."

Calvin was still thinking of his boots.

"Easy money, too," added Hector, "as customs officials almost never resort to strip searches."

5   Of V I sing

In which Calvin falls asleep and
hears the prophets and the
cracking of eggs.

The next morning, Calvin walked Boulevard Victor Hugo in a
new pair of sneakers. At the corner of Boulevard Gambetta, he met
Hector, who had, in fact, managed seventy-six centimes on the franc
for Calvin's train ticket. The *deux chevaux* was parked on a nearby
side street. Though it looked perfectly empty, the vehicle was
expertly fitted with hidden nooks and, according to Hector, was
loaded with contraband.

"She is masterfully fitted," Hector assured. "All the same," he
added, eyeing Calvin intently, "intelligent, mobile hiding spots are
always preferred to dumb, static ones."

Calvin thought the vehicle must have been fitted with a
mechanical thyroid of sorts, for it had effortlessly gobbled up all of
the treasures targeted for its many hidden holds and still maintained
an admirable and svelte – if not overly athletic – metallic figure.

Hector brought the car to life and the two men embarked for
Spain. They stopped briefly in the Var, near Fréjus, for coffee,
croissants, and orange *confiture*, and then continued west into the
heart of Provence, where youthful green fields of sunflower and
lavender stood erect and waited impatiently for summer to adorn
them with their annual celebrity of vivid colours and sweet odours.
Calvin sat at a lazy angle, watching contentedly out the window,
while Hector's voice ran smooth, like an easy endless ribbon. He

spoke of theories and philosophies, things a fellow could count on in a pinch, stories of quick getaways and close calls and all the hot situations that could've gone either way—the things men without women let loose to romp about in the golden meadows of their minds when they are out on the open road, or in the shower, or alone in bed; the things they stand back and watch with admiration and pride; things they label *glory*, or at least recognise as some rich equivalent that can neither be caged nor contained.

The hum of the road and the pleasant drone of Hector's voice had a tranquilising effect on Calvin and he started to doze off. When, somewhere east of Carcassonne, Hector asked him if he had ever witnessed the depth of purple to the waters rising and falling between the Pillars of Hercules and Calvin mumbled drowsily, "Beef. But only if it is lean," Hector smiled, fell silent and let Jacque Brel quietly take over the storytelling on the FM.

Calvin's request of lean beef, however, was not a fading response to Hector's query, but rather a response to a question from the head waiter at one of his favourite restaurants in Barcelona, a man who Calvin had formally met for the first time at a funeral some years prior in a small town near Valladolid, through which ran the river Styx—the same waiter, in fact, who had asked Calvin just moments before Hector smiled, fell silent and switched on the radio, if Calvin knew which plate Victoria would prefer—the fish or the beef. Despite Calvin's response, the waiter brought fish plate after fish plate, all the while assuring with a confident chuckle that the beef was lean all right, almost too lean.

"But she won't *have* the fish!" Calvin yowled with dreamy anxiety.

"Pah! *She* won't have the fish!" complained the head waiter. "*Who* won't have the fish?"

"Why, the parti-coloured killweed who tied-off and dosed outside my garden!" cried Calvin, running into the alleyway with as many fish plates as he could carry. "She, who, for a time, tugged inky velvet *pétalos* over this godforsaken deadbeat Spanish corridor!" he continued feverishly, dropping the plates, all of which conspired to land with a resounding crash. "Ditto-blue in the vein and pale purple from the ankles down, solvent-soaked soul on high, through and through, on and on. *Of V I sing*! And now we must go forth," said he, running wildly up towards the Basilica de Santa María del Mar, "with and without you, Victoria, strapped neither with fate nor intent, leaving no footprints despite the effort. And I must call on *him* now because I have tired of traditional modes of expression, because he knows how to pour a good whiskey and slice a good cheese, because there is no going back and I haven't the faintest idea how to move forward. And because the wailing bastard still reeks of your sweat and saliva, and your tears, and whatever remains of your unclaimed right to winter-weight viscosity, your hightorch blood, your mudbuck fire, your madgoat desire, your tangled woman guts. And because I'm a junkie, still suckered, still hearing it loud – *Mug came in, ear-holed that fool*! *Zap*! Fist-packed pot-shots from Garfield brothers, jacked-up, yoked, nightwound bones, thugs, outrage and crazy angled sadness, goddamn it all to hell!

"Sold out on first sight of those far-gone legs, those vines trained to white-bone Spanish latticework, which did sprout up on fire, bend and arc from black spice and canvas All Stars. You had it all over us. And how we threw elbows, knives, wrestled our way into your front row, spilling wine and blood and all semblance of self respect, side-by-side, the Wailer and the Junkie. A multi-spired tragedy. Poor choices all the way around. We hadn't a clue.

"And so what, then, if you're crying on the shoulder of a washed-up street fighter twice your age? *He* could just as easily be one of those talented young turks who make back-alley art and electronic music and know Rioja from Ribera, and in a tighter size of grey tank. Could just as easily be *me*, Victoria! And you could be clean and together. Here we are nonetheless, in the room where I love you, and where you cry, and where *he* moans a hay-pale colour of *fado*, serenading on legs made blurry after fatal love, all the ways to die. Pay no mind to prior deaths by quiet defeat and silent decay; we are all dandies here, outrageously painted flowers, thin and sticky, exploding fabulously on concrete walls, dying out of little more than spite. Look at *him*—Harlan, with a dark shade of nut: gunshot wound to the head, slit wrists, overdose, cracked skull from bathtub ceramic, splat landing at the tail-end of a great fall, so on and so forth. He masturbates to gauche authors with pretentiousness to match his melodrama. And you, Victoria. *Victoria*! Ha! My, aren't mothers optimistic creatures with their first born. You peel away from him cheek first, to the waist, your hips a crepe-paper fulcrum pinned by high-gloss mitts to Harlan's belt. And there am I, here, trespassing bastard additive.

"'There's a small kitchen there,' you say, emphasising unfortunate form over useful function.

"How much room, I wonder, is required to break an egg?

"'Oh, a kitchen, is it?' I say, puffing weakly.

"Still pinned, you dab at tears with non-absorbent fingertips, such curious oddities. Always *some*thing—the sweats, racing heart, anxiety, insomnia, skinny lines, stepped-on junk, swift backhands, counter punches, *maquillage* with grossly inadequate opacity, ill-designed uncooperative non-absorbent body parts. Your knees dip with a peek towards the door, suggesting motion. But whose wheels shall turn, my dear?

"'I just ate, thanks.'

Damn these shaking inner-city knees and elbows. Try to envision naked winter fingers scumbled onto trunks and canvas, rattling grey bones disappearing back towards goodness, in still life with winter breeze. Thoughts of Gent. Give a boy Gent, though he's never been before. Gent, where he might find laughable far-as-China serenity. Hell, you could be a mother, Victoria, if only you had children. But *then* what?

"'Love is no source of nutrition, *chico*,' Harlan admonishes. He is a variety that comes overflowing, gushing, forever sated, forever famished. A half-spin and backside swat sends the Butterfly V towards the kitchen. 'Besides,' he rails, 'a man without hunger is no man at all. Cook something for me, Victoria, my love, if *he* won't eat! *Duerme con tu orgullo, cabron.* Dulcinea will never be your—'

"But I'm not proud. See here how I need new boots. Let those who think they've something to lose or something to gain, know pride. I am a straw soldier fighting a fire ball of my own creation. I have nothing to lose. Just look at these boots one time. *Yo, Kid! Onetime! Onetime! Drop the gun, fool! Run!* Still suckered after all these years. Harlan slips like Spanish wine into an erogenous zone and twists the knob on the hi-fi. Credit him this: the armadas upon which he drops his sword are not windmills, but armadas. Still, he steals his mottos.

"'You have no *alma*, chico. You have no soul!' he demands, pulling guns knives his fat gut his dick her waist her ass her hair her lips and lips and lips spring-sweet sauterne august taffy stuck in the working jambs of his cock-thick fingers I'll kill the fucking rat bastard I'll kill him dead!

"'A kiss away, you ignorant—'

"'No, *chico*! A *shot*! A shot away.'

"At the bar in el Raval, you mention that you once kept a pet lizard, smooth and not scaly. You said this in response to the reptile-green of my eyes, slashing bluegrass stains devil-dancing on the knees of white church pants. The first time you've honestly looked at me since Harlan, The Great Abductor, returned for you. You were sky high and I ordered another round. Your eyes mist over whenever you place flat palms on the terrains of death, an undeniable Harlan injection, that, a veritable hijacking, a gun-machine spray of his sorrowful grey semen into your soft pink guts and I get a flash to smack the head clean off your shoulders, claim a rocking clap of thunder for my very own, and then walk home whistling a show tune. You promise the neglect is perfectly unintentional and buck up to impress upon me that people, bankers, shop owners, waiters, assessors, bartenders, junkies, should have better judgement than to allow any animal under your care and attention. I order another round and we sit longer and you finally rip the loose button from the blouse you hate so much, and I remind you of the Doberman I saw make strawberry purée of a three-legged cat outside Genova. I'm getting dizzy. Picking at the strangled remains of the thread near your collar, you compliment my chin. You say I could be somebody's reliability, stability, if only I weren't so extravagant. This, as you pick at the mangled blouse you hate, but wear nonetheless; your penance.

"You forget everything; how our paths first crossed during a winter series of farewell parties, pandemic in scope, a real exodus, under the grand chandelier at La Paloma. Two adjacent half-moons of crushed red velvet in the balcony above the dancehall floor framed our first encounter; a slow-rolling collision sequined with all the uncertainties, unanswerable questions and fractured optimism associated with a celebration of ends. Meeting with silent, uneasy mouths, smiles like wayward cracks in city-shocked cement, I take your wrists, poetic slips of silver whisper, and move, move softly, baby-blue and picking up speed, now springing leaks, now pastel-smeared ballerinas spinning backwards towards a forgotten beginning, licking lips, now racing breakneck towards yet another new end.

"'Walking you home that night, high as the moon on hope against odds, kissing away visions of a desperate walk through deep-blue Levi Square, San Francisco, one o'clock in the morning, a dangerous hour to be jacked-up on booze and anxiety and fear – too much night left to kill – December wind and bourbon driving the desperation shakes, having given last farewell and parting kiss to the little blonde girl I married the year before. That same December wind, sucking madly on lips of big brick chimney at a darkwood hotbrass bar, making fire twist devilish and festive for the final good-bye good luck I love you fuck you embrace. Boxfire sucking the life out of steamy green wood, looking back to watch her paint a coat of Christmas red on her lips and pucker up like a showgirl for the next patsy.

"Maybe if we had more in common, Victoria, you and me. Maybe if you were from Garfield or Flint or Gary or even Riverside. What is possible beyond *jamon* and *vino* when you're suspicious of anything on four wheels—but not afraid of Harlan, my sweet kitten, nor of tomorrows, nor of God, nor of shame, nor of needles, you float in sweet brown clouds of self-serve victory. Victoria! What foolish baby pride from my foolish baby mind, to think that we might floor mountains, part seas, change the courses of planets with puckered baby lips and a soft puff upon a cotton bloated dandelion.

"Now tethered to heavy appliances in the small kitchen to keep you from floating away, you search to offer dusty consolation, while Harlan flutters around the room, a broadwinged buttermoth in goldenbulb, knocking into walls, hallucinating, laying down angel dust and heavy syrup, composing and reciting requiems for newborns. Yet in the kitchen you bang no cupboards for me, you slam no drawers, crash no platters, rattle no silverware, and so I sit waiting, waiting to hear the one thing I know you will never offer. Eventually it comes—bacon grease over eggshells. Mine eyes have seen the glory, mine hands have spread wide like open eyes, open wounds, open wrenches, bracing, wet with warm cleansing tears, palming denim covered knees, ducking and weaving as best I can.

"'Thank you, but I've just eaten.'

"'What a waste, *chico*! *Hablas tu*! I would have liked her to spend that breath on song.'

"'I thought the menu might include—'

"'I swear on Gala's grave, you said you weren't hungry!'

"'I only said I've just eaten.'

"When it's time to go, it's time to go. A native of wall-to-wall shag and greasy linoleum, I trip foreign at cold right angles down your Spanish stairway, slate and milky marble, rigid longevity, dumb blindness, low humming laughter in the face of our ridiculous turnover. Never so alone, never so lonely, ducking and weaving and keeping the feet moving, asking only for the old worn wood of my precious peninsula for comfort, humid rotting wooden walls and floorboards to sag and creak under foot, to bounce in time with a scarred gait, wet wood content to absorb ever-more tears and guts, content to moan, content with saturation; shoulderpushing through a golden mudpoem of time and place, a thing forgotten, a weatherworn champion now worse off for time than myself, nursing and caring for it, flophouse floorboards, bedbugs, fat and jolly prostitutes, street-level tidal soup.

"Over to Plaça George Orwell, step one at a time over baby-faced children dirty with grease and dust and third-rate ink, lying prostrate and drug-drowsy, newly born pups ripped fresh off the nipple, stumbling blindly for a sense of belonging. Bells of my tattered blue jeans swish and flap in passing. Having abandoned a home, one is no longer hated, no longer loved, no longer missed or feared or recognised, a benign sceptre in ether orbit, into bar Bahia, shoved to the end, where the flooring fumbles and falls away and happy young elbows swing in the smoky air to catchy tunes, where young flesh waggle crisp cigarettes, where postcards, pierced and with heavy eyeliner wait to be plucked up and taken somewhere, written on, stamped and pushed out the door, where Earthy Senegalese French careens around the barroom, where coffee cups and shredded sugar paper build among the landless with deep stains and blunted horns. A cracked varnish bar top, devil red, licking the limbs of three salty wenches from the Camargue, down on holiday with magic batons, smoking and always on the light, disappearing one after another in hungry fingers with too many joints. Propositioned by the one with glorious tits and cig- and coffee-stained teeth, giving *bisous* and whispering in ears. I suffer this dive for the girl behind the bar, who reminds me of you, only she's not pretty and she trusts her instincts. She has the same candyjack ass swinging in tight arcs, ass like the bells of the *muguet* that bloom on the Mandelieu hillsides, like you, tight and tattooed, ignoring me with frightening ease, curving green, bending on the wet side of the bar, swishing ashes from shadowed corners and phantom cups now that it's time to close and neither of you notice or care. Still, I breathe despite disappearing in fading shades of obscurity, looking in on semi-sec bubbles with black-painted nails, twisting in red knee-highs. How I once devoured whims like you.

"Over and over, skipping record swapped for skipping record, with no bridge in sight, no safety net refrain, we are falling apart, wading through a madman's version of the river. You graduate from kitchen to boudoir to salon, in a darkening progression. Only the *ático* remains between your bedroom and the abattoir, the top floors now reserved for derelicts, students, chemical manufacturers and clients seeking a wild-night freeway launch pad to the next, laced with Pyrex, tubing, electronics-grade clarity, setting up your cot next to the still, the fire, setting up your dreams in parallel with a glass-pipe heaven. And when you awaken, oh my, Renoir's rosy cheeks interrupted by dried beds of salty midnight rivers. Forgive me my sensibilities and relocated weaknesses – a staged eviction aided by smoke and mirrors – they've been kept cordoned and entertained in back-alleys throughout the lesser-known parts of the city. You've settled the dispute with the domestic service provider, gotten the button sewn back on the hated blouse, and I will so gladly forgive you your damages, dear flower, if only you will leave Harlan once and for all and come back before it's too late, before the death rattle comes over us and the hairs on my arms stand ready and the clocks stop cold, before the thunderous clap. For the first time in years, someone is calling my name. It is Harlan, the wailer, sobbing, exultant. *O Victoria*!

"At the end, white lights from heaven reached down in full dripshine, melting the skies and resetting our world to original silence, a gift-wrapped trifle to be shattered with the first bats of our baby lashes. You once mentioned how satisfying it is to watch our pet inventions abiding natural laws.

"I insist upon Harlan, 'We know not what we've conceded.'

"He counters, beaming, choking back tears, 'Don't balk now, *chico*. We prefer our lights blinking with high intensity. They are so much more festive that way.'

"Walking up Muntaner, sweetness and other islands make soft my path, our burden. I reach home, kick off my dusty boots and rest them on a mat of hope and tested faith, a slippery idea to which I lay fragile claim. We could've been saved, you and me. Could've left the cannas long and tall, pushing towards tranquillity, feet planted firmly in the earth of intentional slowness and light. I could've battled Harlan, could've pulled cracked shins up to his pedestal and driven splintered bones through his heart, as he lathered in milky tears. He drove you there, to the river, to the crumbling bridge, in his mad sorrow milk truck, huffing and tipping with ghost vitamins and phantom lactose, your hands gaunt and icy, caressing his big warm butter-muffin mitts still slippery with olive oil, telling him, 'Shh shh shh, there, baby, there.' Consoling him as he weeps and moans, croons your dirge song, begs you to stay during the commercial breaks, the adjusting of the mirrors, the plucking of an eyebrow, the picking of a tooth, the flipping of the dial on the radio, the railing of a symphonic opus swathed mirthfully in high-thorn'd roses, every condensed drip adding to your death pool, and me in the back bench with an unoccupied gun rack and an empty bottle. A playground shove does the trick, puff puff, out of the truck, off the ledge, a red-petal mash rip-tiding you under and out to one sea or another, eventually from our memories altogether, until nothing remains of you but the shadow of your snail trail, glistening, barely visible on the hardened surfaces of our still-beating hearts. Except on days when the smell of summer-warmed wine walks us back to the room where I loved you, and where you cried, and where Harlan moaned, and I can still hear the prophets and the cracking of eggs."

Calvin woke with a start. He was pitched forward with his hands palming the dash of the parked *deux chevaux*, emotionally unnerved for the terrorising dream. The car's engine crackled hot. A hail storm pinged on a pie tin under its bonnet and Calvin frantically chased cracked marbles through the abandoned rooms in the ramshackle tenements of his subconscious. The *deux chevaux* was parked in the gravel lot of a small petrol station on the side of the *route nationale*. Hector was nowhere to be seen. Suddenly Calvin felt violated and checked his mid-section to see if Hector had made off with any internal organs, or, perhaps, hastily sewn some valuable nugget of contraband to the underside of his kidney while he slept. A cursory pat-down revealed no wet incisions, no sutures, though this did little to alleviate the discomfort born of his dream.

Just then, Hector appeared in the rear-view mirror, approaching the car. In his hand was a French vanilla cone. Poking his head in through the driver-side window, he cheered, "You're awake. Hurrah! I thought perhaps you had died. Imagine attempting to cross the border with a dead man for a companion—it would never fly.

And imagine the goodies they'd find during the autopsy! No, no, I'd have to put you on ice in Perpignan. Ha-ha!"

Calvin sat in silence and stared hard at the man in the window frame, studied his rich *vêtements*, his cognac eyes, his lolling red tongue lapping away at vanilla cream. No longer able to contain himself, he lunged from the passenger side and demanded, "Who are you!"

Hector, heel-to-heel and standing tall, yanked opened the door (a *veronica* that would have made Joselito envious) and watched Calvin, the stunned bull, fall snout-first onto the dusty lot. Bending earthward from the waist, Hector spoke. "Dear child," he said, looking deeply concerned, now wiping drips of melted cream from Calvin's forehead, "what has happened?"

"*You* are what happened, you rat!" burst Calvin, swiping at the white handkerchief buzzing about his brow.

"Enough nonsense," said Hector sternly, yanking Calvin to his feet. "What is wrong with you?"

Once again upright, Calvin demanded anew, "Tell me the truth! Do I know you?"

"I see, I see," Hector said with a sigh. "This again. Truthfully, Calvin, no, you don't." He managed somehow, then, to elegantly lick a drip of vanilla cream from a difficult spot near his bared elbow. "But I do know you."

Calvin gasped. The admission sent him stumbling towards an off-register conclusion. Squinting, he looked deeper into the Spaniard, believing that a search through narrowed eyes would allow him to identify Harlon's once-familiar features looking out from behind a transformational disguise called Hector. As though he might coax him out, Calvin, now with wide eyes, whispered, "Harlan?"

"Excuse me?"

"Are you Harlan?"

"I'm Hector," he said, placing a flattened palm of proprietorship on his chest.

"Hector?" echoed Calvin, bewildered, no longer certain of anything.

"Yes. Hector. Harlan's brother."

With that, Calvin fell back into the driver's seat, slain.

Years ago, Harlan had carefully built doors in Calvin's psyche, doors that gave onto rooms of seemingly insurmountable pain and hatred, doors that Calvin had painstakingly nailed shut. Now, here was Hector, Harlan's flesh and blood, his older brother, ripping the damned things open and laying to waste all of Calvin's hard work.

Calvin leapt from the car, intent on delivering his deceiver a proper thrashing. But in the mere seconds it took Calvin to bring himself to a full and fearsome growl, just like that, the fire within him died. He felt no hatred. In fact, he felt no anger at all; neither for Hector nor Harlan. The astonishing fact of the matter is that Calvin, standing there, exposed, for the very first time, before open doors that he believed to be sealing off a vast and active family of monstrous memories, those that would surely devour him if ever freed, found that the demons had withered and wasted, and found in their stead naught but clear blue skies over soft sands, spotted here and there, perhaps, with the harmless calcified remains of dead recollections.

He felt a terrific sense of freedom, liberation. It is true that one never feels quite so new and alive as on the day he first recognises that a deep dark pain has finally lifted. So miraculous is the feeling that one's spirit is liable to commit to conscious, waking memory the flash of great discovery, forever and for all time.

Nevertheless, Calvin had been deceived and he felt it prudent to maintain an edge and a scowl, and he came at Hector with pointed questions and heated accusations. Hector pled guilty, answered all questions directly and petitioned Calvin for forgiveness. He insisted that what Calvin had interpreted as a deceitful plot aimed at ensnaring him in a sickening act of revenge, a wild intrigue or some unsavoury fix, was perfectly innocent and unintentional, if also foolish. He admitted to having taken it all too far. It was a gross lapse of good judgement, to be sure, but by no means was it a pre-penned abstract designed for big-screen thrills or suspense. The *aim* – if one were to insist – was as simple as it was true: Hector wanted to meet Calvin. Was it so inconceivable? Harlan had spoken glowingly of Calvin, and yes, despite his brother's gross disqualifications, Harlan was a sound judge of character. What's more, Hector had new interests on the Cote d'Azur and was aware that Calvin lived in Nice. What chance had he of rapping on Calvin's door unannounced, introducing himself as Harlan's brother, just like that, and inviting him out for a friendly drink? Why, it was an impossibility; it never would have flown.

In his line of business, Hector explained, it was difficult to meet good people. Outside of business dealings, the good people he met were largely dismayed by his calling. Oh, sure, *every*one loves cocktails, celebrations and parades, but not every fellow has the social dexterity to make it as a bartender or an emcee or a grand marshal. Hector got by through atypical, unorthodox means—means the mainstream found inadmissible. So be it; solitude would be his companion and in many ways his saviour. But hell, even the most solitary of fellows are apt to find themselves mired in loneliness from time to time. There was no ulterior motive in offering Calvin a ride to Barcelona, Hector averred. He longed for the camaraderie. He, too, after all, had become inebriated by the unexpected vitality of their conversation at the Rive Bleue, the boyish flexing and posturing born of their mutual enthusiasm. And anyway, theirs was far from the bawdiest arrangement ever accorded in a hotel bar. Why, one enters a good hotel bar in a resort town at night and starts drinking bourbon with a certain notion of the possibilities; just as one enters a Jacuzzi with a certain notion of hot water. Calvin had forever gravitated towards novelty, sport and bright lights. It was ever-evident, and so when he had gone sufficiently far in his rebuke of Hector, the latter put a stop to it.

"Really, Calvin, that's quite enough! I have apologised and I will continue to do so if you wish, but there is no cause for further reproach. I'll remind you that your presence here is due in no part to coercion!"

"You're right," he conceded sourly. "I'd be comfortably on the train right now if I hadn't invited you to sit last night."

"I say!" began Hector, feeling a bit spurned. "Has it really been so terrible?"

"That's not the point! I don't know what the hell I'm doing here."

"Oh, stop!" Hector burst. "Blindness is one thing. Blindfolding oneself and calling it blindness is quite another. Pah! You can't fathom why you are here? Allow me. You are here because a beautiful young woman is anxiously awaiting your arrival in Barcelona. You are here because I am paying you handsomely to accompany me and steward a good on my behalf—a boon you never anticipated, a windfall that will allow you to treat your girl to a holiday otherwise beyond your means. You are here because this is pretty damn enjoyable and your next best alternative is clubbing fish and robbing them of their slimy innards. You are here because you are a man of adventure, because the journey is invigorating, the road gorgeous and the conversation refreshing; because this morning you found a new wrinkle on that handsome mug of yours and felt a new ache in your back; because you are human; because with every passing day, your life sublimates towards the heavens with slightly greater velocity, and will continue to do so until one day you no longer feel your feet beneath you. And you will realise then, as you look down towards earth and see yourself lying prostrate and alone on a cold metal gurney, that your heart has stopped beating. But you know all this already! Don't pretend that you have walked unwittingly into an elaborately laid trap. I should have been more forthright with my identity, but I told you no lies. My apologies; this was not a good idea."

In conclusion, Hector offered to call off the arrangement, empty the car – the side panels, the undercarriage, all of its false fittings – and chauffer Calvin risk-free and in silence, if he so wished, across the border and into Barcelona.

Calvin thought for a moment. In the distance he saw an old stone *mas*. A short stone wall extended behind the house, enclosing a terrace area on which a large white umbrella offered shade. Perhaps there was a swimming pool. Olive trees and scrub oak dotted the grounds. The land was vast, gorgeous; it ran off in every direction, rising and falling in easy green hills.

"You know," Calvin admitted finally, "I found a grey hair this morning."

"Nonsense. Show me."

"Look; right here."

"I don't see anything."

"Look closer."

"There is no grey. Your hair is black."

"You're blind."

"Nonsense I'm blind. Your hair is black."

"Well, it's there. Somewhere. Trust me."

Calvin steered them towards the well rested *deux chevaux*.

"I'll tell you this much," said Calvin. "If I see Harlan, I just might kill him."

"One cannot kill," said Hector, "that which is already dead."

Calvin stopped abruptly, but Hector took him by the elbow and continued towards the car. "Forget it. It was bound to happen eventually," he said. "One can only tempt fate so many times."

The sun was past its apex. The car started on a dime.

"I don't know what to say. I never thought... Hell," said Calvin. "How did he go, if you don't mind my asking."

"Bah, he would want you to know—a fellow does not rig a pyrotechnics fiasco if he wishes to die quietly."

"Pyrotechnics." Calvin whistled. "Your brother had an unequalled flair for the dramatic."

"The colours alone brought tears to the eyes. Fireworks, you know, are called *feu d'artifice* in French—"

"Fire born of Man's artifice."

"Deployed by Harlan with commensurate artifice, in the execution of a *mort spectaculaire*."

> *Through garnet teardrops hanging in the doorway to a backroom. Posters, party flyers for park jams, street parties, taxi cabs on hard-colored streets, steam veil some make ghosts of others. Record albums stack high in crates, long brown leather couch that run along a wall ablaze with color, lines and curves in fat black, red spray for red lips, a red refrigerator with chrome beer spigot fit in the door. I sit on the couch and take Nicki's hands. She stand in front of me between my legs. My hands slide down the backs of her smooth legs and to her knees. Time click thick and viscous, lips pucker like a baby anticipating tender kisses from an unseen angel, my cheek meet featherlike against her smooth thigh, dissolve into her, disappear and disperse throughout her young body, put myself inside her, carry myself in her more capable arms and legs, be her baby, start over, be more reliable. She put her hands on my shoulders, touch my cheek. I pull slowly back, external. I recognize myself. I breathe, I breathe, my teeth click.*
>
> *The old leather couch and her smile fades. I watch the sadness and the hard questions forming in her brown eyes. Her lips move to speak and crush me. A gear catch and hold and hold and then it slip and bang against its housing. Tears pump up somewhere behind my eyes.*
>
> "You ran off to California," *she say.*
>
> *Katie watches out the window, still, silent, face awash in shiny night air and swishing brown hair whipped up devilishly by pre-winter phantoms.*
>
> "You up and ran off, Kid."
>
> *My sweet Nicki. Inside her, a thirteen-year-old boy won't have to worry so much about everything that lies ahead.*

"Kid, I'm talking to you." *She is in my heart and in my head. Got to pay attention. Learn to talk right, look at people when they talking to you.* "Don't leave me again."

Katie stares wide-eyed beyond the tattered edges of an empty November night, off on some bright-white Colorado mountain top.

"But theys death on my hands."

"Don't leave me again," Nicki says. *Pug. He left first.*

"I miss the mark. I know all the things parents say. I hear them." How a boy screw up so much. He don't think enough, he daydream too much, he get into too many situations that only got bad endings. *I hear what they say.*

"I ain't no flower, Nicki. I don't get things right the first time."

"You do just fine, baby. You do just fine."

She put two fingers under my chin, raise my head and watch down at me with a loving smile. "You find a girl to make you them lemon pies?"

I can't remember. Theys oceans, deserts, old piers jut out into the churning bay like rusty teeth, a broken zipper, a mad death rattle shake down to the axels, the world watching and laughing.

"Don't you worry about it none, baby," *she say—she says.* "It's OK."

She smile differently. "Why did you bring me to this record store?" *she asks. She know—knows I want to make flowers.* "One day you're going to yell it loud and sure from up high in those clouds you dream about so much."

We lay on the long brown couch

Surrounded by eucalyptus trees, Laika leaves her car idling in a parking lot of a residence-motel, smoothes a whisper of blond hair back behind her ear and turns a key until she hears the lock

My heart catch and hold and hold and then slip against its housing

Clicking and tumbling. She leaves the door open and the keys stabbed into the lock, walks down a hallway to a bedroom with a neat square bed on which behaves a tight and too firm mattress. All things present are neat and squared and dominated. She sits and writes a short note. Two parakeets in a cage at her side stop their chirping. They, too, are neat and dominated.

Katie, high on a skiing mountain, slender legs go this way and that and she falls on her face. She lifts herself up on two shaky elbows and tries to wipe away snow from her cheeks. She's got sorrow and shame and salty water pooling up in her eyes.

Got to pay attention. Got to learn.

Theys flowers.

Nicki and me, we move together, we make flowers on the long brown couch.

6 Providencia be thy guide

In which Calvin is engaged in a
cold war and eats of the
forbidden fruit.

Calvin had lived a life at sea-level, street-level, which may have had something to do with the fact that mountains made him uneasy, restless. And while there is something of a cinematic allure to border crossings, they are also manned by uniformed authority figures. Calvin had long grown leery of authority figures short and tall, metropolitan and provincial, regardless of post or pay check. And so one might have expected the border crossing on the Mediterranean side of the Franco-Spanish frontier, seated high in the Pyrenees, to rattle his nerves, but that was not the case. It was only after starting their descent into Catalunya, having rolled across the border without stopping or having seen a single uniformed official that his nerves began to play against him. There are concepts, laws, histories that are too spatially complex for the dimensionally challenged minds of young children. Some two millennia ago, according to legend, three men of considerable wisdom tracked, from a desert floor awash in darkness, the North Star to lacklustre quarters in which a virgin gave birth to a child king, or a child prophet, or, at any rate, a child boy. It is a fantastic story from any angle, and *a propos* when travelling an unfamiliar road towards great expectations. With Girona behind them and Barcelona somewhere beyond the horizon, it occurred to Calvin that as a child, he never questioned the biological validity of a virgin giving birth to a baby boy. The tracking of a star by earthbound men without compasses or ladders of light-year length, however, mystified him. Well into adulthood, now, it still seemed to Calvin that all stars twinkled more or less straight up in the sky. As they reached the northern barrios of Barcelona, he wondered whether Klarysa would prove to be an impossible myth that he would accept unquestioningly as a truth, or a complex reality he just could not wrap his head around.

Hector dropped him off at a quiet intersection in el Clot, a barrio hushed from outside noise by the plane trees that climbed high and arched over the streets in leafy congregation. It was Hector's idea. From there it would be a pleasant walk to Klarysa's flat, far enough to stretch the legs, fill the lungs and negotiate a fresh start with the city. El Clot, an autonomous barrio marked by the fragile, sober happiness of South Americans in a land not their own, a barrio that gracefully balanced highs and lows, occupied by solid people who make good in a land that appreciates them for little more than their strong backs and hands and other taxable assets.

Calvin formerly walked those streets with an angst unfitting of his age, wondering when he would finally grow up and shed his thin skin for something thicker and more protective. The notion that that which does not kill a fellow only makes him stronger was, to Calvin, incomplete. One must first define what *strength* is and what *weakness* is—an arduous task that would yield greatly differing results across any diverse population. Just give him thicker skin. That was all he wanted.

Realising he had no gifts fit for a queen, he passed by a florist and bought a lively pot of hot pink cyclamen, the perfect flower when the gardening tendencies of the recipient are unknown, for they are cheap, pretty and nearly indestructible. He left the florist in high spirits, as an odd jingle looped merrily in his head. Continuing his way down a tree-lined avenue, he sang out loud to an unknown tune:

> Butt'n it, my dear,
> You give me the fear
> Though at times
> You send my heart soooaring.
>
> If I gave you the boot,
> Would you still be my *chou*

And kiss my sweet ass
In the mooorning?

Before long, he reached Carrer de la Providencia, the street on which lived his *inamorata*. Why, not even Tirso de Molina or Lope de Vega could pen a dark, ironic fate for a fellow on a street so named. The foreseeing care and guidance of God and nature over the wee creatures of earth—Providence be thy guide and thy shield!

A forged iron web in *verdigris* swung inward before he could ring the bell. Standing there in the doorway stood a frightful vision: a squat, judicial toad with a head of boiled ham, or Leonid Brezhnev – the Brezhnev of Catalunya – manning its post as *portera*, moist in the humidity of its brick and shadow jurisdiction, yellow thighs wrapped in chicken skin on a chequered pond of cool marble, framed by the gilded doorway like the resigned fixtures in Mark Ryden tableaux, poised to apprehend errant flies and sundry lunchtime edibles *volants*.

Passing mucus eyes over Calvin's north and south, it said, "*Rrraauch*. You don't live here!" Then, eyeing the cyclamen, it burped and croaked, "Apartment 3B!"

"How did you know I was—"

"*Estas perdido*—lost! *Rrraauch*. Mind your stay. I am watching you!"

The *portera* lurched into the harsh sunlight with a broomstick of bound twigs and held the sun at bay with a blunt nose shoved in its fiery direction, for a moment of silent accusation. Calvin grabbed the door before it could close. Then, because it was just past the thirteenth hour of the day, the *portera* took to scratching at the sidewalk with short, insolent jabs and berated an absent other, some poor fellow named Cadiz who had apparently fled Barcelona and taken up unauthorised residence in the southern Spanish city of the same name.

"Others far cleverer than *you*," it said, stopping to point its broomstick at Calvin, "have guessed me endowed with eyes in the back of the head. *Rrraauch*. If I had need of them, rest assured I would have long ago evolved them somewhere behind my ears, which don't lack," it added with a broomstick tap to the side of its marshy cranial terrain, "for sensitivity. *3B!*"

"*Señora…*" offered Calvin, bent at the waist between submission and supplication, and let go the door.

On the third landing, he knuckled thick wood designated *B* in tacked brass. In the time it took to pluck a single dead leaf from the vegetative base of the cyclamen, the door opened to reveal a dark minx of a girl. She stared up at Calvin with sublimating patience, as though she had been standing there half the morning. With one hand against the door jamb and the other gripping the spine of a popular book about a bespectacled boy wizard, she said coolly, "Klarysa *no esta aqui.*"

Calvin stared at her thickly; Klarysa had not mentioned a flatmate. The girl's body – that of an unripe teen – somehow managed nonetheless to make a mockery of the concealing qualities of clothing. She and her tea-top had no rapport; the tiny rag looked anxious, eager to disappear altogether and find someone with more of an appreciation for the sartorial potential of cotton.

A student of archaeology, she would later recount with rehearsed solemnity and the averted eyes of the shy and uncertain (of which she was neither) her dreams of excavating with pick and tweezers to further uncover the cultural DNA of mankind in the heralded basins of humanity's birth. Such dreams were legitimate, even noble, though she spoke of them somehow as if they were fruit to be selected from a market stall—"I'll take that one, please. No, not that one, the one next to it without the wee brown spot"—and with the naïve certainty of a six-year-old who proclaims that he will one day make a big-league shortstop, though from time to time he will forget on which hand to wear his ball-glove. "Profit and loss," she regurgitated during several different conversations on widely varying topics, "is a concern of the practical—that is to say the anchored and small-minded." She would go nowhere in life if it were not for those eyes—two almond-cut gems that flashed with fountain-active fire. Against the odds, she would have to make good with the eyes, blink and bat her way across every inch that lay between Barcelona and Mesopotamia, obscurity and distinction. Nevertheless, even from his vantage point in the hallway, Calvin could see that the flat was a sprawling sweep of elegance, of a size and style unfamiliar to all but the most gifted graduate students— gifted, it would seem, not necessarily in any god-given sense, but rather in the sense that might be recorded by receipts and monthly payments.

"*Oye, chico. Hola,*" she sung mockingly as Calvin stared dumbly down the hallway. "*Entiendes?* Klarysa is gone."

"Oh. OK," said Calvin, newly present, smiling pleasantly. "Gone as in *gone*, or just out?"

The flatmate smiled with the evil curiosity of a young boy shouldering a skein of antisocial credits, shifting her fly-weight from one foot to the other, suddenly feigning patience to last through the end of time. She was all eyes and spaghetti straps.

"Why?" she provoked. "Are you worried?"

"Not especially," said Calvin. "Should I be?"

"You wouldn't be the first."

"The first?" Calvin replied, rising to her naked provocation. "To knock on your door? To bring a flower? To find himself temporarily ensnared in the mildewed mental wiring of the Brezhnev of Catalunya? No, I shouldn't think so." It was a decent counter, which did nothing to improve his ground. "Did she leave a message, by chance? She is expecting me."

"Who, Klarysa?"

"No, Brezhnev. Yes, of course, Klarysa."

"It's funny you keep referencing Brezhnev. There are countless Russian cows less attractive than that bull if you intend to take down our beloved *portera* by way of cruel comparison. Take Irena Vostrikova, for example."

Calvin had never heard the name.

"She's at *la casa de* Jordi, in Sant Cugat," said the flatmate.

"Who, Klarysa?"

"No, Irena Vostrikova. Yes, of course, Klarysa."

"Don't you have anything better to do," asked Calvin, "than harass me? Did she leave a message?"

"That *was* the message. And yes, I do. So if you don't mind—"

"Wait. Please," he appealed before she could close the door. "What is La Casa de Jordi? Did she mention that I should meet her there?"

"Not that I recall."

"Can you tell me where it is?"

"Over there." She lifted a cleft chin that hinted at a feisty sexuality, to indicate direction. Calvin followed her line of vision as far as the door marked *A*, on the other side of the hall.

"Somewhere shy of the Portuguese border, I suppose," he said crossly. A bead of wet irritation trickled towards his temple.

Cyclamen thrive in all but the harshest environments. The ones Calvin carried seemed thoroughly embarrassed, wept for the floorboards and attempted to flee his grip for the anonymity of the darkened corridor. The flatmate masticated a piece of chewing gum – a vulgar liberty of the gawky, graceless and uncultivated – and shrugged at Calvin's questions, while eyeing him up and down.

"*Puta*," she declared. "Aren't you a little old for Klarysa?"

"Aren't you a little old," he shot back, "to be reading children's books?"

"It's easy, painless; I understand all the words. Truthfully, I could never manage a tattoo for all the discomfort. Look, no earrings. Self-induced pain is for those who—"

"No problem passing your free time in a callow and obvious experience taken up by millions?"

"None whatsoever. And you?" she said poignantly, with a noxious, foreboding smirk.

"Shut up! Right there! You shut up!"

Her eyes dimmed slightly, like receding waters after the passing of a summer storm, lending her for the first time a soft, human regard. It really was a cruel thing of her to have insinuated. The tea-top, straps still joined at the back of the neck and traversing down over delicate shoulder blades, suddenly lay quiet, like a nursing child in the arms of its mother.

"That was not good of me," she said. "I'm… Look, we are not enemies. Honestly. Come in."

Taking Calvin by his free wrist, she retreated into the flat.

"Bah, let's forget it," he said, and asked if she had a number for La Casa de Jordi.

She did. She skipped into the kitchen and ran a child's finger down a pencil-scrawled list that was affixed to the refrigerator by a magnet shaped in the lasciviously rendered form of a naked sea nymph at play. Her finger slowed at a block letter *J* and came to a definitive stop at the first in a succession of three *Jordi*s. The written name was curiously missing, noted Calvin with suspicion, its commercially connoting modifier (i.e. 'La Casa de'), which, regardless, Calvin had wrongly envisioned with the upper case letters invariably required in signifying proper nouns. He suddenly had the distinct impression, as the flatmate handed him the telephone ("I'm Natalia, by the way. It's ringing." "Calvin. Thank you.") that he was not calling a place of business, but rather…

"*La casa de* Jordi Garcia," said the voice on the line.

Good, thought Calvin—an older Spanish woman; likely apron'd, with a tightly bun'd coif and a pin-stuck nametag.

"*Buenos dias, señora,*" he replied. "I would like to speak with Klarysa Pavlichenko, if you please. I believe she is there."

"Miss Klarysa?"

"That's her. Thank you."

"*Oh si,* Miss Klarysa is here."

"Splendid. Might I speak with her, then?"

"*Ahora, señor?*"

"Now seems a fine time. Grand. Let's do, please."

"O-o-h," she bellowed, as though she had seen another ghost and, as yet, had not quite made up her mind about such sightings. "I am sorry, *señor*, it is quite impossible at the moment.

"How so?"

"Why, she is in the bathtub."

"Having a bath, is she?" said Calvin, as distaste began to climb in his throat.

Natalia stared at him rapt, mouth egg-shaped and hard-boiled, looking as though she had wagered her tuition that fireworks would rocket from Calvin's dome. Calvin stared back with a blank gaze. All he could see was Klarysa naked at *la casa de* Jordi—lower case, private residence, *im*proper as all hell.

"Say!" he popped hotly into the receiver, "Just what kind of racket are you running over there, anyway?"

"*Señor?*"

"I say what gives over there? What are you pushing—Catalan knick-knacks? Tourist-trade doo-dads? Batik scarves, ceramic lizards, ash trays? Tapas? Warm meal? Out with it. A shit, shave and a tub if you're feeling in the mood?"

"*Señor! Por favour! Este es la casa de señor* Jordi Garcia!"

"I'm sorry. I'm sorry. *Lo siento mucho, señora,*" he conceded. "But now please, I must insist that you allow me a few quick words with Miss Klarysa... Come again?... Yes, yes, by all means; do please transfer the phone despite her submersion in neck-deep bathwater. That's correct; we will roll the dice and hope like mad against calamity and electrocution."

Natalia stood left over right, wetting a digit for friction and finger-flipping her way through her book like a savant, feigning great concern for the boy wizard, while silently chomping at the bit to hear Calvin's side of the forthcoming conversation with his seal pup tubbed in bath salts.

"Hello. Hello!" he barked into the receiver, competing with slapping waves of bath water.

"*Mon amour!*" she cheered. "You've arrived! How was the trip?"

"Fine, fine. Where are you?"

"I'm at *la casa de*—"

"I know! But what the hell does that *mean*?"

"*La casa* means *the house*. I thought absolutely *every*one knew that; even many Americans."

"Oh, we're slow on the uptake, all right! What *is* that place?"

"Don't be hard on yourself. You are like a little boy sometimes... Oh, love, no, I only mean to say that you are precious. Since you need to know, I am at my friend's house... That's right, drinking milk and having a bath and now, too, juggling a telephone with soapy hands and shampoo. Isn't this quite likely dangerous? There *is* electricity in these phones, is there not?"

"And where is our mate Jordi?"

"In bed, I suppose. He prefers to sleep away the ill-effects of a late night. I prefer a nice bath, if the tub is right."

Then, as though a prize nut had just fallen from the Great Oak of Revelation and knocked her square on the crown, she said, "You know, *you* might consider taking me to a raunchy jazz club once in a while, lover. Sweaty bodies everywhere, I admit—oh, and the wandering hands! Honestly, do I look like a trumpet?"

Strumpet perhaps, thought Calvin.

"But I suppose," she continued, "that's to be expected, what with all the whiskey and these brutal pre-summer nights. Is that a good word, love: *raunchy*?"

"I'd leave it alone," he advised. "Hell if I didn't *try* to take you to a jazz club—a hot one, no less!"

"Why, you don't mean that smelly cave in Antibes."

He rang off on the spot, almost involuntarily; a meek defensive reaction he hadn't quite recognised until hearing Natalia's voice.

"How did it go?" she enquired.

"About as well as you knew it would."

"Sorry."

Sweating, he said, "Bah, no sweat," and turned to leave.

"Wait," she said. Her book slapped down on the vast granite counter top and her hands came to rest on the hips of what Calvin only then began to identify as a surprisingly knowing and complex young woman. He wanted nothing more than to hightail it to anywhere wet, but she held him in place with a regard of which he hadn't thought her capable.

"Look, Calvin, you've done something to her. This week alone, I've heard her speak with childlike wonder of tree-ripened mangos the size of hens' eggs, dolphins, an island village called Aratuba and something she refers to with tangible confusion as the Eschaton— some strange end-of-the-world obscurity played out with tennis racquets. I've never seen her quite like this. It's something all right. But listen, soft-lining histories of foreign novelty on the innocent edge of her heart, however indelible the ink, will only make you a beloved poet. You underestimate her, as you've underestimated me. She is not a simple girl. Get your hands dirty, *hombre*. You must dig if you want to reach your Mesopotamia."

Natalia invited him to stay and await Klarysa's return. She told him to make himself a drink and relax. Feeling as though the poorly mannered events of the day might run further amok in his absence, he agreed. In an expensive rocks glass, he mixed a drink from the bottles lined on a server of smoked *vitrines* and eucalyptus and then reclined in white wicker on a balcony overlooking a one-way street made catatonic with siesta, while Natalia busied herself with tasks typical of lean young Eastern European women of a certain privilege with idyllic new designs for the bloated old Western world.

Calvin closed his eyes for a moment and boarded a train bound for the sober interior of Catalunya, away from the terracotta crust and cracked lips, away from the imposing coastal fever, towards the green hills rolling west of Tibidabo, where mist and steam did on occasion rise as though from the mouth of a huffing South American jungle, away to snake along the Columbia River gorge from Portland to Hood River and beyond, into a brittle country neglected by all but the sun and the serpent. Always moving, always chasing another untouched opposite, banking on the notion that a well-run journey will always reach a grand terminus, and so too that every man will eventually slow and come to rest upon his own pillow of equilibrium, and that once there, he will harvest his securities, build his home, and embrace his woman, all with his own good reliable steady hands, which will no longer twitch and flutter as they did when he was just a child, summer-tanned, a little boy half-asleep wherever he could, in the backseat of Pop's Toronado, he who drove and passed down regional fears greater than any of the national ones they began peddling, and enough quiet concern to drown all the fish in all the seas, in sideburns this man, and in one ribbed undershirt or another, Pop. Took the train away, away, peeking in and out of Spanish lands running hot and tan like those beyond Hood River, where he and Laika spent youthful days in the back of a red Subaru wagon, leaving behind old Oregon taverns, lying low and kissing, waiting for the cops to forget who and where they were. Took it away, away, now out onto a one-way Spanish street made catatonic with siesta.

"You know when I feel most vulnerable?" he tried, but his words went muffled by the hot leaden baffles of high siesta. And anyway, there was no one present who might listen.

Eventually Natalia entered the salon, bestowing the gift of feminine voice fleeced of concern, nimbly heaving a delicate lyrical axe into the heat and silence, drawing cracks at the outer edges of late siesta and working a wet towel with quick limbs about her wet head.

"It shouldn't be so hot in May," she began, tilting her head to the side and hopping on one foot to get the water out. "It's hard to get drunk in this heat, don't you think?"

"Evidently," said Calvin, "we suffer dissimilar maladies, you and me."

He slipped back the end of his glass and made once more for the server. He crossed the salon, skirting expensive furniture and objects in velvet, glass and dark wood, all of it prescribed by a well-funded designer with an august eye.

"You live well here," he said with the optimism born of the prospect of another drink.

She shrugged, unimpressed, not as an aristocrat from an inherited socioeconomic *niveau* against which she might take loans, but as a stubborn runt with an enduring outsider's lack of esteem for oft-prized household possessions. Natalia was, by design, a black sheep.

"Why not?" she said. "Nothing is free, if that's what you think. Make mine a gin, if you would."

"Your stuff, all this?"

"Ha-ha. Oh, no."

"Klarysa's then?"

"Bah, I don't know. Do you consider the White House, with its directional wings and all its lavish furnishings, the property of your president when he's in office and in possession of executive powers?"

Calvin excused himself, went to the loo and wondered rather randomly what Gem would think of him running illicit goods for Hector; what Hector might say about the beautiful woman who, after all, was not exactly awaiting Calvin's arrival in Barcelona; and what any of this had to do with Gem's longstanding advice on the tenuous topic of fighting when outnumbered, which seemed for some reason to suddenly bear relevance—aim for the biggest and best looking bloke, chances are he will have never been in a fight. And avoid at all costs those with nothing to lose.

Klarysa finally arrived. Calvin, from his wicker'd and balconied vantage point, could sense it without any real proof of life. Call it a hunch, when a gaudy Italian machine sped to abrupt halt below, where it moaned and growled, altogether annoyed at the idea of clogging such an unimpressive one-lane artery. At least the little thoroughfare had awoken and regained a modest post-siesta pulse. More reasonable models – Fiats and Seats and Renaults – stacked up behind it, sputtering and coughing in the heat with unrivalled patience, waiting, it would seem, for precious stones to shimmy loose and spill from the Ferrari's bucket seats *en cuir de vachette*. *Et voila*, Klarysa finally popped from the passenger's seat like a spring-loaded bon-bon onto black asphalt. Calvin half expected cheers from the Spanish gallery, but nothing; only heat and emissions rising like transparent daisies pushing up from Hades, as Klarysa quickly tip-toed across the street to the shaded sidewalk, careful not to caramelise her perfumed sugartoots post-session at *la casa de* Jordi.

Calvin began to count down from thirty, killed the top-half of his glass at twenty-five, bit a nail and searched the sky for the second coming from twenty to fifteen, braced for the flood at ten, stood erect at five, and at zero... No explosion, no deluge, no Dresden-grade firestorm.

"*Mi amor*! I'm home! I'm home!"

All seven syllables rang symphonic and all of Calvin's concerns dissipated thinner than the thinnest wisps of cirrus clouds over the hot Iberian Peninsula. The fear he had harboured was instantly rendered a sweet pea of joy and self-pride upon hearing the bright melody of her flowered voice, for divided love could never disguise itself in such rose-coloured cheer. Klarysa ran and thrust herself into his arms without reserve at a time when the oppressive heat would have served as a handy excuse with which to plead restraint. Divided love could never spring forth with such alacrity. Ha! thought Calvin. To hell with Jordi! Or rather, he amended, invite him round for a champagne lunch at la casa de Calvin!

"Why, it's really you!" she cried. And then with capriciousness to make even the skies of Brussels seem stagnant and consonant—for my honeydove breathes not at all, admired Calvin, if she does so without capriciousness!—she immediately begged, "Look! Don't you want to see my long hair?"

She spun about. Fluttering hands found the neck's nape and with a simple twist released a cascading flow alight in fiery chestnut.

Klarysa stood still, with tender shoulder blades a-blush, waiting, waiting for what seemed an awful lot like approval. There Calvin saw the little girl with whom he had picnicked on a February afternoon near Cap d'Ail, some months prior. Forget everything she was and was not when facing him with cocked shoulders and locked eyes; forget her genuine powers and those contrived and promoted for advancement in times of fear and insecurity; from behind she was not an ounce more than an unsuspecting child.

"What do you think?" she prompted, seeking him out over her shoulder for a sign of good favour.

He was convinced she might have stood there, vulnerable, virginal, until the end of time, waiting for him to annihilate her with word or weapon, or nourish and wrap her in a wash of softness and acceptance.

"It is already much longer than when we met in Nice, don't you think?" she sought. "*And* healthy; that's what is most important. Look."

There was still no sign of fatigue from her. A devil might make her stand there until she dropped of exhaustion so as to glean proof of her dependence on his good favour. The thought alone wrenched Calvin's heart. He would never ask her to wait for his favour. Would a loving parent test a child so? And though he could perceive not a millimetre's difference in its length since their previous visit, and knew no metrics by which to judge its health, he, of course, said with great conviction, "My god, how it has grown! It is gorgeous, my dear—*and* healthy. That, above all, is plain to see."

But just then his mind fell back to Natalia's dissertation, which had run the better of a cocktail and a half, had come free of charge to well-intended knit-wits in the grips of love and despair, and which aimed at illuminating the dangers of erring on the side of simple when calculating the powers of even the frailest of fairies. For, as Natalia had put it, wings and eyes and arse – not to mention fickle chemical impulses and other capital that can't be kissed – are the first mates of a rosy crew well footed in the histories of mutiny and toppled dynasties, forget that one rarely finds such truths unsullied in male revisionist narratives. Furthermore, Calvin recalled the fact that Klarysa had just returned home having left another man's bathtub, having drunk another man's milk, no less, never mind the continental details running inward from those coasts, devil take them whatever they may be. At any rate, he resolved, that was enough romantic sap. There would be plenty of time over the coming days in which to throw roses at her feet.

Facing him now, she clutched his forearms in her kitten paws. "Remember the day we met, *mi amor*? I remember every minute of it. You might not because memory deteriorates with age, but oh, what a day, I swear to you! Don't worry if you've forgotten most of it; men are like that. I shall recall for us both, down to the last detail. I should remember the winter for how kind it was to us, although inside, the memory feels just like summer—and *I'm* not old. How funny!"

She slipped off the ends of his fingers and danced a dreamy step over to the server.

"Maybe my memories of that day are coloured in summertime hues because of all the wine we drank. One doesn't drink wine in such a manner in February, I am sure of it," she said reaching for two fresh glasses. "Februaries are for bourbons and other whiskeys—I said so and you agreed. Anyway, it feels like *many* summers ago; the kind of summers you read about in the old café books. But thankfully we are still young. Or, well, at least… I hope gin is OK."

"Fine."

"I was very happy then, I'll have you know. Surely you haven't forgotten *that* much."

She suddenly hushed the winds and strings of her internal orchestra, squared her shoulders to Calvin from across the room and pre-emptively admonished him with hands on hips and pouting lips. "Why, you haven't forgotten *all* of it have you, Calvin?"

"I promise you," he defended with a laugh, overjoyed by the enthusiasm of his precocious wunderkind in red tartan skirt, "I haven't forgotten even the most frivolous stroke."

"Do not speak of frivolity, my dearest," she said, handing him a drink. "It is unbecoming of men of your season. You'll do much better to leave such talk to your more nimble half."

She sprung like bamboo onto a *repose pied* in garnet chenille. "Why, if I could," she continued, "I should stay blissfully trapped in the gilded frame of that golden February. Oh I'm still happy, to be sure. But now we are so terribly far apart, which is how it has to be, don't misunderstand me. Still, sometimes I think I might die of... Well wasn't it all just a miracle?"

She leapt down onto the parquet and raced back to him, seizing his hands, seemingly convinced that she would crack on the spot without his corroboration. "I believe in them, you know—miracles, I mean. Don't you?"

Forced to choose between lying to her and crushing her hope, he yanked her close and said, "Sure, my love. I believe."

He was about to press his lips hard against hers, when a door swung slowly open at the receding end of the long hallway. Privacy in a shared flat comes at a premium, and although Calvin and Natalia had established amicable common ground after their inauspicious start, he would have gladly traded her for a prized poodle and promptly shot the damned dog. The back-lit figure that emerged from the doorway, however, was not Natalia. Rather, it was a masculine figure, one back-lit so intensely despite Calvin and Klarysa's luminous perspective as to give the impression that the centre of the property lay somewhere significantly closer to the sun, and came pocked with skylights or a retractable dome. Calvin could only imagine what one might find in the guts of the flat—an inner terrace, a city park, the Garden of Eden itself with all its biblical flora and fauna and uncompromising deity?

The darkened figure was smooth; it lacked any of the loose material fray that might otherwise indicate that it felt chilled or self-conscious or experienced any of the banal sensations that typically caused one to wear clothing. Natalia, from another unseen *arrondissement* of the flat, barked orders, words with a distressingly high consonant-to-vowel ratio, driving the shadow back into the bright white cavity from whence it came.

"He claims," whispered Klarysa disapprovingly of the darkened figure, "that clothing restricts his flow."

Matching the H-laden breath of her whisper: "Do you mean to tell me he—"

"Yes, he is an atheist and a beast."

"No, I mean does he always go about... Bah, forget it. Say, you sure live well here."

"Sure," she said, eyeing him from six inches away. "Nothing is free, if that's what you think."

"What the hell? Do you two rehearse these lines?"

The figure reappeared, this time in dungarees, tall and lean, with or without God and *flow* Calvin could not say, and slipped like a greased spectre into the kitchen, where he apparently found Natalia and did *not* underestimate her. The purring that followed vibrated through the floorboards and shook the walls, as though a train were rapidly approaching. In the feverish coastal stretch that is a swelling and pulsating Barcelona, a fellow may sequester himself in any barrio, high or low, between walls as thick as ramparts, and still the sounds of love will make an audience of him; humming and buzzing around the clock, as immutable as the Pacific Ocean. Ebbing with the sun's cyclical defeat of the moon, and flooding with the moon's inevitable reclamation of the night, a faithful and rhythmic shore-pound slams home with clockwork regularity. For some, keeping one's clothes on in such a town was challenging.

The apartment shook. Two brazen conductors, locked and grappling with wild audacity and complete disregard for those standing idly agape on the platform and with nowhere to turn, drove a writhing carnal freight train through the middle of the third-floor flat in broad daylight.

"It's not stopping!" Calvin uttered, dumbstruck, in captive observance. There were likely one million ways, he reckoned, to get to Mesopotamia.

Finally, the caboose went slapping by. Decibels and pitch bent south in accordance with Doppler's mandate. Calvin and Klarysa watched the hallway, dusted in a dreamlike silt of slumber and the smoke of drawn cigarettes. In the ensuing calm, Calvin heard Klarysa babbling trancelike, "...with such punctuality... at the top of every third hour, except on Sundays and holidays, when a late morning bullet train supplements the standard timetable…"

"A train spotter's paradise, hey," noted Calvin.

Just then, there emerged yet another figure from a different, but equally flood-lit doorway in the same hall. One had to wonder if all doorways didn't lead to the same nucleus. This fellow was equally occupied, it seemed, with worries of flow restriction, only he was wider and darker of mane. Another of Natalia's rail mates? Why, thought Calvin, she has neither the frame nor flesh for all that!

Calvin had been planted in Spanish terra for all of three hours and had already been subjected to as many men in various stages of sartorial conflict. No, he had not actually seen Jordi, but one would naturally assume that the rogue followed suit, as it were. He wondered, in fact, if random unclothed men wouldn't start popping out of every nook and water cabinet in the damned flat.

Natalia barked no orders at the second fellow, and so he drew closer. Upon reaching the salon, he raised a big mitt in greeting. Torn boxer shorts hung anaemically from his pelvis, the width of which was thoroughly penned, indelibly, ornately, with esoteric designs in black and deep plum.

Gatsby and like-mannered protagonists of colossal proportions fare well in all situations, regardless of era. Though, to be fair, Calvin was up against a different make of antagonist—his adversaries gave little mind to proper social deportment. What's more, it is a hell of a lot easier to challenge a foe when one knows means. Calvin was forced to face his latest adversary with naught but a fiver in his pocket.

The fellow in boxer shorts looked like a ten-car pile-up, though one that would clean up all too nicely if one wanted Calvin's grim opinion. His hitched, morning-after gait, which belonged somewhere between six and seven in the morning, managed to convey an air of proprietorship even in the late afternoon. With a crooked smile that made Calvin want to smash the fellow's handsome face, he introduced himself as Ferran. Calvin winced with the knowledge that outsiders in Southern Europe did not win many battles against guys with olive skin, wavy black hair, deep onyx eyes and names the likes of Ferran. Oh, one might ball up his fists and knock flat such a fellow, but in the grand social scheme of things, one still lost, and often quite decidedly at that.

Leveraging the momentum born of all the generous exaggerations of literature and cinema, the ease of Ferran's Latin manner was perfectly thorough, and now Calvin couldn't decide which prospect was more disheartening: the bloke as a long-term fixture in the flat, or a mid-day prop booked in hourly increments. Having identified a quality of the Great Dane in Ferran – whereby his stature was imposing to all but his master or mistress – Calvin grew disconcerted by how seemingly unaffected Klarysa was by his presence. She appeared to be dreaming of another salt bath.

Ferran placed a hand on Klarysa's bare shoulder, said something in Russian (*ha!*) and won for himself a *bisous*.

"You are Russian," broke Calvin, eagerly eyeing the classroom that did not exist, thoroughly hoping nonetheless that just one boot-licking student (Anyone? Klarysa?) might pick up on his keen investigative insight and shoot him an admiring wink of encouragement. Bah, nothing. Calvin continued alone, "I am almost certain that was Russian you just spoke, and too Fabergé-accented, I might add, to have been acquired off the nipple. And yet you call yourself Ferran. Isn't that right?"

A Russian on Spanish holiday, with the gall to call himself Ferran, Calvin charged. Confess to the shirtsleeve arrogance of such self-granted license, you beggar!

With his eyes fixed on Calvin, and Klarysa's angled towards Tahiti, or some other distant isle on which there were bound to be fewer territorial bulls, and from where the ocean breeze now parted her lips in a sigh of blanch annoyance, a slowly poured smile spread broadly across Ferran's face. Then, with a flippant shrug, he confessed, "Sure. I am Russian. So what? I am in Spain for one lousy month. Long enough to make a few worthwhile connections, but not so long as to waste precious time and money overcoming the global mistrust attached to the name Adolph."

Klarysa attempted to explain. "His parents are—" but she was clipped short.

"Basta from you, маленькая девочка!"

"How dare you speak to me that way," Klarysa objected. "I've accommodated you in my home for the last two weeks, have I not?"

"*Her* home," he mocked, shooting Calvin a knowing wink, though Calvin knew not what to do with it.

The conflict between Klarysa and Ferran might have encouraged Calvin had it not come across quite so naturally, so domestically. It seemed almost as though one's knowledge of the other was a tract of earth that had been worked and tilled and perhaps even sown with the seeds of... He wisely shut his mind to the possibilities.

"The name Ferran, you would agree," he began explaining to Calvin, "is far easier to work with in Barcelona. It helps one to meet..." sensually rolling an invisible light-weight melon between his palms, "how to say... a certain kind of lady friend, or bedfellow. Do you say *bedfellow*?"

"No."

Calvin steamed. What frustration in having broken down a system or ciphered a code, only to find the mechanics so well engineered that the contraption still ticks!

"Next week in Verona," he continued unabated, "after a long weekend in Monaco with the *surnom* Rainier—a bit bombastic given the celebrity of *monsieur le prince*, I admit, but with a mere seventy-two hours in the principality, it is all or nothing; a fellow goes for gold. Anyway, in Verona I shall circle the coliseum blushingly at sunset as Luciano the Lonely. A kindred spirit, the young ladies will swoon, tragically abducted at birth and stolen away to be raised in *dread*ful Russia. It will be challenging, no doubt, despite being a natural tenor with a natural ear. I had considered adopting the name Leonardo, but thought that, even in Rome – a larger, more metropolitan city, despite all the religion and ruin – to be a bit too pretentious, not to mention the unfortunate cloud cast by the age-old debate as to certain sexual leanings. The susceptibility of the mind to even the most ridiculous suggestions... At any rate, forget it; too many lonely nights."

Ferran extended a pack of cigarettes to Calvin. He took two and didn't smoke either of them. Klarysa lit one, took a couple puffs and extinguished it. She didn't care so terribly much for smoking, she admitted, but loved setting objects ablaze.

"To save you from asking, because I know you are wondering," said Ferran, "my Greek features and complexion come from my father."

But Calvin had lost interest somewhere en route to Verona.

"Which makes Greece an obvious destination," Ferran continued. "But I've no time for Greece this summer."

Natalia and a fellow called Boris ambled into the salon, eliciting informal greetings from Calvin, Klarysa and Ferran, the three of whom had, for the last several minutes, described an awkward geometry of disenthralled vertices, an ill-invented polygon that pitched and leaned with quiet animosity under a pale patchwork of tobacco smoke. The arrival of Natalia and Boris caused a serrated smattering of Cyrillic phonology to careen about the room. Boris said something, laughed low and received a sharp elbow from Natalia for the effort.

"Leave him alone," she said to Boris in English, warning Ferran, as well, by way of a stern glare.

Standing with his feet together, Ferran arched backward with his arms spread wide and blew a line of smoke at the ceiling. "Yes, Boris," he boomed, contorted. "Leave him alone!"

"You're an ass," Klarysa hissed.

Calvin felt the thumping anxiety that comes over a fellow when he is cornered, outnumbered, and in love with mercury. It could be said that all trust and goodwill had abandoned the room, but more accurate to say a thick void of trust and goodwill flooded it—the negativity was active, not passive.

Had the Cold War really ended, or were Reagan and Gorbachev only out for press? Calvin heard the same warning sirens that wailed on the first Friday of every month throughout his youth. Ostensibly, the sirens were sounded to test civilian reaction to approaching tornados, but one precocious classmate evangelised that, in truth, they were intended to test the reaction to an impending Russian invasion. With no school desk to crawl under, he made slowly for the wicker chair on the balcony.

Recognising the rise of another cold war of tiresome posturing and positioning, Calvin gauged his own desire to battle Ferran for control over a verdant island governed by a wily and complex mind that was susceptible to spells of peculiar logic. Would Calvin participate in this latest production of a dreary, ungainly history? Would he engage in destructive battle at the supple shores of this island, in defence of his own foreign ideals and for the sake of his own personal advancement? Hell no, he would not. Let any number of missiles enter her bay. If she wished to throw open her ports like a hot August whore and cavort with his adversaries, let her spread far and wide. He would step freely aside and impose no sanctions. Besides, who was he to say what was best for another? Who was he to invade and lay claim to something that did not belong to him, something he never really tried to understand in the first place?

Gather enough men of power – be their power granted, stolen, or make-believe – and they will distil themselves devils from a vicious soup of greed and intolerance.

Hungry for an ally, Calvin took solace in what he perceived to be a modicum of alliance with Natalia. Though no sooner had he embraced the consolation than she blurted something in Russian that caused the entire room to jiggle with laughter.

"Listen, you gorgeous little brats, I've got a fist of cocaine in my pants, so…"

That, anyway, is what Calvin wanted to say—not that he honestly thought it would gain him any ground. Besides, it was no longer true and in such desperate days, one did not bluff the possession of drugs for risk of being eaten alive.

Klarysa approached and took a seat on his lap. The wicker complained for a count and then fell silent. She put her arms around his neck and looked at him, though it seemed to Calvin more like watching than looking, and he grew self-conscious.

"*What*," he huffed a monosyllabic triton, the three prongs inquiring, declaring and accusing in turn.

"Relax," piped Ferran from across the room. "It's me they're laughing at. I'm an *an*imal."

"Of the vilest sort!" Klarysa added. "Be thankful you're nothing like him," she said to Calvin with sufficient volume for all to hear.

"*Grrrrr*!" from the soi-disant animal.

"Honestly, I de*test* you," said Natalia, who stood with Boris to leave.

As they passed Ferran, Natalia swatted him on the arse. He stuck it out there to give her an easy target. "*Grrrrr*!" she growled back at him and giggled, thus greatly jeopardising the integrity of the honesty she purported.

"Take a good look at this man," Klarysa instructed Ferran, while clinging to Calvin's neck.

Ferran complied, salivating, waiting for the challenge to be cast.

Under slightly different circumstances, Calvin would have stood and took his best shot at denting the fellow's skull with one piece or another of heavy contemporary art, the surprisingly tasteful options within arm's reach not limited in number. But Klarysa's defence of him was debilitating, was warm butter over the soapy lather of his Southside hormones, the ones that fired for evening a score by violent means when low-grade displays of disrespect had given the other party an ill-gained advantage.

"What's your name again?" Ferran asked Calvin.

Klarysa answered on his behalf, and effectively drowned him in boiling butter.

"You could learn a thing or two from the likes of Calvin," she continued in her defence of him. "Why, just look how,"—In the presence of a trench-level foe, only dark mutinous credits are welcomed. All things considered, however, *gentlemanly*, *tolerant* or *dignified* would have sufficed as it concerned the completion of Klarysa's sentence, but it was not to be. "Why, just look how *well-behaved* he is!"

No, there would be no fighting back. The only option remaining for Calvin was to feign death. He sighed miserably and hung himself to dry over the side of the balcony.

The rays of a late-afternoon sun raced from the sky and barrelled down the narrow street, sending colourful waves of salted beef giggling and panting towards curb-side cafés and other shaded oases. There is no singeing the spirit of the Barcelona youth. Down the street was a *cerveceria* with a sun-blunted awning, which served beer and Jerez and *vino tinto*. Men of resignation drank there. Three masons in chalk overalls squinted in silence at a sandwich board, as though watching the majesty ooze from a dying bull. One ordered for all three. A short squat man in a mid-length smock stained purple from a lifetime of trimming and dressing flesh made a companion of brandy in a small snifter and white coffee in a short tapered water glass. When he drank, his smallest finger pointed high and proud towards heaven. Had Calvin not felt like a flightless dodo, he would have flown from the balcony. There was a round pink man wearing an after-thought suit and an after-thought tie, and with plump nervous hands a-twitter, tinkering with a beer in a tall cool *tubo* beaded with sweat, killing it in thirds. There were *bocadillos* filled with thinly sliced meats and hard cheeses, and grannies with pastries and cream and coffee, and hard-edged labourers who snapped newspapers over their knees, made clean folds and called out lines from the news of the day and goings on in mistrusted Madrid. The smocked man stole glances at the pink man in the after-thought suit and ran a flat hand slowly down the front of his smock, smooth—an allegation, an assertion, a gesture of brotherly advice, somehow everything and nothing at all. He watched out of the corners of his eyes as the pink man lifted and killed a new beer in two smooth rushes, while the barman made his change. The pink man lifted a hand, halted the barman, told him to turn the change into another *caña*, which he kicked back presently with just a wee hitch, a hitch deployed with futility in attempts to disguise the hounds of despair that circled him hungrily. Exposed, he looked over at the smocked man, who smoothed his front once again with an open palm and took another sip of regal-glint brandy. Regret and concern reflected from the gesture. The world felt a pang for the man in the suit, what with his unpleasant business, his news to break, his confessions to deliver. What he wouldn't have given to jump into the boots and britches of the smocked man and never look back. The smocked man tipped his glass to the poor man in the suit and slid back the remainder of his snifter. Then one man headed up the street and the other down, never to meet again.

Calvin sat on the balcony, mentally penning his invisible role in these productions of far-off lives in far-off lands. The man in the suit would ramble on, making his way, shaking his way through life amidst the comings and goings of *la gente*, a people that would forever continue to gather on that beautiful arid patch, and all the great patches of wide-open Spanish land.

Brought out of his stupor by what sounded like an electrical storm crackling at his feet, Calvin spied a wee grey kitten working its claws on one of the wicker legs. Klarysa was no longer on his lap. He recognised Ferran's voice mingling with Klarysa's and lamented the fact that he would never understand Russian. There were no deep-rooted obstructions to keep him from learning the language; he simply sensed that it would not come to be, the same way it will eventually dawn on the glove-confused six-year-old that he will never make a big-league shortstop.

Calvin turned his head and saw Ferran plant a quick kiss on the crown of Klarysa's head, drop a short stack of bills on her lap and walk out of the room.

"What's with the money?" asked Calvin when it was once again just the two of them. "And the lip service?"

"Nothing. Just payment for services rendered."

"I see. What kind of services?"

"The worst kind—domestic."

"I trust it didn't entail the changing of soiled nappies."

She didn't respond.

"And the kiss?" he asked.

"The kiss was most probably interest."

"Fascinating. Compounded daily? Monthly? How deep is he into you, anyway? Don't...! I mean how much does he *owe* you for crissake?"

"I don't mean that kind of interest."

"What the hell kind of interest do you mean?"

"But it's true that nothing comes free between these walls," she said.

"It's a regular motto around here."

"I'm not about to start *item*ising for him or anyone else who passes through here, though."

Klarysa was rarely in the same conversational stream with Calvin. She would generally flow towards the same sea, but almost always in her own twisting tributary.

"Good traffic through here is what you're saying," said Calvin, thoroughly piqued.

"I state a price and that's all there is to it. Why, I work any fi*nan*cial interest in with the principle."

She slid open a thin hidden drawer in the *table basse* and deposited the money. It was all too mechanical for Calvin's liking. At that moment, for perhaps the first time, Calvin saw Klarysa as a *woman*—a woman with a keen sense of consequence and with bills to pay and with finely calibrated ideas as to how to get the damned things paid. He didn't enjoy seeing her so deliberate. He rather preferred her more accidental ways.

"Don't you want to finger it a bit?" Calvin grumbled. "Count it? Make sure it's all there?"

"Lord no. I hate counting money. The worst thing a*bout* money is that you have to count it from time to time. Everyone expects you to know how much you have at all times. It's nothing short of exasperating. Anyway, I think I've managed my affairs quite admirably to date. Anyone could tell you so."

"That *is* a fear."

"What is a fear?"

"Pah! That Ferran for starters! Don't tell me you've *been* with that ape."

"Don't be ridiculous," she said with the pensive expression of a girl who couldn't say whether she'd lost that missing tenner or spent it somewhere between the green grocer's and the coiffeur. "You may not believe it, but you are my first."

"Ape or man?" he scoffed with narrowed eyes.

"Is there a difference?" she jabbed.

He growled, then stopped, realising that he was proving her point.

"Oh, sweetest heart," she begged, "don't be cross. I'm not good with jokes. Of course there are *some* differences. *You* are different, for starters. Why, you're no animal—you're harmless."

"Is that supposed to be a compliment?" he asked nastily.

"It absolutely *is* a compliment! Why is it that men assign such value to harmful, brusque qualities? I'm quite serious when I say you are a first."

"The heat must be getting to you, darling," said Calvin. "I'd be tickled breathless if I thought I was one of your first ten."

"From the first to the last, the aggregate number is meaningless. What matters is the *types* of men tried, and that number," lowering her eyes in palpable perplexity, "is all too manageable. Men can be downright nasty beasts. Take my word for it."

"I see. I'm the first of a genre."

"A special genre. Don't tell me you deceived yourself with that ordinal indicator."

"Oh, no, sweetest heart. Not for one goddamned second! Jesus, go easy for crissake, would you."

"But darling, I have – and have had for some time now – certain needs. Nana always said I was precocious."

A fresh batch of questions baked in Calvin's brain, but his attention was suddenly diverted. The kitten was back at his feet, lapping at his ankle with its adorably hooked tongue, and taking the occasional nip with its less-adorably needle-lined puss. Damn if he weren't marked for abuse from all angles in that flat! Having finally accepted the fact that Calvin was not a dead Dorade Royale – he only smelt like it – the kitten quit nipping and leapt up onto the balcony railing, where it froze and eyed him solicitously, as though it were eager to strike a hot deal and time was of the essence. Despite his desire, however, Calvin could be of no help, for no sooner had he noticed the angel-hair pull around the kitten's skinny neck than the line was yanked instantly taut and the feline followed an unforgivingly flat trajectory towards parquet *en bois massif*—a direct descent to challenge even the magical keel that keeps cats upright.

Klarysa, lying in classic recline on the meridian, watched the limp string running from her hand, and then yanked it again, this time not so hard. With loving admonition she ordered, "Come here, Kat!"

She reeled in the reprehended mite with a look of grave disappointment. Appearing on the edge of tears, she pleaded, "Why won't she learn that she can't go rambling about on third-floor balconies! She's not yet old enough to accommodate every instinctive whim and live to purr about it."

"I don't think you have anything to worry about," said Calvin, rather alarmed by the display. "Cats know their limitations."

"They most certainly do not!" Klarysa cried.

The grey wisp was curled and purring on her childish bosom.

"Must they not occasionally slip and fall that we might know they always land on their feet?"

There would always be strings, pondered Calvin, poor puss, with which muddle-headed mothers would simulate errant steps.

"Hell, you can't possibly keep a cat on a leash," he said. "It's perfectly absurd."

Klarysa jack-knifed instantly at the waist and leaned towards Calvin. The cat flew a short distance and then scampered off.

"Listen, you!" she demanded with glistening eyes. "I keep this cat on a leash for *e*veryone's sake! Oh, the richness of you men! Do you have any idea what would happen if I let it off the leash? I do my best to be prudent and responsible, but at every turn, some smarmy devil is telling me to lighten up, relax a little, take a chance. The world is one big contradiction, and the single toughest position you can find yourself in is that of a single woman. You men sure put up some show. You're always quick with the advice, as long as you stand to profit from it. You do whatever the hell you like without consequence. As for me, whether I do or I don't, somebody is there to tell me where I've gone wrong. I may be clumsy at times, and every now and again I might fail miserably, but hell if I don't try my best. I try to be thoughtful, caring, responsible."

Klarysa tried to be a good neighbour to her personal limitations. She admired them the way one who doesn't much care for children admires the freshness of a five-year-old.

"Sometimes my desires get the better of me," she continued. "I'm a champion of freedom, all right, but I try to keep *this* cat on a short leash."

The grey kitten was nowhere to be seen.

"The sweet thing is a veritable lioness at times and controlling it during such moments is impossible. It tries to gnaw its way free, and yes, it does occasionally succeed. You can bemoan that reality all you want, but that's all there is to it! Listen, I have a will—when I'm feeling strong. Have I mentioned that it's the most expensive cat one can buy? I'm keeping the little prize on a string until it's old and wrinkled or until its native instincts run dry. But it's never good enough."

The kitten reappeared, leaping up onto the table. It sniffed gingerly at the cyclamen; then batted and snapped off one of the fuchsia buds.

"I'll have you know I'm not very careful with plants," she said.

"Does precious have a name?" enquired Calvin, at a loss.

"Of course. I named her before she could even open her eyes, much less run about and torment the entire apartment block. It's the most expensive cat one can buy; everyone seems to agree."

It was the most peculiar acclaim Calvin had ever heard used in praise of a pet. "How is it called, then?" he asked.

"Kat," she replied.

Calvin was disappointed in himself for not having guessed as much. He thought to ask Klarysa if she were accustomed to accepting 50-notes to go to the powder room, or if she made weekly visits to mob bosses in Sing Sing, or departed the prison with coded messages cartoonishly wrapped in unlikely weather reports. Thinking all that a bit much, he asked, "You know who else had a cat so named?"

"Sure," she said. "But this one is spelled with a *K*."

"And the name of Holly's tabby was spelled with a *C*?"

"I have no idea. It seems they rarely roll credits for cats in films. You know, you could be an engineer or a lawyer, what with all your attention to meaningless details. It is exasperating at times, but I *do* love you dearly. We must learn to accept each other's intricacies."

"A cat named Kat," Calvin muttered. "Why not? Forget the tautology."

"It might be obvious, even silly," she admitted, "but it is not a tautology. After the last time you used that word, I looked it up. You can't have a tautology with only one word. I learnt that myself. See, I try to make you proud of me, you brute. If you are angry at me for whatever reason, come clean, but please don't be so cruel as to rub my face in the limitations of my *fourth* language…"

Zing! Calvin would have surely gone pie-eyed with awe were he not so consumed by a crush of shame and embarrassment. When a wronged woman has a culprit dead to rights, only the most merciful and generous of them will lift the stiletto from his jugular.

"Or else," she continued with a generous, loving smile, "I'll revert to my Russian tongue and you won't stand a swimsuit's chance in Siberia."

Temporarily wracked with frustration and uncertainty, Calvin had inadvertently committed one of the most frequent and shameful crimes largely specific to mono-linguistic peoples—underestimating the ability of the non-native mind, based on the timber of the non-native tongue.

"Oh god I'm sorry," he moaned. "I'm really very sorry. I don't know what's gotten into me." He looked about the room. "What *is* it about this place? Absolutely disarming! I can barely remember my name and can't feel my legs."

"You underestimate me for starters."

Amazing, thought Calvin, either everyone in this house is on cue cards or I am terribly obvious.

"And that's what hurts," she concluded.

It was not like Calvin to take things for granted. In truth, he had found it rather unbelievable that Klarysa would ever come to profess love for him. He quite simply did not know what had gotten into him. Having apologised profusely, he asked if they might not start over.

With the help of Klarysa's animated fingers, an expensive fruit basket presented itself from under a crackling dome of golden cellophane. A bunch of grapes tumbled lazily over the edge of the basket. Two bananas fell out and rocked themselves to sleep. An energetic orange made a run for it and jumped off the *table basse*. An envious magenta-hued mango wanted to follow, but lost its nerve and came to a wobbling halt at the table's edge. And for the first time all day, a cool breeze blew through the salon.

"My darling," said Klarysa, plucking an apple from the middle of the basket. "Come here."

Calvin complied.

"Let's please don't start over," she said. "Let's instead go forth with what we've learnt, better equipped as such to face what lies ahead. All lives face challenges, but I want you to know that you have no reason to be suspicious—not of me at any rate. You are in Barcelona now. Here it is all ease and beauty."

"I am sorry," he said, his green eyes sparkling under a thin sheen of moisture, "if I seem hesitant. History and its long, swollen fingers of influence…"

"I understand. But you don't need to fear me. I really have such little control over—"

"You have much more control than you profess," he said, walking out to the balcony.

"Bah, control is almost as irrelevant as it is imaginary. What I mean is, the only thing any of us really have to fear is ourselves. We tend to do the ambushing and the sabotaging just fine all on our own. You, for example, fear loss, so you try to self-vaccinate with little doses of the same junk. But all you end up doing is poisoning yourself. None of it is easy of course, but as your own aggressor, you only make matters worse. The past has its finger on you, Calvin. OK, it does most of us. Just don't give in so easily to the handicap."

She tossed him the apple.

"Anyway, none of it really matters so terribly much. I love you and I'm going to help you. Now eat, you must be starving."

Calvin studied the apple. It was firm and shiny. He could see himself on its surface, his features funhouse-perverted. He looked down from the balcony towards the street below. The sun, a blood-orange, owing to the late hour, continued along its line of descent, and all was peaceful. A smattering of pigeons flapped iridescent, then stopped their wings in unison and floated angelically past Calvin's feet on a gentle updraft. Eventually all things find their places in the world. The smocked man had his brandy and his craft, the pink fellow in the ill-fitting suit had his crimes and confessions, and Calvin had Klarysa, at least for the moment, which was all that really mattered. He also had his apple, the convex quality of which caused his reflection to fall away over its hemispheres so that he saw naught but a distorted face. Wishing to see it no longer, he took a big bite.

We lay in silence on the long brown couch.

I wonder with slit and dreamy eyes at the familiar walls that surround. Young whelps stand with arms locked at the shoulders and chins lifted above the horizon, looking down adolescent noses. A camera snap. What lies beyond if these here walls were to tumble down? Oceans? Deserts? Endless expanse of openness? More and more walls? Nicki lay at my side, lay like an exotic mirage between me and the back of the couch, my arm wrap around her naked shoulders, her head lay on my wiry birdcage chest.

Lime-green birds trapped, stacked high in colorful cages, chins lifted above the horizon, bright lights, street horns and street metal, swing they elbows, stomp they feet. A camera snap. So young these boys, watch the strength, watch the courage in they eyes, chins above the horizon. A camera snap. Watch the scars on they skinny arms and faces, defiant mouths bent downward. How they hang from each other in a pack, hardened etchings inexplicable on so young faces. Snap.

Nicki, she feel the far-away chill. She press warmer against me. Thirteen-years-old and I must be crazy. Watch the walls, the sharp edges of life, the concrete, cold metal, sting of hunger, smell of cement—what it smell like when my teeth hit it—city dirt, motor oil, my cheek smack flat on a street and the stars come out and twirl

Don't leave me again

Rattle in my grip, shoe-tip in the spaces between, jump and hit it high, up toward the top cross-bar so the chain-link don't give and sway when I hit it fast, reach up and over, grab another handful of metal and swing up and over to the other side

Pug, he left first

Quick jab steps, for to not slip on the gravel and broken glass and then dig in with full stride, fast as I can. Don't look back, don't look back for nothing. Too much lie ahead. Got to pay attention. Got to learn

This is Garfield. Don't leave me no more

Katie stares wide-eyed beyond the tattered edges of an empty November night, off on some bright-white Colorado mountain top. She's seen and touched something big. Something has me dizzy. I'm sick. Mountainous calluses, stained Two J's, goddamn simple no-account.

The duffle is empty. Dez tuck it away and sit on the cot. It screech under his weight *A lime-green flurry* Looks around him *Confused childlike hallucination* How a brick warehouse becomes a home when a judge declare he drink too much *See what you do to your mother* Got to keep away from his baby girl.

7   The new occupiers

In which a toreador is gored and
a smoke-and-mirrors man earns
his keep.

Calvin sat in a nameless bar in the Musicians quarter, his bar of
choice when in need of a reprieve from the crew and its tendencies.
He sat at the far end of the long bar, amid a number of retreaded
suits and a few tables spotted with local Niçoise peaches sufficiently
dolled and taped-up to get away with it at least until sunrise, and
read a tattered 1955 first-edition novel in which a narrator spoke of
missiles and tanks and other wartime weaponry that had been
decommissioned at the end of the second Great War and turned into
curb-side memorial installations, and whose haunting visual
attributes had soon become so familiar that the citizens of the
American West town described no longer recognised these weapons
as tools of suffering and destruction, but rather cosy furniture-
fixtures to be admired, there in the living room of its civilian
community. That had been the governor's very goal, explained the
narrator—to give new flesh to the notion of war and all its
accoutrements, to disguise the devices of death and destruction as
flag-waving citizens with rights to protection, promotion and
prosperity. In essence, to bring tanks and teddy bears together in the
same emotional sphere, to touch the same warm emotional buttons.
He didn't just speak of these things, the narrator, but spoke of them
sati*ri*cally, *in 1955*, which was something, thought Calvin.

Calvin winced when he noticed Aloysius framed in the doorway and futilely attempted to hide behind seventy-five centilitres of Val Dieux Grand Reserve. Having been spotted, he quickly sacrificed his poor journal to the top of the barstool adjacent him, to give the impression of an occupied seat.

"Calvin!" Al cheered. "What are *you* doing here?"

Al's big mitt clapped down on Calvin's shoulder with a clammy slap. Calvin groaned. "Must you throw those wet blankets over everything in sight? I thought you were getting that sorted out."

Al removed his hand and examined the wet-darkened print left on Calvin's shirt. Al had a rare talent for finding a fellow when a fellow wanted most to stay hidden. He had a canine's nose for sniffing out contentment and a canine's lack of restraint for stamping his soggy paws all over it. Al was a good friend of Calvin's, but the latter had put in a hard week of work and there were times when a fellow wanted to stay lost in his own slow-spinning world. Now here was Al, looking like a lumberjack who had lost his trees, drying his hands in the cottony nests of his flannelled armpits. Al dealt in antiques. It was a delicate line of business that was not necessarily at odds with his size, but with his lack of fine tuning absolutely. At any time, one might think he had just washed his hands and dried them off on a *croque monsieur* or a garage man's filthy boot. His hands were big and meaty and his handshake that of dead fish. He did not shake hands as much as haul out a sweaty stump and hope that his acquaintance would give it a good rub down.

"Hyperactive sweat glands, Calvin. Doctor says there's nothing to be done about it."

"For starters, you might dress in a lighter gage of tent in the summertime."

"Negative. My people like flannel."

Aloysius was equal parts Vilnius and Minneapolis. Under a line of dour circumstances, Al remained an optimist to the end, though he had never been able to inspire optimism in another. It is a precious commodity, optimism, but life is a balancing act in which all things are best pursued in moderation. Al was too roughly calibrated to detect the daily subtleties that shape one's forecast for the future, and his lofty optimism was beyond all reasonable justification. Over time, the combination eroded his credibility and he began to look less like a man and more like a Golden Retriever with too many liberties.

"You live on the Mediterranean, Al. Try to adapt."

"Listen, I sweat. There's nothing to be done about it."

"Fine. But stop touching everything."

"They're my *hands*, genius."

He held them up in the manner of a scrubbed surgeon, for Calvin's inspection.

"How am I supposed to…" he began, but broke off upon noticing Calvin's journal on the barstool. "What's this?"

"You can't sit there," said Calvin.

"Why not?"

"It's taken."

"Negative."

Al took the journal in his big grubby mitts and pawed through the pages as though digging for buried treasure. It wilted in his grip.

"Give me that!"

Calvin ripped the journal away from him and gently wrung it out a bit.

"I can only hope you don't handle women the way you handle books."

"They do melt in my hands, if that's what you mean," said Al, with a lewd grin slashing across his pie-round head. "Just like that precious journal of yours."

"Well, I've tried everything over the years and it seems there really is no getting rid of you. You may as well sit. But don't touch anything for crissake."

"Don't touch anything? Why, I have half a mind to walk right back out the door."

"And don't be a tease. What are you drinking?"

"Vodka. Double."

Calvin ordered the double.

"No, not that one!" Al screamed at the barman. "The other one, the other one. What do you take me for, anyway?"

"Why, he takes you for a big fat bloody Russian is what."

"But I'm Lithuanian."

"That's good Russian vodka, what. You don't even know how it's called, the other stuff. You just like the price of it—seeing as I'm buying. I try to stand you a decent drink and you act like an animal.

That's why your stomach is all burpy and distended—you don't show it any respect."

Al shook his melon-head in mock empathy, "Come on then, Calvin. Tell Uncle Al all about it. What's eating you? Let me help you out."

"A fellow can do without your kind of help. Uncle Al's help leaves a guy with less in his wallet, less in his glass and ready to jump off the balcony."

"*Pro bono* has had its day," said Al. "It's all capitalism from here on out. And I'm all capitalist. Unlike you, I understand the ramifications of... Hey, that bit about jumping off the balcony? Unwarranted if you're referring to Marcel le Dingue."

"If I had the good fortune right now of a balcony and little elevation, I'd show you just how sane sweet old Marcel le Dingue was that night. Capitalist. Pah! There is no demand for your nerve-wracking supply."

"And yet, by the end of the night, you'll have stood me a good few drinks and lent me a couple hundred francs."

"Not a chance."

"I'm already into you for a double and I've only just sat down. Any word on Marcel le Dingue, by the way? Is he OK?"

"Depends who you ask."

"But he's out of the body cast, I mean. I should pay the old boy a good visit."

"His poor wife would draw and quarter you on sight."

"She's upset at me? *I'm* sharing some wisdom with the geezer and *he* jumps off the balcony. I'll not be held responsible for that. At any rate," said Al with lascivious apple-pie eyes, "I'd be happy to have the wife draw me, though I admit the quartering sounds uncomfortable."

"Imagine the poor horses charged with the task."

"What's this?" asked Al, snatching up Calvin's heavy beer bottle. "Order me one of these, hey."

"They don't serve it here."

"Hey!" Al yelled behind the bar. "Let's have another one of these here."

The bartender was a new fellow, a mere child from Nancy, in the North-Eastern department of Meurthe-Et-Moselle. The boy was kind and tender and would have done well to have stayed in the North.

"*Cou cou*," chirped Al, as though coaxing a baby bird from the nest. "Bottle of beer off the wall?"

Uncertain, the barman eyed Calvin, whose look indicated there was nothing to fear, that Al was only a harmless dolt.

"But we don't have any Belgian beers, *monsieur*," chanced the barman tentatively.

Al turned to Calvin. "The child says they don't serve the stuff here."

"There you have it."

Al smiled. He detested such games, but Calvin let him off the hook anyway. "I bring my own bottles," he explained, "and tip well for the authority to do so. Everyone is happy."

"Make it another double, then," Al told the barman. Then to Calvin, he said, "For an ascetic, you sure are fond of complicating matters. Where'd you get this, then?"

"A friend of mine. A guy I know from the Rive Bleue."

"Bullshit."

"What?"

"There's a tourist industry to protect around here."

"Do the world a favour, Al—spend less time with Sandoval."

"Do they really let you in at the Rive Bleue, Calvin? But they're trying to sell fantasies, right? Not nightmares. Hey, I like your sneakers. You get those new?"

Al killed the second double in a single go. "How'd it go in Barcelona, anyway?" he asked. "Sandoval says you're up to your neck. Look, Calvin, you have to take control with a gal like that."

"A gal like *what*?"

"You have to go to her, take her in your arms and say, 'Now look here—'"

"Wasn't I just in Barcelona?" Calvin defended.

"Well, how'd it go over?" Al blew air. "I'm asking you here."

Before Calvin could respond, Al grabbed his glass of beer and took a gulp. "Say, that is *some* grog. What'll you take for three fingers of it? Name your price. Though it must be said, Calvin, that grovelling over money among friends is uncouth."

"That's what I'm told," replied Calvin. "Of course you, Al, hide out on the credited side of any deal. You, Big Al, are what they call a bad debtor, a black hole, a money pit."

"Hey, you can forget it if you want me to grovel. It's not my calling. I deal in an*tiques*, remember. Used to, anyway. Is that what you want me to do, Calvin? You want me to grovel?"

"No, I don't want you to grovel. I want you to contribute once in a while. I don't care if it's five goddamned Lithuanian shillings, I want to see you slap some hard currency on the table every now and again."

"Con*tri*bute?" Al spat. "But I already told you I'm a capitalist. Moreover, I haven't a centime on me."

"Well, what the hell gave you the idea of coming into a capitalist establishment without any money? Don't you know how the model works? You have no right to be here."

"But I had a hunch *you'd* be here," said Al, appearing genuinely hurt. He filled their glasses with the last of the beer and shoved Calvin's at him with a serious nod that said *No, no, trust me, it's good, you'll like it.*

The two touched glasses.

"*Santé*," said Al.

"*Santé*," said Calvin.

Al kicked back his glass like an American lad at a Mexican wedding.

"What do you mean," said Calvin, "you *used* to work in antiques?"

"I got the sack," Al admitted. "Believe it or not."

The two watched each other in silence. Finally, Al said, "It's all for the best, really."

"Sacked," said Calvin with a degree of surprise.

"That's it."

"How about that. Boss Man couldn't tolerate you any longer, hey?"

"Not another day."

"What happened? You warp all the fancy antique wood with those watermelon hands of yours?

Aloysius once witnessed a very large woman bonk a fellow square on the crown. Young Al objected, "Stop, Marta, you brute!" "It's *Boss Man* to you, little Al!" said the very large woman, who then delivered Al a similar blow. It was *Boss Man* from that moment forward, not only to Al, but to everyone. Boss Man stood a cool six feet, two inches tall, and weighed not a stone less than her shoe size, which would have been the largest on the squad had she been a member of the Lithuanian men's national basketball team. The worst of it for Al was that Boss Man was not only his boss, but his mother.

"Sacked by your own mother," Calvin commiserated. "I'm sorry to hear it, Big Al. I really am. What are you going to do now?"

"I'm not certain. I have an idea, though," he said unconvincingly.

"Can't deal in electronics; you'd short out all the circuitry. Nothing involving paper products, that's for sure. Hmm. Have to think *wet*... Lifeguard!" blurted Calvin. "Can you keep that body of yours afloat long enough to do anything positive with it?"

"No. You're not listening," said Al, drained of his signature optimism.

"OK, OK," said Calvin. "Tell me, then. What's the trouble?"

"I'm thinking of starting a new firm, see."

"What did you have in mind?"

Aloysius swallowed hard. "Russian artefacts, rare treasures," he said looking sickly at Calvin.

"What's the problem? Boss Man?"

"Oh, sod Boss Man! I slip the Russians a little cheese, they'll protect me."

"You'll have to move house. No more bedtime stories. Sunday brunch will never be the same."

With concern and sincerity, Al asked, "Calvin, don't you ever worry about things?"

"Sure. Like what?"

"Bah. Forget it," Al retracted. "There are big things in store for a guy like me. But you want to know why she sacked me? I won't lie, Calvin," he said, drying his hands on his ribcage, "I don't feel comfortable talking about this."

"Are you in trouble, Al?" Calvin asked pointedly.

"No. Not yet. A fellow has to eat, though."

"Is that all? No problem. You want work? I can get you work, Al."

Calvin said as much, but he wasn't entirely sure. There was plenty of work on the coast for quick-witted, quick-limbed blokes; the lean fellows, those who learnt quickly, worked hard and knew how to scramble—in essence, any from a gamely group that did not include poor Aloysius. Al was big and slow and cumbersome and when Calvin suddenly perceived such an ill-equipped fellow lagging behind in the merciless world, it mattered little if he was a member of the crew or some random dumb pup, Calvin welled-up with protective juice.

"Look, Al" he said resolutely, "I can *get* you work. I can."

"Hell, you don't understand, Calvin. I'm not smart like you lot."

"Oh, sure – Gem, Arbuckle, Polish, Manx, the Butcher, Marcel le Dingue – we're a regular bunch of geniuses."

"Don't patronise me, Calvin. You *have* something. You know how to get by. Maybe not Marcel le Dingue, OK. But what do I have?"

"Hell, you have us geniuses," said Calvin, unimpressed, "if nothing else. We're one big family, crack-pot as it may be."

"You know why she sacked me?"

The words were stuck in Al's throat. He couldn't get them out.

"There's a guy, see."

He ran his wet palms over his ribcage again. Finally, his words came dislodged and ran like a stream from his big round gob.

"Lord knows anyone on the coast can be bought. The poor, the jobless, the forsaken; they can be bought with heart alone, and this guy's got heart all right. He's got much more than heart. Hell, take a guy like me. What have I got going for me? I'm not smart like you lot, Calvin. The only thing I have going for me is I know my limitations. It's worth the risk for a fellow like me to latch on to someone like… Hell, what have I got to lose?"

"Someone like whom?"

"It's not important—anybody. But *this* guy, he's not just anybody. He brought a crate into the shop. He wanted to store it in the warehouse." Al lowered his voice and looked about the bar. "I really shouldn't be telling you this, Calvin. This guy gets around, see. *You* probably know him."

"Me? I don't know anybody. French guy? What was in the crate?"

"What was in the crate? Hell… What was in the crate?"

"That's what I'm asking—what was in the crate? Is he French?"

"Of course *I* don't know what was in the bloody crate."

Al looked about, picked up his glass, shoved his snout into it and mumbled, "Russian artefacts. Maybe. I don't know." He killed the glass. "He's not French. Look, I *rea*lly shouldn't be telling you any of this. That's why Boss Man sacked me."

"Because you stored a crate of Russian artefacts and Boss Man hates the Russians. Is that it?"

"No, that's not it. But yes, she does hate the Russians."

Had Al slunk any lower, he'd have been under the bar. "*Stolen* Russian artefacts, Calvin," he whispered hoarsely. "Russian *trea*sures. Although I can't be certain. Hell, Calvin, you let some of the sorts around here get their hooks in you... We do just fine with armoires, bureaus, chandeliers; we don't need any cursed Russian..." Al's dark eyes sparkled with rapture. "Calvin, have you ever seen a Fabergé egg? I mean an honest-to-god Fabergé egg? In person? Ever hold one in your own bleeding hands?"

Al squared up to Calvin. Sweating profusely, he lifted his cupped hands, as though he were raising an invisible chalice. "The Danish Jubilee," he revelled, lost in an antique dealer's dream. "One of the eight lost Fabergé Imperial eggs. Its outer surface of light blue and white enamel, ornamented with gold and precious stones. On top sit the armorial bearings of the Danish Royal Family, supported by heraldic lions. *I* held it, Calvin—in *these* hands!"

"Damned unlucky egg. Sorry, Al, you lob a steak to a hungry mutt..."

But Al was beyond hearing petty jokes. If the astonishing intrigue had lodged itself in Al's arteries for months, confiding in Calvin was the cathartic stent that freed the blockage. He was suddenly exultant.

"Some old hen brought it into the shop for an appraisal. She hadn't the slightest notion what an impossible treasure she possessed. Said she'd picked it up at a *vide grenier*—a stinking rubbish sale! Ha! But first it came from that crate, I'm certain of it. That was over a year ago."

"A *year* ago? What did you do about the blooming egg?"

"Told the old lady it was a dandy little knock-off. Told her to put it in a curio cabinet and admire it during the holidays. She smiled and gave me fifty francs for the consultation. I bought a beer at the port with the fifty francs, then threw the beer – glass and all – into the sea and washed my hands of it. I didn't sleep for three weeks."

"Why, you could've had that egg for a song."

"I expected such disapproval from Boss Man—*that's* why she finally came round to sacking me. But Christ, Calvin, don't *you* play daft!"

"What?"

"You honestly think a fellow stands to profit by getting his hands on an Imperial egg, when it's not *his* bloody Imperial egg, for crissake? Pah! It's a death sentence is what it is. Listen, I've noticed plenty other rare gems around town since then, all of Soviet origin, none of them in Soviet hands, much less in the hands of collectors. Of course," finished Al with a regard that suggested prudence was a luxury of the wealthy, "now I'm jobless."

"Oh, *bro*ther. You're not thinking of—"

"Listen, he wanted the crate stored. I stored it, for a whole year, no less. I'm reliable. Maybe there's an opportunity for some work, there," said Al with shining eyes. "What have I got to lose?"

"Your goddamned legs for starters. Jesus, Big Al, you just said so yourself—you know how things work around here with the bloody Russians."

"Says the man who's *da*ting a bloody Russian."

"Which means I might actually know a thing or two. And Klarysa is Ukrainian, not Russian. And you watch your mouth. Look, Al, you want work, I'll get you work. *Hon*est work. Work that won't leave you with debts you can't clear."

"Hell, I'm not getting any richer telling you all this. Loan me two-hundred francs, for starters, Calvin. I'm good for it."

"Loan *you* two-hundred francs. For *star*ters!"

"I'm good for it. You just said you'd get me work."

"And not a single one of you can fathom why I need a night alone from time to time."

Just then, the front door was thrown open and the two lads went wide-eyed.

"Good lord," said Calvin.

"Boy oh boy," added Al, thickly glazed. "Look at them, would you!"

Taking Al's meaty arm in the manner mothers do their babies when passing leashed dogs on city sidewalks, Calvin said, "Not to-night, Aloysius. Not here. Please. I'm asking you."

"Get a load of the *udd*ers."

"Bulls," Calvin corrected, "don't have udders."

"Those ones there sure do. Top heavy, those ones, like all good bulls." Al was already in a trancelike state. "Large humps. Shimmering, sequined sea-bulls at night port. If Hemingway were alive, he'd be bawling his eyes out. Bring in the *picadors*."

"And the *banderilleros*," added Calvin with steadily mounting fear. "On the double. In waves of twelve."

Al rose from his seat and looked at Calvin, alive with new optimism. "Leave me go, Calvin," he said bravely. "I'm up to the challenge."

"There's two-hundred francs in it for you if you can steer them away from here. But for crissake make it quick!"

"*Cou cou*," called Al.

"Oh god," groaned Calvin, "we've been spotted."

Fore-hooves scratched heavily at the old floor and suddenly the two beasts charged forward with flaring nostrils. With nowhere to turn, Calvin grabbed his pen and dove into his journal, making as though he were rewriting the bible. As the bulls drew nearer, Al advanced and met them in the centre of the ring.

"Hey, doll," burped the sweaty anti-hero.

"Hey, yourself," flirted the one called Emma.

The older of the two charged on and skidded to a halt at Calvin's side. "Are you leaving?" she snorted, appropriating the barstool Al had given up and encroaching to within inches of Calvin's face.

"No, I'm not leaving!" he growled, standing his ground. A circular sweep of his open palm indicated a claim staked, a camp established. "What on earth gave you the indication I might be leaving?"

"Why, I assumed you were signing the bill. I see now that you have a little journal. It's not often you see a chap writing in a bar. Go on then, what's it about?"

"Love in the time of cholera," said Calvin, his shirt pulled up to his eyes, like a frightened toreador hiding behind his cape. "Death in the afternoon. Take your pick."

"Poor darling," she said. "Either way you're too late; those stories have already been written."

"Leave me with my failures then, you well-read beast! Aloysius, I've been hit! O sweet *cornada*!"

The elder bull was called Susan. She walked away from Calvin with the vague confusion of an accidental murderer, extracted a red handkerchief from a red handbag, and wiped away the viscous smear of blood and plasma that coated her huffing snout.

"Done with me already?" cried Calvin deliriously. "Very well! On to the next! My right eye for a slick, silver blade!"

Al said to Emma, "Excuse me for just a moment, dear," and raced over to Calvin. "How are you, pal? Whatever you do, don't panic."

"I *am* panicking!"

"They can smell fear."

"I've been gored by a British bull. Hurry up, you!"

"Relax, pal. Say, did you smell her cologne?" Al asked excitedly.

"French!" exclaimed Calvin.

"Classy, what!"

"I swear," said Calvin, "sometimes I think the French would have been better off siding with the occupiers. This place is a goddamned zoo!"

"Why, you self-loathing—!" accused Al.

"Not quite. Rather uneasy over the last half-century, though, sure. Just look at those two. Look at us for that matter! Hell, *we're* the new occupiers, them and us."

"*Occ*upiers? You've lost it. We've no tanks coursing along the Champs Elysée! We are long-term tourists who speak the language, contribute to the economy and pay taxes. Our hosts lay down the terms of the deal, so don't get weepy for the French. If it weren't for us they'd be speaking German."

"I swear to God, if I hear *that* line just one more time! Instead, they're speaking *Eng*lish! What's the bloody difference?"

"Surrender your soul if you must, but keep your legs—you'll need them to get to the *boulangerie* each morning. *There's* your difference, Calvin."

"You're deplorable."

"Handsome! *Hand*some!" Susan blared.

The child bartender stopped and turned towards the call, fearfully placing an index finger to his chest.

Emma joined Susan at the bar.

Aloysius urged, "I'm talking about survival here, Calvin!"

"Sur*vi*val? You can start by saving that poor miserable bartender!"

"Yes, you," said Susan to the barman. "Who else?"

The Nancy lad stood no chance.

"You *are* handsome," they crooned, as he turned sea-green.

"Oh, don't you worry," said Emma, "I don't fancy you. I'm with him," she said pointing a finger towards Calvin and Al.

Calvin shuddered visibly.

"Not *you*!" she shrieked. "The hunky one."

Al said, "I can really draw them in, hey, Calvin? Like bees to honey."

"Like flies to carrion," said Calvin, who began kicking and shoving him in an attempt to induce motion, but Al did not budge.

"Stop it," he said. "Hey, look!"

Susan had honed in on the overmatched bartender, sighting him between two sharp-tipped horns.

"Oh, man," mumbled Al, as though watching a car wreck in slow motion. "She's going to scatter fluff and meat throughout the Vieux."

"*Avez-vous choisi, mesdemoiselles?*" trickled the barman, like a leaky faucet.

"Atta boy," encouraged Calvin.

"Good," Al agreed. "Cloak yourself in your mother tongue. And *fight* this time, for crissake!"

"Look at that smile!" demanded Susan.

The lads could smell blood rising to the barman's surface. Just then, a dark sticky liquid began to drip from his ear. His anaemic lips were pulled back in a wan smile. He hung still and peachy white, like the underside of the soft sad perch that Calvin used to pull from the cesspools that lay between the Chicago Skyway and the steel mills. Poor things, reflected Calvin. They have no fight. Dead in the water before you even bait your hook.

Susan leaned in close. "What beautiful teeth you have!"

Baby teeth. Uncut. Sweet pearls. Translucent cocktail onions. Far too pretty to offer any protection.

"Get your chin up!" urged Al. "Stick out your chest."

"*Blanc de poulet*," wept Calvin.

The barman spoke, "*Alors*, you would like...?" knowing immediately that he would pay for the unfortunate sentence structure.

"Oh, yes!" they hooted ecstatically. "We would like. We would very much like! But the night is young—drinks first. A glass of claret for Emma and I'll have a Margarita."

"*Merci*," said the lad, retreating behind the bar.

"Mercy," moaned Al strangely. "Choose your battles carefully, retreat when necessary, live to see another day."

Calvin braved his eyes away from the bulls to address Al's strange tone. Maybe it was the drink, maybe a filament had blown in Al's cranium. He went suddenly bleary-eyed and slipped into a low trance. Hell, Al had fallen in love.

"Look at that!" he said, awestruck, disgusted, enamoured. "A ruby-sequined vessel hinged somewhere near the high middle, jack-knifed towards shimmering bottles of booze, forearms like flying buttresses, to take the weight. The legs, the arse, high and firm, peaking majestically over two tapering haunches of milky white granite, great mother of pearl, alabaster fresh from the purple depths of the North Pacific, a great whale dump of wet mountain snow, rounded and sculpted with crevassed pass, inverted Alpine mountains of haunch."

"What the—" said Calvin. "Al. Al!"

Al could not be diverted. He narrowed his eyes towards the sum of her and peered through a thick Lithuanian forest of eyelashes. "Log cabins and frosted speculoos," he mumbled, lost in a lecher's dreamy haze. "Holiday spice and pine, thick creamy rugs before a crackling fire, cold grey stone, falling snow, berry schnapps, hearty meals, stewed venison and potatoes, leg of lamb, blood-red wine, bestial winter colliding, the slamming of heavy sun-starved animals."

The dim lights twinkled on her sequined backside as she leaned in over the bar. Rubies suspended in Plato's fiery midnight sky hooked Al with a million lascivious winks and silver-red kisses, teasing him erotic.

"Al, you're scaring me," pleaded Calvin. "Wake up!"

With an animated huff, the great mountainous bull of Al's desires licked seismic lips and erupted volcanically towards the helpless bartender, "You look like... Why, I bet your name is Pierre."

Further tipping the cosmic balance to the disfavour of decency and fairness, she hit the mark. To the defenceless barman, utterly betrayed as he was by the gods of good fortune, it was a mortal blow.

"I'm right!" she yowled. "I knew it! I could just tell. I said as much to Emma. Ask her if you don't believe me."

"She did," corroborated Emma. "And she's right, Pierre; you *are* very handsome. Do you know that? Why, come here, you..."

A grotesque tactile crunch rippled across the bar top, sending shivers through Calvin. Pierre's peachy-pink ear had gone missing, viciously ripped out by the roots and gnashed into *wurst* by the bone-crunching machinery of Emma's gyrating gob, leaving a red-black crater, a half-eaten plague-ravaged pomegranate where once protruded the tender appendage. The iron smell of blood and fear mingled with that of burnt tobacco. The night was overwhelmed by rouge.

German is a coarse language, Calvin considered. Nobody ever said speaking German was like kissing the air. However... No, no, he disallowed the thought; they simply had to be vanquished.

"I love your goatee, Pierre. Do you groom it yourself?"

"Do be a dear and pour this into a new glass, this time with salt on the rim. And remember who taught you the proper way."

"...Take you unannounced. Take you by storm. Attack!" Al hadn't stopped fantasising. "With your consent, we evacuate immediately, silently, and get to task. Without your consent, I seize your neck with both hands and squeeze. When your eyes bulge and your mouth flies open, I ram a felled tongue splintering down your purple gullet."

"Jesus, Al! Three-hundred francs! Make it all stop!"

"Ram a cinderblock fist between those quaking arse cheeks, uproot all the ridiculous lies and disguises; those horrific costume sequins! You enormous whale of a crock! I know what lies beneath. I know your insides—diseased pudding. We shall descend directly; go beyond, deeper, to the alabaster. Puncture and drill and reap my sweet reward!"

"*Aloysius!*" Calvin hit him in the head and dropped elbows on his back, but Al was still spellbound. "Do something!"

Blood from Susan's chin dripped and splashed in coagulating puddles on the bar top. Glittering chips of broken glass and white shards of bone peak jagged, like piranha teeth, from her bottom lip. Now bringing in the lip, curling it into her puffy gob with vacancy and furrowed brow, her horse teeth came together to the tweeze human barbs and spit them with mild annoyance onto the hardening skin of the crimson puddles.

A *cornada* does nothing to contradict or diminish a toreador's greatness. In the ring, the best of them hold firm to a tight line, without betraying honesty and grace. But Aloysius was a magician, a smoke-and-mirrors man, and magicians are never gored. Nor do they ever come to know glory. Al might surrender his soul, but he would always have his legs. He blathered incoherently, in twisted tongues. From a middle distance, he cursed the two bulls in what sounded like a mad mash of Lithuanian, Euskadi and English.

"Four-hundred francs, Al! Hurry!"

That did it; four-hundred broke the trance. Al silenced himself and started back towards the middle of the ring. Bloodied, yet still conscious, Pierre reached in over the horns to give the sword thrust, but aimed poorly and struck bone. The great bull lurched, its rack described a short violent arc and its left horn hooked the barman, piercing and ravaging the chest.

Soon it was over and the habitual hush retook the bar. The air reeked of blood and faeces and expensive perfume, and in the middle of it all, only Al stood tall, almost elegant. Occupier or occupied, it mattered little to Aloysius. He was not a proud man, nor was he quick of body or mind. But he knew how to plod forward, even if he didn't always believe it himself. The citizens of Vieux Nice were so adept; they would always find a way to get by. And Al, among them, for better or worse, would always be one of the last men standing.

He latched a meat hook around Emma's waist, corralled Susan in the other, and the three sauntered punch-drunk towards the door.

"Hey, Calvin," Al yelped, pausing tall before the door, towering like a magnate, looking altogether fictional. "I'll come by tomorrow for those four-hundred francs," he said, flashing a wide kielbasa smile. Then he clucked and offered a showman's wink.

Calvin screamed, "Out, you beggars!"

Al accepted the order without question and began barking sternly at the full women in his full arms, "Giddy up! You heard the man! Let's go! *Andale*! Out! Out! Out!" The women complied without a whimper.

Al would have his way with them that night, and in the morning, they would be shot and dragged over the edge of the *Grande Corniche*, because all bulls that gore in the ring must be destroyed.

Winter come down sharp over the city, like razor blades and bad intentions, whip through the streets, icy-white crystals twinkle in headlights, make street-level stars. Kid, he go into a store on the way home from school *Cigar, razor stubble against my cheek so high in the air* The moon shine brightly against a silver-gray pre-dusk sky. He cling to a cold gallon of milk, pass a man shivering in a wheelchair outside Haussmann Shelter, who hunch over a lit cigarette, who don't wear but a shirt and pants in a winter like hungry razor blades. "Too cold to be out on a night like this here, son," that man say. "Hustle along 'fore you catch your death, boy." Headlights from metal monsters scan the horizon for a way out, through the bleak snow-covered park, a frozen light sit atop a metal pole on top court *Take him, Sugarbear. Take him.*

"*I'm home, Ma. I got the milk for you.*"

"Take off your boots before you come in the house."

"*I got the milk, Ma.*"

"Did you take off your boots?"

He lift the jug of milk and shake it to see if it started to freeze up on the way home.

"Give your mother a kiss."

"*Oh, ma!*"

"The furnace is out again."

"*But, ma!*"

"Give your mother a kiss. Don't mind my hands."

Her hands are blue, her lips are blue.

"What was the price of this milk?" *Her hands are ice cold, her lips are blue.* "You don't know? How do you know you got the right change if you don't know the price?"

His thin gray socks soak up a small puddle of melting snow.

"You need to start knowing! People living on the street don't know!"

Got to start paying real close attention. Got to remember.

"Can't even buy milk at this rate." *I feel sick. Ma can't lick it.*

I sit in the chair wiv a cuppa tea and watch the lad struggle. "Kid," I say, "somebody is downstairs. Hear the bell?"

He's trying like hell to remember the price of that milk. He can't let go of a history, an unfinished idea. He raises his arms out to his side *Looking on the mountains and the sea You're a rat!* to display the rag of his body, only it's not a rag at all.

"*Look at me, Pug. Look hard, now.*"

His arms are lean and carved, a deep furrow like in a plowed field run between his biceps and triceps, run to his forearms where it branches into a tree of veins and gripping tendons.

"*How I'm going to take visitors when I'm all full of holes!*"

A little blonde girl *The kind you want to scoop up and squeeze until your last breath. I need to explain to her some things about the past* She already knows the past, you slag. A girl wants to know about the future *I can't know about the future* Make something up and dazzle her, mate *I can't see the future* Promise all your plans are going to beat the world like. A girl wants to be dazzled *I can't see the future*

History is where a boy go to find the future. Got to remember things. Got to pay attention.

"Turn up the goddamn heat, Pug, and leave me alone." *It's so cold. My poor ma and her blue lips.*

"Your mum says there's a little blonde girl at the door, Kid."

"Bring her to me, please. I have to explain some things."

"It sure is cold in here."

"It's the sickness, Pug."

"No. It's the furnace. It died again."

"It's the furnace!" his ma yell from the basement.

No, please, no.

"It died again, boy!"

I feel sick and ashame. Ma, she can't lick it.

"Let me look, Ma." Her blue lips.

"I said it died, boy! What can a ten-year-old child do about a dead furnace?"

Got to pay close attention. Got to remember things. I be the one to lick it.

"Tell her about the future, Kid. Make your plans to beat the world."

"Not the furnace again," he say into his hands.

"What do you mean not the furnace again?" his ma say.

"This is the *real*, boy!" say his pops. "What do you think? This ain't California, now! This is Garfield!"

Pug left first. Got to start remembering things.

"No, this ain't California, Pop. This is Garfield." He stand in wet gray socks on linoleum.

"Take off your boots and kiss your mother."

"Ma, your hands!"

"Don't mind my hands. Give your mother a kiss."

"You got to start thinking, son," say his pops. "This is Garfield." *She got blue hands and blue lips.* "You must be sick, boy. Irma, come feel the boy's head. Check if he has a temperature."

"Take my mittens, Ma. I will peel the potatoes."

"Check the boy for a temperature, Irma. And call the repairman for that damn furnace."

"I'll peel potatoes. Take my mittens, Ma. Please, don't call!"

"Don't call? You think I'm going to let my baby freeze?" His ma point a potato peeler at him. "Put that coat on, now. This isn't California."

"Irma, call the repairman!"

"Please, now, Mama. I'm sorry! I won't go nowhere."

A wolf in sheep's clothing show up. He go downstairs.

"I'll pay attention. I'll stay home and be real good!"

A wolf go down to the basement.

You don't have a necktie I could borrow, do you, mate?
Theys lambs about with blue hands, with blue bleating lips.

Kid, he sit in the doorway in thin gray socks. He sit and watch where the carpet meet the linoleum *The carpet fall over the edge into the kitchen* Footsteps come heavy up the stairs *A scissors would do the trick* A wolf in sheep's clothing *Supposed to take his boots off. The carpet is green like Christmas, like parakeets. It fall like grass at the edge into the kitchen.* Kid pull at the carpet strands.

"But it's got to be fixed!" his ma cry.

"Not that furnace, ma'am. That furnace is shot."

"What do you mean not that furnace? You have to fix it!"

Kid pull up a strand of carpet near the edge *It shape like a V. There's a small kitchen there. It got dried putty at the fold where it come away.* He pull away another strand.

"I'm sorry ma'am. It's shot."

"But that furnace is only ten-years-old!" *Ma press her blue hands.* "The man from your office assured me you could fix it."

"The man from my office don't know what he's talking about, ma'am."

So many strands of carpeting pulled, he got a small green pile at his feet. *The color of Christmas, in a fort of Christmas-green where I take off my boots and bring money for ma and give her a kiss on her warm rosy cheek and she kiss me with red Christmas lips. Laika Laika Laika! A hellish scream fills the car. Don't balk now, chico.*

"Well, listen here!" his ma say. She watch down and straighten her apron. "How much is it going to cost? I mean…" she can't hardly bring herself to say it. "I mean for a new one. We can't…"

So many strands pulled from the carpet, theys a hole in it. He focus on a Christmas-green fort instead of paying attention. *Green and green and milk money and no hard white van.*

"But we can't afford that!"

Ma's blue lips.

"But we don't have that kind of money! We have to *eat!*"

The back door open and close.

"I'm sorry ma'am. You need a new furnace and that's the price."

Theys a wonderful cigar smell. I feel razor stubble against my cheek high up in the air. Do it again, Pop, do it again.

James come home from work *I can smell cigar* The Christmas-green strands won't go back into the carpet. They won't stick. They ain't no getting them back in. He going to get a whooping for it. He get lost in his head and don't pay attention.

His ma, she go weak. She wonder what margins got to do with a hard-working family trying to keep warm in the winter.

"Everybody in Garfield a little bit cold and hungry during winter, ma'am."

"You look pretty well-fed there, bub," James say. He appear from around the corner *He smell like cigar* A hand wrench around his bicep like he checking it for good use. He got a brow jagged like a mountain pass and big hands that never come to rest, always grinding away on something. "What's your name, son?"

Now we going to see what all about this seven-hundred dollars.

"Name's Dez, sir." That man Dez just grow two inches taller than James. "We both from Garfield, sir," he say to James. "You can talk plain. If you mean to say my business is good, say it. If you trying to say something else, go on and say it."

I feel sick.

"What I'm saying is what do you mean by seven-hundred dollars! Can't you see how cold it is in here? It's winter, man!"

Pop's face contort and his muscles strain to a breaking, but he can't lick that old tree stump in the front yard. He try and try, his face turn red and his arms about to explode, but he can't lick it. It don't matter of a damn axe and shovel. He can't lick it. He can't lick it! Kid watch his pops struggle with an axe and shovel, but a eight-year-old can't help for nothing. He watch his pops' face turn red in the front yard for all of Garfield to see, but he can't lick that tree stump. Kid race away like a jangling bolt to his bedroom, where he gnash his teeth and cry bitter tears, so bitterly angry at his pops for failing.

"I'm aware of the season, sir."

Kid, he feeling sick, his heart pumping hot.

"It's freezing in my damn house!" James say.

A gear catch and hold and then slip and bang into its housing.

"Please, now, I'm asking you!"

Pop, he begging like a dog! Got to do something! Got to get that stump! He can't lick it! He can't lick it! The gear hold and hold and then it slips. *Bang!*

Like out to where the Sacramento and San Joaquin rivers flirt and twist and come winding together brown and fresh before making a hard push, there builds an overflowing river that carries me helplessly toward a breaking point; a raging approach full of unconscious, split-second calculation. My body is heavy and nauseas, and the gears all hold and hold and then slip. BANG! when the brain chews and chews, weighing the upsides and downsides, the possible outcomes, the justifications, all the disappointment on all the faces of loved ones, the disgust in their eyes, the consideration of another trip to the hospital, to the lock-up, the past, all of it churning turgid and cumbersome. It holds for a beat and then slips. BANG! furiously toward the breaking point which says stop or go, until the point is crossed and there is no going back, and the weight of the world dissipates and I am light and clean and innocent and nothing can be lost. Everything goes stark and bright white and crystalline and Laika, she loves me. Laika Laika! Bring the general a necktie!

A slanderous word slide thick and leaden from Kid's young lips. His mouth twist down low and ugly. His eyes fix on the repairman, fill with bitter tears and the whole world go silent *Beyond all the white suburbs and brown pueblos and Mexican cantinas green and red, with Christmas green and red lips she kiss me. Milk money and Christmas red lips and no hard white van.*

"What did you say, boy?" James lift him by an arm so that Kid's shoulder higher now than his head and he only barely touch the ground by tip-toes and James drag him to his bedroom. Kid throw himself down on the bed and listen to the door slam. He cry hot syrupy tears and throw punches into the mattress. *He can't lick it.* No money, no heat. So simple as all that. A ten-year-old boy can't help for nothing. Kid taste a full mouth of bitter anger.

Got to pay attention. Theys lemon trees in California. I be the one to lick it! Theys lemon trees beyond these walls.

He press his ear to the door.

"Please, now, I'm asking you. Look at my woman's hands!"

Kid sob and rip at his hair *Left the Delta burning and consumed, vultures circling overhead. Burn the whole city down.*

"Come on, now, I'm asking you! Look at her hands!"

He can't lick it. He put his lamb on display before a wolf. Poplar trees flapping madly, the nausea.

"What can you do for us, brother?"

"I'm sorry." *I'm so sorry, Ma.* "I got a family to feed, too. Look, you get the money, you give me call." Dez button up a thick sheepskin coat.

A hellish scream fills the car.

I'ma kill him, Pop. I'ma kill that mug.

Irma jump at her husband. "James, you let that man leave!"

"Don't look like that, now! Damn it all, Irma, he's a working man. These here are tough times!"

"But James, it's freezing in here."

"It ain't either! Let's get some food on this table now and forget it!"

Wind whip and whistle like frozen ghosts through the holes in rusted cars that line the streets. Street signs twist and rattle on they stakes *Laika with two lime-green parakeets, a lime-green flurry, emerald green and yellow in the springtime like a living snake, and no white van.*

8   A Gross of Schizophrenics

In which Calvin's day is altered
by the validation of a hazardous
manuscript.

Calvin was loyal to one *boulangerie*. It was not unlike him to go twice a day, such was his love for the baguettes, *fougasses* and *mounas*. Yet, despite his devout patronage, his baker rarely agreed to extend him credit for a mere croissant on the rare occasion when the brakes touched metal. Though Calvin had come to find a comfortable niche, he hadn't much influence in Nice. Gem, on the other hand, was lousy with influence and sent his skipping from one end of the Mediterranean to the other by way of hand-selected emissaries, as though the sea were but a wee wash basin.

One day in June, while Calvin was enjoying a mid-afternoon session of Jerez and sweet nothings with Klarysa, on a terrace in the barrio of el Borne in Barcelona, a dark-skinned Roman youth, who was all knuckles, ankles and elbows, and who stunk of the sun and the sea and all the sea's creatures, appeared at their table.

"For you," said the Roman to Calvin, pinching a folded slip of paper and sliding it under the ashtray, as *camareros* do bills. "From Gem, in Napoli," he added, lustily eyeing Klarysa.

"Hell, man, did you *swim* here from the other side?" Calvin replied, piqued by the lad's hungry stare. "Ride, perhaps, in the belly of a stinkwhale?"

The Roman was a fisherman, too, and Calvin's response betrayed an ancient understanding between men of their trade—no odour jokes. The lad's head was wet and beads of an unknown liquid – sweat, sea water, fish juice, olive oil? – trickled past his temples and down his neck.

"What's your catch?" asked Calvin, in reference to their mutual trade.

"*Gambero rosso, vongola verace, cozza.*"

"Shell guy. I see. Which ports?"

"Roma *a* Napoli, *inclusivo.*"

"Fine. I like you," said Calvin, flipping the lad a silver coin for his troubles. "Now go scrub up and find yourself a cold beer. And next time try to keep your eyes in your head."

The Roman bit the coin in a mock test of its authenticity and with a wry smile flipped the coin back to Calvin. Clever boy, thought Calvin! A singular counter, that.

When the Roman left, Calvin picked up the note and deciphered Gem's hand-scratched glyph. There was another prospective flat in Nice. The proprietor, a certain Daniella Rossi, would be expecting a call from Calvin, to arrange a rendez-vous.

On the morning of the day on which Calvin was to see the flat, he sat for a coffee and a *tartine* at a café on Cours Saleya and watched a mix of tourists and locals shuffle among the colourful mass of bouquets at the flower market. He ran a number of errands thereafter and at noon, decided to have a cold *demi* at a bar on the Rue de l'Opera. The bar was empty. Taking a seat at the window, Calvin watched the sun further fade the cobbled street and made tentative plans for a weekend with Klarysa in Biarritz. There were good cafés and bars along the Atlantic, and good restaurants and good wine, and long-boarders riding the gentle breaks and girls on the beaches.

Calvin was weighing certain holiday determinants (the girls on the Atlantic beaches were not as dark and lovely as those on the Mediterranean, but then again neither were the men) when the front door burst open and in rushed a lanky fellow who looked two hours late for the West Haven homecoming. Hysterical and hell-bent for hideout, the lad raced behind the bar and made a rail-thin shield of Gary the bartender, who awkwardly tipped and shuffled, juggling maraschino cherries and cocktail onions the while.

"Quick, Gary, weapons!" shrieked the lanky fellow. "Rosenbloem has really mucked it up this time! Furnish me with your most intimidating corkscrew and bottle of anything at all!"

"At your service," replied Gary in dithering confusion.

Gary was kind and docile, ever a volunteer, never quite certain as to the labour of his subscription. He watched out over the empty bar with squinted eyes, as though from a crow's nest off the coast of a deserted isle. "Identify your man Rosenbloem. Point him me and we'll fit him out as best we can."

At that moment, another intruder, an enormous raging Italian in all black and swinging a motorcycle helmet above his dark head, charged into the bar, cursing violently.

"Stop!" called the lanky lad from behind Gary. "My apologies for the actions of that abject scoundrel. I assure you Rosenbloem feels a great deal of contrition and regret for having squeezed that gal's ample bosom!"

"Here's a bottle of Chianti," said Gary, hopeful, ever behind the curve. "It's a good one, this, a 1990. What else did you ask—a corkscrew?"

"Not the Chianti!" protested a short fellow with a monk's broken halo of curly hair, who at that moment hung off the back of the raging Italian, with feet dangling above the ground, perfectly unnoticed despite flapping about like a bulky cape in an epileptic wind. This fellow was known as Polish Pete (though he was not Polish and his name was not Pete). "Don't you waste that Chianti!" railed Polish. "Not a '90, for crissake! That's a good vintage."

"Great contrition and regret!" repeated the lanky fellow. "Still, how could Rosenbloem know to whom that bosom belonged?"

The pinched bosom, of course, belonged to the Italian fellow's girl. She had been waiting for him in front of the opera house when the lanky lad passed by and grabbed her.

"You'll pay in teeth for your fetish!" the Italian scowled. "*Capisce?*"

"Here's a corkscrew," said Gary in deep concentration. "A very nice one at that."

"Damn it, Gary, I said in*tim*idating. That one's in the shape of a stripped harlot! Rosenbloem needs a weapon, not a degenerate magnet! Though in a less tenuous situation—"

The Italian growled and stepped forward.

"Stop! You've got the wrong man!" the lanky one cried anew, ripping apart the legs of the erotic corkscrew. A pig-tailed appendage that was at odds with the corkscrew's gender extended benignly from the crotch. "I hate to be a rat, but I am innocent in the matter. Rosenbloem is the fellow you're after. Why, he's incorrigible!" he said, swinging the wine bottle by its neck. "On all counts, I am innocent!"

"Drop that Chianti!" demanded Polish, whose ineffective chokehold was further failing for the Italian's hair tonic. "Hit him with a bottle of white for crissake!"

"*Inn*ocent? That's the guilty hand right there, you cowardly dog!" averred the Italian, pointing at the hand with the corkscrew and slowly advancing.

"Right hand, wrong man!"

"*Ebbene*, then I'll only destroy the hand."

The lanky fellow tried a new tack. "For all his social blemishes," he began, attempting an offensive, "Rosenbloem has friends in surprisingly high places. He and his are prepared to thrash you rotten!"

The Italian was not deterred.

"Oh dear, oh dear, this is all flying grossly against the script."

"*Tu sei pazzo*! Nevertheless, you will pay—"

"*Pazzo*?" clipped the lanky fellow, acutely sensitive to claims made against his sanity. Stepping out from behind Gary, he continued, "You think *I'm* crazy? Bah, it has all been scripted. Listen here, you…"

Dropping the corkscrew, he rooted about in a satchel and extracted a nest of bound papers, mumbling the while, "…One ample-bosomed Italian lass is the deceiver in this wicked plot, and evidently *you*, sir, are the deceived."

He flipped through the first few pages, cleared his voice and passionately recited:

"Rosenbloem
O my Rosenbloem
With fingers like thorns
from a rose in bloom
Oft soused on strawberry ripple
High king of tatty-twist and tipple
Yours true to-day

Yours true to-morrow
Yours true from first
pinch of the nipple

"That one is entitled *Love Poem No. 4*," he said, raising the collection of papers and flapping them about, like a lunatic prophet. "There are volumes more where that came from."

The odd poem miraculously triggered suspicion in the mind of the Italian. Could it be true, he wondered? Was it possible that his girl had fallen for this mad fellow and granted him consent by way of a series of love poems? Had she feigned outrage at having been pinched only because the Italian had arrived on his moto at that very moment, to witness the indiscretion? Why, she had, after all, recently taken up poetry courses.

The striking coincidence would astound all but the lanky lad, who had long ago come to believe in the prophecy of his work.

"Now then, I will apologise one last time for Rosenbloem and the unfortunate events of the day. However, my deceived Neapolitan puppy in olio and mange, you might attend to your own *giardino* before barging pell-mell into Rosenbloem's and making vulgar threats."

There was no novelty to the scene for Calvin, who idly watched the altercation play out while trying to extract a gnat, which had bumbled its way into his beer glass. Even a wee gnat, thought Calvin, deserved a drink every now and again, though he didn't want the bugger flying up his nose at next swig. He finally got the beer-wet gnat onto the tip of his finger and it eventually flew away, a happy drunken little bugger.

The intentional semi-schizophrenic poet behind the bar with Gary was none other than Stanley Arbuckle, at the moment a virtual windmill of papers, corkscrews and wine bottles.

With the grim look of a struggling chemistry student who couldn't quite visualise the three dimensions of certain molecules from their two-dimensional textbook depictions, poor Gary flipped studiously through the phone directory, but came up with no listings for a Rosenbloem.

The Italian, lost for a moment in deep contemplation, finally cracked under the strain of Arbuckle's manic suggestions. "The two-timing wench," he angrily spat. "But... *Mio dio*!... She cheats me with *you*?"

"If it makes you feel any better," offered Arbuckle, "the affair does not begin in earnest until the third book. And for the last time, she has not fallen for me, but for Rosenbloem." He ran a handkerchief along his jaw line and checked for blood. "Mighty strange means of expressing her love, that one, what with the working of those talons. Women," complained Arbuckle. "Rosenbloem will never understand them."

When enough was enough, Calvin stood and intervened. "Let go, you ineffective mongrel," he said to Polish.

More bored than fatigued, Polish finally relinquished his grip on the big Italian and dropped to the floor.

Calvin offered his apologies to the Italian on behalf of one and all. "Don't worry," he added in closing. "In all likelihood, your woman is true to you."

"Either way," the Italian warned Arbuckle, "I'll be back for you."

Finally turning to leave, he bumped squarely into Polish Pete. "Who are you?" he demanded.

"I'm the guy," said Polish with a fractured chuckle, "I'm the guy that was hanging from your neck just now."

Frustration flashed across the Italian's face. "You're all delusional," he said and, shoving Polish aside, disappeared into a wash of sharp sunlight.

"Let me see that!" barked Calvin, confiscating the papers that contained *Love Poem No. 4*. The stained and wrinkled cover page read:

A Gross of Schizophrenics: 144 Eye-Popping Pursuits

- or -

Desperate Times Call for one Renard Rosenbloem

"Hmph. Just as I suspected," said Calvin, "another of your manuscripts. Why, that fellow's girl didn't write *Love Poem No. 4*."

"Of course not," said Arbuckle. "I've never seen that girl in all my days. But there she was and Polish and I have a lot of literary ground to cover," he said with the pride of a stern parent to the manuscript itself, as though it were his beloved, if unruly, child. "Listen, transforming the pages of pure fantasy into a work of non-fiction is *not* for the faint of heart, Calvin, especially when the protagonist is none other than Renard Rosenbloem. My advance apologies to those in the wrong place at the wrong time."

Arbuckle was an unconventional writer of atypical range and pursuit, whose acclaim was heavily burdened by volumes of unpublished and unpalatable manuscripts and misdemeanours beyond enumerating. As it concerned income, he worked contract jobs for firms that paid him to write jingles, blurbs, reviews, specifications, service descriptions and the like, all for products he was loathe to consume, services that failed to serve, machines that were engineered to break down, five-star resorts he had never been to and six-star resorts that were yet to be built. Outside the office, he touted himself the world's most daring Physical Meta-Sensationalist to have never been published. It was an irrefutable claim, as he was the only disciple of the self-defined school and, to be sure, he had never been published. *We will very literally tear down your walls and pee in your sink.* That was the motto of the Physical Meta-Sensationalist School.

"All the same," Calvin advised, "you had better hope you never again cross paths with that Italian fellow."

The advice drew a long sigh from Arbuckle. "How ponderous. Look, it's not *me* he's after, it's Rosenbloem."

"Yes, yes. Fine. But look here, Arbuckle, you can call yourself Rosenbloem, Rosenbuckle or Bucklebrickle, but—"

"What Calvin is trying to say," assisted Polish, "is that an Arbuckle by any other name is just as susceptible to chain whippings. Right, Calvin?"

"Thank you, Polish. These bones of yours," said Calvin, taking Arbuckle by the shoulders, "under any name you might assign them, will be snapped like kindling if that Italian fellow finds you again. *Capisce?*"

Arbuckle nodded his concurrence and said, "Get yourself a decent disguise, you gorgeous bandit."

The odd instruction rendered Calvin speechless.

"Not you, Calvin," Polish postulated. "I believe he is recommending a disguise for himself. Because to go about town without one—"

"Please," Calvin halted Polish. "Do you mean to tell me Arbuckle is verbally advising him*self* to get a disguise?"

"Ha-ha. That would be funny. No, Calvin, I rather believe it is Rosenbloem advising Rosenbloem to get a disguise. You see, his—"

"Whose?"

"Sorry; Arbuckle's. His characters are wont to berate themselves in the second-person—self esteem issues, sociopaths and certifiable maniacs the lot of them. Arbuckle himself, however, stays rooted in the first- and third-person perspective."

"Oh, it's *me* all right, Polish," Arbuckle interjected.

Polish looked deeply into Arbuckle's blue eyes and asked, "Rosenbloem? Is that you?"

"No, you half-wit! It's *me*—Arbuckle!"

"Ah, yes. How about that, Calvin," Polish conceded. "You were right. It was Arbuckle advising Arbuckle all along. How avant-garde of him. Let's listen."

"I say, can't a fellow try out the second-person narrative every now and again? Oh, sod it; it's a fruitless endeavour when one is constantly surrounded by... Look, all I mean to point out is that *I* should acquire some manner of disguise before *we – Rosenbloem and I –* make it to page seventy-eight of *A Gross of Schizophrenics*—not a sentence beyond chapter six at the very latest. A racy and ribald number, that chapter seven! I shan't be entirely surprised if its validation results in the mobilisation of a be-torched and pitchfork'd mob against one Stanley J. Arbuckle III, ever the poor mis-fingered scapegoat."

"You see there, Calvin; third-person perspective. You'll find that's more typical."

"You're a bit crazy, hey, Arbuckle?"

"Crazy like Karloceski," he endorsed with a gamey wink.

"Who's that?" asked Calvin.

"Syphilitic mental patient," Polish answered, with his head tilted pleadingly towards the afterlife, "turned politician—"

"No great leap there," defended Arbuckle. "Barely a hop, really."

"—Who wins the presidency of the United States in the pages of Arbuckle's most recent failure."

"*Fail*ure? Failure like Frogmalian, perhaps," he contended with a dancing brow.

"*Frogmalian?*" cried Polish, horrified. "How dare you, Stanley. Few failures – indeed few misdeeds in the frightening history of mankind – have been sufficiently deviant as to warrant comparison with the sickening failures of Frogmalian. Erf! Why, the name alone makes my skin crawl. Do *not* ask, Calvin."

Polish Pete was Arbuckle's best mate, his literary agent, his counsellor, his legal adviser, bookie and bail bondsman. Upon completion of any given manuscript, Arbuckle raced about town, assuming the name of the lead protagonist and carrying out his every action, as Arbuckle had penned for him, thereby transforming what would otherwise be a work of fantasy into a historical record of non-fiction. Were a sceptical reader to challenge the veracity of the phenomenal events that Arbuckle had fleshed out within the pages of his works, the author needed only to reach for the respective police report, hospital record or court record to defend his integrity and that of his work. He called this part of the process *validating the work*, and by validating his writing – the most critical step in the unconventional process of creating non-fiction – he found that he validated his very existence. Meanwhile, Polish tried in vain to impede the production and keep Arbuckle out of trouble, out of hospital, out of courthouses, prisons, the grave, et cetera.

"What," asked Calvin, "did your man Rosenbloem do to make the Italian so irate?"

"Why, you heard the poem—he gave the lass a wee pinch. She *has* professed her love for him on several occasions."

"The validation of love affairs," assured Polish, "has proven a very tricky business."

"I don't know what went wrong to-day. It seems poor Rosenbloem is star-crossed. It is all laid out in black and white," said Arbuckle, with a ruffling of the pages, "and the scene runs like a hot cutlass through butter, here on page three."

"Page *three*? Thick controversy, that, for page three, Arbuckle. Rosenbloem gets right on it, hey."

"Rosenbloem does not salvage for to-morrow," confirmed Polish, "what can be destroyed to-day. I'm trying to encourage reflection."

"Reflection," said Arbuckle, "is for pansies, lilies, narcissists and—"

"You mean Narcissus?"

"I'm not talking botany, Calvin. Reflection is for dandies and cream puffs," charged Arbuckle with a sudden look of dejection, "and well, maybe you are right, Polish. Maybe reflection is overdue for Stanley J. Arbuckle III, the great blooming failure, who—"

"Who, unlike any of his misfit characters," Polish interjected, reaching up to lovingly tussle Arbuckle's boyish doo, "*could* make a

simple decision to walk the straight and narrow, to amble the streets and live freely, not out on bond, but on the same platform of civil liberties and freedoms extended to every citizen of the Republic." Polish was Arbuckle's single greatest supporter, despite everything. "You, Stanley, could be a publishable and profitable author if you would only show a degree of restraint in the pursuit and an ounce of respect for socially sanctioned literary formulae. Why, you swap the switchblade for, say, a butter knife and we could get somewhere, you and me."

Calvin cut to a flagged page in the manuscript and read a few lines in which a character named Sirloin Q. Pantz, looking to spark a revolution, commandeered the storming of a foreign embassy in Yemen and, once inside, carried out plans no career-loving publisher would consent to publish.

"Bold stuff, Arbuckle."

Polish piped, "For the love of God, Calvin, do not encourage him."

"He's a fountainhead of courage all on his own, Polish. All the same, Arbuckle, if you prefer to go on writing within the friendlier confines of this free world, as opposed to within a state-run hold for the sick and twisted, I advise you to restrict the dark actions of Mr. Pantz's nightmares to the secret sprawl of these here pages."

Arbuckle refused to dip his literary toes in fictional pools. "The fiction in my life," he demanded, "must begin and end with the corporate documents I author, lest my whole blessed life be one giant work of fiction."

Arbuckle's personal writings knew a limitless colour range. His lines and chapters were strung together like urban theorems—hypothesised in the study and proved on the streets. For his manuscripts to pass as works of non-fiction, he was obliged break laws and shatter social norms. He approached his finished manuscripts the way some do the bible—with the blind abandonment and unquestioning commitment of those who know neither will nor options, who absolve themselves of all personal responsibility, who throw a fool's blind eye at the symbolism and artistry penned by human hand (in Arbuckle's case, *his* hand), not to mention the emotion and ego woven into any human work, and who grope desperately, not between the lines, but at the very lines themselves, for all the printed black-on-white answers to life's (in Arbuckle's case, Rosenbloem's life) infinitely coloured riddles and

concerns. It shouldn't surprise, then, that Arbuckle would often refer to his current work-in-process as the Good Book, or that *he* was often referred to as a blustery and dangerous fool.

"Why not tone it down just a bit, Arbuckle?" asked Calvin.

"I'll tell you why—I can't help myself. It's like when you're sick and the body is craving vitamins and minerals. I go from one crook's office to the next writing glowing reviews of hotels I've never seen. I gush over equipment and machinery that's designed to quit on you, about functionality that will never be engineered. I lavish praise on food that has no right to be called food. It's all fiction, you hear? It's all a goddamned pack of lies! My head is sick and it's craving truth. My manuscripts are some of the last vestiges of known truth—in *my* life, anyway. You rascals go make your own truths. Some of my characters might pick your pocket or rattle your brain, but they don't lie about it. I shoot straight."

"Straight as a crooked arrow."

"Shut it, Polish. I don't skirt my debt, either. You think that Italian goon is the first of his kind? I look both ways before crossing streets and it's not for the lorries. Believe me; I'm paying every penny of the bill for my dissention."

"I keep begging him to have a go at writing something along the lines of what Ashley Burberry is turning out, but nothing doing. He's too good for it."

"Ashley Burberry! The nerve of you, Polish! You know the fellow, Calvin. Lock me away for good if you must, but do not ask me to defend my aversion to such sugary garbage. The very best of it is cotton candy. And no, I'm not too good for cotton candy, Polish. Just don't try to pass it off as *crème brulée*. Ashley's is the stuff of carnivals and free fairs."

"Bah!" Polish countered. "That Ashley is one sharp fellow."

"Sure he is," agreed Arbuckle. "And he might actually write a decent book if anyone did him the favour of smacking him good in the mouth once or twice. Fellows like Ashley Burberry have no idea how much better off they'd be with the occasional smack in the face. I'm not kidding. It keeps a man honest. Lends the body some weight. Keeps the feet on the ground. These days a little wind blows people off the pier."

"But Stanley," pleaded Polish, "Ashley's work *sells*. They can't keep it in stock."

"Bah, if that's what the public demands, let me eat brioche! Ashley Burberry—phooey! He follows all the rules, not as helpful guidelines to creating a decent piece of art, but as sound fiscal policy. I bet you his writing courses were offered through the school of business. Hell, he's more economist than artist. What do you make of a bloke who writes a book every six months, every single one of them between a hundred-ninety and two-hundred pages in length? Or a bloke who thinks every prostitute in the world is short on intelligence, but long on street savvy and toughness? Or who thinks Bukowski was a misogynist and Miller a pornographer? Ashley Burberry is stock and boring. The only bloke better looking than his protagonists is Ashley himself—the best looking bloke in the world! He writes lines for his characters like he's falling down in love with them, assigns them popularity in exchange for their approval and good favour. Every one of them over-educated and born into walk-in closets crammed with cardigans and khakis. All white males, all bloated with self-pity, all struggling to cope in a white-male dominated world, despite their innate genius. Writes without a speck of blood on his hands – no nectar, either – he wears white gloves when he writes. Reading a book by Ashley Burberry is like supping with an old bourgeois clan—no food fights, no knife fights, nothing substantial to tuck into, nothing worthy of tucking away. Oh, the food is well prepared, but by midnight you're starving and you can't remember where the hell you ate or if you missed the meal altogether."

"Hmpf! Honestly, Stanley, *some* of us don't need our blocks knocked by a hammer to feel moved and alive."

"You don't, I do. That's the way it has to be, I suppose."

"But I'm *hun*gry, Stanley!" Polish whined.

"What does that have to do with anything?"

"Everyone is piecing together something that sells. Why can't we? I have a family to support."

"Then go get a real job, for crissake! *You* go crank out the five-and-dime fiction if you're so in love with it. Or go be a copywriter. I know an outfit that markets every gadget under the sun. Go spin a web of fantasies for them. The more fantastic the better!"

No one would consider a hike to the top of the average staircase a terribly satisfying accomplishment. On the contrary, generally speaking, the more challenging an ascent, the more rewarding, as a bolder climb tests a fellow's wits and abilities. Similarly, it seems in human relationships that the bolder a fellow's personality, the more vigorously he is tried and tested by those around him. Arbuckle was something of a slippery, craggy mountain and it seemed to him that those around him longed to validate themselves by scaling and conquering him. In the name of love, he made the typical compromises required of a fellow, but it was never easy for him. Every additional sacrifice consumed another tiny parcel of his soul and he feared there would soon be nothing left of him to sacrifice if he did not make the occasional stand. It helped marginally, therefore, to allow his literary characters to lead domestically unencumbered lives.

He felt himself tugged in multiple directions and he struggled to reconcile who he was at any given moment with who he wanted to be going forward, who Polish Pete wanted him to be and who Nadine wanted him to be. The various Arbuckles for whom each party vied were not, by word or habit, mutually exclusive entities, but the commonalities were few and Arbuckle had a hell of a time trying to expand the overlap. Polish desired a slower, gentler, more commercially viable Arbuckle. As it concerned Nadine's desires, Arbuckle said, "And then there's Nadine, the poor misguided bull-headed vixen. For whom does she pine? For whom does she wet the bed with briny tears? Why, none other than *me*, Stanley Arbuckle!"

"What's the problem, Arbuckle?" asked Calvin. "You're a lucky fellow; your wife loves you."

"*My* wife? Are you mad?"

"Why... Are you and Nadine not married? I thought..."

"Never! Fine woman, that Nadine. Not my type, however. Oh, I've been cornered and coerced into a relationship with her all right, but married? No, sir. Goodness, Calvin, evidently you did not know that she is spoken for, married long before I ever set eyes on her."

"What—she's *mar*ried?" begged Calvin in disbelief. "To a*noth*er?"

"Solvang is the fellow's name."

Calvin sought Polish for corroboration, but the latter was occupied, in quiet conversation with his own voice, which echoed mild encouragement from the bottom of his beer-poor stein.

Calvin ventured, uncertain, "Solvang?"

"*Doc*tor Solvang."

"Danish fellow," contributed Polish, now listening to the sea in the bottom of his stein. "Has a private clinic in Rapperswil. That's in Switzerland."

"You never met Doctor Solvang, Calvin? Good friend of mine. Anyway, Nadine should do what's right—fill her boots and stay true to the man she married. Poor, poor Solvang. The shame of it all."

"I had no idea," said Calvin in disbelief. "Switzerland. Old friend of yours, this Solvang?"

"Indeed. Though we met Copenhagen, Solvang's hometown. He eventually moved to Zurich, which is where he met Nadine. They met, fell in love and were soon married. I could not have been happier for old Solvang. However, as is too often the case, their bliss was short-lived. Well, I shot up to Zurich to pay a visit, show my support. Calvin," confided Arbuckle, "I've committed many a gaffe in my days, but that was one of the worst, for it was there that I met Nadine. I found her pretty, despite her purple complexion and the silver thermal wrap—terribly inauspicious circumstances, really. Tragically for one and all, she fell in love with me on the spot and the rest, as they say, is history. Oh, I don't say ours is a unique story, but there you have it. Such is life, Calvin, such is life. I shouldn't blame old Solvang if he detests me. I am innocent in the matter, but the fact remains, I *am* living with the man's wife."

"I'm sorry—you say she was *pur*ple when you met?"

"Allow me, Stanley," said Polish with a hint of pride.

To the crew, good stories were currency, and recounting an unknown story was a jovial flaunting of good fortune. And as poor decisions almost always make for good stories, the majority of the crew knew untold wealth.

It was a story of crime and of passion, a story of love—both of falling in and of falling out. As much as anything else, it was a story of teeth. Young Nadine's were the source of countless compliments, a source of income – she began as a tooth model and ended up a dentist – and on more than one occasion, a source of protection. It is no great exaggeration to say that her teeth were her first great love, and Dr. Solvang, likely, her second. Though, as Arbuckle had pointed out, the relationship soon soured.

One night while asleep in bed, some small movement belonging to the waking world teased Nadine towards the edge of consciousness. She thought to open her eyes for a beat, as one does to reset the material world before delving back into that of the dream. When she opened her eyes, however, there was Dr. Solvang, lurking rather invasively above her. Her sudden regard startled him and sent a metallic flash racing back beyond the ripples and folds of the duvet. The implement met the parquet floor with a clatter. Solvang claimed to have awakened in the night innocently craving kisses, as another might milk and biscuits, but Nadine would hear none of it. He had been acting altogether strangely of late and that was the last straw. Still perched above her, he had resolved to abandon his nocturnal pursuit, when suddenly a glimmer of moonlight waltzed in through the bedroom window and danced winningly on the high-buff edge of her then poised and sparkling teeth. In happy reaction to what he wrongly perceived as a smiling sign of willingness, he leaned in for a kiss and was presently sent off howling and clutching a mangled ear. Nadine berated him, packed a bag and drove off in the middle of the night. Solvang tried everything to win her back – poetry, promises, tame stunts – and eventually she did consent to seeing him. Reacquainted with his Swiss miss on a bridge over the Limmat River, Solvang took her hands in his, apologised profusely and finally asked of her, "My dear Nadine, did I really so offend in my attempts to coax thy eye-teeth—"

Here Polish veered from the story to enquire, "Tell me if I am mistaken, Calvin, but *coaxing* is strictly a verbal endeavour, correct?"

"Not necessarily, Polish," replied Calvin.

"But I mean, surely, *no*body *coaxes* with pliers and monkey wrenches, right?"

"Let it go, Polish," Arbuckle puffed. "It will never stick— Doctor Solvang is a Danish physician, not an English professor."

Said Solvang to Nadine, "My dear, it is only natural that a couple share their riches amongst each other. Besides, will space not be needed to properly accommodate wisdom teeth?"

Nadine consulted a compact mirror in verifying the perfection of her thirty-two gleaming first-place trophies.

"Nevertheless," continued Solvang, "here we are, together on the Bahnhofbrucke; I, tolerated if not forgiven, with left ear stitched together like the finest winter quilt, and fully leveraged against lightning striking twice, that I might be granted the winning kiss so resolutely denied me on that dark night."

Moved by pity and something close to love, Nadine acquiesced. But when she approached and he leaned in with puckered lips extended, she spied in his grip the same monkey wrench with which he had, on that dour night so many months ago, aimed to de-root her teeth as she slept.

A warm smoky growl shivered not unpleasantly in Solvang's ear and then his lobe (the right one this time) was pulled into the red-rimmed meat grinder situated just south of Nadine's pretty nose. This time she took the lobe clean off. As she picked metal loops and rhinestones from her teeth, Solvang gave her a Copenhagen shove that sent her headlong into the February-chilled river. An unoccupied gendarme, who had watched the scene unfold from the Walcheplatz, whistled for backup and Solvang was immediately descended upon by a gang of coppers with nothing else to do.

Several hours later, at the Commissariat, with Solvang behind bars and Nadine still wrapped in the silver foil used by medics to thwart hypothermia, the latter requested a quiet moment alone with her perpetrator-husband. Alone in his presence, she berated, "You horrendous man! You..."

But almost instantly her words fell away, so profound were the changes in the caged man. He stood tall with sparkling eyes. He did not slump like Solvang, or peek out with muddy eyes from under a ledged brow. Even his mouth was heroic, was that of a general on the eve of the perfunctory final engagement that brought to a close all swift and victorious campaigns.

"Nadine, you're alive," he said with the subdued celebration of those accustomed to winning. "Oh, thank God. I've been worried ill about you. You sure are a sight for sore ears."

Nadine was taken aback by the transformation. The caged man continued, "Dearest Nadine, what can be said? Are there no words to bloom rosy your deep purple cheeks and bring spring to your indigo winter hands?"

It may have been the advancing fever, it may have been the stranger's comely handling of himself, the way he threw back his shoulders, making vulnerable his unafraid torso, as though to display the tools with which he might shield her from additional abuse, were she to allow him the honour. Whatever it was, she felt suddenly convinced that the caged man was not her husband. She was furthermore convinced when he said, "Pardon me, Nadine, I know it is not my place to say so, but that scoundrel of a man should hang for tossing you into the icy river like so much felled timber."

"Oh, don't *you* dare apologise, good sir," she demanded. "My husband is a rotten conniver!"

In the adjacent office, a gendarme, who had earlier that day spotted nine potted geraniums overgrowing and dominating a residential balcony, asked if they mightn't apprehend for such an infraction. "What is this, Salzburg?" mocked another gendarme. The room erupted in laughter. "Nine is not ten and laws must be observed. Book the deviant!"

Gingerly fingering the mangle of flesh that had once served so aptly as an ear and a cushion to many hand-crafted, pin-backed rings, the caged man said with a flirtatious wink, "Why, I do believe you've the mouth of a blue-ribbon bull terrier."

"The tooth," said Nadine coyly, "is a dentist's most cherished asset and trusted weapon, and I've four more than most."

"But how is it possible?"

"I've had all four wisdom teeth in since before my fourteenth birthday."

"Only four! I'd have guessed that puss of yours triple-breasted with opal beauties. As perfect in form and function as a bale of razor wire! I trust you've registered those pearlies with this lot," he said in reference to the gendarmes.

"Oh, my! Do stop!" she cried in full blush, ever a pushover in the line of toothy flattery. "I *do* take great care of them. Who *are* you, anyway, stranger?" she asked in a sultry manner, the colour returning to her cheeks, "And what have you done with my depraved husband?"

Said the caged man with a deep and dramatic bow, "The name, fair lady, is Stanley J. Arbuckle III. As for your husband, Dr. Solvang, he has been," said Arbuckle, playing his cards wisely, "put down, like a condemned dog."

Calvin gasped, cringed. "Impossible!" he cried. "Arbuckle, please tell me Dr. Solvang isn't another of your rogue characters."

"As much as I wish I could, Calvin, alas, I cannot. Had you said villainous, I might have challenged you. But rogue? That is a rather adequate descriptor."

"Born of a manuscript," confirmed Polish, "entitled *Lousy in Lausanne.*"

"Imprisoned and short of options," said Arbuckle, "Solvang had no choice but to turn to me. You'll agree I'm the most diplomatic of all egos vying for these bones. As for the Swiss, do not confuse political neutrality for social tolerance—nary a qualm as it concerned Nazi Panzers sunning themselves in the Luxembourg gardens of Paris, but park an unwashed sedan on a Suisse-German street, or encourage a gal to take an invigorating dip in the Limmat, and it's your neck."

Naturally, most any woman would be devastated to learn that her husband had been withholding libraries of personalities—gentler and less offensive ones notwithstanding. So eager was Nadine, however, to have Solvang euthanized that she shed no tears and demanded no explanation from this man who called himself Arbuckle. Instead, with urgent eyes, and separated only by the rat-grey bars of his jail cell, she elucidated a rather simple deal. "You put Solvang down for good and you and I will dance."

"I'm afraid that is not an option," said the imprisoned Arbuckle resolutely. "Solvang and I have a history together. Sure, his edges are rough, but at the end of the day, he's a top mate. Won't you consider giving him another chance?"

"Oh, no. Never!"

"He'll be devastated. You have his heart, you know, infested as it may be."

"Hmm. Pity," said Nadine. "I know how much you'd hate to see Solvang charged with attempted murder—although *you* would likely find a conviction many orders of magnitude more uncomfortable than he."

Just then, a gendarme approached and enquired of Nadine, "Well, Fraulein, will you press charges?"

"Oh," responded Nadine, content as a daisy in a Swiss meadow, "I am quite happy to leave the decision to Mr. Arbuckle."

"To whom?" begged the gendarme.

"Or to Doctor Solvang," she said. "Either may speak as he sees fit."

"Oh, Nadine!" erupted Arbuckle, on the spot. "The night is old for some, but it has only just begun for you and me. Let's let great Danes lie and us two poodles to go romping together through the sterile streets of Zurich."

"Why, nothing would please me more," said Nadine. "*Mein guter kapitän*, I implore you to release this man to me at once!"

Arbuckle was soon freed, and standing anew on the Bahnhofbrucke, it was now Nadine who forced herself on the familiar frame of her former husband. Grabbing him gamely by the bum, she whispered breathily, "Now then, where were we?"

"I'm sorry—*we*?"

"Oh, of course!" she played along. "I mean, though we've only just met, kind sir, won't you please kiss me?"

"Bah, not a chance," denied Arbuckle. "You are a married woman and Arbuckle is not that kind of fellow. And you sure as hell won't get a kiss from Dr. Solvang—not while we stand in Swiss territory, at any rate."

Sufficiently bolstered by her small jailhouse victory over both Solvang and Arbuckle, Nadine preceded to list for Arbuckle, in short order, all the ways in which she would torture Dr. Solvang were he to muster up the nerve to show his id or ego ever again. She promised to inflict a realm of pain so otherworldly as to invoke visions of a nightmarish mega-dentist with an aggregate pain potential of all the demonic dentists in the world.

"For Nadine," concluded Polish, "it must be Arbuckle all the time, or else."

"No Rosenbloem, no Karloceski, no Frogmalian. *Cer*tainly no Solvang!" Arbuckle corroborated with a shiver that shook the bottles behind the bar. "Just me. Just Arbuckle. Go figure."

"Bah, you should be thankful to have some part of *you* consumed by a real woman," said Calvin sternly, "instead of just your literary devils—a real woman with real hands and hips and ideas. Nadine is a dream and you take her for granted. Hell, Arbuckle, the fact is, the air around you goes cold when you're all alone—cold as winter, even in the middle of a Barcelona summer."

"Oof!" the two lads puffed in painful unison.

"What now?"

"Sandoval said you were in over your head."

"He told you two rats, as well?"

"Not me," said Arbuckle.

"Nor me," echoed Polish.

"Well who'd you hear it from, then?"

"Rosenbloem," said Arbuckle, "threw dice with Sandoval over at the port last weekend. The two then shared a delicious Italian pie and a bottle of Barolo."

"And then Rosenbloem," said Polish, "told me."

"Hell if my news doesn't dance across rotten wires. That Sandoval! Go on and laugh, you two, but there's no way around it—I'm in love with this girl."

Calvin heard his words and, dropping his head, noticed his hands. Love, he thought to himself. Hell, what right have you to good and proper love, idiot child?

His hands, those that only made themselves known during times of uncertainty and recovery, frustration and aggression, now lay idle on the tabletop, empty but for the beer—empty, scuffed and nicked, occupied intermittently, only ever with fish and beer, fish and beer, fish and beer—invisible in all but difficult moments.

To his surprise, however, there was no derision, no mocking from Arbuckle or Polish. Instead, they congratulated him with good cheer and blessed him with hugs. Gary the bartender, sweet willow of a soul, popped a cold bottle of champagne and filled four flutes. His voice creaked like an old staircase, as did his back when he bent to softly say, "That is very fine news, Calvin."

"Thank you, lads," he replied. "It won't be easy, though."

"For whom," asked Polish, "has it ever been easy?"

"Sure, but Klarysa was such a sweet and easy child when we met. Now I rather believe her to be no child at all."

"A woman, after all," accused Arbuckle.

"And a challenging one at that."

"She's going to make you work," asserted Polish. "Is that it?"

"I'm not afraid of the work, Polish. A fellow needs to work to keep the bus in motion. No, I'm eager to work. It's the *kind* of work that concerns me. I'm a physics guy, see, a motion man. Just let me crank out the horsepower. I'll swing hammers for her, dig ditches, break boulders, rip phonebooks. It's the steering I fear, the mental work, the strategising. I can't seem to time the green lights with her. I'm stopping and starting all the time. Just last week in Barcelona, Klarysa and I were enjoying a late dinner. I excused myself to go to the Gents', but before I could stand, she grabs my hand, looks at me with those big sienna eyes of hers and begs my swift return. Can you imagine? The only other time in my life I was begged swift return was when Pop knew I had his change after a trip to the market—and there was sweet little begging, I promise you. But this angel, Klarysa, she begs me to hurry back. She says she wants to know everything there is to know about me and it's already almost *mid*night. Ha! A live summer night in Barcelona, the whole shimmering world at our elbows, young people up and down the street, everybody vibrant, warm with motion, everything twinkling red and green and gold, there on Carrer de Verdi, and this girl Klarysa was blind to all of it. She only saw *me*! Only wanted to know about *me*! Bah, something must be wrong with her."

"How did it end?"

"It was a perfect evening. And hell if we didn't wake at six in the morning in a gorgeous tangle on one of the benches in Plaça de Rovira, not fifty meters from her building."

"Too nice an evening to spend under a roof," guessed Arbuckle.

"I suppose your right, Arbuckle, though it was never discussed. It just happened that way. We woke, sat up, stretched luxuriously for a minute or two and then stumbled a mere twenty paces for coffee and croissants."

"I must admit," said Polish suspiciously, "none of it sounds overly taxing, Calvin."

"I'm not done! To be sure, it was one of the most effortlessly beautiful nights of my life. But now, I was only there in Barcelona for three days and quite naturally, I was hoping for some manner of sequel the following night."

"How did it turn out?"

"I'll tell you how it turned out—rotten! The sequel was buggered before it could begin. Damn if I could even locate the leading lady. She disappeared with some *bloke* during siesta! Ran off while I stole a quick kip. I woke alone, figured she had run out to the *tabac* or something, so I jumped in the shower and thought nothing of it. So blindly hopeful was I, that I even whistled atrocious Spanish pop tunes in the shower. Then I took a glass of wine on the balcony before dressing for dinner. Only Klarysa never came back."

"No!"

"Oh, yes! She finally rang. It was going on nine o'clock. The sun was dying outside and everything beyond the balcony had turned cream and cinnamon—"

"But what did she say?"

"What did she say? I'm going to tell you what she said. She said she was drinking Rioja *blanca*. You want to know where? In the Plaça Real—in *Zaragoza*!"

"Zaragoza?"

"The capital city of the former kingdom of Aragon, for crissake. Half-way to Madrid!"

"You're a rotten liar," declared Arbuckle.

"Strike me dead if one word is contrived. She told me that she'd run out for cigarettes and met some bloke named *Vic*tor at the *tabac*—oh, I've no idea; apparently some cannibal she once dated. She swore it was a perfectly innocent and aimless excursion out into the desert in search of white wine. Evidently the stock in Barcelona isn't good enough for old Vic! She encouraged me to go out and enjoy myself, have a nice dinner. She said she'd eventually meet me back at the flat."

There was a brief moment of silence before Arbuckle trained his gaze to Calvin's eyes and demanded with rare gravity, "Enough of this. Now I want the truth, Calvin Stony. Is that all true?"

"To the letter."

Another short moment of silence ensued.

"I see. Well... In that case..." said Arbuckle, stymied and flinching, as though teams of bubbles rose at random in his chest and shoulders. "I mean. *Pfff.* If you think about it..." he mulled, rolling the story over in his mind and slowly getting a grip on what he had heard. "Why, I'd have to say... To be honest... Why, that was some move on her part. Wouldn't you say, Polish?"

"What's the confusion?" said Polish. "Hell yes it was some move. *Sing*ular, actually. Hands down."

"He's right, Calvin—*sing*ular. Ha-ha!" Arbuckle was gaining momentum. "How about that, hey? Some move, that! Some gal, she! Hell! Impressive, what!"

Polish, too, had whipped himself into full lather. The two could barely breathe for all the laughter.

"You have to hand it to a broad like that!" choked Polish. "The nerve! *Couilleuse!*"

"Fine, fine," said Calvin. "That's it. Let it all out, boys."

"Sorry, Calvin," said Arbuckle, catching his breath and wiping away the tears. "My, that's rich. Well, so, in the end, how'd you get on that night?" The two burst anew into a fit of laughter.

Calvin had followed Klarysa's advice and went out that night. What's more, he enjoyed himself. He shared a table at a crowded and jubilant café under the stars in the Plaça Del Sol and watched as the barrio pleasantly expanded and contracted its colourful lungs. After only a *caña* or two, his sour mood began to lift. There is something wonderfully bracing about standing tall in a foreign land after having weathered a good shot from one of its own. Young, alone and in love, smacked about, but standing firm and tall in Catalunya—hell, thought Calvin, there were far worse fates. He could, in fact, think of few better.

Despite Klarysa's rotten desert run, he felt damned good. The ebullient sounds of young life filled the old stone *plaça*. Threadbare boys scrapped for change to buy beer. They laughed and sang and spoke loudly. Some of them fought. At a nearby table sat three young girls. One of them lamented the burden of her own inconvenient and ill-timed tears; the other two did their best to console her by speaking harshly of an absent other—surely one rambunctious boy or another. They drank *cañas* from small glasses and when the glasses were finished, they quickly ordered three more. Calvin pondered all the hurting people in the world – millions upon millions of them – some worse off than others, but few of them with his resources to wield for comfort.

Calvin sat and absorbed the ambiance with great consciousness of his blessed life and those blessed surroundings that had long ago agreed to adopt him. If he could, he would see to it that there would never again be ice, never again the dirty slushy snow that piled high in the inner-city streets, no more rusted and frozen vehicles that coughed arthritic and refused to start. Somehow a busted lip and the resulting tears were manageable in summer, while the same violent fate on a bitter-cold winter day might destroy a young fellow. Calvin sat with a sense of gratitude and joy. He was not an outsider in Klarysa's city. He had long ago extended the boundaries of his existence to include, in some loose way, the very seat in which he sat. Until vacating that seat, it would not be a borrowed seat, but his own, and all the folks around him would accept his place among them. To be sure, it is a lot to ask of a place and its people. But then one is never a visitor to Barcelona the way he is to Stockholm; never a guest the way he is to Lisbon; never a tourist the way he is to Paris or Rome. In Barcelona, each is a small verse in the never-ending lyric that defines the city.

The conscious acknowledgement of his own good fortune opened his eyes to a startling realisation. Good lord, he wondered, when did I lose my will to fight? He quickly concluded that the time spent hacking away at himself as punishment for his failure with Victoria had left the best of his tools blunted and dull. The handicapping, however, had gone on long enough and he decided right then and there to change course. Instead, he would fight for

Klarysa. He would fight for her using the same verve with which he fought victoriously in his younger days. He would win her time and win her heart and drive all Victors and Jordis into a deep ravine of obscurity!

Arbuckle and Polish hung on Calvin's every word.

"I hate myself for even thinking this," said Polish after lengthy deliberation, "but it seems to me you might benefit from Arbuckle's brand of conflict resolution through a well diversified portfolio."

"Of perso*nal*ities?" begged Calvin in disbelief.

Having inspected his fingernails and found everything to his liking, Arbuckle raised his eyes and said with a shrug, "Until there exists a single tool to work all grooves…"

"But I thought you were against all this, Polish?"

Polish grimaced. "Truth be told," he confessed, "we are considering a series of seminars."

"I'll give you our best price, Calvin."

"You'll give it to him for free, Stanley," ordered Polish.

"By *best price*, I meant free," Arbuckle submitted. "Now then, Calvin, in the future, should the little snippet choose to run you through a similar gauntlet, simply leverage some ideas from *Schizophrenics*."

Arbuckle slid the ratty manuscript across the marble table and added as a word of advice, "You're a smart fellow, Calvin. Stay within your means, you hear? This here is powerful stuff. And don't you go appropriating the namesake or actions of even the most minor of characters. This is only to give you some ideas."

"Don't just throw the book at him, Stanley," said Polish, as giddy as a salesman closing his first deal. "Recommend a page or two."

"Well, now, let's see," Arbuckle pondered. "*Love Poem No. 127* packs a hell of a punch and comes highly recommended."

Arbuckle's words sent Polish tipping backward in his chair. Scrambling to all fours, he pleaded, "Forget it, Stanley! Not *127*! If you love Klarysa and value her kidneys, Calvin, you'll steer well clear of *127*. For crissake, *any*thing but *127*!"

9 Haemorrhaging skies

In which a scheduling conflict
presents itself and vengeful tears
are dispatched from Oran.

The lads sat and drank and discussed until additional wait staff appeared and began preparing tables for dinner. It is a sombre moment when a good bar tucks in its shirt and shows its more serious side towards accommodating a dinner crowd. Too late to order another round and too early to eat, Arbuckle, Polish and Calvin fell into the street, a trio of pups, all legs and bellies, the opera house frowning upon their drunkenness from under a curiously yellowing sky.

Calvin's errands had once again failed to run themselves while he sat at the bar. As such, there was work to do. The conversation with Daniela Rossi had been brief. She was looking for a flatmate, the price was within Gem's budget, might they meet in front of her building in Cimiez at seven o'clock.

"Oh, Stanley," began Polish, "it's been such a fine day. Mightn't we take the remainder of it off and accompany Calvin up to Cimiez? We could buy a bottle of wine, play eye-games with the *trompe-l'œil*, marvel the ruins…?"

"You mean without the manuscript?" Arbuckle frowned. "Why not?" he finally conceded. "We haven't had a night off in ages."

"Oh, thank you, Stanley!" Polish beamed. "You don't mind, do you, Calvin?"

"It's a fine idea, Polish."

Polish asked if he might first run home for a shower and a change of clothing. Calvin and Arbuckle waited for him on the Rue d'Hotel de Ville, tossed pebbles at a beer bottle in the street and spoke of women. When Polish finally reappeared, he modelled himself with arms spread wide, like O Christo Redentor atop the Corcovado.

"Looking on the mountains and the sea," sang Arbuckle, "oh how lovely you aren't."

"You're a rat, Arbuckle," said Calvin, rifling a buckshot of pebbles at him.

The action triggered a battle of slinging stones and pebbles until Polish could finally negotiate a truce.

"Don't be deterred by this rat, Polish. You are a vision."

Polish donned a freshly pressed Mexican *guayabera* that was randomly ornamented with souvenir-stains from a Tabascan fiesta, during which the shirt absorbed countless off-target tequila slammers, among other more indelible liquids. Along the crown-line of his otherwise bald dome sprung a neatly coiffed crop, which sprouted from his bean in short brocaded wavelets of thick black pasta. He smelt as though he had rolled in a patch of rich spring hyacinth.

"I'll be," said Polish, transformed by the rare holiday that Arbuckle had granted him.

He tugged lightly at the bottom of his *guayabera* and ogled the dusty pastel beauty of the Mediterranean architecture. Skinny palm trees stretched high into a strangely humid sky. "So this is how the other half sees things."

"Other *half?*" said Calvin. "You mean the other ninety-nine percent. Dear Polish, you and Arbuckle lead the lives of the one-percenters."

Life with Arbuckle and company was one lived on the fringe, one of steep odds and sucker-bets, a constant tempting of boots and bats, of thugs and coppers.

"Look about you, fellows," said Polish. "Dazzling! I've lived too long without noticing. Just to-day I flew right by the opera house and failed to recognise the splendour. Why? Because I was clinging to the neck of a big Italian moppet, that's why—trying like hell to preserve a few of Stanley's remaining teeth," he said, his head aimed skyward, like a good mutt, sniffing the wind for a tasty clue. "I've never noticed the golden hue of the sky."

Arbuckle craned his neck towards the southern horizon and saw a scrum of clouds building in the distance. "I can smell it," he mumbled.

The yellow sky had begun to further bruise. The air was infused with a heavy stillness.

"It won't be long now."

"Strange," said Calvin in acknowledgement of the atmosphere's sepia stain. "It feels as though bombs might well begin to drip from the sky."

"Wrong!" exclaimed Polish. "To-night, we trade chaos for calm, anarchy for art."

"I'm afraid there's nothing to be done about it, Polish," said Arbuckle. "The bloody tears of Algeria have been dispatched from Oran. I fear they are marked for Rosenbloem—payback for indiscretions committed in chapter twelve. It has been written. Big red swollen Algerian tears."

Despite protests from Polish, a pallet of sickly colours – those used to portray infection and doom – had smeared the skies beyond the coastline.

The trio started off for Cimiez and soon came to the correct address. It was a typical Cimiez holiday apartment block, with large glass eyes giving onto long balconies lashed with burnt-orange awnings.

Affixed to the door was a note on cardstock of an economy and class that accompanies rose bouquets. A certain tempered seriousness to her voice, as noted by Calvin over the phone, was now visually confirmed by her hand—a biting sans serif ribboned with a signature that was at once baroque and exceedingly legible. There was little doubt in Calvin's mind that Daniela Rossi would prove to be fit, snappish and demanding. So too, per the note, late. Unavoidable circumstances, she wrote. Would be there shortly. Please wait for her.

Daniela's tardiness created a rare scheduling conflict and Calvin's thoughts shifted suddenly to a gated villa noted for its stout columns and towering scruffy palms—shabby for neglect, the villa, though a former glory still peeked through the cracks of its peeling paint. It would not be a complex drop. Over the five or so weeks since meeting Hector, Calvin had made several such drops on his behalf. They were always a simple matter of following simple instructions. This one was no different: at the stroke of eight o'clock, ring thrice the bell, enter through the gate, lay the package at the front door, turn and leave. Any imbecile might do it. Even Arbuckle. The drop was the more critical of the two tasks, but it was also dead simple and far less risky, for only a fool would recruit Arbuckle for a task through which Renard Rosenbloem might be tempted by yet another *Italiana*. Arbuckle was liable to unleash Rosenbloem in Daniela Rossi's presence, to test her willingness and eligibility as Rosenbloem's unfortunate love interest. Absurd as it was, prudence demanded one consider such impossible insanities. Though it was clearly in Calvin's best interest to make the drop himself, it was in the best interest of all mankind to disallow the lone presence of Daniela Rossi before Stanley Arbuckle.

Calvin explained the situation to the lads. "A simple delivery is all," he concluded.

"No way," said Polish flatly. "No way."

"Gladly," countered Arbuckle.

"But Stanley," Polish pleaded, "you promised no work to-night!"

"I promised we'd leave the manuscript at home."

"But the Roman ruins, the *trompe-l'œil*…"

"Roman ruins!" Arbuckle huffed, unimpressed by any ruined remains for which his characters could not take credit. "You go sit in the amphitheatre and stare cross-eyed at the *trompe-l'œil*. I've done nothing but sit on my arse all day."

"Ho-ho! Very well! You are on your own then, Stanley! I'm not following you, you hear me? One night off is all I ask. You're on your own!"

"I am terribly sorry, Polish," said Calvin. "There's really no—"

"You're on your own, Stanley!" Polish boomed. "You hear me? *Ans*wer me, goddamn it!"

"I hear you. Why, the whole goddamned *quartier* hears you. Now off with you, Polish! I do fine all on my own."

Calvin handed his satchel to Arbuckle. "It's in there," he said. "Ring three times, drop it at the door and leave. Got it?"

Arbuckle nodded and marched off down the palm-lined hill. Polish nodded, as well, and marched off in the opposite direction in the miserable *guayabera* that broke Calvin's heart. Polish stopped almost immediately, however, and looked back over his shoulder. His shirt bloomed patches of sweat. He dabbed with a humid handkerchief at his brow.

"Please go, Polish," encouraged Calvin. "He will be fine. Please. We will join you shortly."

Polish turned and continued up the hill in silence. Then, finally, red as a beet, he turned and came huffing down the hill in double-time. "You. *You!*" he cursed Calvin as he passed. "*You* are liable for to-night! Consider yourself notified!"

Calvin watched Polish disappear after Arbuckle around the bend and sat himself on the curb to await Daniela's return.

Sadly, the street was desolate. Cimiez was silent. The sidewalks were unburdened by pedestrians. Every now and again, an expensive car would race past. Cimiez was no place for Gem. Gem, like Calvin, was fit only for the old town. Gardens, driveways, and automobiles meant encumbrances. Those who climbed stairs to reach their homes, thought Calvin, faced fewer demands, fewer expectations.

As Calvin was in love, his thoughts did not stray far from that which had captured his heart. He made a game of pretending Klarysa was near. He daydreamt that she had hidden herself nearby, to watch him as he went about his day. He derived childish pleasure from consciously following the banal movements of his own body, as though he, too, were watching from a distance. He watched himself as he jerked the filet knife up the belly of a fish and scraped out the insides, and considered her gaze when he dove into the sea at the end of the day. He thought of all the ways he might please her, all the ways they might be happy together. He spoke all the words she might like to hear, even when she was not present.

He had decided to give himself fully to Klarysa, to commit himself without his traditional reservations. It was a decision that meant approaching the relationship without the numerous escape hatches and contingency plans that were otherwise at his disposal, should a relationship turn sticky and uncomfortable. Past strategies had failed him. He had refused to place full trust in Victoria and his refusal catalysed a similar lack of trust within her. Their mutual distrust became a co-dependent phenomenon. Either of them might have broken the chain, but each was stubborn, too foolishly proud and too hurt to make the simple concessions that were needed to break the loop. A single word, a single touch might have sufficed. Many were the nights they spent apart, each in misery, each angry at the other, each wanting nothing more than to be consoled, loved, embraced by the other. In a painful trance, they held their breath, and held their breath, and held their breath, and before long they drowned in a pool filled only with the fear of drowning. (There once was a government that, in a stroke of genius, decided to use the threat of foreign invasion to strip its citizens of their civil liberties. The citizens complied without question because it believed an invasion would ultimately lead to a loss of civil liberties. Despite the fact that the fear of loss is almost always more debilitating than loss itself, when one willingly concedes victory merely to alleviate the fear of losing, one is doomed.)

Despite her bold and challenging actions, Klarysa had been truthful with Calvin. And though he might not have yet fully trusted her, he wanted and needed to, and he hoped that giving himself over to her without reservation or contingency might arouse in her a trust for him that he might then kindle, in kind, for her. He might, he considered, unwittingly give her reason to not love him, but he would not give her reason to distrust him.

To be sure, the offspring of their communion was, at that moment, little more than wet, nested potential. Calvin bade himself to remember that his fledgling relationship with Klarysa had not yet seen enough sunrises to extend a birth-wet wing, much less test its potential for long-range flight. The assimilation of their individual life cultures, he acknowledged, need not take place immediately. They need not consume one other. One might say that the days Calvin spent with Klarysa in Barcelona represented an opening of the eyes (a precursor to spread wings) to a reality that would prove challenging by necessity, for the two were young and dynamic, and significant accomplishments were never constructed simply or without some degree of difficulty, contention or strife.

It helped that the occasional fog born of Klarysa's curious manoeuvres was almost always burnt away by the heat of her honesty and affection—and, sweet Hephaestus, what energy did fuel the forge of her affection!—but that, too, posed a challenge, for the girl was virtually insatiable. As such, her special hunger was a gift when he was near, but a curse when he was far away. After all, will a hungry fellow not eat, Calvin reckoned, just because his restaurant of choice is closed for *congé annuel*? The French say *les absents sont toujours tort*, and never before had Calvin so fervently begrudged his absence.

It was the *petite belle huitre bien couronnée* that accused Calvin of negligence when he was not near; a *petite belle huitre* that he had come to love and admire completely, though it might punish him mercilessly from afar; a centrepiece jewel; a crown jewel without armed guards or glass encasements to turn back dirty mitts—*les absents sont toujours tort!*—a precious gem to accompany Klarysa to the grave, and from where the seeds of exotic flowers would take root, sprout and push up through strata of earth and stone, through the casket itself, to bloom naked and glorious in eternal commemoration. Not a centime to its name, the *petite belle huitre*, the slippery little devil, yet in possession of wealth immeasurable. Only once did it fail in its omnipotence, once during an erotic stroll through the valley of angels, when a red ambush seized the party. How she blushed and bled and tried to distract him with idle frivolities—talk of booze, dinner, mumblings of barred access to the slick of thick nectar then dominated by rich, pungent runoff. There would be no battles, no war, no victory. No concerns during the dry season, honest men ordered about like peons, massacred one and all. Though the slightest whiff of the approaching monsoon caused the queen to twist impotent, incapable, depressed, liquidated of power, abandoned of influence. Nary a spot of perspiration to cockle the signed death decree, and would not stand for a drop of blood when the blade slammed home. But then her eyelids fluttered epileptic, her head rolled in seasonal schizophrenia when he drove through the piddling waves of piddling deterrence. The great blue bull whale lunged forth in blistering pursuit of its silverfish. Bullhorn boomed in an ink-blotted night, flood gates and barricades peeled back from their foundations and the moon's mottled craters reflected silver on a split shell, a shucked shellfish. So began the feast of wounded fish, quivering, whimpering in fish-netting, pearls, salmon, pickerel, herring, mackerel, sardines, *boquerones en vinagre*, bending, twisting, diving, sucking on a bed of seaweed, suspended in salted air, arching, coming and receding, embarrassing the pace of lunar tides. Nets and netter sated, the netted devoured, an unquestionable keeper of seas, a miserable failure of a taxidermist. Stuffed flounder, stuffed sea bass, stuffed briny sea slug, stuffed *belle huitre*. Stuffed and stuffed and nailed to the wall again and again with white-hot bolts, incessant and still wet, still slippery, still eager to flop down off the wall into one lap or another, to beg unabashedly for undivided attention, at least until the roosters crow in the silent still-dark morn. Mercurial, sighing *belle huitre bien couronné*, embedded in its worthy throne. Never enough stuffing, never enough guts. Ever more wadding, ever more guts. Always poised for another course, three-course, four-course, never a meal too large, never enough tripe, never enough guts. "Do *finis*, my boy!" snapping, moaning. "Will be no sunrise to-morrow if all is not devoured to-night." More stuffing! Flooding and shifting, rocking and waking, clashing bodies, riverbeds overflowing, continental textures, turned-earth over bone and gristle, mud slides waking in Bordeaux, beet juice sediment, seasonal clockwork ecosystem, internal weather patterns of a pagan goddess on which no man may put a finger. More wadding! More guts! Feast through the New Year and into the maddest blackest nights of winter. Towards the end, she looked down upon the aftermath and gasped, "Oh my!" One felt ashamed, chastised for failing to notice the sole green bean that survived the feast under the cover of napkin. "*There is so much blood!*" "Bah! But a drip! If it be more, so much the better. Let it drown us all!" Bathe in the wake, jungle lepers! Seek the blood of God through the mouth of the Amazon. Suck it up with straws, like so many starving Spaniards over a shallow bowl of gazpacho. Ye shall all be moved! Dive into earth and wine and DNA where it gives way between high friction and resistance, pain without complaint. An unquestionable keeper of land. A miserable failure of a poacher! Stuffed pig, stuffed savannah jackal, stuffed vulture. Stuffed and stuffed and pounded high on the wall again and again with hot iron rivets non-fucking-stop! Still twisting, still charging, still sucking sour air, still eager to flop down off the wall onto one plate or another, to demand without remorse unrequited attention, at least until the roosters fall silent entering the still shivering night. Where toil is the greatest gift, we shall all be moved!

What Calvin first identified as the patter of Death's drumbeat, proved, upon waking from his unintentional curb-side kip, to be the approaching footsteps of Arbuckle and Polish.

"You, Calvin Stony!" bellowed Polish, "Ho! *You!*"

"Oh god," Calvin groaned. "Oh god."

"Had a bit of a snag, it's true," admitted Arbuckle, beaming.

"Just tell me you made the drop," begged Calvin. "Just tell me that."

Polish, mumbling gibberish, unstrung his belt, like a beaten sheriff relinquishing holsters.

"Affirmative," Arbuckle confirmed. "Mission accomplished."

"Good, good," Calvin settled. "You put the package on the doorstep."

"Precisely. Just as instructed."

"And then you left. You turned and walked away."

Rather anachronistically, Calvin hoped to verbally coach free the barb, there in the present, which had apparently caused snags in the most recent past. "No, no, that's fine," he said assuringly. "That's the way it was to be. Everything is quite right, then."

"Ha!" popped Polish. "But he *didn't* turn and walk away, Calvin. Therein lay the snag. Pah! The misfortunes of a broken enterprise cannot be undone with wishes and novenas!"

"Here is the confounding thing about Polish," shared Arbuckle wondrously, "he is often quite right."

"But surely," said Calvin in full grimace, "this is *not* one of those times."

"It is entirely."

"No, no, no, Arbuckle!" Calvin bleated. "But why? Why didn't you leave, as instructed?" Calvin's eyes grew wide with revelation. "Why, if that Rosenbloem had anything to do with this…!"

"No, Calvin. No," said Arbuckle calmly, offended only as Rosenbloem. "You might try casting your blame instead upon the bloke with the golden gun. He had the devil's angle on influence."

"What! Golden gun? Impossible!"

"One might reckon," Arbuckle agreed, "and yet it is the truth. Listen, Calvin, I did my very best, you see, but a disapproving fellow in possession of a gun has a distinct edge in most neighbourhood negotiations."

"Impossible!" Calvin repeated. "A *golden* gun?"

"Charcoal-grey, if you must."

The contradiction brought Calvin to the edge of cracking.

"Calvin, Calvin," Arbuckle plied, "spies and similar proxies must be granted license to embellish, if only for the sake of intrigue."

"There was no lack of intrigue, Calvin," promised Polish, restringing his belt. "A near-black pistol is plenty intriguing, e*spec*ially when poked at one's own snout."

A shiver of electricity climbed Calvin's spine, like a shooting firework. His shoulders shook when it exploded and stars bloomed red in his head. Of the few deliveries he had made for Hector, none of them had called for human interaction. He merely picked up a package from Hector (blissfully ignorant to its contents) and dropped it at a designated spot at a designated hour. All parties preferred it that way. One time the drop spot was the water cabinet at an Italian restaurant in Fabron; another time it was the front passenger seat of a parked Fiat; that day it was to be the doorstep of a seemingly vacant villa.

"What the hell happened?" Calvin demanded.

Said Polish critically, "Had any of this been decreed by Stanley's implacable pen, I shouldn't be shocked. But *you*, Calvin? Well, let me tell you I *am* shocked, sir; and furthermore appalled to learn that you and Stanley draw water from the same polluted well."

His words rendered Calvin momentarily speechless.

"Come, Calvin!" shot Polish with slit-eyes. "Or do you prefer the moniker bestowed by your new handlers? Oh, *do* say something, Blanche Neige!"

"Personally," Arbuckle interrupted, "I've never considered validating any of my female characters. And I've never dreamed of writing for fairytale figures," he added with mounting admiration. "You and I, Calvin, must compare notes."

"Enough, you maniacs!" clipped Calvin. "This is no joke!"

"No joke, indeed!" Polish concurred.

"What on earth are you raving about, then? Arbuckle, did you make that goddamned drop or did you not?"

"I did, indeed."

"We are raving about you!" burst Polish hotly. "And this pre*pos*terous new job of yours!"

A fellow who wittingly undermines his own good judgement is often particularly ill-disposed to another's unsolicited critique. "Don't *you* worry about *my* jobs, Polish," warned Calvin.

"Would you not solicit the aid of others," Polish shot back, "I might not have to!"

"The bloke with the gun said he was expecting Blanche Neige," explained Arbuckle. "That's not you, is it, Calvin?"

"Me? Snow White? Of course not! What's wrong with you?"

"Pah!" Polish puffed.

"At any rate, he was none too pleased with the substitution," said Arbuckle. "But see here, Calvin, you are getting all worked up for nothing. For just when it looked like the end of the line for one Stanley Arbuckle, who should appear at the property's edge? Why, none other than your man DeTorche!"

Arbuckle's face lit up to match Calvin's, only Calvin's failed to do so. His remained mired in a dark bog of confusion.

Every sailor knows that the wind wins invariably—it is a non-negotiable force. A similar axiom was understood by the fellow who spent any amount time with Arbuckle and Polish. And so Calvin drew a deep breath, closed his eyes, exhaled, opened his eyes and questioned calmly, "Who, if you would be so good, is DeTorche?"

"DeTorche? Why, the boss, of course. An exceedingly excellent fellow, your DeTorche—"

"I've never heard of the man," cried Calvin. "*Do* stop assigning him to me!"

"Never even heard of him?" condescended Arbuckle, who had a proud and splashy history of crowing with the top brass. "Inacceptable, Calvin. A real gentleman, he. I tell you, one suffers too few gentlemanly acquaintances," added Arbuckle with overblown wistfulness, "in this modern life. It was all very cinematic. 'Where is Blanche Neige?' grumbled the gunman. 'Indisposed at the moment,' replied DeTorche, leading me towards the gate and freedom and perhaps eternal life, let's see. 'Not that you need concern yourself,' continued DeTorche to the gunman, 'and *do* put away that re*pug*nant weapon – with the wellbeing or whereabouts of my reports. *I* am here, after all, and you have your package.' Then he looked at me and sternly questioned, 'He *does* have his package, right, son?'"

"Stanley could only nod," said Polish, who had witnessed it all from a hidden vantage point in the hedges. "And in an absolutely *fawn*ing manner at that. Stanley was struck dumb; a fool in love."

"The backs of his hands," said Arbuckle, undeterred by Polish's censure, "was the peachy down of baby church mice, and he carried a regal cane of a black wood. The handle was carved of a stone the colour of the Baie des Anges, fashioned in the shape of a duck's head."

Polish corroborated the entire story, though that which Arbuckle had ascribed to DeTorche as majesty and excellence was perceived by Polish to be peril and portent.

"The poor gunman," continued Arbuckle, "was rendered bumbling and impotent in the presence of DeTorche. Ha! You should have seen his sad face, Calvin, when DeTorche told him you were currently indisposed."

"But Arbuckle," said Calvin. "I'm not Blanche Neige."

Arbuckle took Calvin by the shoulders and said mockingly, "Calvin Stony by any other name is just as susceptible to—"

"Oh, cut it out!"

"Anyway," concluded Arbuckle, "here I stand before you," raising his arms that all might better view the sum of his person, "without so much as a dent or ding."

Disaster appeared to have been averted. All the same, Calvin would be obliged to apprise Hector of the situation.

What began as a bruised congregation of clouds heading north from Algiers had mutated into a maroon army, dark on the rise and with battered kidneys. There was sickness overhead, a thick sickness that appeared intent on touching down upon the heads of the begging and the begged and everyone between. The Sirocco had arrived. The skies opened and haemorrhaged pale-red rain, and in an instant, every exposed body was coated in the finest African silt. The Mediterranean turned as brown as the Mississippi River. Muddy waves peeled off in all directions and pummelled the break walls. The fountains in Place Massena became mud baths, the pink and white Hotel Negresco a melting mound of Neapolitan ice cream.

Through punishments big or punishments small, all scores are eventually evened.

Daniela Rossi never did show. The wild turn of events caused Calvin to half-wonder if she truly existed.

The lads took cover at a café. Though they could not wait out the storm – as it would last for days – they had hoped the twin bats of beer and whisky might help them beat back the guilt and other creeping discomforts born of their minor crimes and lack of umbrellas. Having eventually re-entered the browning flood, Arbuckle suddenly lost verticality, as a rangy wirehair popped out of the crowding darkness and dropped him with a cement fist. Polish and Calvin restrained the puncher.

"*Hé*, Rosenbloem!" he spat violently. "*Tu souviens de moi, mon vieux?*"

Arbuckle, as defiant as ever, moaned in mixing puddles once pale, now increasingly decisive in their reddish hue.

"The name's Arbuckle, you maniac! You've got the wrong guy!"

"*Boh, désole, connard.* My apologies. Do us a favour and give this to Rosenbloem next time you see him!"

Though a heavy boot may not make a swooshing sound when it ploughs through the air, it will often produce a deep thud and crack at the end of its path to the ribcage.

To be sure, all scores are eventually evened.

10   A move to Manchester

In which Viola Jean Killebrew
meets John Rush among the slap
and clatter of a Salford Quai.

One day in 1970, John Rush, a hard fellow who was born and
raised in a hard borough (Salford) of a hard town (Manchester) in
England, fell in love with the first soft object he set eyes on—one
Viola Jean Killebrew (no relation, though she claimed otherwise on
several occasions, when it appeared advantageous to do so). Viola
was a quiet girl from small-town central Ohio whose build was so
slight and disposition so mild that these aspects of her seemed to
contribute rather convincingly to her complexion, which was a pallid
china-blue, or the colour of skimmed milk. Viola had studied
mathematics at a small university near to which, in the springs and
summers, she would earn paltry wages posting dark metal placards
with white-painted numbers in an old-fashioned scoreboard beyond
a centerfield fence, for teams with enticing names like the Swing
and the Zips and the Mud Hens. It was a lonely way to pass a
summer afternoon, which was just fine with Viola, for she had been
a lonely girl long before her love affair with baseball. What's more,
she harboured an avidity for all numbers great and small. She felt, in
fact, a certain sympathy for the feebler ones, those so often reached
without computational aid, those so often taken for granted in
societies – like her own – which ardently maintained that more was
invariably better than less. Viola found it scintillating to post, for
example, before a cheering home crowd at the end of a stellar

inning, a twin-petalled number 8. What a numeral, she thought, the number 8! So graceful, what with its infinite fluidity and grand potential for biaxial symmetry, and yet so often neglected outside figure-skating and billiards circles and the superstitious Orient.

Between innings, Viola knitted and crocheted scarves and English-style beer mats with the nicknames of the various teams for which she kept score. Her passion for mathematics was exceeded only by her passion for knitting, crochet and various forms of embroidery. And hers was no conservative lily-white passion. On the contrary, it was a bold needle-tipped passion, which some may have considered adventuresome and others masochistic—at least in her dreams. The semi-erotic dream-reels that were projected onto the screen of her subconscious each night involved rhythmically rushing parts—flying shuttles, spinning mules, jennies and looms that clapped and slapped and slammed back and forth in never-ending cycles. So, too, she would daydream, her hands involuntarily following the classically hypnotic motion as she turned out scarf after scarf, mat after mat, each bearing one or another of the most manfully notional nicknames of the teams that passed through town. There were the Crushers, the Nuts, the Dukes, the Joes, Bulls, River Bandits, so on and so forth.

One sultry afternoon, early in the summer of '69, Viola temporarily slowed a lifetime of momentum towards solitude, in order to make a play for the visiting River Bandit who played centerfield. Viola suffered a weakness for centerfielders; they tended to be the best athletes and maintained the best figures. This particular centerfielder also batted clean-up, with a four-seventeen average and twelve homers—and it wasn't yet July. Besides, from her station beyond centerfield, it was the only player-position with whom she might effectively flirt. She had hoped he would whisk her away to some mysterious and romantic riverside den – if lucky, the kind she had read about in The Arabian Nights' Entertainment – or wherever it may be that river bandits so chose to cavort. But when she cast a hesitant line his way, he turned and saw naught but two horizontal rows of digits, the bottom of which was consistent with zeros (a shutout through eight) and end-capped by an oval pallid china-blue zero framed by a small rectangle of ninth-inning darkness. The home side went down without a fight (three Ks, two of them looking—they were a truly embarrassing side) and the River Bandit hustled back into the dugout without her; and then, one had to assume, back to the river to rob and steal, never to been seen again, at least until the next three-game road-swing. Viola hung the ninth '0' for a home crowd that had mostly packed it in before the seventh-inning stretch, and sighed a bleak and lonely sigh.

At any rate, yes, under a frail and placid exterior coursed a hot appreciation for hands-on industrial-style power and might. So much so that after graduating from university, Viola packed her valises and boarded a trans-Atlantic ocean liner for England—Manchester to be exact, or Cottonopolis, as it was called by folks with interest in the world's most important cotton spinning and textile manufacturing hub during the Victorian era, and was still called one hundred years later, long after the city's diversification, by one Viola Jean Killebrew. Disembarking the ocean liner, she hitched a ride on a smaller vessel that chugged its way to the end of the Manchester Ship Canal, some thirty-six miles east of the Irish Sea, and eventually took a small clammy room near the Salford Docks. There, Viola perched herself like a nesting dodo between warehouses and sat for hours at a throw among the blissful beat and clatter of giant looms and the rumble of industrial carts, knitting under the gloomy skies that shrouded a paper-wafer sun. The sun would mottle itself in grey and gild itself in orange depending on its humour and that of the prevailing cloud cover. Having lost her easy access to baseball teams and their strapping centerfielders, she contentedly took to knitting into her fustian scarves and mats names more domestic to her new surroundings. She chose big broad-shouldered English names dank with Dickensian fog and gravity; names like Ordsal, Agecroft, Broughton, Langworthy, Hartshead Pike, Irlams o' th' Height, Hundred of Salfordshire. Hundred of Salfordshire! What tantalising, potentially frightening thing, she asked herself, might a *hundred* be when figuring in the name of a town!

One remarkable day, while wrapped in a scarf that bore the simple yet sturdy name *JOHN* (after two textile heroes—Kay and Wyatt) in bold block letters, and finishing another woven with the name *ASTLEY GREEN*, it dawned on her that for the first time in her life, she felt at home. England was old enough and sober enough to let a lonely girl be, as opposed to back home, where every young thing, eager or awkward, aged two to twenty, was expected to sing, tap dance and baton twirl in sequined singlets, and otherwise vie for the Corn Queen crown. She was mulling over such liberating notions, when out of the smoky canal-side vapours lumbered young John Rush, coal-dusted from tip to toe except for the reversed-out raccoon eyes so marked by mining goggles. John Rush was returning home from his last ever day of work at the Astley Green Colliery, which had been flagged for decommissioning. John spied Viola, the lovely wraith, the translucent angel. He introduced himself, not failing to notice the scarf she was wearing, the one embroidered with his name, nor the one she was knitting, which bore the name of mill from which he had just been released. The miner pronounced the incredible details of their meeting to be the stuff of divine intervention, while the mathematician postulated in nervous and love-bitten silence that it was all perfectly viable, considering the tens of thousands of chances for coincidental manifestation in any given city, on any given day—all perfectly viable, both statistically and mathematically, that they should meet in just that very manner, without the slightest influence of some higher power.

John Rush, for what it is worth, had never played baseball – had never even played cricket for that matter – but it made no difference to Viola. He asked in disbelief if she had been waiting for him, specifically. She answered directly—yes. Yes, she had—specifically. He apologised for his appearance and went on to speak of the colliery, her eyes growing wider with every additional detail. Upon mentioning the twin shafts, which the colliery knew during its heyday, she fairly squealed in delight. Later, he drove her out across a flat sea of green to Chat Moss, to view what would to prove to be the only surviving headgear and engine house in Lancashire (home to Europe's largest steam winding engine, an enormous three-thousand, three-hundred horsepower twin tandem compound beast). Viola fought the urge to clutch her loins, and very nearly fainted of excitement.

John and Viola married a mere moon phase after their meeting. They would have liked to stay in Salford, but John struggled to find work. Instead, they begrudgingly moved to the Midwest US, to a town happily entangled in the supply-side silk of Detroit's expansive web of employment and no-frills opportunity. There, Viola gave birth to the couple's first born, a son whom they called Willie Mays Rush, after the man whom Viola considered the greatest centerfielder to ever play the game. With the unconditional love for which all good mothers are known, Viola accepted Willie's rejection of the Brooklyn Giants (and apple pie) in favour of anything bearing the name of his father's hometown football club, the Salford City Ammies (and bread pudding).

Three years after Willie's birth, on the eve of the summer solstice, Viola gave birth to a second son. Despite the precession of the equinoxes and the resulting misalignment with the constellation, they called him Gemini.

John Rush was a workingman. He was a man of few words, of fewer dreams and of fewer yet, entitlements. He was a survivor, a man of great resolve who did not bother with the small details unless the small details made threats. Though known by all for his kindness and sensitivity, he very often *meant business*. Willie and Gem knew when their father meant business, and when he spoke, they damn well listened. The understanding was crisp and precise. John never needed to tell his sons the same thing twice. They saw the meaning in his eyes and in the set of his jaw. But when John's eyes flashed hot and his jaw locked tight, his sons knew it was only a reflection of anger or annoyance or some other from a range of emotions which solid and steady men, like John Rush, might embrace intensely for short moments and then quickly purge from their systems without the slightest trace of lingering residual. The boys might steer clear of him until his mood changed, but flashes of anger or disapproval never frightened them. The only thing that frightened John Rush's sons was the impossibly rare and subtle look of fear in their father's eyes. *That* was frightening, certainly far more frightening than any prospects of his belt lashing their backsides were they to fall out of line. So rare was the look of fear in his father's eye that Gem could only remember having seen it once in his lifetime—on the brutal, remorseless morning when John Rush learnt that his first-born son, Willie Mays Rush, had been shot and killed on the rude winter night that preceded it. Living in a manic land, where it seemed that all disputes, regardless of nature or complexity, were only ever resolved by gunplay or litigation, John's worst fear had become a reality. Finally, he uprooted the family, reduced by one, and moved back to Manchester having confirmed the American Dream to be the risky and nightmarish proposition he had always figured it to be.

11   Debt recovery

In which much is made over lost
cellos and lost Australian boat-
hands.

The telephone rang one Tuesday night, rattling in its cradle for the first time in many weeks, shrieking as though it had been holding its breath since spring. Calvin was suffering an early-evening nightmare in which Arbuckle fanned out his entire collection of wayward characters into one hideous paper-clipped army that marched forward and unleashed a torturous regime of abuse upon Calvin, while the rest of the true and living crew looked on with Sunday-morning smiles and pushed various horse-toothed buttons to inflict additional pain and injury. Polish was there, as were the Butcher and Eddie, Manx, Big Al, Sandoval and Tiller. Even Gem pulled a lever or two—payback, Calvin supposed, for all the low-grade abuse he'd likely subjected them to in *their* dreams.

The phone sounded like a doomsday alarm. Calvin jumped out of his chair with the jerk and jab of a prize fighter asleep on the job between rounds, called now to action for another circuit of pummelling. He stabbed at the phone, picked it up to make it stop screaming and stood, gripping the receiver, distrustful of the reclaimed silence. Finally, he put the phone to his head, to see what all the fuss was about. It was Gem. He was speaking to someone on his end of the line. Eventually, he turned his attention back to the phone and questioned it, "Ellow?" he asked and then insisted,

"Ellow! Ellow! Calvin, is that you, me wee Yankee tart? Say somefing!"

For the creatures that were brought to frenzy by the wildfire of Gem's day-to-day, his departure for Italy each winter marked a return to self-possession and wound-licking. And whereas the songbirds of spring signal new beginnings pinstriped with optimism, the first chirps from Gem's cracked beak each summer signalled a more dubious chamber of beginnings. The ring of his voice through the line had the effect of smelling salts.

"I'm home, Calvin. Knock over a beer wagon and run the booty out to the beach."

It was already nearing midnight. Calvin countered Gem's idea with an offer of a few homecoming drinks at the Ghost bar.

Calvin left the flat and walked over to Rue de la Barillerie, around the corner from *l'eglise* St. Suaire and the *accueille de nuit*, where the homeless and crippled rested their ravaged bones each night, next to one of the most rat-infested corners in all of Nice. One could tip-toe quietly down from Rue Droite after all the bars had closed and at the word *go*, watch the asphalt shatter into squealing hunks of four-legged darkness, watch waves of silver-pocked shadows claw and scratch themselves blindly down into the catacombs. And the meek, they say – God help them, one and all – shall inherit the earth.

Calvin arrived at the bar, rang a silent buzzer and was brought into a vestibule not appreciably larger than a phone booth. Entry was granted or denied at the discretion of a staunch Russian doorman who manned his post in sharp contrast to the French sprites that fluttered about in the smoky inner din. The outer door closed, an inner door opened and Calvin was flushed into the bar, a low red-ceilinged joint with green vinyl booths in which gangs of foppish youth chequered with angst and optimism affected an overall display of contentment that was as admirable as it was very nearly believable. Conversations ran the standard course—scooters, sex, friends and enemies. The striking visual uniformity from one booth to the next was proof that chatter among the young was far from idle. A slender platinum-headed Austro-Croat ran needles deftly over dizzied vinyl.

Calvin sat invisibly at the bar, the glass in his hand the only proof that his presence was at one point detected. Now, however, there was no signal to prove his existence. Upon first arriving in

France, the anonymity frightened him. America (where to age was to sin) had conditioned him to fear the prospects of personal irrelevance. In short order, however, he came to savour the anonymity, which helped when the consciousness of a fellow's aloneness might otherwise become an unwelcomed bar-mate.

Yes, I am invisible, thought Calvin with curious contentment, in a land of invisibles, which allows for some hope that when the invasion is launched, we in Vieux Nice might all go blissfully ignored. Back home, Calvin pondered, such irrelevance was considered a sign of defeat, and the conscious acceptance of such irrelevance was a far worse crime.

European societies did not feed the Spectacle the way American society did, and its citizens did not, in turn, come to be the dominated subjects of such a fantastic glittering beast. Neither was contentment for any one man so decided by relational comparisons, nor a fellow made to feel like a fringe element shoved to the margins of society for lacking the desire to compete by the terms of corporate-capitalists run amok. The French socialist society, which was – at least in theory and legislation – predicated on cooperation, demanded a certain industriousness and generosity of its citizens, that every man, woman and child might prosper. The American capitalist society and culture in which Calvin had been raised, on the other hand, was predicated on competition, and while it demanded an even greater level of industriousness of its citizens, it also very much demanded failure for a vast contingent. Losers and outcasts offer the relativity that is required of a capitalist society in defining its victors. A capitalist society cannot exist without relational comparison, for it is the sole means by which the capitalist gauges success and failure. The capitalist society is a collection of competing assets. These assets do not know to feel, do not know to look inward to define their self-worth. Rather, they look outward and use measuring sticks and figures to calculate whether or not they have succeeded or failed, and in turn, whether or not they have a right to satisfaction and contentment.

To be sure, in such a society, the losers are every bit as important as the victors, and if necessary, the losers will be engineered, their failure mandated and organised for them. The lesser of any two must perish, for a victor must be crowned, and a coronation without the vanquished present to bear witness to the Spectacle is no good. In the zero-sum meritocracy of Calvin's

America, for example, it had long been determined that the vanquished did not merit – among other fundamental courtesies – basic healthcare, though they may well be newborn babies, tax-paying patriots or loyal veterans of any of America's countless wars. When the leaders callously bellowed *God bless America*!—forget the brazen self-importance of voicing such a command from the pinnacle of the global power structure in an interconnected world of suffering—what they meant was *God bless the victors*! Under the bell curve, every score that denotes success must be counterbalanced by a sibling score that denotes failure. In a room full of geniuses, some must be designated dunces, some must fail. When failure refuses to identify itself organically, the least of the successful will be pinched and squeezed to the far left margin, for failure is not optional—it is mandatory. Where failure refuses the judges of society their derision by virtue of failure's non-existence, it will be created in the lab and manifested in the streets. The victors must not be deprived of their hatred and derision. They must be able to quickly identify one another. They shall not be made to waste time and money on discovery through face-to-face interaction and exchange. Only provide them with black-and-white reports that they may know without burden of effort whether to love or hate, nourish or starve, worship or crucify.

Gem finally arrived.

"Why, look what the catfish dragged in," said Calvin, as the two embraced. "Welcome home, Gemmo. When did you get in?"

"Last night, mate. Or was it the night before last? Hell, you know I'm useless at time-stamping terrestrial comings and goings, dear boy. Sure, the seas may adopt a surface tension to make a mockery of steel, and throw temper tantrums to madden a herd of goats. But this *land* of ours—perfectly maddening, relentlessly difficult! No, no, can't be certain as to when I arrived, Calvin. Me gauges tend to fall out of calibration the moment me feet run aground," said Gem, tilting his head back to where the moon and stars might be consulted had the lads not reunited under a smoky ceiling.

"Six monfs in Napoli," Gem continued, "and of all those nights, mate, on only two of them did I sleep with the *f*elines—"

"Bah! *You*?" challenged Calvin. "Only two nights with the ladies?"

"No, not *women*, Calvin—*cats*! Whiskered, tailed, fishy of breath, four-legged—the lucky ones at any rate. More cats in Italy than people, mate, that's a fact. You spend a night on Italian soil, you're sleeping wiv the cats! Absolutely de*test* water; can't stand the sight of it. Aye, all but two nights spent on the boat. Why? Because I can't figure fings out on land, mate. I don't understand how fings work, see. Now that I'm back home, I fear the bed; I'm not sure baby will be able to sleep wivvout the shifting sea to rock me cradle each night."

"But have you not even been to the new flat yet?"

"Can't say that I have, Calvin. But then I've only just gotten in, haven't I."

In the course of New Year's Eve festivities, the Finnish are known to drop a small charge of molten tin into a bucket of water, to foretell details of the coming year. Gem performed a similar ritual on a daily basis. Upon entering the bar, he immediately spilt the contents of his pockets onto the bar top and stared for a moment at the constellation of fortune-telling junk.

"But where did you sleep last night?" asked Calvin, though he knew it to be a silly question. Gem hadn't slept and Gem did not deign to answer. "Whatever was the point of me finding you a flat," begged Calvin, "if you're not going to *vis*it it occasionally?"

"Calvin," began Gem, extracting from his satchel a little black book, which provided tidal charts for the world's one-hundred and fifty most popular ports. Where the average fellow checked the time and then consulted a tidal chart to know the water height at a certain location, Gem was extraordinarily sea-tuned and could discern the water height in his various bodily joints and junctions. Then, in a manner of reverse referencing, he would check his chart to calculate the hour. Gem did not trust mechanical timepieces. They were made by men, and men were fickle. A fellow could count on the moon, he said. The moon never lied. Startlingly accurate, Gem knew all of the tolerances of his curious corporal gauges, such as the tendency of his right ankle to over-indicate by as much as three inches at the Antibes port during mid-summer quarter-moon neaps. "Calvin," he said. "It's twelve-fifty in the morning, which means we only pulled into port some forty hours ago."

"But Gem," said Calvin, shocked by his mate's unprecedented miscalculation, "it's already past one."

"Off by half an hour, am I? You may need a new battery, mate. Anyway, wot've I got to race off to bed for?"

Gem required amazingly little sleep. It was never fatigue that pushed him towards bed on any given night, but rather an attrition of company. He was an untiltable pinnie for which rest was the unfortunate result of all prospective players having dropped dead or run dry of coins. When there were no more bells to ring or lights to flash, and no more electric bumps and reverberations to keep the humming run warm and colourful, he shrugged his shoulders and lumbered off to the closest bed willing to accept his mad glowing bones. At that moment, up for the better part of two straight days, Gem looked as though he had just wrestled a rhino and drawn at least a tie in the affair, which is to say old Gem looked great. Or so thought Calvin, at any rate, who was of the mind that a fellow looked his best when he looked his truest. Gem was a madcap adventurer, a veritable Argonaut for whom victory and defeat were of little import. What mattered to Gem – though he may never have been fully conscious of the fact – were the rhino and the wrestling match.

"Wot'll you have, mate?" asked Gem, rubbing his slate-flat tummy and cocking his noggin towards the chance guttural acoustics. "I do believe it's white-capping in there, Calvin, though we haven't yet reached peak flood."

Gem flagged down the barman and two whiskeys were soon placed before them. They toasted Gem's return, the young summer and the elation known to those who find themselves precisely where they want to be, doing precisely what it is they want to be doing, if only for a brief moment in time.

"Napoli agrees with you, Gemmo. That much is evident."

Gem's reddish blonde curls were trimmed close. His forearms were a thin layer of tanned flesh stretched tightly over a knotted grouping of wire cable.

"Working seven days a week, mate. Making sure it all comes togevva real proper like. Six-and-a-half-million-quid boat, mate. Hottest vessel on the Mediterranean. Last fing you want is some Italian geezer mucking about wiv your German engineering. Know wha' ah mean?"

Gem killed his whisky as though it was the first drop he'd had in the dying week, and flagged down the barman anew with one hand, while the other took its familiar place on his tummy, as though he were being sworn in and his flooding midsection were the holy entity upon which he would solemnly swear to tell the truth, the whole truth and nothing but the truth, so help him, God.

The two discussed forthcoming summer plans and highlights. Despite the occasional summer madness, it was difficult for Calvin to spend time with Gem and not have his mortal concerns dissolved away by the solution of Gem's carefree spirit. Calvin was encouraged by how well Gem got on despite all his blown fuses, his crooked gait and all the devils that lined themselves up like knock-down circus punks elusive with fringe in the misfit carnival of his past—all the weighty burdens that should have kept him anguished and on edge. Such ponderings made Calvin wonder what the hell it was *he*, himself, was so concerned about, what with his high-buff clockwork peach of a life. Gem hacked his way through the jungle of modern life with blunted blades, handicapped by shortcomings that became more prominent with each graduating class, each new invention, each passing year of so-called progress and advancement. Most folks were startled upon discovering to what an alarming extent Gem relied on instinct. And yet Gem managed to rise almost unfailingly to any occasion, with generosity, kindness and selflessness. Only minutes had passed since his arrival at the bar and Calvin felt fresh and alive and ready to try it on. Gem may very well bring the end of me, thought Calvin, and should it come to pass, so be it.

Calvin wanted to hear more about Napoli. "I hear the food is wonderful."

"Best food in the world, Calvin," replied Gem, though he suddenly seemed clouded by a shadow of sadness and uncertainty.

Tomatoes and mozzarella were certainly not issues of great concern, but from his countenance, Calvin wondered if perhaps an authority figure had sold Gem on the idea of Neapolitan cuisine and he wasn't quite sure he wanted to commit. Gem was aware of his limitations. He knew that he often relied on the good faith of others to not be taken advantage of. There were times when Gem simply didn't know who to believe. In such times, a cloak of self-consciousness might enshroud him as readily for his lack of knowledge on a topic as benign as Italian cuisine, as it might over a topic of consequence. And though Gem was able to conceal his embarrassment as admirably as anyone Calvin had ever known, his embarrassment was often potent and heartbreaking.

"Everyfing is fresh, mate," Gem said. "Every day and every night, fresh fish and fresh veg."

He ran a hand, palm down, over a vision of a fine Neapolitan spread, the thumb and forefinger of his other hand swiping clean the jambs of his mouth. Calvin was certain that Gem hadn't eaten a crumb since the boat docked at port some forty hours prior.

"Seasoned just right, Calvin. And everyfing cooked wiv olive oil—*vir*gin olive oil. Know wha' ah mean? Real good for the heart, aye."

Gem was not one to offer such reviews, certainly not as it related to cuisine, which convinced Calvin that either Gem was oddly inspired or something was amiss. And there again, Calvin watched the same far-away look of confusion mar Gem's pensive features. What the hell did Gem care about olive oil and whether or not it was any good for the heart? The line was not Gem's, and Gem was not one to leverage lines. It made Calvin wonder if Gem hadn't recited such words to some hidden benefit, to impress, to appeal to someone, that he might be the beloved fellow who caused another to dream and to hope. Calvin was uncertain, and there sparked within him an old vigilant flame, which combusted on call and guided him successfully through many defensive stands. He wondered what slick devil had gotten his hooks into Gem and the horns of his protective instincts began to sprout. Such were the times when he longed simply to assure Gem of all the things he held dear.

"Sounds wonderful, Gemmo," said Calvin. "Maybe I could go with you next winter. I could get a job at the port and bring home fresh catch to grill with all those nice herbs and that good olive oil."

"*Vir*gin olive oil," said Gem sullenly. "Say, Calvin..."

"What is it?"

"Wot does it mean, *virgin* olive oil?"

"It's a fine question. Hell if I know anything about olive oil," he said, casting a sidelong glance at Gem.

Gem said nothing. He took a pull of whisky. Something was amiss and Calvin suddenly realised it had nothing to do with olive oil or Italian cuisine.

Gem looked at Calvin. With his eyes narrowed to convey his seriousness, he said, "Did I ever tell you, Calvin, that I'm the only bloke in the yard in Napoli? The only bloke managing all these Italian monkeys. Me boss, he trusts me to make sure the work is done good and proper like, yeah? It's all on me, mate. Know wha' ah mean, Calvin? Look, mate, I've been a right fock-up me whole life, haven't I. Me dad, mate,"—damn near denting the wooden bar top with his index finger—"Me dad broke his focking back to get me off the streets, didn't he. I have to be better, mate. Know wha' ah mean, Calvin? I have to do the fings right."

Life is a battle and Calvin felt lucky to have made it that far with all ten fingers and all ten toes attached and intact, and with his spirit still charged and with a sense of identity and direction. He had tools at his disposal – in his head – weapons. He knew how the business man and the elected official waged war with text and technology, logos and law suits. He knew how they killed unseen enemies, whether the enemy were picking coffee beans in South America or rice in Southeast Asia. Calvin had been taught well. He had come up through the education system devised by the victors and championed throughout time by men like Roosevelt and Van Buren and Jackson—men who loved the battle, men who lived for the slaughter. If absolutely necessary, Calvin could be a pig and roll about in filth with the swine who maintained the power structure. If worse became worst, he could be a shit-eating pig.

But Gem, thought Calvin—why, Gem was pure! His brand of fighting was that of children decked out with swinging fists and forearms and motorcycle chains. Big, burly, frightening street children, granted, but children all the same when you only consider the range and reach, the capacity for destruction of the monsters that wage war. Gem got along in the streets as adeptly as anyone anywhere, but like most of his lot, Gem was only capable of fighting off the single-count rats that scrambled within arm's reach, while elected pigs snuffed out a hundred targets per breath (10,000 per cocktail) with their hands-free long-range weaponry, their fear tactics, their lies. Calvin's great fear was that as the world continued to sell out to corporate interests and cash in on war, fellows like Gem would be flushed from their simple dwellings into the blaring, xenon-lit next century, to be annihilated with the rest of the so-called rats, from long-range, without ever knowing what hit him.

Gem was never far from what some considered trouble, others sin and others merely adventure—it depended largely on the laws to which one gave precedence: those of the magistrate, those of the church or those of the street. During his Manchester youth, Gem blew in and out of trouble as frequently as he did the terrace-house door, which was, in part, intended to demarcate internal, familial order from external, community chaos. Order and chaos did occasionally bleed beyond their boundaries, though the direction of the bleed was rather consistently inward.

One night, having showered after a long day of factory toil, John Rush wrapped himself in a thin grey towel and went rummaging about the house in search of his favourite boxer shorts. He had maintained an athletic waistline and Viola, dispassionate towards her archaic role as resident launderer, had long given up trying to discern her husband's boxers from those of her son. John eventually found his shorts in a wadded bunch at the back of Gem's bureau.

Later that same night, Gem returned home to find his father seated at the kitchen table awaiting his arrival. John invited Gem to sit, and proceeded to entertain him with a short and foggy dissertation on parental concerns, the ulcers they induced and the importance of sound decision-making, in general. When he had finished, he escorted Gem to his bedroom and wished him a sound night's sleep. The following day, noted John Rush, would be the first day of the rest of Gem's life, and John, for one, was keen to know if Gem would choose to make his life a long or short one. Then he switched off the light and closed the door. Gem, still fully dressed, stood confused in the dark for several moments.

The next morning, John Rush woke his boy at a painfully early hour, brought him down for coffee and presented him with two gifts. The first was a second-class train ticket to Cornwall, the coastal territory that formed the tip of the south-western peninsula of Great Britain. Though Gem would have preferred a Spanish destination, he was excited by the prospects of any holiday at all. The second gift, said John Rush, was *direction*, which struck Gem as odd, for Cornwall was more or less due south and he would, in any case, rely on the conductor to both drive the train *and* navigate.

"Anovva cuppa coffee, son?"

"Fanks, dar," said Gem.

John explained to his son the difference between *directions* and *direction*. John's father, Gem's grandfather, was one to give direction with a brisk palm, and on several drunken occasions, closed fists. John Rush, however, intended to give Gem direction by way of a softer, gentler tack—a mariner's word, *tack*, and if Gem didn't know what it meant, he soon would.

"Ye do know how to swim, don't ye, boy?"

Who could know? In all his days, Gem had never been in water over his ankles."

"Bah," it didn't matter either way, said John. "The idea is to stay *in* the boat."

"The boat, dar?"

John then handed Gem an envelope stuffed with bank notes. Gem promptly misinterpreted the money as yet another gift. It was, in fact, a loan, the terms of which were simple: Gem was to repay the full amount on or before the third anniversary of that very morning, accompanied by interest equal to the amount of the loan (i.e. one-hundred percent), regardless of any early payback—high-risk investments, insisted John Rush, who had just entrusted Gem with the bulk of the family's savings, demanded exorbitant interest. Upon reaching Cornwall, Gem would report to a certain reputable captain who headed a reputable sailing school. The loan would cover room, board and instruction, though Gem would be required to go short on the room and board, and long on the instruction, were he to meet the demanding terms of the loan.

Gem put forward with a wrinkled mug that the whole arrangement seemed awfully little like a holiday and an awful lot like a burden or misfortune; one – if he were to be completely honest – he might wish to refuse altogether. John Rush would be the man to catalyse Gem's transition from hood-rat to responsible adult, and by producing at that very moment the brick of hashish he had found in Gem's bureau while rooting about for his boxer shorts, he effectively brought the solution of change to a rapid boil.

To his credit, Gem took to his new trade like a fish to water – albeit one that had knocked about in the bottom of the boat for a good while – which is to say eagerly, if rather pie-eyed with fear and disorientation. In short order, he found his sea legs and discovered a keenness for the application of Man's dominion over the world's mercurial seas and waterways. When Gem returned to Manchester three years later, he had clean money in his pockets for the first time in his life. He paid off the loan from his father and the modest household brimmed with familial pride.

Gem completed his coursework on the temperamental English coastline and honed his skills on various vessels from Helsinki and Gdansk, to Lisbon and finally Nice. He worked hard and eventually established a tangible something in which to be proud. He would always navigate life with a thirst for edgy action, but where he once saw no future, he now saw the outlines of possibility. When a poor reckless fellow finally comes to identify at least one thing of beauty in his life, something to cherish and protect, something to lose, he comes for the first time to know certain limits and, in Gem's case, a slightly more conventional aversion to risk.

One day, while on leave in Manchester and regaling his mates at the local pub with seafaring tales, Gem was approached by a sprightly lass in pigtails and canvas boppers. When she introduced herself as Mira, his mind trained to a vision of Shaky Dale, just another poor Salford lad who hadn't a John Rush in his life that he might have otherwise taken direction and changed course. Mira, once Shaky Dale's awkward younger sister, was now a brotherless girl who, owing to the grace of some twenty summers, had become the perky little blade standing firm and taut, there before Gem. Unabashed in the presence of all the lads (none of whom had yet begun, with any tact or skill, to reconcile their aggressive masculinity and their seedling notions for wooing the gentle sex), Mira confessed a long-standing love for Gem. The lads jeered, but she stood unflappable. Over a couple of lagers and shepherd's pies, Gem apologised for the lads' brash behaviour. He needn't apologise, she said, gamely putting forward that, as she had taken over the business made available by her brother's earthly departure, she was well accustomed to the clicks, grunts and guffaws of lads who hadn't yet learnt how to express themselves before women.

Gem dropped his fork and knife simultaneously, dramatically, with the effect of a loud clattering in his empty bowl. Had she just admitted to taking over Dale's business? She had. What of it? *What of it?* Had she forgotten that Dale was shot down in the street over a mindless business dispute? She hadn't. But had *he* forgotten that Dale was a careless dolt? He hadn't. But did *she* not know that the most damning evidence supporting her condemnation of Dale as a dolt was in fact Dale's decision to engage in such heedless business pursuits in the first place? She did, but did *he*...

When the argument had reached a crescendo, Gem fairly vowed to bind her, place her in a duffle and whisk her away to Nice before an equally nasty fate could befall her. *Et voila*, Mira's ruse worked like a diamond. To set the hook, she stuck out a nubile chest and demanded to know if Gem's words comprised a promise or a threat. Not a week later, she found herself on a terrace in Vieux Nice, applying a fresh lemon and garlic marinade to red peppers and Dorade Royal over an open grill.

It is not uncommon for Man to stroke himself in the glowing penny-credit of any good deal, while his woman contently extols the rare breadth of his admirable qualities from the treasure-bursting background. Gem styled himself a hero. Mira was only too happy to have him believe it. And in a way, she knew he was.

An old vinyl pressing of Indigo Blue spun flat and black at the Ghost bar. Calvin and Gem sat elbow-to-elbow, soaking up bourbon and bridging the islands formed by the rising waters of distance and lost time.

Calvin asked after Mira. "I bet she's glad you're back," he concluded.

Gem replied, "Have you seen her?"

Calvin had called on her several times over the winter, but had never found her to be home.

Their conversation was interrupted by the approach of a striking fellow whose bald head appeared to have been kiln-baked for battle temperance and attached to the body of a steel-belted bull. His eyes – brilliant blue gems – were tucked under an exaggerated ridge, which would have been chiselled away immediately and without consultation by any apprentice sculptor with even the most distant and underdeveloped mind for refinement and modernity. If it were not for the disarmingly alert eyes, one might stare rudely, in awe of the archaic bone structure. With the common knowledge that Man evolved away from his heavier skeletal structure as he evolved away from a daily existence that demanded such a brutal physique, one could only assume that this fellow had been warring for millennia and did still actively hoist and swing the paraphernalia of Iron-Age combat. As for his block head, it seemed not as though he were opposed to smiling, or that he lacked the emotions that most typically brought one to smile, but rather as though the physical durity of his face disallowed such fluid action. And so, as a youngster with two left hands will eventually move away from the piano, so too did this fellow from smiling.

He extended a big mitt to Gem. Gem then introduced him to Calvin, who thought he could feel the history of mankind in the fellow's stone grip. Calvin was ever-impressed by the breadth of company that Gem kept.

As though Calvin had been caught in a plot of deception, Fitim said to him directly, "You are American."

There is a certain soapy cleanliness to Americans that is readily discerned by those on the make. Shop owners, labourers and barmen all took Calvin for a Brit; but thugs, dope dealers and international businessmen – the speculation and manoeuvrings of the latter three legions being startlingly similar – discerned his nationality straight away. Calvin was one to accept that which he had no control over, though he wished certain truths were not so readily perceived—the government of his homeland seemed to be doing its damned best to make sticky the street-life of its citizens overseas.

Calvin confirmed what Fitim had suspected and returned, "And you? What is your nationality?"

Fitim did not respond immediately. Finally, he said, "It is a compelling question. Where I come from, a region in which borders and political regimes are in dispute, identity is the central concern of a man's existence. And though in his heart every man knows his nationality, sometimes he must fight to legitimise his truth, that he may live a full life with adequate representation. Most identify me as Serbian…"

Had Fitim been any less grievous of stature, or had the United States military not promiscuously bombed all hell out of Serbia and the Balkan Peninsula for the better part of the decade, the blood may not have run cold in Calvin's veins. Realities being what they were, however, it did.

"But why," asked Fitim, "are you so nervous?"

"Why so nervous?"

Calvin would have him know that foreplay as a prelude to violence was an especially sick undertaking. He then cocked his head to give his aggressor a clean shot at the mandible and demanded, "Go on! Get it over with for crissake!"

But to Calvin's great surprise, peace prevailed.

"Relax, relax," said Fitim. "I align with the other side of the conflict."

Calvin remained tense. There were a thousand different sides to the global polygon of political conflict and the vast majority of them joined others at acute and conflicting angles to those of the US. Anyway, thankfully, Fitim's mind was occupied with other business.

He and Gem volleyed pleasantries back and forth noncommittally for a brief moment before Fitim cut hard along a new line, "So, where is Martin Hamblin? Tell me."

"Martin Hambone!" jumped Gem. "Since when, mate, do you concern yourself wiv wankers?"

Fitim was not one to entertain rhetoric. "I cannot remember a time when I did not concern myself with wankers," he said. "But isn't Martin Hamblin a friend of yours?"

"Used to be, didn't he. I housed him, fed him—I was the one who got him his first job on the boats."

"And the one who got him fired," Fitim pointed out, "from that post and the one that followed."

"Martin Hambone is focking lucky I didn't..."

Gem stopped himself. He looked positively ill, like a scarecrow nailed together in all the wrong places and jammed rudely into hard earth. Overly conscious of all his ill-fitting parts, he poorly feigned an appearance of control.

Fitim calmly expressed his annoyance over Martin's sudden departure; then, in a show of proprietorship and territorial leverage, he had two drinks slide to a halt before Gem and Calvin. A chill struck the air. If the lads hadn't known before, they knew then that they were drinking on borrowed time and borrowed turf.

"Martin Hamblin owes money," said Fitim heavily.

Apparently, noted Gem, Martin had several outstanding debts stemming from several poor decisions. Gem took what he was owed out of Martin's backside.

A cat-and-mouse game ensued, through which Calvin learnt that Gem had slipped back from Napoli unannounced in early spring and waited for Martin Hambone to report to work at the port in Beaulieu Sur Mer. On his arrival, Gem gave him a "right proper slap, aye." Only with Gem, a slap was never a slap. That specific slap put Martin on his back, a position from which he bawled and claimed to have been struck blind. Gem let him know that the beating had not yet begun, and that when it did, it would be a nasty little course that would likely last a good stretch. And then, without further ado, it began.

Martin's most critical error was the lack of foresight he showed as it concerned the extent of reprisal ordained by Gem's world for improprieties such as Martin had committed. The captain of the yacht on which Martin worked had witnessed the beating and sacked him on the spot—a reaction that raised no eyebrows, for it was widely understood that one could not have such antics taking place outside one's boat, regardless of who was at fault.

Fitim admitted the first beating was warranted, but having analysed the details of Martin's second beating in as many weeks, he pointed out with a queer sense of chastity that while death was quite often funny, beatings were almost always ugly. Some believed that Martin buggered off back to Australia shortly thereafter.

The problem now, as Fitim explained, was that Martin owed Monique an exorbitant amount of money for failed dealings that would otherwise have delivered to Monique the supremely rare 1867 Stradivari-patterned C.A. Miremont cello for which she had paid Martin.

"It's going to take a lot of time and effort to find Martin and get that money back."

"Sorry, mate," said Gem, "but—"

"No *but*. It's going to be damn difficult."

Gem, sparking mad and not sure what to do about it, barked at the barman for two more drinks.

"Sorry, mate," Gem spat anew. "*But—*"

"*Stop* that," Fitim demanded with a raised index finger. "You must be more careful who you knock about, see."

The drinks appeared. Desperate to regain some ground, Gem nodded at the bartender as Fitim had done previously, but it had none of the desired effect. The barman wanted cash. Gem huffed angrily and began digging for payment, but before he could extract his wallet, Fitim gave an imperceptible nod and the bartender disappeared. With that show, the scarecrow Gem came unhinged.

"Martin *fock*ing Hambone sows his criminal seed in me woman," Gem howled, "and I'm supposed to run my plans for retribution by *you*? That focking moppet—you just don't do somefing like that, mate! Where I'm from, mate, you will get a right smacking for shagging someone's ol' lady! You will literally get your focking legs rightly *focking* broken for shagging someone's ol' lady, mate!"

Fitim was unaffected by Gem's explosion. "Calm down, mate," he said firmly. "It's going to be difficult to get that money. That's all I'm saying."

Having made himself clear, he bid them farewell in the French manner, shaking Gem's reluctant hand and then shaking Calvin's. As he departed, the house lights came up.

Gem flapped jagged like a poisoned crane, jerking his wings with ill possession, working the joints, reading the clicks and hitches, then flipped open his tide chart and proclaimed, "*Clo*sing time? But it's not yet two o'clock!"

Calvin looked at his watch; it was almost three. "Let's go," he said. "To hell with this lousy place."

They walked down to the beach. It hadn't been the same spirited reunion they enjoyed in summers past.

"Rotten news, all that," said Calvin. "You could've told me, you know."

Gem didn't respond, so Calvin kept quiet and each man walked alone.

Standing at the edge of the Mediterranean, Calvin threw white-grey stones, one after another into the still water of a late night. High upon the chateau, the spot-lit waterfall cascaded silently past pine and rock. From the lads' vantage point, the spot-lighting and the pooling of water somewhere unseen gave the picture a kitsch lacquer.

Gem laboured to calibrate his joints. He tilted his head towards various constellations and appealed to the inner ear with the heel of his hand. Something required dislodging. He tightened his belt and gyrated through broken arcs of motion, loosened his belt, removed his shoes and kicked his legs out to the side – first right, then left – epileptic. He was all-consumed.

Calvin's body warmed with the long-arm motion made famous by Viola Rush's heroes—warm, fluid, whip-like. He trusted the motion the way some do science, and others religion—it produced infallibly. The stones landed further and further out to sea, where each smooth grey egg was plucked from the viscous blanket of night in a tight splashless slurp nearly unseen from the shore. Some have science and some have religion; Calvin long-armed beach stones into an endless night-blackened sea.

At length, Gem broke the silence. "He's right, mate. The first beating was well deserved, aye. The second one… Somefing is off. Seems me gauges are jammed like."

Gem wondered if the years at sea hadn't completely salted away his acumen for the scabrous terrain of a life lived on land. His nights were increasingly interrupted by a recurring dream in which he traded limbs and lungs for fins and fish lips in becoming the better part of a gorgeous blue fin tuna. And fish, as all mariners know, end up gutted and grilled—or, in any case, gutted. Crimped internal conduit seemed to be restricting the drainage of certain poisons that now inundated Gem's nervous and vascular systems. Had he consulted a doctor? Four of them, actually. Unfortunately, from one to four, they were, to Gem, all incompetent. The blockage continued, jamming his joints and drowning his ability to negotiate day-to-day responsibilities. There was appetite loss, anxiety, difficulties sleeping. He had even lost his ability to gauge the tides, and what in Neptune's name was the value of an artist with no feel for the only substrate on which he knew to design and draft himself?

Calvin gave heave to another silver stone and the sea plucked it from the sky with a tight kiss. "I'm afraid it's much worse than mere poison, Gemmo. Why, you've got a broken heart."

"Same shite prognosis from the doctors. Load of bollocks. I expected a fair bit better from you, Calvin."

It might be argued that there is a fine-line difference between revenge and retribution—that revenge is motivated by the will of Man, while retribution is ordered by the cosmos. Gem had never known an appetite for vengeance; the first beating handed down to Martin Hambone was straight retribution, and retribution in any neighbourhood worth its name was a duty, unsavoury as it may be at times, ordained by the cosmos. Now, among other complicated developments, and as Gem had consistently proven incapable of leaving his instinctive itches unscratched, he feared the plague of retribution that was likely to spread from his hands to the corporal collective of Martin Hambone's crew, a sniggering pack of oafish boaties that had been provoking Gem from a afar – the ratty crew's preferred proximity to those they heckled – ever since the Mira-Martin debacle. Try as he may to buck the life-long trend, Gem followed his instincts like an army ant in blind queue. As for Calvin, Gem's best mate, all he could ever do was ask for fair warning and weather the physical fallout as best he could.

Eventually the lads came back round to the anthropological wonder that was Fitim. Said Calvin, "Who *is* that guy?"

"Monique's most recent bloke, for starters, isn't he."

"You mean *our* Monique?

"You thought, perhaps, another Monique equally endowed to pursue priceless cellos? Yes, one and the same, Calvin, mistress of your favourite blue-haired terrier. Though probably best to refer to her from now on as *his* Monique."

Calvin looked out to sea, as though the future could be consulted there. Boredom was the likely explanation for Monique's union with a fellow the likes of Fitim. One could never tell what enterprise might be launched when a fickle dame like Monique felt the shadow of boredom shading the white toes of her excitement. Unfortunately, Monique was frequently bored, and the bored are often quick to develop insecurities in the company of the active and the engaged, of which Fitim was both.

At first glance, one could easily identify the commonalities that encouraged Fitim and Monique's engagement, but closer analysis revealed a dubious match. Sure, both were highly skilled specialists, but while she drew a cellist's octagonal pernambucco bow with an ebony frog, abalone slide and a French pearl eye, he drew a flat-black Kalashnikov. Both were resourceful—she could kill softly on a cellist's stool with her song; he could kill softly from a cell if a stool didn't sing. Both were cultured—think Shostakovich amidst Baroque marble friezes, gold leaf, cherubim and nymphs (her); and the cinematic lust for the victorious bouquet of morning napalm (him). Both were financially independent, but while her independence came courtesy of an unbroken multi-generational chain of inheritance, his came from... Well, he simply seemed to have no need for legal tender; each nod of his big stone cranium seemed a ready substitute for cash.

Calvin was certain the sea concurred with him—it could turn messy.

What might happen if Monique needled Fitim the way she had her other beaux? Might he not reduce her collection of cellos to splinters, destroy all her bows, devour that mutt of hers? And then, once again, she would be *their* Monique, only a wronged and petulant version that would oblige the crew to cheer her, and such a version of Monique cheered neither easily nor cheaply. The lads would be required to show her about at all the posh cafés and expensive clubs on the Cote d'Azur, which in and of itself was not terribly taxing, but oh how in times of grief that near-bursting wallet of hers did snap tight like a frightened little clam!

"Don't worry about Monique, mate," said Gem. "She's built like a doily, but she can handle herself all right. She's a woman, after all, isn't she."

"She needs a *job* is what she needs," prescribed Calvin. "Nothing too demanding, of course; something to occupy her days. Why don't you get her a job on one of the boats?"

"Because it's a focking 'orrible idea, isn't it."

"She'd make a fine purser."

"She'd make the worst purser. The fing about most jobs, Calvin, is they involve work."

"Hey, how about Aloysius? Think you could find a job for Big Al?"

"Big Al?" questioned Gem, wrinkling his nose.

"Hell, get *some*body a job for crissake!"

"How about you?"

"I've *got* work. And I told you a hundred times I'm not a boat guy."

Calvin never understood the appeal of boats. He could admit to an attraction for those that stayed docked at port, but dropping anchor out in the middle of the sea? Then what?

"Besides," Calvin added mindlessly, "I can't be away for months at a go, on some boat. I've got a girl to protect and serve."

Gem lashed out, "Not anovva jumper, I hope," and at once felt his heart slip.

"What?" Calvin dropped a handful of select throwing stones. "What did you say?"

Gem inhaled. A hot orange dot flared in the darkness before his face and then fell away. "Who, then?"

"Go to hell," said Calvin, grabbing a new handful of stones. "How dare you? Go straight to hell."

"A Ukrainian lass." Darkness concealed his regret.

"*San*doval told you? To hell with the both of you," said Calvin and let one fly.

"Yeah," said Gem. "I suppose so."

Again Calvin let the stones fall. He turned to face Gem. "You were back here in the spring and you didn't tell me? You came back and scattered Martin Hambone's teeth all over the port, but you couldn't call over to say hello, see how I'm doing, pay me a lousy visit?"

"You would have tried to stop me from doing wot I had to do."

"Oh, no I would *not* have! I stand clear of all your nonsense until summertime!"

"That's only because I'm not around in the spring," said Gem wretchedly. "I have dreams, Calvin."

"Far be it from *me* to muck up your goddamned magnum opus."

"Not those kinds of dreams."

"Look," said Calvin, "you know I didn't mean anything by mentioning I have a girl to protect. It was a stupid thing to say. I wasn't thinking. I mean really – *me* – protect someone! And anyway, hell if *she* would allow it. Hell if I even know what I'm doing with that girl."

"Bullocks."

"No! That goddamned Sandoval is right: I probably *am* in over my head. But look, you have to let me know when you're in town, Gemmo. I'm your best friend, for crissake. You just have to."

"I know, mate."

With blown and blurry edges, the lads sauntered across the Quai des Etats Unis and back into the old town. The street cleaners were spraying down the alleyways, creating the nightly illusion of cleanliness. Lamplight reflected in the wet alleyways as morning began to rise in the east. They stopped before an old Niçois building and talked a moment longer.

"I think you're going to like your new flat," said Calvin, looking up towards the window and finding a crescent moon hanging there. "And look," added Calvin hopefully, "you're just down the alley from Manx."

"Want to go kick in his door?" asked Gem, feigning heart. "Burn a Rizla on his forehead?"

They heard the hard spray of street hoses in the distance, the comforting sound of homecoming at the end of a long night.

"It's damn good to have you home, Gemmo." said Calvin. "I'm sorry about everything. It's going to be all right."

"Of course it is, mate," said Gem, gripping his left elbow and kicking his right leg out to the side. "Come on up for a final whisky?"

"I better get to bed."

"Come on, mate—last one."

"Bah, I can't drink another drop," said Calvin guiltily. "You go see the flat. You're going to like it."

Gem clutched his elbow a bit harder and kicked his leg again; then consulted the tide chart. "Wot time have you got?"

"A little after five."

"Nearly there, mate," he said, but Gem was the worst of liars.

Calvin had a change of heart about that final whisky; it was the first he had seen of Gem in six months. But then he heard the hoses and the seagulls crying and suddenly felt rather run down and sorrowful.

"I've a load of fish to process in a couple hours. Meet for lunch somewhere afterwards?"

"Ring the bell," said Gem. "If I don't wake up, kick in the door."

Calvin smiled—for the first time, it seemed, in hours. "Sure," he said. "I'll burn a Rizla on your forehead."

"No you won't. You haven't got it in you, mate."

Gem was right. There were few mysteries between the two of them.

Calvin headed up Rue Poissonerie, wishing, unlike ever before, to find Klarysa asleep in his bed upon arriving home. The impossibility of it all made his heart ache.

Suddenly, Gem called out to him.

"Tell me, Gemmo," replied Calvin.

"Is she all right, mate? I mean is she good to you like?"

Calvin stopped and turned to face him.

"The Ukrainian bird, I mean," said Gem, as if Calvin didn't know.

"Sure," he said. "I suppose so. Sure."

"I told Sandoval he could go fock himself, didn't I."

Calvin smiled, waved and stumbled on, took the jog onto Rue Benoit Bunico and was nearly home, when he tried to conjure up Klarysa. Squeezing both eyes tightly shut for several steps, he became dizzy from drink and fell over. Lying in the alleyway, laughter rumbled in his belly and worked its way up to his grinning face. He hoped to hell the magic trick hadn't worked. What kind of impression would he have made, after all, had Klarysa materialised and found him there lying drunk and prostrate on his back in the wet alleyway?

He heard footsteps. Klarysa? Impossible. The sound was too heavy, besides. The footsteps slowed as they grew louder and closer, and stopped altogether at the top of Calvin's head. When he finally reopened his bleary eyes, he did not find Klarysa, of course. No, rather he saw two silver herding dogs, frozen in time and floating upside-down in a brown herringbone sky, waiting for Calvin to make a move. Interesting, thought Calvin. He squeezed his eyes shut once more and tried again. But nothing. No Klarysa, and even the dogs had moved on.

A thin-lip man in a wheelchair flick away a dead cigarette and notice he stuck on a icy sidewalk. He cough up a sick laugh and look up at the moon. Moon wink down at him and laugh, "Come on, old man, give it me!" Wheels spin and spin, he wear a shirt and pants outside in a winter like hungry razor blades and start to cry out for help. The moon watch and laugh and laugh.

Kid trudge through Garfield Park. He pass under a lone frozen light post at all the wrong hours to meet a boy shrouded in a dark winter coat.

"He just mad," I say. "Leave him go walk it off."

"No, no," he say and spit a wad of sunflower seed husks. "Better keep an eye on him."

"*He going to pay.*" Streetlights wince and blink. Snow blanket the streets, muffle the sound of the few brave cars that lumber by. "*He going to pay.*"

"What are you thinking of doing, Kid?" The boy in the winter coat pull a red hat down over his head. "Why don't we just walk it off…"

In my head the tinkling of a song sorely out of place and I got no time for a grievous annoyance.

"*Going to teach him a good lesson is what.*"

Legs go in different directions and Katie falls on a high white mountain. Her face is wet with cold snow and warm tears. A Garfield girl don't belong at a ski resort.

"This ain't California, now!" say his pops. "This is Garfield!"

But theys Tennessee boys in the goddamn ocean! You see how I start to remember things. I be the one to lick it!

She's got snow and tears on her face and she watches prep-school eyes come down suddenly before her

Heaven-blue eyes and a gold-medal smile there in the back of a white van

Takes away a long lock of wet hair from Katie's face. "Please, never get good at this," *he says. His mouth sends shivers of excitement all through her. He got a voice like liquid leather.* "I want to rescue you forever."

"Who is responsible for his death, if not you?" a judge demand. "Nonsense! You crawl into the night in search of blood! Flowers in one breath, cuss words the next. Flowers and fists! You can't believe yourself, child!"

"What did I do, your honor?" Irma cry from the kitchen. "What did I do to have my son end up like this?"

He knows the answer. Might be the only answer he do know. "*You ain't done nothing, Ma!*"

Skinny arms and a belly that hang over his belt, his hands white and weak. "He's going to be a fine boy just as soon as he—"

"I try, your honor! Oh, how I try. I'm always telling James—"

"That's enough, Irma."

Feel his razor stubble on my cheek high up in the air when he lift and kiss me.

"Your language, boy!" the judge cry.

"Goddamn right these boys of ours."

"I know, I know."

"*I didn't want nobody to die, sir.*" *He smell like bacon and perfume and sweat and he make me sick.*

"Address me as your honor!"

"*She called the repairman, but I already remembered what was going to happen.*"

"Everybody, everybody! Here before you is a ten-year-old child who can remember the future!" the judge mock and everybody laugh and laugh.

Kid, he unable to let go of a history, an unfinished idea. *History is where a boy go to find a future.* Make it dazzling *I can't see the future.*

"*I'm very sick, your honor.*"

"Sick indeed, boy, but that won't save your neck."

He cry hot syrupy tears and throw punches into the mattress *Her keys stabbed into the lock, Laika sits on the bed and writes:* No one can cage me. Not you, not my father, not anyone. Not ever again. *She raises a bedroom window and raises the door to the birdcage and two parakeets screech, flap in a frothy lime-green flurry and fly free. In a moment they are perched among green leaves in a stout eucalyptus tree.* Freed cage-birds, *she thinks*, are like confused childlike hallucinations.

"This is Garfield, boy!"

She smile whenever I talk about them lemon pies, she kiss me with Christmas red lips

Laika leaves the note and the empty cage, climbs back into the station wagon and aims for San Francisco.

Calvin is on the roof throwing stones out into the bloody sea. I join him and spark up a fag. "Feeling any better, mate?" Wiv me one hand, I open the window and a long train of opals and pearls shoots out into the night sky, each gem bursts in a fine silver mist high over the

Baie des Anges, creating a midnight rainbow of silvers and golds that stretch wide from Nice to Monaco.

"Not anovva jumper, I hope," I say. Me heart skips at once.

"What? What did you say?"

A hot orange point burns in the darkness just off his face and then falls down.

"Who, then, mate?" I ask. "Laika? Katie?"

"Go to hell. How dare you? Go straight to hell."

I got death on my hands.

Calvin is in shackles on the rooftop, throwing stones out into the bloody sea. He smiles an incredulous, wondrous smile, despite his chains. *"There is a sea right there,"* he says in joyous disbelief. He starts to laugh quietly, as though he might be going mad, *"A sea,"* incredulous, smiling, reluctant to going mad if only because the sea might then disappear.

"Was I found guilty? Was I convicted?"

"You are as free as a bird, mate."

Sharp November air, smoldering leaves, gasoline and 10w-30, young-girl perfume on humid young-girl skin in snug woolen sweaters, cherry lip gloss, barreling down neglected backwoods roads, tight-skinned in Jack's tough black '78 Chevy, Darcy and Katie half-asleep, lazily stretched out long and dreamy like shadows across the back bench seat. A tangle of industrial rail lines.

Sneak us a half jar of whisky. Richie's dad, a closet drunk, had pints of cheap stuff under the drop-ceiling in the basement. We knew all the hiding spots. Down at the bus station time stand still gray and lonely, empty warehouses pile up across the river, blunt-nosed steelhead, ugly sturgeon, burnt red brick, 1920s names high and white with authority and promise across their sides, see the power clear from the highway. Mickey, he came through, too. When Stan was in a rare good mood and he wasn't beating shit out of Mick, he'd run down to Two J's and buy us pints of Mohawk. You would've loved it, Gem; we were little kings on Friday nights. Detroit Hemi under the hood and a bottle of forty-proof in the glove box. We pick up Darcy and Katie and head anywhere out of the way. Excited lips, baby-white teeth eager to bite, cherry scented from head to toe, chomping the bit for every green light, pedal to the metal. Go faster, Jack! Make 'er growl!

Down at the bus station and the stretched iron rail lines, shiniest silver you ever saw lying sad and dormant under broken patches of Midwest rust. Find way to market rust, Gem, you make a millionaire in Garfield. Electrical wire run sleek and lean, no fat, dip and run slick and silver-gray from towering skeleton castles, bone-metal whiter and sadder, leaner than ashen cliffs of Dover—I suppose you could confirm or deny, Gem. Garfield patchwork rust webs like a loving cancer.

Down at the bus station with whatever we could get our hands on, Blatz or Hamms or Schlitz, cheap stinking beer, hanging around in ripped canvas tennis shoes, throwing stones and green glass bottles. Watch them shatter with high cheer on rock and concrete, shards pick up silver flash off those worked rail lines, burst in fiery Christmas green and bet each other ragged dollar bills worn thin like old linen with torn corners to see who can hit the flashing rail lights red and green on the other side of the yard. The girls lean against the car painted bright like Russian dolls and princesses from wealthy Heights. Cheeks and hips, they talked and made plans for university. Katie would grow bored and sling around flattering lines about Danny Meredith and John Meadows, any of the prep-school athletes from North, old as money gets in Garfield if you recall, appliance descendants, wide streets with old maples, ivy-covered turn-of-the-century brick, our rivals, the enemy, best watch you don't cross south of Portland, for if we catch an ivy sprig in Garfield, you never feel so far from home. Katie knew that such talk set me off and I'd race over and rip her away from the car hard and fast by the waist and pin her up against my body. Arched and suspended, submissive, her long brown hair falling helplessly earthbound, mouth poised slightly agape, wet sticky candy, hanging on the edge of pain, excitement, anticipation, so close I could smell her baby's breath, breath mixed with shimmering cherry gloss. I'd lay out heroic promises to all adversaries current and prospective and press my mouth and body long and hard against hers.

Down at the bus station, sadness and nostalgia take hold of me these years later. Damned rail lights that never stop blinking. After all the years and cans of beer and spilled whisky, still blinking, still trying to clear away the welled-up tears before any sodden rail-junkie passerby takes notice.

Jack takes the turn into the parking lot with the same high-adrenaline arc of old, snapping the tail hard and fast like a heavy black-metal Chinook in midnight fight, making tires scream, leaving long black-rubber semicircles on Union. I spot Katie before Jack brings the Chevy to a halt, his sentimental maneuvers seem mistimed and sorely out of place.

"Goddamn, look at her!" *I say.*

I had an iron-clad confidence in the old neighborhood. Pot holes, front stoops with broken handrails of musty rotting wood, generations of thick green paint peeling, exposing rot, burnt motor oil blacker than black, salt-stained Grand Torinos, stretch Galaxies, rusted Imperials a block long. But that confidence was untested in the real world, the one run by Northies. Here we are twenty-one-years old, and I can tell you, Gem, my Katie is no longer a Garfield girl.

"She took the bus back from Denver," *Darcy says,* "because she wanted to see countryside."

I laugh and Darcy laughs, too. Hurt and mistrust still lingers from Katie's decision to go to college half-way across the country. Why couldn't she go to a Midwest school like everybody else in the entire world, save for you, of course, Gem. You left first.

I'm the last out of the car, made leaden by lack of preparation and newly discovered insecurities. Jeans and heavy boots, ripped t-shirt black on stained white Two J's under long-sleeved flannel, hard shiny-blue welt and yellow eye from last weekend. I lope up to greet her and all three of them are searching me for answers and directions. Mountainous calluses, rough snagging skin stretched tight over knuckles, rusty iron netting, goddamn simple no-account. I ache for a shot of anything strong and harsh and come up ashamed at how much ache there is wrapped up in it. Jesus, Katie. Jesus! She's seen and touched something big, an awareness. She's poked around with curiosity and contemplation at life beyond this city. There is a sadness to her beauty, knowing any attempt to explain her visions would only make us all uncomfortable.

We all climb into the car after the uneasy embrace. The scent of her perfume follows me, so different than the stuff she wore to the homecoming dances. It makes me sick and small inside. The walls close in around me. Oceans, deserts, endless expanses of openness, more and more walls. A silver-green bus pulls slowly out onto Union, the first bus I've ever seen come or go. Rail lights still blinking across the yard, still blinking away brilliant red and green tears. I feel sick. She once loved me, she once kissed me with Christmas red lips. Learn to talk right, speak right, speak well simple no-account. I pick up a stone and let fly

I could use a sea to pick it from the night sky with a silent invisible kiss

I miss by a mile

We once lay together in silence on a long brown couch and all the walls close in around me

Jack drives out of the lot with all four tires touching asphalt.

"How is school? How is Colorado?" A thick salty deluge having never been west of Chicago. I watch out the window, thinking and forgetting and then remembering that Pop taught me to look at people when talking to them. I missed whatever it was Katie might have said. Her hand is on my leg, her hand comes to rest gently on my leg. Turning to face her, I find my old girl smiling softly. Take her hand, take her hand, it seems ridiculously sad and sentimental. I feel small and thick but at least I am a goddamned brute. I lay my hand on hers, ashamed to look at her, she's so beautiful, pieces fitting flawlessly without flash. She is miles and years ahead of me. She got eyes that look back and tell me to relax, but I can't catch up, caught on each thought that comes to mind, resuscitating myself with reminders You

was all-state, Kid, you was all-state. Each iteration bringing wet shame and the realization that she has touched something big, the ocean, the desert, an endless expanse of openness, something beyond the walls and walls. She looks back at me, tries to bring me along with kindness and patience and something that looks like love, but I can't catch up

I can't see the future

But it feels a hell of a lot like pity. Watching out the car window, aware of the bleakness, speeding forward much faster than what the Chevy can take us

Got to pay attention, got to remember

Unconsciously wrap my hand around my bicep and work it slowly in contemplation and then stop and remember to look at Katie when she talks

Following rail lines south, out of the city, away from the red brick warehouses and all the cracked cement to the low flat farmlands. Shoot past 118th, then slow and turn down a brown dirt road that leads nowhere. Climb out of the car without question. Back between the walls, I find sad comfort. Things change even when you stand still and hold your breath. People and places pass by. Jack takes a pint of rye whisky from the glove box and the four of us lean up against the Chevy. Flat and gray in every direction, a dark endless stage, the players all fallen exhausted, home to bed. Autumn corn fields low and stake-like, jagged and bruised a bluish-brown, chopped down at the ankles at the end of summer run long and effortless to a falling horizon in they own sweet time. Every half mile sits a tired old barn, a small box house, a dirty white clapboard addendum for weathered men and women. Two miles up the road sits Southern High football stadium, gray skeleton bleachers peek up from blue-brown earth. Thanksgiving is a time to be thankful and praise God and knock your neighbor's teeth out on the football field, pound out violent, low-margin victories. The air is cold. Lights from the stadium twinkle with a fine-line brilliance that only comes from a long-distance light dancing its way over frozen air. Frost will come heavy tonight.

Watch the short row of farm houses that border the far edge of the field and think how sad and beautiful it must be to look out across a harvest-cut field, frosted silver and twinkling crystalline below a frozen orange-pink sunrise. Cold and loneliness creep up under my pant legs and dig in with a sharp-toothed grip. I take a long draw from the bottle and feel the rush of warm biting silk slide down my throat and go to work and shoo away the chill. A shot of courage runs through me and I am big and old, though somehow still just twenty-one. I sling an arm around Katie and pull her close and remember very little

Make it dazzling

Theys oceans and deserts

And Katie is smiling. I take another pull of whisky.

She smile when I talk about those lemon pies she going to make

Two lime-green parakeets alight on ankle-high stakes of blue-brown earth

The lights twinkle with fine-line brilliance and rail lights blink, blink red and green

She once kissed me with warm Christmas red lips.

I take another pull and offer the bottle to Katie. She utters no words, just smiles softly and brings her head to rest against my shoulder. I look up at the moon, its silver outline digging in harder against the gray night, and take a big gulp of cold air.

"What say, how's that bottle, Kid?" Jack! He and Darcy are wrapped tightly around each other, though you know Jack is never cold. Never cold. He rolls down Randolph in the dead of winter, dirty downtown snow piled high on the sides, one hand keeping the Chevy straight, the other lopped out the window, flannel rolled up to the elbow like Labor Day. Big goddamn bear, Jack. I never appreciate the sound of his voice ever so much as right now. I lean across Katie without letting go and pass the bottle to Jack. He takes a good pull and cracks the silence like a hammer on glass.

"Southern's going to win state this year."

His words are always too loud. The air is dark and cold. A far-off cheer reaches us in tight frozen bubbles from the stadium, on the tail of a chilling breeze.

"We'd have crushed 'em," *Jack says like a hammer and spits.*

I watch Jack, lost as he is in a dream of past glory, watch the signature flame dance in his eye. The boy did lay out punishment on a halfback in his day. Those quick brown boys with lithe tapered muscles hate to get hit by Jack. They bones crunch and groan and you see the hit big and white in they sad beautiful brown doe eyes. The frost will come heavy tonight. I feel sick. Tears pump with each heartbeat, up into the edges of my eyes.

Jack snaps out of his reverie like a livewire. We all climb back into the car, slick black leather already gone cold and stiff. The girls are in the back seat and I'm in front. All is silent in understanding.

Back toward the city, Jack shoots the Chevy straight and true, a flat black comet. I watch Katie sixteen-years-old all over again in the haunted side-view mirror, Go faster, Jack. Make 'er growl! Wipe red hot tears from my secret eyes, shoot a hard northern line, rising, past 104th, 94th, 82nd, 74th, signs of life, movie shack, adult bookstore, drive-in, bail bondsman, 66th, 62nd, 50th, pot hole at 46th can't stop us, roll past Fat Bob's, pink lights on Vegas-style sign half-dead, neon tuna no longer dance for Fat Bob. Through the intersection at 38th and past the Feline Bar, Tae Kwon Do school, Schafer's Club where Ma and Pop danced orange and gold, orange and gold. Under the train trestle at 32nd, heavy sadness in every pound of rusted-out train trestle, lean *forward, jam a tape into the deck, slowing down now, city limits, struggling neon, hard-white lights, dirty brick. Past 26th, Chiu's market, RJ's Lounge, the music comes up. Randolph becomes North Randolph, soup kitchen, shelter, dead hotel and boarded up warehouses, Serpent Club, Haussmann Shelter, beat down whores in patchwork of fake fur cackle like possessed chickens, drinking from paper bags under electric-yellow streetlight at Franklin and I turn up the volume on the radio to hear Bon: "It's another red-light nightmare, another red-light street, and I ain't too old to hurry, 'cause I ain't too old to die, but I sure am hard to beat." Jack nods hard approval, cranks down the window, lops out a giant paw and points the long black Chevy up North Randolph. Cold night air hijacks the car with bitter force. In the back seat, Darcy is sound asleep, beautiful, oblivious to all that has come and gone and all that is yet to happen. Katie watches out the window, still, silent, face awash in shiny night air and swishing brown hair whipped up devilishly by icy pre-winter phantoms she thought she'd left behind. Stop abruptly for red light at Hamilton, cast-iron toughs hitch their way across the street, Chevy's head lights blink hard as they pass, cut like diamond through frozen meat. First midnight snowflakes of the season swirl in the oily black sky, swirl lost and confused, soft white feathers perish on oil-packed asphalt. Bon wails with whisky'd hope, desperation from the radio and I get a good look at Katie in the momentary stillness, staring wide-eyed, she watches herself beyond the tattered edges of an empty November night, off on some bright-white Colorado mountain top where the sun shines golden and true, with some guy I hope never to meet.*

12   The tourists

In which Calvin is warned, a
metals man faints and Janice
finds her Phoenix.

Calvin leaned over the side of the balcony and peered down towards the alleyway, but saw nothing that might confirm or deny the Butcher's suspicions. The Butcher had rung from the Bar des Oiseaux voicing concern for the shopgirl who ran the boutique in the alleyway below Calvin's flat. Calvin had carried out the occasional reconnaissance effort on the Butcher's behalf. He begrudged all it entailed, but without aid, the Butcher was liable to blot out a fellow's sun with Northern woe and depression. It was in everyone's best interest to lend aid.

Nothing seemed out of sorts downstairs. There was the usual gathering of dark-eyed youth and the resplendent chaos of John Coltrane's Newport '63 caroming up between the buildings from the boutique, which, like countless others in Vieux Nice that were zoned commercial, lacked the types of wares that lent shops an air of commercial viability. The boutique was primarily a hangout for scooter punks and other makes of punk with a penchant for chain-smoking, modifying the exhaust systems on whiny two-stroke engines and contributing to the high-gravity inertia of the group's low-intensity loitering. All of it was carried out with an indefatigable persistency—attention deficit had not yet come to afflict the youth of Vieux Nice. At any hour of the day, the shopgirl could be found flipping records, smoking loose-tobacco cigarettes and duct-taping secure all the rattling parts of her old flat-black Vespa. She wore faded jeans and high-top sneakers and had the suspicious countenance of one who has been consistently disappointed over extended periods of time, though she was in fact surprisingly ebullient and affable. She had rich hair that fought back in times of humidity, eyes of smouldering black ash, cloud-berry cheeks and an off-plumb nose that lent a depth of character that intimidated the Butcher, who consistently sold himself short and failed to impress outside shallow pools, as a result.

Calvin had resolved to go down for a closer look when the telephone rang. He sighed—the best part of an early summer evening interrupted by a stalker who was too lazy and insecure to do the stalking himself.

"Hold on a bleeding second, will you, Butcher?" Calvin said into the phone. "She's still a*live* for crissake. That's all I can tell you just now."

"Calvin? Is that you, old sport?"

It was not the Butcher, after all. It was, in fact—

"Jim. Jim *Cren*shaw! You OK? *Say* something, old man!"

It was not the sound of Jim's voice on the line that rendered Calvin silent; it was the clarity of his voice, which signalled close proximity.

Calvin and Jim had spent time together at the same outfit in San Francisco; Jim writing and drafting, Calvin archiving innumerable reports on metal parts that fit together with (and sometimes within) other metal parts, so on and so forth until eventually the metal parts, together, became one variety or other of metal product that the world couldn't possibly survive without. That was years ago, back in Levi Square, where, at the office, Jim successfully generated Sierra-sized mountains of paper, up and down which Calvin failed to adequately traverse. A cold midnight avalanche, the very phenomenon Calvin had been hired to mitigate, finally buried Calvin and sealed the death of his employment. The coroners said it was an unfortunate accident. Only Calvin, who left the office giddy and bright-white, knew it was a form of blissful suicide.

Calvin hadn't seen Jim or Janice since the wedding. It was a memorable affair, a Southern affair staged at a distillery just off the Kentucky Bourbon Trail. Aware as Calvin was that he only experienced déjà vu as a foreshadowing of troubling times, a tendon in his neck pulled taut when Laika approached the alter, as Janice's maid of honour, locked arm-in-arm with the Knoxville stud turned California surfer, who acted as Jim's best man. Having grown up in pastures of iron and heavy metals, Calvin suffered cellular-level distrust for surfers (what with their oceanic sense of ease and comfort) that no geographical transplanting could shake. Ironic, his distrust—not so much for the fact that Laika, Calvin's chosen one, was also a surfer, but because, therefore, so became Calvin.

Might one fellow, wondered Calvin to himself at the wedding, as he sat alone in the church pew, claim to spot impropriety building like a thunderstorm in another fellow's eyes (especially when they're so damned bright and blue), and pre-emptively bust his fucking skull for it and *not* fashion himself a maniac and sociopath in the eyes of the congregation? Not likely. So Calvin abandoned the idea altogether, sauntered out of the church well before the 'I dos' and conducted a ceremony of his own, making a congregation of the charred oak barrels in the brick storehouse and playing groom to a tin-cup bride of undiluted barrel proof whisky. "Very nice to meet you. Name's Calvin. What's that? In times of sickness and in times of health? Oh, I most certainly do."

Gulp, gulp, gone. 'Twas a beautiful and pain-free arrangement, he thought, as she glowed warmly in his belly and in his head. He wasn't so tipped as to think all marriages might be so clean and easy.

Soon after the wedding, Jim accepted a(nother) promotion and whisked Janice off to London, where they began working on a family with the same great alacrity that Jim applied to all business ventures. He was an overachieving type who was always cracking and on-form and succeeding at the highest levels. He only ever referred to another as *old man* or *sport*. He was the type to sneak up on a fellow in a crowded bar and sock him in the arm to see how much of the fellow's drink he could spill. Then he'd scan the bar to see which of those present had profited from his genius and comedic savoir-faire. As infuriating as it was, Calvin bit his lip and accepted it, knowing that such acts were not just born of Jim's notion of boyish fun, but so too his notion of brotherhood—a fraternity-house grade of brotherhood that was, therefore, pitiable. Every occasion on which Jim met an acquaintance, he acted as though it were the first time he had seen the fellow in years. His enthusiasm was admirable, only the poor acquaintance could still feel the knot in his arm from the last time he saw Jim, the prior evening.

"Why, Jim Crenshaw," said Calvin, trying to muster heart. "Can it be?"

"You OK, sport? I won't lie," said Jim, as though he were capable of it, "you sound wretched. What a curious way to answer the phone."

"No, no," said Calvin. "It's just... It's just a joke."

"A joke, hey? I'm doubled over."

"Anyway, it's great to hear your voice, Jim. Why, it sounds as though you're just down the street."

"Funny you should say; old Janice and I checked into the Méridien this morning. You know the place, I suppose. I'm calling from the front lobby. I'm waving my hand—can you see me?"

That was Jim's idea of high humour.

"Great news," said Calvin. "What's the occasion?"

"Seems old Janice had a miscarriage..."

Old Janice? It *seems*? Such language was part of Jim's pat strategy for emotionally insulating himself from women and (their) tragedies. He would speak of Janice as though she were one collegiate pal or another, and the miscarriage as something that may or may not have actually happened, so let's not everyone get all bent out of shape.

"I'm very sorry to hear it, Jim."

"Well, yes. Thanks. Janice is quite torn up over it—no pun intended."

No man had ever called on the pun as frequently as did Jim Crenshaw. Never, of course, were they intended.

"So we flew mother over to manage Zoe and decided to get away for the weekend."

Zoe was considered an angel, a gift from God to Jim and Janice after her first miscarriage.

"And where better to spend a weekend than Nice?" questioned Jim. "Or so they'll have you believe."

Calvin absently arranged three candles on the *table basse* and encouraged Jim to spend a relaxing weekend with Janice in the gardens and walking the Promenade, just the two of them. Jim interrupted to inform Calvin that they had already been in Nice for half a goddamned day. They had suffered an hour on the godforsaken rocky beach, ate a mediocre and over-priced meal on the Cours Saleya, shuffled along from one end of the *zone piétonne* to the other, and Jesus, wasn't there anything to actually *do* around there? And by the way, what the hell kind of re*sort* town can't manage a lousy sand beach? And wasn't there some manner of internationally sanctioned watchdog organisation to monitor such low-grade scams? And well, if there *wasn't*, there *should* be. With a grin, Calvin asked if they hadn't yet stopped for ice cream and Jim replied that yes, smartass, they had.

Finally, they arranged to dine together. Calvin was to meet Jim and Janice at the hotel.

Jim was a good guy, Calvin reflected as he washed and shaved. What fascinated Calvin was that he had forever identified Jim as one of the world's biggest idiots. He liked Jim; they had spent many fine times together. But it was truly perplexing just how well Jim got on in life. Calvin kept waiting for the punch line, for the velvet curtains to be pulled back and the mechanics of the trick exposed. But every time he talked to Jim, or gleaned a bit of information about him from a mutual friend, he learnt that Jim had just closed another big deal, or had just accepted another big promotion, or had just gotten back from an all-expenses-paid holiday courtesy of some big outfit, which, if *it* had any say in the matter, would adopt the big lug and give him a key to Kansas City.

Jim was Ivy League educated, achieved high marks in a rigorous engineering program and captained several intramural teams. He had memorised arguments, some modern, some archaic, for just about any topic of conversation. Against topics that did not readily lend themselves to successful debate through rote memorisation and statistical analysis (e.g. the Arts), he armed himself with shallow, bull-headed arguments and discounted the topic at hand as the concern of the idle and masturbatic. He caustically scoffed at Jackson Pollock, labelling the artist a demented paint-dribbling drunkard, and considered Mark Rothko a phony, a mortification of his Latvian ancestors and contemporaries alike. Calvin might argue that Pollock and Rothko were mad ravaged geniuses, but pointing, for example, to the mammoth Seagram Murals that hung forebodingly in their own *salle* of the Tate Modern, he could not articulate with any eloquence why they were the works of a great master.

Owing to his well-intentioned heart and the years spent in Northern California, Jim was an arm's-length social liberal. Owing to his white-pillared Southern upbringing and his determination to keep every single penny of the money he had worked so hard to obtain, he was a diehard fiscal conservative who harboured all the greed, aggression and mistrust that bode so well in the making of rich men and ardent competitors. Jim could reel off five reasons for anything at all, and used his fingers to keep count as he steamrolled through any attempt at interjection. One critical flaw in Jim's mechanics was that he was so bound to his rigid convictions that he no longer thought, he only recited. He was fixed, like a printed encyclopaedia—impressively thorough in scope, but lacking in coverage of any new discoveries. Jim embodied all the colourful mystery and intrigue of a computer punch card—manila, square, slotted, able to recount a story with pinpoint accuracy, though completely bereft of character and texture. His synapses fired strictly in mapped habitual patterns, triggered responses to trademarked household stimuli.

There are brief moments of time in any Niçois summer day when the air hangs charged with regal electricity under which even the destitute awaken with a certain flickering sense of luck and optimism. Calvin descended the stairwell and stepped out into an evening air so charged. He was suddenly excited to see his old friends.

The carousel in the Jardin Albert 1er was lit with taffy-coloured lights and spun slowly to an organ tune from yesteryear. Having crossed to the other side of the garden, Calvin arrived at the reception just before nine o'clock and asked to have a call placed up to the room.

"*Bonsoir, Monsieur* Crenshaw," purred the receptionist into the house phone. "*Monsieur* Stony *est arrivé à la reception.*"

A short stretch of silence ensued. The receptionist held the phone to her ear and looked seasick. She tried again. "I say zat Meestur Stony eece ear een zee receptions fau yoo, *Monsieur* Crenshaw."

"Oh, for crissake!" steamed Calvin under his breath. "Goddamned barbarian!"

Calvin fought to suppress a wave of distaste and anger for Jim. Some outfit paid that bastard two-hundred grand per annum and he couldn't decipher the simple announcement of Calvin's expected arrival at the hotel. Calvin smiled meekly and thanked *mademoiselle*; then spun about and wiped the goddamned hamburger juice from his chin.

Moments later, the elevator doors parted and out bounded Jim and Janice. They were handsome in a way Calvin could not have expected—good enough to eat, in nostalgic southern shades, perfectly dressed for morning mass in the middle of a pleasant Nashville summer. One solid bite, thought Calvin, might reveal a warm and tasty filling.

Jim was embarrassed in his costume. Clearly, Janice had laid it out for him, likely as payback for paces through which he had put her. He looked like a lumbering priest, excommunicated and dipped in Easter dye. Janice, on the other hand, was ecstatic, a fit little whisper of cotton candy, a breathless puff of cirrus moving gracefully about in the skies over planet Jim.

Calvin's excitement heightened with each passing second. What an impossible treat to witness Jim Crenshaw stuffed into powder-blue polyester. Calvin was certain he had never felt so comfortable in his own skin, or felt so content with his thin understanding of certain realities. Life was really only cruel for those whose expectations outshined the lights of their realities.

"Good to see you came dressed for the occasion, old chap," said Jim critically, looking as though he'd been left in the oven too long.

"Leave him alone, cretin!" Janice protested excitedly. "He looks *won*derful. Why, he looks like our Calvin. Besides, *we're* the ones on holiday."

The town of Nice conveyed conflicting messages to holiday-goers. There were all of the icons of grandeur one expected, but then, after strolling among the yachts at port, Calvin would escort Jim and Janice down streets so contaminated with canine excrement that city officials passed legislation to try to curb the problem. Still, no one would bat an eye were a giant mastiff to empty itself in the middle of the alleyway and its owner ignore the fallout. *Le lutte contre le pollution de chien*! The battle against dog shit! Jim and Janice would have to tip-toe their baby-blue way through the warrens of a polluted minefield, and invariably, before the night had died, one of them would likely tread on a bomb. This, from the same proud nation that reared the likes of Voltaire, Sartre, Baudelaire, Verlaine, Rimbaud. *Bienvenue à Nice!*

Calvin rocked back on his heels and spread his arms, as though he might burst into gay applause. "Janice!" he cried with inflated wings. "I say; if you're not the very picture of fairness and beauty!"

Calvin approached and exchanged *bisous*. As he pulled away from her, his shoulder absorbed the inevitable wallop from Jim.

"Hey there, sport," he said.

"Great to see you, Jim," replied Calvin sincerely.

"*Ça fait longtemps*," said Janice, beaming, eagerly unveiling her shiny new skill set.

Janice hailed from Louisville, Kentucky and smelt wonderfully of warm cream cheese and powdered sugar.

"She's been studying *French*," Jim accused.

"*Tais-toi*," said Janice.

"That's right; *ta gueule, connard*," added Calvin, and the two tittered and creamed, like children, on the half-shell of their extemporary co-conspiracy.

Calvin was suddenly overwhelmed by the sparkling recognition of his own happiness and wellbeing. He recognised the love he felt for his two old friends. A feeling of carefree confidence engulfed him. What power there was in such emotions. That was real freedom—freedom no administration could grant or deny. In such moments, he thought aggressively of Klarysa. He knew he would win her heart. And were he to fail... Hell, failure held no threat for the truly content and grateful. There before his wet lips and dancing fingertips stood his old mate Jim, he who was meant to be Calvin's superior in every way, stuffed tightly and uncomfortably, like a big baby in a soiled nappy. And wouldn't Jim buy dinner that night, as well! Calvin anticipated the moment when Jim would wrench a fat wallet from his back pocket and produce the candy-coloured French francs—this from a man with rabid loyalty for the greenback. What a gift! The playful pastel notes were sure to boil Jim's pot.

They decided to walk along the Promenade before cutting into the Vieux and settling down somewhere to dine.

"Listen, Janice," said Calvin, as they departed the hotel. "I'm sorry to hear about... I mean I feel horrible about your..." Calvin drew a blank; what was the appropriate euphemism for *miscarriage*?

"My what?" she asked.

"You know, honey," Jim assisted, "the *bah-bah*."

"Oh. I see. I'm OK, Calvin. Thank you."

Loss—that was the euphemism for which Calvin searched. He suddenly felt out of touch and felt a flash of anger that euphemisms were necessary among old friends. Three old friends, mused Calvin, strolling down the Promenade—two Easter lilies and the gardener's dirty fist. He would have liked to ask Janice a question or two about the miscarriage. Had she detected something amiss during the pregnancy? Was there a physical or emotional sensation that caused alarm? Or was the problem discovered during a scheduled examination? He would have liked to ask what it felt like to lose something that was growing inside of her, something that was a part of her, reliant on her, something that was to be the centre of her universe. But the *bah-bah* euphemism meant the topic was not to be discussed—at least not as adults.

Calvin was convinced that he, too, had suffered a miscarriage or two in his time. He could feel the rough knotted scar tissue from having had a budding something scraped from his insides. In the best of times, Calvin was able to admit that his miscarriages may have, in fact, been abortions. Nevertheless, there were times in his life when a translucent, helpless something counted on him for nurturing and protection and the poor thing died on his watch. He chased off a cold chill. It occurred to him that words such as *miscarriage*, *abortion* and *death* were already adequately euphemistic to emotionally diffuse the hard realities so often associated with such life occurrences.

Moving on, Calvin asked, "How are you finding London, Janice?"

"Oh, it's fine, I suppose," she replied. "Just like any other big American city."

Jim corrected her, "Just like any big American big city, you mean. Or just like any other big city."

"No, not at all. It's absolutely nothing like Tokyo or Rio or even Zurich for that matter. I just *love* Zurich!" she exclaimed. "Did you know, Calvin, that Zurich is considered the cleanest—"

"Well, because," Jim interrupted, unable to contain himself, "your words imply that it's an American city."

"Zurich?"

"No, London. You can say *other* or *American*, but you can't say both in the same sentence."

"Fine, Jim, fine." Then back to Calvin, "London simply can't compare to Zurich when it comes to—"

"Because, of course, it's *not* an American city, you know."

"Yes, Jim," said Janice. "I am rather aware that London is not an American city."

"But you said any *other* American city. Which it is not."

"My god, will you *please* not be an ass for once."

Jim couldn't help himself. To Jim, right was right and wrong was wrong, and who could imagine a person not wanting to improve *her*self. Catching someone in an error was like pepper to the nostrils, and to refrain from voicing a correction was like trying to hold back a sneeze.

"Huh, Calvin?" he said, jerking his thumb towards Janice, abandoning his correction to take up the next best angle of criticism. "You should hear how she goes on about Zurich. Have you ever been?"

"No."

"Smart man. Stay away. It's the worst!"

"Of course, Jim has never actually been to Zurich," Janice clarified. "He only hates it because I love it. It is a matter of course with him."

"Did you know you can get arrested in Zurich for not washing your car?"

"Is that right?" said Calvin, having decided that involvement was his only chance of steering the line of conversation away from the cliff.

"Of course it's true," said Jim. "But does *she* consider such things? No way. *She* thinks Zurich is the greatest city on earth."

"And if you think," defended Janice, "that I'm going to apologise for it—"

"Who's asking for an apology? For not washing your *car*, Calvin—ar*rest*ed. It's insanity."

"That's not at all true," said Janice.

"Well, just make goddamned sure you don't call *me* when you're locked away in a Swiss prison for having a dirty car!"

"I don't even *have* a car."

"As I've pointed out many times, Janice, you're not exactly cut out for driving."

"Fine, then," concluded Janice. "If you simply *must*, then by all means go on and be an ass."

"I know a guy who spent time in a Swiss jail," said Calvin desperately. "First he tried to extract his wife's teeth in the night with a monkey wrench; then he pushed her into an icy river. It's OK, though, she fairly bit off both his ears."

It worked; that took the air out of the argument. Jim didn't like being an ass; he simply couldn't help himself.

Suddenly his lily petals went erect and he blurted, "Hey, look at that!"

Down one of the narrow streets that shot off the Promenade, two youths squatted low around an old Renault.

"Why, they're stealing the hub caps!"

"Looks as though they're planning to leave the wheels," Calvin deadpanned, having come to grips with the prevalence of rats in Nice.

Calvin knew a fellow who had once gone out to his old BMW in the morning, only to find it propped up on cinderblocks and stripped of its wheels. Another time, the same fellow had innocently parked across the street from the Jewish temple over on Rue Gustave Deloye. When he returned to the car, he found that the gendarmes had ripped out the door locks and broken in, apparently in search of pipe bombs and the like. One had to recognise that from time to time, the small rats would get you. And if they didn't, the big rats would.

"The nerve!" said Jim. "Oh, sure, in the US they'll shoot a fellow in the head, but at least they have the goddamned decency to not steal the shirt off his back."

"*Hub*caps," mused Janice, picking an invisible piece of lint from her dress, "Who cares? I'd rather be pick-pocketed than shot."

"Oh, horseshit!" Jim steamed in his baby blues. "Hey, punks! Move away from that car!"

The kids looked up, grey and nonchalant, blinked a couple of times and went back to work, picking up the pace just slightly. It reminded Calvin of a midnight walk down the Colaba Causeway in South Bombay. The east side of the street was lined with cots just wide enough for a sleeping body, side-by-side and perpendicular to the curb for what seemed the length of the causeway, like the skinny teeth of an endless comb. The street was dark and heavy with sleep, except for a congregation of rats that had gathered at the next street corner under a tight circle given off by the streetlamp. A pack of small dachshunds, thought Calvin with a squeamish grin, waiting patiently, as though for the start of the hunt. He anticipated watching them race for cover when he drew close, only they did not race away at all. They were perfectly unfazed by his approach and he was forced to veer around them or risk rat guts on the soles of his dusty shoes. It was undeniably impressive in a foul, pestilent sort of way. The filthy buggers would have been impervious to Camus' plague.

Every city has its rats, thought Calvin—they that rule the streets. One may try to eradicate them, but they only keep breeding, keep multiplying. The streets belong to them before anyone else – before the city officials, before the coppers, before any would-be exterminators, certainly before any hack tourists – and they come in all shapes and sizes.

Calvin, Jim and Janice passed under an arched tunnel and entered Vieux Nice by the Marché aux Fleurs. At the edge of the Place du Palais-de-Justice, Calvin spotted Gem, who appeared to be en route from the last pint to the next and who was accompanied by a curvaceous Lyonnaise with more dark curls than a man could reasonably hope for.

"You there, Gem!" Calvin burst hotly, foregoing all introductions. "What gives, brother! Did we or did we not..." he lowered his voice and cast a sidelong glance at his unintended audience, "did we not have a certain arrangement last night?"

He steered Gem off to the side, though the debate would continue well within earshot of the others.

"Apologies, Calvin. Had a bit of an emergency last night, didn't I."

Calvin braced and then wilted and then braced again, for Gem's history of emergencies was a bottomless grab-bag of unimaginable events that nevertheless fizzled as often as they exploded.

"You see, mate," Gem continued, "I was on me way over to yours, wasn't I, when I got a call from Anissa."

"Anissa," said Calvin. "Who the hell is Anissa?"

"Why, she's a bird, isn't she," said Gem with a look that was intended to jog Calvin's memory without divulging all the racy details before their company.

"I rather gathered she's a bird," said Calvin. "What I mean is *who the fuck* is Anissa when—"

Calvin met Janice's riveted eye and grinned sheepishly. Again he lowered his voice and said heatedly, "We had *bus*iness to attend to, Gem! Serious business."

By no means had Calvin recommitted the earlier error, whereby he enlisted the aid of an outside other to act as a replacement in making a delivery, though any fellow privy to the details would nevertheless have labelled his latest arrangement with Gem another lapse of good judgement.

"Right, mate," said Gem. "And I thoroughly see your point. I do. But she told me to meet her at Galleries Lafayette, didn't she."

"No!" Calvin gasped. "You mean… You mean *that* Anissa."

"The one."

The Lyonnaise fidgeted impatiently and smacked her chewing gum, never deigning to acknowledge the presence of Jim and Janice. To Janice, the Lyonnaise was an irritant and a distraction. Janice, a loving but no-nonsense mother on holiday, and there removed from domesticity and her own demanding brat for one lousy weekend, felt a sudden urge to smack the gum clean from the child's gyrating gob.

"Anissa," voiced Calvin, as though referring to a vaporous myth. "And she was *work*ing?"

"She was until I got there," said Gem with a cluck and a wink. "Know wha' ah mean, Calvin?"

"I see. I see," he pondered.

By and large, a fellow is allowed great leeway when he has an honest shot with a dame the likes of Anissa Montserrat, it's true.

"But look, Gem," said Calvin finally. "That's it. No more. You can't break an accord like that. You of all people understand the gravity of the situation."

Gem professed a deep understanding, apologised once again and explained that he had only gone to Gallieries Lafayette to tell Anissa he was unavailable. When he made to leave, however, she thrust him into a changing cabin for the handicapped and ripped off all his clothing.

Jim and Janice hung on every word of the terrific exchange and constructed God knew what kind of images of life in that Latin quarter. The last efforts of dusk illuminated the Palais de Justice and its massive stone columns. White water arched and splashed in the fountain and the cafés bustled with life. The air was infused with the pungent smell of burning hashish, and the unleashed dogs of the homeless snarled and snapped at each other and at the night, there on the steps of the *palais*. Janice would later confess (when Jim had strangely fainted), that one did not brush up against such action when pushing a stroller through Kew Gardens and the other lush parks and quiet neighbourhoods in and around Wimbledon.

Jim strongly disapproved of the nature of Gem's recital. He opened his mouth towards Janice, but she snapped her hand up to his face and said, "Hush!" before the first word of rebuke could escape.

If Gem had for a time shown concern for company ears, he could no longer be deterred, and recounted the rendez-vous with Anissa down to the finest detail. In closing, he yelped ecstatically, "If you fink about it, mate, I could've had her ticketed for parking in the handicapped! Could've had her arrested on charges of rape, is wot I could've done!"

"One must *resist*," Janice interjected, "to make rape charges stick."

All eyes turned and came to focus on the powdered southern belle.

"*Jan*ice—" Jim gasped, putting two fingers to the knot of his tie.

"Still," Gem conceded, "at the least, I could've had her sacked on the spot."

"Sure, but you don't want that, do you," Janice advised. "Not if you hope to *get* a piece from her in the future."

"Janice, please. I say!"

"Plus, next time she's in heat, hoist her up onto a glass display case, put her ankles behind her head and—"

"Janice, I insist!"

Janice shrugged, Jim blushed, Gem licked his chops.

Introductions were finally made. A gamely current seemed to have found oddball psychic bridge between the antipodes of Gem and Janice, as though the two were reacquainted siblings. Gem continued like a buzz saw through meringue, recounting details from the history of his previous twenty-four hours, pausing at various junctions only to ask Janice's advice. It was a standard session with Gem, the kind that left adventuresome audiences broad-shouldered and three inches taller.

At long last, Calvin forced the farewells, as the kitchens would soon close, and because Gem's rendez-vous with Anissa meant that Calvin would be obliged to excuse himself from Jim and Janice for a brief moment.

Calvin took his visitors to dine at a fine restaurant on Rue Pontin that paid homage to the gay quarter of Paris by way of its name and the weightlessness of its staff.

The restaurant was a warm, dimly-lit aviary with beautifully hued exotic birds gracefully flapping about. As Calvin perused the menu, Jim and Janice watched an attentive pink flamingo, an émigré from the Camargue, sporting a sprig of succulent sea lavender, perched lovingly over the adjacent table, regurgitating pre-digested servings of steak tartar into the gullets of four crimson chicks, slight-of-frame. Gay Nice, noted Janice, as Jim shifted uncomfortably in his seat, was lithe, fashionable, feminine.

When they had ordered drinks, Calvin promptly stood and excused himself. "I'll be back before the drinks arrive."

"But…" began Jim, running a handkerchief over his brow. "But where on earth are you going?"

"*Calme toi*, Jim," tamped Janice, sitting primly and consulting her compact mirror. "He said he'd be back before the drinks arrived. You'll be OK."

Calvin put a hand on Jim's polyester shoulder. "Listen to your wife, Jim," he said. "She knows a thing or two." And then he left.

Jim puffed helplessly and loosened his collar. "Who *are* you?" he questioned his wife helplessly.

"Things are different here, darling, that's all." She snapped shut her compact and looked at her husband. "You can see that."

Just then, a fire-orange butterfly flapped past. "*Mademoiselle*," called Janice, snagging the butterfly in mid-flight. "*Du pain, s'il vous plait. Et de beurre.*"

The butterfly beat iridescent and started off.

"Oh!" thought Janice aloud and nabbed one of its fluttering wings (twilight butterfly dust glowed mandarin at the tips of Janice's painted fingers). "*Et apportez-moi un couteau – bien pointu – d'accord? Le plus pointu celle que vous avez.*"

"What was *that* all about?" Jim asked, turning flush.

"Bread."

"All that talk for a basket of bread?"

"And butter."

"And butter," Jim groaned. "*Jesus.*"

A menacing outline of vague defeat danced teasingly before Jim—an outline he could neither erase, nor fill in with one of his stock definitions, that he might then obliterate it. He hadn't really lost anything, but his meters, his senses, his gears, inexplicably failed to find traction in that part of the world. It might all have been OK, had his wife not flown the coop and unexpectedly found her Phoenix in the ashes of Vieux Nice. Had she not, wondered Jim, noticed the rocky beach, for crissake? He leaned back in his chair and attempted to focus on anything weighted and sedentary, anything that embodied the reliable qualities of any serious metal. It was no good. Caged in a southern menagerie, where birds, bees and butterflies flitted about unaffected by the nausea of weightlessness – never at rest, never fatigued, never touching down, always a-tinkle in the naked kiss and rush of diaphanous French and celebrated genitalia, Jim grew thick and dizzy, hands now pushing sharp quills, quills now flaring toucan plumage, the wife a fiery blur of downy muff, feathers of sapphire and *jaune*, flick flick flicking her thumb repeatedly against the long blade of a great knife, and appearing to have, through the rainbow fog of his humid vision, slipped it deftly into her handbag.

Calvin, now on the move, one alley removed from his drop point, pushed his way gently with the current, through the night flowers that coursed slowly, crutched and without teeth, towards Place Rossetti, where they would say prayers for the unfortunate, among the night hawkers of gelato, long-stemmed roses and blinking sunglasses. He slipped around the corner, into the next alleyway and crept forward towards the pertinent address. The lights dimmed, as they tend to do in passageways deemed inconsequential. Layers of shadow ganged-up in the doorway through which Calvin intended to pass, determined to promote darkness and ambiguity. There would have been absolutely no cause for alarm had the stalwart figure-*oscuro* poised there not appeared so intently positioned. Still, he may only have been a tenant or proprietor out for a smoke. Calvin involuntarily wondered aloud, "Decoy or deterrent?"

"Perhaps both," voiced the darkness. "Draw you in that I might scare you off. Have you ruled out the possibility? Mutual exclusivity is rarely..." the dark figure sighed heavily and said no more. The sigh conveyed disappointment with the youth of the day, they who took so much for granted, they who expected all things in life to be packaged neatly and placed at their feet.

My, thought Calvin, thankful that the fish he handled down at the port were not as slippery as the deliveries he made in Hector's employ. "How about randomness in three dimensions?" he challenged the voice.

"Pah!" scoffed the shadows.

Calvin could make out no face, no physique. Only the weight of the presence was tangible. A wet toothpick fell from the apex of the obscurity, catching the advancing moon light as it fell.

"Randomness? Really?" admonished the darkness. "If you are referring to my presence here, no—by no means is this is a chance encounter."

The darkness shifted in the doorway, shaking free some of its night coverage, and the opaque figure of a stout man materialised in the divisional lighting.

Sometimes a fellow stumbles upon a vaguely familiar picture show in three dimensions and wonders if it isn't déjà-vu. He paddles for it, as though before a wave that may or may not break, coaxing along the sequence of forthcoming frames for verification of something previously witnessed without consciousness; a thing never experienced, but nevertheless recorded somewhere in the mind. The man appeared to be wearing a brown herringbone coat. What little light there was had gathered and reflected off the silver pin that adorned his lapel—two expressionless herding dogs, each with what looked like a saliva-catch surgically attached to its muzzle. In the insufficient light, it looked as if twin border collies were smoking gentlemanly pipes. Calvin was certain he had never seen anything like it, and yet the pin looked strikingly familiar.

"Have we met before?" asked Calvin.

The man in the doorway said nothing, though he may have smiled. Finally, he offered, "It was an unconventional encounter, if we met at all; though you needn't concern yourself with that. I should rather – were I you – concern myself with the answers to more critical questions."

"Such as…"

"Can the eye in the sky be blinded? Can the house be beaten? When the bell tolls, do my psychic secretions drip onto Ruskie shoes?"

Calvin's face showed distaste.

"It's a metaphor," said the man with the lapel pin.

"Not a terribly attractive one."

"You'll do well to not mistake me for a poet."

"Who are you, then?"

"To be sure," said the dark figure, ignoring Calvin's question, "your Whitman – God rest his miraculous soul – could not have penned metaphors to sufficiently narrate the discomfort you shall face should such questions go unfavourably answered. How much money, sir, would you require to feel comfortable, knowing your name resides at, or near, the top of a Russian hit list?

"I'm afraid you've got the wrong man," said Calvin, unsettled by the trajectory of the conversation.

"I sincerely hope that's the case."

"I can assure you I don't mess with the Russians. Furthermore, I give them no cause to mess with me."

The dark figure knowingly poked, "And the Serbs?"

"The Serbs!" burst Calvin in a hushed voice. His eyes darted towards the darkest corners of the alley, convinced that Fitim had reconsidered his stance and was now ready to spring forth and strike him down.

"Of course not!" Calvin urged. "Listen, I'm no representative here. I'm clean. I washed my hands of American foreign policy years ago, if that's what you're alluding to. If you have a beef – and who doesn't? – I suggest you queue with the rest of the world and take it up with Washington."

The mouthpieces of the Superpowers, thought Calvin, decried enemy retaliation through civilian attacks. But in real life – life in the streets – how in God's name did they honestly expect the suffering war-torn nations of their making to respond to constant attack? Or were the invaded expected to lie like dogs and take it? How could one possibly worship missiles, manufacture and deal them shamelessly throughout the world, and then denounce those who responded to such high-tech attacks with crude homemade weaponry and the occasional baseball bat?

"Well," said the dark figure, "I am pleased to know you have not taken lightly my words. It would be bad of you to underestimate the gravity of my warnings. You have, however, misunderstood me. If I've referred to nationalities, it is only to spare you the personal exposure and liability that accompanies even superficial knowledge of certain dangerous figures. I do not speak from a political perspective. Look, politics needn't be the province of greedy, self-serving monsters, but there you have it. Still, since we have found our way onto politics, I would advise you against allowing political shame to drive you towards unsavoury ties with men who are as ruthless as any of your world leaders, and who are proximally much better positioned to dominate your existence."

"But I've no ties to the Russians or the Serbs or anyone else, political shame notwithstanding. Why, just who do you think you're dogging, sir?"

"I am not yet entirely sure," said the man, raising a featureless face to the ever-darkening night. "But I can assure you of this: when the whistle blows or the gunshots ring – matters not the trigger – I'll be there to see how you salivate. Were I you, I'd be damn well sure not to slobber on Russian boots, if you know what I mean."

"But that's the whole problem; I *don't* know what you—Wait!"

It was too late. The figure in the doorway ducked his head as though it were raining and pushed off, disappearing almost instantly into a heavy bank of newly formed shadows.

Back on Rue Pontin, three sweat-beaded glasses of white wine stood neglected amidst much flapping and fanfare, as Janice and two pale-pink flamingos worked to revive a slumping Jim.

"Sorry I'm late," said Calvin. "What happened to him?"

"He fainted," said Janice, showing concern, albeit the kind of concern one might expect had the revived fainter been the kindly septuagenarian from whom one bought flowers at the flower market, and not the father of one's child. "He started mumbling something about birds and bloody murder, went flush and fainted."

Calvin bent low, to get a good look at Jim. With his hands on his knees he asked, "You OK, bluebell?"

"Screw you, Calvin," said Jim weakly. "This is all your fault."

"What's my fault?"

"*All* of it, of course. Janice, let's have that knife."

"Hey now," said Calvin, with mock theatrics. "There's no call to get violent."

"I'm not going to slice you open, you rogue, though you probably deserve it. Now hand over the knife, Janice."

"Relax, Jim," eased Janice. "You're delirious."

"De*lir*ious!" he attempted to counter, but the effort rendered him woozy. "Janice…"

"What's he going on about?" Calvin asked.

"Who can say? He's delirious." Janice, tapped of patience, settled it. "Sit, Calvin. We're going to drink. He'll come round soon enough."

They each bolted down a glass of wine; then ordered a fourth glass to go with the third and drank those two at a more civilised clip. When they had finished, Calvin said, "We'd better get him back to the hotel."

They flanked Jim, supported his weight as best they could and started off towards the hotel. The two pale-pink flamingos spotted them for the first few paces, then let them go and stood watching as the three shuffled around the corner and disappeared.

"Poor dame," said the paler of the two flamingos, "fixed to such a *grue*some anchor of a man."

"Indeed. Poor thing," said the pinker one. "I wish you wouldn't have given her that knife, though."

The paler one shrugged. "She asked for it."

"You could have denied her. We are a restaurant after all, not a gift shop in a house of wonders."

"But she needed it. Why, she'll win a place in heaven for her time with that husband of hers. I'm glad she took it. I regret keeping it for as long as we did."

"I hope she'll put it to good use."

"She would do well to sheath it somewhere in his backside."

"It was a gorgeous piece, really."

"Silk is gorgeous. Leather can be gorgeous. Metals are never gorgeous. Not ever."

"You're too delicate," said the pinker one, the bolder of the two. "It is an antique no doubt, and I regret you casting it off so flippantly."

"That nasty-edged instrument? I was prepared to throw it out with the rubbish this very evening, I promise you."

"Poor, poor thing. Lovely in an exhausted, frazzled, American way."

"Smelt good enough to eat, no?"

"It's true," said the pinker one, bringing together the feathered fingertips of one hand and rubbing them together for inspiration. "Exuded an essence of warm shortbread."

"What did the albino say about the knife when he gave it to you?"

"Al*ban*ian; not albino."

"Albino, Albanian…"

"Honestly, he could pass for a Greek god. Orestes, perhaps—he who conquered mountains."

"Orestes was *not* a god; he was a mortal—a mortal who slay his own *mo*ther for that matter," jealously corrected the paler of the two. "Orestes was coarse and your Albanian is equally as coarse. Gods have never been coarse. They may be ornery, vindictive and vengeful, but they are *never* coarse."

"The Al*ban*ian didn't say anything at all. He enjoyed his meal—said it was the best he'd eaten in Nice," proudly said the pinker. "Before leaving, he asked if we would accept the knife as a token of his appreciation. That's it."

"My, if *that's* not coarse!"

"Mysterious? Absolutely. But far from coarse."

"Whatever it is or isn't, I'm relieved to be rid of the dirty instrument."

"You're too delicate."

Calvin and Janice were still supporting Jim when they reached the Jardin Albert 1er. On the other side of the garden, the Méridien sparkled white against the black sky. They stopped in the park and took a seat on a bench under the palm trees. The air was warm and still, devoid of all tactile qualities. They positioned Jim so that he lay on his back with his head in Janice's chiffon lap and his feet planted, flat on the ground. Janice smoothed his wiry hair with her fine southern fingers and softly caressed his face. This, thought Calvin, was the time of night when a mother's brilliant facets shone most impressively. Like all good mothers, Janice worked her loving magic instinctively. She was a good mother, so her love was inevitable, but what impressed was that, despite all of the daily realities of life, she made it look effortless. Jim laid there, blissfully helpless, very much like a child, very much in a state of respite born only of Janice's inherent strength and creative grace. Good old Jim, asleep there with the faintest of smiles, looked almost angelic.

Calvin and Janice, each held by their individual occupations, had been silent until Janice said, "Do you want to tell me what happened?"

She looked at Calvin when she said it and voiced her question steadily, so that he need not feign ignorance or make with silly denials. He became conscious of all the times when, as a child, he tried to fool his mother with one pointless lie or another, and all of the times she let him believe he had succeeded.

"It seems as though I've been implicated in something," pondered Calvin aloud. "Or rather that I'm about to be."

"What's the nature of it all?" she asked.

"I don't know. Apparently something to do with the Russians. I'm to consider myself warned."

"Russia," Janice sighed wistfully, as though longing for the Cold War and the sobriety and gravity it lent, and so too all the grand parties that bloomed gaily from the anxiety of such serious rot. A good party, thought Janice, was easy. But a great party? Greatness required resistance against which to juxtapose itself and shine. Only having fought through resistance could an idea or entity burst free and extend its soulful amplitude to the point of recognition as a grand accomplishment, a thing of greatness. Success without resistance was a given, a gift. It had no amplitude at all, it was a flat result. The wars of to-day, she ventured, were all terribly phony, all studio-staged and pixie-presented. And death – certainly death on foreign soil – was no match for the lights of stage and cinema. The Cold War was manufactured and propagated, but that was more or less her point. What's more, Americans were truly fearful during the Cold War years. As Janice saw it, the leaders of to-day no longer bothered to manufacture conflict; they simply declared that it existed somewhere or other and something drastic had to be done about it. Nobody cared, anyway. Americans certainly no longer feared war— wars had the fairytale convenience of always taking place a million miles away, in towns and territories with funny names, which no one was sure really existed. Americans didn't fear anything anymore; they were just on edge over a million different things and were ready to champion anyone who promised not to disturb them in their anxiety. No, in Janice's mind, there would never be another great American party.

"Isn't Klarysa Russian?" she asked.

"Ukrainian."

"Forgive me—I know they are not one and the same, but isn't that close enough?

Those in denial tend to have short fuses. "Close enough for what?" he said.

"I don't know. I wasn't the one issued a warning."

"Sorry. It's all a bunch of nonsense anyway. I don't know any Russians. And I don't know any Serbs, either. Well, one, but I have no involvement with him."

"Serbs?"

"Yes, I'm to stay away from the Serbs, as well. Something about psychic secretions and the soiling of shoes."

"Gross."

"It's a metaphor."

"Still."

"I know, right?"

Calvin looked at Janice; Janice looked at the Méridien and caressed Jim's head. After a moment, Calvin asked, "What's the tougher job—being a mother or being a wife?"

Janice said that if there were differences, she hadn't as yet been apprised of them. All her life, men had vied to construct their pet-projects inside her—their hopes and fears, their expectations and dreams, their babies, sundry endeavours more and less tangible. Try as she might, she couldn't stop them. Eventually, they came to invade and pollute her to the point where their projects no longer took root within her. Ironically, this was when friends and family began to credit her as being a strong woman, when in truth it was only a question of fertility. The men in her life had over-sown and left her unfertile. Janice spoke openly about physiological failings and their psychological price tags. The doctors told her cold hard truths in a cold hard manner. Jim, a metals man, appreciated their forthrightness, but rejected out of hand most truths that disagreed with him. Her parents and in-laws were soon involved and together they battled equally over her womb and her less tissued parts—her mind, her soul. Many were the moments – not just dark moments, but in fact many of the lighter, more hopeful moments – in which she had decided they could all, as far as she was concerned, go straight to hell. Janice had never eschewed her motherly instincts or responsibilities, per se. She had, for example, accepted Jim's defection from his own mother that he might make a child and husband of himself to Janice. Jim could be a handful, and just how many big fat babies was she expected to raise? She didn't particularly want to be a mother for a second or third or n^{th} time thereafter. Zoe was nevertheless born and Janice became a different kind of mother, and a particularly good one at that. Janice was a natural, a fact that frightened the hell out of her, for once you break the seal... And sure enough, after little more than three hours together with Calvin, it became evident that he would be the next child she'd be made to protect and pamper.

"Did God choose you for motherhood?" she heard him ask. Did he mean women as opposed to men, or her as opposed to any other woman?

"I'm willing to consider the existence of a god," she replied, as though reciting a prepared piece, "but the notion that He created Man in his likeness, or that He is even a shade more concerned with Man's fate than that of the black worm is as egotistical as it is ridiculous.

"Look, Calvin," she said, pulling her eyes away from the hotel to look him in the eye. "We can be your mothers if we must. But we can't be your saviours. One can only ever be a savoir to oneself, and no other. You've conditioned us to absorb your fears and your guilt, and to reflect all of your desires, but that's where it ends. Don't deceive yourself; don't look for a saviour in the doctored reflection of a man falsely stripped of all flaws."

He said he thought he understood, and she confessed out of the blue to having pencilled in Zoe's birth like a four o'clock business meeting, confessed to having demanded that if the baby was not born prematurely, it was to be cut from her belly on the hour of the ninth month. She looked down towards her lap and saw her Jim sleeping soundly, peacefully, and she was grateful for his peace.

"You've got a new girl," she continued. "A Russian girl—more or less." She smiled. "You're a lucky man, Calvin. Do be mindful. And do be careful."

Though he listened intently and took to heart her every word, he wasn't sure of what he was to be careful. He said, "I will, Janice," and resolved to try to be more careful, in general.

The next morning, the air was lovely, still cool, as Calvin stepped into the alleyway. He walked to the edge of the Vieux and began his way across the Jardin Albert 1er towards the Méridien, to meet Jim and Janice. Mulling over the events of the previous night, he eyed the park bench on which he had sat with Janice and her sprawled baby boy not so many hours prior. He sat momentarily on the bench, leaned back and looked to where Janice no longer sat, as though trying on an old shirt that was once a favourite and that once lent certain powers when worn to bars where young women convened. He sat for a moment, but there was nothing. The conversation, thought Calvin, would have been impossible under an illuminated late-morning sky. There is an obviousness to daylight that tethers the lambs and lions of the imagination, stakes its subjects to stillness, chases dreams to the far frontiers of the psyche, where they are slow to tempt and slow to torment. The pines and palms, which ran dark-on-black towards the end of vision's short leash only hours before, were now, in the new morning, electric green on blue so thick it capped the sky and blotted out the heavens with vibrant, violent opacity. Awash in heavy sunlight, the hotel squatted, bulky with immobility, while under the gauzy quiet of night, the moon-lit Méridien looked as if it might just twinkle-toe its way nimbly, ever so quickly into the deep blue sea. Just then, a young boy of perhaps three years, dropped a strawberry cone in the dirt, looked excruciatingly at Calvin and began to wail. Then, still wailing, he picked up the cone, which was now coated in dust and dirt, took a desperate bite and wailed still louder until his mother shook the filthy cone free from his sticky hand, at which point the wailing reached a shrieking crescendo and held steady for an astonishing duration.

Jim answered the door to a top-floor suite, wrapped in a monogrammed robe of fine Charmeuse silk. His smile was toothy, the pint glass in his grip brimming with garnet Bloody Mary. Jim wore no slippers. "Morning, Calvin!" he boomed with Southern gusto. "Come on in, old boy."

Calvin entered and dodged a swinging left fist. Jim took another, lighter, consolation shot and connected.

Said Calvin, "Glad to see you're back on your feet, pal."

"No problem. I am brand new this morning," said Jim, filling his lungs. "Not sure what happened last night."

"It was the heat and the wine."

"I didn't have any wine."

"It's a mystery, then. You mix that yourself?" asked Calvin, nodding at Jim's drink.

"There are ten different ingredients in here," he said, eyeing the glass with a preposterous amount of pride. "Like me to make you one?"

"As long as one of the ten ingredients is vodka."

"*Two* of the ten ingredients are vodka, no less. One is pepper-flavoured. The other is—"

"Busy yourself, then, if you don't mind," said Calvin.

Jim lifted the hinged lid of a leather travel bar. In the bar lay bottles of various shapes and sizes. There were hot sauces, Tabasco, a variety of ground peppers and salts, Worcestershire and all manner of knives and strainers and a stainless shaker. The horseradish, the cocktail olives and the onions he kept in the mini bar. One drank well in Jim's presence, if he could afford it.

Jim stabbed the collection of bottles one at a time at the bottom of a pint glass and said to Calvin without looking up from the task at hand, "That was some production last night."

"Production?"

"Janice says I lack tact. I say if you can't be direct with your pals... All of it—that was really some show. The goddamned circus is less contrived."

"And you haven't yet seen the live homeless man who pisses on my doorstep each morning," said Calvin. "Rest assured, pal, we're all here for your entertainment."

"Homelessness and crime—that's your and Janice's idea of the highlife, all right. Colourful little town you've got here, though. It really is."

"Where is the dear girl, anyway?"

"On the terrace. Go on out. I'll be right out with the best drink you've ever had in your whole sodden life."

"Morning, Janice," said Calvin, stepping out onto the terrace.

The view was stunning. The sun kept rising, the beach was filling in down below, Janice extended herself on a luxurious chaise longue.

"Good morning, dear!" she said from behind black horn-rimmed sunglasses.

"Some day in the making, huh?"

"Why, you can see clear beyond Cap d'Antibes."

"You're lucky; such a clear view in the summer is rare."

They spoke for a minute or two of idle coastal observances, until a break in the conversation allowed each to apologise for actions pursued, situations witnessed and words spoken over the course of the prior evening. Mediterranean summer nights quite simply had a way of emboldening a fellow and bringing him to consider what so much of the listless world considered extravagant and impossible. Anything was possible on a Mediterranean summer night and each insisted the other had no cause for apology.

Calvin lost himself in thought. How true it seemed that a fellow advanced through life, hour by hour, day by day, inching along so gradually that the ride seemed all but stationary. Only at a point of crisis, or at a seemingly critical crossroads, did a fellow perhaps recognise that the sum of the millions of infinitesimal movements of his life – all of the inches and fractions of inches to have shifted, all of the raindrops and teardrops to have fallen, all of the atrocities to have been committed and the kindnesses to have been rendered – all had indeed laid themselves out beyond his heels at the moment of their manifestation, their flashing and fading presence, to create a winding historical path of such indescribable length and complexity of character, that it had in fact, ages ago and without the fellow ever having known it, formed the only and truest definition of that woman or man. And that at some point, the man and the path he had blazed became one and the same, each defined by the other, and of which – the man and the sum of his actions, his path – no distinction may be made. And in recognising the inseparability of a man and the definition of himself and his life through the history of his actions, the idea of breaking the path, though it may well be the sane and logical choice, was nevertheless a sort of death, a potentially harrowing death. What then of the fellow who committed to memory his history that he might spare himself the doom of its repetition? What of such a peculiar suicide? In the final analysis, was he any less doomed for his efforts? Had he essentially safeguarded himself against equal pain and suffering in the future? Was he any less vulnerable to a different and potentially worse fate?"

Janice was speaking, but lost as he was in thought, Calvin did not hear her.

"Calvin," she called, feeling neglected. "Won't you say something?"

He abandoned his thoughts to find Janice still stretched along the length of the chaise longue, still in her white one-piece interrupted at the waist by a stylish black belt, and still donning her black horn-rimmed glasses, but now too curling back fire-red lips, to reveal her bright-white teeth (poised, they were, as though to take a greedy bite out of something moving) and brandishing a gleaming knife that looked frighteningly serviceable in her tanned and raised grip. The sun raced instantly to gather at the blade's edge in blinding, twitching congregation, until a flick of her wrist sent it leaping back towards the heavens.

"What," said Calvin, "is that?"

Her teeth no longer bared, Janice looked disappointed. She had, it seemed, hoped that the sight of the knife – a likely implement, she thought, of Calvin's clandestine persona – might trigger an instinctive rise to the dark and scintillating role to which she had assigned him in her mind. Lowering the blade, she said, "Why, did you not hear a word I just said?"

"Oh. Sure," he said—though he hadn't. "You mean…"

"Oh, I know it's crazy," she began, now sitting on the edge of the chaise longue. "I just thought I might be able to help. Last night, I mean. You know, if that's what it came to." Then adjusting her grip on the knife. "Not that *I* could ever…"

"You did help last night," said Calvin.

The line was meant to console and encourage, as much as to bring her away from such dire occupations. And he meant it. "You helped very much."

She did not concur. "You don't mean with all those *words*," she said. "What is a life when it is reduced to so many words and theories? Words can't fix…"

She deftly spun the knife in her palm and extended the handle to Calvin. "I just thought if it came to that, perhaps I could help."

He felt as though he had somehow let her down.

"Here," she said. "I can't conceivably keep this."

Calvin took the knife from her and wondered if she mightn't be cheered by a solemn promise to slay some devil in a dark alley. But he said nothing.

"It goes without saying," said Janice, "we'll not have Jim see that."

"No, ma'am," he obeyed.

Calvin shakes loose of his shackles, climbs off the roof and back into his bedroom. The note on the bedside table read: For all the flying I've done, I would've made a cage of your heart and flown into it of my own desire. But where were you?

Confused childlike hallucination flap in lime-green flurry. Could be somebody's reliability, stability, if only I weren't so extravagant.

Kid run from his bedroom and into the hallway, where he nearly knock over Nicki *The long brown couch sit empty and beat.*

"Don't go," Nicki say. "Kid, you promised."

"*I have to go. They all know about the death.*"

"Forget all that, fool child. They don't know nothing."

"*I got death on my hands, Nicki. I ain't no flower.*"

"You *are* a flower."

"*I miss the mark. I don't get things right the first time.*"

"You do just fine, baby," Nicki say. "You do just fine."

The long brown couch sit empty and beat. A needle obey a different groove.

"*Theys oceans,*" he say. "*And deserts. Ain't they oceans and deserts, Nicki?*"

"Oh, God, no! Oh, God, no!" *somebody ma cry out.*

"Pay attention, boy. You going to learn. You going to learn." *Got to remember to forget.*

Irma, she peel potatoes at the kitchen sink. *She kiss me with red lips.* A whole sink heap full of peeled potatoes.

A little blonde girl rings the bell; the kind of girl you want to scoop up and squeeze until your last breath. I need to explain to her some things about the past.

"*She said she would have made a cage of my heart, Ma. Only where was I?*"

You don't know? People on the street don't know. You got to pay attention, boy!

Ma points her potato peeler at the window. I climb up onto the countertop and bump Ma's elbow. She drops a potato onto the floor. "Oh! I'm sorry, Ma!"

"Shhh, it's OK, baby," *she say.* "Don't you worry a shade. It'll wash right off. Look at that. Good as new."

I pause at the window and squat down on the countertop. "*Hey, Ma.*"

"What is it, baby?"

"*I've seen a sea.*" Kid smile in disbelief of his own self and look deep into his ma's eyes. "*Theys oceans and deserts, Ma. Theys lemon trees. What do you think? Do you think so?*"

His ma's eyes mist over. "You're a good boy, son. You're a good boy."

Ma points her potato peeler at the open window. I step out onto the ledge. Just before I jump, I feel her hand on my ankle.

I turn around and look upon her. "*Hey, Ma,*" *I say.* "*How do you know which is the one?*"

His ma smile back upon him. "You're going to see her from across a crowded dance floor and you'll know. You won't have to worry or wonder. You'll just know. So simple as all that."

Kid, he bend down close and she kiss him with Christmas red lips.

I turn and jump.

13   Russian delicacies

In which the crew is nearly
spared a night soused on
Kronenbourg brew.

Andre Lemmonier was better known to the crew as Manx. The
name was not borrowed from the renowned cat from the Isle of Man,
nor was the name bestowed upon him because Andre Lemmonier
hailed from the Isle of Man—because he did not; he was quite
French. Rather, the name was inspired by the Manx Rumpy chicken,
an indigenous fowl of the Persian Gulf region, which *does* take *its*
name from the tailless cat of the Isle of Man. See here, the Manx
Rumpy chicken has no tail, no rump. It lacks the necessary vertebrae
possessed by most chickens for such accommodation. Similarly,
Andre Lemmonier was a chicken, which is to say, a coward. And he
had no backbone, no spine. Andre Lemmonier allowed himself to
believe the nickname was given him because of his contemptibly
undersized derriere. He had no idea that it was due to his wretched
lack of fortitude and guts.

Manx lived on Rue Poissonerie, four flights above La Banane
café. The crew could often be found chez Manx, horsing about,
drinking, throwing rabbit punches, needling one another with darts
(most typically verbal, but so too, on occasion, metal-tipped). There
was a time when they gathered weekly to play Bézique, Whist, Ruff
and Honours and the like, but divergent levels of focus and
conflicting definitions of cheating and gamesmanship led initially to
hurt feelings, then to fisticuffs, and finally to a disbanding of the

weekly card game. Sandoval had once brought along a fine edition of Edmond Hoyle's *A Short Treatise on the Game of Whist*, but it was run through the shredder in short order. None of them knew how to shuffle properly and there were constant misdeals. They required four new decks for every gathering, as the cards were folded, bent, torn, oil stained, or lost altogether. By the end of any evening, there may have only been forty-four cards remaining from a fifty-two-card deck. Of those, the queen of diamonds might have lost an eye, the king doubled-over and creased during a sidebar magic trick run afoul, the valets wrinkled and twisted, the ace of clubs dotted with clover-shaped cigarette burns.

As he approached Manx's building, Calvin saw Fitim and Monique sitting at one of the small café tables outside La Banane. The metal café chair under Fitim appeared stressed to the edge of exhaustion. Calvin didn't recognised them until he had drawn quite near, at which point his gait hitched and he felt a burst of adrenaline flash in his head and heart. Monique's presence, however, did a great deal to sooth his initial nerves. Besides, no accuser could contend that a chance early-evening encounter outside a café entailed a manner of illicit engagement. And anyway, who was Fitim to Calvin? Monique's fellow and not an ounce more. Khali the blue-haired terrier writhed like a worm in Fitim's stone lap, offering its underside to his caresses. Calvin and Monique gave *bisous*, and then the men shook hands.

It was the first time Calvin had seen the two together. They were as odd a match as he had envisioned. Fitim proved decidedly less business-minded than he was during the encounter at Ghost bar. To Calvin's relief, there was no mention of the fugitive Martin Hambone, money due or cellos lost. In truth, he seemed to Calvin entirely pleasant. Calvin noticed the tattoo on his wrist and said, all but involuntarily, "The end, the last, the ultimate limit."

Fitim looked quizzically at him, as Khali nipped sharply at his thick fingers.

"Your tattoo," Calvin clarified. "The Greek omega."

Fitim's eyes seemed to smile, though his lips did not. "The end, the last, the ultimate limit," he echoed. Then he added not unpleasantly, "I suppose most Americans would consider that misguided intent, defeatist ambition."

"It is true," admitted Calvin, "we've been conditioned largely to value firsts, not lasts."

"Such focus is symptomatic of deeper issues."

Defending modern American ways before citizens of ancient cultures was tenuous – like carrying water in a paper cup – for although the water was contained and moving forward more or less as intended, it was all but impossible to believe in the system's long-term viability. The walls of America's paper cup had been deteriorating for years, and although everyone was aware of the fact, the stress and anxiety that accompanied the realisation – which, if consciously addressed, might have gone a long way towards mobilising a unified drive for change, for the desperately needed system overhaul – was instead suppressed by daily doses of mind-numbing Spectacle.

"Continue," said Calvin.

"I mean to say that there no intrinsic value to being first," said Fitim. "Why, before one can be declared the first, an arbitrary finish line must be set. But it is just that—arbitrary."

Fitim's words struck an immediate chord with Calvin. He had forever tried to put words to similar sentiments before Sandoval.

"Naturally, family is the top priority of every good man," said Fitim. "And now consider any man who calls himself a patriot. A true patriot knows that over the course of time and history, there is no distinction between his family and his country. His neighbours and countrymen are his brothers. This conviction is the very backbone of the patriot. And what is a country if not its culture and its values?"

Fitim flicked Khali once in the snout and the mutt stopped its nipping.

"Take, for example," he continued, "the French patriot who, when speaking of family and country, proudly reserves a place in his home and heart for Jeanne D'Arc. Joan of Arc—the patriot's mother, his sister, his daughter. Proud and noble men see far beyond themselves. The patriot lives selflessly, for his family and for his nation, understanding that to do well is to work and sacrifice, to ensure the mental and physical health and prosperity of his brethren for the millennium to come.

"The wisest of men understand that they are nothing compared to their history and those who came before them, and that they are equally insignificant compared to the future and the generations that will follow. The wise man embraces his history that he might make better the future. He understands that the present day is small and insignificant, fleeting and fragile, constantly dying with every tick of the clock, whereas antiquity, like the future, is perfectly endless. The wise man, the selfless man and the patriot live out their ambitious, dying days content in the knowledge that their glory will come after they've departed this world, when those who follow are prospering through their past efforts and sacrifices and propagating their noble ways and philosophies. They value sustainability and longevity. They design their systems not for their own benefit, but for the benefit of future generations.

"Where is the value in being first to such men—men who identify their own blood in the blood of their families and in the blood of their neighbours and in the land on which they have all lived together and loved together and fought together for the last thousand years and the next thousand years to come? To be sure, the idea of *firsts* can only carry relevance for selfish beasts that sense an apocalypse hurtling from the sky like a comet. Some are fond of saying that *time is short*, but the truth is that time is short only for the self-concerned and those who are short of vision."

Speaking of dubious firsts, thought Calvin, it had been determined that his generation would prove to be the first in American history to not have bettered the bouquet of life entrusted to it by the previous generation. His would be the first to have taken more than it contributed. The walls of the paper cup were wearing dangerously thin.

"Unfortunately," said Calvin, "the ideals you speak of were crushed long ago under the wheels of modern capitalism. The machine disallows any concern for tomorrow. If it can't be mass-produced and merchandised today, we're not interested."

"It has been said that capitalism will eventually collapse under the weight of its own contradictions."

"And America has been laughing at Marx ever since."

"That is my very point," said Fitim.

"You're boring me," said Monique. "And I'm thirsty."

"The only man with the gall to laugh and ridicule any thinker," said Fitim, signalling a waitress, "is the man who is convinced that a final verdict has already been reached on a matter; that some arbitrary finish line has been established and crossed and a victor declared. It is a notion of the simpleminded—only a damned fool would attempt to portray the dynamics of world existence in racing terms. To be sure, the only man secure in his gloating is he who is focused solely on the present; he who stares with a fixed and isolated gaze, in blissful ignorance, at the frozen finish-line photograph in his grip, and who is content in his blindness to all of the whirling and shifting movements that continue to reverberate over and across the planet. Such a man is both a dangerous and endangered fool."

"True," agreed Calvin, warming up to the conversation. "But again, the overriding American psyche has been weaned of all consideration for anything beyond the here and now. It focuses its energies and resources on maximising wealth in the immediate term. The governing components of the current power structure, self-interested as they are, must be able to show – and take credit for – measureable material gain before a constituency with an over-developed sense of entitlement and a rapidly deteriorating attention span—one that demands immediate returns. The culture has been sabotaged such that America now only values the immediate term, the here and the now. Decision-makers declare their actions to be direct responses to the needs of a demanding public, but it is a ruse. They know that they, themselves, have engineered the needs and the impatience of the masses, and that they have done so for their own personal gain. The sermon broadcasted from the top of the power structure teaches that the masses are entitled to the immediate accommodation of their every whim. And by believing it, the masses have willingly sacrificed their only true entitlement—longevity, fairness and decency for their children and their children and their children, ad infinitum. That is the one true entitlement of every society.

"However, to ramble through the hard grind of life while maintaining such determined consciousness and selflessness requires strong faith and trust in one's fellow citizens, one's leaders and one's god. This is where the American psyche fails to deliver. It is suspicious and disapproving of its neighbours, it despises its government, and for all its praise of organised religion and its professed faith in God, it is shockingly afraid of death and rejects the notion of death as an inevitable fact of even the most beautiful and blessed life. To be sure, it is damned difficult to sacrifice for the future, or even discuss hopes for, and a vision of, the future, when one is deathly afraid of death."

Two drinks were brought to the table.

"Will you have something?" Fitim asked Calvin.

"No, thank you," said Calvin, shrugging the case of beer he carried and poking his nose up towards Manx's flat. Aloysius was watching down from the window above, like a Kilgore.

"And is it true," asked Fitim, "that Americans fear death?"

"Is it true? Why, death has been fashioned the Great American Tragedy, a national sin, high treason! Despite widespread religious convictions and the promise of heaven, we revere birth, condemn death, and ardently cordon off our existence and the existence of the entire world between those two occurrences. Despite the notions of timelessness and endless life professed by our revered holy men, we view births and deaths as polar phenomena that denote beginnings and ends, lightness and darkness, good and evil—bookend events that mark earthly existences rendered thin and linear by a lack of curiosity, wonderment and true faith. As it is widely held that God made Man in his likeness, a fellow falls asleep at the end of each day – dies, in essence – and the universe dies with him. He is reborn the following morning and his rebirth, alone, triggers the rebirth of the universe, just moments before, while he rubs the sleep from his eyes, in order to celebrate his rebirth and to accommodate his every whim. We are largely a people who require precisely defined beginnings and ends. We cannot conceive of moving forward without what so many, in the context of their lives and their emotions, call *closure*. But OK, it is a young country and it is only natural that it should experience growing pains."

"Your America," contended Fitim, "is suffering the skinned knees of a country crawling about in the infancy of its time. Entire nations benefit when it coos and grins. And when it is tired and cranky, entire nations suffer. But it is not the age of a country that matters, per se. What matters is the age of the culture. Your country is young, but so is your culture. The culture of my people is very old, and yet we are still waiting and fighting to be the ones to deliver the birth of our country."

"I am bored beyond death," repeated Monique. "Give me my dog."

"I'm sorry, kitten," said Fitim. "Why don't you take a short walk."

"Why—! You would prefer it if I never came back!"

"Don't say hurtful things," said Fitim calmly, "especially if they are not true. Here, take this. Buy something nice." He placed before her a wad of franc notes.

"I don't *want* your money," she said, snatching it up from the table with blinding quickness.

She started off with Khali, but was hooked by a Balkan mitt. She acquiesced. Fitim pulled her close and kissed her. "Don't be gone long," he said. "We have reservations."

"And then," she assured him, "we will talk of something less drab."

"By all means. Anything to win your favour. Now go."

Monique skipped away, restored of hope and cheer, some thousand French francs the fatter. Fitim watched affectionately after her and the dog. When they had disappeared, he turned his attention back to Calvin. "Men kill," he said coldly. "They always have. World leaders portray their adversaries as instruments of evil in order to justify their eradication. But in the final analysis, no killer may claim righteousness over another. This one kills his devils, that one kills his. And I kill mine."

"The *birth* of your country," said Calvin, avoiding the bold conversational shift. "I don't understand. You said you're from Serbia."

"No. I said that most people would consider me to be from Serbia. I am Kosovar Albanian and the birth I seek is that of the Republic of Kosovo as a self-ruling independent state."

Calvin recalled the warning he received from the shadowy figure in the alleyway. "I see," he said with relief. "You're not Serbian at all. That's what you meant by the other side of the conflict."

"Yes. You are familiar, I think, with the KLA."

A more daring fellow might have cheekily ventured, "The KLA! Fine, but now remind me of your current status on the world stage—are you considered terrorists or freedom fighters?"

Calvin said simply, "The Kosovo Liberation Army. Sure."

The KLA was a Kosovar Albanian guerrilla organisation that sought independence from Yugoslavia. Since its formation, it had been recognised by the US and NATO members as a terrorist organisation. In 1998, however, in a sudden reversal of stance, Washington removed the KLA from its list of terrorists. (It is, perhaps, worth noting that American intelligence admitted to having covertly helped train members of the KLA while it was officially listed by Washington and its allies as a terrorist organisation.)

"The baby coos," said Calvin, "and grins in your direction."

The delisting of the KLA as a terrorist group allowed Washington to cultivate open diplomatic relationships with KLA leaders and supply them with CIA intelligence, weaponry and training. Through fervent lobbying, Washington pressured Britain and France to follow suit, which of course they did. Washington didn't give a damn about Serbs or Albanians, ethnic cleansing notwithstanding. A maniacal Slobodan Milosevic in Belgrade simply offered an adequate excuse for Washington to champion the KLA, a previously condemned terrorist organisation, which, with the right amount of help, might fracture the power structure in the Balkan region.

Washington was not about to openly back the cause of a few jilted Kosovar Albanians. There was no benefit in it. But once the KLA established itself as a significant force in the region, Washington picked the moment, reversed its position on the KLA as a terrorist group and went public with its plan. Right or wrong, the KLA fought aggressively for its freedom from Belgrade. And due in part to Belgrade's alliance with Moscow, Washington jumped at the opportunity to supply the KLA with weapons, intelligence and favourable Press coverage. The plan was simple: champion the cause of the KLA that they might wreak sufficient havoc to destabilise the Balkan region. In essence, level the playing field for maximum death and destruction. With the region in chaos, NATO could easily justify its intervention and Washington would bolster NATO dependence on American military might.

As though in anticipation, Fitim said, "I am a soldier. Every day of my life, regardless of where I rest my head, I am a soldier. Like you, however, I have chosen a life beyond the frontier of my homeland. I assure you, in no way does that undermine the integrity of my patriotism or the value of my involvement in the fight. Understand that the same war may be fought on several fronts."

A familiar canine yapping from up the alleyway signalled Monique and Khali's imminent return. In bringing the conversation to a close, Fitim said, "Many around the world resent America, not necessarily for its actions, but for its arrogance and hypocrisy. Your government paints itself as a collection of selfless angels, though it murders men, women and children, the sick and the simple, across all points of the globe, without pause or remorse. It bombs schools and hospitals and casually dismisses such tragedies as the unfortunate consequences of pursuing a greater good. But I am not one such critic. The United States is a dirty murderer, of that there is no question. But so too are Britain and France, Russia and China, Serbia and Iraq. Kosovo, too, when she is finally born, will be a killer. And a killer is a killer."

Monique arrived carrying several small wrapped packages. Generally, she preferred her purchases gift-wrapped, even if they were not gifts, even when she purchased them for herself. She excitedly presented one of them to Fitim. "Open it!" she cried joyfully from her place on his lap. "It's for you."

"Oh, kitten," he said, touched by the gesture. "What have you done?"

Calvin bid them farewell and ascended the stairs to Manx's flat. The staircase wound like a collection of old grey dentures. The slate had worn thin from generations of falling feet. Manx's flat was grand, with high ceilings and deep archways that connected several vast rooms, a kitchen and a full bar. Manx had inherited the place. It hadn't been redecorated in decades. There was no end to the precious junk piled high on the shelves that lined most walls. There were top hats, hub caps, bicycle parts, mechanical clocks and wind-up animals, old oil lamps, soldering guns, implements for measuring various parts of the body, books, surgical antiques, so on and so forth. And there was a ping-pong table in the salon and two young Moroccan girls who were constantly at play. And Aloysius, too, could be considered another of the many fixtures.

One never knew what manner of action one might find chez Manx. Once, while validating pages from Arbuckle's *Nursery Rhymes for the Famished and Depraved*, Arbuckle and Polish smuggled six live magpies into the flat, pre-heated the oven to two-hundred degrees Celsius, and attempted to enclose the birds in a crust-lined casserole, with a delicate pastry lid. It was a culinary and wildlife disaster, both, which sent the entire crew scattering and dodging insensate magpie beaks and slimy droppings.

Upon arriving at the top-floor landing, Calvin kicked open the door and sent thick wood slamming into the stone wall. The two Moroccan girls, accustomed to such announcements of arrival chez Manx, did not flinch. They were university girls, friends of Manx's whom the Butcher habitually chased about the room, desperate and depressed, until he had them good and cornered and their claws came out and the tables turned.

"Big Al!" cheered Calvin upon entering.

"Hallo, Calvin."

Manx entered from the kitchen yanking his hair and pleading wildly into the telephone.

"It's the plumber," Aloysius explained. "Manx has been without hot water for days."

"Hey, Manx," pried Calvin. "What do you know about Monique's new fellow? Quite a character, that one."

But Manx was occupied with the plumber.

"I can tell you anything you want to know," said Aloysius from under a greasy sheen. "I suppose you'd like to go into business with him," he added jealously.

"What?" said Calvin. "What are you talking about now? With whom?"

"Why, with Fitim Kaleci, of course. I saw you down there, carrying on like a couple of thieves. I'd be careful if I were you. I shouldn't tell you this—"

"Then don't," Calvin cut him short. "In fact, I re*fuse* you to tell me."

"He's KLA, Calvin. There, I said it. You've no idea what you're getting yourself into."

"I know he's KLA, you harebrain! He just told me so. You don't have to worry about me. There are a lot of people out in the world fighting battles, Aloysius. I'm not getting myself into anything. Lord knows I've got my *own* battles to contend with."

"He *told* you?" said Al, crestfallen. "But they're a terrorist organisation."

"Not anymore they're not. Not in the US, not in the UK, not in France. We've championed them, practically made them a Balkan extension of the United States armed forces. Why, old Fitim has been given the Allied stamp of approval – trained and armed and ready to murder – all courtesy of our boys in Washington."

"All these years," began Aloysius incredulously, "you've shuffled cautiously about these alleyways, ever-conscious of your nationality. Now you learn Washington has delisted a terrorist organisation to spite Serbia – *a Russian ally* – and you're suddenly carefree? For crissake, Calvin, have you forgotten who runs the show around here?"

The Russians. It was a damn interesting point.

"Now you're best pals with a KLA operative," he continued. "Pah! And you think *I'm* a harebrain."

"Oh, stop it, Al. I had a lousy conversation with the man. I've chosen no sides. I'm still neutral."

"Listen to me, Calvin, your new pal is out to get the Russians. That's the truth and I'd be well careful if I were you."

"Look here, Al, his war is in Kosovo."

"Then what the hell is he doing in *Nice*?" Aloysius demanded astutely. "Have you asked yourself that?"

"Wars, Aloysius," answered Calvin, feeling rather urbane, "are fought on many fronts."

"*Quelle richesse!*" Al popped. "Aren't *you* sophisticated! Tell the truth, Calvin—*he* told you that, didn't he?"

Exposed, Calvin demurred, "Hmph!"

"I'll grant you this much," said Al, "Fitim Kaleci is not your average soldier. He is a philosopher, a romantic, a vigilante, possibly a politician. He is waging war, all right. I can feel it. He may be with the KLA, but he is not at war with Belgrade—not from Nice, at any rate."

"With whom, then?" challenged Calvin. "What kind of war?"

"Who knows, whatever kind of wars vigilantes wage—those driven by vengeance? A sense of righteousness? I don't know."

"*Right*eousness. Funny how war offers the gaudiest displays of irony."

"This coastline is rife with small-time scumbags, Calvin. Fitim Kaleci is not one of them. See how he carries himself around the Vieux. See how he dresses. He is gentle, generous, respectful. He keeps the undesirables away."

"You're not convinced," Calvin guessed.

"Oh, he'll shake your hand and look you in the eye, all right. He doesn't mince words."

"What—you think he's holding something back?"

"Everyone is holding *some*thing back, Calvin. Honestly, what the hell is a guy like that doing in a place like Nice?"

"Sunshine and one hell of a fine beach. Hell, *you*'re holding something back, Aloysius. Since when do you—"

"*Every*one holds something back, Calvin. Didn't I just say so."

Manx was finally off the phone. He entered the salon sweating, still tugging at his mane of black hair. "That convict refuses to come back and fix his mess. Meanwhile, I'm stuck with cold showers! '*Ce n'est pas grave,*' he assures me. And yet it is—it is *per*fectly *grave*!

He'll be back next week if he can fit it in. Next week! Come have a look in here, you two."

The three of them went into the kitchen. Manx and Al dove under the sink to consult the pipes and trade theories. Calvin grabbed a Kronenbourg from the frigo and quietly stole off the same way they entered. Gnip-gnop, gnip-gnop, sounded in the salon. Calvin snatched up a free ping-pong bat and spun a pointless waltz about the table, swatting as he went at the ghosts that trailed invisibly behind the little white ball. One of the girls plucked the ball from mid-air and hissed at him. He replaced the bat and slinked away to straddle the windowsill, dangling a foot four floors above La Banane.

Shortly, Calvin spied Miroslav Kováč coming up the alleyway. Miroslav stopped at the café to speak with Fitim and Monique, and, in what Calvin considered an act of treason, caressed Khali affectionately on the head as they talked. The bloody traitor, thought Calvin. He dropped a bomb in the form of a single fuchsia geranium petal. It fluttered earthward and veered off course. When it landed in the alleyway, there was a hard clang and a soft explosion.

"Get in here, Calvin!" screamed Manx from the kitchen. "Hurry!"

The clang, of course, had come not from the geranium petal landing in the alleyway, but from the violent communion of the wrench in Manx's grip with the metal conduit under the sink. The explosion that followed emanated from the throat of a violated coupling that failed to withstand the abuse. Cold water gushed from under the sink, as Manx and Aloysius cursed and scrambled to reverse their fortunes. Calvin grabbed another Kronenbourg from the frigo and sneaked away, back into the salon. He reinstalled himself at the windowsill, but Miroslav could no longer be seen down below.

The door was suddenly kicked open and the crew's resident Slovak stood poised in the doorway. "Catch!" he said, and tossed a flat glass jar in Calvin's direction. Calvin jumped to make a fine catch and kept the jar from going out the window. How apparently effortless it was, he pondered, to drop a bomb. Retaking his seat on the sill, he read out loud from the label on the jar, "Russian Osetra Caviar."

"Fitim gave it to me," said Miroslav.

"You know Fitim?"

"We just met downstairs. He seems like a sound fellow."

Calvin braced, winced and ever so carefully twisted the metal lid from the jar. "Look at that," he said. "Nothing."

"Nothing?"

"Bah, I thought it may have been rigged, booby trapped, a cluster bomb or so."

"Calvin," replied Miroslav, producing a second jar, "it is caviar. You *eat* it."

"I know, I know," said Calvin, making a face and pointing towards the kitchen. "That big Lithuanian in there has gotten into my head. He thinks Fitim is waging war with the Russians."

Manx appeared from the kitchen, satisfied, drenched and towelling off, as though after a big match. "Success!" he said.

"You two harebrains fix those pipes?" asked Calvin.

"Still need a good plumber, of course," Manx admitted, "but we've saved the entire building from certain inundation."

In the great wide world, Miroslav Kováč was surprised by exactly nothing. "War," he said pensively, as though suddenly convinced of it himself. "That explains the gun."

"What gun?" asked Manx.

"He has a gun?" said Calvin.

"A Kalashnikov!" yelled Aloysius from the kitchen. "A *Russian* make, Calvin. You're in over your head!"

"You're not at war, too," ventured Miroslav, "are you Calvin?"

"Silence!" Manx burst fearfully. "You lads mind your gobs!"

Beside Manx sat a large crate of monkey skulls.

"What is it with you fellows, anyway? You show up and in no time at all, there's a KLA operative in my life!"

Calvin and Miroslav stared guiltily at their shoes.

"Would it be so terribly difficult for you fellows to engage in a noble pursuit for once; some honourable hobby?" he begged of them, shaking an orang-utan skull in their direction. "I'm sorry, but if you insist on cavorting with third-world thugs, I'll have to ask you to take it up elsewhere. Why, *I'll* not be the man who knew too much!"

Just then, for the third time in thirty minutes, the door was kicked nearly off its hinges, and in sauntered Arbuckle, Polish Pete and the Butcher, the former most carrying a white corrugated carton.

"You'll want to get this door fixed, Manx," advised Polish, with parental concern.

Asked Manx in defeat, "Can't any of you animals open the door in the manner we humans do?"

"Why, don't blame the door, Polish," said Arbuckle critically. "That door is just fine. The lock, however, is like putty."

Manx groaned, lifted a wire basket from one of the shelves and began picking through a collection of deadbolt locks. "Can't we agree, fellows," he petitioned, "to keep a lid on the madness, if only for to-night?"

"I second the motion," said Polish eagerly.

The Butcher smouldered in the direction of the ping-pong table and heard not a word of it.

"Relax, Manxy," said Arbuckle. "We've come armed for a sophisticated evening."

"Sophisticated," echoed Manx, mollified and hopeful. "Now we're getting somewhere," he said, raising his bottle of beer, to bind them all in contract.

"Not so fast," cried Arbuckle. "*Kronenbourg*! *E-e-ech*! Don't let's toast with such swill."

Arbuckle flopped the white carton onto the ping-pong table and withdrew jar after jar of caviar, and bottle after bottle of champagne. The lads stared in joyous disbelief. Having torn away the foil sleeve, Arbuckle made the first bottle pop.

Manx jumped at the sound. "But Arbuckle," he ventured uneasily, "that must have set you back several thousand francs."

"Nary a *centime*! A gift from the flying Dutchman downstairs, upon whom our fair Calvin," he teased with bobbing eyebrows, "has evidently made a *ve*ry fine impression."

"Eh?" grunted Calvin in confusion.

"'For Calvin and crew,' is what the man said, right Polish? Not your average pilot, that fellow, I dare say. Not terribly jovial, a bit stiff, statuesque, really. Swell fellow none the less. *Good* for Monique!"

"*Pi*lot?"

"*Dutch*man?"

"Mo*nique*?"

"Yes, yes and yes," confirmed Arbuckle. "A career KLM man. I had no idea you kept such bountiful company, Calvin. Have you any *blinis*, Manx? Gentlemen, fetch your flutes!"

"Here's another jar of caviar, Arbuckle!"

"How come he didn't give me anything?"

"Here, kitty kitty kitty!"

"What's a *blini*?"

"*Hsss. Hsss. Aller pour les yeux, Sophie!*"

"*KLM*?" Manx managed to cut through the rising din.

"Koninklijke Luchtvaart Maatschappij," expounded Arbuckle in his best Dutch. "The Royal Aviation Company, the national airline of the Netherlands."

"You fool!" cried Manx. "That fellow is with the KL*A*, not KL*M*!"

"KLA? But aren't they a terrorist organisation?"

"Not anymore they're not."

"At any rate," Arbuckle conceded, "I shan't argue over one trifling letter," he assured, running a sleeve over his salivating gob. "Least of all when there is a tsar's spread before us. I called for flutes, lads! On the double!"

Miroslav ran into the kitchen and splashed about in search of glasses. A meaty howl escaped the dark recesses of the flat, where the Butcher was busy having his eyes gouged out by the Moroccan kittins.

Polish palmed one of the bottles. "Odessa Sparkling Wine Company," he read. "*Sovetskoye Shampanskoye*," he mutilated. "Who knew the Russians produced champagne?"

"That's Ukrainian wine," someone corrected.

"They don't!" denied Manx, wielding a bottle. "Champagne is French!"

"Clearly, the fellow has a hell of an affinity for Russian delicacies."

"Negative," Aloysius contested. "Fitim Kaleci detests all things Russian."

"Who on earth considers Kalashnikovs a delicacy?"

"That gun is more of a delicacy than this *Sovetskoye Shampanskoye* rot!" Manx howled.

The Butcher finally appeared with self-applied plasters. The girls filled two flutes, retook their ping-pong bats and continued their game where they had left off.

"It's an attempt to erode the value of Russian luxury items by developing black-market demand," Aloysius postulated. "That's all this is."

"Running black-market swill does not describe an affinity," agreed Manx.

"Merely a wartime effort to undermine the Russians."

The onslaught of musings continued. The lads launched into hypotheses and theories and soon began to tip and sway under the seductive weight of inebriation.

Calvin pulled Aloysius aside. "What is it with you, huh? Lighten up a little!"

"Lighten up a little," Al scoffed.

"He's a *bloke* for crissake, Al. A bloke in love with Monique and her damned dog. And why the hell not? Who's the worse for it? No one here," he said in reference to the crew, "has done anything wrong."

"Nothing wrong! This is ludicrous. Really, Calvin, have you seen anything like this in all your life?"

"So what!" said Calvin, with waning patience. "So Fitim smiles and shakes hands. Big deal. He is courting Monique, not us. Go give out to her; she's the one in bed with the guy, not us. We have no affiliations. We are the free. I assure you, Al, no fellow shall buy me with a smile and a handshake, for crissake."

A wry baloney smile cracked along the surface of Al's face. "We've been gifted several thousand francs of Russian champagne and caviar. That's one hell of a handshake. That's some bright smile. Don't look now, Calvin, but you are officially the courted. Do you feel special? You think *they* do?" Al challenged, nodding toward the lads, as they launched into a rousing ditty of their own drunken creation:

> Three cheers for the Vieux!
> Three cheers for the crew!
> Three cheers for the lad with the KLA blues!
>
> We ain't ones to gripe
> We ain't ones to rue
> Still, he spared us a night soused on Kronenbourg brew
>
> So to hell with your politicos, leave 'em die on the pitch
> 'Less they vie for our hearts with Slavic delicacies rich
> This crew can be bought with fine Russian wine
> Sent westward to France o'er the Danube and the Rhine
>
> Aye, approach your man gently as a matter of course

Might win you with kindness or physical force
Maybe blinis under sturgeon eggs shining Ruskie red
Maybe Kalashnikov slugs: *bang! bang!* now you're dead

Mother Russia, have mercy
We know not what we do
Three cheers for the lad with the Kosovo blues!

No longer able to heed his own warnings, Manx took a bite from a *blini* covered with caviar. His eyelids fluttered with ecstasy. "*C'est bon,*" he uttered dreamily. "*Oh, c'est trop bon.*" Then, reverting to a more vulgar tongue, he snarled, "Oh, sod it, you snakes! Give me a flute and fill it!"

Manx drained the glass in a single go. "*Encore!*" he demanded.

Said Aloysius mockingly to Calvin, "You shan't be bought with a smile and a handshake, is that it? Hell if this crew can't be bought in its entirety for a song."

"Even if that were true, Al," Calvin conceded, "we have no commercial value. We have no position, no influence. No fellow can benefit by our purchase."

"Don't play dumb. You've got able minds, you're all talented—unorthodox as your minds and talents may be. You've got fists and boots. Every warm body may prove an asset to one running for office or assembling an army." Aloysius threw back his head and drained his glass. "There's something else," he said. "Between you and me, yeah?"

"On my word," Calvin complied.

"Remember the night of the British bulls, the goring of that unfortunate young barman from Nancy? Remember I told you about a bloke who asked me to store a certain crate?"

Calvin choked and nearly sprayed champagne all over Al's flannelled chest.

Two summers prior, Fitim Kaleci entered Al's antiques shop. He was not there to buy, nor was he there to sell. Al followed him into the yard, where three fellows, all of whom fairly dwarfed Fitim, flanked a wooden crate that was covered by a tarpaulin. Said Fitim, "I need storage space."

Said Al, scratching an armpit, "You're in luck; there's a lot of it for rent around town. As for us, we're an antiques shop."

Fitim looked at his watch, looked at the corn-blue morning sky, looked at Al. He complimented Al's affinity for straight talk and vowed, going forward, to speak more directly. Then he stepped forward with flickering temples and said, "I need storage space."

Al – or rather Bossman – was paid exceedingly well for having temporarily diversified their service offerings to include storage. A year or so later, Fitim showed up unannounced and removed the crate. Bossman declared it the end of the story and ridiculed Aloysius his burnt nerves during what was, by all measures, a lucrative year of services effortlessly rendered.

Shortly thereafter, Russian treasures began trickling into the antique shops of Vieux Nice—an ancient urn, a scroll of text, an original Alexeyev and yes, incredibly, a Fabergé Tsar Imperial Easter egg.

The rumour mill among antique dealers, which typically ground limited fact into the grist of fantastic speculation, began to rattle and buzz. Variations on the single intrigue were as numerous as the whispering mouths that propagated them. Though the details blurred and ran in all directions, the principle threads converged and peaked at a single point of concurrence: such exceedingly rare and precious artefacts only ever wound up in the hands of private individuals as the result of dangerous and illicit plots.

Some years prior, according to Aloysius, a priceless private collection of unconfirmed antiques and artefacts was in transit from Moscow to an unknown location in France, when, somewhere east of Warsaw, the heavily armed convoy was intercepted by a paramilitary group of unknown origins. The Press was believed to have been silenced and all traces of the carnage eliminated, as the affronted collector could not submit to identification, nor have the ill-acquired contents of his collection pursued and discovered. The power and influence required of an individual to silence the Russian national media and thereby, in effect, alter the records of time (for without record, there is only lore), was nearly inconceivable. Such a man would require a seat among the highest ranking members of government or the mob. Such a man would find and reclaim his collection without official aid, and he would relish the hunt. As the heist was never officially chronicled, the countless crafted details were soon embellished with legendary flair. Some indeed considered it myth. Al was seized with fear and paranoia when certain artefacts began finding their way to his shop. Each treasure brought in had been acquired through grandmotherly means and none of them were rightfully owned. A layman might come across an ancient urn and think it a handsome replica, but no antiques dealer found in possession of such goods could plead ignorance. Unquestionably, such a fellow would, in effect, consign himself to a untidy and uncomfortable fate.

When Aloysius had completed his recital, Calvin, nodding slowly, reached out a hand and rested it on Al's shoulder. "I appreciate your confidence, Al," he said. "I do. No part of what you've just said, however, makes any sense."

Al knocked his hand away.

"You want me to believe," said Calvin, "that Monique's boyfriend – the fellow downstairs – intercepted an illicit shipment of ancient artefacts and murdered the armed transporters, only to give it all over to *you*, and finally cast the invaluable lot out into the streets of Nice with *his* name tied to it, like so much cheap parade-route candy."

"The fellow who declares war on an adversary places no stock in shielding his name," said Al confidently. "The heist was intended to provoke and torment, it was not organised for personal gain." Al, retiring towards the kitchen for a beer, concluded, "That's what I believe, at any rate. You can believe whatever the hell you want."

By midnight, the champagne and caviar had been exhausted and the crew, despite predilections and proclamations to the contrary, had yet again gone soused on Kronenbourg brew. Suddenly, there was a knock on the sober side of the door and the party fell silent.

"This can't be good," spoke Arbuckle on behalf of one and all. "Any well-intentioned fellow would have kicked the door in straight away."

Manx nodded his fearful concurrence.

Ashamed of her association with such a paranoid bunch, one of the Moroccan kittens opened the door. There stood Gem, half-way up Mount Olympus and still rising. Relief and good cheer rippled throughout the flat and there was a boisterous return to revelry and speculation. Gem sauntered in to applause. Once inside, he emptied his pockets onto the ping-pong table and studied the spill.

"How does it look?" asked Arbuckle

"Don't encourage him," cried Polish.

"The wolves are coming," said Gem gravely. "Hold onto your hats, lads."

"Fitim Kaleci," whispered Aloysius to Calvin.

That did it. Manx could take no more. "That does it!" he bellowed. "Everyone out! Let's go! Get out!"

14   Crossed wires

In which Calvin bears witness to
a foreboding conversation.

Having been turned out and into the alleyway in the frantic, abortive manner to which they had grown accustomed, the fellows resolved – as they too often did when the Vieux's more respectable contingent aimed for the restorative comforts of bed – on a session at the Whales. Calvin told the lads he would catch them up, and ran home to change into his mudders, check his messages and throw back a shot of something flagrant, for courage—a typical campaign, really.

Having changed his shoes and killed a shot of Slovakian *slivovice*, he checked his messages. There were none, though just as he was putting down the telephone, a masculine voice came through the line. And then there was another. Calvin was about to say something, but nothing came immediately to mind and he instead found himself tuning in to a conversation that would have translated into English very closely as follows:

"Patience, patience. It won't be long now."

"You, sir, have patience to outlast granite. What little remains of mine is wearing thin."

"I know you've been stung by the barbs of my obsession. For that I am sorry. But beyond offering you my apologies, what can be done about it? Indeed, what makes obsessions so antagonising – and the obsessed so anguished – is that they cannot be reasoned away. One day you shall be the boss, Fiston, and a fine one you shall make.

For now, however, I am the boss and you have much to learn. There comes a time in a man's life—"

"When he must detach himself from the harness and jump."

"Quite right. And such a man, upon jumping—"

"Either flies or dies."

"You've heard this before."

"Once or twice, sir. And I reiterate: I should not like to see you die."

"The Omega is out there, Fiston. And as long as that remains true, I shall spread wings and pursue it.

"But are you truly flying, sir, or is the ground – that is to say the foundation upon which your life and your entire existence was built – simply falling further and further away from you as you continue to plummet? I am concerned for you, sir, that's all."

"And if I should die? What then, Fiston? Is life so precious as to live it to the end without knowing what it is like to jump? And if you insist that life is indeed so precious, might I not equally maintain that its preciousness alone justifies the bold and daring actions of a man driven by a cause? Dear Fiston, don't let my words get to you. I voice them more for myself than for you. Doubts creep in at the damnedest moments. One must stay focused and motivated."

"There are other lives at risk, sir; more than just yours."

"Look, I have designed and built myself around this pursuit. The pursuit defines me. Whomever I may have been to another at a previous point in my life has likely died. And if that version of me is not dead, hell, I shall argue that success as it concerns the Omega is my only hope of winning back that which I've come to accept as lost. I have long passed the point at which I might have considered cutting loses. To be sure, all is lost, save for the Omega. I regret the pain I have caused you and my family. As fantastic as it may sound, you lot are my tie to sanity, the resistance that keeps me from falling on my face, the reason that lets me know that I have not yet gone mad."

"You mean to say that we are your enablers? Do you honestly expect us to share your blame?"

"No, no. You simply make it all a little less agonising."

"I won't respond to that. I should not like to be reprimanded for my insolence. Allow me to make it unequivocally known, however, that you are a slave to this."

"If you must, Fiston, if you must. Some men gaze at the vectors of their lives from the perspective of an astronomer tracking the stars—as a far-off observer marvelling an inexplicable phenomenon, one he'll never fully understand, one he'll never begin to influence. I've never been such a man. There have been times when I've hedged bets, cheated, strategized and played games, but such strategies have failed me. You want me to say it? Fine, I am a slave to this. Yes, I have jumped. You see with your own eyes the reasons I wish for you a life free of obsessions. No man is more self-critical and loathing of himself and his internal concerns than the obsessed. And no man should suffer such terrific self-criticism and self-loathing. Nevertheless, here we are with a job to do."

"Very well, sir, but how can you be certain the Omega is nearby?"

"Much like a wartime occupier, obsessions take up unwelcomed residence in a fellow and leave him suspicious and anxious. The aural horns that trumpet the arrival of the Omega trigger destruction, both for its pursuers and the innocents caught in the wake of their collective rush. Look about this town—so many steeds grinding their bits, fighting against the reins, as if a demon flow were descending the Southern Alps, for the coast. Why, I only hear the name *Omega* and my hair stands on end. We pursuers have been conditioned through the course of our pursuit – Pavlovian beasts, the sorry lot of us – each unable to say with any confidence whether his behaviour is the sum of a series of wilful actions or merely a string of triggered responses."

"But isn't it possible, sir, that the destructive behaviour we've noted is not related to the Omega at all, but to the blaring of another horn, so to speak? To be sure, a fellow is liable to rattle himself mad with all manners of psychological weaponry, and over anything at all—haunting memories, ominous forecasts of the future, even a lover's harsh words. After all, it seems to me that obsessions are little more than the manifestations, or surfacing, of acute and irreconcilable fears of failure."

"It is a fair question. But you'll have to trust me. If signs were cobblestones, the roads built of their assembly would lead to Nice. I can't explain it, I can only feel it. Speaking of which, DeTorche has returned to France. I want his every move monitored, understand? And stay close to Blanche Neige."

"Yes, sir."

"We are out at the crack of dawn greasing the streets, eventually someone will slip and fall. We continue to watch and listen, turn up the heat and gauge reactions. We will have our answers when we discover our suspects' purposes."

"Purposes?"

"Indeed. Every organism is guided by a purpose, Fiston. It matters not if one is conscious of one's purpose or not. Some beasts are content to slobber at the twang of a tuning fork. And then, of course, there is Man—conscious of motives and morals, a compulsive goal-setter. Yet, for his highfalutin brainstem and all his so-called miracles rendered, he is unable to identify a single purpose worth living for.

"Don't you mean to say worth *dying* for?"

"Certainly not; Man will die for any penny-ante trifle, though no man lives with death as his purpose. It is his failure to identify a golden purpose that renders a fellow fragile and vulnerable to death, and so too drives him to kill that which he identifies as lesser entities with lesser purposes."

"But will a man not sometimes consign himself to death, that others may live?"

"No. Decorating oneself in death and calling it heroic sacrifice is despicable. The momentum of martyrdom on this planet is as phony as it is appalling. Any fool can die, but to live consciously requires great strength and courage. Why, when a man's purpose is pure, he will not merely die for it. On the contrary, he will live for it.

"But would not you kill for the Omega if you came within striking distance?"

"By all means, but I've never said that mine is a pure and golden pursuit. It is indeed a violent and gruesome one. I am not proud of it, Fiston, but as you have pointed out, I am dominated by a certain fear of failure. Some contend that we have been conditioned away from introspection and towards the raging world to which we have been consigned as transparent wisps of temporary energy bereft of extensible purpose. Wisps, dear Fiston, do not self-contemplate, nor do they ask questions. And fewer questions posed means fewer challenges and greater control for the power-hungry, whose only real demand is that we slaughter each other and die in the streets, like dogs, the world over, over nothing at all and for no conceivable gain. Ah, but what is the value of such digressions. Back to work. The lad said that when one trumps another's play, the next move belongs to the aggressor. But I had no intention of trumping his purpose—"

"Oh, no?

"Look here, Fiston, I am extending him the benefit of the doubt. I am not out to slap him on the wrist for his poor judgement, unless it interferes with my pursuit. I have a purpose—a very well defined and constructed purpose, uninspiring as it may be. No, it does not delivery me to any special heaven – my father was murdered after all, and in a way, my only son is fatherless – but my purpose got me out of bed this morning and perhaps it will do so again to-morrow. If it does not... The beauty of the dog, you see, is that it can be invariably conditioned to perform any task within the range of its abilities and live happily with its menial purpose. Men, of course, are not so fortunate. You know, I've developed an affinity for the lad. When this thing comes down – and it most certainly is coming down – I hope to hell his hands are clean."

"You've given him fair warning, sir."

"Because affinity or no, if the boy comes between me and the Omega in even the slightest, most unintentional of ways, he will come to know unbearable regret. Take it from me, Fiston, even the smallest of regrets can be a crippling burden. I must be going now, but first, the restaurant—what do you think?"

"La Baie d'Amalfi? I suppose you are not referring to the menu, sir, though they do serve one hell of a fettuccine vongole."

"I am not enquiring after your opinion of the food, Fiston, no. But you are absolutely right, the marriage of the garlic and white wine—"

"And the shallots, sir. Do not forget the shallots."

"And the shallots, Fiston. Nothing short of a dream."

"A dream, sir, that's what it is. Do you think the rendez-vous at the restaurant will bring us closer to the Omega?"

"I have given up assuming and hoping, both. This is simply another wall that must be knocked down. The lads have reserved a table for ten o'clock. We shall be waiting for them."

"We might book a table early enough to partake of that delicious vongole, might we not, sir?"

"We just might at that, Fiston."

"What you haven't yet told me, sir, is how you propose to verify the lads' involvement. Because if we jump them and they prove to be innocent, we are sunk. Our covers will be blown."

"Not at all. Up until this point, we have engaged in a chess match. The application of psychological pressure buys time and is less… sticky. If our covers are blown, however, too bad—we then abandon the chess match and strike with hammers."

"I need not remind you, sir, that I am no glutton for spilt blood."

"The man in possession of the Omega lays false claim to a treasure of Russian heritage, one that was crafted as a show of gratitude to French emperors, the Champenois and the General Chapter of the Cistercian monks. Every fellow knows that a usurper's steps are perilous steps, and none know this better than the usurper himself. When the lads enter the restaurant, I shall take to whistling the melody from the exquisite Song of the Swans leitmotif from Tchaikovsky's Swan Lake, the most famous Russian ballet of all time. To the innocent, it is merely a delicate and lovely tune from a popular ballet. For the fellow in wrongful possession of the Omega – paranoid as he must be while in possession of an invaluable and ill-possessed treasure – the tune will have the effect of a wailing doomsday siren. The notes will ostensibly announce Swan Lake, but his paranoia will reassemble them into a Butterfly's Lullaby—that is, the final tune. One wrong twitch will betray an unblessed liaison between the lads and the Omega."

"It is as though you are the legendary piper from Hamelin, sir, and the lads enchanted rats."

"Bless you, Fiston."

"Thank you, sir, though it wasn't such a lofty compliment."

"No, the blessing was in response to your sneeze."

"But I didn't sneeze, sir. I thought you sneezed."

"If I didn't sneeze and you didn't sneeze…"

Click. The line went dead.

15 A night at the Whales

In which Calvin dances with the
girl in white and Gem loses his
wallet.

The Whales was deep, narrow up front, wide in the back,
disjointed. It was a late-night bar with no windows and no
ventilation. Pungent air hung, as though in the belly of a great beast
with no brain or diaphragm to belch it out and draw a fresh breath.
Of the young bodies that gathered within, some were bared to the
hot summer night, some teased, some advertised gauzily veiled
curves that might later be traced and followed, all of them tacky for
the perspiration and tipped show drinks. They came into contact,
sometimes by chance, sometimes with the intentions of friends or
lovers, sometimes as foes. There was heavy drinking. The hanging
air smelt of sweat and sewage and perfume. And there was the wait
staff, a darting set of fickle youth who were quick to admonish the
living and inanimate alike, over hell's range of infractions. "But *you,
monsieur*, put us at this table!" "*Tant pis! Bougez vos culs! Vite!
Vite! Vite!*"

A long-haired band grinded and wailed through hard-edged
covers on a cramped stage. The bands that played the Vieux Nice
circuit took few chances, opted for sure-fire rock numbers and got
by largely on volume and nostalgia. Off-duty barmen gathered next
to the stage, jerking their bodies in time and slapping savagely at
bass guitars that did not exist. A dreadlocked front-man, a black man

in black leather, screamed Helter Skelter into a mike. The hard metal version would become anthemic by the end of the night.

Calvin arrived at the Whales to find the lads swarming about the bar, like a beard of bees. They swung elbows and jockeyed for position in attempts to order the next round. Calvin lagged back and considered the conversation to which he had just bore witness. Fantastic enough to have picked up his own telephone in his own home and overheard another's rather foreboding conversation. But that he could not truthfully proclaim every word of it foreign produced an entirely different degree of shock and unsettling within him. He might have explained it away as a technical glitch and hung up, had he not been arrested for the second time in several weeks by the peculiar names of DeTorche and Blanche Neige, two names that now rang in his ears with unwelcomed familiarity. What an alarming occurrence, thought Calvin. He scanned the bar as though he might find an explanation for it all, there in the bowels of the Whales.

A bar is only as good as its clientele, and the reputation of the Whales suffered for its many fixtures, one of which was a washed-up English mariner called Captain Stu. Mickaël was also there, seated at one of the café tables near the stage and the band, with several shadowy unknowns. Mickaël was stitched together of rich Polynesian and European fabrics, was long and liquid brown and strikingly handsome. He was also lazy, arrogant and ignorant. Days were numbered for the fellow who took the preposterous risks Mickaël took. At the same table sat a girl in a tight white sleeveless top, one that ran stressed and then slack, here and there, in all the right places. Such close proximity to Mickaël, in general, thought Calvin, tarnished the finish of any otherwise peerless image.

Captain Stu had trapped a pair of holiday doe. "The code of the sea," he demanded before them, "is as binding as it is ancient, which means every last one of them was due a flogging. Aye, and a *prop*er flogging at that! Are you girls paying attention? Say something. *Blink*! Calvin Stony, come here!"

Calvin approached on the prescript of the Good Samaritan, offering the girls a distraction, of which they took immediate advantage and scampered off into the foliage of a sweaty, adolescent fray.

"Flogging! I say, has the word no meaning on land?" Stu begged of Calvin. Spotting the cotton-white tails of the fleeing doe, he aimed and lets loose a round of verbal buckshot, "*Flog*ging, ladies! Flesh ripped to ribbons! *Ripped to ribbons!*"

"Unorthodox approach to courtship," noted Calvin.

"Unorthodox devil," piped Stu with a rising chin that signalled self-pride. "What this town needs, you see, is a good public execution."

"That would be something," admitted Calvin. "Right here in Place Rossetti."

"As good a place as any, I'd say. Pull this town out of its stupor is what it would do. This entire country has been in decline since the days of *Dick*ens."

"Dickens was English," Calvin pointed out.

"What's your point? Social reform is the focus, am I wrong?"

"I see. You were serious about the executions, then."

"Oh! Are such considerations suddenly taboo? I promise you there were no such restrictions in Sicily, when those mutinous dogs left me stranded among the *Stiddari* in Gela? Ha! Imagine, an Englishman of my complexion and standing, cast away in Gela. Only a stone's throw from Palermo and that pederast Marchese with his room of death on the Corso Dei Mille. Oh, the garrottes! And not those limited to the cinema of my worst nightmares, but the honest-to-God wooden ones lacquered with the human varnish of Corleonesi rivals; fitted here and there, no less, with blades and spikes to facilitate the snapping of spines. That's *their* idea of generosity! An Englishman of my post, cast away in Gela! The dead dissolved in acid, or diced and fed to the blind and gaping purple sea that lay between the battlefields and Malta. *Lupara bianca*—white shotgun! Corpses destroyed beyond all recognition. *Excellent cadavers*! *Gela*!"

The girl in white stood out like cut diamond. Calvin had no intention of making eyes with her, much less furtive eyes. It had seemed to him, however, that she was staring at him from across the murky stretch, and in verifying the unlikelihood, found himself staring right back. Working girl, thought Calvin. She was too striking, too alert, her comportment too purposeful to be in the Whales at that hour, ignoring the band and, in fact, ignoring everything and everyone, it seemed, but him. A pity, he pondered further—biding her time with Mickaël, slogging through the social foreplay that would precede a lacklustre main event and a handsome purse. Mickaël kept his hair in glossy black braids. They made him look tough—to each his guise. Still, Mika knew people. If it weren't necessary, a fellow did not want to provide punks with too much time – even lazy punks – a cause.

Suddenly, she stood before him, the girl in white. "*Bonsoir*," she said.

The sound of her voice was snuffed by the noise of the band, but there was no burden whatsoever for the fellow forced to read her red lips. And even there, in the guts of the Whales, did her eyes know rare fire.

"*Bonsoir*," said Calvin.

She moved closer, in order to be heard. "*Comment tu t'appels?*"

"Calvin," he replied simply.

"*Je m'appels—*"

"No, no, no!" he urged, raising an index finger between their two bodies.

"What is it?" she asked, startled.

"*On dois rester des inconnus*. It's better that way."

"Better to remain strangers?" she asked. Any onlooker would have concluded it was not the first time Calvin had disappointed her. "But you just told me your name."

"True," said Calvin. "An unfortunate credit to your wile and feminine trickery." She had it in spades.

"Trick you? I did nothing of the sort," said the bruised peach.

"You did and I wish you hadn't. You can't come into this place looking like that."

"Why not? Looking like what?"

"Looking nice. Too nice. You don't belong here."

Tears may or may not have been poised to plummet upon his next brusque word. "But why don't you want to know my name?" she asked.

"Look, I've known for some time that I'm not the cleverest fellow. But I'm finally beginning to realise that may not be all bad. It's not good to know too much."

"But you don't know *any*thing," she said.

"I won't argue with you, though I suppose I should wish it weren't quite so obvious."

"I mean about me. You don't know anything about *me*."

"You're a *pute*, aren't you."

She slapped him hard across the face.

"You're with Mickaël, aren't you."

"Who?"

Of the two accusations, thought Calvin, the second was the more offensive, the one that warranted a good slap.

"That guy," said Calvin, pointing. "The one you're sitting with."

"Him? I just met him an hour ago. A fellow can't *move* in here for all the bodies. He made space for me at his table."

"I'm sure he did."

"Bah, he's a simple kid," she said.

"Simplicity on its own is bliss, but add heavy parts envy and ignorance and you're liable to get your bean split, especially around here, where it's tough to make out the blades for all the ice cream and succulents."

"You seem to know a lot for a guy who knows nothing."

"No. I only know that Mickaël is going to catch his one day. That much I know. And I know you don't want to risk being at his table when the day comes."

"I already told you I have no attachment to him. Let's you and me find our own table."

"I can't do that."

"Why not?"

"Because I don't want to," he said. "My girl would not approve."

"Oh!" she exclaimed and fairly jumped and Calvin was surprised to find her somehow in his arms. More wile and feminine trickery, thought Calvin.

"It's OK," he said to the warm collection of tight curves, and added, "She's not here."

Looking into his eyes, she said, "I'm sorry."

She made the apology sound much more like a greeting.

"You have a girlfriend, then. But what foolish girl would leave you alone for even a minute?"

Calvin noticed that he hadn't quite let go of her. "Most all of them. Now stop it," he said and stepped back from her.

"But where is she, this girlfriend of yours?"

"She's in Barcelona."

"Barce*lona*?"

"That's right. She lives there," he said. "That's where she lives."

She looked at him as though she were awaiting the rest of the story. When it was evident that he had said all there was to say, she concluded, "Why, that's in another *coun*try."

"Sure," he began, as if he were no longer entirely certain, "but the Barcelona in Spain, right?"

Dear Klarysa, he thought somewhat miserably, where are you now?

"Not any of the ones in South America," he clarified.

"It's funny," she said, taking him playfully by the wrists and coyly examining her grip, "how all boys think they can take care of themselves."

"It's a neighbouring country, for crissake. Shared frontier and everything. A lousy six-hour drive."

"Six *hours*," she marvelled, imagining herself on the eternal stretch of highway.

Time, thought Calvin, positively crawls for the young.

"Some of us do quite well for ourselves, actually," he said. "You'd be surprised."

"Some do. Sure," she conceded. "What do you drive?"

"SNCF. Second class cabin. OK, fine—ten hours."

"And others," she said, sliding her hands down his wrists until she was holding his hands, "need help. Silly boy, that's not a girlfriend."

"Oh, no?"

"Six hours by car? Ten by train? *Elle est ta maîtresse.*"

"Mistress! She can't be my mistress; I'm not married."

"You must be married to *some*thing," she said evidently. "Or else why are you not with her? Look, I'm here—I could be your girlfriend."

Something was amiss and Calvin knew it. Women like that did not approach guys—much less *French* girls like her; much less guys like him; much less in stinking dives like the Whales.

"What is it?" she said in response to his narrowed eyes.

"You work for them, don't you," he said suddenly. "Tell the truth."

"Who them?"

"Don't lie."

"Bah, *who?*"

"The guys on my goddamned telephone line, *that's* who," he said. The words jumped involuntarily from his mouth and gave rise to an immediate and unexpected cathartic rush. "Or the man in the alleyway. Or the goddamned fiends in Cimiez with their canes and guns. Or are all of you part and parcel of one big network—"

"Baby, please," she begged. "Please; I don't know—"

"I'm not your baby," he said coldly.

Such a reaction should have deterred her, caused her to turn and leave or perhaps even deal him a second blow. But it did not. Not that girl. She stood before him and looked pleadingly upon him with a regard of deep concern. She was not frightened, nor did she relinquish her grip on him. These unlikely truths further startled him. Gone was her playful, almost childish air. It was replaced by a seriousness and intelligence for which Calvin was not prepared. Her hands locked around his wrists as though she had captured him. Again he recalled the phone conversation and it occurred to him for the first time that he was in a situation.

"Who are you, anyway?" he demanded. "Let go of me!"

He jerked his arms away and broke free of her grip. Finally, she flinched and the fire in her eyes died. Calvin was free.

"I saw you and thought," she began, stopped, found new confidence and said, "I liked the way you looked at me. You looked kind." Her lips were certain of nothing. "Obviously, I was wrong."

She turned, as though to disappear very quickly, but Calvin, as uncertain as her quavering lips, caught her nonetheless by the arm. "Wait," he said.

"Go to hell!" she cried. "You're a horrible man!"

"I said wait! Hell, you're a sensitive thing, you. Look, I don't know what you're…"

But he could not manage another word. It had been a long day. Exhaustion had set in and, in any case, he knew not how to complete the sentence. She hung in his grip, watching his eyes, waiting. A strand of dark hair had fallen before her face, partially obscuring her vision. She dared not move. It *had* been a long day. Klarysa seemed to him much further away than ten hours by train. He conjured a vision of her, but like those that are remembered exquisitely as long as they are not focused upon or studied closely, Calvin, in trying to specifically picture her button nose and her white polished teeth, realised that he could not, to his great dismay, picture her nose or teeth or eyes for that matter any more clearly than he could those of any other fellow.

There they hung in a fragile spot of silence. She watched his eyes; he watched the contours of a workingman's grip in possession of an object of workable weight and resistance, though one privy to a shape and beauty unknown to the workingman in the sphere of his métier. Calvin jerked his hand higher up on her arm, closer to her armpit, testing the full weight of its possession, challenging gravity its claim. (At that moment, in the countless recesses that pocked the dark globe, lovers praised their gods for the constancy of gravity, without which life would be but a feverish, hellish eternity of weightless futility and impotent petting.) The movement produced a sound from her parted lips, and caused her to lurch closer to him. This arm, he thought, should not feel so substantive. By god, a man could live off it! He pulled her closer still, this time less brusquely, until there was nothing left between them. What live action in that woman's young body—*action*, he meant, in physical, almost mechanical terms, very literally her *push* and her *pull*, her glorious resistance. Now body-to-body, he breathed in the scent that rose from her skin; breathed in near to where her hair met the nape of her neck, where the slightest touch of his lips made rise fine humid hairs and a tender chill; breathed in the fine bitter scent of her crushed-crimson lips. Her immediate proximity to him alone was a fortune. His free hand found her waist and attempted to pull her closer yet, but there was no space left between them to eliminate. He gave into this, wanting nothing more in the world than to put his face against her and breathe deeply, to bury his face in the heat that emanated from her humid, miraculously present body, and breathe. A sudden, rabid urge came to a boil within him, and now he longed just as achingly to feel the resistance of her body, her hips, her waist, her neck, to pull her and push her, to tug on her and bend her, to feel the resistance of pushing her away and then pulling her close again, to grip her high on the throat and wrap his fingers around her cheeks and jaw, to pull her by the waist up and into him, to grip her tightly, battle the earth's pull for her mass and immediacy, to win all of her, to have her know and feel just how desperately she was needed at that very moment.

Some will say that the body is but a temporary shell occupied by the soul, until it withers and quits and the soul takes to flight. But healers understand that the body and the mind are interdependent and indivisible in the context of true health. Lovers know that this same interdependence and indivisibility exists in terms of a fellow's arduous, punishing pursuit to prove and validate his own existence. In the US – where obsolescence was engineered across the board, where destruction and creation in all their wild mutations chased one another in a vicious spin – burden, fear and pressure could tack a man down where he stood. But there, in Europe – where they had somehow found a way to make sure nothing at all ever happened – a man was liable to go mad, go feather-light and blow away without a warm body to which to cling, with which to bunk down and help fend off the weightlessness, a body to crush madly and by which to be madly crushed, a passionate thing to give him his name—for Calvin, by god, a warm thing on which to fix and settle his arrhythmic, thumping heart, a body against which to verify his existence and anchor him to the earth, for it is true that he began to feel himself slipping, and was no longer certain that his feet were at all times under him and making contact with the cobbled streets. An unjustified anger for Klarysa welled up within him. Damn her distance, he cursed. He drained his anger almost as quickly as he recognised it, however, reminding himself that no fellow should be denied his practiced independence, for absolute aloneness is life's greatest inevitability. Indeed, though one may surround himself, during all his days and nights, with dependents and glittering personalities, every man is but a singular closed loop that eventually comes unhinged of itself and lies down flat, finally, alone, for all time. And only then did one's struggle and one's aloneness finally end. Only then did one achieve genuine communion. Life's inevitable pills, Calvin found, were always easier to swallow.

What the hell, he told him himself. I am still in control. And I will, at the end of the night, for better or worse, go home alone.

Then, to the live and present body in his full arms, he said, "Let's dance."

They danced and drank and Calvin feared that her legs would be the next drug to demand constant consciousness of him, were he to evade their addictive hooks. There was a hell of a lot of Westmalle behind the bar and that never bode well for the fellow who was trying to maintain his resolve. She wore tight ripped jeans and Calvin's fingers found skin where one might have expected an under-layer of silk or fine cotton. Her breath, when she mouthed words, hung sweetly before him like ripe Spanish fruit. She said many things to him, things he could not hear or did not understand, reminding him in some strange and wonderful way of a long-lost summer night in a Paris that was gone forever, in which he, lacking experience and metropolitan savvy, grappled humidly in a hidden patch of grass behind the Hôtel des Invalides, with a bright-eyed girl who had precociously professed to have, by the age of twelve and a half, flatly denounced all administrators, officeholders and authority figures, citing a profound distrust for whatever common disease boiled within them and fuelled aspirations of obtaining such provinces in the first place; and who had, the following morning, after a breakfast of croissants and exotic fruits, thrown open the sixth-floor windows, wearing naught but a fuchsia scarf *en cachemire*, and on tip-toes to better view the full fall, tossed out into the street, one at a time, three bright-yellow lemons, kissing each before the release, just to watch them fall, and then marched in humming satisfaction to the bath, casting off her scarf en route, to sing unabashedly (though not without an uncanny ear and a decidedly robust voice for a sticky-fingered seventeen-year-old), French classics in the shower.

Said the girl in white to Calvin, "Meet me to-morrow."

"I can't do that," he replied.

"On the beach at Gambetta," she said. "Meet me there at noon."

"Doesn't anyone work in this town?" he begged.

"Then come afterwards, in the night-time."

"I especially can't do that."

"I know," she said, pouting. "You want to stay strangers."

Other women may pout, but they are only borrowing from the French.

"Don't be that way. You're just not used to it, that's all," he said gently, referring to rejection. "You never will be—rejection is not something you'll come to know with any frequency. Anyway, I can tell you it's not so bad."

Although they still held each other close, Calvin suddenly felt emotionally detached. Not only detached, but now, too, rather ecstatic. Yes, ecstatic and heartened by a sense of defended love and fulfilled responsibility towards Klarysa. He sensed his love for her filling his chest, burning ever-brighter within. Mistress? Ha! Everyone needed a kick now and again to keep his head clear and ready, to open his eyes to the urgency of a situation. It was all Calvin could do to keep from racing home without further delay and laying out plans for an imminent move to Barcelona.

"You are in love with her," noted the girl in white.

"Yes. All the same," he said kindly, "I shall never forget the girl in white."

"Bah, I am not bound by any one colour, regardless of my name. And whether you like it or not, we are no longer strangers. You've shown yourself to be a gentleman, and if by some misplaced stroke of serendipity I've fallen in love with you—" she interrupted herself to challenge his reaction. "What? Oh, you find it unreasonable?"

"No... I..."

"You find it impossible that a girl might have fallen in love in your arms just now? I, too, am here holding *you* don't forget. I saw your eyes, your mouth. I felt your chest and your arms. I felt your body tremble. Will you deny having loved me, if only just a little?"

"No, I won't deny it," he assured her out of a sense of duty and fairness to her intuition. "I did."

"Very well," she said, restored of faith, for intuition is the beginning and end of a fellow's line on self-preservation. "And if I do love you, why would I want to ruin your good standing as a gentleman? This is silly; my name is Blanche and that's how you will call me."

'*E-e-ech*!'

The name careened sharply through the corridors of Calvin's head.

"Did you say *Blanche*?"

"Yes. What now?" she said.

"What now indeed, *Blanche Neige*!"

"Honestly," she sighed. "Snow White? I thought the world would have fatigued of that joke sometime before I left primary school—"

"Spare me! I'm no schoolboy and this is no schoolyard run-around!"

"—Though I shouldn't complain; there are far worse complexes. Had I been born in America, for example, they may have called me Blanche DuBois. To be sure, Tennessee Williams did *her* no favours."

"Oh, stop! Don't think for a second that I've forgotten the Cimiez drop. I don't know who you are or what your involvement is, but I took a *lash*ing for that and poor Arbuckle nearly ate lead. Listen, you little vamp, you stay out of my affairs and I'll stay out of yours!"

"Affairs?"

"Two men on *my* phone line to-night spoke specifically of *you*, Blanche Neige—*affairs*!"

"Authorities," she provoked, "might want to monitor the intentions of men enjoined in intimate late-night conference over fairytale figures. Were I you, I'd be cautious, lest you—"

"Lest I what? Implicate myself? Pah! I've already been warned by your man."

"What man?"

"The man with the lapel pin, of course. Look here, I'm eager to leave everything well enough alone, although what it is exactly I'm to leave alone has not, as yet, been elucidated by any of my accusers. You spooks are the obsessed. I'm just trying to love a girl in Spain!"

"But—"

"As for Tennessee Williams, he did not create Blanche DuBois as much as Blanche DuBois created *him*."

"What does that mean?"

As a Gemini with capital polarity, who found himself frequently cleaved into competing hemispheres, Calvin reserved a soft spot in his heart for schizophrenics and walking contradictions.

"It means we all have histories, Miss Neige; some of which are *gen*uinely burdensome."

Both the labour and the art of life, then, Calvin believed, were found in trying to keep afloat a future on the ocean of one's turbulent past.

Just then, Arbuckle appeared. "Hello, brother Calvin," he sang in a knowingly playful manner. "Come, join us upstairs for a wee drink and a crossing of the cues."

"Arbuckle," burst Calvin, "I present to you the heretofore unknown Blanche Neige!"

"Let it be known here and now that I am sorry," Arbuckle pre-emptively excused. "And that under different circumstances, I would, by all means, launch an exhaustive fact-finding inquisition to deliver justice to this young lady for the wrongs suffered her at the hands and hearts of one or several of the literary ruffians under my charge. Realities as they are to-night, however," he said, eyeing the ceiling with grave distrust, "I pray, Miss, you'll accept a thoughtfully abridged blanket apology and call it an arrangement. Now then, Calvin, they have conveniently installed a staircase directly behind us, which works wonders in attaining the second floor."

"Arbuckle, this is *Blanche Neige*, she whose absence in Cimiez created such a scandal! Has the excitement of being held at gunpoint worn so thin?"

"Ah, so! Blanche Neige," affirmed Arbuckle. "By all means. A pleasure to put a face to the name. Thrilled, too, to discover for once that Rosenbloem and his lot require no pardoning from yourself or the local authorities."

"Are you both quite certain you're OK?" she asked, thoroughly unconvinced of her identity and role in the dubious exploit.

"Do, all the same, my dear," advised Arbuckle, "file away the apology just offered for any forthcoming day with bite. One never knows, the horizon is rife with them."

At that, Arbuckle hooked Calvin by the elbow and made to lead him away.

"Arbuckle!" Calvin protested. "What is your problem?"

"Why, I would like to show you an underappreciated invention designed to bridge vertical distances by dividing them into smaller, more manageable distances called *steps*. An architectural miracle, really—"

"Let go of me!" cried Calvin, shaking free of his grip. "What gives with you?"

"Well, you see, upstairs—"

"Quickly!"

"It's Gem."

"No, no. What now?"

"It seems as though he... The thing is, you see..."

"Out with it!"

"It seems he has lost his wallet."

"No. No. No," objected Calvin, drifting towards the front door. "No, no, no, no!"

"This way, this way," soothed Arbuckle, steering Calvin towards the staircase, like a dim and beaten bovine in escort to the abattoir.

"Where is the rest of the crew?" Calvin pleaded.

"All gone to bed. All but Polish."

"But I've a new shirt on..."

"Take it off."

"I just bought it *yes*terday."

"Quit your whinging."

"But it's *white*! And I'm feeling no pain!"

"Oh, do stop it."

Submitting to Arbuckle's lead, Calvin called back to the blank-faced beauty who, prior to that evening, was sure she had seen and heard it all, "I'm not done with you! Stay there! Don't you move!"

But Calvin knew that she would move—that pretty much everyone would move.

Absurdly, there was a pool table in the tight room upstairs. It had either grown there from a seedling, or management had greased the walls and stairs and had the table slammed home into place. There were no other options. Playing a game of pool upstairs was a contact sport that required skilful deployment of cue, elbows and arse.

The lads climbed the stairs through compressed bodies as wet as pickerel, and strata of cigarette smoke so thick they lodged in the back of the throat. At the landing, Calvin eyed Gem across the room, shrugged and mouthed, "What gives?"

From the far corner, Gem, with arms akimbo, yowled, "Calvin, where is me wallet!"

"You're going to see her from across a crowded dance floor and you'll know. You won't have to worry or wonder. You'll just know. So simple as all that."

He bend down close and she kiss him with Christmas red lips.

I turned and jumped and hit the ground hard and rolled into a dense patch of yellow tangleweed mean with snags like angry treble-hooks. They ripped at my clothing and plucked holes in my skin. She said that she would make a cage of my heart, Gem, but where was I? I pulled myself up and looked around.

A hot California valley extends in every direction.

That funny girl, Gem. She broke my heart. I broke her heart first, though, so I guess we're more or less even. How does it go when that big powerful pain comes rushing with end-of-the-world immediacy into stomach and lungs, and sucks all the wind and life straight out of them, when you're not prepared for the things you find in life, in dark streets, in words, mostly in the wide dancing eyes of something you ache for— your lover, your girl. What do you reckon you might do in a similar grind? First off, pinned here to this California valley that takes no time and gives no thought to a weak animal like Man. San Joaquin. No bigger, lonelier place on earth in the middle of a disciplined August than out on the far gone edge of Contra Costa county, farther though, so that you roll dry and cotton-mouthed beyond all the white suburbs, to the brown pueblos and Mexican cantinas green and red, and the sad fringe markets with dusty canned goods and wonderful homemade tamales, dim flinching fluorescent lights and low-slung Mexicanos who you can see in their beat shoulders and cheeks and eyes full of true Western sorrow that they know they got the shaft. Out toward Lodi and Stockton and the big college you'd never guess was sitting there baking away on the valley floor. Out to where the Sacramento and San Joaquin rivers flirt and twist and come winding together brown and fresh before making a hard western push, together, past Fairfield, a town with a cover of emerald green in the springtime, like a living snake slithering along with silver-green skin over serpent muscles, and a river through it with wavelets that ripple smooth, as though over a million china-fine bones, into the bay and under the Benicia bridge stacked up with cars, heavy-metal pollutants, good old broad-shouldered boys from Vacaville and second-generation Houston imports shuttling between the refineries and chemical plants and out-of-the-way track housing. And then the mad-flowing water running into the San Francisco Bay and, finally, tirelessly out to the great wide Pacific.

I've spent my time out here, Gem, and I got no business with this land. The river throws up blinders, not even giving a hard blink to any of the things dead or dying around it. Tall stems and reeds shoot up from the rock at the water's edge – in the water – and they're death-brown, too. And I, too, throw up blinders in this game of wits, this battle of attrition. I don't trust anything or anyone out here to keep me alive and my heart beating, and I know that if I don't keep everything pumping and moving along on my very own with great consciousness, I'm going to die on hot jagged rock, alone, of heat stroke and heartbreak. The heat, boy! The heat and the heartbreak! Goddamn I can feel them both in every burnt intention lying dead around my feet, in the dust blown into the cracks and crevices of the land of my own body, in the dirt and stones under my feet, in the stingy barbs that stab into my boney ankles, see it buoyant even on the dusty surface of the river and feel the sucking action fixed just off my mouth and lungs, goddamn. And now walking with a dry wrenched back, I wonder why this country don't explode in flames each year. Nobody fights the Devil in his own schoolyard. Just get to your business and act like you don't see him watching you. No matter what the body might happen upon, keep the head straight and the heart beating, do what you come to do; keep it beating that you might live to enjoy another cold beer and a fine brass band, dark, wet and weary in San Francisco. One day, anyway, after all.

Every minute I keep one nervous eye on the low western ridge, where the fertile ocean land and everything remotely moist and hopeful finally stops struggling and dies – the ridge that separates San Francisco and the coastal gods from this Delta devil. The other eye watches and roots in vain for that hopeless rebel cloud, so pale and translucent, inching its way over the ridge, now leaking thinner and thinner by the second, dying a wispy tattered death high above the valley even before it can drag skinny humid shoulders to peek over the edge. I stand here, motionless, with a hand shielding my neck, hoping and wondering if that defeated cloud shed some misty tears or at least some humid intentions on Pacheco or Pittsburg before dying, and if maybe there are others, bigger and darker and more athletic, that might bully their way across the ridge and stretch all the way out to my dusty hands and shoes, so dusty to give shrieking chills like dry white chalk in your cracked hands and up under your fingernails. But they never come, those homecoming clouds, after all.

I stand here still with a hand rubbing the back of my neck, looking for that little blonde girl, the one so adorable you want to scoop her up and squeeze until your last breath, the one that I married one true day so long ago somewhere in Sonoma Valley, Christmas green all over, that fine day, except for the burnt orange and dark red summer snapdragons – dark dark red and yellow and burnt orange – those fuzzy and dense with that unique deep quality to their color that remind me so much and in fact only of Garfield summers, when Ma would drive us in the Oldsmobile out to a cool shallow lake by the farms, tucked away, under trees giving shade to white summer cottages with old piers of rusty pipe and gray slat wood and the small lakes which look so big and rich and tender at eight-years-old, lakes with friendly silver minnows taking shade in the edges made cool by deep green grass that curls over the sandy lip above the water, and picnic tables in the tall grass for eating Ma's wonderful sandwiches.

And still with one eye on that nasty ridge that you can barely make out for the heat ghosts rising up in front of your eyes, and that same ridge that sure as hell don't care for nothing about how hot and dry it gets out in the valley for a hardened man, much less a dumb lost child like me, a confused childlike hallucination, a mirage of a man. So that with so much heat and not enough bleary eyes to keep watch on everything, my head and neck get so hot and start to sting and ache and almost get me sick in the stomach. Here I am, Gem, worrying and wondering to hell and back where that little blonde girl is and why when she says she'll be right at the river's edge, just cooling out and letting go of all the mad suspicions we have on each other, I still can't find her.

I do my best to stay hopeful, a fool child trying to entice a merciful vision, a vision of standing there looking out over everything and for everything in that bad-tempered heat, and in my vision comes a heavy rolling cloud, thick and plum purple and big like a good ol' southern mama moving in over the horizon all loving and sad and hopeful and rich with wetness. She's been through it all, this mama. All of it. Through so much in her time and cried so many tears, all she's got left is big wet love and protection. Been through so much that I feel ashamed for being so desperate and afraid. But she says it's all right and you go on, boy, you go on and cry and cry all you want. She takes me up in her big brown arms and puts my head in her big brown bosom and she rocks me so soft and heavenly I get to believing that nothing bad can ever happen, so that I don't cry out for fear of anything coming, I just shut my eyes real tight and cry to let out all the sad and painful past, all the things I remembered and all the things I remembered to forget, and disappear helpless like a newborn baby with his mama. But after all, she's just a sweet vision, a hallucination that starts to rain down on me real nice and hard and cool, wiping away all that goddamn furnace-red heat and making the sky and the air dark blue, deep and wet. And all the dust washes out of my hair and my clothes and my eyes, and oh boy, how I wipe it all away with scrubbing hands, washing in the rain and getting heavy with it and so no matter what I find out here on the godforsaken Delta, nobody can tell the tears from the rain and I still look a man, or at least a dumb boy with a straight back and fists and some pride to yell out with. Only, as nice as that vision is, as comforting as it is, I push it away real hard and squint my eyes over everything thin and hot, lest I go weak and submit to my fears and start to tremble in anticipation alone, which is never anything to tremble over unless you are really bad off.

But I'm not so bad off. I just need to find my love, my Laika. Then everything will be all right. Maybe I cry just a little bit then, but only because I'm so happy to find her and because I love her so much and maybe too just a little bit to release the sadness. Just need to find her, goddamn it. Then everything will be all right, I promise. Maybe I'll even go into the river with her and we can wash away our sins – all the things we remembered and the things we remembered to forget. But now with every fruitless minute that passes, I trade hope for fear, and not even the soothing notes of a memorable song help me to recognize my feet and hands, which, for the mounting fear, seem far away and borrowed. The happy tinkling of a song sorely out of place in this arid hell and I got no time for it and so suddenly the tune becomes a grievous annoyance for taking up precious space in my searing mind. Kill it!

This is Garfield, boy!

Don't mind my hands. Give your mother a kiss. Theys lambs about with blue hands, with blue bleating lips

And just then, lucidity rushes tinseled and wet to my aid. Fresh wet adrenaline courses through me, kicks in the doors like back-bar thugs eager, blood-covered and aching for more battle. Whoa! I rise large on a serpent's tail, soaking with electric adrenaline, shed a dusty cracked shell and writhe free now, a hideous wet reptile, dripping wet, with bulging eyes and flicking tongue sniffing, searching wet and ready, flick flicking, sniffing, ready to strike.

Irma, come feel the boy's head. Check if he has a temperature

Ho now! The familiar tinkling tune coming not from my head after all, but from the hard white van parked beyond the jutting patch of high-reaching weeds off the water and down in the burnt up ravine.

Footsteps come heavy up the stairs. A wolf show up in sheep's clothing.

My hands race back to me. Look! See how they come to me! See how they obey, these loyal gripping defenders, these greased wrenches, these wet metal hooks! I watch them curl and knot at my command, pull tight on stretched wire tendons.

Who got a necktie for the general?

See how they behave, my hands! Working now, gripping, flex and release, and my jaw too, and my arms that respond in kind, pumping now at grotesque angles. I smell burnt stars, burning in my head, shooting sharp-edged from childhood atmospheres that died long ago for me—the first taste of warm sticky blood coating the mouth and lips and baby teeth, thrust into adulthood, ready or not, the first hearty slam of an older boy's fist felled squarely onto my virgin mouth, struck dumb for a count, producing slow-motion showers of numb colorful sparks before my warm stunned eyes. We are never so brave and true and challenged as then, seven-years-old on a cement playground, learning to cope with the inevitability of fear and violence.

But it's got to be fixed!

Not that furnace, ma'am. That furnace is shot

No arbitrators, no foremen with which to file a grievance, no ma, no pops from whom to seek protection. Seven-years-old, can't look beyond patched-up flannel and corduroys for protection and comfort, and realize that that's OK, that that's all you really need.

Carpet falls like grass over the edge into the kitchen, it is green like Christmas, like parakeets. I pull at the carpet strands while bad news get delivered

Salty water run down my cheeks because I ain't old enough to touch rage and pain with tender child-hands and heart without coming to tears. The door slam and I cry bitter tears, throw punches into the mattress

But those childhood atmospheres exist for me only in the clouds that die trying to crawl over the western ridge. So here I stand, Gem, out here in this goddamned California valley, seven-years-old all over again, but now in the weeded body of a thistled twenty-five-year-old man, feeling hot vibrating waves of rage and pain emanating from the center of my bones. And these anxious hands that I can't put brakes on swipe down over the sides of my corduroys, teeth set on edge, recognize that old hot-metal taste in the back of my throat, and start to lean and fall forward toward that hard white van, and just like on the playground, when a boy accepts for the first time that there is nowhere to turn, nowhere to run, and realizes he can't shake what's in front of him, can't stop the inevitable, everything spins golden and summertime-slow. And there, that boy comes upon a strange and wonderful version of himself, a version he can bet on. This is where I find her, Gem, that lovely little blonde girl, my love, my Laika, alongside a golden Knoxville stud turned California surfer, with heaven-blue eyes and a gold-medal smile, there in the back of a hard white van. She lay there in his arms, a lime-green flurry, a confused childlike hallucination in a brand new cage.

This ain't California, Pop. This is Garfield.

Hey, Pop, you watch. I be the one to lick it!

Polish had sniffed thoroughly about the sticky floor for Gem's wallet, though to no avail.

"So help me, Calvin," said Gem, "Where is me bleedin' wallet?"

"Do *not* do this to me, Gemmo," said Calvin with the pleading hands of an Italian footballer. "When did you last have it?"

"I put it right here on this table," he said, making the table jump with his knuckles.

"Say again!" barked Calvin, stupefied.

"You heard me, mate. This table right here."

"I *did* hear you," Calvin steamed, "and clearly you don't know what you're saying. Surely, you mean your wallet was in your pocket!"

"Me *pock*et? Surely, I *don't* mean it was in me pocket," said Gem defiantly, "because it *was*n't. I put it right here on the focking table!"

Arbuckle and Polish surveyed the room, investigated sight lines and potential traps, calculated odds, angles of attack and lines of retreat. Gem blinked hotly. He was sufficiently self-critical of his error without Calvin's sarcastic reprimand. He despised having to take precautions to avoid being victimised. Gem contended that constructing walls around one's property was an act of defeat, and that doing so reinforced the notion that thievery was an irreversible force of life, and furthermore gave a manner of license to, and even encouraged, the asocial behaviour one was attempting to thwart. And also, Gem could never remember to stow his wallet.

"Don't be a prat, Calvin," warned Gem. "I put me wallet right here, and that's the fird and final time I'm going to tell you."

"OK," said Calvin. "Fair enough. I guess that's it, then," he concluded. "Arbuckle, Polish…"

The lads gathered round. Calvin looked at each of them and said, "Let's get this over with."

The three of them turned to Gem. Calvin took another deep breath and gave him an almost imperceptible nod. And with that, Gem bellowed to one and all, "All right you focking thieves! Which of you tasty bints wants to cough up me wallet like?"

There was no rhetoric in Gem's question, and when the only responses were disapproving sidelong glances, Gem dropped his hands onto the closest two or three bodies and went to work, searching, assaulting, working each over in a manner not dissimilar to the technique he had shown Calvin down at the port for handling big fish.

Adrenaline burst quickly through the manifolds of Calvin's machinery and brought him to a warm and familiar place, a place one generally prefers to avoid, though he may relish in some dark, thrilling, competitive manner when no choice is left him. Calvin and Arbuckle covered for Gem using knotty forearms and triceps to pin down small bands of resistance. Calvin's hands closed around shirt collars and necks and greasy layers of epidermal scruff. His forearms pressed against cheekbones and noses. Arbuckle, wiry and bent like pipe-cleaner, crackled under a crazed veneer, lunged at targets, took hold, twisted and debilitated bodily branches. The three were blind and deaf, guided only by heat, instinct and Polish Pete, who ran interference, howled threats and acted as the diminished crew's eyes and ears. The lads, frighteningly outnumbered, knew their only hope was that the element of surprise would render their adversaries – which amounted to the entire top-floor of the Whales – frozen in stupefaction long enough for them to regain the wallet before anyone came to with heroic notions.

The prospects of reclaiming the wallet and getting out quickly were never good. Calvin knew before climbing the stairs that it would prove to be a lost cause, but Gem paid no mind to luck or odds. His psychic drive train was powered by a single piston that furiously pumped out culturally defined static impulses. There was no wrenching his foot from the gas pedal. For Gem, at any such moment, there was one problem and one action-heavy solution for alleviating it—as pragmatic as bread for hunger.

Having found nothing incriminating on the first lot, Gem advanced to the next table and accosted those around it in kind. Calvin fended off a rush of blows from the rising swell of resistance. Arbuckle savagely swung a beer bottle, while struggling to keep at bay a corner of multiplying monkeys.

They were racing towards an ugly tipping point, a point at which they would have to concede the wallet and flee down the stairs and into the street as fast they could fly. The room reached a feverish flux. Bodies scattered, chairs and tables were toppled and heaved, pool balls flew, cues snapped, knees and elbows and dark intentions flexed and jerked with fiery angularity. The volume of the tumult thickened, escalated towards a bulky peak and then overflowed with viscous howling, guttural accusations and threats. The whole cumbersome sweat-box scene was perched hopelessly on a tight precipice, ready to hurtle downward at a sickening speed towards total violence and anarchy. The lads were seconds away from a full on barroom brawl, at which point they would be trapped and consumed.

Just then, as if recalled from a dream by a far-off alarm, the three came to at the repetitive wailing from Polish, who signaled the point of imperative retreat. With that, a tremendous scrum began sloshing down the stairs towards the band and a quickly shifting mass of dancing bodies. The band never missed a beat, only picked up pace and pitch. The mob spilt bruisingly into the street, diffusing a charge of white-hot energy from the capacitor that was the belly of the Whales.

The froth in the alleyway was thick. Gem still cuffed a few wet fish. Arbuckle and Polish were nowhere to be found. One particular bloke caught Calvin's eye—a mighty-looking fellow, thick as a Roman column, with a scorpion in prison-blue ink crawling up from his neck to the back of his shaved head.

"Wallet's gone, Gemmo!" yelled Calvin. "Time to go!"

Gem dropped his catch and ran up the alleyway towards Place Massena. Calvin raced after him, elated.

They flushed from the alleyway and into the verdant expanse of Place Massena, with its turquoise-blue fountains and its manicured lawns and flowered gardens. Calvin, breathless, laughed the lunatic laugh of the giddy, grateful as never before for the freedom of motion, easy breathing, clear vision and thumping pulse. Place Massena dazzled under the stars, birds of paradise glistened with dew, the cafés patiently awaited morning's bloom under the glow of golden streetlamps.

"Beautiful!" exclaimed Calvin, overwhelmed by the bounty of gifts. "Opulent!"

What pity for the fellow who failed to recognise each day one thing for which to be immensely grateful, or the man who, while cognizant of that one thing, nevertheless failed in his gratefulness.

It was too soon, however, for laughter and forgetting, for Gem was still out one wallet and had apparently not yet conceded the loss. On the contrary, he had rushed to Place Massena specifically for armament, for no sooner had he reached the garden than he launched a swift attack on a broad, squat palm. Calvin, now frozen in wild wonderment, concluded Gem punch drunk, and watched as he tore free an enormous frond, which was evilly lined with needle-sharp barbs. With his Excalibur in toe, Gem raced off, back towards the fracas, to finish the job. Jerked once again from a fragile state of tranquillity, Calvin gave chase.

By the grace of all gods and four gendarmes, the alley-side charge had been further diffused by the time the lads made it back to the Whales. In the mêlée, the glass door of a neighbouring restaurant had been smashed, and the damage supplanted the brawl as the focal point of attention. Gem, arriving with the palm frond, went completely unnoticed. Several of the youth, who had been punching and grappling only minutes prior, were now filing in and out of the dark restaurant, tip-toeing over shattered glass, all – astoundingly – under the watchful eyes of the gendarmes, who appeared bored and drowsy as they fielded unrelated questions, shrugged shoulders, blew air through puckered lips and advised care as it concerned all the broken glass. Gem was piqued by the thickness of neglect, while Calvin rejoiced in the fact that they had been spared flesh and hospital time.

In the calm of the pre-dawn morning, Gem recognised a pleading shining in Calvin's green eyes and finally dropped the palm frond.

The alleyway had been abandoned. Two gendarmes remained to watch idly over the restaurant until the proprietor arrived. They leaned languidly against a stone façade, smoked cigarettes, talked football and flicked ashes over glass embers still aglow with lamplight. An old man on a second-floor balcony sat in his briefs and undershirt and whistled *cantos degli Italiani*. In another hour the sun would begin its ascent to its morning station above the old chateau. Nothing ruffled the far southeast corner of the Republic.

Ambling off slowly, the lads decided to check in at Arbuckle's before turning in. Calvin assessed his damages, dabbing at his face and head with another ruined shirt and reading the results. For all of the crew's faults – and lord knows they had plenty – the manner in which they put their necks on the line for one other was admirable. Damned fortunate was the fellow with mates who lent him money in a pinch, stood him a proper meal or gave him a place to sleep when in need. But the fellow whose mates stood with him side-by-side in battle understood a deeper brotherhood. A fellow who is willing to chance a chunk of flesh for another—well, that is something. And when one walks the streets at night, he either knows he has a brother at his side, or he knows he is alone, which is not to say that there is merit in leading one's brothers into a slaughter. There were times when Calvin begged, screamed, cried, tackled Gem to the ground, even took swings at him in attempts to deter him from pursuing what seemed a certain suicide mission. Diffusing a hot situation or turning and running were consistently the best options. But whatever a crew might happen upon, it was addressed as a crew, not as individuals. And if one went down, the others rescued him or went down trying.

Calvin and Gem found five undamaged knuckles between the two of them and rapped gingerly at Arbuckle's door.

"Hello, gents!" issued Arbuckle in a hearty whisper. "What a grand sight you two make!" he said, emphatically embracing one and then the other.

All three of them winced and moaned in painful delight.

"I had to get Polish out of there. We just put him to bed," he said, stepping into the alleyway and easing the door shut behind him.

The lamplight gathered and kissed the many points of Arbuckle's face that were wet with damage.

"Handsome," said Gem. "That Nadine sure does fine needlework."

"That woman is something else!" demanded Arbuckle, beaming as can only the man who had long taken for granted one treasure or another and who finally came to realise the error of his ways before it was too late.

"We stumbled motley through the door, Polish and I," Arbuckle explained, "but Nadine—hell, she never batted a lash, only reached for the vodka and the first-aid kit, poured us three fingers each and went to work."

"How is Polish?" asked Calvin.

"He'll be OK. In his deepest delirium, he said he had never seen so many stars in all his Arabian nights. Nadine cleaned him up and stitched him good and I read to him from Cervantes until he fell asleep."

Arbuckle stood with a hand on his hip, hitched as a crooked walking stick, with a shining smile and eyes twinkling, strong and bright as Christmas Eve. When everything had been said, Arbuckle sent them home, told them to make a pot of coffee and clean up as best they could; Nadine would wake shortly and come round with the needles and thread.

16   All the Russian treasures

In which Klarysa packs her bags
and Calvin chases down a great
mammal.

Why are you not with her? As difficult as it was for him to
reconcile the strength of his desire and the distance that divided him
from the object of his desire, it was a question that stabbed at Calvin,
waking him in the night long after his bodily wounds had healed. In
bed beneath the stars, when logic loops and loops and cracks, this
object would blur, morph between elusive body that could not be
pinned down (or even be made to sit still long enough to be outlined)
and graspable idea that lay motionless for interview and inspection,
like an old dog awaiting the caressing hand of its master to fall
lovingly upon its belly. At dawn's break, just before rising, on yet
another plane of wakefulness, one unfettered by expectations, the
object was openly challenged—was Klarysa the object for which
Calvin's desires burned, or was it all the qualities that she could
offer a lonely fellow, those which might be afforded by any other
healthy young woman? Come the light of day, adequately distracted
by the cacophony of stimuli that at once bolsters the world and
drives it batty, Klarysa was clearly his answer, clearly the object.

Despite his conviction, there were questions that only time
could answer. And though he was still prone to committing to
unachievable star-spangled causes, Calvin was beyond the age of
doubling down with conviction merely as a fool's attempt at
influencing something ultimately beyond one's control. But if brain

blisters from nocturnal ramblings were the analytical counterweight that balanced Calvin's mental lever and resulted in the sound psychological physics that some call wisdom, then his failure with Victoria was the dark art that jumped from great heights onto the amatory side of the teeter-totter (the one occupied by unmitigated risk and blind commitment) and blasted sound science and logic into outer space, where it could not needle a determined lover, nor hinder him from shooting down a youthful path of decidedly little resistance. To be sure, Calvin still lost sleep at night, but not a minute was lost over uncertainty concerning a commitment to Klarysa, for he had long ago decided that he would eventually badger her, if that's what it took, until she agreed to live with him.

He approached the telephone for the first time in a fortnight – the first time since the great telephonic invasion – with a pinch of paranoia, and eyed it with suspicion, mulling over the chances that it might once again bite if he put his ear to it. This time around, however, there were no spies, no codenames, only the normal droning dial tone, a mono-tonal aria to Calvin's tentative ears.

"Oh, lover, you can't possibly move to Barcelona," Klarysa retorted. "Not just like that. One doesn't just move cities on a whim, you know; much less countries. There are considerations— electricity, phone service, mail. Why, whatever did you envision in the way of work?"

"Gutting fish, I suppose. Never enough fish gutters," he mused, "in any decent port town."

"Fish? Oh, no, not in *these* waters," she said.

"No fish around the Catalan bend, there?"

"Not that I'm aware of."

"Rather certain there might be."

"By all means, no."

Well, hell, Calvin didn't particularly care to leave Nice anyway, but in instigating talk of a move, he did feel inclined to show willingness towards effort and motion.

"I don't suppose," he began with little hope, "you'd consider a move to Nice. I've plenty of room here for two."

"Are you asking me to move to *Nice*?"

"I am."

"Really? You know how I love the Baie des Anges. Oh, do you remember, my love, the gorgeous afternoon we shared above Cap d'Ail?"

An unexpected dagger of hope ripped through a thick canvas of mental cloud cover.

"Of course I still remember," he declared. "I've never forgotten—despite my age, as you like to say, ha-ha! Well, what do you think?"

"Wow! Just think of it," she cried, "*me* on the Cote d'Azur!"

"Say the word and I'll send you a ticket."

"To tell you the truth, my love," she began, and then paused to dab pre-emptively, or so Calvin speculated, at the gathering tears of joy, "nothing would make me happier."

"Oh, Klarysa, consider it done!"

"If only, only, only such an arrangement were re*mote*ly plausible."

"Wha?"

"Can I say that? Plausible?" she sought, apparently not quite attached to the gist of the conversation – that of spending their lives together – in the same manner as was Calvin. "Well, can I? For you I want to speak a native's English."

"Yes, fine, fine, but—"

"But nothing, I'm afraid. You know as well as I do that it's simply not possible, *or* plausible for that matter. In fact it's *im*-possible. That's what it is—utterly and completely im*poss*ible."

Calvin was at a loss for words. Unsure as to how to carry on from there, he mumbled nonsense in an irked manner until she pointedly informed him that she was quite certain no native speaker could make heads or tails of such gibberish.

"Look, I miss you," he clarified. "I want to be with you. I want you to be more than my mistress."

"My love," she passionately replied, "I miss you and want to be with you, too. But please, I'm not your mistress," which did make him feel marginally better, until he realised he wasn't exactly sure if she had said, "I'm not your *mis*tress," or, "I'm not *your* mistress."

Calvin found himself falling down a demoralising well in which certain phrases that were unequivocally spoken to convey broad and powerful swaths of love produced absolutely no feelings of love whatsoever—a torturous well in which, on the contrary, every subsequent love-line only served to drag a fellow deeper into despair. And at that point, it was hard to know who, if anyone, was to blame—"You know," he said, "I might not be around terribly much longer."—and furthermore led one to reach desperately for corny, melodramatic lines that are no sooner blurted than regretted.

But words can never be unsaid, and fearing the reproach due Calvin-as-clammy-brat, he fled defensively into a colourful pastiche pulled together of local anecdotes, conspiracies and cabals through which Klarysa, with audible restlessness, suffered. With no signs of abatement, Calvin blathered on about a bleak personal future, as verbally and symbolically forecasted by gun-flashing thugs, cautionary alley-side henchmen, knife-bequeathing flamingos, stolen wallets and mounting violence, charted steps by no-account spooks from whom he, Calvin, apparently lacked approval for perfectly benign café-side chats with a caviar-pushing, Kalashnikov-strapping, Ally-approved Balkan representative, et cetera, et cetera, so on and so forth. And how funny, he continued, that Nice should be found more than suitable for dwelling by half the bloody citizens of Russia and their godforsaken artefacts, antiques and treasures – not to mention their Danish Jubilees – for crissake; but oh no, not good enough for her, Klarysa, his little Ukrainian sugar-bunion.

And there did fall at some point during his verbal unravelling, on Klarysa's end of the line, a steady calm, followed by a perceptible hum of attentiveness, followed by vocal chirps of interest. These chirps and tweedles of hers did once or twice precede a curt, "*What?*" or a "*What did you say?*" And though he repeated himself clearly after each interjection (these that were so uncharacteristic of a generally incurious girl), and enunciated his words slowly and to the point of tongue-tapping, lip-smacking absurdity, she stabbed yet anew, "*What!*" with the brassy *T* of a high-hat cymbal and diction that favoured exclamation over interrogation. And so at that point, not only still dejected, but now, too, annoyed, it was his turn to respond, "*What!*" (his *what* favouring accusation), to which she replied, "Oh, nothing. Nothing at all, dear," and, "Don't you worry, my love," and, "But shouldn't I be moving to Nice, and quite as quickly as possible at that?"

Stunned by her sudden change of heart, he managed only a bewildered grunt.

"My love, my love," she applied, "I had no idea the trials you're up against. Why, it seems you're perfectly lost without your sugar-muffin. I must come directly, you poor thing. Do send a ticket at once, won't you?"

He sent the ticket the following day, and she arrived the day after that—a decidedly tight and calibrated little twig, her, alert and ready to spring forward towards some undeclared objective. "Ah," breathed Calvin deeply. "The verve of youth!"

What by all counts must have been the first ever taxi van to snake its way into the cobbled heart of old Nice and onto Rue Benoit Bunico, dropped Klarysa at number 22. Calvin, having raced down from the balcony, made to pay the driver when a second taxi van pulled up behind the first. Both drivers jumped with untold alacrity from their pilot positions and turned stevedores, unloading their voluminous holds with port efficiency.

"Thank you, my love," said Klarysa to Calvin, curling closed his fingers around his pale and laughingly insufficient two-hundred-franc note. "It's taken care of."

"Look at the size of that crate!" he exclaimed. "Should I not at least tip them for the handling? What's in there, anyway?"

"Crated things, of course. It's taken care of, dear."

At length, the oversized taxis were emptied. The sweating drivers thanked Klarysa profusely, as though for miracles rendered. They eventually regained their driver's seats and pulled away, sounding their horns long after they had disappeared.

With good cheer, Calvin began hauling Klarysa's belongings up the four flights of stairs. There were two stuffed suitcases, both nearly splitting at the seams and heavy as lead. Then there were the trunks, the chests, the crates, the boxes, the bags and the satchels.

"If your flatmate Natalia is packed away in one of these, perhaps she could walk from here, ha-ha!"

"You don't regret having asked me to come, Calvin, do you?"

"Hold that live tongue of yours! Don't even toy about such things."

After countless trips up and down, with limbs on the edge of bursting and his back half in the bag, Calvin solicited the aid of a young turk in the alley to help him with Klarysa's big-ticket affairs.

"In the future," the child advised Calvin, "call my cousin. He owns a removal company. He'll give you a sound deal next time you're moving flats."

"Moving flats! Wonderful! I had no idea. I thought this was to be an out-patient operation."

With the move completed, Calvin had taken to icing down hoofs and haunches, when Klarysa, who had busied herself with the task of taking inventory, noticed a single box was missing.

"Ah, yes," Calvin concurred, "the one I used to prop open the *portail*. Not good, not good. I'd better hustle down."

"Wait!" she cried, intercepting him at the door, lacing her hands behind his back and pulling him gently closer. "Thank you, my love. I mean for everything. I'm thrilled to be here. Oh, the places we'll go, the treasures we'll find!"

"What a great pleasure it all is," he agreed, kissing her warmly.

He slipped through the door and closed it behind him. There he paused for a count to let shoot the head-rush of love-rockets that quite literally blinded him, and let flow the blood that had slowed in his numb, iced feet.

With clearing vision, Calvin saw before him a large brown walrus, which, upon spotting, spun an abrupt about-face and waddled away down the short landing, towards the head of the stairwell. No need to run off, thought Calvin. In singular spirits, he bade, "Good evening, sir. You were coming to see me, were you? How may I help?"

But the man – yes, now with eyesight fully restored, Calvin identified the receding beast as a man, rather than marine mammal – neither returned the greeting, nor broke stride.

"Hello, sir," Calvin shot anew. "We are indeed home. This way, please."

Nothing.

"Well doesn't that just strike you," he mumbled to himself. "The English!"

It was not uncommon for proprietors to let their flats to tourists throughout the year, and Calvin was fascinated by the manner in which different nationalities responded to a friendly *bonjour* during chance encounters in the stairwell. The French did not speak until spoken to, and then echoed every voiced sentiment with sober politesse. Germans gave a hearty *bonjour*, offered a brief weather report and an unknown fact about the town or region. Americans locked down their fears and insecurities linked to linguistic deficiencies and cross-cultural inexperience, and did their nervous best to make it through unscathed. Italians smiled wide, asked humorous questions for the fun of it, shook hands and gave compliments. The Irish greeted with civility and reservation, courteously answered any question in three words or less and moved on. Aussies were surprisingly aloof and suspicious. And then there were the English, who tucked their chins to their chests and made a run for it, frightened to near death, it would seem, at the prospect of having to greet a stranger in the stairwell.

But as has been established, Calvin presently enjoyed a full red heart, and so he shrugged, and without any further appeal, allowed to disappear down the first bend of stairs the sullen broad-backed figure in the brown herringbone coat.

Brown herringbone coat?

Much easier to break out in a cold sweat when one is already iced from the waist upon encountering his spooks, and indeed there was Calvin with an instantaneous jungle humidity flourishing about the cheeks, chest and temples, as he fell forward and hobbled after the man, down the stairs, uncertainly, on still-icy stumps.

At the third landing he shouted after the man, "Hello, sir! Excuse me! Please, a quick word with you if you would be so kind."

A brown herringbone coat, he thought—there must be hundreds worn in the city each day. At the second landing, he implored, "If you won't stop, perhaps you could slow your pace just a titch, that I might catch you." Oh, dippy optimism, he had to admit.

At the first landing his *sang froid* had turned hot—good for the toes, bad for the brain. "By god, if that coat is stuck with a lapel pin... *Arrête*! Stop!" he demanded, gaining ground on the assailant.

On the ground floor, just before the front gate, Calvin reached out, grabbed the man by the shoulder and spun him about. And sure enough, confirming his mounting fear, there they sat, squarely on the lapel—two twin herding dogs cast in silver, each with a saliva-catch surgically attached to its muzzle.

"You again!" Calvin gasped, dizzy with shock. "Who are you!"

But Calvin's catch was the size of a deep-water Pacific halibut – that is to say the size of a side-by-side refrigerator-freezer – and with a fervent yank, he freed himself of Calvin's grip and disappeared with a burst that was impressive for his age.

17   The loneliest place on earth

In which Calvin has a thought to
draw blood from the golden calf
and vultures block his sun.

Calvin woke in the morning, flat on his back. He had laid his
head on the pillow some hours past midnight and hadn't so much as
twitched until morning. The prior evening – the twenty-first to have
passed since Klarysa's move to Nice – was another one for the
books. He stared up at the highway-like network of cracks in the
ceiling that led from town to town (dimpled plaster impressions) and
city to city (intersections where the cracks had caused the plaster to
give way and fall) and dreamt of swan-diving through whatever
rabbit hole might let him ride one of those cracks away to a new
town, where he might have a fresh go at things. He would be sure to
steer well clear any of the towns adjacent to the curl of paint that
peeled away from the ceiling-sea near the corner of the room, for it
resembled a breaking wave of white-water, and seaside towns, he
concluded, take a damned hearty toll on a fellow.

The mid-morning sun salivated through the top-floor window,
devouring Calvin with fork and knife, while Klarysa lay cool and
clean on the other side of the bed. Were felines, he wondered, ever
uncomfortable? He stood, he stretched, he tried to feel invigorated,
tried to sniff out any small victory. Poking his head out the window,
the buttery scent of fresh croissants came wafting up through the
void between the buildings. Traditionally, for Calvin, whose greatest
strategies and efforts went towards avoiding the nets of modern life,

which he was convinced were wide and active and sought to catch a fellow and put him on ice, croissants and a cup of strong coffee in the morning usually sufficed to steady his vision and set the world straight. That morning, however, the croissant and coffee would have their work cut out. He moved to the kitchen and prepared the kettle, then put needle to a Serge Gainsbourg record and moved to the balcony. Leaning against the balcony railing, it occurred to him that in America, life was lived only for the future, which, of course, was always at least a day away; whereas in France, there was no future. There was only a past, which was kept in an ornate gilded frame, and more days to follow—endless days, but no future; simply more and more days, stretching towards eternity. Both realities were flawed.

Calvin and Klarysa decided to spend the day at the beach. They crossed over the Promenade, descended the stairs of the break wall and spread two towels over the grey stones just down from Castel Plage.

Ten o'clock in the morning was the finest hour on a Mediterranean beach. One thought of crystalline sugar – sharp-lined, refractive, everything sparkling thin and new – versus the afternoon hours, when the aging sun was not so good-humoured, and everything under it turned glazed and meaty. There, sometime before noon, the pulse was energetic, the mood young and elastic.

Calvin and Klarysa lay on the communal bed of beach stones and argued points from the prior evening. With the sun lasciviously licking her softness, she said to him, "Fine, but you can't very well blame Donato. That club will raise the devil from a fellow, what with all the skin and that Latin music."

"Donato. The fellow has a name."

"I suspect it was given him at birth," she provoked. "They do that in Calabria."

The prior evening, Klarysa was sprawled out on the divan, flipping through a picture book of cats (a veritable kindle of kittens in a fisherman's flat, thought Calvin) when she cast aside the book and said to him, "Calvin, darling, I'm bored. Cheer me up."

"What would you like to do?" he asked. "Want to go out for ice cream? Take a walk around the port? We could go dancing."

Bingo. Klarysa decided she wanted to dance, and when Klarysa wanted to dance, one took her dancing. She wanted to dance, she said, like they did at La Paloma in old Barcelona. There was no choice but to take her to La Bodeguita del Havana on the other side of Place Massena. She liked the name. She was convinced that all the right people would be dancing there and that the band would play all the right numbers.

"And what if I blame *you*?" he challenged.

"Absurd."

"You, after all, were the one baring so much skin."

"It's a backless dress, Calvin, what choice did I possibly have in the matter?"

He had lost her at one point during the evening. Having returned from the bar with a couple of Rusty Nails – she was mad about Drambuie – she was nowhere to be seen. At long last, he found her in a dark corner with a dark young fellow, speaking very closely. Calvin had convinced himself, while granting her the thin benefit of steep doubt, that such closeness was indeed essential for any old humdrum conversation, due to the pitch and volume of the horns in the hot Cuban number that, for the love of Satan, blared on and on and on.

"It is a *fright*eningly sexy dress," she admitted, as though startled by the sudden realisation. "I'll grant you that. Anyway, it didn't mean a thing. You men are all alike—you want to cage a woman."

"That's not fair. I've never tried to cage you."

"Not you; *him*."

"Oh, he wants to cage you, does he? You weren't exactly flapping for freedom. It looked a hell of a lot like you know that guy."

"He's from around town, if that's what you mean."

"No, that's not what I mean, unless you mean to say you know every guy in town."

"Of course I don't know *every* guy."

By god, he thought, what was the little hellcat doing all day while he was out scraping fish shit and picking scales from his eyelids—carousing?

"I couldn't find the Ladies' room," she defended, "so I asked Donato. He's a chef at one of the Italian restaurants. He told me I was *la cosa più carina pictola* he had seen in a long time—that means *the cutest little thing*. I don't speak Italian, but I *do* know that much." She was beaming.

"Is that right? And did he know where the goddamned toilets were?"

She deigned to respond.

"I tell you quite often you're the most beautiful thing I've ever seen."

"That's just hyperbole," she dismissed. "Besides, you're my boyfriend."

"It's the cross I bear, I suppose."

At any rate, thought Calvin, no bloody trumpets could justify the closeness that followed, there in that dark corner of the club. "Calabria," Calvin mumbled to himself. "Diana—goddess of the hunt. Dionysus—god of wine. Donato—god of my fist in his fucking face."

Just then, no longer able to contain her emotions, she spilt herself onto Calvin's chest like a wavelet that lapped up from nowhere onto an unsuspecting shore, and cried passionately, "Oh, darling, quick—tell me I'm gorgeous!"

"Why—what?"

"Promise you'll never say I'm cute. It's a tragic word. Rather, tell me I'm *gorgeous*," she gushed, pressing moist lips to his. "Now there's a word – a *gorgeous* word – my favourite in all your language. Oh please, Calvin, say it. And *do* make it quick."

In love with her and her odd little quips, he chuckled and complied, "Let there be no doubt, *mon petit canard lacqué*, you are gorgeous."

It was a lie. Klarysa could claim any number of flattering adjectives, but *gorgeous* was not one of them. Gorgeous belonged to a woman of greater deliberation, one slower to fire, slower to freeze. The points of combustion and freezing that marked the polar extremes of Klarysa's behavioural scale were but a kitten's breath separated. Gorgeous belonged to a woman with a depth of beauty that one may in fact miss upon first glance, but that becomes more evident with each subsequent encounter, whereas Klarysa's beauty struck a fellow like lightning, then diffused and resided epidermally, on the tip of her button nose and in the rose-pink of her cheeks. To be sure, gorgeous belonged to a woman of greater physical stature than that of Calvin's fiery little sprite. A lioness is gorgeous in a way that a best-in-show Abyssinian can never be. A sixteen-year-old may be considered gorgeous, but only if she can pass for twenty-four, and although Klarysa (of twenty-four years and karats, both) was alluring, tantalising and adorable, she did not qualify as gorgeous in part because she could barely pass for sixteen. She was the first woman Calvin had ever seen refused drink at a French café. (It should be noted, however, that it was only a matter of four seconds, three bats of the lashes and two pouting lips before the barman rescinded his refusal, after which she drank expensive champagne until closing, on the barman's offer, while Calvin sucked on cut-rate lager and earned a bill for his efforts.) To be most precise, Klarysa was cute—cute as sin. Calvin had always preferred cute to gorgeous, and that was a contributing factor in his demise, for cute women were constantly trying to prove themselves as women, and the most direct route to womanhood is, of course, through the body. To put an end to this nonsense, let it be said that while Klarysa was a pixie of angelic visage and flawless proportions, she was clearly a good six inches shy of gorgeous.

"Well," she began, abandoning his chest for her towel, "I know *you* don't think I'm gorgeous."

It was bait, and poor bait at that. Calvin said nothing. He knew well enough not to bite, so she resorted to the equivalent of a big-game rifle.

"And *nei*ther," she continued, watching him askance, "does the handsome butcher at the corner."

"What do you mean the butcher at the corner?"

Et voila, she brought down a big dumb beast.

"He says I'm too small to be gorgeous."

"You mean *the* Butcher? *Our* Butcher?"

"Oh, sure, *that* lout," she said sarcastically. "Of course not. No, the handsome, dark-eyed butcher downstairs. He's a *real* butcher, by the way, not a peddler of cheap smut to a bunch of bloodless Brits. Why, don't tell me you haven't noticed him, what with his dark curls and big black eyes. Oh, hell," she boiled, "what does he know about beauty, anyway; hacking away at dead meat all day."

"Is his opinion of you really so vital?" asked Calvin, prepared for a long, drawn-out slog through which she would argue that he was overly jealous and he would counter that he simply had no desire to discuss all the compliments she had successfully solicited about town.

But to his great surprise, she paused for a beat and then declared, "Oh, you're right."

She spun back towards him, as instantly ebullient as a pouting four-year-old upon finding a shiny nickel.

"You are absolutely right, Calvin. Who is *he*, anyway?" She rested her chin heavily on his chest. It hurt like hell, but it was a loving pain. "You know how to make me smile don't you, my love? I do love you so."

"I love you, too."

Calvin propped up his head with one hand. With the other, he guided back behind Klarysa's ear a long strand of hair that had come loose of her ponytail. "All relationships have their challenges, you know," he cited, "and ours—hell, we've been separated for most of it. We have a lot to learn, but I know we can be good for each other. We just need to—"

"Besides," she bubbled anew, "the man at Sephora said I'm abso*lute*ly gorgeous and *that* man has class."

"For the love of—!"

"He is a real gentleman. One can tell by the way he puts his hands... Well, it's quite simply evident. Also, he wears a jet black suit with a crisp white shirt and a black tie. So very handsome."

"Interesting," Calvin steamed.

"Everything is always interesting to you. There is no single thing in this wide world that you don't find interesting."

"It doesn't seem to mean anything to you when I extend you such compliments. Do you not believe me?"

"Forgive me if I don't believe you, lover. You find me *cute*, and that's the extent of it. It's not terribly enticing."

Calvin amazed and disappointed himself by how deeply he allowed himself to be pulled into such sinking arguments. "So," he began, despite himself, "the handsome butcher and I have fallen out of your good graces, is that it?"

"You two and the fellow at the casino."

"I see. You couldn't negotiate gorgeous with him either?"

"If you're insinuating that I fish for compliments—"

"I am."

"Nothing could be farther from the truth."

"My apologies," he said, embittered. "Which casino, anyway?"

"Casino Ruhl."

"And I know for a fact that they wear black suits, crisp white shirts and black ties at Casino Ruhl. They *must* be gentlemen."

"Please," she snapped. "Don't let's compare a lousy croupier to the manager at Sephora. What now?"

"I didn't know they employed men at Sephora."

"They do sell men's products."

"I did not know."

"If you wore cologne once in a while," she tried without conviction, "perhaps you would know."

"I do wear cologne and you often tell me how much you like the scent."

"It is true; I adore the way you smell, my love. Most of the time, anyway... Whenever it's not *eau de poisson*."

She planted a long, heady kiss on his lips.

"*You* really are gorgeous, mister, even though you don't think the same of me."

"But I—"

"It's OK, I still love you terribly." With that, she slipped off him with a nettled sigh. "It's bloody hot to-day. You know, *you* might consider buying a tie of some sort. It might lend you an air of credibility."

"You don't say."

"What a strange expression—I *do* say."

Calvin rose and eased his way over the hot stones, down to the water's edge. She detested his strings of silence, the ones with which he bound his forked tongue when the urge was there to lash out with something cruel and hurtful. He filled his lungs with clean briny air and stood for a moment, envious of the sea's easy repose—blue-green perfection as far as the eye could see, some thousand blues alight in softly sighing concert. The sea could be temperamental, he pondered, but it never spoke nasty words to a girl. He stepped in, to the knees, and dove smooth and long, as he had done a million times, long and shallow, and then angling deeper as the seafloor fell away and the blues became darker and cooler. He came to the surface and used long athletic strokes to pull himself out towards the far buoys, where the voices of mankind could no longer be heard. The only sound was that of the sea – long a friendly and soothing language to Calvin, if forever incomprehensible to the city boy – interrupted here and there by the soft whir of one far-off propeller or another. Looking back towards the crescent shoreline, he saw the holiday mirage depicted on picture-postcards, the soft swell of pastel structures capped by burnt-orange rooftops rising along the rim of a grand, antique bowl of yesteryear blue. The vision was perfectly still, peaceful. He resolved right then and there that all things were so simple wherever he was not.

It wasn't nearly always this way, he thought. The last couple of years had been largely filled with sea-days, those that flooded and ebbed without effort, blue and cool. There was the loss of Victoria of course, which resulted in a stretch of sleepless nights promoted by relentless critique and self-reproach. But even then, after the deepest darkest nights had been survived, there arose an intense sun that smiled and winked brilliantly over the rebirth of a strong young man who looked with wet, new eyes upon all the vibrant objects shivering joyously around him. There came new edges to previously amorphous tendencies, craftily conceived mechanics worked into long swaths of time that had been filled with foam and idle stuffing, and bold new intentions unveiled with great optimism. Why, not long ago, while alone on a typical aimless weekend walk about town, Calvin found himself awestruck by a simple and wondrous sight—a golden dome set majestically against a ripping blue sky. The Mistral blew down through the Rhone Valley and made a heady breeze along the coast, driving whitecaps beyond the protected edge of the bay. Select runaway clouds, wispy dreams of lace, hurried past on the cooling breeze.

Calvin could sit and stare trancelike at clouds for unbroken hours, filled with ecstasy and a wild nostalgic joy that contained all the days and memories of his lifetime. The sky and its clouds filled him with the invincible hormonal joy that only those far younger than he knew with any consistency. It almost frightened him how much he was taken by the clouds and the manner with which they melded and shifted, so alive, so knowing, silently reflecting through some inexplicable means all of the details of his worked life—so high and bright in the sky, so full of sunny afterlife and optimism. And so, too, how the nostalgia ravaged him upon his discovery that all the lost days of one's life lived on in the vast blue sky. That after all the failed head-smashing and tearful attempts to grab onto something solid, to halt the entropy, to finally find meaning and open an inner eye to wakefulness, one could – *there in the skies* – recapture and relive, not the visions, but the sensations and emotions of one's ecstatic days, in stunning familiarity, if only for rare sparks of time, slippery partial seconds.

What fellow, after all, could anticipate arriving at the day when he would recognise a perfect love affair with the sky and clouds, especially when he was young and on top and had the flash in his eyes, when he was engaged in digging the dark night with fists and boots and claws—those wild, slash-eyed days and nights when one made all the big decisions that went to forming the root structure of a man's existence? Why, by the time one realised the depth and ardour of his love for sky and clouds, all the biggest decisions had been made, the biggest battles already fought, and one was more or less stuck with the *wheres* and *whats* and *whos* resulting from all those mad decisions and battles. Kicking himself for all his unconscionably foolish and wasteful antics, one was stuck with what one had—and what one did not have, like the most precious angel he had ever known and who loved him to the core and so far beyond. And it was only then, when he was lying slipshod and prostrate on the bed, helplessly in love and trying to contain a bulging and bleeding heart, a heart that was nearly exploding for the far-reaching skies, his long-lost youth and his long-lost girl—yes, it was only then, when he was far beyond his hammering prime that he realised with great lucidity just exactly how wonderful it might all be had he the foresight back then, goddamn it, to have done things the right way, to have valued nothing more than that girl and those *fin du monde* clouds! And then maybe, just maybe, instead of lying there on the brink of asphyxia and breakdown, he might know breath – and with his girl at his side, no less – as he gaped shiny-eyed into that dreamy god-filled endless sky.

Full sunlight struck the golden dome, like a hammer, sending blinding rays back into the endless blue. And there stood Calvin, frozen, captured, staring into something enormous, overcome by an indescribable joy. He tried, in his state of ecstasy, to put a name to the sensation. It was, after all, only a dome and a blue sky. But oh, what the vision catalyzed within him!—something nameless, something beyond description. A manner of ecstatic perfection that one experienced perhaps no more so than at the age of four or five, while sitting and scratching at a sun-warmed sidewalk with a rock, or watching a single black ant crawl into and out of a jagged crack of broken sidewalk cement, completely lost in wonder, eclipsed and done in by golden fantasy without limit, without end. He stood there, frozen by awe, and so too *recognising* (something not possible for the four-year-old) the chance opportunity and the god-blessed wherewithal to experience that boundless youthful bliss.

The miracle sensation hit him in a flash. He stared, lost and elated, basking in the glow of the feeling; then took his eyes away and looked about for relativity; then looked back at the dome and looked away again. Life burst in colour all around him. All sounds were symphonic, not in the sense of an orchestrated beauty, but rather in the perfection of their appropriateness. In childlike wonder, at the centre of one's universe, simple yet brilliant wonders abound—the wonder of sun on a green awning, the wonder of a sunny street curb, the whirl of a bicycle rolling past with sunlight reflecting madly off its chrome parts. He looked back at the dome, the blue sky raged beyond; in it burst the sensational essence of his greatest days. He looked away again, inhaled deeply to tie the experience to the aroma of the day, felt the hairs rise on his arms, came very nearly to tears with the knowledge – a knowledge truer, fuller and more powerful than any he had ever known – that this rare and fleeting moment approached a manner of nirvana, that this very moment was *everything*. The sensation born of the gold dome shining against the blue sky was the very beginning and the very end. There was nothing more and never would there be anything bigger, more powerful or more important.

Though, too, he recognised the need to focus on the sensation and coach it along, keep it flowing. He could otherwise sense a fear, there, standing at the crisp, brilliant summit, knowing that it was a fleeting moment, that the sun would soon shift and the reflection would die and the world would return to its pallor and thickness. And then, suddenly, it was gone. It had to come to an end—of course, the planet would not sit still. Though never could he have predicted the speed and violence of the plummet from such great heights. Lowering his gaze from the dome to street level, everything had returned to its monotony of decay. The nausea rushed in. Death hung everywhere—death in stillness, death in motion, madness, mayhem, tears, fear, the mounting pain of the world wrapped in shades of grey and epoxy. Anxiety rushed in and took hold. Having witnessed it all in a single moment – free release, the purest essence of other-worldly bliss – how was one to move forward? How was one to climb the stairs to an old flat? How was he to keep his feet on the ground? How was such a fellow to ever again reach for a newspaper, much less read the timeless drivel that filled its pages?

How was he to engage, to concern himself with automobile sales, or property values, or insurance policies, or consumer indices? How was he to vote for one lying politician or another, when each was a ravenous self-promoting criminal? How was he to go through the paces demanded by this decrepit, dying world? Oh, God, there was simply no choice but to shut down, to turn off, to – in a sense – kill oneself. Not shut down the body, but deceive the heart and spirit, tell them lies and abuse them, try to convince one's heart and soul that this is simply the life of modern man in the modern world. But shy of that, before throwing in the towel and conceding victory – and life itself! – take every conceivable measure to stay connected to the sun and the sky and the clouds and the truth and endlessness contained therein.

My god, thought Calvin suddenly, rising to revelation—my fish! My fish, my chopping block, my gutting table under the sun, in the unfiltered air. That was the answer! What a blessing! What treasures! Rejoice all fish mongers, all gardeners, all ditch diggers—you are only a step away from heaven! Some judge harshly this modern world, but what demands can be made of the dead and their dead leaders? Where was the living element of life to the fellow who ripped himself up from bed in the dark of night and strapped himself in behind a wheel, to cough and choke and curse and honk his way down gridlocked streets and highways, only to lock himself in an office where he – from the mail boy to the chairman – was nothing more than an implement, a tool; and where he strapped himself blank-faced and indebted to all his shiny death mechanisms, day after day after day? Why, such a man is obliged to murder himself every single morning, whip and beat and murder himself, at least until there was no curious, rosy matter left twitching inside him. Dear God, begged Calvin, only allow me to gut fish, to dig ditches for the rest of my days! Under the blinding sun and the running skies, where I might breathe, huff and swallow the whipping winds! Where my arms and legs flex and grip and lift and thrust! Where my head flies freely in and out of far-flung dreams! Let my skin blister and chafe, let my bones crack, if that's what it comes to. But grant me the sun and the clouds and kindness and truth!

Oh, poor dead West! he raved. You that cry dead tears for the living! You that project your emptiness onto those with so much, having never left your plush, isolated bunker that you might have otherwise noticed the rest of the world shimmering brightly! You whose tunnel-vision has become so clogged and cynical that you are unable to comprehend the lives led beyond your borders, those lived in full rich colour. You that scramble in desperation for the next gadget after the failure of yesterday's gadgets to bring meaning to your life. The nausea overwhelmed him. Please, God; please, God; oh, please God, only keep my back straight and strong that I may dig ditches for the rest of my sweet days!

The earth shifted, the vision was gone and the slog began; a slog during which he would be ridiculed by anyone privy to his manic internal ramblings. A manner of paranoia moved in, realising the failure he would come to know, were he to ever try to articulate what he had just experienced in staring at that dome against the blue sky. Anxiety riddled him, as he stood weak and alone, a condemned lunatic who failed time after time to defend his truth before folks like Sandoval, whose fathers had – just as their fathers had, and their fathers had – convinced them that freedom was measured by the ease with which a man could found a business. But hell, for that briefest moment before the sun had shifted, as he was staring up and watching like a helpless, gurgling, knowing child – *watching himself watching* – well hell, the lad knew that he had indeed lived. And beyond that, for what more, really, can one ask?

But now, yes, and rather suddenly, too, it seemed, the once benevolent old town had developed pointy edges that took to poking him when he rounded corners, dark or light. Flowers now snapped at him, forks now pricked him, not to mention the animate objects that took to heckling him. He once sang freely and laughed heartily, but of late it was all whispers and hushes, screams and cries and defensive stands made both verbally and physically.

Who was this man with the lapel pin, he whose silver canines might wait endlessly, dogging Calvin high and low until... until when—until he went mad with paranoia and confessed to everything? Hell, he would confess right there and then, at Castel Plage, only he had no idea of what he should come clean. Still, he could not absolve himself of some nebulous culpability. He tried to speak with Klarysa about the matter, but she was not vulnerable to such pecking concerns and could not empathise with those who were.

He swam back to the beach, rinsed off under a cold shower and rejoined Klarysa. She had cooled off under a shower while he was out to sea, and was still wet. He stood above her and watched a million and one tiny rainbows refracting through the droplets on her golden figure. (The golden calf, he pondered.) An aggressive idea materialised in his mind, to lick her dry and take a piercing little bite while he was at it; draw a spot blood and watch her bleed, the sharp little fawn. He shook the unnerving thought from his head and laid himself out across his towel.

After a moment, Klarysa said, "The Butcher was here."

"You know what," replied Calvin, "you do whatever the hell you want. I'll take care of myself."

"No, I mean *the* Butcher," she clarified, and then added in a manner of unsavoury submission to Calvin, "*our* Butcher," and with it, made an unsavoury face.

"Oh," he said. "I see. Did he have anything to say?"

"Not a single word," she said.

"Not one word?"

"I just said so."

The Butcher was English and out of shape, and Klarysa was Eastern and spoken for. They were perfectly irrelevant to one another.

"He stood right here for a whole minute, in silence, looking out to sea, like a dumb dog waiting for his owner to come home." Then she pointed and said, "Now he's up there."

Calvin looked and saw the Butcher sitting slumped and alone on the break wall.

"Oh, brother."

"What's he doing up there?" she asked. "He looks awful."

"It's the valium."

"He looks like a beach ball, only without the colour and the air."

"Don't you worry about it," said Calvin defensively.

"I hadn't the slightest inclination to."

Calvin stood and gathered himself. Klarysa lay motionless beneath his stare. A bolt of dark energy shot through his static stance, bringing a threatening edge to his frame. He was wired to something acidic, but couldn't define the source. He only knew he needed to move.

"I'll be back," he said. "I better make sure he's still breathing. Would you like anything from the bar?"

She thought she'd like a Campari and soda. Calvin bent down and put his mouth to hers, kissed her and took her lower lip ever so temptingly between his trembling teeth. And then he released.

"Very good, my love," he said. "Back in a bit."

Walking over to the bar, he swung his arms wildly, one after another in windmill fashion, trying to loosen the valves, release a little of the acid.

"Butcher!" he shouted when he was within range.

There sat the Butcher, high upon the break wall in a valium daze. The sun beat down on his unprotected British skin. A plump tomato cooked whole in a southern oven, a burnt plump tomato waiting for the slightest break in its thin blistering skin to release a weeping flow of boiling juices.

"Goddamn us one and all," mumbled Calvin to himself in frustration. "Butcher!"

Calvin felt fearful and helpless. He could only just take care of himself. What could possibly be done with a depressive beast that needed to consign himself to comatose on sparkling days, there in one of the easiest and most beautiful corners of the world?

"Goddamn it."

Despite everything, the moribund bull was one of Calvin's best mates. How much longer would the luck last with him? How many more fortuitous run-ins could they count on? Calvin feared that one day they would miss each other, perhaps only by seconds, and there would be no reeling the old boy in.

The Butcher rented a top-floor flat above the *toilettage* on Rue de la Prefecture. Calvin called on him one winter's eve, unannounced, breaking one of the many unspoken understandings that guided their friendship. The Butcher's silky baritone came crackling to life in the *parlophone*.

"Butcher?" said Calvin, stupefied. "Is that you?"

"Yeah."

"Why'd you answer the buzzer?"

"Dunno," said the Butcher, equally stupefied. "Why'd you ring it?"

"I don't know." They were both stupefied. "Hey, since we're both here, what say let's go for an ale?"

"Thanks, but I think I'll stay in to-night."

The Butcher was almost always 'staying in'. Then, two hours later, Calvin would see him about town, drinking at one bar or another, and the Butcher would shoot him a half-cocked smile. His eyes would say *that was an admittedly ratty move on my part*; the twinkle in his eyes would say *but you're a fool if you think you're going to stick me for it.* Then he would say something farcical that both he and Calvin just had to laugh at, though the Butcher would be the only one laughing.

The Butcher got on best with other English expatriates. They would slag each other off, ask nothing of each other and leave one another alone. Were they to bump into each other in the streets, they might talk football results for a breath or two, and then bugger off, each in his own direction. If, in parting, one were to, say, turn and get run over by a lorry, the other would shrug and keep walking. But once in a great while, the Butcher would invite several of the crew round for dinner and a film. On such nights, he would outdo himself, cutting no corners to make sure everything was just so, all the while unable to suppress hearty bursts of genuine laughter over just how grand it all was.

"Staying in to-night?" said Calvin through the *parlophone* on that winter's eve. "Fine; more ale for me. But hey, listen, Butcher, I'm dying to use the loo. What say, let us up quickly?"

"I thought you said you were going for a beer."

"I am going for a beer."

"Well can't you hold it?"

"No, I can't, for crissake! Be a pal, open up!"

The Butcher sighed in defeat. "OK. But don't touch anything."

"For crissake, who do you think you're talking to—Big Al? Well, make sure the goddamned *seat* is up and you have yourself a deal, you rotten bastard!"

The buzzer sounded with reluctance and the heavy door gave way. When Calvin arrived at the fourth floor, the Butcher was standing in the doorway. "Make it quick," he said.

Calvin ran in and took care of business. When he came out, the Butcher was still standing at the open door. Just to chafe him, Calvin walked the opposite direction, into the salon, which brought out a deep and sorrowful sigh from the Butcher. Calvin had been in the flat on several occasions, but now something felt different. What had changed, he couldn't say at first. There were still the leather-bound history books and the volumes of poetry, the old framed maps, the original schematics of ocean liners, the antique globe, the oil lamps, the stained-glass light fixtures, the framed oil paintings. Ah, there! On the stone hearth above the fireplace sat two magnificent lead vases with cream calla lilies standing tall, spring-green and erect. The elegant callas, there on the masculine hearth of old beige stone, struck a fine crisp balance. The arrangement was that of an artist with a keen eye for colour and line.

"Wow, Butcher, who arranged those beauties for you? They look expensive."

"What do you mean? I arranged those. Fifty francs for the lot, down at the flower market."

"You're a liar and a thief!" said Calvin in cheerful disbelief.

"Neither one nor the other," said the Butcher, beginning to jiggle with laughter, barely able to believe himself.

"No joking—*you* did that?"

"No joking!" he managed, nearly doubled-up and rippling with laughter.

"Well, I'll be," said Calvin with his hands on his hips, thoroughly impressed and bolstered by new ideas that the Butcher just might make it.

The clean, dying light of winter's dusk began to recede from the large picture windows. Calvin spotted an edition of Candide on the coffee table. "What's this?" he said, taking it from the table and flipping through the pages.

"Put that down," said the Butcher, taking several steps forward, but it was too late.

"You bastard," said Calvin. "Why, this is a French edition!"

The Butcher muttered something indiscernible.

"You deceiving bastard," he redoubled. "You speak French!"

"I *read* French."

"Goddamn it all, Butcher. I don't get it. Somewhere..." he extended his arms towards the Butcher with upturned palms, "somewhere in there, you care!"

"Oh, don't start."

"But you do. One cannot decorate a flat like this, arrange flowers like that, enjoy these books, devour that poetry, value these paintings and learn this language," he said, shaking Candide at the Butcher. "You can't do all of these things if you don't *care*, if you don't *feel*. You pretend not to because it's easier that way—no expectations. Isn't that right? Hot damn, now I know why you never allow anyone up here—you don't want anyone to know there is real depth to you. You don't want anyone knowing that you feel. Bah, don't worry, you sneaking bastard," said Calvin admiringly. "Your secret is safe with me."

Behind the jowls and the smarmy sarcasm and the cheap smut, the Butcher was an artist! Boy, thought Calvin, just when you think you have a finger on an Englishman, he'll surprise all hell out of you.

The summers were more difficult for the Butcher. Depression on a cold, dark day is manageable. On a warm and sunny day, when the rest of the world is laughing and celebrating, it can be unbearable. The Butcher suffered in part from a type of withdrawal. Many of the crew had been raised in their home countries on a steady diet of state-administered dread, and were now trying, among free and easy breezes, to wean themselves from the divisive regime. Many arrived on the Mediterranean coasts conditioned for chaos and mayhem, and the abrupt withdrawal from daily doses of doom left them disoriented and anguished. Calvin had recently come to be haunted by visions of the Butcher dangling by his soft white neck from the beautifully restored rafters of his gentlemanly flat.

"Butcher!" he yelled again from point-blank range.

"Oh. Hullo, Calvin," he called down from atop the break wall. "You all right?"

"No," he said decidedly, still working his limbs. "Hell if a menacing fear hasn't taken me by the neck."

The Butcher rumbled low and hard with laughter. So steeped was he in his own angst that anyone else's concerns, be they trifles or traumas, were comedic and unbelievable.

The Butcher looked dangerously unwell. "Come down to the bar with me," said Calvin. "Let me buy you a cocktail."

"What, to drink?"

"Sure, they make horrible pets, after all. Come on. Get down here. Let's go. Now."

Calvin spotted Eddie lounging under the canopy at the bar and raised his voice. "Don't make me drink alone with that depraved scamp Edward," he said, and again the Butcher rumbled heavily with laughter.

The Butcher shifted, grumbled a bit and floated softly down to the bar. Calvin led him over and anchored him to a shaded *chaise longue.*

"Hello, chaps," said Eddie, from the bar, where he lustily admired his tall and frothy cocktail.

"Get me some water, Eddie," said Calvin.

"What you want," said Eddie, "is a Ramos gin fizz."

"Let me describe for you," began Calvin, loath to agree with Eddie on even the most irrefutable of truths, "what kind of imbecile orders a cocktail with egg in it on a thirty-five-degree summer afternoon…" But that's where his words died, so salivating and choked up was he over the prospect of a cold gin fizz.

"God bless America," Eddie replied, overjoyed by the daftness of such a comment from Calvin.

"Sure," said Calvin with disinterest, as he struggled to position the Butcher, to avoid him from spilling onto the floor. "Why not."

"Say, Calvin," began Eddie, eyeing a nearby table of four. "You must be handy with a knife, relieving fish of their innards as you do all day. Perhaps you could teach your compatriots there some table etiquette. They're turning my stomach. Look at them. Watch how they muscle their fork tines through their meat with genuine sweat and real American gusto. You are gluttons for a battle, that much can't be denied."

"An Englishman giving out to another about the application of force and a thirst for battle—that's rich."

The Butcher, now slowly coming to, stretched wide his arms and knocked over an empty martini glass. The fragile glass broke on contact with the wooden decking.

Calvin winced. "It's OK, it's OK," he eased.

"My word," continued Eddie, "are they somehow unaware of the knives at their disposal, alongside their plates? Clean and untouched they go, like shiny little army reserves."

"Order those goddamned gin fizzes and get a carafe of water for this man. And make it quick."

"Yes, yes, but just how is it that your America has become so proud and defensive of its bumbling corndog culture and lack of refinement?"

"Eddie, goddamn it, I'm warning you."

The Butcher wavered. Calvin felt like an overmatched parent. "Snap out of it, Butcher! This is unacceptable!"

Said Eddie, "I'm impressed that you were able to get him down off his pedestal. I couldn't do it."

Pedestal! Calvin cursed Eddie. Why, thought Calvin, a fellow mired in anguish hoists himself desperately onto the chopping block, like an abject pig giving himself up to the slaughter, and how does his best mate respond? He tells him to wait just a second; then he preheats the oven, shoves an apple in his mouth and tells him to slice away. Hell if this isn't the loneliest place on earth.

"How did you get him to come down, anyway?"

"I told him you were standing us drinks," said Calvin. "Don't make a liar out of me, mate."

"Did you not refer to me only minutes ago," asked Eddie while signalling to a waiter, "as a depraved scamp?"

Eddie leaned back in his chair with rare contentment. He revelled in any situation in which he appeared in a brighter light relative to anyone at all, even to a version of the Butcher a-glow in the low-watt luminance of a slow-motion valium bog.

"You heard correctly."

"So I thought. My hearing is impeccable. God bless America— *twice*."

The drinks arrived. Calvin woke the Butcher and forced a tall glass of water down his throat; then gave him a sip of gin fizz. The Butcher opened his eyes a bit. Encouraged, Calvin clapped him on the shoulder. "Atta boy, Butch," he said. "We're going to be just fine, you and me."

Calvin poured another glass of water for the Butcher, and then leaned back on a *chaise longue* and finally relaxed a bit. He sipped the thin head of froth from the top of his drink and looked out over the beach. The aroma of grilled shrimp and garlic wafted past, followed immediately by the standard scent of sea and coconut oil. A tinkling accompaniment of silver and stemware overlaid bop jazz. Necks of wine-bottles jutted above the icy surfaces of silver ice buckets. Calvin watched his feet roasting nicely on the teak decking of the bar at the canopy's edge.

The Butcher, with a broad, sleepy smile, said, "Why don't you two have a game of chess?"

"Morning, sunshine," said Calvin, happy to see the Butcher alive.

"Drink that," said Eddie, pointing with accusation at the cocktail, "Drink it before it gets hot."

"What, the cocktail?"

Calvin smiled, coerced Eddie into ordering another round of drinks and then proceeded to lose in embarrassing fashion on the chess board. Eddie made it known that he had never won so quickly in all his life, and added, "Come back anytime you feel like taking it up the arse."

Calvin ordered the Campari and soda for Klarysa. Taking a quick seat next to the Butcher, he said quietly, "Take it easy now, Butch, huh? We're all in this fine mess together, you hear me? All of us, even Edward here. Nobody's exempt. Got it?"

The Campari was brought out. Calvin approached the bar, picked up the drink and warned Eddie under his breath, "For crissake, Eddie, look after him a bit, won't you!"

"I'm not paying for the Campari."

"Yes you are."

Calvin headed back to the towels feeling a hell of a lot better for the encounter. As he was walking away, Eddie bellowed after him, "God bless America!"

When Calvin returned to the spot where he had left his sunning buttermuffin, he found a well-tanned beach-jockey propped up by a thin, athletic elbow (on Calvin's towel, no less), trying his Latin best to have a go of it with Klarysa. It's always the same around here, thought Calvin—any young girl alone on the beach is a mark. The vultures lined up on the break wall and panned the landscape for a slab of unaccompanied meat. Then alone or in packs, they would swoop down and pick away at the sweet, tender bellies.

Calvin handed Klarysa her Campari and tried to shelve the temper that consistently brought him to the edge of trouble. "Look, Romeo," he said to the Latino, "I don't so much mind you chatting up my girl," he lied with a wrinkled kisser, "but you're on my towel, see, and that won't do."

Nothing. The lad rattled off clever lines, anchovy whispers and oily nothings to Klarysa, but didn't move an inch. Calvin fired off a cracked glance at Klarysa, which let her know the countdown had begun.

"Look," she said to the lad, "you had better slide over a little, darling," steering him as a patient school teacher might a dim kindergartener. In reference to Calvin, she added, "This one flips at times. Why, you should have seen him last night at La Bodeguita. Oh, my!"

Calvin popped, "I warned your man Donato *three times*. That's two more warnings than he would have received where I come from."

The kid scooted off to the side and squatted like a catcher behind home plate. "Where do you come from?" he asked Calvin.

The lad was painfully pretty, fine as a matador, with dark sparkling eyes and long black lashes. Calvin lay back on his towel and a stone met squarely with his spine. It seemed to him that every time he was at the beach with Klarysa, rocks were stabbing him in the back, flies were landing in his drink and one slick rogue or another was licking chops and blocking his sun.

Calvin tried to flatten out the bed of stones with his palm and said, "Look, kid, you and your kind rattle my nerves. She is with me. Surely, you can see that. Why, if you tried this type of move in—"

"Calvin!" Klarysa snapped. "Stop it at once!"

"Why do you do this to me?" he demanded.

"Do *what* to you?"

"Entertain these clowns when—"

"*Aie!*" said the lad, taking umbrage and protesting with open palms.

Calvin yanked himself around and shot the lad a menacing look. "That's right!" he said. "And don't you interrupt me when I'm talking to her, got it?" Then to Klarysa, "Honestly, is it too much to ask? Can we not come to the beach just once, you and me, and spend an easy day together without me having to share you?"

"Oh, you want *hon*esty? I left behind a wonderful life in Barcelona to be here with you. And I have no regrets—I love you. But if you think you're going to keep me from making new friends; if you think you're going to define who I can and cannot meet, why, you had better tell me right now!"

"OK, OK," eased Calvin. "Let's calm down."

He glanced back at the Latino, whose palms still appealed to the vast blue sky. The lad smiled, shrugged, appeared somehow genuine. Feeling carved up yet again, Calvin flopped back on his towel and silently bemoaned the sting of yet another defeat. It was a defeat handed down neither by the lad nor Klarysa, but by his own rigidity and insecurity. Such defeats were not altogether uncommon. A fellow leaves home for a foreign land, romantically prepared to cope with the foreign values and rules of engagement that he will invariably encounter. Though perhaps without even acknowledging it, he fully expects that in situations of consequence, if worse comes to worst, science, reason and universal truths will settle all disputes, regardless of culture. Never did Calvin expect to feel so impotent at times, when battling wits on foreign turf. The beach scene was yet another step along the thorny path towards acceptance of the fact that there were extremely few universal truths. If a fellow is to survive in a foreign land, with its foreign culture, he must accept the fact that one plus one will occasionally equal three.

"Tell me," began the Latino with a sudden burst of loquaciousness. "Where are you from in the States? Texas? *Bang bang*, you're dead! Ha-ha. I love Texas. I saw three men shot dead in one weekend, while in Texas. Saw it with my own eyes. Do what you like in the States. Here we're up to our eyeballs in bureaucracy."

"Christ, these beach towns," moaned Calvin. "Let's go for a drink."

The three of them crossed over the Quai des Etats Unis and onto Cours Saleya. Calvin was struck dumb by his willing self-inclusion in the engagement and cursed his legs as they moved in time with Klarysa's and the Latino's.

"Where shall we go?" the Latino asked cheerfully. "Might I suggest—"

"La Civette," said Calvin flatly. He knew people there. It was about the closest he would come to home turf on French soil.

The terrace at La Civette was packed. They sat down at the only free table under the broad awning. The Latino looked at Klarysa and then at Calvin and said, "Champagne?"

Before either could respond, he had ordered a bottle.

"Champagne? In this weather?" Calvin challenged. "A fellow of any mind would at least wait until sunset."

"Do you think?"

"Having just left the beach? Not before having a shower, at any rate."

The bottle arrived. An ice bucket was hung from the side of the table. The waiter filled three flutes and shoved the bottle into the ice bucket. The Latino raised his glass and held it up against the bright sky. "It is only wine, sir," he said to Calvin.

Klarysa gasped at the words of certain blasphemers.

"It is not only wine," said Calvin.

"No," agreed Klarysa. "It most certainly is *not*."

She drained her flute and pushed the empty glass towards the ice bucket.

"It is only money, at any rate," the Latino amended. "Easy, darling, you're liable to get drunk."

"I should think so," she said. "I have every intention to, after all. And rarely do I fail when I set my mind to something."

"Very well," he condescended, "but I'll have you know that too much champagne makes for an excruciating hangover."

"Hmph!" she snorted. "A Frenchman advising a Ukrainian on the subject of drink—how droll. Why, would a Frenchman submit to a Bolshevik's lecture on cheese or perfume or the art of submission? You, dear, taught us how to make the wine. That much is true and for that we are grateful, but we learnt how to drink it all on our own."

"Ukrainian, hey? I had no idea, my dear."

"I was practically nursed on champagne. I was bathed in warm vats of the stuff."

"I don't believe all that."

"Believe what you will."

"What are you doing in Nice?" he asked.

"Many things," she said. "Living with him, for starters."

"How is that going?"

"Grand, when he's not throwing people out of windows, or getting thrown out of them himself. I've no mind for nursing."

"Yes," he said, turning to Calvin. "That eye of yours looks nasty. Apparently your man Donato got his licks in."

"He most certainly did *not*," jumped Klarysa. "That eye is from a prior evening, one which began as an elegant soirée. There was, however, entirely too much booze for it to remain classy deep into the night. For the record, I don't condone the actions of the head waiter, leading me away as he did, through the crowd and the kitchen and into that dark *vestiaire* that smelt rather strongly of men."

"That's quite enough, Klarysa," said Calvin.

"Why, footballers aren't supposed to use their hands *at all*, right? Much less like—oh, look!" she exclaimed. "A pocket."

Yes, she discovered a delicate little pocket in her linen blouse.

"This place is lousy with connivers," the Latino confided gravely in Calvin.

"You're telling me," shot Calvin.

"Say, you haven't yet told me where you're from."

"Midwest."

"Is that right? I have an uncle in Chicago."

"All the things you love about Texas there, too."

"Don't I know it. Wonderful place, Chicago. I saw a guy beaten with a length of black pipe in Chicago. Broad daylight, too. They took his shoes before fleeing the scene. Left his wallet; took his shoes! Wonderful place. How do you find life in France?"

"Grand."

"Is that so?"

"Except for the connivers."

"This place is lousy with them. I prefer the Southwest. We are in airplanes, see. Well, I'm not, but my father is. We have property in Toulouse and a house here, in Vence. My father says I'm too taken by women. I can't deny it, really. Bah, who would care to?"

"See here," said Klarysa to the Latino, "you're the one getting drunk, darling. Pour me another."

"I suppose I am. Give me your glass."

"Women are fine," contended Klarysa. "We're too complicated to build a life around, though. Just ask Calvin here. He'll never admit it, though. I do make life terribly difficult for him and it breaks my heart. But airplanes—there's a racket around which a fellow could build a life."

"Just tell me how many you would like, my dear."

"You haven't the beginnings of enough."

"Enough *air*planes?"

"Personally, I've no mind for aviation. Still, you don't."

"Oh, but I do."

"Oh, but you don't. Besides, I'm not in it for the airplanes. If I were, do you think I'd have fallen in love with a fish monger? Calvin and I are more into affairs of the heart. Isn't that so, my love? It is exasperating at times, but there's nothing to be done about it— affairs of the heart *and* champagne, of course."

"How about that? I am taken by women, and you, sir," said the Latino to Calvin, "you are taken by fish. It takes all kinds, doesn't it. Truer words have never been spoken—or written. I write a little, too."

"What do you write about?"

"Women mostly. A man can learn a lot about himself by writing a book."

"Calvin here has a million stories. He's been around."

"Has he? I, too, have been around. Perhaps not as much as he, but then—"

"Yes, he is a good deal older than you. Hup!—just *look* at those flaring nostrils of his. I've seen them before, darling. I *would* be careful if I were you. Anyway, I'm always telling Calvin he should write his memoirs."

"Oh, no. Not memoirs," denied the Latino. "There's not much to be learnt by chronicling one's own history. Fiction, darling, fiction. That's where a man finds himself."

Calvin got up and walked inside the café, past the bar and into the Gent's. Like every other washroom in the Vieux, it was cool and musty and smelt of a permanent sewage. He splashed cold water on his face and looked in the mirror. Calvin looked too closely at history as an indicator of the future. As such, he suspected the Latino of harbouring designs on making off with Klarysa, throwing her in the back of a van down at a burnt up levee and having an orgiastic party for two.

He tried to forget those dark remembrances, those that stained hands and heart and future. He looked into the eyes of his reflection and advised, "Buck up, for crissake."

Maybe the Latino was onto something with regard to memoires. Forget histories. Draw up a fantastic future instead and have a go at it.

Calvin patted dry with a paper towel and went out to the bar. There he spotted the owner. They greeted each other warmly and talked for a minute about the heat and the summer and business.

"You ever see that guy about?" Calvin asked, flipping his chin towards the Latino.

The owner shrugged and turned down his lips. "They come and go during the summer. It's impossible to say."

"He says his old man is into airplanes."

"Good looking lad."

"Say, does Klarysa ever come around during the day?"

"Now and again. It is summer. And it is a good terrace."

"Yes, yes."

"She is a nice girl," the owner said, knowing worry when he heard it. "Women, you know, *monsieur*, are little miracles." He added empathetically, "Difficult little miracles, of course."

Calvin smiled. "Men, too. We are all bloody difficult, aren't we."

"Oh, yes, *monsieur*. Men are much worse. But now it is summertime and those occupations are best saved for the off seasons. Bah, she loves you, that one, *monsieur*. You don't need to wonder."

"How can you be sure?"

"In part because you are a good man and you worry that she might not. In part because I have heard her say so many times. Have faith; you are young and it is summertime on the *Cote d'Azur*."

"It *is* a good terrace," Calvin concurred.

"*Bah oui, monsieur*. One of the best."

They shook on it and Calvin walked back outside. At the table, the Latino was leaning in towards Klarysa, elbows on his knees, lips pressing passionately towards one youthful conclusion or another.

"The French are never ugly and never beautiful," he was saying. "In France, we are all too satisfied. Look about you; not a single concern amongst the lot of them. Then there's the US—richest nation in the world, yet no man has enough of anything, everyone is miserable, everyone is starving to death. Wonderful! All or nothing, I say. Bah, France. You know in Bombay they cut each other's fingers off for spare change. Can you imagine? Now that's something!"

"Speaking of cutting, darling, if you were a little less into airplanes and women, and a little more into knives, we might get somewhere."

"Is that right?" he asked, looking at Calvin and then back at Klarysa. "Wild about knives, are you?"

"An*tique* knives."

"That's easy; there are more antique shops in Nice than there are *boulangeries*. He ought to know that," he said to Klarysa, throwing a thumb in Calvin's direction.

"A good friend of mine is an antiques man," Calvin defended.

"Bah, the one who supposedly *held* the Danish Jubilee?" Klarysa mocked. "Why, that sweat-lined Cossack trader wouldn't know a knife from a *shashka*, nor a Fabergé from a hard-boiled. I want a knife!" she cried, sitting on her hands and kicking her feet.

"If a knife is what you want," said the Latino excitedly, "hell, I'll get you a knife."

"Oh, you will, will you?"

"Sure I will."

"Fine, you impotent little prince!" she blasted impatiently. "Go, now, and bring me the knife that killed my grandfather!"

The Latino was silent for a beat; then burst, "That's the spirit, darling. Yes, demand the blade that slain your forefathers! Why not? Here in France, our forefathers are still running the damned country.

Too satisfied, France, I'm telling you. Take Moscow, darling—guns ablaze as though it were Philadelphia. Sibling rivalry," he said to Calvin. "That's what it is."

"Sibling rivalry?"

"America and Russia, of course. Children of the same mother, seeded by different fathers. Forefathers forsaken, slain one by one, all of them spinning in their graves. Why, you two can't be a couple. It's incestuous. You," he said to Klarysa, "should be *my* girl. And you," he said to Calvin, "should adopt us both. And I'll fly us all to Los Angeles. Wonderful!"

"*L'addition, s'il vous plait*," said Calvin to a passing waitress.

"Who said anything about forefathers?" said Klarysa. "I said *grand*father."

"Oh. It wasn't a metaphor?"

"She doesn't speak figuratively," said Calvin, getting up from the table.

"Waste of time," said Klarysa, following Calvin's lead.

"Wait. Where are you going? Listen, I need to rape and be raped. Your homelands are good for that. Here there is neither laughter nor tears. Only handshakes and diplomacy and a mild disregard for rules. Come back! You lot destroy one another and scramble for the shoes of the dead! I've witnessed it with my own eyes! Wonderful! It's no good for me here. Wait! Come back!"

Back at the flat, with the heavy wooden shutters thrown back, late afternoon light flopped inward, soft and old-fashioned through the open windows, like overripe magnolia blooms. Klarysa was fresh and scented, *après-plage*, in a gossamer gown. Calvin had showered and was shaving, chin pointed at the mirror. She called to him from the salon, "Funny how a hot day on the beach will leave you pleasantly chilly after a nice shower."

"Yes. It is a good feeling."

"You should feel my skin."

"I intend to."

"It is *very* soft at the moment."

"It is always very soft," he said.

"It is at that," she concurred. "Oh, darling, I *do* give you headaches, don't I?"

"I don't get headaches."

"Well, black eyes I mean."

"Oh. I see. Well. It might be easier, it's true, if we were both a bit... what—calmer?"

"How come," she asked, "you don't know how to fight like a gentleman?"

He envisioned top hats, paces and revolvers, and realised he had little notion as to what made a gentleman. Might a homeless man with impeccable manners and sense of etiquette qualify as a gentleman? Or was social standing required?

"Do gentlemen fight?" he finally ventured.

"No. They do not," she said. "They used to. My father did. And my grandfather did. Back then it was the only way. But they were gentlemen."

He said seriously, "I suppose I was never taught how to fight like a gentleman."

"Now it's all death," she said. "I mean everything. Don't you think? Everything used to be about life. Now it's all about death."

"You are far too young to be entertaining such notions."

"Latin men can be awfully pretty, don't you agree? Much prettier even than the women."

"Perhaps," he said.

He finished shaving and entered the salon with a towel around his waist.

"Now where's that soft skin of yours?"

"It's here," she said, trying it out for herself. "Feel."

"Here?" he asked, kissing her there.

"No, here."

He kissed again.

"Yes. And here. And here. Oh my, here it's softer yet."

When she could not find a softer, smoother spot on her body, he grabbed her good and kissed her hard and she kissed him back with equal fire. After a moment she pulled away. "Darling, stop. Please. I can't take it. Would you like me to faint?"

"I'll catch you."

"Later. But now, won't you please make me a Negroni? The night will soon come down. Let's sit on the balcony and watch."

"Sure," he said happily, walking back to the bedroom. "But I thought you were quitting gin."

She put her nose to the air in deliberation. Having come to a verdict, she said, "You're right. But I simply can't get enough Campari."

"A Negroski, then."

"No. I couldn't possibly drink vodka to-night. I'm overwhelmed at the moment, can't you see? Do you think that Latin child would stand any chance of locating my grandfather's knife, what with all the airplanes he purports to have?"

"I don't know how he possible could, love."

"He *has* airplanes, doesn't he? Well, does he or doesn't he?"

"Who knows."

"Who *cares*. After all, it is somewhere in France," she cast roughly, looking over her shoulder at him, though he was still in the bedroom.

"What's in France?" he called.

"Why, the knife, of course!"

Calvin exited the bedroom buckling his belt. "Really?" he asked with surprise. She had never divulged the belief.

"Yes, really!" she scolded.

"What?" he begged. "What is it?"

"What *is* it? What on earth do you *do* all day besides... Oh, sod it! Bourbon, then!" she cried and heaved a heavy sigh.

"*Bour*bon," he echoed with a lifted brow and put himself forward to listen to what she needed to say.

She refused the implicit invitation. "Why not," she snapped. "You're always going on about it so."

She needed to fall apart and he knew it.

"Come. What is it?" he said. "Tell me, my love."

With the expressed license, she leapt from the divan, ran and launched herself into his arms. "Oh, Calvin, kiss me!" she begged.

He complied.

Pulling away, she said, "Oh, Calvin, you *will* help me find that knife, won't you? I *do* love you so."

He assured her – of what, exactly, he knew not – and poured her a rum shot to take off the edge. Then he ran out to pick up a bottle.

In the alleyway, he ran into Manx. Calvin told him he was out for a bottle. "Klarysa's a bit..." He held his hand out, palm down, waggled it like a tipping raft and whistled. "She wants a Negroni, but she wants it with bourbon."

"Unconventional little twist, she. You have to hand her that."

"And I admire her that, I do. But she also wants it topped up with champagne."

"Brassy little lass."

"You don't know the half of it—put me through hell's paces to-day down at the beach."

"You see Eddie, by chance?"

"Did I ever. He handed me my arse on the chessboard."

"One hell of a chessman, that Eddie."

"I wouldn't know; I'm a pushover."

"There's no shame in losing to Eddie. All the same," said Manx, "I've never lost to him."

"Of course not. You're a chess prodigy, just like everyone else I know. You're not the worst of them, but you're pretty damned close. Everyone mind the fanning feathers."

"Say what you will, but I can't recall having lost a chess match."

"No, none of you can. Just don't tell me gentlemen wage battle on the chessboard."

"Gentlemen? Rather certain they don't go slapping about talented young *sous chefs* on the dance floor, at any rate."

"That particular *sous chef* wasn't on the dance floor and he sure as hell wasn't dancing. What's more, I warned him three times.

"Which is two more warnings than he'd have been afforded where you're from. It's the same old line with you, Calvin."

"Yeah, Manx? Well, it's the same old scoundrels."

"Stop it. What is the matter with you, Calvin? You're losing your grip, not to mention your boyish glow. One of these times your eyes are going to remain purple, your nose bent and your lips split."

Manx's words cracked Calvin's thinning veneer. "By god, you're right, Manxy," he swooned. "I'm falling apart! I can't get on top of things lately. Oh, sure, I'll always be obliged to take lumps for Gem and Arbuckle and the rest, but see here, Arbuckle is on holiday in San Tropez with Nadine and Polish, Gem is captaining a tour of the Isles de Lérins, and *I'm* here nursing fractured ribs and licking wounds. And not just topical wounds, but now, too, psychic! I'm exhausted. Look here, I can't sleep at night for the men in the hallway and the spooks awaiting me in the alleyway each morning. I'm losing it, Manxy, I'm losing it! Why, just the other day—"

"Pull yourself together, man!" Manx demanded and issued Calvin a bracing slap.

"Thanks, Manxy, old pal. I needed that."

"Surprisingly exhilarating, that," Manx said of his rare violent outburst, now practicing his follow-through. "Anyway, it had to be done."

"You're right."

"I say, Calvin, have we righted the ship?"

"We have."

"Very well. With that behind us, I come to tell you that I've a mind to host a small party to-night. Interested?"

Calvin brought himself to full height, dusted his brow, thumbed his nose, sniffed twice to beckon courage and said, "Why, naturally, Manxy. Of course. You can't recall having lost a chess match and I can't recall having turned down an invitation to a party."

18   The Great Ebb

In which Calvin finds an ally
and Klarysa awakens to the taste
of musk and cheap talc.

Coyness was to Klarysa what self-restraint is to the obsessed—a waste of valuable time. All the same, she had a go at it for Calvin's sake. Lowering her gaze, she bit a lip and said to him, "Oh, I don't know, perhaps this new dress is taking things too far."

Such a line leads the mind towards the risqué, but in fact it may have been the first time since she moved to Nice that Calvin could not make out the suggestive Georgia O'Keefe-inspired tattoo on her backside for the concealing layer of slippery garnet viscose. That night Klarysa governed her sex-appeal to that of a housewife at the close of the second Great War – a time in history when winters were cold, drinks were honest and flags meant something – a housewife, nevertheless, that might have advertised cooking lard or any number of home appliances in the glossy magazines, or professional-grade garage tools in a more conservative wall-calendar. She wore red like no woman he had ever seen. The dress was a simple number that knew its way around her curves. It was sexy and yet classy, matched her lips and the fiery glints of her dark hair, and for once, left the imagination something to nibble on.

"Too far?" said Calvin. "Nonsense."

"Hell," she said, as though conceding failure in an ill-conceived theme costume, "I would make a miserable Muslim. How does one cope with all the fabric?"

Taking her in his arms, he said, "You look stunning. You look…" It was almost a major gaffe, but he caught himself and choked back the word and did not tell her that she looked *appropriate*.

"Why, you are positively gorgeous." He said it and he meant it, and she lit up like a celebration.

Her hand was a whisper in his as they stepped into the alleyway. The night had come down and made the evening dark and velvety with the ease of spilt ink. Awnings extended from the restaurants and cafés on either side of the alley and met in the middle to form a long tunnel of ochre and magenta. All of life gathered under the canopy, lured by the light and the laughter, the seafood, the roasted peppers and the garlic. Through a kitchen doorway giving onto the alley, a pizza chef in all white slid a pizza sleeve into a deep brick oven and pulled a bubbling pie from its belly.

Calvin and Klarysa took a table on the terrace of L'Abbaye in Place Rossetti. The Cathédral Sainte-Réparate was lit golden. The scent of candle wax and fresh linen lingered subtly under an open sky, a sky under which a fellow might affirm vows and make declarations.

Calvin watched, enamoured, as Klarysa mindfully smoothed her dress after she had been seated, to avoid adopting any errant wrinkles. "It is," she admitted, "a luxurious shade of red."

Calvin found himself suddenly ribbed by a tickle of regret and he thought back to the days when he shared quarters with the majestic Doberman. Both susceptible to bouts of obstinacy, oh how the two could engage when their differences of nature did clash. There was the time in Italy, idly tracing the Corso Italia Boccadasse, not far off the Marina Porto Antico in Genova, when Calvin and the Doberman chanced upon a three-legged tabby sunning itself in a terraced garden of cacti and sundry succulents. It was a grotesque mismatch for any canine worthy of the classification. In a flash, the dog broke free of its lead and, somewhere behind a blind of chalk-blue agave, made a fine mess of that poor handicapped tabby. The dog returned to Calvin's side with a blood-fixed beard of feline fluff and gristle, expecting the praise and glory due a local hero, though instead received a devil's reception. The poor thing recoiled as though it had stepped into an ambush. It recoiled not from the pain that any curses and open-palmed swats to the rump might affect, but for the sheer surprise at Calvin's vehement disapproval. The dog hadn't anticipated the reprimand. It had absolutely no idea what it had done to warrant such reprobation. But only seconds passed and the hound had forgotten all about their dispute. In no time at all, it was eager to play ball, go for a run, love Calvin fully and completely. Calvin marvelled the beast's ability to bury a grudge. Was it an uncanny ability to forgive? Unconditional love? Or was it simply the upside of having a frighteningly dreadful memory? Whatever it was, he was certain that such hopeful beasts needed protection—sometimes from others, but mostly from themselves.

Similarly, Klarysa seemed to have no memory of the disputes she and Calvin negotiated; or else she could let them go completely and immediately. For Klarysa, every experience was distinct. She lived each moment independent of all those that had passed and all those that were yet to come. Calvin, on the other hand, recorded and catalogued, rather against his will, all accounts of their fights, including the pains and sorrows associated with them. And while he was apt to shut down and shield himself from the sting of her anger, she raced back to him fully exposed to the angry words with which he might lash out at her.

Extraordinary—at any given time she was one or the other: a shrewd enchantress or a helpless child, though even she seemed to have little control over which persona might dominate from one moment to the next. At the restaurant that night, it was the gentle child that sat across from Calvin. Child-proud in her new red dress, she smiled with an authenticity and purity of hope that made him feel a bit ragged and broken. When the waiter brought their plates, she lifted her eyes to Calvin's and celebrated with a very tiny, noiseless clapping of her hands; then savoured the first bite with eyes closed. She worked on one quadrant of her pasta at a time, using the edge of her fork after each, to lightly scrape up the last remnants of sauce before moving on to the next. Gently stabbing a baby shrimp, she brought it to her mouth with fork-tines turned down, convinced that if a meal allowed it, using a fork in such a manner showed an element of grooming (though such action with a spoon during dessert was both immature and uncouth).

She was too full for a proper dessert after the meal, so she made one of her coffee by adding an extra lump of sugar and drinking it daintily with the miniature spoon that accompanied it. She brought in her lips when she felt eyes on her, and scrunched them to the side when searching for a name or working out maths in her head. Out of the blue, she said, "I once saw a young jazz singer in San Remo. This girl had it all—looks, voice, *ev*erything. That was years ago, though. She's probably a big star somewhere by now."

At the end of the meal, a yawn escaped her. And then there was another. Each time, she fluttered her hand over her mouth, as if to tamp it down or shoo it away, and she would furrow her brow just slightly as if it were the oddest curiosity, and if only the peculiar little nothings would stop pestering her so.

After dinner, Calvin settled the bill and they crossed over Place Rossetti. A man at a table on the terrace of La Claire Fontaine was standing and delivering a toast. When he finished, his company raised their glasses and cheered. Indeed, it was sky under which victories might be launched.

"What," began Klarysa, "should we bring to the party? A bottle of something nice, I should think."

"Whatever you would like, *mon cœur*."

They passed the bar Les Idéales. It was heaving inside and there was not a free spot on the terrace. A group of Marseillais threw dominos, which cracked like firecrackers on the hot marble tabletop. Inside, a television showed a football being roped into the back of the net. The bar erupted. Italy had equalised. Men sang traditional fight songs, while their women sipped Monacos and Panachées and moved closer together, the better to hear one another.

Calvin and Klarysa continued down Rue de la Prefecture, en route to the old bottle shop. The shop was busy, abuzz with a symphony of voice and motion. The walls were lined with heavy glass. A million bottles, each with a classy etiquette typecast in gold or silver or red or black and with necks decorated in thick colourful foils, reached high toward vaulted stone ceilings. Overhead, the bugs of summer buzzed benignly in the glow and hum of high lamplight. Only a hopeless fellow could go unaffected for the better by the ambiance of a good bottle shop. Three generations of artisans conducted business efficiently, though without haste. The eldest acted as *conseiller*. The youngest worked the low front counter, filling jugs of all sizes with provincial wine from the spigots of large barrels. Calvin grabbed the two bottles that Klarysa had pointed out (both of sky-blue glass, both with gilt-edged labels and gold lettering) and moved to the counter to pay. The man at the till motioned them over. A spark danced in his eyes and his hands were active.

"*Et avec ça, monsieur.*"

"That will be all, thank you."

"*Mais non*! What of this ravishing young woman you're with? Does she not deserve champagne to-night, sir?"

"Sure she does," confirmed Calvin good-naturedly—he appreciated a merchant who showed a measure of character. "Champagne and much more. But she has chosen these."

"But mademoiselle, don't you like champagne?"

"Who me? You've no idea."

With this, the merchant looked disapprovingly upon Calvin. "Sir," said the merchant, "you buy her champagne to-night, no?"

The mirth, which to be fair hadn't really amounted to much to begin with, disappeared from the merchant's eyes altogether and Calvin could no longer gauge the temperature of the exchange.

"Thank you. There will be plenty of champagne where we're going. We'll stick with these."

The merchant grabbed a champagne bottle by the neck. "But the green of the bottle will be striking against the deep red of mademoiselle's dress."

Calvin looked at Klarysa. She shrugged.

"The golden bubbles," he continued, "startling against her full red lips. And undeniably sexy," he said, reaching for Klarysa's hand, "among the curves of mademoiselle's supple—"

"OK, that'll do, Baudelaire!" Calvin yowled, thrusting a small wad of bills into the merchant's hands and ripping away the bottle of champagne. "Keep the change!" he said, and huffed off with Klarysa in toe.

"Oh, darling," she said to him, "you shouldn't allow yourself to get so worked up."

"My, that fellow sure offers a lot of lip service for a wine merchant."

"Yes, but it's a holiday."

Calvin looked at her, uncertain. "It's not a holiday."

"No, it's not," she demurred, "but it feels like one and that is what matters."

"I swear," he mumbled to himself, "this town has it out for me."

They headed off towards Manx's. The length of Rue Poissonnerie was lit, as though for a fiesta. A patient mob lined itself three-deep for ice cream at Fennochio's and the terraces of Les

Ponchettes and La Civette were bursting where the alley met Cours Saleya.

Fitim and Monique were sitting outside La Banane. Fitim was holding Khali. The clammy mutt yipped at Calvin as they approached. *Bisous* were given all about.

No paper sack could deceive Monique. "Moët!" she gasped.

Champagne brought out the best in Monique, and the best in Monique was something to behold. Her eyes shone with an infectious light that every fellow wanted to preserve for the duration of the evening.

"There is a whole army of them upstairs," said Calvin. "You're coming up, right?"

"I wouldn't miss it for the world," said Monique. "We'll only need to run home first and freshen up."

She looked at Fitim for concurrence, but he didn't seem to hear her. He was intently eyeing Calvin, who immediately regretted having deployed the military metaphor in Fitim's presence. A good party was no place for debating international conflicts and political objectives.

Fitim said, "Calvin, do you know what a *çiftelia* is?"

Calvin's mind raced to dark conclusions.

"Oh, darling," pleaded Monique. "Not now."

"No," Calvin responded doubtfully. "I don't know."

"It is an Albanian instrument of wood and stretched metal strings."

The description matched the image in Calvin's mind. He swallowed hard and muttered gravely, "A medieval Albanian killing device."

The women looked at him in horror.

"Calvin!" Klarysa rebuked.

"Honestly!" added Monique.

"Girls, girls, please," said Fitim. "Americans are taught to distrust foreign words and pronunciations. No, Calvin, it is an acoustic instrument played by Albanian folk musicians."

Monique said proudly, "Fitim is learning to play. He shows great promise."

"No, no," he said bashfully. "She is too generous. But," he continued hopefully, "I must admit that when I play, it makes beautiful sounds. My father tried to teach me when I was young, but I was too angry to care about music. Now I understand why he wanted to teach me. Now I can hear the beauty. It is hard to believe," he added, acknowledging his big stone mitts, "that these hands can produce such beautiful sounds."

"That *is* something," said Calvin, and received a swat from Klarysa.

"I wonder if..." began Fitim, but then lost his nerve. "No, it is too much to ask."

"Go on," said Calvin. "What is it?"

"I wonder if I might bring my *çiftelia* to the party."

"No," said Monique resolutely. "Darling, you will be a laughing stock. It's simply not the place."

"Hell, why not?" said Calvin. "I think it's a fine idea."

"No," Fitim conceded. "Monique is right. It is not the place. But maybe another time I might play for you."

"By all means," said Calvin. "Anytime time at all."

Calvin and Klarysa ascended the stairs to Manx's flat. Calvin looked to Klarysa and said, "That Fitim is all right, no? I like him."

"He is a gentleman," she replied as a matter of fact.

"Yes," Calvin concurred. "I suppose he is."

On the landing, Calvin eased Klarysa aside.

"No, no," she denied. "How come you always get to?"

"Sorry. I had no idea. Please, mademoiselle," he submitted, stepping away with a slight bow, as Klarysa slipped out of her heels and took a step back. She shimmied red viscose up around her thighs, and with a concentrated brow and a clever yelp, charged across the two-meter sweep to deliver a bare heel to the heart of the wooden door. Had the door eyes, it would have rolled them, but it opened all the same, to reveal a party in full swing.

"Goddamned animals!" Manx shouted from somewhere within.

"Good," Calvin critiqued, as Klarysa slipped back into her heels. "A little closer to the handle next time."

"Hey, hey!" someone shouted from within. "Look who's here!"

Calvin and Klarysa were pulled inside. The bottles were ripped from their hands in exchange for kisses and hugs and smacks on the back and rabbit punches.

The Butcher was there. He stood with ping-pong bat at the ready, bouncing on the balls of his feet, anticipating service at the near baseline of the pine-green table.

"Hey, Butcher!" cheered Calvin. "You're alive!"

The Butcher, with red lips glistening, chortled like a happy goose. The two Moroccan kittens hissed and spat at the far baseline. One of them served and it was the Butcher who turned catlike, showing an efficiency of movement, a lightness of step, a grace and agility incongruous to his ample mass. The short volley came to an abrupt and violent halt when the Butcher rose up on butter toes and smashed home a passing winner. Having had their catlike ways appropriated, the girls scrambled about for the ball like disorganised mice, knocking into each other and guests alike. Their side of the table had become tacky with spilt drink. The Butcher looked at Calvin as though it were the first time he'd touched a ping-pong bat in his life and in doing so found his new religion. The Butcher emitted an ecstatic clap of laughter and crouched in anticipation of the next service.

Klarysa rolled her eyes and slipped further into the party. The lovely, gentle persona was most likely gone for the rest of the night. She would never understand Calvin's draw to the likes of the Butcher. Calvin, himself, hadn't always understood. He maintained visions of the Butcher mulling about by himself down by the flower market, wandering from stall to stall, looking for the perfect bouquet, so that he might take them home and live alongside the cut and dying beauties for a few days. Calvin rooted incessantly for underdogs and the Butcher was another mutt barely getting by in the world's immeasurable and over-crowded cage of underdogs. Calvin was never so happy for the Butcher as when he allowed himself to be a part of something joyous, a little light-hearted enjoyment, out from under the dark shadows of some heavy barbiturate.

"How you move with a paddle, man!" Calvin roared, causing the Butcher to nearly collapse in laughter.

Between bursts of giggles, he choked out, "Stop it, Calvin, you're going to make me give away a point!"

"Give 'em hell, tiger!"

The humidity in the salon was thick. A loud Latin beat jiggled the chandelier. All about the room there was a great clinking of glasses, after which heads were thrown back in concert and glasses relieved of their golden burden. Whisky ghosts and tobacco smoke mingled, forming sweet amber clouds in the immediate sky, that which was capped by high crowned ceilings.

Two men in the *entrée* stood arguing and waving tobacco pipes. One said to the other, "...*He* was the finest tobacconist in all of

Alexandria and it shan't be argued to the contrary. Hollingshead you say? *Holl*ingshead? Come, his grandfather was a *lum*berman, for crissake!"

"You have a point, John Doffing, but that was during the Antebellum—"

"Yes, Hodgetts," said John Doffing. "You're damn right it was!"

"But John Doffing—"

"Negative, Hodgetts."

And with that, John Doffing rapped the bowl of his pipe against his palm until a wad of dead ashes fell into the planting pot in which was rooted a giant banana tree. A third guest looked disapprovingly upon the action.

"Chastise me now if you must," said John Doffing to the disapproving guest, "but at next bloom, this baby will sprout fruit to feed a full-grown gorilla."

Calvin spotted Sandoval and Tiller across the way. And there was Felix, who had cornered some unsuspecting young woman and was in the act of murdering her with his patent manner of suffocating kindness. Three Danish lads unknown to Calvin bounced like blonde bobbers on a dark sea of inebriation. The Butcher spun a deft pirouette and drove home match point. Niko and a spotted leopardess, both dancers with a local ballet company, slid hip-to-hip from one side of the room to the other. Like graceful, copulating sea-slugs, they left libidinous juices glistening in their wake.

Calvin was working his way towards the bar when he ran squarely into Louis MacCovey. Calvin and Louis were old friends from their days of working yacht parties in the port of Antibes. Calvin attended bar, while Louis attended skirts. The right personality got away with hell's own agenda at a yacht party, and Louis MacCovey had one such devilishly fine personality.

"Hallo, Calvin!"

"Louis MacCovey, you lovely old dog. How are you?"

"Fine, fine. Long time, Calvin. No drink yet? Let's fix that."

They made a concerted push for the bar. Louis dove into the icebox and pulled out two bottles of beer. They were ice cold. He popped the caps off them with a cigarette lighter and handed both bottles to Calvin."

"Two beers?" asked Calvin.

"Sure. I've already got one."

"What do I need with two beers?"

"How can I know?—it *has* been a while. Why don't you tell me all about it, sweetheart."

"Look here. You take one of these," said Calvin, returning one of the bottles of beer. "And now *you've* got two beers."

Louis MacCovey looked at the bottles in his hands, as though he had no idea how they got there. "Why, take a look at that," he said, overjoyed by the new arrangement. "Grand! Say, Calvin, do you remember Roberto Bolivia?"

"Boy, do I. How could I forget? Gosh, Roberto Bolivia. It's been ages. I'd pay the devil's ransom to know what Roberto Bolivia is up to these days."

"So would I. And I'm convinced I saw him last week at Charles de Gaulle."

"Is that right? Roberto Bolivia? Of *Her Majesty's silky underpants* fame?"

"I'm almost certain of it."

"What did he look like?"

"Why, he looked like Roberto Bolivia, only older. I haven't seen him in what—ten years? Not since the weekend in Dieppe. Still can't grow a decent beard."

"You didn't say anything to him?"

"I wasn't entirely sure it was him. Then, as I was on the verge of saying something, I noticed he had a French passport and a beauty mark on his cheek. So you see, it couldn't have been Roberto Bolivia."

"But why not?"

"Because he's from Bolivia, for crissake. He can't have a French passport."

"He's not from Bolivia, you loon. He's from Vancouver."

"Is that right? He's a Canuck, is he? How about that," Louis pondered, taking a long last draught from his first bottle, and killing the top third of the new one. "Hey, that's cold! Roberto Bolivia. And all this time I thought he hailed from Lake Titicaca. Why in God's name do we call him Roberto Bolivia if he's a Canuck? We might do better to call him Roberto Canada, or Canadian Robert."

"Hell, Louis, that's the man's name."

"Is that right? Bolivia is the family name? How about that—Bolivians in Canada."

"Boliv*ias*, not Boliv*ians*. A family, not a people."

"Probably at least a few Boliv*ians*, as well, though, no? Toronto maybe. Who would have guessed?" Louis said, diving back into the icebox. "Here, have another cold beer. Still, he can't have a French passport."

"Sure he can. His father is French, you know."

"Roberto Bolivia? His father is French? I did *not* know."

"I'm not sure he had a beauty mark on his cheek, though."

"Roberto Bolivia? Sure he did, didn't he? For the life of me I can't remember. Nothing beautiful about him, at any rate."

"Not while we were in Dieppe, anyway. That much is certain."

"That much *is* certain."

"My god, cider was never intended to be drunk like that."

"Nor glasses intended to be shattered like that."

"Nor fires set."

"Nor the fair Dieppoise..." said Louis MacCovey with a shudder. "Why, he very nearly got us all homicidally murdered!"

They both drained their beers.

"Wow," said Calvin. "Roberto Bolivia. Probably best you didn't say anything to him."

"Right. Only, a fellow does wonder. Spitting image of our man Roberto Bolivia. Absolutely spitting. Anyway, I should think another couple beers will help us get to the bottom of it."

"You want to get to the bottom of something?" said an active fellow from behind the bar. "Do yourselves a favour and get to the bottom of these," he advised, putting forth two martinis.

"Evening, Dash," said Calvin to the fellow tending bar.

"Evening, gents."

"Awfully kind of you, Dash," said Louis MacCovey. "Won't you join us with one?"

"Oh no, not me. I've a beggar's backlog of regrets to work through and I'm just beginning to make good. It would be imprudent of me to add new ones just yet."

"That's admirable, Dash," complemented Louis MacCovey. "The missus must be one proud dame."

"The missus?"

"Yeah, your missus. She must be proud of you."

"Didn't you fellows hear? I traded in my wife for a dog."

"Stop it," said Louis MacCovey. "Is that right? A real live dog?"

"A real live dog. No kidding," Dash said, and then added, muttering, "The black-haired, long-whiskered, yapping mutt."

"Why, that sounds like a horrible trade, Dash."

"Horrible trade? Like hell! I got a gorgeous yellow Labrador in exchange for her. One hell of a fine trade, actually. And the crazy thing," Dash explained while holding two martini glasses upside-down over two uncapped bottles of Cinzano blanco, "is that I ended up keeping the dog. It's a hell of a lot brighter than I anticipated, and a man is not a man without something to protect and defend. What's more, I haven't the stomach for gunfire."

"And what about your wife?"

"One can only hope for her sake that the fellow who traded for her is equally squeamish when it comes to guns. Now, see what I'm doing here?" said Dash in reference to the glasses he held upside-down over the Cinzano. "You only want the most determined vapours to coat the inside of the glass. When the vodka is good, a martini should be drier than summer in Sevilla. Now you two line these toothpicks with olives while I get more vodka."

Calvin and Louis MacCovey went to task, carefully lining each toothpick with four small dark-purple Niçois olives. Dash returned with the vodka and shook two more martinis, then dirtied them slightly with the harpooned olives and slid them in the direction of two dark lynxes in black.

One of the dames said to the other, "...You mean jumping out of *air*planes? Oh, no, that's not for us. Alpine skiing—that's our big thing."

"Really? Roger and I love to ski. We *must* all go together next winter. We prefer Chamonix. Where do you prefer to go?"

"Oh, we don't go. We haven't been in ages—absolute ages. I very highly doubt I could make it to the bottom of a beginner's *piste* without breaking my neck. Excuse me for a moment, won't you?" she said, and then turned to Dash.

"I say, barkeep, this *is* a good martini. Do tell us what you call it."

"Depends who's drinking it—anything from inebriating to deadly, I suppose."

"I'm being serious here."

"Hell, I've no idea, lady."

"Well shouldn't you do?"

"Why, I've a long history of drinking them, not naming them. Look here, why don't you have a crack at it if you're so keen?"

"Fine. How about the *perle noire* martini?" she suggested.

"The black pearl martini? That's not half bad."

"It's tremendous."

"Sure. Why not. You know, we could go places, you and me."

"We could, but we'll go nowhere if you insist on harbouring such guilt of drinking."

"Why, is that all?"

Dash scanned the bar top. Having spotted an abandoned low-ball glass, he picked it up and killed the lining of dirty shish at the bottom of it, and then drove it home with authority on the bar top and said, "Well, my dear, it's a start."

"And a vulgar one at that," she said. "Though I like you more already."

"That's fine. To whom do I owe the honour, my beautiful little frog?"

"You don't owe anyone, and I don't extend credit. Never have. Debt is at once the crutch and the noose of little boys, I always say.

"That's not so in the least," he retorted. Dash fancied himself one hell of a shrewd businessman. "It takes money to make money," he said. "And sometimes the cheapest money is borrowed money."

"I'll say it for the last time—only fools work on credit. Who do you make yourself out to be anyway, Warren Booffay?

"You mean Warren Buffet?"

"One and the same."

"Why, of course not. I only—"

"Then don't try to impress with such guff. It's boring *and* dreadful."

"Look, my little lake perch, I only meant to enquire after your name."

"Very well, but going forward, you might say what you mean directly and stop wasting your breath on snappy jingles and—"

"Listen here, I mean to shortly rush you off to my hideous little den and have you climbing the walls by sunrise! Now then, what do you make of that for directness, my resplendent little bluegill?"

"Well, you're a quick learner. I'll give you that. As for your salacious mind—"

"Pay no mind to that, sweetheart. I'm a pussycat, I tell you."

"I say, do let a gal finish her lines, kitten—I *was* hoping for a tiger to-night."

Dash roared. "I can make like a tiger all night long, if that's your wont. Don't worry a lash, love, only tell me your preference—Siberian or Bengal."

"Little difference to me—Asia be damned." She paused to drink of her martini. "Divine! All the same, we still haven't been properly introduced. I'm called Miranda. Miranda Sotheby."

"You mean *that* Sotheby?"

"Please..."

"Call me Dash."

"Please, Dash, do you honestly think I would be found *here* if I were *that* Sotheby?

"Listen, Sotheby, money can't buy you pulse or personality, and if you've got either, you can't do a hell of a lot better than this joint—if you don't mind all the animals, that is. It's a goddamned petting zoo in here, am I wrong?"

"Oh, I've no complaints there. Especially now that I've got my hands on you. You *are* a bit of an animal yourself," she said, reaching across the bar and giving his chin a gamely waggle.

"I say, you're an odd duck all right. I like you immensely. By the way, whatsoever gives you the wild idea that I have a complex about drinking?"

"Why, I've heard you bemoan the effects on three different occasions this evening."

"Oh, that," he said, sliding a purple olive between her red lips. "That wasn't guilt. No, that was just self-deprecation. Now *that* I have a problem with. You know I can't take a compliment? Never could take a compliment. I know I'm a decent fellow, but I can't believe a nice word anyone has to say about me. What do you think of that?"

"Oh, my! That's even worse."

"Sure it is. It's much worse. What's more, drinking is the only way I know to get over my poor self-image. Of course the drinking leads to all manner of regretful situations." He reached over and killed the rest of Calvin's martini in a single shot. "I'll have you know I traded in my wife for a dog. But guilt? No, I'm guilt-free. Why, a decent dose of guilt might save my liver *and* limit my regrets. But what the hell, nobody's perfect."

"Tragic! At least you can be honest about it."

"I've no problem with honesty—except for all the times I feel compelled to lie. Queer, isn't it, my *petite cressonnette*."

"It's neither here nor there to me; I find you disarmingly handsome."

"Haven't you heard a word I've said? I'm a mess!"

"Oh, I don't know. There's a lot to be said for honesty, so long as one doesn't lie while he's at it."

"You're an odd duck, all right." Dash jerked his thumb toward the dance floor. "Say, you want to shake it up a bit?"

"I'd love to."

"Calvin," called Dash, "you know how it works back here. Do a fellow a favour and take over for a while, won't you?"

"You know," said Miranda Sotheby to Dash, as they headed arm-in-arm to the dance floor, "my husband is the worst sort of drunk. He's always going on about—"

"Forget about him. To-night let's do something we'll both feel guilty about in the morning."

"You're incorrigible."

"You've no idea, lady. Say, how do you feel about yellow Labradors? You might try trading in your husband for one."

Calvin was behind the bar serving a drink to Manx when Fitim and Monique appeared in the doorway. Monique carried Khali in her arms. The dog was fitted with a blue bow to match its crop of blue hair. It sniffed at the air with disapproval, and then yapped at the two Moroccan kittens who, in turn, hissed back.

Manx turned a sickened shade of pale at the sight of Fitim.

"Relax," said Calvin. "He's OK."

"But his affiliations," contended Manx.

"Quit your worrying, Manxy. This is a great party and affiliations are checked at the door of every great party. Relax. Enjoy yourself. I'll mind Fitim."

Calvin caught their attention and waved them over towards the bar.

"It's on your head, Calvin," warned Manx. "That's the last I'll say of it."

Fitim sidled up to the bar like a wide-berth tugboat docking itself for refuelling.

"Fitim Kaleci," introduced Calvin, a bit loose for the drink. "Your host for the evening, one Manx Rumpy."

Without missing a beat, Fitim said, "Like the chicken."

"It's not my real name," said Manx with visible discomfort.

Misidentifying the source of Manx's discomfort, Fitim said, "It is a lovely bird. Lays eggs in a variety of colours—white, blue, brown, green. And that chicken will defend itself if that's what it comes to. It is a name you can be proud of." He finished with an extended hand and the shadow of a bow. "A pleasure to make your acquaintance."

Moved by the unexpected gentility, Manx smiled and shook his hand. "The pleasure is mine," he said. "Do make yourself at home." Then, to Calvin, as he walked proudly away, he said, "There's your gentleman—the pearl before you lot of swine."

Klarysa and Monique, together at the bar, engaged themselves in a coquettish game whereby on the count of three each would raise a topped glass of champagne to her nose. She who withdrew her glass first, lost.

"I win!" one declared with glee.

"The bubbles are too ticklish!" the other giggled.

Fitim watched them with a smile. Calvin watched Fitim.

"It is good to be young," said Calvin. "I have a keen memory for those days."

"Come, you are still young."

"No. I am not old, but neither am I young."

They slipped into conversion. Calvin recounted certain memories, not for the sake of recounting memories – which tend to carry significance only for the one beholden to them – but as a means of connecting with Fitim on a common plane, in a common language, to evoke the emotions that are tied to fond memories and that are somehow as universal as they are unique. Fitim listened intently, squinted an eye or shrugged his shoulders when he did not quite agree, and turned down his lips and nodded heavily when he did. He recounted surprisingly similar stories and memories, despite origins half a world away. It was an enjoyable exchange during which both men moved comfortably between the bulky and the blithe.

Fitim was put together of an economy that was too austere for another to label him charismatic. To be fair, the charisma he had was somewhat blanketed under his limited range of facial expressions. Nevertheless, he did possess an underlying magnetic something. He was the kind of fellow whose acquaintance made one feel a bit daring and proud, as feels the fellow who is on belly-caressing terms with his neighbour's exceedingly large Rottweiler.

Modulating to a more business-like tone, Fitim asked, "Would you be interested in a job?"

The question caught Calvin by surprise. He realised that the confidence Fitim had earned from him was young and untested and had its limits. There had been much said about Fitim that was yet to be validated or disproved.

"Thanks," said Calvin. "I appreciate the offer, but I… Well, I just couldn't. Not at the moment."

Klarysa and Monique came bounding back to the bar to freshen their glasses. Monique said to Fitim, "Why does Calvin look like that? What did you say to him?"

He replied directly, "I asked if he wanted to help me with a job."

"Here? Now?" she nagged.

Fitim had conceded to her disallow of the *çiftelia*, but her latest reaction brought him to smoulder. It was a matter of jurisdiction.

"Sure. Why not?" he challenged.

"Because it's a party, that's why. Bah, you do what you want; *I'm* going to dance and drink Moët."

"Anyway, I really can't accept," said Calvin in an attempt to appease. "I'm really very busy these days."

"It will be a quick, Saturday job," Fitim persevered. "A one-off, with some prior coordination."

"But I process fish on most Saturdays."

"Good luck!" said Klarysa, making a fish-face. "He's in love with those fish. He loves them more than he loves me."

"That's not true," said Calvin, laughingly.

"It *is* true," redoubled Klarysa. "He's devoted to them. He won't leave them for anything!"

A smattering of good-natured laughter followed, but Calvin sensed the shadow of a certain raggedness and rejection descending.

"Will you gut fish until you drop dead, Calvin?" asked Monique with genuine mortification.

"No, no. Not forever," he replied meekly.

"He *will* gut fish forever," demanded Klarysa. "Until the seas run dry of them! Just you watch. Why, I'd consider settling down with him, but he can't think beyond to-morrow. He doesn't understand that a girl wants some stability in her life."

And with that, the girls ran off to follow the course of their desires, which was green and gold and lined with bottles of Moët.

Fitim said, "It's OK, Calvin. I understand."

"You want the truth?" asked Calvin.

His carousel of concerns was in constant motion of late, each of his tormentors occupying one or another of the colourful seats. And oh, how his dear Klarysa did occasionally choose to joyously mount a gorgeous wooden stallion with terror in its eyes, coloured in peppermint-stick and trimmed with gold enamel, and gallop round his heart in a rising and falling manner, kicking up clouds of anguish.

"Only as it suits you, my friend."

"I'm at my limit right now. Up here," said Calvin, tapping his skull. "I'm at the edge. I can't take on anything else. If anything I need to cut back, pare down. I don't know where I am anymore. I don't know what I'm doing. In times of need, Gem advises doing what you do best. For me, that's gutting fish."

"What is the matter?"

"That's just it—I don't know. I can't make out the sun anymore, or the colours it once made of things. My vision is muddled and blurred. Everything I touch snaps at me. I can't sleep at night."

"Hmm. That's not good."

"It's very bad. Look here, this stays between you and me, yeah? I go entire nights without a wink of sleep. Sometimes, if I turn on a bedside lamp and keep my eyes open, I can unleash my thoughts and eventually I'll doze off for an hour or so. That's a *good* night."

"Klarysa doesn't mind sleeping with the light on?"

"I turn it on after she falls asleep."

"It doesn't wake her?"

"*That* girl?" begged Calvin, shoving a finger in her direction. "That one there sleeps like the dead and buried!"

"But when was the last time you had a decent night's rest?"

"Last night was the first in weeks, and that was only because of an unexpected *work*out at La Bodeguita. Hell, a fellow can't be expected to knock heads all night just for the sake of some shut-eye. And that's not all. Look here," he said, exhibiting his open gob.

"Oh!"

"You, see? I've chewed holes in my cheeks. It's a nervous reaction, I suppose. I can't seem to stop it. Sometimes I'll be walking down the alleyway and realise my jaw has been clenched shut like a vice, for hours. My teeth ache. Other times I come to and realise I'm grinding my teeth to bits. Sometimes, in the morning, lying in bed, I find I can barely pry open my mouth for all the pain in my jaw."

"That's not good."

"It's very bad."

"You might see someone about that. You need to relax, slow down, take it easy."

"You know, it's funny—all his life, a boy is told to be tough, to fight for what he wants, to take a stand for what he believes in, lest he get run over or taken advantage of. Then he becomes an adult and he's told it's no good; he's got to compromise, be patient and flexible, lest he go mad."

"OK, but what is to be done about it?" asked Fitim with a timeless regard. "How is it with Klarysa?"

"Exasperating, challenging, exhilarating, occasionally gentle, wonderful." Calvin eyed her on the dance floor. "My god, man," he exclaimed. "Look at her!"

Perhaps it was a rush of juice to the head, or perhaps the room really was suddenly turning in slow-motion. What did it matter and who gave a damn? There she was, all in red, shimmying and shaking on the old hardwood floor under the great chandelier, the music rousing, her long hair loose and very nearly everywhere. The entire room shimmied and shook with dance and not a single soul gave a sweet goddamn what the morning might bring. Just then, Klarysa caught Calvin staring at her, star-struck, and she waved to him, joyously, lovingly, as though it were the first time she had seen him since that first miracle week together. She blew him a big kiss that made his heart race, and then she shook it good in the middle of the room.

Fitim followed Calvin's line of sight. "Yes," he said. He understood. "Yes."

"Hey, barkeep!" someone shouted, breaking Calvin's trance. "Hey, Calvin! How about a few Margaritas this way?"

Calvin shot back, "I'm on it, Hazel!"

"Make them Cadillacs, won't you?" screamed Hazel.

Calvin plucked five or six limes from a basket toppling with them and took to squeezing the juice into several rocks glasses filled with ice. While he worked, he continued to Fitim, "For every hour spent with Klarysa, fifty minutes are pure bliss. The other ten are like trying to catch and tackle a very tempestuous cyclone—it is impossible and you take some kind of beating for the effort. But hell, how I love that girl."

Every good bar has Grand Marnier, and when a fellow finds it, he uses it—especially in his Margaritas. Calvin poured the Grand Marnier into the glasses, after having properly dosed them with good tequila añejo; then capped each in turn with a nickel-plated shaker and shook.

"My best shot at clarity," he said to Fitim, "comes down at the port, outside in the open air, under the sun, all the boats coming in and going out. A fellow can clear his head a good bit down at the port. He can try to anyway."

"Don't worry, Calvin, I will not pressure you. Before I drop the subject once and for all, however, I should mention that if all goes well, the job will pay handsomely. To-day, you make a career of the fish, and they help to fix your head. But to-morrow, maybe the fish are just a nice hobby, and you can still go to the port whenever you like—to fix your head."

"Sounds like a lot of dosh for one Saturday's pay."

"Boh," Fitim puffed. "Details are important. Very important." He leaned back on his barstool and shrugged his shoulders. He looked well-fed and content. "But sometimes one is forced to grab the hammer and swing it without gloves, and worry about the blisters later."

"All the same, I think I'd better leave the hammer lie."

"That's fine. Not another word will be spoken on the matter."

"I hope I haven't disappointed you," said Calvin. "In any case, I don't qualify for much beyond fish duty."

"Monique says you are a good man. I see with my own eyes that you are a good man. If you change your mind—" he caught himself. "Not another word will be spoken on the matter."

"*Oye*, Tio Calvino!" It was Quentin Hazel again. "How in hell could you deny a fellow another round of those fine Margaritas?"

"I'm on it, Hazel!" Calvin confirmed.

"Make them Cadillacs, won't you?"

"Go to hell, Hazel!"

"Do you think," asked Fitim, "you could teach me to make a cocktail?"

"What?" said Calvin. "What do you mean?"

"I would like you to teach me to make a cocktail. I have never made one."

Calvin threw down his barman's implements in disbelief and searched the Albanian. "Say that again."

"I have never made a cocktail."

"Are you telling me you've never made a cocktail?"

"That's what I'm telling you."

"You're a no-good liar. Go on, try again!"

"Honestly," said Fitim. "I have never made a cocktail. I don't know how to."

"How about that! I guess it's true, then. Hell if it's not your lucky night, big fellow."

"Can you make a Manhattan?" asked the big Albanian.

"Now you're going to insult me? Dry, Ruby, Brandy, Perfect, Latin, Cuban—you just name your Manhattan."

"No," he said with a sudden change of heart. "Teach me to make a Margarita. Monique likes them very much."

"Very well, you are going to make that girl the best damned Margarita she's ever had."

"What is that?" Fitim asked, pointing at a bottle of Triple Sec.

"Rule number one," said Calvin, "no Triple Sec. Grand Marnier if you have it—no one expects you to have Gran Gala—Cointreau if you don't. Triple Sec only if you're in a beggar's pinch."

"Why not Triple Sec?"

"Listen, we may be poor, but we are principled. If a fellow can't afford good tequila and Grand Marnier, he can't afford the Margarita. Use only the best ingredients; then it's called a Cadillac."

Calvin coached him through it. When he had finished, Fitim stood proudly and asked, "What do you think?"

"That there," said Calvin, "is a drink a man can be proud of."

"And you think Monique will like it?"

"Hell if she won't."

Fitim headed off with the drink. Calvin yelled after him, "Don't forget to tell her it's a Cadillac!"

"Oh, barkeep! Oh, Calvin!"

"Tell me all about it, Hazel!"

"I do believe that tequila is sick and tired of the masquerade. Send the bottle over directly and we'll take her straight, without all the damned make-up!"

Quentin Hazel was on holiday in Nice, after having recently moved to Oaxaca, Mexico, home of the lucky girl who thought she'd fancy a go at making an honest fellow of him. The wedding was to be a no-expenses-spared winter affair in Acapulco. Most of the crew would be in attendance. Calvin plucked a dancing daisy from near the bar and sent her over to Hazel and company with a silver tray upon which was steadied a tall sapphire-blue tequila bottle, a siphon that twinkled with red rhinestones, a six-set of hand-blown shot glasses and a bowl of sliced limes.

"Here's the tequila now!" Hazel cheered. "Now listen, fellows. Gather round. Now look here—come January, if you boys want to have a good showing before the Mexican contingent, you're going to have to work hard and show that you want it." He grabbed the tequila bottle by the neck. "Now let's see what you got. Look alive, what!" And with that, he took to pouring out shot after shot.

Someone asked if there would be cigars at the wedding.

"Cigars? Hell if we won't blot out the Acapulco sun with clouds of Cuban smoke. I only hope the Mariachi band at the pool won't choke to death—you know, Mexican attorneys and what not."

"Well, that settles it!" exclaimed Wolfe, smacking his palm. "I've been searching for the opening scene for my biography and I believe that'll work famously."

"Someone working on your biography, Wolfe?"

"No, not that I know of," said Wolfe drunkenly. "If someone is, he hasn't informed me of the project, in any case. You heard anything?"

"Negative. You know, Wolfy, you might try *do*ing something first. Give a fellow something to write about, hey. That's the trick."

"Why do you think I'm so flared up over this wedding of yours? Say, how shall we dress? Myself, I'd like to wear linen in a shade of champagne," Wolfe said gallantly, "and I shall wear a like-coloured blossom in my buttonhole, which I'll bestow upon the maid of honour at the moment of my choosing, during the reception."

"Bring a hundred and twenty bouquets, but leave your buttonhole out of it."

"I might just do it, Hazel—the bouquets I mean."

"Hell, bring an entire nursery of rosebushes, thorns and all. Of course, there won't be a maid of honour per se, but rather a sprawling parlour lined with tequila-fuzzed Mexican beauties."

"I'm in love already!" Wolfe swooned.

"Sure you are. And at the end of the whole affair, you know where will you'll find yourself?"

"I haven't an idea," said Wolfe, hanging in anticipation.

"Why, you'll find yourself on the sidewalk in a torn sombrero, with *chilaquila* stains down your bare chest and twirling a flute of bubbly while howling and blinking at the Mexican sunrise."

"Hot damn, Hazel! And where will we stay?"

"You'll stay with us, of course. Everyone is welcome. The house is nice and big with excellent light. I mean really excellent light. And if all is going according to plan back in Acapulco," said Hazel, consulting his watch, "the swimming pool is being filled as we speak."

"Isn't that something! You know, Hazel," said Wolfe, suddenly looking terribly concerned, "I reckon there's an awfully good chance I'll become famous down there in Mexico."

"Is that right?"

"Did I mention I'll be wearing linen in a shade of champagne?"

"You did."

"And I mentioned the part about the like-coloured blossom?"

"You did at that. In your *butt*onhole, no less."

"So, you know," concluded Wolfe with an air of satisfied resignation, "it stands to reason."

"Have you a back-up plan, though, Wolfy? Because I recall that your champagne linen never paid dividends on this side of the pond."

"That's the crazy thing—you're absolutely right. And yet I'm all but certain I'll be a big hit down in Mexico. Why, I'm a respectful fellow!" he demanded, while staring down the barrel of a shot of tequila and nearly tumbling over. "Don't you think I'll be a big hit down in Mexico, Hazel? Don't you think I'll get on well over there?"

"Like a wildfire, Wolfe, like a wildfire. Just try to keep your legs under you, for crissake," said Hazel, trying to steady Wolfe.

"Why, you really seem to be getting on well down there."

"It's not bad, even if I stick out like a sore thumb. It all seems very reasonable at this point. I'm in good with the owner of a bar down the street and he's extended me a tab, so there's that. My only problem now is I have to find out how to make a goddamned wedding ring. I tell you, it never ends!"

"It sure is going to be a grand week."

"A grand week? Stop it, a grand week. You're coming down for the entire month of January, if not the whole bleeding winter. And you're going to bring the whole bloody crew with you, as well. Of course, I can't guarantee any of you will make it back to Europe in one piece."

"Arbuckle and Polish, too? Are they invited?"

"Mexico is not ready for the likes of Arbuckle," Hazel confided.

"You don't think? The country is jolly with dereliction and delinquency."

"Still, they are a solemn people, dignified. They have enough problems without the likes of Arbuckle running about and raising hell." Hazel kicked back another shot. "Bah, what the hell, bring those two monkeys along. The Mexicans are a lovely lot. I've never seen them opposed to a good stirring-up."

Hazel and his court continued on in such a manner for some time, drunken and swaying arm-in-arm, like a band of brothers who knew they would have to part ways at sunset and go off to fight in the war. For now, they stopped only to sing another song and tip back another round of tequila.

Calvin, still behind the bar, suppressed a sudden burp that bubbled up acid. It hung somewhere high in his chest and burned like red rockets. He stood tall, threw back his shoulders and winced. The burn subsided. One of the tall windows that gave onto the alley, which had been open all evening, blew suddenly shut with a bang.

"Hell," said Calvin to no one. "Slack tide."

The evening had reached a high-water mark and every additional minute spent bleary-eyed and upright would only contribute to, and prolong, the oncoming ebb. The sensation that had come over Calvin was not a novel one; it was not specific to that evening. It was a sensation that had begun to creep up on him with quickening frequency for some time. It was a harrowing sensation, a death-like sensation and one he no longer attempted to skirt by youthfully pushing forward or pushing limits, for he had come to understand that long-term damages most typically inflicted themselves in the waning moments of any good fight or celebration. The phenomenon, as Calvin felt it, was a socio-psychic one that he was at a loss to explain. He referred to it simply as the Great Ebb. The Great Ebb was characterised by a loss of excitement, verve, wonder and curiosity, and Calvin predicted that if left unaddressed, it would slowly and silently deconstruct the crew, until the long-time friends were apathetic strangers given to lethargy, cynicism and broadcast programming. The window floated open and again banged loudly shut.

"Slack tide and a summer storm," he declared. "All at once."

There was a time when Calvin knew that every party would be followed up in short order by another. But those days were gone. Any party, now, he decided, might be the last. When the evening at hand came to a close, would the crew ever again come to know those golden moments when it swung, one and all, as a unified group; a boisterous, jockeying, elbowing crack-pot family that knew only good health and fresh colours, ecstatic love and bright eyes? Hell, who could know for certain? Perhaps not, if left to chance. The crew vowed one another its collective back, its unified jaw, its braided fist, but the Great Ebb was the one threat against which Calvin failed to trust the crew in its defence of self. They struggled to communicate with one another over his obscure notion. The crew didn't understand what Calvin meant by the Great Ebb, and he was unable to adequately articulate his feelings on the matter.

"If you can't *feel* what I'm talking about, goddamn it," he would plead, "we are doomed! Do you not recognise our... our steady loss? We are losing, it is all falling away and coming apart. It is all running empty!"

The word *loss* shook free and fell consistently from his wooden jaw.

"But what loss?" they replied. "What is your fear?"

"The Great Ebb!—the very cursed phenomenon that drove all our heroes to *murder themselves!*"

But it was no use. He tried to explain and they tried to understand, but both sides failed in their attempts. Love him as they did, they did not share a common psychological platform that might otherwise make common their fears and foes. Any two men with diverging hopes may maintain an eternal closeness, but two men with diverging fears become strangers with startling quickness. Such was their divergence and it left Calvin feeling alienated and frighteningly alone. The crew knew not what to think or how to react. They feared for Calvin, but were powerless to help him. They thought him to be taking on water, and the diagnosis, irrespective of its accuracy, convinced Calvin of their collective capsizing. In an earlier day in his youth, when life was still flooding – ahead of the ebb – Calvin would gather the crew and whip them into a state of exuberance and elation over little more than their collective presence, but he no longer harnessed the energy to catalyse such a state. They were all a little heavier, a little slower, a little older.

Calvin looked out over the party, which would maintain its ebullience for a short while longer. It was slack tide after all, the illusion-time between high tide and the start of the ebb, when further ascension is impossible and the young and foolish, those still wonderfully deluded by notions of invincibility, try desperately to climb higher, to touch an illusory heaven—and when the sad and broken beasts who know better, who have been stripped of their illusions, look about obtusely and recognise the death of an evening, an experience, and maybe even an era, and see themselves suddenly and clearly for the clunking and irrelevant bodies they have become.

Calvin perseverated, as romantics will on the backside of a good high, despite themselves. Lunar ebb tides are offset by flood tides, in and out, back and forth forever, like the mainspring action of a clockwork machine designed for perpetual motion, forcing wheels and cogs with little friction or deterioration, driving the imperceptible sweep of the hands of time, the constant motion that contributes to the illusion of stillness. The crew, however, faced a different kind of ebb, an ebb that was not generously balanced and offset by an eventual flood. A child standing at the edge of the Grand Canyon is unable to fathom the idea that a paltry, dirty green vein somewhere down below and out of view had carved the great crevice over the ages. The crew's was a constant ebb, an ebb as present and as evident to Calvin as the rushing Colorado River when standing on its red sandy banks; a river-like ebb, which, over time, would twist and turn and carve its way through the heart of the crew.

At any moment, the revellers, choking themselves at the ends of the leads that restrict Man in his efforts to destroy himself, would attack the bar for one final drink, for one final shot at Glory, most of them failing to recognise that they had been prancing and canting about with Glory all evening long.

All of the remaining guests were blown. Broken stilettos littered the edges of the flat. Hazel and Wolfe, arm-in-arm and well out of tune, suffered a great spill. The window slammed like a gunshot every now and then, and no one noticed. A once victorious sky had been turned back at some celestial point of attack and now, with bruised ego, made no further promises. But the storm was not theirs. It was a foreign storm that bullied about somewhere south and spun out before arriving on the shores of Nice. And so the winds did not whip as much as they pushed and shoved in concert with the sea's waves, which pounded the coastline with great violence, racing voluminously up the beach and battering the break wall, sending white water high into the night, as high as the rooftops of the hotels that lined the Promenade. Each crashing wave drove beach stones up and over the break wall, over the Quai des Etas Unis and into the old town. Before long, the gendarmes had blocked off all access to the Promenade and the Quai, the junior-most of the force wielding shovels in an effort to turn back the rising beach. But none of the partiers heard the wash of rocks rushing madly over cobblestone.

Two blokes stumbled up to the bar and asked for a round of whisky. Calvin ran back to the kitchen to see if any bottles remained.

"That's some hot dance floor," said the fellow with the bent nose, wiping his brow. "What did you call that step? The Lindy?"

"No, Lindy was the girl's name."

"Which girl?"

"*Which* girl! Honestly?"

"Oh. You mean the one that…" He pointed a finger toward the ceiling and twirled it about while whistling.

"That's her. At this rate, someone will go out the window before sunrise. I'm sure of it."

"Worse ways to finish a party than going out a window. There is something admirable about a fellow going out a window. It shows character."

"Sure. But let's finish our business before it all comes to the point of going out windows."

Calvin found a final bottle of whisky and ran back to the bar. As he cracked the seal on the bottle, he heard the tall man say in a low voice, "Hell, if I go out a window and end up dead in the alleyway come morning, you'll wish we had finished that conversation."

Calvin poured two glasses and filled an old Ricard decanter with water, as the tall man had requested.

"Right," grunted the other. "And you're no good to me dead. I want the info. After that, the devil take you."

The window slammed shut again.

"Well," said the tall man to the man with the bent nose, "what do you think of what I told you so far?

"I'm still here aren't I? Look, I know this town like the back of my hand. I know people. A man needs to know the streets; then he can start making claims about knowing people. How many are you in the organisation, anyway?"

"Ten. No, make that nine. There was a problem with Gonzalez. But there's no problem anymore, is there."

"What was the matter with Gonzalez?" asked the man with the bent nose.

"He couldn't keep his fat trap shut. Keeping your trap shut is paramount in this line of work, see?"

The tall man searched his rocks glass, turned it about on the bar top as if he were slowly dialling a combination lock. "Still, the man had a wife, didn't he. And a kid," he said and quit dialling.

The tone of the conversation made Calvin's heart thump. A group had danced their way to the bar and ordered a round of Cosmopolitans. Calvin went to work near the two men so as to better hear their conversation.

"Can you back?" asked the tall man. "We're doomed without good backing. Have to be able to resist all hits, all blows."

"Don't worry none about that; I can back."

"And I heard you strike well."

"Yeah? Well, you heard right."

Calvin had encroached too closely. The two men eyed him. He seized up and dropped a loaded martini glass. It shattered on impact, leaving glass shards glittering in a sticky pool of rose-pink.

"Good," said the tall man, regaining the conversation. "Because when we strike, we strike hard. Pieces must be taken out swiftly, cleanly."

"*Pieces*, hey?"

"It's an impersonal term and that's how we prefer it. Beauty is addictive, and it's nothing but beauty on top of beauty around here. Every now and again one of the lads will get attached to a piece and that makes things dicey."

"You don't have to worry about me getting attached."

"They say you're rather cold-blooded. Fine. You do what you're told, you're in. You got a weak back, you don't like the hours, you're out. Simple."

"What's the boss like?"

"He's not the boss for nothing, is he. He can be intimidating. Some say he's ruthless. I say he's an artist."

"He must be good."

"Good? There's no talking about an artist in terms of good and bad. When you get down to it, there are only two kinds of artists—the one who is celebrated for the miracles he creates, and the one who tries to create works that will pass as miracles, or will at least win him bread to pay the bills."

"Hell, I don't care if he's a bloody dictator. I need the dosh."

"See here, his latest line of lapel pins—gun dogs. Absolutely exquisite."

Lapel pins! A chilled spike shot up Calvin's spine and sweat instantly moistened his head and chest, as had become his conditioned reaction.

The tall man reached for a summer-weight coat. "Have a look."

Calvin spun about and saw, there on the man's lapel, a corded standard poodle cast in precious metal and poof-studded with brilliant-cut black onyx. Its face and legs were contrasted with miniature white diamonds.

"How about that," said the man with the bent nose. "The poodle's carrying a polka-dot parasol."

"Sure. The parasol is sterling silver, the polka-dots genuine rubies."

It was just the conversational banana peel to rob Calvin of his psychological footing. "Spooks!" he cried. "Spooks! Keep away!"

He spotted a bottle of *sucre de canne* and clutched it by the neck; then instinctively coiled himself into ready position and paused for the breath that would spring his catch and set into motion a violent whirlwind blitz.

"Spooks?" challenged the man with the bent nose, "Hold your tongue, child. We are artisans."

It was sufficient riposte to give Calvin pause. "There may well be an artistic angle to your espionage," Calvin put forth, "but calling yourselves artisans—Pah!"

"See here," said the tall man, putting the lapel pin on display. "We make jewellery."

"Save your breath, you proper devils! I've seen the herding dogs with saliva catches. They haunt my head, chase me through the alleyways and the halls of my own building! I see nothing else as I lay in bed each night. I know the boss, the man in the herringbone coat!"

"Herding dogs with saliva catches? Why, that's the Pavlov collection."

"You want Pavlov's dog?" boomed Calvin. "Here I am! Go on, ring the bell and watch me clear the house!"

"Hear me good, bigh," said the man with the bent nose, unsheathing a thick Limerick accent. "Swing that bottle once again and I'll claim ye."

Calvin railed blindly, "Think you'll take me out swiftly and cleanly like you did Gonzalez, hey!"

The music wailed. A wan and dishevelled crowd had gathered round. The dancing was still feverish.

"Hold on, son," said the tall man, using a flattened palm to restrain the man with the bent nose. "Take you out like Gonzalez? Gonzalez wasn't taken out; he was sacked. Our clients have a right to their privacy."

"*Sacked*! Sure!" Calvin spat. "A moment ago it was all striking and backing. You boys think I'll make a fine *piece*, do you?"

"Look, a lot of our pins are hand-stamped. That's the striking. And without the backing, how on earth would a pin stay on a fellow's lapel? You don't like the term *piece*, call them whatever the hell you like. Only mind yourself and leave us be."

Calvin heard none of it. "You sons of bitches got *noth*ing on me!"

It was an undeniably queer scenario for all those present. Paranoia had driven Calvin to hallucination. For all the scuffles, dust-ups and brawls they had seen and been a part of, this was the scene that would be recounted time and time again, through correspondence and at the crew reunions that would follow over the years, long after they had split and the winds of change had blown them to the far-gone and foreign stretches of the globe.

Sweat stung Calvin's eyes and blurred his vision. It can be argued that survival is the most fundamental instinct guiding any organism; and that madness is what happens when the integrity of that guiding force is breached and the prospects of death, of the end, lobby successfully for a valid voice within the living system. Madness, however, is unnatural, and as an immune system battles germs, so battles natural instinct against unnatural madness. The battle for sanity is waged by bombarding the burning brain with clean, lucid thoughts (a certain aspirin to break the fever) in hopes of calling to action the will to live, that it might then carry the subject off to some safe haven for repair and calibration.

Now, through all the heat and chaos of the moment, there was one lucid thought that was determined to cool Calvin's searing mind, and finally succeeding somewhere deep within, Calvin recognised the obviousness that these two fellows were not spooks. He had made the wrong read and he now knew it. The admission, however, did nothing to placate the clash at hand, for Calvin's afflictions ran much deeper than any one conflict, any one incident. The acknowledgement that the two men before him were innocent artisans did nothing to alleviate his dread over the spies he believed were tailing him, those he believed to have bugged his flat, those tracking his movements in the hallways of his own building and the alleyways of his own quarter. So while he fell silent and no longer flashed the bottle of *sucre de canne* at the two artisans, per se, he did indeed continue to threaten and accuse and brandish the bottle menacingly at the men as two effigies that stood in representation of all of the scoundrels, spooks and anxieties that had come to hound him of late.

He had made the wrong damned read and this troubled him greatly. Although he knew he would never have standing in the world, he had been able to count on his wits to get by in certain comfort and style. A fellow, he always believed, had nothing to fear so long as he had his wits. On that night, at Manx's party, his wits failed him. He had made the wrong read, and that is what frightened him most. It had, in fact, been a troubling trend of late. And so, despite the external menaces, which were indeed palpable and plenty, he was forced to consider whether the greatest threats to his mental and physical wellbeing weren't now rising up from within himself, the creations and failures of his own addled mind.

But as it were at that moment, standing there madly poised with a bottle of *sucre de canne*, he had gone too far to cut losses, reverse course and save face. He could only push forward with still greater force at the risk of losing everything.

"Calvin! Calvin!"

The sound of his name reached him and hit like a bullet. Only then did he recognise that Klarysa had been screaming at him. "Calvin, stop it! Stop!"

Just then, a pretty young buck appeared and slipped his arm around Klarysa's waist. "Come on, baby," he said. "Forget that maniac. Let's see you shake it some more." And he whisked her away.

The timing could not have been worse. In the receding vision, Klarysa's dress bled a red wake to match the hot flood in Calvin's head. He needed her at that moment unlike ever before. She was the one thing that might have saved him, and her abduction in his time of need, by yet another local bloke, was the final inequity that pushed him over the edge. Seeing only red, he erupted with a guttural noise and swung blindly with all his might. The result was an alarming cacophony of smashing glasses and shattering bottles.

The man with the bent nose looked sickened and determined and seemed to be seeking out an angle of counterattack, but the tall man held him back nervously.

"You raving lunatic!" cried the tall man with a quavering voice. "You should be locked up!" He struggled to restrain the man with the bent nose. "Let's go, George!" he said. "George! Let's go!"

George eventually began to shuffle off, against his will, with the tall man still wrapped around him.

Manx finally pushed through the crowd and appeared at the head of the scene. He clutched his head in his hands and moaned from his midsection. Several of the crew calmed Calvin and examined him from a very close distance, as one does a fallen rider thrown from a fast-moving scooter. The music cut, the dancing stopped, the floor sparkled dangerously with a singular wet brilliance.

"Go home, Calvin," said Manx almost inaudibly.

"I'm going."

Manx erupted. "*Go home and don't ever come back!*"

"Go to hell, Manx."

Calvin crunched his way through the stunned crowd and towards the door. At the back of the gathering mass, he found Klarysa. The bloke who had whisked her away stood close, but no longer had his arm around her. Call it a flash of good judgement.

"Come on, Klarysa," said Calvin. "We're going home."

"*You* go home!" she said. "I'm staying. Just because *you're* a worn out animal, don't think that I'm—"

"Come on," he said quietly and reached for her hand.

"Hey!" piped the bloke with whom she had been dancing. "The lady says she's staying."

So much for good judgement.

Calvin, with his glistening bloodshot eyes and his bamboo limbs and his roadmap face, stepped to the lad so that their chests were nearly touching. He leaned in and whispered something low in the fellow's ear; then stepped back to Klarysa and calmly said, "Come on, Klarysa. Let's go home."

"I'm not going anywhere!" she insisted.

Her response was expected. Calvin looked over at the young bloke (as did Klarysa, the shameless rubbernecker, now wide-eyed for a bloody car-wreck), but the formerly quick-tongued fellow with the once-fine complexion had turned the colour of diseased chicken fat and said not one goddamned word. And then in one deft movement, Calvin bent and scooped and slung Klarysa up and over his shoulder like a good Moroccan lad with a prized rug, and made for the door. Klarysa tried to resist, but it was no use.

On the landing, Calvin and his payload ran smack into Fitim, who had stepped out for a moment and was returning to collect Monique. Survival instinct flared anew and without a hitch, Calvin shot at him, "I'm your man."

Fitim was at a loss.

Said Calvin testily, "Well, are you looking for someone to help you with a job, or aren't you?"

"I am."

"Very well, then."

"But—"

"But nothing. I need an ally around here. Good night."

Fitim stepped aside, blank-faced, and let them pass. Klarysa's cursing voice receded down the staircase.

Once in the alley, Calvin put her on her feet. Like a flash, she slipped out of her heels, raced off down the alleyway, rounded the corner onto Cours Saleya and disappeared. Calvin moaned in defeat and huffed off after her, but as he reached Cours Saleya, she was nowhere to be found. He had heaped all blame upon himself even before Klarysa's feet had touched down in the alley, and as he pursued her, he knew his punishment would be severe; for Klarysa understood that those like her, who were willing to put themselves in harm's way as a means of punishing a loved one, made for deliciously cruel torturers.

To be sure, it was an ill hour for any young girl to be walking the streets in viscose and bare feet—even a girl as savvy as Klarysa. Good lord, thought Calvin, grant her the good sense to not drift too far west. And for crissake, keep her off the goddamned Promenade. At that hour, the Promenade was a hot vein spotted with all the wrong types. Every corner was occupied by painted ladies and men who passed themselves as painted ladies, and all slick dogs were juiced and cruising, not so much for whores, for they cost money and didn't scare easily, but for any pretty little untagged doe to have wandered inadvertently out from under the protective glow of the old town's ice-cream vendors and panini shops.

Calvin combed the area at a good clip for a quarter of an hour, and then looped back to see if she had returned home. No luck. It was his punishment. And if she were eventually found molested or worse, in some dark corner, that too would be his punishment. There was little choice but to walk the streets until he found her. And if it meant walking the streets for an entire week without pause, perhaps to finally find her one shining day on a sunny terrace, in sunglasses and a broad-brimmed hat and drinking champagne with a dark-haired blue-eyed fellow, that too would be his punishment.

He headed back out into the alley, his search made difficult by every point of light, tauntingly crosshatched as they were with great yawning Xs for the welling water that refused to stop blurring his vision. How wet those eyes that kept drawing the attention of his moist wrists and fingers and shirt sleeves. A desperate, animal moan bellowed low from his chest and throat, and then, too, a fresh flood of saltwater and more bright-white Xs yawning, yawning between frantic batting black lashes.

He pushed his way thus, down the Promenade, which was, by the grace of all gods and the southern storm, blocked off and sheltered from the typical manmade night action. Never so relieved was he by the presence of uniformed gendarmes, who would be clearing beach stones from the street until long after sunrise.

Eventually, the skies lightened. A meek star rose behind a prevailing mass of clouds, somewhere east of the chateau. Calvin looped around yet again and aimed himself back towards the old town. Near the Place du Palais-de-Justice, he caught sight of Klarysa. Arbuckle and Nadine were with her. The three of them walked slowly, gingerly, Nadine supporting Klarysa through her bare and tender steps.

"Hey!" Calvin yelped, catching them up. "Hey!" It was the only word he could manage.

Klarysa looked a wreck. Her hair was a knotty tangle, her face filthy with the dusty trails of dried tears.

Arbuckle and Nadine, having returned from San Tropez, found her like that, walking trancelike back towards the Vieux. For a moment, no one said a word. Finally, Calvin attempted a question, but was cut short by Arbuckle. "Not now," he said. "Just get her home."

Calvin took her gently, without another word, as Arbuckle advised, and guided her home.

It was another new low.

> How many versions of yourself will you meet tonight?
> *How will I greet myself?*
> *I Left the Delta burning and consumed, vultures circling overhead. One-hundred-six degrees, a burning hell. I rise high on the Bay Bridge and realize I've been unconscious for the last sixty miles, watch in the rearview at the wide bank of toll booths not knowing if I've paid to pass or slammed my way through, dip and shoot through the Treasure Island tunnel and climb again on the foggy SF side, the Embarcadero lining the concrete edge of the city. Old piers jut into the churning bay like rusty teeth, a broken zipper ripped apart by salty surfer mitts, my love, my Laika, a mad death rattle shake down to the axels, the world watching and laughing, I napalm every goddamned thing in sight.*
> "I've been barred from the Birds. You know that, Kid."
> "*Yes. I know. But I'm sick, Pug.*"
> "You just panicked is all."
> "*I ain't panicked.*" Pug, he know about death. "*I'm a wolf.*"
> "You wasn't convicted."
> "*I'm a wolf and you know it!*"
> *I need to lie down.*
> Footsteps come heavy up the stairs. *A wolf in sheep's clothing.* In the hallway, Kid run into Dez.
> "We got work to do, boy!" Dez say.
> *Not tonight. Not tonight. I'm real sick. I need to lie down.*
> "You a wolf, boy! See how cold it is up in this house! You a sure enough wolf! Theys work to be done!"
> "Don't mind my hands, boy." *My ma and her blue lips.*
> Black slander slide thick and leaden from Kid's young lips. His mouth twist down low and ugly. Dez, he rear back with a big fist and smack Kid good in the mouth. He crumble to the floor and smell burnt stars. His tongue run warm with sticky blood over lips and baby teeth and he recognize that old hot-metal in the back of his throat and his hands swipe down over his patched-up corduroys.

"What are you thinking of doing, Kid?" He pull a red hat down over his head. "Let's just walk it off…"

The door slam and I cry bitter tears, throw punches into the mattress. I be the one to lick it.

"*Going to teach him a lesson is what.*" A confused childlike hallucination in a brand new cage.

"Oh, what did I do to have my son end up like this!"

"*Somebody tell Nicki I'm gone.*"

The judge, he stand up. He slam down a gavel and shout, "Bury him where he falls, Desmond, if that's what it comes to!"

Laika walks back to the front seat of a hard white van and takes her handbag. She takes a leaf of stationary and writes: You got what you had coming to you. You deserve everything you got. *She takes a matching envelope, stuffs it, seals it, poises her pen to write an address on the envelope, only she doesn't know who to send it to. She puts the pen and the paper and the envelope back into her handbag and starts walking up the dusty levee road*

I left the Delta burning and consumed

"He going to pay."

"But what are you thinking of doing, Kid? Let's just walk it off."

A sudden burning urge overtakes me, an urge to fly right back out to the Delta and finish the job, only Laika doesn't know who to send the letter to and I don't know who to finish off

I can't lick it. My god, I can't lick it!

A hellish scream fills the car. Tangled hands find the steering wheel. Dusty hair falls onto dusty floor mats. Some big confused part of me watches me helplessly

A childlike hallucination

Peaking now on the Bay Bridge, San Francisco has never looked so bland and aloof and accidental. Skyscrapers gather and stack ridiculously. Burn the passive lot down. Good rude city stomp a boy good

You got what you had coming to you. You deserve everything you got.

"*I'm a wolf.*"

"But you wasn't convicted!"

She doesn't know who to send the letter to. She puts it back in her handbag and walks off, down the dusty levee road.

19   If lust and violence foretell rotten endings

In which Klarysa leverages
astrology and religious myth and
Calvin meets Richard.

Klarysa had shown great resilience in rebounding from the
graceless denouement to Manx's party. Calvin, on the other hand,
had not fare so well. And though one might argue that generally
speaking his burden was more cultivated than hers, another might
claim that resilience has less to do with one's burden and more to do
with one's youthfulness or, as Klarysa would point out for Calvin in
a show of back-handed comfort, his lack thereof.

If such a thing were possible, Klarysa was greedy with her
youth, and at the limber age of twenty-four, she was convinced her
best days were distant memories. "For my kind," she once said,
"every day beyond twenty-one years belongs to *le Grand Cirque*." It
was a statement that confused Calvin on a number of levels. What
did she mean—sad? Clownish? Gauche? There was, she replied with
a sigh, no sense in explaining it to those who weren't of her kind. Of
what kind, he ventured, but was informed that if one had to ask, one
did not qualify. Calvin wondered crossly if she weren't referring to
the impertinent kind that perceived the benefit of youth to be naught
but that which absolved its company of the culpability (and
subsequent sentencing) otherwise charged at the tail-end of all the
callow and foolhardy acts they were apt to commit.

A week had passed since Manx's party and Calvin had spent a good day down at the port. The fish had cooperated marvellously, lying motionless, offering their necks, their soft underbellies to his gleaming sun-struck blade. Sure they were dead, but as difficult a go as Calvin had had of late, no good fortune was taken for granted, and he loved the little creatures all the more for their willingness and exaggerated lack of opposition.

After cleaning up, he traced the Quai de Lunel up around the Monument aux Morts, around the chateau and over to Castel Plage, where he traded his dungarees for swimming trunks and treated himself to an after-work dip in the sea. He had once heard that salt water helped to wash away the lingering fish oils and softened the skin, the latter advantage accommodating what had become the very least of his concerns. At any rate, floating about in the warm blue sea had a wonderfully pacifying effect. He was still unable to sleep at night, but what startled him more was the fact that the sleeplessness hadn't slowed his motor any. He was eating less, too, though he hadn't lost any weight. It was as though some calorific strain had come to occupy his belly and was now serving as a mutant source of sustenance.

After the swim, he rinsed off under a shower along the break wall and towelled off; then walked down to the Rive Bleue to meet Hector, who had arrived the night before, from Milano. They embraced, they sat, they drank whisky and recounted summer plums and highlights. Nearly a month had passed since they last sat face-to-face and each was happy to see the other.

Calvin was not a particularly proud fellow, but he felt a certain pride when in Hector's presence and a certain serenity in associating himself with that fellow's propriety and charm. He felt similarly about his acquaintance with Fitim, though there were prominent differences. Some London pubs have a main bar, the one entered into by the front door, and a back bar, which is typically entered into, by those who tend to occupy it, from a lesser-known side door, off a side-street or alley. Some such back bars are sunken, less brightly lit, have lower ceilings, and are frequented by blokes with thicker bones, broader backs and more colourful tongues than those at the main bar. And though both Fitim and Hector were accustomed to having their way regardless of room or setting, Fitim was clearly the tough with whom one wanted to knock about in the back bar, whereas Hector was the gentleman with whom one wanted to glide gallantly through the front door.

Hector was tall and slender. His swarthy skin promoted the best of everything the Mediterranean had to offer. With his fine linen suit, his year-round summer complexion and the silver hairs that feathered subtlety at his temples, he was the picture of good health and easy living. A pleasantly rich scent exuded from him. He smelt worldly and wealthy—wealthy with knowledge, and no lousy textbook knowledge, but rather a live and rambling knowledge; wealthy with experience and confidence. Mostly he reeked wonderfully of contentment. Not any conservative, stay-at-home manner of contentment, mind you, but an active contentment, one that shimmered like a fat wet snake winding its way under equatorial sunlight.

And although until recently Calvin had been conscious of, and grateful for, a sound personal grip on that rare gem called contentment, he never quite harboured the confidence to maintain the degree of contentment privy to a fellow the likes of Hector. It wasn't, for example, only for a lack of finances that Calvin preferred a cosy, intimate flat; he was never one to feel he had the character to adequately occupy and fill large spaces. Hector, by contrast, had no need for a flat whatsoever, his lavish Catalan spread notwithstanding. Hector knew a sense of adequacy, confidence and contentment to make a travelling home of all Europe and Asia, all the continents' vast and open spaces, their valleys and mountains, and likely those of the rest of the world, as well. At present, there was little gamble in wagering that Calvin envied Hector his contentment more than he had envied any other man his treasure.

The two never lacked for conversation, for each was innately curious. Their verbal threads did not narrow towards ends, but rather branched into networks of topical tributaries that ran off in countless directions. It was not rare to see one or the other jotting down notes, the easier to regain a certain bend in a conversational stream, and from there follow a thought from which they had temporarily deviated. Each had a lofty level of respect for the other, and each man's desire to impress the other brought out the sharpest in him. Interesting, too, was the remarkable unspoken familiarity evident between the two of them, which may have contributed to the slightly disarming sense of exposure each felt when in the company of the other, as though there were little chance that even the most closely guarded secret might make it through the end of any visit unexposed. The queer presentiment of naked transparency was somehow provoked by the fact that each identified in the other certain admirable qualities and facets that he neither possessed nor, nonetheless, coveted. Calvin was, for example, astounded by the unabashed swagger of the venturesome trader-trafficker who, for all intents and purposes was only ever one incriminating wrinkle removed from being seized and indicted. Meanwhile, Calvin's sense of restraint in the face of golden opportunities rather astonished Hector.

Lastly, there was the unaddressed subject of trust, and the fact that neither knew exactly how much of the stuff he had for the other. For when one got right down to it – moral judgement and legal relativity aside – two intelligent men between whom the most tangible bond is a mutual engagement in illegal activities stood sweet little chance of establishing much in the way of joint trust. And as void contracts are void *ab initio*, which is to say from the start, so too, perhaps, are the friendships hatched under suspect stars.

When they had just about talked themselves out, Calvin asked of Hector, "You're sure you've never heard of this fellow called DeTorche?"

"DeTorche," echoed Hector. "No, not since the last time you asked. I did once spend a number of stormy nights, however, fumbling about in a darkened houseboat, looking for a torch with a girl called De Toren—I believe you call it a *flashlight*—related one way or another to the South African wine family, or so she claimed. Certainly had the wine collection to back up her claim, at any rate. I can recall many racy moments from that trip, but can no longer remember what she wanted in exchange for her wine. Doesn't matter. That was in Rotterdam, by the way, and the search for the torch was a ruse—she believed it was the lightning, but it was I who shorted all the fuses. Who is this DeTorche, anyway?"

"I don't know," said Calvin. "Some stripe of spook or villain, though. Of that I'm certain. Well slick fellow by reputation; powerful, too, if you believe the legend."

"Legend, you say?"

"You're quite right, let's not embellish. I'm sure he's only a man. I say, you look somehow hurt. He *is* just a man."

"I wouldn't know one way or another. All the same, a man may be considered a legend, might he not?"

"Of course not. Extravagant to say a man of flesh and bones is a legend. An exceptional fellow may earn legendary status, but legends are mythical. What now? Are you disappointed?"

"Don't be ridiculous. You see concern and nothing more—the words *spook* and *villain* are twenty-five-cent words in my line. You know that."

"Sure, but *legend* is the word that made you glow."

"*Legend* is a fifty-cent word. Listen here, Calvin, I am a man, and a damned motivated one at that. And like all motivated men, I am deterred by deterrents, but motivated by prospects. If that sounds elemental, that's because it is. For better or worse, motivated men seek action, results, movement. They have no mind for inaction or stillness, and no motivated man is brought to a point of inaction by deterrents. Deterrents merely compel the inactive man to remain inactive. Proponents of correction-through-punishment fail for their inability to understand that. The concept of negative motivation is oxymoronic to all but the risk-averse, and the risk-averse are already voiceless and immobile."

"Hell, he may only be an aristocrat," said Calvin, narrowing his eyes.

"I see; a don," said the proud Latino.

"No, not a don. Surely, not a don," Calvin denied with the satisfied look of a tenured man who had just ripped the stripes off the uniform of an audacious sub-official. "Not with a name like DeTorche. And you call yourself a Spaniard."

"I call myself a Catalan, and there are many fair-haired among us. Could be an assumed name, a faux *Néerlandais*."

"They say his hands are as smooth as church mice."

"Lucky fellow. Legendary hands."

"You know," said Calvin with a lift of his chin. "One might describe your hands as having the smoothness of church mice."

"How kind of you," he said facetiously. "I do take care of myself. You'll come to discover it takes more effort with every passing year."

"What do you think of swimming in the sea? I am told saltwater makes for soft skin."

"Are you?"

"I am."

Calvin held a sportive smile. Finally, Hector said, "Is there anything you'd care to unveil and discuss, my boy? Otherwise I'm happy to go on comparing beauty secrets deep into the night. I've all the time in the world."

There was a short silence, which Calvin gamely burst, "Bah, what boring chatter! Go on, then, tell me what you have for me."

Hector let hang a silence of his own, and finally said, "Hair tonic. If you're still onboard."

"Hair tonic? I wouldn't have guessed hair tonic might qualify as contraband."

"This tonic is different than most. It contains marmot urine."

"Marmot urine is illegal?"

"No, but the extraction method is. If you're still onboard," he repeated.

The sparring left Calvin fatigued. Sincerity was all that was left him. "I don't know, Hector," he said. "Honestly, I don't think I'm cut out for running."

"I understand. There is a strong element of stress to what we do. I recommend a break, if you don't decide to pack it in altogether. You do a fine job, Calvin. You are dependable and I... Well, you are trustworthy," he said with sincerity. "But it is true, you don't look quite well."

"I haven't slept in weeks."

"I believe it. You once looked like a Spaniard. Now you look like a Frenchman." He finished with a friendly wink and the two friends laughed.

Calvin walked a case of hair tonic over to the studio of a local stylist, and with the idea of eliminating two birds with one stone, flopped down in a chair for a haircut and a shave. Women have their manicures and pedicures; when a man wants to treat himself to luxury, he goes for a steamed towel and straight-blade shave.

The sun was setting by the time Calvin returned home. Klarysa was stretched out on the divan, studying a fashion magazine.

"Darling, finally," she said without looking up from her magazine. "Where have you been?"

"I met Hector for a drink and then went for a quick clip."

He kicked off his shoes, emptied his pockets and ambled into the kitchen. "I told you this morning that Hector was in town, no?"

"This morning was days ago. Darling, you know I prefer you to come straight home from work."

"That's sweet of you. Did you miss me?"

"Plus," she replied, "there is work to be done to-night."

"Work? To-night? Impossible. I'm laid out. Did you eat already?"

"I ate days ago. Any news of a certain knife?"

"No, but I've asked Hector to keep an eye out for it."

"Who, that Catalan trafficker?"

"Sounds awfully cheap when you put it that way, but I suppose that's the long and short of it. I told him all about the knife, so… What work, anyway? Can it wait until to-morrow?"

"Not likely. What did you tell him?"

Calvin sat at the kitchen bar with a bowl of *soupe de poisson*, a slice of *tête pressée* and half a baguette. "Bah, I told him your grandfather had fashioned a knife and died by its blade. I told him you're looking for it. Told him you believe it to be somewhere in France."

"It *is* somewhere in France."

"He seemed interested."

"Pah! I'm sure he did. Can you trust him?"

"In what sense? To not stab me with it should he find it? Are you OK? You're on edge to-night."

"Oh, darling, it's true," she said, slapping aside the magazine and finally looking at him. "Oh!" she gasped, but maintained her course. "I'm a basket of nerves to-night. I am. But you first; what did the Catalano say?"

"He didn't say anything. He choked on a swig of whisky and excused himself to the loo. By the way, I told him I'm done running."

"You did? But why?"

"I don't feel right about it is all. Do you have any idea how marmot urine is extracted?"

"What do you take me for? Honestly. But why quit now? You make so few deliveries as it is. He pays you well, does he not?"

"He does indeed," Calvin admitted, and added with perplexity, "And he just doubled my rate."

"Really? I say, you're a fool to quit."

"I'm a fool all right," he mumbled into his soup.

"Did you quit, then?"

"No, I didn't quit. Didn't I just say I'm a fool?"

"Would it offend you greatly," she began, retaking her fashion magazine, "if I said that hairstyle is all wrong for you?"

Klarysa had no need for religion. Having identified little difference between the provinces of religion and pop-culture, she looked conveniently to cinematic productions and the lifestyle magazines of London and Paris not only for her amusement, but for her moral foundation and direction, as well. Both provinces, she posited, demanded the suspension of disbelief, depicted good and evil with childish simplicity and promised happy endings for all but the less-attractive supporting cast. It was only a matter of audience, she said—religion being the most effective means of reaching the gullible and fearful, the elements of pop-culture being the most effective means of reaching the idle and fashion-forward. One could only be so critical of her brash assessment. By all means, pop-culture was trivial, sensational and corrupt, but it never served as reference material for promoters of organised intolerance, mass murder and genocide.

"I hope," she added in reference to his haircut, "the consultation did not cost and arm and a leg."

Despite what all the waifs at the studio had said, Calvin was not convinced that a tipped bowl of chopped salad constituted a hairstyle.

"The consultation," he said to her, unruffled, "came free of charge. The stylist called me fatal."

"And what did he mean by that?"

"I've no idea, but it came across as a compliment. It would seem he fancies me."

"It's going around," she mumbled. "Clearly, they are putting something in the water."

"How do you mean? What is going around?"

"There are a lot of queer fish in this town," she said. "Anyway, that stylist rendered you a madman."

"You are on rare edge to-night, dear. What gives?"

"Don't worry, we'll get there. It looks as if you may well murder someone."

"I called him a follicular deconstructionist. For what it's worth, the Belgian youth apparently call this *destroy*."

"Destroy," she repeated pensively, studying the glowing tip of her cigarette and then rolling it between her fingers, sculpting the silver ash into a perfectly domed nub against the inner rim of the ashtray. "There was mention in to-day's horoscope," she continued.

"Something of Sodom and Gomorrah. I forget what exactly—fire or destruction or some similarly dark forecast."

"I didn't think you took stock in any of that."

"Astrology or religious myth?"

"Either."

"I'm just like any other fellow," she said. "I'll believe absolutely anything if it suits my needs."

"Who benefits from religious myth?" he asked, for she often gave wonderful responses to such questions.

"The fearful and those who are too lazy, or otherwise unable, to take responsibility for themselves."

"And astrology?"

"Why, the fashion-forward, of course. Ask anyone with an eye for fashion; they're even more superstitious than the Asians. Why, a fashion designer in Tokyo may read as many as one hundred horoscopes per day."

"Is that right? Where did you hear that?"

"It's impossible to say, really, and anyway it doesn't matter. Bah, attributing curses to black cats and broken mirrors, for example, is your own American dilemma. But the fable of hellfire and brimstone for the Pentapolis on the Jordan—why, that's practically universal."

"What's your point?"

"My point," she said, "is that every town is guilty of misdeeds and transgressions, just like Sodom and Gomorrah. And if lust and violence foretell rotten endings…"

"Lust?"

"That which comes before sex."

"I thought that was foreplay," he said jokingly.

"What's more, you've received your warnings, have you not?"

"You mean the spooks? OK, but unlike Lot, I've housed no angels. Are you implying that we should we leave town and not look back lest we turn to pillars of salt?"

"Ha! You joke, but which of us is so righteous as to forestall the fire and brimstone? What with *your* violence and *my*—"

"Lust?"

Calvin sensed a little blue flame flickering in the deep recesses of his internal boiler.

Klarysa drew from her cigarette and held it, gazed wistfully away with narrowed eyes towards a faded horizon, affecting the look of a mid-career veteran who had not only come to realise that there would be no gratitude for valorous sacrifices rendered, but that there was no real justification for the sacrifices in the first place, and who now slogged unbelievably through a self-prescribed role of martyrdom, rather than investing the energy to cut losses and make a fresh start.

"Lust," she managed thinly. "That which comes before sex."

"OK. That does it. Out with it!" Calvin demanded. "What misdeeds and transgressions have you—"

"Oh, *do* go see yourself in the mirror!" she excitedly interrupted. "You are the very image of a madman! I know you should like to kill me, but stay away! Don't you touch me! Don't you lay a finger on me!"

"Good lord," he said calmly. "You dramatic little mouse, whatever has gotten into you? I've never laid a hand on you and I'm not about to start."

With that she leapt from the divan and ran to him.

"Please hold me, Calvin!" she implored. "Quick! Oh, I know I said not to, but I need you to. I hate that I need you to, but I can't help it. When you touch me I fall apart. I so badly need to fall apart right now and never come back together."

He held her and rocked her gently.

"My, my, my," he said. "There, there. Come, let's sit down."

They went to the divan and after a moment Klarysa calmed down. Calvin said to her, "My love, you're all over the place tonight. What is the matter? Ever since Manx's party, you've been manic."

"It's true, Calvin. That night changed everything."

His heart sank. "How so?" he ventured.

"Just everything."

"Including me?"

She nodded sadly and said, "Yes, you, too."

"Oh, no," he said directly. "Please don't say that, Klarysa. I'm sorry. I can be better. I promise."

"Oh, Calvin, don't you see it's too late for change? We can't help who we are. And anyway, this really has very little to do with you.

"I can change, Klarysa. I can. I want to. I *need* to. Just give me a chance."

"You don't understand, my love. I don't want you to change. You should, of course, find a way to fight less, but—"

"Yes, yes, of course," he concurred. "I will."

"You must stop agreeing with me! I'm not one to be listened to. I don't know what I'm talking about. You are lovely, Calvin. You are passionate. I love you just exactly how you are."

"I don't understand. What, then, is the matter?"

"Don't you see? People don't change."

"But I *can* change, Klarysa. I can be better."

"My, but you don't listen! I'm not talking about you. *I* am the broken one. *I* am the one who is no good! You must hate me."

"That is not true. Don't say that. Please."

"I am broken!" she demanded tearfully. "I can't be fixed and you will come to hate me if you don't already."

She was determined in her self-flagellation, and so Calvin sat quietly for a moment, in part because he did not wish to further excite her, in part because it is terribly frustrating to watch a loved one torture herself with one's hateful feelings when one's hateful feelings simply do not exist. Klarysa was an erratic baby bird, to be sure; one prone to chance panic attacks and fits of insecurity, but he had never before seen her in such a state. He searched their conversation for clues, stumbled over the word *lust* and was mentally circling it in red ink for closer inspection when she pulled away from him, looked him in the eye and said, "I must tell you something. The early morning following Manx's party, when I ran away... I may have betrayed you."

"Betrayed me? How?"

"*How*? Why, how on earth do you think? It's true, you *are* fatal. You are! You leave it all out there, you foolish, foolish child! When are you going to learn to not be so open? Such abuse you invite! You throw those fists of yours at every tinkling of a bell, but you have absolutely no idea how to protect yourself! Will you never learn?"

Klarysa's words produced a cartoonish sound of fried electronics in the house of Calvin's head, and suddenly all the lights in his great glassy green-windowed eyes popped and blinked, on and off, on and off.

"Calvin. Darling. Won't you please say something?"

"You *may* have betrayed me?" he said dryly.

"I was completely soused and desperate. You had gone mad at the party and outside the night was so gorgeous and dangerous and demanding. With every crashing wave against the break wall, I felt a little weaker and a little more liberated—helpless, but without even the smallest concern over my helplessness. With help from the waves, all the rocks from the beach were throwing themselves up and onto the Promenade. I had a mind to climb down the break wall between waves and let the next swell stone me dead. I relished the idea and the only reason I didn't pursue it is because I realised there were countless streets in Nice which I had not yet walked, and shouldn't I see a few of them before dying? One block over, I discovered Rue France. The name leads one to think it might be an old and beautiful street, so I followed it along. But it isn't beautiful at all. It is big and new and terribly dead and lonely. The only source of life is the girls that crowd each corner. My, there are an exorbitant amount of girls working in that part of town. Soviet girls, the closer you get to the airport; before that, gorgeous Africans."

Calvin listened in silence, as though from within a warm womb flooding heavily with anaesthetics. The world had come to a halt. The alleyway below, an incessant cacophony of revving motors and clanging chaos, had fallen silent and still. In all the world, there was only Klarysa's voice.

"Some girls," she continued, "took pity on me and advised me to go home, but the night was jumbled and ripe and I wanted to walk along and watch the buildings under such battered lighting. Two men in an expensive black sedan followed me for a while. They ridiculed me and shouted horrible threats, but at that moment, no one could hurt me, no one could touch me. Finally, I stopped and looked at them and listened to all their hateful words and eventually they drove off from boredom. I doubt I would have offered the slightest resistance had they attacked me. When they had driven off, I turned around and directly into the arms of strapping white Russian. I don't know what happened after that. I may have fainted, it's impossible to say. But my, what a filly!" she finished with a look of dazzled wonderment.

Calvin's hands swiped down over his trousers. His teeth were on edge and he tasted hot-metal in the back of his throat.

"I'll kill him," he gurgled like a waking geyser. "I'll kill him!"

"Who him?" she demanded impatiently. "I said *filly*. Are you listening to me?"

"I am, you little trollop! You said *filly* all right, only a filly is a *female!*"

"If you're going to play schoolteacher," she lashed back, "do at least teach me something I don't know! It's hurtful how little confidence you have in my English."

"What cruel nonsense you talk! Do you mean to tell me you've betrayed me with another woman?"

Oh, the ill feeling that befalls a fellow upon discovering that he has carelessly overlooked a perfectly reasonable possibility.

"I've already told you," she said, "I don't know what happened. I may have fainted. I woke in a crummy white box of a flat with bevelled mirrors and plastic-framed Nagels on the walls and cheap vertical blinds of a yellowing fabric drawn over the windows. Many people in this town have remarkably bad taste! Beyond that, I only recall the faint taste of cheap musk and talcum on my tongue when I left the flat."

"Sweet Mary Margaret!" Calvin cried, with his hands in his hair. "Strike me down!"

Then, distracted by the thought of how tormented she looked when he had finally found her supported by Arbuckle and Nadine on that blustery morning, he said, "But you looked as though you'd been crying for fear of your life."

"Bah, you might also come to tears if one day you realised you may have wasted the best years of your life with foals instead of fillies."

She meant *colts* or *stallions* – not *foals* – but it was not the time to dispute the taxonomy and naming conventions of equines.

Calvin recalled a time not far back, when he had found in the street an old, ornate wooden door that someone had discarded. Thrilled with the find, he hauled it up to the flat with the idea of restoring it or putting it to artistic use, but Klarysa balked and nearly laid eggs over the matter.

"You found it in the *trash*?" she screamed. "Get it out of here at once! It is most probably diseased. I don't care what you do with it, but remove it on the quick!"

She would not suffer a discarded antique door in their bedroom, but had absolutely no qualms waking in the bed of an unknown tart in a flat lousy with Nagels and bevelled glass, and with a mouth afoul of cheap musk and talc.

With downcast eyes and little-girl hands, she said, "You're angry with me, aren't you?"

Calvin collapsed on the divan, and like a worked bull in a bloody ring, was all the more dangerous for his proximity to death.

"I'm tired," he said in exhaustion. "I'm so fucking tired. I haven't slept in weeks. I love you with all my heart, and you kill me time after time."

"Now you understand why I always kept a string affixed to Kat's collar."

The situation could not have been worse. Had she been with another man, Calvin might have killed him. Had she been with a different mammal, a canine, a filly or foal, he might have thrashed it. But a woman? There was nothing to be done about it. His battle tactics – the majority and most effective of which called for the swift deployment of bottles, boots and fists – were null and void against such a nemesis.

"Go to hell," he said flatly.

"I should have known better than to think you might handle this like an adult," she said. "I'm as confused by this as you are, you should know. Anyway, I'm sure I'll figure it all out when I'm gone."

"Gone?"

Despite all he had just heard, the word *gone* still stung.

"Yes," she said sadly. "I'm leaving you."

"You're leaving me?"

"I've almost finished packing."

"Like hell you're leaving me!" he roared.

It was an asinine thing to say, but across history, the mad have been known to take certain license. Not, however, on Klarysa's watch.

"Listen up!" she said, taking control. "I'm leaving you and I'm leaving you to-night. Do show some dignity, for crissake."

"You're leaving to-night are you?" he answered. "And where in hell do you think you're going?"

"I don't know. I've been so busy packing, I haven't given it much thought."

"I shouldn't have guessed you might."

"Don't be crass, you selfish bastard. I may return to Barcelona. I may well stay in Nice." Then, lifting her gaze towards the ceiling, as though she had long ago found a hidden door to paradise somewhere in it and had been keeping it a secret until she needed it most, she said, "Or maybe I'll move to Paris."

"Paris!" he blurted. "And just who do you think is going to bankroll a move to Paris?"

"I have no need for financial assistance," she said. "I am my own woman. I'd have thought you bright enough to know that by now."

But with that, she blinked and began to fiddle with a small silver ring that circled her littlest finger, and she looked as though she had come just a breath shy of believing herself. And that is what ripped Calvin's heart out. He loved her dearly. What a price he would have gladly paid to see her ride a strong hard line straight through the argument and onto victory. Instead, that subtle seam of vulnerability would haunt him. In his saddest and loneliest moments after she had left, he would see a little girl with downcast eyes, twisting a sad silver ring around her finger as she tried to explain her fears and confusion to an old injured beast. He might survive her departure if he could only manage a hatred for her and cling to it. But he could never hate her, certainly not after she'd failed to mask her vulnerability and doubt.

Nevertheless, a caustic mixture of anger, sadness and desperation continued to pool in the pits and valleys of his psyche, and so he reloaded and shot, "You're your own woman, hey? *I'm* the one working every day. *I'm* the one making all the goddamned money around here!"

"*Money*!" she scoffed. "Ha! What a fine little boy you make, spouting over your ridiculously overvalued currency! Recount for me even one occasion when a lack of money kept *me* from what I wanted!"

The rebound was admirable, and made him wonder if the vulnerability and doubt he had identified weren't in fact a projection of his own weaknesses onto her.

He narrowed his eyes and flung wickedly at her, "*Yours* is a depreciating currency, my dear. As you've pointed out, your days belong to the *Grand Cirque*. I advise you to consider Cannes."

Cannes, thought Calvin viciously, where a whole lot of washed-up freaks and circus-folk chased the vapours of bodily assets that had sublimated from them years and decades ago. He thoroughly hated himself for his words, knowing how they would sting her, and they did. The sad fact of the matter, however, is that such was the objective of slinging such cruel lines. To a pained and love-sick idiot, dirty-pool is an effective means of dealing with rejection, for such means render one hideous, and it is much more frightening for one to think that another despises a fair and decent version of oneself.

"I shouldn't mind if I make it no further than Cannes," she said, wholly uncertain. "One never knows, perhaps I'll find fame on the *Croisette.*"

She couldn't help but smile at the sad comedy of such a line. The kid, thought Calvin, could win any sprint, but didn't have the foresight required of stamina.

"At any rate," she continued with a deep breath, "Richard won't let me drown."

But the girl was good. Her latest words shot through him like a bolt.

"Richard?" Calvin pronounced it like the French: *Ree-shar.*

"He's not French," she informed him, "and he prefers the English pronunciation of his name."

"Duly noted, sweetheart! And would your man Richard prefer the English or French version of his teeth caved in?"

"French, naturally," she said.

Even during the worst of times, she couldn't pass up an opportunity to stick it to the French. "I imagine the French version yields no greater damage than that of a hard kiss, no? Anyway, he finds the English pronunciation to be less pretentious than that of the French. It's a ridiculous thing to say, but I don't question him on such matters. He's a gentleman, you know."

"Why, of course he is."

"I'll miss nearly everything about you. May the devil, however, take your sarcasm."

"Oh, stop it," he said, though he knew she was right—sarcasm was a cheap and lazy scheme best left to the defeated and the English. "Who is this Richard fellow, anyway?" he continued. "One of your many suitors, I assume."

"A suitor," she echoed with a sad, dreamy smile, testing the timbre of the word.

Calvin, with his face still slightly shadowed by the lingering clouds of recent bruises, tried to imagine what she must have been thinking—perhaps a suitor would be a gentleman. Perhaps a suitor would approach me with some semblance of softness and a greater understanding than that possessed by the band of tactless hacks that currently paw at me like so many fumbling savages.

Calvin had failed and he knew it.

"Oh, please, Klarysa," he said, beside himself with grief. "I'm so sorry. I can be better. Please give me a chance. I can be better."

"Oh, my darling, you must stop with that. It won't work between us."

"But you're killing me, Klarysa, don't you see?" A thought occurred to him and he sat up bolt-straight. "Bah, you don't love me. That's it, isn't it? Hell if I'm not a blind idiot! You just don't love me. It's as simple as that!"

"How dare you, Calvin!" she burst, at the edge of tears. "Don't you dare say that! I *do* love you. I love you like I've never loved another. The killing, as you call it, is a different thing altogether, and I am terribly sorry for that. I am. But I love you and I love you plenty! The unfortunate reality is that love alone is not nearly enough to keep two people together."

Every now and again she would slay him with surprisingly mature observances.

"Now buck up," she said. "Richard is coming round to help you remove my things and you don't want to look such a mess."

"Like hell he is! Just let him try to make it through the doorway. Just let him try!"

"Why on earth are you yelling? I'm right here. Now listen, I've asked Richard to help you with my things. You're going to let him in and you're going to act decently towards him." Then, without the slightest hint of rhetoric or provocation, she asked of him, "Why do you say you won't, when you know you will?"

Hot damn, he thought, the girl is pure! He considered explaining to her that when couples fought, they rather often chose to hurl about false, hurtful, or nonsensical statements out of anger and spite, and with the direct objective of denying or injuring the other. But he thought better of it, knowing it would be impossible to explain without coming across sarcastic and ridiculous. What's more, only a cynical cad would knowingly introduce such a sad and bitter tactic to one so innocent.

"Of course you'll let him in," she repeated, surprised by what she perceived from him as a startling lack of self-awareness. "You know you will. You are too kind and too considerate to do otherwise."

"How kind and considerate was I with your man Donato and the rest of them?"

"They were a lot of fools and each got what was coming to him. You know me, and you know this time it is different."

Again Calvin felt somehow sorry for her. He was bowled over by her lack of gamesmanship. She might prove, he thought, to be a major factor in his ruin, but in no way was she a conniver or an impostor. By the grace of her youth and good looks, her prospects at the time were limitless, but there exists a strange and steep opportunity cost in relying too heavily on such fragile, dying resources. Klarysa could afford to be frivolous for a while yet, but brokers who dealt in her kind of currency walked a thin line that only stretched thinner with the passing of time. They were eventually forced to make good on a least one big deal, or face a hard and uninspiring reality in the later years, when the bright lights of outward physical allure shut down and relocated to shine over younger, fresher stages. As such, even when Calvin and Klarysa were at each other's throats, Calvin felt a guardian's sense of duty to help her along, to set her up to-day so that she might have a puncher's chance to-morrow, were they not together, and should she fail to close that one big deal. Though at that, there were the times, admittedly, when he felt ludicrous for accommodating her every whim, while she was currently the wealthiest woman in the world.

There in the desperate down-slope of their relationship, Calvin professed a great need for her. She corroborated his need for a woman, in general, but dismissed his assertion that it had to be her, specifically. She assured him that there was a whole world of young bright-eyed girls who would be forever drawn to guys like him. He disagreed, citing that women feared his way of life, and added with certainty that he would die miserable and alone. She countered that his fatalism would prove, for many girls, the most magnetic of his many attractive characteristics. He didn't understand.

If left alone, she explained, men would destroy each other within a day or two, tearing one another limb from bloody limb. The presence of women, however, kept men relatively civil. Women were to credit for largely limiting the carnage of men to that which crossed national, political and religious borders. Women were the links that came together and chained men to reason and sanity. Man tore everything apart and Woman put it all back together. Still, despite the impressive rate at which Man killed and destroyed, it was

Woman who suffered a hardwired sense of guilt and shame, a burden no man would ever understand. It had something to do with Eve and original sin—one of the few religious myths that suited Klarysa's needs. And because the propagation of mankind rested squarely in the womb, the taming of Man with the idea of saving him from himself was not only a form of penance, but the equivalent of saving the world—or rather preserving Man's presence on the planet, that he may go on killing and destroying, and that Woman may go on repairing and suffering. Calvin did not necessarily disagree with anything she said on the matter. All the same, he did lobby on the side of Man for his role in the seeding of the womb.

"Ha!" she rebuffed. "Don't fool yourself. If ancient Woman had been given half a second to breathe, without her boneheaded male counterpart constantly pinning her down and shooting his guts into her, she surely would have developed a self-seeding womb. Men are useless and pointless and the decent among you will be the first to admit as much. You are so flawed and embarrassed that you had to invent a universal scapegoat to take blame for all your endless messes. But as no ordinary scapegoat could withstand such eternal abuse, you made him untouchable and invisible and called him God. But that wasn't enough. It wasn't sufficiently self-laudatory, so you assigned Him omniscience and omnipotence. And every generation taught the following generation that God created Man in His likeness. How rich! For the life of me, I can't fathom how you men can maintain a straight face. Your motives are all self-serving, of course, so I shouldn't be surprised. Still, it is one thing for Man to promote his all-powerful and ever-present god, but a completely different level of absurdity altogether to then push the idea that He created the earth's most arrogant, ungrateful and glaring error in His own likeness! Why, you can't exist without women. Conversely, do away with the lot of you men and see if we don't go on living and propagating a superior breed, in perfect bliss. Russians and Chechens, Chinese and Japanese, Serbs and Albanians, Israelis and Palestinians—we'd all get along famously if it weren't for you men. It's you, the greedy, fearful gender who foul everything up; you who live to invade and destroy, and then look to us to bandage you up and make you whole so that you can get right back to the bloody front. You don't exist without us. You grow within us. Hell, the only thing growing in Man's fallow insides is bile, hatred and intolerance. What a gorgeous, bountiful, peaceful planet we would have if only it weren't for your wayward, no-account gender. You run amok with drool dripping from your chins and loins, ravaging, ruining, killing, destroying every decent thing in sight."

Eventually making her way back round to the notion of Woman's desire to save Man from himself, she said, "You know the routine—a woman identifies the funniest, wildest, most outgoing fellow in the room and then sets out to marry him, put the screws to him, clamp him down and chain him up; do whatever she can to change his life, to keep him from doing all the things that make him the man he is. Why, you ask?"

He hadn't—Calvin was gob-smacked, frozen in silent rapture.

"Because she wants to get knee-deep into you, set up camp in you and save you from yourself, with hopes that by doing so, she will spare herself the wrath of your vengeful god and earn the right to forever glow in some celestial light."

"But why," Calvin finally managed, "would a man concede to such domination?"

"He concedes because he subconsciously believes that by doing so, by submitting to her designs and playing his role in her game, he is effectively assuring himself that he'll never have to give in and alter his destructive behaviour. It is simple—by consigning himself to the sanatorium, a madman effectively secures the right to his madness. But Man is an obvious beast, and there is, of course, a far more obvious answer to your question."

"What's that?" he dared.

With a look of exasperation she threw her arms out to her sides and ran her eyes over the length of her tight, curvaceous body. Calvin realised instantly that the obvious answer to his question was Woman herself – the ultimate trophy, the ultimate territory, Man's true saviour in the flesh – not some invented vapour in the sky. It was all terribly convoluted.

Klarysa, however, was different. She did not suffer the burdens of guilt and shame, and she was not out to secure her place in the eyes of Man's god. Klarysa never believed that any single human organism was so precious as to be saved at the expense of all the other organisms it encountered on its egotistical path towards mortal glory, especially when humankind was such a late addition to what was, at the time of its arrival, a lush and verdant planet. She found Man to be a self-aggrandising animal that was constantly congratulating and celebrating itself. And yet, at the close of any day, he stumbled home and up the stairs and watched himself in the mirror of his lavish bathroom and quietly saw himself for what he really was—a worn-out and bewildered beast. Only the most determined of the charlatans were able to continuously dupe themselves into denying the glaring fact that what they did all day, and in fact what they did every day, was grovel in the muck and the pollution and the slop; one grand gathering in the global pen of godforsaken swine, rooting and rummaging about in the filth of their own making, with the sole purpose of seeing another day, fornicating and propagating the rotten, stinking breed, just like every other organism, no matter how seemingly grand or pathetic.

And therein, thought Calvin, sprung the source of Klarysa's strength—she did not grovel on her knees that she might save herself, or save Man, or propagate the species. She did not hoist her privates onto an altar and pass them off as sacrificial offerings to a god unknown. She did not try to whip a man into shape and coerce him with her powers of persuasion. She did not manipulate the supply and demand of her most valuable assets. Her assets, for better or worse, fluctuated on the free-floating market.

"Let's face it," she said. "There is no greater threat to Man than sexually liberated Woman. Man knows he is doomed if it all comes to that."

It would be, she explained, much like the flooding of a market with its dominant currency and triggering inflation. With his trophy and territory depreciated down nearly to nothing – which would also mean the destruction of that which saved him from himself – every man would need ten women to feel as dominant as he did when he had just one. Without trophies to win and borders to defend, there would be no wars, no destruction, no killing. Man would no longer have his ballast, his protector, his nurse, and without her to keep him in check, his very outline and form would blur and bleed into the atmosphere. And then poof—Man would no longer exist. It was, indeed, all terribly convoluted.

"You contend," Calvin challenged, "that without Woman in Man's life, he will have lost his motive for destruction, but so too, he will have lost that which defines him, breathes life into him and protects him from himself."

"Woman is at once Man's blessing and his burden, his protector and his enemy, his treasure and his trash. At every turn, this world is one big conflict. Man cannot live without pain and chaos and that is his greatest flaw. If he truly wanted peace, he would have it tomorrow, but he has proven himself incapable of it. Conflict is what keeps Man pegged to the earth. It is what keeps him from floating away into outer space."

Klarysa stood up, signalling an end. "It's all a big game," she said, "and a not very clever or subtle one at that. I find the whole engagement deplorable. But such as it is, even the strongest and wildest of you are willing to curl up at my feet in front of the fireplace, like beaten mutts and whimper until I give word, each of you hoping I'll stay home and keep my most prized possessions swathed in cotton and lace for you and you alone. It is sad – pathetic, really – but what's to be done about it? Men are weak and hopeless and, you'll admit, not terribly bright."

She smiled again. "Men gauge intelligence with speedometers and altimeters and calculators, by how small their gadgets are, by who can build things that go fast and go boom and kill the most men. It would be comedic how blind and dumb you all are if it weren't for how rotten you make everything for the rest of us on this planet. Here's your intelligence for you—put any two men in a room and when I twirl my little finger, watch them tear one another apart with their bare hands. Oh, dear God, if you do exist, bow your head earthward and get a good look at your Man, your supreme creation, the one you made in your likeness. Ha! Brilliant, that. To the devil with the lot of you."

Calvin sat silent, slack-jawed.

"Enough of this," she said finally. "Richard is downstairs at the bar. Another man, I know, but again, what's to be done about it? Anyway, he's waiting for you."

Richard! The name yanked Calvin out of his stupor. He reckoned all Klarysa had said was more or less on the mark, which was all the more reason to dent Richard's dome.

"*Wait*ing for me? The nerve of this guy!"

"He wouldn't dream of calling at your door without having met you first. I told you, he's a gentleman. Oh please, darling, don't let's continue to argue over Richard."

She took his hands in hers, prompting him to stand up. And then looking up at him with those big brown eyes, she said, "My darling, I love you. You must have faith in me."

"But I'm a man."

"Yes, but you are one of the good ones. One of the best I've ever met." Her eyes glistened with the building of tears. "You do trust me, don't you?"

"Trust you with what?"

"With your love, of course. With your heart."

What could he possibly say? She hadn't lied to him; she hadn't fed him false hope. On the contrary, she had been painfully open and honest with him. He could angrily demand that she prove her love for him by staying, but that condition of love had died decades ago. And if he were to beg her lasting presence and fidelity, would his pleading be an exhibit of love, or simply an exhibit of selfishness in the face of fear and sadness?

"I don't know what to say," he admitted. "I'm perfectly crushed."

"Oh, *please* don't say that, my love! I swear it will be the death of me, don't you see? There really is no reason at all to feel that way."

"Oh, but there is."

She gripped his hands tightly. He looked down at her, down at the tears growing in her eyes and watched two break free and fall instantly away.

"Goddamn," he whispered. "Do you really love me?"

"My god, Calvin." Two more tears slipped and fell away. "I couldn't possibly love you any more if I tried. You must promise me you'll never worry about such a thing."

He nodded meekly. She brought her hands up to his face; her kiss was long and meaningful and affectionate.

Some kind of rare girl, that Klarysa. She had delivered him hard, knock-down truths, and then built him up into something bigger, better and more beloved than he was when he had arrived home that night. There are many ways to grow and learn, and very few of them are painless. Anyone to have witnessed the scene without context would have been convinced that he had done her some great service for which she was infinitely thankful. And as far as she was concerned, by nodding and having affirmed, however meekly, his trust in her, he had indeed done her a great service. In her own bold and unorthodox manner, Klarysa loved Calvin very much.

"Now please," she said at last, "do hurry down to Richard, won't you? He's waiting."

"OK. I'll go," he managed. "But I can't promise you I won't roll his goddamned head down the street."

One lone fellow was seated at the bar. Otherwise the place was empty. No music and not even a bartender in sight. There never was. The proprietor was a miserly sort who sat in a hidden cave behind the wall of bottles and glasses when he wasn't suffering the poor luck of having to serve a customer.

Calvin walked in off the alleyway and a brass bell affixed to the door announced his arrival. The fellow at the bar nodded at him unsuspectingly and Calvin nodded back. Deciding to put off introductions until he'd had a beer and summoned a degree of heart, Calvin took a seat near the door and waited to be served.

Good-looking fellow, thought Calvin. Young, too, though something had stripped him of the typical lustre of youth. He looked out of place, there in the dank Southern establishment. Calvin was one who liked to sit at the bar, but he was conscious of the slouching that went along with most barstools. But now here was a fellow who sat at the bar and looked exceedingly comfortable, and he did not slouch at all, and Calvin was not at all certain he could trust a man who maintained such an easy and distinguished pose on a barstool.

It would be some years yet before Calvin reached his competitive peak. He was perhaps a half-step slower of foot than he was in his younger days, but he was two steps quicker of mind. At one's competitive peak, the slight physical advantage of a younger adversary was easily overcome by wits and battle experience. To the battle-ready, the estimating of a potential adversary is a split-second calculation and Calvin immediately established that he would split the boy's bean if it came to that.

He was the only bloke in the bar, but Calvin could have picked him out of a packed stadium. Calvin had only ever witnessed the typical coastal clowns bumbling around Klarysa since her move to Nice, but just as she had said, this fellow was clearly different. He had a pedigree. He may have been from Warsaw or Prague or St. Petersburg – somewhere east, likely a capital city. He held himself far too comfortably, there, alone in a foreign territory, to be from a small borough or hamlet. His hair was the colour of sandalwood, his skin a fine porcelain grey and he exuded a sense of serenity and composure without a whiff of pomp or pretence. Despite his pedigree, he had not lived a privileged life, though there was little doubt he had a firm understanding of what made for one. His eyes were kind and distant and looked as though they might disappear altogether, like soft brown mirages.

He lifted his gaze now and again towards a small dusty television that was riveted into the low stone ceiling and drank from a glass of cheap German lager. Thought Calvin in his misery, he probably has no idea the beer was poured from a can. Not that he would likely care—to most citizens of the world, bad beer was nothing to get wrinkled over. The proprietor made a habit of loading a cargo van in Ventimiglia with cases of cheap lager and driving it in over the French-Italian border. It was the only beer he served and he advertised it as draught beer. He would have a fellow know the taps were in the back room, but one could hear the cans popping on the other side of the wall and out would come a tray of pale lager.

Just then, there was an aluminium pop somewhere behind the bar, and the proprietor brought Calvin a glass of beer without uttering a word.

The fellow at the bar smoked an expensive brand of cigarettes and sat on the barstool with one leg draped over the other. He shifted slightly in his seat and Calvin noticed a crack in his veneer. He looked out the window, likely looking for someone to enter the bar and introduce himself as Calvin. At his feet sat a travel bag of an old worn leather; an old travel companion. Calvin was suddenly taken by the idea that the fellow was unanchored and decidedly alone; a man with all the time in the world to attend to his few belongings, to keep them in good working order, in part because it was the right thing to do, in part because sometimes assigning oneself domestic undertakings, like order and maintenance, allowed a fellow time to forget and time to heal. There was a dark spot on his neck, a reddish patch the size of a two-franc coin. With that, Calvin decided that the lad was not only alone, but ill. How pensive he suddenly appeared. Something weighed heavily on his mind.

Well goddamn, thought Calvin. Despite the nature of the business at hand, he couldn't help but take a near instant liking to the fellow and he immediately cursed himself for always feeling so goddamned sorry for everyone.

Calvin watched him and crafted a history around him. He was an injured animal that some powerful woman had left alone to drift and wander, perhaps upon learning of his illness. And now he was going to have a go of it with Klarysa. Calvin identified, with sinking hope, a pre-defeated calm about the lad that indicated he might just fare well with her. He was rather well attired in worn tan trousers and a worn white oxford that was tucked loosely into his trousers and which somehow contributed to his air of managed illness. His shoes were of a fine oxblood leather that time and experience had thinned and scuffed, now dusty and ripe and aged the way only hand-crafted objects made of quality materials can age—with dignity. He had suffered the expectations specific to families that knew certain status, and having had enough of it, packed it in, forsook it all and walked away, to live closer to the land and its peoples, closer to his heart, closer to his lovers. He was dead to his family and that fact also contributed to his illness. And while his independence brought him strength in his youth, it would likely kill him over time. Such were the conjectures of Calvin's working mind, at any rate.

Calvin had him occupying a single high-ceilinged room in Krakow or Vienna, vaulted winter space, a room made cold and Spartan by a lack of furnishings and décor, empty but for an old desk at which to write and read and a bed in which to sleep and make love during times of prosperity. The vision reminded Calvin of a time in Trieste. Trieste, the relegated beauty that once demanded love and attention; she who sparkled before Venezia stole the show and became the starlet of the Adriatic. No city displayed a greater mix of petrified grandeur, seclusion and loneliness; a thoroughly sad and lovely city into which one descends from above by way of winding roads, if arriving by land from the northwest. Dropping into her by night, with a chilling autumn breeze blowing through her body, where legs run down and slip into the sea, will rob a man of all cheer and supplant it with worry and concern and uncertainty that the sun will rise at the dying end of the night. Still, she begs one's presence that she might be remembered and celebrated for past performances. She does not place herself above one's charity. She longs for the warmth of a fellow's body, but she won't begrudge him for slipping out under the cover of night, never to return.

Once, en route to Dubrovnik at the end of a late September evening, Calvin and Victoria drove into Trieste and she chilled them to the bone. The two held each other as they moved briskly down her majestic streets, those empty of light, bereft of life, those stripped bare of body and breath, and took the first hotel they came upon. The room in which they stayed was the same room Calvin had assigned the young man seated at the bar, with the ill-looking patch on his neck. Calvin dropped their bags in the middle of the room. Victoria took a smaller bag from within hers, kissed him and drew a bath. Calvin laid down on the bed. The room had been frozen by time, locked by history. There was a distinctly immobile quality to its cold and loneliness. For all its magnificence, it could not manage a degree of warmth, and Calvin could not stop thanking God for Victoria. Thank God for her—her skin, her legs, her entire being! Thank God!

They had arrived by car from Barcelona, side-by-side for sixteen hours, fatigued from the journey, and now Victoria lay in a warm tub on the other side of the bathroom door. Sixteen hours side-by-side, but in the cold of that room, Calvin was overwhelmed by her absence. He was nearly eaten alive by a need to see her, to kiss her face, look into her eyes, hear her voice, pull her close and tuck into her good and strong, to lock her up in his arms and legs. He called out to her and she answered. Her voice reached him through the door, like a miracle, so eerily certain was he that he might never see her again. They spent the night tangled up in each other, with honest hopes that they might knot up and never be pulled apart, fervently whispering words at point blank range, naked vines clinging tightly in hopes of binding their defences and fending off the fear. In the morning, they picked up their bags, which were still sitting patiently in the middle of the room, and scurried out of town.

Calvin was now aware of his sad fascination with the fellow at the bar. He could not divert his eyes. The fellow did not wear his shoes as much as he consented to having them take place around his feet. He made the same allowance for his aloneness and illness, appearing in fact to be a gracious host for anything or anyone that might want to take part in his time on earth. There was at once a pride, a generosity and selflessness to him. Every parcel of his visual presentation, from his clothing – the obvious quality of which had been stressed to a point just shy of shabby – to his expensive cigarettes, the royal slope of his nose and the fullness and contour of his plum lips, the discoloured patch of illness on his neck and the concerns that occupied him. His image filled Calvin's mind with rich stories, some sober and some fantastic, of faraway lands and classic beauties, of rambling hope in the midst of suffering, of brief joys and extended heartaches, of Oriental fantasies snuffed out by Occidental realities.

On the static-stained television, a nameless footballer put the ball in the back of the net. The fellow at the bar jolted upright for an instant and let slip a slight cheer. Then, as blokes will when watching sport in the company of others, he looked over at Calvin, for indeed, the shared recognition of another's physical prowess was the lifeblood that coursed between all red-blooded men. His smile was apologetic, his eyes flat with sincerity, and all of it—this man with his travel bag and ill patch, the black-plastic television, the cheap yellow beer, the fact that Klarysa was leaving—all of it, the whole stinking scene, conspired to break Calvin's heart. What a rotten night. Calvin raised his glass towards the lad and managed a miserable smile.

"Some goal, hey?" said the fellow at the bar, with far more spirit than Calvin had anticipated.

"Some goal," Calvin concurred joylessly.

With the subtle shade of shame that one feels upon breaking the boundary of another man's solitude, the fellow ventured, while eyeing the bottom of his glass, "It is not the best beer in the world, is it?"

"It's terrible beer," said Calvin. "The worst."

The fellow nodded at a small chalkboard behind the bar. "It says draught beer, but I believe I heard…" he silenced himself, lest he wrongly accuse. "At any rate, it is cold."

"No, you're right," Calvin confirmed. "It's canned beer. He drives it over from Italy."

"I see," said the fellow. "I suppose it is less expensive that way."

"It's a damned lousy way to run a bar."

"I suppose so," he said, empathetically adopting Calvin's misery. "Still, a second round can't be worse than the first, right? Since we don't have much choice, I mean. It's on me."

That did it. The act could be taken no further. Calvin pulled himself up and approached the bar with an extended hand. "Richard, right?" he said.

"Calvin?" asked Richard incredulously, as though with untold luck he had happened upon a long-lost friend. He took Calvin's hand in his two and moved all three up and down with far more esteem than was due.

"That's right," said Calvin. "Klarysa's… Hell, Klarysa's friend."

Few things will sink a man as will the first time he hears himself refer to his ex merely as a friend. No longer a husband, or a boyfriend, a partner or lover, a defender, a hero, or protector—just a friend. Far less traumatic, he thought, to label yourself her victim, enemy or murderer.

"But why did you not introduce yourself sooner?" asked Richard, with a look that referred to all the good time that had been lost.

It seemed that Calvin's failure to introduce himself had saddened Richard, and therein Calvin found selfish heart—perhaps Klarysa would drive the poor guy into the ground after all.

"We could have had a beer together," he said, and then realised, "We still can."

"Sorry, mate," said Calvin. "It was poor of me. I wanted a good look at the guy who was stealing Klarysa from me."

It was a gutless line that embarrassed them both.

"Ah, hell," said Calvin. "Forgive me, would you."

"Please," Richard replied, "you needn't ask such a thing. You've done me no wrong."

"Let's get the hell out of here. Come on up and we'll have a real drink. We're all going to need it."

A cigarette butt lay cold and dead. A dying man try to make skinny gray tires grip a glassy Garfield sidewalk. A last cry for help come and gone, slipped away like a lover's unheard whisper. Winter claim another one and it going to claim more. The silver moon thrust elbows back proudly into the dark bed of night and nestle in deeper still to watch with sleepy satisfaction a familiar cinema.

Without thinking, I veer off at Van Ness and ricochet down to the bottom of the Fillmore. Fog hangs just above the dumpsters lining the street. In times of need, do what you do best. That's what you told me, Gem, so I'm parking and going to get drunk. Need to kill what's killing me, out to poison the anxiety that's bringing the walls in heavy and tight, suffocating all around me so I can hardly breathe. If it can't be done, maybe I'll keep trying until I sublimate light and white and finally clean beyond these sticky rum-soaked walls and piss-stained toilets and this lazy silver city with its lazy layer of milky tourist fog, all of it, the burnt up Delta, Laika, everybody!

I'm a wolf, Pug. I'm a wolf.

"You are not! You weren't convicted! Now stop it, you slag! Get out of there, now. Come to France. You stay with me, now!"

Pop, he come in from the garage and taste Ma soup. "Irma," *he* say. "You do yourself proud with this here soup." *Pop, he stand with a momentous look and ask what all make that soup so tasty. He wink and smile at me. I can smell cigar. He pick me up and I feel razor stubble high up in the air when he kiss me. Pop! He grip his bicep and wrench it good and maybe he going to find all the answers there.*

20   Painful reservations

In which Calvin finds a pressure
valve and faces his ultimate
affliction.

Klarysa curled herself luxuriously into the heart of the divan. Richard sat on the very edge, at an awkward, removed distance from her, and flexed his leg muscles slightly to keep from spilling onto the floor. He kept his elbows pinned to his sides and his clasped hands in his lap. Having admired Richard's easy posture and presence at the bar, Calvin knew that his uncomfortable placement there on the divan was in deference to Calvin, who sat across from them on a rigid wooden chair, in his unenviable position. Calvin appreciated the gesture.

Given the context of the evening, Richard's presence in Calvin's home was a poor idea and both were made miserable by the arrangement. Poor ideas, however, rarely registered with Klarysa, and neither fellow was terribly adept at denying her caprices. Calvin wanted to tell Richard to relax, as the latter had been sufficiently generous in his show of deference, but he could not quite put tongue to the words. There may not have been any well-drawn winners amongst them, but Calvin was the clear-cut loser. His heart had been whipped, his ego licked, and Richard had the empathetic wherewithal to place himself beneath Calvin—a submission that was as gracious as it was wise. Calvin had noted in Richard a highly likable quality. There was much the two fellows might have discussed, were Klarysa not present. Hell, under different circumstances, they might have become close friends.

Calvin's composure before Richard would have come as a great surprise to any of the crew, who had known him to have a short fuse around disrespectful flames. But although the blade of the sad situation had cut dangerously deep and Calvin was dizzy with pain, he had not been wronged or disrespected. On the contrary, Klarysa's honesty and Richard's deference reflected the considerable respect each held for him. In any case, he hadn't the strength to fight. His insomnia had not improved. He slipped in and out of sleep for a broken hour or two each night and it was beginning to take a heavy toll on him.

Calvin held true to his core values, but he generally preferred to avoid conflict while doing so. He was not one to fight against rushing currents, or attempt to reverse the course of engines that knew great downhill momentum. He was only willing to fight against an opposition for so long before cutting losses and moving camp. He cast very few anchors, believing that there would always be a place – someplace, somewhere – where a soul could relax in peace, without friction or great effort. He put his best foot forward towards success, and when his best was not good enough, he was content to concede victory. He rejected all talk of fate as it concerned success and failure, though he often had strong inclinations as to when an endeavour was not meant to be. He accepted the blame in times of misfortune and deflected credit in times of prosperity. Despair would only seize him when he knew that he failed to put forth his best effort, and despite all his determination and effort as it concerned Klarysa, he was convinced that he had failed. And so once Klarysa had spoken her mind and professed her desire to leave in no uncertain terms, the only action that could have pained him more than letting her go would have been pathetically begging her to stay. It was not, therefore, with a valiant summons of strength and grace that he let her go, but rather with knowledge of the futility involved in any attempt to change her mind. He accepted the fact that there would be no salvaging the bridge back to her, nor reaching the other side of the wide and rushing divide that had swollen between them. Instead, he clung to his dignity and self-respect for dear life, hoping that by the virtue of their buoyancy, he might wake the following morning with his chin above the flood line.

Calvin walked to the refrigerator and grabbed the lone bottle of champagne. He had been saving it for a special occasion—those jewels that had once been so easily claimed, and that had recently become decidedly active and skilful in their evasion. It seemed a poor concession to drink the bottle on such a dour occasion, but opening it at any later date, he reckoned, would only serve to dab the evening's knifepoint into what he hoped would be – at some currently inconceivable future date – a healed wound.

He popped the cork and filled three flutes, but though the bubbles did rise (don't they always, those gorgeous golden beauties) the spirits of those who imbibed did not follow. Despite their best efforts, they could not overcome the weight of the situation. The harder Calvin worked to hide his misery, in an attempt to show himself as a good loser, the more conspicuously did Richard reveal his, in an attempt to show himself as a gracious winner. The room was wet with misery, and try as they might, they could not find the means to dry it off, so they finally shut up and anxiously drained the bottle in near silence.

Klarysa tipped back the last half of her flute and cried, "Done! Well, shall we get to work?"

The lads, eager for motion, jumped from their seats and bounded into action. Men improve with motion, and so, therefore, did the moods of Calvin and Richard once taking to task. Every now and again, however, as Calvin handled Klarysa's packed belongings, the burr of her scent or the hook of a vivid memory would ensnare him and lead him away to a cherished oasis and there, cruelly thrash him. When Klarysa was good, by god, she was very good, and as the dreamer in his darkest and weakest moments turns masochist, Calvin had acquired, during his short but intense tenure with Klarysa, a quiver of impeccable memories with which to whip himself raw.

And just like that, she was gone. Gone. How quickly they had removed her. Standing there in the middle of the salon, alone in the flat for the first time in several months, Calvin could not recall the details of the previous hours. During his sleepless nights, the ocean of his head was home to many bizarre creatures and strange considerations. He often stared at the ceiling and wondered: at the stone terminus of a fall from towering heights, were a fellow to land feet-first, would his death be delayed, if only for a fraction of a second (while the legs crumpled up and into the torso), versus the fellow who landed head-first, and who, clearly, died the very moment his tender dome touched down? Calvin decided that, indeed, death would be delayed for the fellow who landed feet-first. At live speed, of course, the difference would be too brief to recognise. However – and this was the gist – even if it were possible to slow the passage of time so that one hour were to pass between the moment the fellow's toes touched down and the moment of his death, the lad would already be unconscious and unable to contemplate that impossible, excruciating hour, for the mind – Calvin knew from experience – shuts down some goodly amount of time before traumatic impact.

There stood Calvin, newly alone and unable to remember carrying down the last of Klarysa's belongings, or bidding the girl farewell. Nor could he recall any final words with Richard, or any details of the man's appearance. At that very moment he could not, in fact, truly say one way or another, with any degree of certainty, whether or not the gentle fellow had set one foot in his flat, or even existed. Coming slowly to, he was perfectly uncertain as to what had just transpired, and he half-expected Klarysa to come bounding through the door and give him a long heady kiss, as she had always done upon arrival home. How, he suddenly wondered with some anxiety, would he explain to her the disappearance of all her belongings?

On the kitchen bar he found a near empty bowl of *soupe de poisson*, a half-eaten serving of *tête pressée* and a dry stump of baguette, and vaguely cursed the inconsiderate fellow – whoever he may be – who hadn't the decency to clean up after himself.

Soon, however, the reality of the situation came racing back to him, and with it, so too, visions of Klarysa at various points of her future life. She would go on living! A banal notion perhaps, but was it not, in fact, the only consideration of any consequence? Yes, she would go on living, and she would do so without him. She would grow older and amass countless experiences. She would learn to relax, she would fall in love and dedicate her life to one special person, she would give birth (and how gorgeous the precocious little buggers would be), she would mother a family. She would live a full and complete life, and Calvin would not be about to witness a single stroke of it. He would likely never see her again. It was a perfectly suffocating thought, which caused him to gulp desperately at the air, as though he were drowning. It was an excruciating feeling, and true to his propensity for violence, he demanded his waking conscious to grapple and toil with all those horrific ideas until the tips of their slick, nicking blades worked themselves dull and rusty against the wet bone of his psyche.

She was gone. Gone. And gone, too, were the clutter and mess. Gone were all the boxes and crates and suitcases, the shoes and the hats and the strewn magazines, the plastic bottles and tubes, the jars and the compacts. Calvin had gone to great lengths after Victoria's death, to preserve her memory. There were too many aspects of that relationship – most of them specific to him and his involvement (or, more accurately, lack of involvement) – that he could not bear to forget. And having met Klarysa, he put forth great effort to be mindful, to remember, to pay attention, to provide her with reasons to live, and reasons to live with him. But now, without further thought, he dropped to his hands and knees and gave the entire flat a proper scrubbing, so fearful was he of living with Klarysa's scent and memory.

When he had finished, it was just past four o'clock in the morning. And then she was thoroughly gone. Gone were the long hairs that occasionally clogged the sinks and gathered in the corners of the flat, gone were the crumbs and the unwashed dishes, gone was the toothpaste spittle that tarnished the bathroom chrome and spotted the bathroom mirror. All of it gone. And in the newly restored order and cleanliness, he saw piled high in every corner, behind every door, and in every cupboard and cubby of the flat, all the harrowing remnants of still greater failure and emptiness.

Thankfully, there were fish to process down at the port the following day, and the day after that, and the day after that. But the day after that, there were none, and Calvin was quietly frantic over how to occupy his day and night. Having, for the majority of his days, lived life with a certain easy grace, despite all the knocks and setbacks, he suddenly found himself entertaining the idea that he would never again know care-free contentment. Failures could always be viewed as aberrations during one's youth, and should an unfavourable trend emerge, one could comfortably place his hopes in the future, believing that there would always be time enough to turn the tide, to buck the trend. Trends, however, are not so easily bucked later in life, when inertia adopts the heavy, rigid qualities of concrete and lead.

News of Klarysa's departure had spread, and several of the crew had reached out to Calvin through invitations to dinners and various engagements. He declined all such invitations. At a dinner, he would be obliged to talk, obliged to drink and be social, and none of it could he handle just yet. His rejection of their invitations, however, only added to his despair and sense of incapacity. In slogging through low periods, every fellow needs to put on a face and fake it from time to time. The inability to fake it for a few hours among one's closest friends was a discouraging sign.

A sudden craving for one strong drink burst in his belly. Sometimes a fellow cannot fathom a drink in the name of affiliation, but might, in his solitude, deal directly with the devil for one in the name of courage and survival. Calvin made his way to the other side of Place Massena, away from the sea, in search of a bar at which he could be certain not to find a familiar face.

There were few good bars on the north side of town, but he found one; a corner café outside of which was assembled a moveable jazz band, one complete with brass, and a guitar and an upright piano, jangling away, there on the broad sidewalk. The café and the jazz band outside provided him with a small shot of encouragement. Few circumstances brought about fear and anxiety like the experience of loneliness alongside an inability to engage socially, and a good live performance was a socially binding engagement that could be enjoyed anonymously and in silence.

Under deep awnings, the terrace was crowded. The women were in dresses. The men wore ties and coats. The crowd had convened at the café to pass time between a wedding ceremony and the reception that would follow. All of the wicker chairs on the terrace were occupied, though the most engaging of the crowd remained standing. They gathered in smart and clean-shaven groups, tapped their shoes on the sidewalk, chased down cocktails, launched into engaging anecdotes and offered sound advice and can't-miss prognostications. Some danced and some watched those who danced, and some laughed and cheered.

Calvin stepped inside to the bar. The bartender asked him if he was with the wedding party, though he hadn't a tie or a coat and looked nothing like those in the party. They talked for a brief moment and somehow the interaction with the bartender lifted his spirits. Here was another vulnerable fellow who must have had his own sufferings, and yet continued to push forward with hope and a smile for his clientele. Calvin tipped the man generously and then went out to the terrace with a Sazerac.

The late day was hot and bright. The sun had fallen west, but still did its part in painting the tops of the awnings and creating cool shadows under them. Sweat beaded on the bald head of the piano man, as he hammered out an attractive rendition of a Jelly Roll Morton number. At Calvin's elbow, three sharp girls in floral-print summer dresses, all of whom were drinking tall cocktails made snake-green with Pisang Ambon, chattered excitedly. The girl in the hibiscus print spoke, with dark enchantment dancing in her light eyes, of Madagascar and the Mascarene Islands.

"That was precisely what precipitated her fall from grace," she said, her short blonde hair shining with her eyes. Her skin was healthy; tropically influenced. "It was a grace," she advised, "which she had no business knowing to begin with, so don't be crushed. True story, though."

"I don't believe it," said the girl to her right. "It just *can't* be true."

"And yet nothing could be truer, Fiona. That's what makes drama dramatic."

"But she was married to the Malagasy," attempted Fiona, the prettiest of the three, who also proved to be the dimmest.

"She was *not* married to the Malagasy," denied Hibiscus. "Therein lays the scandal, Fiona. She was married to another—a *stadt*holder, no less."

"A *stadt*holder?" echoed Fiona with heightened disbelief. "But aren't they—"

"Wait a minute, Muriel," said the third girl to Hibiscus. "You're contradicting yourself. Why, just last night you told Anne-Marie that he was a lieutenant, not a stadtholder."

"So I did, Margot, so I did. But at the time I thought he was French. Tommy set it straight—he isn't French at all. His people came from the Republic of the Seven United Netherlands."

"Dutch!" said Fiona with a delicious squeal, biting down on the suspense and on her straw, and fluttering her feet joyfully.

"Hell," said Margot, ill-accustomed to being the recipient, rather than the deliverer, of toothy island gossip. "A steward is a steward, wherever he's from."

"A steward, dear Margot," denied the hibiscus-clothed Muriel, "is most definitely *not* a steward!"

"Hmph," Margot snorted, feigning disinterest in stewards of any nationality or station.

"He was no mere governor, my dear. His great, great, great somebody or other," said Muriel with a flurry of her impatient hands, to help her advance beyond the trivialities, "was appointed by the Dukes of Burgundy."

"Not the Dukes of Burgundy!" gasped Fiona.

"Why, of course," said Muriel. "Which others? That's what Tommy said, and Tommy has a keen nose for such things—quite possibly the keenest on the island."

"Imagine," said Margot with haughty disapproval, "a Rose Hill man with a tramp like *that*. I watched her perform the séga in Pointe-aux-Piments and let me tell you..." But Margot had no intention of telling.

"It *was* scandalous," Muriel corroborated.

"But what did her husband do when he found out about the Malagasy?" asked Fiona.

Muriel and Margot looked at each other significantly; then turned the collection of their four eyes on Fiona.

"You don't know?" said Muriel finally. "He never *did* find out. He was the only one on the island who didn't. The poor man was snake-bitten—"

"Snake-bitten. Nonsense," said Margot, being difficult—it was clear she had no idea. "He was one of the lucky ones. He lived a life of leisure. Why, you just said he was a stadtholder. Snake-bitten. Hmph!"

"Hmph yourself! I mean it quite literally. He stepped on a snake while settling a dispute in the cane fields and the rotten thing bit him."

"And he was poisoned to death!" demanded Fiona in great excitation.

"Of course he wasn't poisoned to death. But he *was* required to see a doctor for it, which made him late for a production at the Port Louis theatre. He only arrived during the *entr'acte*, and hurrying towards the theatre from his car, he was flattened by a passing *camion*."

"No!" said Margot.

"*Yes!*" said Muriel.

"And he died then and there, on the hot pavement!" demanded Fiona anew, finally getting something right.

"Yes, Fiona—dead on the spot."

Calvin finished his drink while the three girls continued to discuss the fates of the Malagasy and the séga performer. He was surprised to find that he enjoyed the moment. He enjoyed listening to the girls in conversation, enjoyed the intrigue and possibility associated with their scandalous stories from the southern islands. There was something innately enticing about scandal among palm trees and trade winds. Inwardly, he smiled meekly and mumbled to himself with his hands on his belly, "There is hope in there somewhere."

But soon, with the Sazerac drained and the stadtholder dead, there was no reason to continue listening. With reluctance towards the solitude that awaited him back at the flat, Calvin took a long, aimless route back toward the Vieux, winding his way unhurriedly down quiet back streets, in the waning light. He turned down Rue de Docteur Balestre and onto Ruelle des Prés; then down a little-known alleyway and onto Boulevard Dubouchage. Turning the corner, he nearly collided with two flapping fellows. He was excusing himself when his eyes met the gaze of friendly recognition.

"Ah, *bonsoir, les gars,*" he greeted the two pale-pink flamingos from the restaurant on Rue Pontin, where he had last been with Jim and Janice.

"Oh, it's only you," said the paler one, pressing his hands to his heart, in hopes of securing it.

"*Bonsoir,*" said the pinker of the two. "*Ravi de te vois.*"

"Nice to see you boys, as well," Calvin concurred.

"You haven't been to the restaurant in a while," said the pinker.

"Not since the night with your American friends," added the paler, still tending to his heart. "That poor, tragic woman. I can still smell her," he said dreamily, with closed eyes. "Warm shortbread."

The lads were en route to a dinner reservation at a nearby restaurant and Calvin walked along with them. They had only gone another block and crossed to the south side of Rue Pastorelli, when the paler one let go of his heart and announced, "Here we are."

"La Baie d'Amalfi," said Calvin.

"Best fettuccine vongole this side of Rimini," claimed the pinker.

"That's what I've heard," said Calvin uncertainly. Where he may have heard such a review, he could not say. "Well, *bon appétit.*"

They shook hands and parted ways. Calvin stood on the sidewalk and watched the lads through the window as they announced themselves to the hostess. Their smiles were wide. People were very often the best versions of themselves at a favourite restaurant. Sadness reclaimed Calvin. To be sure, he never loved Klarysa as much as when they were sharing a meal together somewhere nice. How that girl appreciated a good meal. She hadn't a harsh word for anyone while at a dinner table. Upon finishing a nice meal, she would often pretend it was a holiday and ask Calvin to please play along and not break the spell and let her go on believing it to be true. Calvin suddenly wished he had fed her more often.

The lads were seated. The house was full. Calvin stood watching through the windows. He saw a table of four fumbling teens on a double-date and remembered the enormous, awkward, nervous thrill of young love. Many of the tables were surrounded by jocose Italian families. At a few sat tentative middle-aged couples who were staying at the surrounding tourist hotels. There were several parties of reserved Frenchmen, and a table of four gentlemen sitting just inside the window. At that table of four, three of them were a good deal younger than the fourth. The fourth was the age of a first-time grandfather, though he appeared to lack the stoutness of ease that comes with the joy of having passed the parental torch to a son or daughter. Grandparenthood was a second childhood for those fortunate enough to know their grandchildren, those lucky devils who hadn't been slandered by a spouse so that one's son refused to bring around one's only grandson on the occasional weekend or even just once a year, during the holidays.

Perhaps those four men had met at that restaurant once a week for many years, a lads evening out, away from their women for a night. Perhaps one of them no longer had a woman from which to ask leave for the evening, because she could never come to accept life with a determined man of great passion and desire for justice, so that eventually she came to accuse him of harbouring an abnormal and dangerous obsession of a kind which none of her friends' husbands were guilty and why, oh, why on earth could he not be more like them? But he couldn't, and so she abandoned him. And she slandered him.

Calvin may or may not have ascribed these exact life scenarios to all those he viewed through the restaurant windows, but that is of little import, for the lad went suddenly ashen and his heart now beat erratically. The edges of his vision burned hazy and white so that all that remained identifiable before him as a genuine proof-object of his existence in his crumbling world, was framed there in the restaurant window. From his vantage point, the gleaming features were for a moment indistinguishable, but as he fell involuntarily forward towards the window, the twin hounds, with their frozen deadpan expressions and their surgically attached saliva catches, twinkled knowingly, mockingly for him from their pinned station on a broad sea of brown herringbone.

"It's him," said Calvin, pie-eyed, as though he had cornered Father Christmas ankle-deep in soot and ash, and with no available angle of retreat. "It's him. My spook. My man. It's *him!*"

Calvin considered turning and running, but then what? Would his spooks not continue to dog him in those very streets? Calvin's fears were tied to the prospects of loss, and the simplest way to combat a fear of loss is to relinquish one's current holdings and limit one's acquisitions. The only acquisition that might come from rushing into the restaurant and making demands was answers—and perhaps lumps and lacerations, too, though Calvin was able and slippery and physical pain for him was most typically an acquisition with a short half-life.

Besides, every now and again, the curious and the desperate rolled the dice on physical pain, took a shot at getting lucky and hitting it big. And if the roll came up snake-eyes, a fellow could at least coddle the animal pain and forget about his lousy and over-celebrated human heart, what with all its torturous feelings and emotions, at least for a moment or two.

What's more, the man with the lapel pin had not shown any tendencies towards aggression. Quite to the contrary, at last sighting, he had fled from Calvin. Though now he was in the company of large men, and looked entirely different than he had when fleeing down the stairwell of Calvin's building. Calvin remained unnoticed, though he stood gaping and separated from the man by only a thin glass pane. How deep that man's wrinkles, how heavy his brow and bone-structure. And how queer his pose, thought Calvin, and that of his cohorts; the angles of their broad backs and thick necks, how each held his individual mass at a pitched and ready position. Statuesque in their stillness, they were nonetheless unmistakably bristling for release.

Gem had always said that the most dangerous men were those with nothing to lose, and though Calvin was not so damaged by Klarysa's departure as to consider all hope and reason lost, at arm's-length sat the man he felt convinced was the primary source of his anguish, paranoia and insomnia, and the moment to act had presented itself to him. Regardless of how impossible the odds, a man may writhe and sob in an effort to reverse his fate if he feels there is the slightest opportunity left him. When all chances and choices have been unquestionably removed, however, an eerie calm befalls him. Such a calm befell Calvin. A steady tranquillity came down around him, a certain cathartic liberty, so long had he suppressed his fears and uncertainties. For the first time since the arrival of all the strange troubles he had come to know, Klarysa was not there to distract him or deflect his attentions. She was not there for him to protect or defend. He sensed a rich and powerful freedom. Inside the restaurant sat an opponent, an opponent that would at last be confronted face-to-face. The consideration alone brought relief. He felt the sorrowful, distraught freedom known by those with nothing to lose. He calculated and accepted the odds that he would wind up prone on a hospital bed for his efforts – the calculation took place in the span of a batted lash – but physical confrontation was the only course that would preclude any need of future hounding by his spooks. He may wind up half-dead, but he would be free. Free! And there, beaten, half-dead and laid up in hospital, he might finally come to know once again what it was to sleep through the night. He was granted a pressure valve and by god he was determined to twist the damned thing wide open.

With the first twitch of motion, the first step toward the door, his calm instantly dissipated. His blood pressure rose, his pulse raced, his head pounded. He turned suddenly rabid—desperate and rabid. Many men will fall away at the brink of a bloody stand, sell short and run, but for the man who had recently suffered substantial losses, such an opportunity, frightening as it was, was a gift, a tourniquet, a means of stopping the bleeding. Calvin would get his answers if he had to beat it from his adversary. A threatening howl emanated from his body where the neck meets the torso. Here was his release. He would bite and bite hard, until the thing burst, until it all broke open, red, wet and flowing. He would bite and gnash until the pressure gave way, or until his teeth splintered and fell, sharp and jagged, from his howling gob. By god, one way or another, there would be a moment of truth! He pushed through the doorway. His heart thumped and banged. A black-fanged jackrabbit trapped inside his chest fought all hell to kick and rip its way free.

The hostess bade him *bonsoir*. Calvin never saw her, never heard her, only fell forward into the main dining room. He had forgotten all about the pale-pink lads seated in the far corner, so riveted was he to the four men, pitched forward in their seats like plaster statues at fun-house angles, nearly tipped over towards the flamingos who were then sipping aperitifs. Calvin continued falling forward on amped and shaking legs, as the man with the lapel pin pursed thick lips and blew several bars from a classic tune. So loud, so incongruous and penetrating was the melody that Calvin froze mid-step, nearly all of the diners mid-bite, and the whole house turned toward the bullish foursome, including the two flamingos, who, having found the impromptu performance invasive and perfectly uncouth, no less at a place of fine dining, flapped mad feathered wings and voiced, if only to one another, their furtive disapproval.

Calvin regained his stride and aimed himself with tight fists towards the man with the lapel pin. Just then, one of the four men noticed him.

"You!" he scowled low.

The man with the lapel pin, with eyes only for the flapping flamingos, growled violently, "*Prenez-les!*"

At his command, the four exploded from their table. Calvin howled a war cry of his own, raised his fists to fighting position and braced himself for the imminent brawl. There was an exceedingly brief moment of silent stupefaction, after which the entire room was awash in chaos. Four unified parts of a single tsunami crashed down equally over the living and the inanimate. Chairs, tables, glass and silverware chased after, abused and in some cases outraced fleeing bodies, and smashed heavily before them against stone walls. A writhing congregation formed on the floor in the far corner, where effeminate pleading followed masculine threats, where masculine grunts preceded the delicate, eerie sound of uncommon breakage – a sickening breakage with the visceral timbre that gives even hard men chills – followed immediately by the sounds of intense human suffering.

Calvin knew not how much time had passed since he raised his fists and started howling. He only knew that he was still howling and still throwing his fists wildly, in a frenzied manner, madness on madness; and that, in all the chaos and wreckage brought forth by the man who Calvin had pegged as his ultimate affliction, he stood untouched, unscathed and perfectly neglected.

Astonished and frozen by his lack of involvement in the bloody mêlée – a scene which he had planned to detonate by way of his own hands and feet – he eyed the lads' pale-pink plumage scattered about beneath a writhing scrum of hot coercion and falling fists. The lads were on the receiving end of a savage beating.

Calvin came to with the splashing sounds of pooled water, laughter and barking dogs, with a night sky overhead, with his elastic legs churning with motion, eating up cobbled ground, distancing himself by leaps and bounds from a horrifying scene at an Italian restaurant on the other side of Place Massena. He reached the Place du Palais-de-Justice and stopped running. His hands found the weathered stone wall of the fountain, and there, he all but collapsed amid the light mist, the fountain's sparkling waters falling in delicate necklace arches into a cool green pool. He stared into the pool, flood-lit white from the bottom, and devoured the night air with burning lungs. The sound of glass shattering on cobblestone was heard on the terrace of the Bar de la Degustation, where raucous cheering and song ensued. Three mangy mutts snapped and snarled at each other on the steps of the Palais de Justice, and were barked at in return by tattooed teens with black-grease Mohawks.

Staring into the fountain, Calvin began to process what he had just witnessed. The scene was singular; singular to mock the uniqueness of fingerprints and snowflakes, and yet there was a shocking familiarity to the details. He tried to make sense of it all by mentally retracing his steps—the pale-pink flamingos, the Italian restaurant, the man with the lapel pin poised for destruction, intently whistling a tune from a famous Russian ballet. Leaning on the edge of the splashing fountain, Calvin spoke aloud, with his own mouth and his own voice, words that he knew were not his own: "Song of the Swans from Tchaikovsky's Swan Lake."

The details looped in his mind, and with each iteration, became increasingly familiar. The familiarity was not the kind that comes with repetition, but rather that which comes with the observation of an occurrence foretold in fine detail. It was as though an unseen prophet had previously whispered all the details in his ear: La Baie d'Amalfi, the fettuccine vongole, the Song of the Swans *leitmotif* whistled as a musical tripwire.

"*E-e-ech*!" Calvin suddenly spat.

It all started coming back to him, like a night's buried dream beginning to reluctantly unearth itself the morning after. And then it hit him—the telephonic invasion! He remembered it all, everything he had heard that night from the two men who conversed mysteriously over his phone line. Everything had played out exactly as they had planned.

The fountain giggled and splashed, another glass shattered, more voices cheered drunkenly, the mongrels on the steps of the hall of justice snapped and howled. Calvin hoisted himself erect on trembling limbs and ran for home.

21   Shameless, carnivorous beauties

In which a number of rabid gulls
tear away at the gutted flesh of a
trapped rat.

How quickly a home becomes a hold – and a man the kept
object of it – when one passes the hours largely counting them. The
anticipated moment of truth at La Baie d'Amalfi was instead, for
Calvin, a stillborn affair that only served to send him deeper into
confusion and despair. What had he learnt? Only that he had
underestimated the man with the lapel pin, and that he was being
watched, monitored and eavesdropped upon by a band of men who
were wont to strike with exceeding force. Such discoveries only
spawned further questions.

"Why on earth did you flee the scene?" Calvin demanded of
himself into the base of a listless and thoroughly unresponsive
coffee mill. "You had your man right there!"

His psyche came to his defence, and delivering the mill an
abusive shake, he cried, "I'll tell you why! Because one does not
stand idly about watching mushroom clouds billow, does he!"

And after sixty or seventy such counted hours in trapped and
raving seclusion, the questions one poses tend to double-back on
oneself in an unconscious attempt to validate or deny one's grip on
sanity. The result is a self-perpetuating cycle wherein the more
questions asked, the more questions that require asking.

"Oh, you think I'm crazy?" he further demanded of himself.
"You think I'm over the edge? Pah! Just because I stand here

berating household items and kitchen fitments? Am I not justified in doing so when *they* are the ones to have started all this bugging and badgering?"

It was a cycle which, by virtue of itself, provided an inauspicious diagnosis as to the overriding question of one's mental health. Under all but the most extraordinary of circumstances, raving at length into the recesses of coffee mills and other household appliances stands as an undeniable attestation of ones madness. Calvin, however, was certain that his flat was bugged and that a listening audience was bunkered somewhere nearby. And in his mind, the existence of an audience lent credibility to his ravings and defended his claim to sanity, if, ironically, at the very same time, threatening it. For better or worse, the coffee mill did not talk back, but only peppered the floor meekly with leftover grounds. Its silence led Calvin to the delusional inkling that he was finally the one calling the shots and doling out the intimidation. In his more impertinent moments – after a goodly amount of bourbon – he cursed and yelled threateningly at the light fixtures and electric sockets, and in the temperate moments that followed, he pondered the thin line that separated the cuckoo from the sane.

He knew that he was being tracked and monitored, and that his pursuers would soon come for him. He was convinced that he was the next to be descended upon, that the violent scene at La Baie d'Amalfi would prove only to be the ominous prelude to a horrific main event. He locked all the doors and counted the hours leading up to their arrival. He ached to speak with Klarysa, but knew not how to reach her. Lacking a telephone number, he instead set himself to writing, frantically filling page after page with bluster and harangue, only to realise that neither did know where in the world she might have settled with Richard. He paced, he pitched pennies against the wall, he hung out of the windows and drank. After three full days, however, the only thing to have descended upon him was boredom. It was an oppressive boredom that displaced much of his fear and he came to wish that his Four Horsemen would hurry up and get on with it—invade, bring on the apocalypse already.

Early the next morning, as he sat gloomily down to a meal of coffee, croissants and Corsican fig jam, there came a knock at the door, and his heart fairly seized up. After all the waiting and mental preparation, he found himself frightened quite to death when the hour of their arrived had come. Perhaps the greatest impossibility in life is the free fellow's ability to comprehend the capitally sentenced fellow's grief upon hearing the death-rattle of keys as the warden, priest and executioner make their final approach.

There was a knock at the door, true. And yet – and *yet!* – he thought, no one had sounded the buzzer at the *portail* down below for entry into the building! Good chance, then, that the knock was only a neighbour. A shard of hope shivered in his heart, and that heart fired suddenly bright for the first time since Klarysa had left—perhaps (and this realisation shocked him rather greatly) for the first time since meeting her, some eight months prior. It might be anyone at all knocking at the door, he considered with an ecstatic hopefulness—a neighbour shy of eggs or sugar or pastis. It might not be his executioners after all! He recognised the sunlight for the very first time, though it had had poured in through the open windows and filled the room for the duration of his sequestered days. He was suddenly shaking with energy and hope. He could not, in fact, recall having felt so energetic, so youthful, so hopeful. He was young and healthy, harnessed a strong heart, knew long limbs rippled with lean muscle—*capable* was the word to describe Calvin. Good hell, there was a whole world out there yet to be explored and experienced, and he would do it all if given just one more chance. He remained completely muddled as to why he was being pursued in the first place, but it no longer mattered to him; not in the least.

There was a second knock at the door. He regretted denying a neighbour in a time of prandial need, but by god, ignore he would. He would remain motionless and silent until the egg or sugar was sought elsewhere, and then he would race immediately to his bedroom, throw together an overnight bag and flee; take the first available train to Rome or Lisbon or Valencia—anywhere at all. Oh, yes, he would quit Nice and start anew! He would find a new port with new fish, set up camp under new night skies lit by new stars. The crew would come and visit him. There would be grand reunions and easy holidays. He would host his mates proudly and without reserve. Perhaps he would start drinking Fundador and go to the bullfights. He would be softer, gentler, less concerned, more accepting. He would try to forgive himself and the crew their collective quirks. He would try to collect memories that one could recount without having to lower one's voice and check over one's shoulder, memories that one might recount without reserve before children and those who wore khakis and shirts with cuffs and buttons.

There came a third knock.

"*Merde!*" Calvin quietly cursed.

It was a slower, heavier knock; one that expressed with waning patience: *We know you're in there.*

Calvin boiled nervously. "Go to hell for your goddamned eggs!" he wanted to scream. But every fellow knows that a neighbour never knocks thrice—certainly not for breakfast ingredients.

Calvin ran half-crazed into the bedroom and shoved a handful of random clothing into a bag; then leaned out each successive window and scanned feverishly for an escape means—any pillowy congregation below that might make possible a fourth-floor leap. He raced into the salon and leaned out over the alleyway. Any fair character of ink or screen, he thought, would flop himself onto the awning below, but it was no time to go losing one's head in the cartoonish exploits of fiction.

Just then, what seemed like a huddle of metal ants began to scratch away at the insides of a metal clock. The sound grew louder and more determined and then it stopped altogether. There was a short span of silence, after which the door to the flat burst open with a startling crack, causing the morning's gathering of white gulls on the orange rooftops across the alley to shoot off in a mad and snowy flurry. Calvin, bloodless and unable to move, heard the discharge of an enthusiastic cheer from several unseen men gathered in the entryway. The brief spike of cheer flattened into a heavy hush and a gang of ominous men lumbered its way into the flat: one, two, three, all thoroughly decked in dark-blue, save for the black boots. The fourth and last man to enter the flat was me. With my lock-pick in one hand, I bent down and took hold of the long splinter of wood that had ripped free of the doorframe.

"How about that, sir?" said my man Fiston, taking the splinter of wood from me. "Who would have guessed it so easy to kick in a door? This one here is as thick as my fist."

The worst moment for any fighter is the moment just before the opening bell. Once the bell rings, however, all fighters find their feet. Calvin was a fighter and the maxim held true for him.

"It has only to do with the lock," he said, "not the thickness of wood, you challenged goon."

"Therefore, kick closer to the handle," I said, fingering the silver pin on my lapel, the one that had come to haunt Calvin so. "That is what you teach, is it not, Mr. Stony? Or did Fiston here botch yet another bug?"

"No, sir," denied Fiston, the youngest and most promising of my crew; a little less bull-like in stature, if only for age. His shoulders were wide and his back broad; in time his belly would grow. "*That* bug," he insisted, "was installed correctly the first time. You have my word, sir. Kick closer to the handle. That's how he instructed her, all right."

"I was only joking, dear Fiston. It was a bad joke. Forgive me. You do fine bug work when you put your mind to it."

"The *first* time?" Calvin questioned with disgust. "As opposed to the bugs you poorly installed throughout my flat, which needed correction. I heard every word of your conversation—I hope the vongole was to your liking."

Fiston reddened before Calvin's critique.

"I suppose you," Calvin continued derisively to me, "were coming to correct his errors on the night I chased you down the stairwell."

"You will come to know that we are very good at what we do, Mr. Stony. But we are not perfect. Yes," I admitted, "I had come that night to fix the bug. It was careless of me to have come when you—"

"You don't have to, sir," Fiston interrupted, disappointed in himself and embarrassed for us both.

"No, Fiston, it was careless of me. I won't deny that. Patience, Mr. Stony, is a commodity of the elderly, but extraordinary circumstances sometimes catalyse... Bah, I don't need to tell you that every stage in life has it curses. The curse of the young," I said with a gentle eye for Fiston, sorry for having to draw reference yet again to the botched bug. Truths, however, are truths even when they are ugly, and they only become uglier when we refuse to acknowledge them. "The curse of the young is that they know not what it is to be mortal. That's right. If one has never carried a baby in one's womb for nine months and pushed it out wrinkled and screaming into the bright white world, one cannot comprehend what it is to give life. So too, if one has not come face-to-face with the signs of his own mortality – if he has not witnessed the uninvited webbing of wrinkles that come to traverse the contours of his own drawn face, felt the aching of winter joints, coped with the incessant ringing in his ears, fought through inexplicable early-evening fatigue, fallen lost through the gaps of a failing memory, forgotten his way forward, recognised his irrelevance in a world that once danced for him, recognised the loss of command, the loss of voice, the loss of family and friends – in short, if he has not experienced such autumnal turnings, he cannot begin to comprehend what it is to be mortal. He is, conversely, for all intents and purposes, immortal. What is a penny to a millionaire, Mr. Stony? And what is an hour to the immortal? What is one missed opportunity when it is believed that great waves of opportunity will forever follow in neat rhythmic sets? Where is the sense of urgency for the immortal youth, Mr. Stony? Why, it does not exist.

"On the other hand – let us not deceive ourselves – a life led unaware of one's mortality is a roaring and vivid life. The young know not what it is to be mortal, and that is life's most miraculous and fleeting gift. There are gifts to growing old, I suppose. None of them, however, are miraculous. And so we are left to manufacture our own gifts, our own reasons for wrenching our tired bones up from the bed each morning, our own prospects for miracles, minor as they may be and paltry as they may appear to the young and immortal. I have my reasons and my prospects—bet the devil I do. And how about you, Mr. Stony? Bah, but you are still young! You still belong to the set that largely finds my motivations to be... All I mean to point out is that Fiston, too, is young, and sometimes, God bless him, he lacks the sense of urgency required to execute a task with precision the first time. Nevertheless, I am the boss, and I take responsibility for the botched bug. I have a hard time delegating, though I am told it is necessary. I am learning."

"You delegate plenty well," said Calvin, "when it comes to beating hell out of helpless boys, not to mention kicking in doors. What is it—don't care to dirty your hands?"

"No, that's me," jumped Fiston, his deep brown eyes silently begging my continued calm and reservation. "I am an intelligence guy—science, numbers, psychology. I am not one for violence."

"Ever see hands like that on a numbers guys, Mr. Stony? I dare say he could shred an inflated football with those hands. Could extract unimaginable lots of information, too. He only needs to learn how to use them, believe in them. Isn't that right, Fiston?"

Said Fiston to Calvin, "Sir believes our physical strengths are as valuable as our mental strengths, and that I'll be more effective on the job when I learn to trust the tools of my physicality. I do what I am told and unfailingly follow sir's advice, but it is unnatural for a man of my pacification to call on aggression. And therefore, if you do not mind terribly, Mr. Stony, I'd like to ask that you please do us all a favour and cooperate."

"I say," Calvin began hotly, "you kick in a damned fine door for a pacifist!"

"I am sorry for that, but as I told you, I follow orders unfailingly. It would have been good of you to open the door when we knocked. Still, I don't mind force, so much," Fiston admitted. "Blood is my weakness. I am a boy at heart and despite the fine marks I made in school, like most boys, I never cared much for studies or homework. Sir says that we must learn to mitigate our weaknesses, however, and I would not be at all surprised if he had me beat all hell out of you purely in the name of homework."

"That's quite enough, Fiston. Our apologies for the door, Mr. Stony. Normally this," I said in reference to the lock-pick, "does the trick. And thank goodness, really, as it is an expensive piece of equipment. Furthermore, kicking in doors obviates all chances of a clandestine arrival. But you are a clever lad, Mr. Stony; I am sure you anticipated our visit. There was no need for tip-toes to-day. I'll have you know, all the same, that we are not accustomed to knocking. We did extend you that courtesy."

"Of course I was anticipating you," said Calvin, tossing aside his overnight bag with defeat. "I waited for three days."

I took the liberty of pulling up an old wooden chair and asked Fiston to do likewise. I required my other two lads to stay standing.

"Then," Calvin continued, "not five minutes ago, I swear, I had the genius epiphany to pack a bag, run off and profit from the joy of never seeing any of you ever again."

Calvin stood awkwardly, looking as though he might yet opt for a leap through the window. "It took me three whole days before I arrived at the idea to run. There's clever for you!"

"Don't be too hard on yourself," I said, and then baited him, "running is instinctive."

I paused there for a count, intending to lock knowing eyes, as rams do horns, but the runner's eyes fell quickly away. Calvin turned white and haggard.

"Don't worry," I continued. "I only mean that one doesn't often give thought to running until long after the legs are in motion—or until one is caught standing still, gathering moss. The curious thing about running is that bystanders tend to assign value to direction. Running away, they'll tell you, portends weakness and destitution. Run towards something, however, and they'll say you are motivated and determined; though, clearly, the emotions driving the displacement may be identical regardless of direction. Take me, for example. I have lived the world over, constantly on the move. I have loved, lost, seen everything there is to see, acquired many skills and learnt many languages. How do you find my English, by the way? Though it is my first language, it is only one of many to have fought for my tongue's attention since the day I was born. I have learnt English the way one assembles a puzzle—piece-by-piece. Some pieces, you will find, are still missing.

"Still they beg of me: from what are you running? I explain that I am not running *from* anything, but rather *towards* something, and this appeases them for a short while. They do not need to know that the motivations that drive me forward are troublesome and controversial and no less hazardous than the motivations that drive away the fellow who flees into the dark of night as fast as he can and without looking back. Desperation does not abide starting points or end points. Nor does it discriminate, ravaging as it does both the righteous and the sinister."

"Now you are here," responded Calvin, "and I suppose that is best. I've not slept in weeks because of you lot, and I reckon you'll finally help me out along those lines—the dead, I should think, sleep rather soundly. By the way," he said with sudden poignancy, his tired green eyes shining brightly, "Who in hell *are* you?"

An charge of laughter escaped me. "Who *am* I? Brilliant! I'll not lie to you, Mr. Stony; since the day we began monitoring you, I've thoroughly enjoyed your innocence. We do not come across a hell of a lot of it in our line."

"I'm glad you recognise my innocence," he said flatly. "That's a start."

Feeling more secure for having established a certain footing before those who had broken the boundary of his private home, he provoked with competitive pride, "I know you've bugged the place, but I do lead a rather full life, most of it lived outside these walls. What makes you think I'm so innocent?"

Try as I might, I could not suppress a wide smile. "You need not feign cynicism and world-weariness for us, Mr. Stony. We've been watching you. There is a refreshing innocence about you. It is something to be embraced, not disguised or forsaken. You asked who I am. In the darkest hours, only the innocent ask questions that are unanswerable with words and are, furthermore, pointless."

"*Point*less?" he said, offended. "You, sir, kicked in my goddamned door! Do I not have a right to the identity of my aggressor?"

"Oh, you probably do. Or rather," I corrected myself, "I appreciate the fact that you think you do. Don't be upset. I only mean to say that I appreciate your innocence. Why, a band of unknowns invades your home and turns it upside-down—"

"But it hasn't been turned upside-down," he interrupted, as though to assert control.

"And it doesn't have to be," I clarified, "though they do typically end up that way. It is entirely up to you. But let us not get ahead of ourselves. Point being, you find yourself on the distressful end of a violent invasion and your first thought, more or less, is to ask after the name and title of your perpetrator, whose presence is augmented, no less, by significant back-up and firepower. Tell me, how would Klarysa have responded to our invasion, were she here?"

The name hit him like lightening. So hurting was he after her recent departure that he would have jumped at any opportunity to discuss her.

"Why, Klarysa wouldn't have looked up from her magazine as the door was sent flying into the kitchen," he said fondly of her. "Upon recognising you, she may have told you to help yourself to tea and biscuits."

"Wonderful, wouldn't you say, Mr. Stony, the actions of the innocent?"

He seemed to think nothing of our sense of familiarity as it concerned Klarysa. With her departure, she was once again a world-possession.

"We *are* innocent," he said. "Both Klarysa and I."

"In a sense, yes, though let us not refer to innocence in terms of a lack of culpability. That's the wrong type of innocence. Do we understand one another? To be sure, you are culpable—that is to say, guilty."

The souring of Calvin's face told me that there had indeed been a misunderstanding.

"The innocence to which I refer," I clarified, "is that of a man who unconsciously harbours hope where others cannot—in the darkest, most uninspiring of moments, the kind in which, if I may be frank, you currently find yourself. In that sense, you are indeed innocent. You ask who I am, but what does it matter, Mr. Stony? As you have astutely noted, I have kicked in your goddamned door. Or rather, Fiston has. Would it be any less broken, or your privacy any less violated at this moment were I the president of the Republic? I've long lost my innocence. It is true, and of that I am not proud, though it is all but inevitable for someone of my age and métier. As such, were a band of men to kick down *my* door, my first and only question would be: *What do you want of me?* That is the one essential question. Who I may or may not be is of no consequence."

"Fine," Calvin began dryly, his confidence having been stripped by the accusation of guilt. "What do you want of me?"

"Look at that, Fiston!" I cheered. "There is hope yet for your bloodless encounter. I hope you know, Mr. Stony, that there is no celebrity in our line of work, no glamour. There is no joy in watching a young man's innocence drip and puddle in dead, shallow pools on the floor. For once it is gone—"

"Don't patronise me. What do you want of me?"

"It is a shame, really, how all innocence does eventually die."

"What do you want of me!"

"I want the knife, Mr. Stony, since you are asking."

The world stopped spinning for a count.

"Give me the knife."

"What knife?" he asked.

"Fine, fine. I agree; let's not just yet. Knowledge of certain histories will make this easier. But do please sit, Mr. Stony. Might I suggest a seat there, on the divan? No? The chair, then. Sit and let us fill in the picture, starting from your original question. Let us try to appeal to what remains of our collective innocence. *Vous, les gars,*" I said to my men, eager as they were for action. "*Au boulot.*"

Turning my attention back to Calvin, I said, "You ask who I am. Let me ask in return: who is any man, Mr. Stony? What is any man? Is he a name and a title? Is he a product of his environment? Is he the sum of his experiences? The depth of his passion? The ardour of his obsessions?"

Of my two men, one began to tear apart the kitchen, rifling through the drawers and cabinetry, smashing any object with concealing qualities. My other man headed back to the bedroom and did similarly.

"Hey!" Calvin objected. "What the—"

"If a man lives long enough, Mr. Stony, he begins to recognise that life is a continuous loop of recurring events. That is the problem with mankind—we are a sadly predictable lot. Only consider our current scenario here to-day. You demand answers, I give them to you, you feign confusion, your home is turned upside-down. As I told you, it tends to be the way.

"Who am I, Mr. Stony? Forgive me for having laughed at the question just a moment ago. I assure you it was only with joyful surprise and admiration that I did so. I found the timing and sincerity of your question refreshing. But, yes, the question is valid. Who is any man? Who are *you*, Mr. Stony? Understand that we are here because of your magnetism. All roads lead here, and we would very much like to know the real you. You are, for starters, a fisherman. Many men define themselves by the métier of their keeping, but you involve yourself in many... diverse activities."

"It's true," Calvin ventured carefully. "I bartend, I work the boats on occasion, I do estate work from time to time, gardening and the like. I enjoy the change of pace, the change of scenery."

"But you work so well with the fish. It is what you do best—your words, not mine. Why do you choose, then, to get mixed up with the likes of Fitim Kaleci?"

Calvin sparked upon hearing the name. He had come to view Fitim as just another of the many curious characters known in the streets of Vieux Nice, and had taken a sincere liking to him.

"Mixed up with him?" begged Calvin. "How do you mean?"

"Have I misused the expression? Does it not befit the context? You recently worked a job for Mr. Kaleci, did you not?" I said, fingering the damning evidence in my coat pocket.

"I did."

"Well! I must say I am surprised by the quickness of your confession—"

"But listen here," said Calvin, "you *have* misused the expression. I am not *mixed up* with him, and I've confessed to nothing whatsoever."

"We do have ways of making people talk."

"You can keep them sheathed. I *am* talking after all, and if you will stop issuing threats long enough to listen, you might hear me when I say yet again that I have done nothing wrong."

"All things in time," I said. "Though I do hope you will not test me."

The contents of another cupboard came crashing to the floor.

"*Comment ça va, les gars?*" I demanded, wiping away a trickle of sweat from my forehead.

"*Rien, chef.*"

"Nothing! Well!"

A blast of heat burst through my head and dizziness overcame me.

"*Ne souciez pas, chef. On le trouverai!*"

It is always the same, I thought—don't worry, we will find it! But for all my efforts, all my sacrifices, what has changed? Absolutely nothing! The years pass, my patience wanes, certainty precedes nought but ever-greater disappointment and failure.

Lost suddenly in a synaptic firestorm, indistinguishable mutterings bobbled between my cheeks.

"Sir!" I heard Fiston cry. "Sir, your fingers!"

I felt Fiston's fists dropping heavily on my back and shoulders.

"Sir! Sir!"

Called back from the edge of panic, I found four of the fingers from my left hand hideously bent at frightening angles. I let go of those abused and abusive fingers and worked a fist to usher back the blood. My vision soon returned and I saw other than unholy darkness.

"Thank you, Fiston," I managed from somewhere beyond myself, while choking back black bubbles.

A sticky iron wash coated my throat. I felt a flapping sensation in my mouth and realised that in my brief black moment I had gnashed a sizable hole in my tongue. I swallowed back the hot wash, but not before a trickle of blood escaped the corner of my mouth.

"Who are you, Mr Stony?" I finally continued, wiping my sleeve over my chin. "Yes, upon reflection, I find this to be a fair question. And as you asked first, I will oblige your curiosity."

Calvin, the poor lad, was clearly stunned by the sight of my red lips and teeth.

"As I told you, I have lived the world over, and so one might think that I am a citizen of the world, that I am from everywhere, or that I feel at home wherever I lay my head. But although I may blend in anywhere, speak the languages and engage in the culture as would a native, or else wrap my arms around it all quickly and with little effort, the truth is that I am from nowhere at all. Wherever I lay my head, I am, above all else, a stranger and an outsider.

"I was born in a third-class coach on a rail at the frontier of two nations, born to a woman from Wales who failed to make it home from the Crimea in time to give birth among family. It is ridiculous how quickly and carelessly we adopt stock notions of a fellow based on his nationality, though the determining factor in his nationality may only be a handful of hours or kilometres in one direction or another. I hold passports from three nations, but what is my nationality? My parents moved to Marseille when I was seven-years-old. At seventeen I moved to Toulouse, an angry, stubborn young man—the teen years are trying times for a lad grappling with the mechanics of adult crimes and vengeance. From Toulouse I came and went, moving about the globe for the better part of three decades. Am I French? I cannot say for certain. In some ways France is as foreign to me to-day as it was when I first set foot upon the platform at Paris Gare du Nord; just a wee lad, hands stuffed shyly into the front pocket of the *Telogreika* my mother had woven for me during a winter in Yalta.

"If I feel a certain allegiance to France, it is only because a fellow needs, from time to time and for some inexplicable reason, to feel spiritually tethered to a patch of land, its people and its histories, be that land verdant or parched, its people valorous or fearful, its histories meritorious or shameful. Funny, isn't it? Some folks, reliant on the milk of their mother nation, never leave the teat. Some, though they may wander far and wide, carry forever in the soles of their boots the soil of their birthplace, and long for the day of their return home. I am no such man, Mr. Stony, despite the countless hours spent wishing and praying for nothing more than to know that sense of belonging.

"Who knows, it may all prove to be a contrivance, these efforts of mine to make a home of France. Nevertheless, here I am, drawn to her, led back by the actions of corrupt and malevolent men. There is business to attend to and I have willingly given myself over to it, all my days and nights. All the same, I take it as an encouraging sign that this affair has brought me back to the land of my youth and the land that provides for, and gives shelter to, my son and grandson.

Bah, I do not dwell on such concerns. Not yet. Upon accomplishing what I must accomplish, however, I will fill my every pocket and the very shoes I walk in with her earth and pray that she will anchor me solidly to her slippery confines when the winds of justice, or of defence, or of simple curiosity, once again temp my bones away.

"In a given day, a man may sleep for eight hours and work for another eight, or sometimes twelve or more. And when a day is gone it cannot be reclaimed, save for within the webbing of one's memories. The aggregate of our days, months and years, therefore, and all that those years comprise – including our families – exist largely by the grace of the memories we have of them. My family does not need me, Mr. Stony. It is an excruciating admission, but I've already given you my mind as it concerns wilfully unacknowledged truths. Though I am a stranger to them, however, there will come a time for atonement. For now, I continue to sacrifice a relationship with them to-day, that they may have opportunities to-morrow to make indelible memories similar to those that I cherish, and from which I profit. We are nothing without our memories, and theirs I will defend to the end. Someday, perhaps, who knows, they may even have fond memories of me to recall and cherish.

"Understand that it requires of a man the better part of a lifetime to truly understand all of the feathery intricacies of a given place, the dynamics of the million-count orchestrations that conduct themselves inexplicably, invisibly over the course of any given day, across its streets and sands and within the involuntary minds and souls of its peoples. Yes, the better part of a lifetime, though it takes only a few short years of absence from a beloved land before even some of the larger, more obvious ways and movements become strange to him. The disorientation is not only a function of the changes that force themselves upon a given land while a fellow is away, though that, too, will contribute. More influential, however, are all of the foreign stimuli that come to tickle the curious and open mind of a man in a new land. The horizons of such a mind are stretched and expanded by exposure to previously unobserved wonders, realities and philosophies, some of which may contradict those that forever seemed flawless and essential, and which may, upon acclimation, be seen as perfectly valid or even vastly superior alternatives.

"There are, mind you, certain treasures that are specific to one place and one place only. Such treasures become the very backbone of a land. They are unique and inimitable, as much so as are a fellow's own sons and daughters. They represent the land more so than its name, which may not be known by all in its official entirety; more so than its flag, which flaps willy-nilly over stolid administration buildings. The treasures of which I speak stick with a man no matter how long he is away, no matter how far he may wander, in part because he is achingly in love with them. They mark the man and the land both, for all eternity. But like anything of value, even a sacred heritage is vulnerable to attack by unscrupulous others who aim to profit from a stolen identity.

"There exists here in France an old and well-intentioned organisation – fumbling and daft as it may be – charged with the protection of such national treasures. Their strategies are based largely on delimiting geographic boundaries and regulating proprietary processes. It is a government bureau called the Institut National des Appellations d'Origine, and if you are not familiar with the organisation, you are likely familiar with their most vital certification—the Appellation d'Origine Contrôlée. The AOC, as you know, is a certification granted to French regional treasures—wines, cheeses, butters and other agricultural wares that contribute to the unique genetics of this country and its culture.

"Our song and our flag – La Marseillaise and Les Couleurs, respectively – do not worry themselves over cheap pilfering. They, sir, can defend themselves. But take, for example, *le beurre de* Charentes-Poitou, a butter born in the ateliers of a select clustering of West-Central departments. How can a delicate provincial butter, Mr. Stony, with its gentle hue of jasmine blossoms, defend itself and its honour against biopirates that know nothing of twelve-hour biological maturation, or the delectable chastity of a butter crafted by artisans who would sooner perish than attach their names to one with the clownish colour of a torrid, greasy sun, or one with the gaudy shelf-life of those injected with age-defying conservatives? Why, it cannot! *Alors*, should some rogue attempt to profit by distributing its yellow cooking grease under the exemplary name of *le beurre de* Charentes-Poitou, the INAO intervenes and sees to it that justice is served.

"The equity in a name is often critical to the survival of a people—*Basmati*, for example, to South Asian farmers. So too, when one pays the price for, say, a kilo of *jamón* Ibérico, one deserves genuine acorn-fed *pata negra*, not a shank of cheap, compound-fed white pig! Moreover, the farmer who invests his time, resources and heart into producing a delicacy of such superior quality deserves protection from soulless organisations, so that he may reasonably lie down at night and rise the next morning safe in the knowledge of *who he is*. And by god—!"

"Sir, please," said Fiston nervously. "Please."

"—By god when one fills an elegant flute from a bottle labelled with the majestic name *Champagne*, the most beautiful name in the world—*Champagne*! Say it, Fiston!"

"Champagne, sir."

"*Champagne*!—a centuries-old marriage of produce and place. By god, when one fills a flute from a bottle labelled such, why, he does his duty!"

"Sir, I beg of you—!"

"He does what is right by himself and his family, as a protector of future memories! He does what is right by the master vintner, by those who came before him and those yet to come! He does what is right by making damned well certain that the bottle carries the nectar pressed from fruit of *le grand terroir de Champagne* and that place alone—*not* the proletariat pressing from grapes off some poxy Russian slope!"

I rose up before Calvin in quite a startling manner, like a roaring brown bear, huffing threats and heaving abuse at criminal subjects thousands of kilometres away, pounding damning fists like twin gavels, eyes bulging from my skull, spittle dotting the old tiled floor. I would explode thus from time to time. I am not proud of such explosions, nor am I ashamed. I came to in the typical manner, bound in a straightjacket of my team's cabled arms.

"*Lachez-moi*!" I roared. "*Lachez-moi*!"

My men forced me down onto the old wooden chair and backed away.

"Back to work, you two! Fiston, sit down!"

Oh, what a fiery bull I was in my younger days. I began employment at the INAO when living in Toulouse, during a time when I was engaged with the rugby club, Stade Toulousain. Off the pitch, my opponents were unscrupulous biopirates. On the pitch, although one's opponents are men worthy of respect and admiration, violence is torrential and it storms over one and all as naturally as do the rains over my mother's Cardiff. How difficult it was for me then, as an idealistic and hot-tempered young man of great passion, who was constantly goaded by arrogant industry criminals, to refrain from deploying the same violent strategies that had proven so effective on the pitch.

"Deep breaths, sir," Fiston advised. "*Calmez-vous.*"

"Look, Fiston, I am breathing deeply. I am calm. Now, sit."

I looked at Calvin. The short episode had a troubling affect on the boy. It had rendered him a silent, fearful mess that could not meet my eyes.

"I apologise for that unpleasant episode, Mr. Stony."

I am calmer to-day, though I need only ponder the notion of Russian scoundrels slopping piss and grape juice into dark-green glass and calling it champagne, and the devil begins to climb my spine.

"What I want to point out to you," I finally continued, "is that although the INAO exists ostensibly to protect trade and industry, it ultimately serves to protect the authenticity of an experience. And by doing so, it protects the authenticity of one's memories, the essential elements of every life, which must be protected at all costs—not borders or flags or political systems and theories, but the authenticity of one's experiences and the resulting memories that one will cherish for the rest of one's days. Without them, what does a border demarcate? What does a flag represent?

"This is the objective, Mr. Stony. As I have said, the INAO is well-intentioned. The essential problem, however, facing, say, a French organisation that wishes to engage a Russian industry, is a jurisdictional one. Oh, there is the World Trade Organization, of course, but the WTO... Bah, the fact of the matter is that the INAO is poorly positioned to enforce its decisions. To be frank, Mr. Stony, the INAO is a toothless organisation. That is why I quit them, many years ago now. Working within an organisation that ultimately has no authority to enforce its decisions will bring an impassioned man to an early grave.

"Forgive me such digressions and let us return to the question at hand. Who is a man, Mr. Stony? Who is any man? I will answer as follows: define in your mind who or what you want to be, and then lead your life according to the principle truths, the innermost nature of that which you have defined. Give your heart over to it, breathe life into it and let it become the substrate upon which your convictions and the manifestations of those convictions will take root, blossom and bloom—lest, God forbid, you make a loathsome and beggarly impostor of yourself. Let it be a disposition, a profession or the embodiment of a philosophy. Anything, really, though let the factors affecting your decision be noble ones. Let your heart dominate your mind, but practice sobriety and sound judgement. Do not allow false motivations, such as prestige or compensation, their undue influence. Let it be a thing of truth, something that harmonises with your truest self. Make it a source of pride, something you will openly defend. It need not be grand or superlative. It need not please others. *But!*" I said loudly, bringing my fist down upon the *table basse*, "Do *not* appropriate another's identity!"

A rapid boil returned. I was helpless to cool it.

"Do *not* falsely claim an identity over which a man and his people have painstakingly toiled to perfect, an identity that erupted from hearts in a molten flow of passion and inspiration, and eventually cooled and solidified over the course of decades and centuries to become the very backbone of an existence! Why, you look altogether ill, Mr. Stony! Would *you*, sir, unfaithfully accept the tutelage and guidance of a *maître* – a master, a god – acquire a certain paltry proficiency within the sphere of his godly craft, and then proceed to shamelessly pirate and poach the very name and identity, not only of the treasure that your master and his lineage did for centuries sculpt to perfection, but also the name and identity of the land that was your master's ancestral home and the birthplace of that treasure? *Speak*, Mr. Stony! I have posed a question of you!"

"Sir, please," begged Fiston. "You are giving way—"

"*Tais toi, Fiston!* Would you, Mr. Stony! I demand an answer of you!"

"No," Calvin mouthed, pale and voiceless.

"No! You heard him, Fiston! He would not!"

My vision went grainy for a moment and then left me altogether. "There is only one wine worthy of a king's coronation," I moaned as my vision slowly returned. "Only one worthy of thy name, Champagne."

Man does not abide natural laws, those that decree justness, respect, dignity and righteousness. The world has always known the atrocities of remorseless criminals, but there was a time when the criminals admitted what they were. To-day, our devils tell us that they love us, that they care for us, even that they represent us, our families, our communities, our values, our dreams. And we have wilfully aligned with them. What then is the value of the life of a man who wants for nothing but to protect the future memories of his son and grandson? What is the value of the life of a man who longs only for a return to justness, righteousness, dignity and respect? We are asked to believe, but must we align our beliefs with those of the white raging river, of those soulless giants who propagate and suck madly from their own raging momentum? We are asked to commit, but must we commit to the tawdry, facile and plentiful? If I am judged a hoary old berserker for the antiquated convictions that I will nevertheless defend to the death; if I am judged a failure and a danger to society at large, then by all means let my judges take me by the neck if they can and damned well crucify me!

Having once again calmed myself, following another furious disclosure, there was little left for me but to come to the heart of the matter as it concerned Calvin and my forced presence in his home. In doing so, I recounted to him a history involving two wine estates, two of the first founded in the Black Sea port city of Odessa, in southern Ukraine, towards the close of the nineteenth century. The first of which, the Odessa Sparkling Wine Company, was a tsarist franchise establish under the master charge of Henri Roederer of the House of Roederer, renowned champagne estate in Reims, France, capital of the province of Champagne and former coronation city-site of the kings of France.

The OSWC combined Roederer expertise and grapes from the vineyards around Odessa to create a sparkling wine that dazzled Tsar Nicholas II and his imperial court. It was a Russian product, still they stuck out their impertinent chests and called it *champagne*. It was a low and treasonous decision by Roederer. He was a genius, but he had no legitimate call to produce wine in Russia—he founded the Russian estate merely as a means of avoiding French export taxes associated with the sale of French wine in Russia. Roederer's proved to be a financially minded muse, and well chronicled, indeed, are the offences of great artists turned businessmen.

Shortly after the founding of the OSWC, a lesser-known French vintner was hired by a young Odessite to found a rival estate. The young Oddesite was called Oleksander Pavlichenko.

"Yes," I said, confirming Calvin's supposition, "Klarysa's great grandfather."

The estate was called the Odessa Omega Sparkling Wine Enterprise, and was widely referred to as the House of Omega. Sufficient demand existed to support the side-by-side growth of both the OSWC and the House of Omega, and each did flourish. After twenty years of pursuit and profit, they had become two of the most recognised symbols in the city of Odessa. The October Revolution of 1917, however, which saw the Bolsheviks swept into power, kicked off a riotous period of volatility that brought the rush of production and prosperity to a feeble drip. French vintners fled Russia and their work was continued in piecemeal fashion by their Russian apprentices. In the early 1920s, with the Soviet state driving new development, the government encouraged Russian winemakers to devise a sparkling wine for the masses. The result was *Sovetskoye Shampanskoye*, and as is true of most things designed for mass appeal, it was far from triumphal. Soviet champagne—a cheap imitation, a godless impostor.

With INAO credentials, I confronted Soviet politicians, diplomats, vintners and journalists. I begged, cajoled, grovelled and finally demanded that they discontinue their indecorous practices. But I was refused at every turn. Many of the former Soviet states claimed that France had granted the Russian Imperial Government the right to dress their impostor wines in champagne disguises, in perpetuity. The INAO decided it had exhausted its meagre arsenal of persuasion tactics and recommended my reassignment to a case with greater prospects for success. I pleaded for more time, but my pleas were categorically denied. I was reassigned to a case that involved the infringement of an embarrassing imitation on the good name of the *Bleu d'Auvergne*. Indubitably, the reputation of such a fine cheese warranted a swift offensive by the organisation, but I had eyes for only one lady and I would not be deterred. Over time, the must of my frustration fermented into an order of delirium. At length, no nearer to any favourable result, my focus and methodology degraded towards barbarism and reprisal.

The complaints lodged against me by numerous foreign diplomats on the basis of my "frighteningly unorthodox methodology" resulted in the addition of my name to the organisation's shortlist of teetering liabilities. I had taken up the cheese assignment at a functionary's pace, and began using every free minute of the day and night to formulate what the organisation had committed to permanent record as "horrific schemes and highly unauthorised persuasion tactics of a disturbingly medieval character", designed to encourage conformance within the Russian wine industry. Naturally, this marked the end of my tenure with the INAO. I'd have been sacked long prior had I not done the work of ten efficient men. Finally, I took the opportunity granted me to resign and avoided the stigma of a sacking.

The OSWC pressed on as best it could between the October Revolution and the German occupation of Odessa during World War II. Of the two estates, the OSWC was better suited to cope with industry volatility, due in no small part to its Roederer-inspired image as a French wine estate. The House of Omega, lacking a famous French figurehead on which to hang its hat, was less equipped. In due course, having come to the conclusion that prosperity was best designed by youthful minds and best built by youthful hands, an aging Oleksander Pavlichenko stepped down and entrusted the future of the estate to his only son, Kostya.

Kostya was never the wine man that Oleksander was. Although Kostya was equally educated in the oenological sciences and demonstrated an artistic flair that would raise the ceiling of success beyond that which science alone could affect, Kostya's childhood coincided with an era during which wine production was halted now and again, for any number of years. In the idle time, his hours and energies were competed for by several burgeoning passions. The visual arts finally won his favour. From a very young age, Kostya showed a cultivated eye and steady hand for modelling and sculpture, and at his pleading, Oleksander had a small wooden smithy with a bloomery-style furnace erected at the back of the estate.

Kostya was a judicious student of the smiting process. At the age of eight, long before he had the physical strength to handle the hammer, the ore and the bloom, he showed an exceptional acuity for the science of smelting, and directed with patience and faculty the two burly Ukrainian twins employed by the estate and assigned to his charge. The precocious child-foreman directed the lads through the addition of ore and charcoal, once the bloomery was hot. He would huddle between the two, encouraging each to lean in closely and listen with bent ears to the marvellous snap and crackle of the roasting ore. Then he would scurry down to the bellows and stoke the flame, controlling the temperature, like a pastry chef, to keep the ore from excessive carbon loading. Finally, after the bits of molten iron had fallen and collected at the bottom of the furnace, he dropped his head dramatically and brought his gloved hands together twice, briskly, producing two muffled claps that served as the eagerly anticipated signal. The twins, both of whom loved and admired young Kostya (and may have slightly feared his proclivity for temperamental pre-pubescent outbursts), invariably stood rapt and hanging on his every word and signal, and fairly dove for their hammers when bade. Kostya would then cast off his gloves, take his place atop an old tree stump and with a dried willow switch in hand, proceed to flamboyantly conduct the final task in astute animation, to the self-sung tune of Rossini's famous William Tell Overture. The twins obeyed the rhythm that was set by their conductor and hammered in perfect syncopation all hell and slag out of the glowing porous bloom.

Kostya guided the twins through the varied production steps and stages, to manipulate the iron they produced and manifest his artistic visions. Of the first-effort works they produced, a sentimental favourite of Kostya's was an elaborate weather vane inspired by Leo Tolstoy and the Demidov family of blacksmiths and ironmasters – famous patrons of the Russian administrative centre of Tula Oblast – which came to ornament the top of the smithy. The piece was a trifle bloodshot and brittle with phosphorous, and the hammered portrayal of Tolstoy suffered a nose more closely resembling that of de Bergerac or Durante, but it obeyed the winds all the same and the slag was used to fertilise the estate's grape vines.

Years later, as a young man at the reins of the estate, Kostya recognised the need to diversify beyond wine if the House of Omega were to remain viable, and he wasted no time in bringing forth sweeping change. Among the rolling hectares of vines, he had a second chateau built in the style of the original. The new chateau boasted a professional-grade kitchen to which worthy mid-career chefs and confectioners from all corners of Europe were extended residencies; a restaurant worthy of critic-stingy stars; and a fine-arts gallery that won the esteem of discerning artists and collectors alike. Under Kostya's creative direction, the estate established itself as a trend-savvy winery, eatery and art house, and the preferred scene of a certain set of artists, dandies and *excentriques branchés*. *La vie était belle.*

One day, a humble French cutler arrived at the gates of the House of Omega. He introduced himself as the grandson of the estate's original vintner, the man recruited by Oleksander to help found the estate. The broad-backed young cutler had made his way to Odessa from Thiers, France, home of the renowned Marjacq folding knife, of which he spoke ingloriously of himself as a master craftsman. Having spent the majority of his youth in Reims, the cutler was at home among grape vines and was well-versed in the mechanics of winemaking. He expressed to Kostya that he was seeking employment – any task, critical or menial, would suffice – and listed the ways in which he might be of service to a diverse estate like the House of Omega.

The cutler struck a golden chord with Kostya when, in reference to the ornate iron gates running the circumference of the estate, and the fixtures and ornamentation adorning its grounds, he touched upon his welding experiencing and his general capacity for making iron obey as gracefully as any Bolshoi ballerina. A skilled metallurgist, the cutler's *savoir-faire* was borrowed from the General Chapter of the Cistercian monks, the leading iron producers in Champagne from the mid-thirteenth to seventeenth centuries, and honed in the ateliers of Thiers. Kostya took an instant liking to the brawny lad and hired him on the spot.

The arrangement was a resounding success. The cutler proved highly skilled, selfless, industrious, and devoted to the success of the estate. He and Kostya developed a winning kinship. When the winery was operating, Kostya directed the efforts in the vineyard and the winery, while the cutler made purr all the machinery that wanted to otherwise rattle and shake. On spring and summer evenings, after long hours of viticultural engagement, the two took wine out to the smithy and talked what was for each of them a more passionate brand of shop.

Their contrasting personal histories were such that each approached the creative process from a different angle. Kostya taught the cutler how to smelt iron from its oxides, shingle the sponge and forge wrought iron. The cutler taught Kostya the materials and finishing techniques of bladesmithing and other crafting pursuits. One might say Kostya knew how to make the diamond and the cutler knew how to give it fire and brilliance. While Kostya had been a willing slave to the trade and had made the very most of his god-given abilities, it was evident that the cutler was a natural. To Kostya's up-stream insights the cutler joined his finely cultivated finishing skills and an innate and almost celestial talent. In no time at all, he had collared a complete mastery over the process, from ore to bloom to polished finished piece.

It was a volatile era and before long, perversion in the form of world-war brought winery production to yet another halt. Kostya divided his time among the restaurant, gallery and finances. The cutler was free to devote his time in full to ironworks.

About this time, despite the cutler's objections (for he was nothing if not a modest man), Kostya consented to allow a young Odessite, a patron of the estate and an aspiring curator who had instantly spotted the cutler's rare talents, to organise a show of the cutler's ironwork on the estate grounds. As can happen, however, when a student's star outshines that of his lauded professor-peer, Kostya became reluctant towards the cutler's swift advancements and accomplishments in the way of sculpture, and he came to view the impending exhibition as an opportunity to publicly remind the cutler of his proletarian status among the Pavlichenko family and the estate's esteemed patrons.

The theme of the exhibition was centred on a denouncement of the Russo-Japanese War and the Nanking Massacre of 1937. It consisted of an exquisite collection of metal Chinese octopi, iron of chassis and wonderfully blotched with Verdi Gris-stained brass and bronze and various effects of controlled oxidation. Each of the tentacles of the eight octopi wielded one form or another of gleaming blade, and each of the sixty-four sharp-edged implements was unique. Among them were a Samurai sword, a Dacian knife, a Patton saber, a Filipino balisong, an Indian katara, a Swedish broadaxe, an Argentinean *cuchillo de paracaidista* and a resplendent seventeenth-century rapier the likes of which Pallavicini advocated and which the cutler embellished with a florid hilt resembling a robin's nest of delicately spun sugar. The curator had cleverly stationed the octopi along the cobbled path that ran through the rose gardens that stretched between the estate's two chateaus. The targets of a blistering octopoda anger was a wrought iron band of Imperial Japanese Army generals disguised in the white dress (courtesy of an undisclosed ferroalloy that lent a whitish-silver sartorial hue) of sushi chefs, now flabbergasted and fleeing, now emboldened and plotting a counterattack against their octo-bladed prandial adversaries.

Kostya was astounded by the collection and silently judged the ironwork to be that of a rare master. The concept was ingenious, humorous, farcical—the perfect frivolity for juxtaposition against the backdrop of a world at war. Having assumed that the bizarre and extravagant pieces would never sell, Kostya, with an artistic wink, tagged each piece with a mind-boggling price, thereby hinting with jocularity at the exorbitant price of seafood that came armed and ready to fight back.

To everyone's great surprise, a Chinese art collector and eccentric who was sloshed on *Tokutei meishō-shu* and giddy with joy over the tormenting predicament facing the Japanese chefs sculpted in the likenesses of Tojo and Hirohito had, by the end of the *vernissage*, bought every piece in the collection. News of the sold-out show spread throughout Odessa and the Crimea, and the cutler was rendered an overnight celebrity. Kostya laughed and laughed, ostensibly pleased by the sale, but the flatness of his eyes belied mounting displeasure and jealousy.

The cutler addressed his new fame with mixed emotions. He had given himself to his craft, and as the works he created were the property of the estate – as were the proceeds of all sales – he was pleased to be giving back to the estate and contributing to its success. He was, however, exceedingly uncomfortable with the celebrity heaped upon him by the estate's patrons. Above all, the cutler recognised the negative impact of his success on Kostya. And so the greater the cutler's celebrity, the more fervently he sequestered himself away from the public eye. The cutler's discomfort in addressing his unsolicited fame – fame that Kostya longed for, though would never himself garner – angered Kostya more than did the fame itself and triggered a relentless allotment of mockery and ridicule from him.

The only person with the grace and dexterity to ease the cutler's burden was a spirited lass from Anglesey, the British Isles, whose four years with the House of Omega were split between the vineyard and the restaurant. A striking girl was she, with good colour, blue eyes that crystallised towards white, invisible freckles and million-colour hair, like that of a heath when nose-close, and which from afar was the colour of driftwood or beach grass on a snowy Sunday in January—soft-flecked and heather. Her visage was put together of fine features that conveyed sharp expressions, a visage that drew stares, exclamations and compliments. The cutler was her physical opposite. He was broad, with rounded edges that blunted and muffled all but the most explosive of expressions. Stepping out from between rows of spring-green vines on a windswept afternoon, wrapped in Icelandic-blue under a threatening Russian sky, her eyes reflected the racing grey. She was a sprite to be trapped and captured, and the cutler was the first and only man to entice her, devoid as he was of any desire to trap and capture her.

She was called Catherine and was part of the young foreign help hired by Kostya before the war. He had staffed the estate based on two main criteria—keen artistic acumen and hands-on farming experience. It was a difficult combination to find in a person, no less so during a run-up to global war.

Catherine was proud and bold, which allowed the cutler to comply with his natural tendencies for modesty and reservation. She told him what to do and when to do it, and to each command, he responded, *"Volontiers, mon cœur."* All the same, she was sensitive to his gentle nature, and wanting never to suppress his spirit, she developed a subtle way of crediting him for all her good ideas. On off occasions, when he was adamantly against an idea of hers, he would roar like a vexed brown bear and she would hiss back from a near distance, like a determined wildcat, eyes shining blue and fiery as cut gems. Eventually, he would coax her close enough to snatch, hissing as she might, and in no time she could be found purring in his big arms. To be sure, the cutler had an uncanny knack for making things purr.

Marshall Zhukov represented the Soviet Union in Berlin, as Nazi Germany capitulated to the Allied forces, signalling Victory Day and the end of World War II. That morning, on an unassuming patch of land between the vineyards and the smithy, Catherine and the cutler were wed without splendour or spectacle. By the spring of 1946, they were no longer a family of two, but of three, as Catherine had given birth to a baby boy.

In 1950, the House of Omega fully reopened, including its winery production. By that time, the cutler had acquired widespread renown for his sculptures and blades, and had regularly received commissions from wealthy patrons throughout the Soviet Union, Europe and Asia. As a show of his loyalty to Kostya and the estate, the cutler marked every finished piece conspicuously with the house insignia: the Greek letter omega.

In an attempt to retard fame's flame, the cutler refused all high-profile commissions and all exhibition invitations, such that the more elite the gallery or museum, the quicker and more fervent his refusal. A stranger to popular economic models, the cutler failed to recognise that the fewer the works he produced and the less he gave of himself to the public, the greater the demand for both his creations and his presence. Citing the supply-and-demand model, Catherine tried to convince her husband that the only way to reduce demand was to create more, though her encouragement was rather obviously born of a desire to spite Kostya over his increasingly abusive and unreasonable behaviour toward the cutler.

Catherine was unsuccessful. The supply-and-demand model belonged to the social sciences, not the sciences of matter, and the cutler was confused by sciences that were dependent on human emotions. In his confusion and disappointment, he asked her to model the direct relationship between his love for the estate and Kostya's scorn. There was, of course, no model at her disposal. It was an affair of the heart, and there was no model to explain the mix of emotions that might emanate from that mercurial muscle. So, with the winery up and running, and his talents needed there, the cutler abandoned the smithy altogether.

Catherine appealed to Kostya, who only laughed and defended the cutler's right to make his own decisions. "He is free to do as he pleases. Who am I, ha-ha," he giggled, "to strip a man of his will?" His pettiness infuriated Catherine.

Whispers carried beyond the boundaries of the estate and before long, certain influential patrons fairly demanded that the cutler be granted free rein to create. Kostya, who was now given to frequent fits of a type of laughter that hinted at delirium, howled, "The estate is all his! He is free to do as he wishes! Why, he carries the key to the smithy in his own pocket! Go duplicate the Eiffel Tower, lad, only cover it in wrought iron octopi and give it a clever name, hee-hee!"

But the cutler refused to return to the smithy and he hoped that in time, Kostya would come to trust in his devotion. The dispute rippled with electricity through Odessa and the Crimea. Some patrons showed their disapproval by boycotting the estate, its events and its products. The more daring of the patrons and collectors hurled threats upon Kostya. "Give us our artist, or else!" they cried.

It was at this time that the House of Omega was approached with a commission request that threw the entire region into frenzy. It was neither the piece nor the price that widened eyes and dropped jaws, but rather the man who had commissioned the job—one Lev

Mikhailovich Degtyaryov. Kostya was in no position to refuse the commission. Stalin himself, it was whispered, would dare not refuse a request from Lev Mikhailovich. Although Kostya silently begrudged the cutler's return to the smithy, he came to view the commission as an opportunity to heighten the level of estate celebrity beyond that of the artist community, and likewise, by way of controversy, cultivate a previously unknown facet of notoriety.

In accordance with his most renowned mastery, the commission called for the cutler to craft a single exquisite blade. He was provided with rare ores and metals to craft the piece and gems to adorn it, and given license to create as his most colourful dreams dictated. Upon completion, the cutler would be required to present the piece in person to Lev Mikhailovich, in Moscow. The cutler found his tools and took nervously to the smithy. Rumours of the intriguing commission could be heard in bohemian, intellectual and political circles across Russia and the Ukraine. What would the humble cutler create for such an eccentric and feared patron? In cafés they argued, gambled and fought in wild debate.

Facing constant pressure, and conflicted with every heavy breath, Kostya fell sick and was confined to his quarters for several weeks. In bed, his days were dominated by wicked visions, his nights by feverish dreams, those that vacillated between giddy extremes of glory and demise. He awoke one night in the middle of a raucous dream in which he flatly refused Lev Mikhailovich his commission request—more precisely, he doubled Lev Mikhailovich over bended knee and blistered his bottom with a Swedish *pesäpallo* bat, sending the feared Muskvich lad on his way, bawling and bow-legged for his welts and soggy pants.

If the commission had ever been within Kostya's authority to refuse, the time had come and gone, for the knife-blade had been forged. Still, when Kostya finally rose from his sickbed, he appeared before his staff and patrons dishevelled and craze-eyed, like a crazed goat from under a forgotten bridge, and vociferously asserted that the commission would not go forward; Lev Mikhailovich and his lot of ill-defined connections be damned! Those present to hear Kostya's startling proclamation bowed their heads and sadly committed to memory the day and hour on which they bore witness to what was unanimously considered a death knell or dirge song for a once revered and beloved benefactor who had clearly lost his mind.

Some weeks later, with all of Odessa crackling with gossip and wagering on the means and timing of the reprisal due the House of Omega, those who parlayed arson as the means and the seventh of October in the year 1951 as the timing, hit their bets and collected their winnings. That night, flames licked lasciviously at the chateaus and outbuildings and ran savagely through the rolling sweep of autumnal vines. Despite frantic calls to the police and fire stations, neither man nor truck was dispatched. By sunrise, all flesh and fat had melted away within the gated confines of the estate, leaving felled remains blackened among mineral ruins. The vast, undulating sea of vines was reduced to grey hectares of cinder and ash.

It was indicative of Kostya's welling madness that he had run helter-skelter amid the burning trelliswork with soaked towels, in attempts to salvage some small portion of his dead father's dying vines. But although it was a madman's effort from the outset, it was neither smoke nor flame that took Kostya's life, but rather a sleek silver knife that was shoved hilt-deep into the man, tacking him to the charred earth like a *pense-bête* pinned to corkboard.

Word of murder spread faster than did the wildfire through the estate, and by noon the region was horrified and drunken with fresh rumour and conjecture. The authorities did eventually shuffle in to investigate the remains, but by the time of their arrival, the murder weapon, the Omega – as the great knife was known thereafter – had disappeared.

A hushed café contingent whispered its way to near-unanimous condemnation of Lev Mikhailovich, though a far more vocal and violent faction emerged almost immediately and gained momentum through counterarguments and claims that it was not Lev Mikhailovich, but the cutler's hot-headed missus who had committed murder. Hadn't she become increasingly outspoken in her contempt for Kostya and his decisions concerning the cutler? Hadn't she come to despise the man for his inability to conquer his insecurities and jealousy? Hadn't she been heard to issue bold threats against him? Well, no, actually, she hadn't. The urgings were perfectly unsubstantiated. The suppositions brought forth through the mere voicing of such damning questions, however, were often sufficient to condemn a fellow in the minds of those thirsty for intrigue and controversy.

"Klarysa's grandfather," whispered Calvin, lost in reflection. "Murdered!"

"You must have known," I said.

"Sure, but details tend to disagree with Klarysa, or elude her altogether. How does it end?"

"The fire reduced the estate to a burnt swath of wasteland that was eventually ceded to Kostya's sister and sold for a paltry sum."

"The cutler, Catherine and the boy," said Calvin. "What became of them?"

No evidence, incriminating or otherwise, had materialised to support the claims against Catherine, and with the Allied world still inebriated from post-war victory celebrations, the idea of bringing such unsubstantiated charges against Allied subjects would only kill the buzz and marshal a hangover in the form of a foreign-relations fiasco. All the same, the cutler and his young family fled west, for the British Isles. In Cardiff, Catherine was reacquainted with her family, and there, for the first time, her parents had the long-awaited pleasure of making the acquaintance of their son-in-law and only grandson.

It was a transitional period that was not without its difficulties. They missed their lives on the estate, their friends, their freedoms, the sprawling land with its verdant vines, the vastness of the Soviet skies, the chateaus, the cafés and the smithy. So too, they missed Kostya. It was only then that they began to reflect upon the tragedy that brought a horrific end to their lives in Odessa.

They had passed a year in Wales, when a letter from a trusted friend in Odessa informed them that a patron of the House of Omega had been convicted for the crime of Kostya's slaying. It was a curious conviction, a source of quiet controversy, but then no one honestly expected Lev Mikhailovich to be implicated. Although the news served as a further reminder of the tragedy that uprooted them from the lives they so loved, it also lifted a great and theretofore unrecognised burden from their collective psyche. So often, it is only after a storm has passed that one recognises how exposed one was to its lashing elements, and how soaked through one is for it.

In no time, they found themselves absolved of all emotional encumbrances. The conviction in Odessa brought the episode to a close and they were free to follow the winds of their choosing.

By that time, their young son had seen seven spring seasons. The boy took from his father a name – Jean-Louis – passion and a powerful physique. From his mother he inherited intelligence and a fiery temperament. The boy was active and talented. By the age of seven, he had already known an admirable command over the Ukrainian, French and English languages, and could not be found without a sporting ball under one of his incessantly bruised and bruising wings.

The young family heaped its few belongings into a second-hand Opel and followed the Rhone Valley down towards the southern end of France. They settled in a small house near Marseille, on a dry but willing patch of land on which the cutler planted rows of sunflowers and several olive trees and nursed sufficient vines to produce annually a dozen or so cases of good wine. The cutler's smelting days were behind him, and though he did continue to shape and weld metals, the finished pieces became the fruits of less ambitious visions. They were conventional, a propos only of home and garden – a sundial, a watering can, a garden frog – in accordance with his resolution to never again create something that might give wayward inspiration to the mind of a deranged other (though it must be said that even a feather pillow in the wrong hands may promote death).

"What is it?" asked Calvin at my pause. "Won't you continue?"

"Look, Fiston," I said with a sad laugh. "He bids me to continue."

Fiston turned away, as one does from things unsalvageable. I stood and walked over to the windows that gave onto the alleyway.

"They criticise me, Mr. Stony," I said. "They call me old-fashioned. They say that I am out-of-touch. But I am misunderstood. I have lived the wide world over and have seen a great many things, beauteous and tragic, both. And yes, I am prone to violence when I feel violence will facilitate a desired end. Hell, perhaps I am ruined, but might it not ruin you, too, Mr. Stony, if at the tender age of twelve you discovered your own father lying dead on his back in the family garden? Might it not ruin you to find his head forced down – by what manner and number of determined hands I cannot imagine – onto the triangular metal gnomon of a sundial; to see the halo of dried blood staining black an unholy bed of parched earth so soon humming with scores of hungry horse flies? It is no way for a father to die and no way for a boy to alight upon his teen years. *Live by the knife, die by the knife* read the note, in an ugly and uneducated Cyrillic hand, which his murderers had pinned to his shirt."

"The cutler was your father." Calvin's mind raced. "And the knife he crafted was the knife used to kill Klarysa's grandfather."

"Kostya Pavlichenko was a beloved man—a beloved man with many connections.

"They misunderstand me, Mr. Stony, though that is nothing to lament, for no man may truly understood another. They say I am angry and bitter. They say my methods are dated and obsolete. That's fine; let my critics howl. I only want the knife, on behalf of my father and that of France. I joined the INAO to protect France against biopiracy, and left, you see, for an organisation with more teeth."

I reached into my breast pocket for my credentials, the sight of which had a profound effect on Calvin.

"Interpol? You're with Interpol?" He cheered with relief, "Ha-ha! Why, God bless you, sir! God bless you one and all, you mirthless animals!"

Calvin gushed, began to shake with laughter, nearly came to tears with relief and joy over the discovery that we were affiliated with an organisation that lay on the right side of the law. Standing at the open window above the alleyway, I allowed Calvin his moment.

"Interpol!" he cried again, full of laughter. "Wonderful! *Won*derful!"

As he laughed, I watched a flapping mess of blue and silver on the opposite rooftop, where four rabid gulls, donning sanguine masks of darkening rouge and screeching drunkenly on happy murder, tore away with beaks and talons at the gutted flesh and entrails of a trapped rat. Shameless, carnivorous beauties. I drew inward the heavy wooden shutters and closed the windows. A darkness consumed the flat.

"My intentions for joining Interpol," I explained, "were identical to those I had for joining the INAO—to protect France and her culture against piracy. My credentials, however, have become little more than a license to pursue my father's knife, the Omega. I am not proud of the fact. It was never my intention. For years I wanted nothing to do with the business of the Omega or the death of my father and that of Kostya, but a man changes over time, and it is especially difficult for a proud man to perceive the gestation of an obsession within him.

"The Omega is more than a murder weapon, Mr. Stony, more than an artefact. Its blade reflects the histories of two proud nations, France and Russia, not to mention the history of my father and his beloved mentor, my godfather. Yes, Klarysa's grandfather Kostya was my godfather. The Omega is symbolic of the birth of the Russian wine industry, an industry developed on the back of French culture and ingenuity, and one whose boldfaced naming conventions remain a source of contention and a detriment to the Republic. And now, after decades of controversy and lore, after decades of giving chase, here I stand before you. *You*, Mr. Stony, of all the people in the world! How incredible that the mad tangle of history's roads should lead us here to you. You, who refused to open the door to me; you, who considered leaping from the window to avoid our inevitable confrontation. But enough of this! Where is the knife, Mr. Stony? Where is the Omega?"

Calvin, who had for so long appeared indelibly marred by darkness and confusion, lit up with gemlike brilliance, having finally grasped the point of our entire clumsy affair.

"Oh!" he cried with great excitement. "I see! You think *I* have your Omega! I see, I see."

New laughter percolated within him and bubbled over.

"I see!" he kept saying, while slapping his goddamned knee. "You mean all this," he said, joyously waving an open palm towards my men and the mounds of their destruction. "Fine! Fine! But you see I don't have your Omega. If it should interest you in the least, I've been given a knife, OK, but it is cocktail jewellery, *bijou fantaisie*, if you will. Why, the knife I have," he managed through rebounding laughter, "was gifted me by my friend, a tourist from a backwater place called Ken*tuck*y. Can you imagine?"

"I know that! Calm yourself!" I demanded. "And it was given to her by two local lads on the night you dined with her and the husband on Rue Pontin."

"The flamingos! Is *that* why you brutalised them so? Ha-ha! Poor little buggers. No, no, that knife is but a costume prop, a tourist trinket."

My vision ran black again. I wrenched wide my mouth to stretch the jaws and clear the head. The room fell suddenly silent. When my vision returned, I saw that Calvin had turned pale and I realised all my teeth were aimed menacingly at him, my molars grinding in production of a horrific mineral sound.

As calmly as I could manage, I said, "I warned you against a relationship with Mr. Kaleci. I *warned* you!"

"Fitim Kaleci?" he asked. "But are we abandoning the knife already?"

"Not on your life! You had better start paying attention."

"OK," he said uncomfortably. "Talk about Fitim, then."

I retook my seat on the wooden chair in front of Calvin. "You do not want to make my life difficult, Mr. Stony. Trust me finally."

"Quite correct!" he popped. "But I don't want to make anyone's life difficult! And now you've returned to your codes and riddles. What is it with you?" he cried, showing signs of exhaustion. "You warned me against fraternising with the Serbs. I assure you I have no intentions of being difficult, sir, but Fitim Kaleci is not Serbian. He is Albanian. He is from the Republic of Kosova."

"The Republic of Kosova," I screamed, "is a secessionist state unrecognised by all but Albania! If you think a successful defence will be won by the splitting of hairs, you are sorely mistaken!"

"Bah! You're mad! You labour for half an hour on the differences between this ham and that, one butter and the next, and then accuse *me* of splitting hairs? I'm talking about a people without representation, sir! But enough, I already told you I have no interest in politics. The point is, I did not understand your warnings in the past and I do not understand them at present. Fitim is a fine man and that is all I know," said Calvin defiantly. "He is my friend!"

"Careful, Mr. Stony—we are the company we keep."

"Holy Aesopica! Listen here, you who came bashing his way through my front door—we are our ob*sess*ions!"

"*Touché*," pipped Fiston.

"*Tais toi*, Fiston! Hold your tongue!"

"Anyway," Calvin added, "I cannot imagine what Fitim Kaleci has to do with any of this. Why, if you only…"

Calvin paused in sudden recollection of the tête-à-tête with Aloysius, during which Al accused Fitim of spearheading an infamous heist of Russian treasures.

"What is it, Mr. Stony? What are you hiding?"

"I'm not hiding anything!" he cried nervously, clawing at his head. "I just remembered something I was told about Fitim."

"There's a good lad. We save ourselves much discomfort by recalling details on our own. But allow me to further jog your memory—"

"Hush! Don't you rob me of a shot at redemption!"

"Don't be simple. I only wish to bring us more quickly to the heart of the matter. You are delusional if you think your redemption can be won through storytelling.

"Not long ago," I continued, "I was in Russia with a team of men, closing in on Lev Mikhailovich, now an aging crime lord who had long ago, via corrupt and violent means, come to possess the Omega. We were informed of a heavily munitioned orchestration by which Lev Mikhailovich's most prized and ill-acquired affects were to be translocated from Moscow to an unknown destination somewhere between Nice and the Southern Alps. One wooden crate was believed to hold the Omega and other artefacts of untold value. On the eve of our raid, only hours before we were set to descend upon our target, an unidentified band of black-jacketed militiamen armed for doomsday intercepted the moving convoy. The ensuing battle left a small regiment of dead, and reduced an armoured van to scrap metal. The Omega was newly gone."

Calvin looked sick.

"Fitim Kaleci," I said, "led that band of militiamen."

"But you said they were unidentified," he tried sickly.

"Wake up, you damned fool!" I exploded, again bringing my fist heavily down upon the *table basse*. "You have run a grave risk by affiliating yourself with Lev Mikhailovich's most despised enemy. You don't seem to understand that! You sit there laughing, celebrating my credentials as a defender of justice, but I haven't the means to protect you against Lev Mikhailovich. You have wandered arrogantly into a dark, dark wood, despite my warnings, and still you show no recognition of the danger you face. The innocence I identified in you may only be ignorance! See here, Interpol does not involve itself with trivialities and trifles, Mr. Stony. We are engaged in a race to secure an object that has for four decades lured many bold and daring men to death's door. I assure you our presence in your home is no cause for laughter. You should have kept to your fish, as I advised. You have no idea what you are facing, stumbling about blindly as you are in the dying eye of a wicked storm."

"But how many times must I tell you, I've done nothing!"

"Contradictions! Only moments ago you confessed to having worked a job for Fitim Kaleci."

"Sweet Jesus, yes! I unloaded bags of cement for the fellow!"

"*After I warned you* not to get involved with him, goddamn it!"

"But where is the crime in unloading bags of cement?"

"*Crime*? You damned brainless idiot! Who here has spoken of crime? You refuse to listen! Look at me and open your fucking ears! You have squarely affiliated yourself with Lev Mikhailovich's arch-nemesis. Do you not understand that? Crime? Do you believe I am here to charge you with a crime? Pah! Idiot! How small you think! How narrow your thoughts! Were that the aim, I'd have plucked you raw from the alleyway. I wake every morning to defend my father's honour, the culture of my country, the future of my grandchildren. And by way of some frightening lapse of good judgement, I am trying to save your pathetic neck. But you! You, child, have a death wish! What is wrong with you? What happened to you? Bah, it is of little import. *Fiston!*"

Fiston sprang instantly from his seat. "*Oui, chef!*" he barked in his native French, knowing that all opportunity to negotiate on Calvin's behalf had long passed.

"Mr. Stony!" I stood and announced with volume. "Some seventy-two hours ago, three armed men carried out a hit on the Palm Beach Casino in Cannes. Evidence suggests there may have been a fourth man. The take approached two million francs, a wretchedly small sum over which to risk one's neck, but then monetary gain was never the motivation. The gendarmes have captured these three. One of them – the point-man of the operation – was again your friend, Fitim Kaleci."

"But... But," Calvin stammered. Wanting badly to call a bluff, he bucked up and said, "I don't believe you!"

"Fool!"

"But why," Calvin began, grasping at straws, "Why would he do such a thing?"

"You are running well short of opportunities to save yourself, son! Tell me, fool child, do you believe you know Fitim Kaleci? Will you subvert your name and your future to back a man about whom you know nothing?"

"*Back* him?" begged Calvin. "I only just met the guy. Sure, I know all the rumours, I've heard all the conjecture. I *tried* to dislike him, OK? Does that improve my stock at all in those black and bitter eyes of yours? I tried to dislike him and I've never felt so ashamed for the effort, you horribly jaded buffalo! In the end, I extended the fellow a smile and a handshake, and at every turn he proved himself a gentle, kind-hearted fellow."

"History has known its likable villains, Mr. Stony, though only impetuous fools follow them beyond their inked accounts. Fitim Kaleci is a dangerous man."

"But it makes no sense. What is the point of knocking off a casino, if not for the dosh?"

"Revenge. Fitim Kaleci ticks in time with an irrepressible rhythm for vengeance. Serbia and Russia, as you must know, have been bedfellows for more than one-hundred-fifty years. In the framework of this long-standing affair, Moscow backs Belgrade in all its efforts to dominate Kosovo, and contends that any support for Kosovo's unilateral intentions is support for the devil himself. In the late 1980s, Moscow appointed a special envoy to Serbia to keep watch over Balkan developments. The envoy was downgraded to *sui generis* by nervous officials, and eventually disclaimed altogether, for the artistic bent of this man's ruthlessness was ghastly and inhumane.

"Of the hideous, nightmarish losses to have scarred Fitim Kaleci's young soul, the most foul – familial losses – were delivered by tooth and nail of the Russian *sui generis*."

With the windows closed, the room was hot and humid. I ran a palm over my forehead. The sweat trickled down my wrist and into my sleeve and my heart raced.

"I've given you far more than you are due in the way of history and explanation, Mr. Stony, and my patience is wearing thin. I will finish this beastly history by telling you that Mr. Kaleci has an obsession of his own, the sight of which places crosshairs between the eyes of Russia and her devil, the discharged *sui generis*. It is a profound and intricate hatred."

Calvin suppressed a bodily shudder with denial and volume, "How long I have heard these accusations! So intense is his hatred for the Soviets," the poor boy sarcastically mocked, "that he gifts Russian caviar and Ukrainian wine to the alleyway youth of Vieux Nice. Come! Klarysa is Ukrainian and he treated her like a queen!"

"His is not a social or cultural hatred, but a solitary and political one. A man can detest a country without detesting the people who walk its streets. Politics, Mr. Stony, will bring the end of the world, despite the tremendous span of fine individuals on this planet."

"Oh, stop it! Where are the politics on a craps table? Why knock off a casino—a *French* casino?"

"I have tolerated your naïveté and accommodated your curiosity because I like you, but we are nearing the end of the line, Mr. Stony. I am tired of playing your educator. Listen to me, the Russian *sui generis* was Lev Mikhailovich. Yes, it is understandable that you have gone pale—mass homicide is shocking. The casino job had nothing to do with monetary gain, just as the militiamen strike on the armoured van had nothing to do with acquiring collectibles and riches. Fitim Kaleci knows to strike an enemy where it hurts most. Lev Mikhailovich is an old eccentric, a perverse fiend and a devil. The prospects of death are nothing to such a man. However, strip him of his cherished baubles, run helter-skelter over his territories, colly his property and make a mockery of his jurisdiction—this is a course that will tease him to the brink of madness.

"But where is the connection between Lev Mikhailovich and the casino?" Calvin reflected for a moment. "Oh," he said. "Russian mafia."

"Personally, I concern myself more with actions than affiliations, but there you have it. Fitim Kaleci has a heart filled with hatred and a head afflicted by memories of terror and loss, but I assure you he is not imprisoned at this moment for character flaws, Mr. Stony. His crimes are well documented."

"Then have him sentenced accordingly and get the hell out of here! I'll not be indicted for showing civility before the pained and afflicted."

"Why, you ungrateful little—! You shall be indicted for much worse than that! And by men who do not bother with interrogation!"

"Un*grate*ful? I am sorry about your father," said Calvin. "I am. But you've enlisted yourself for battles that do not involve me. You follow me through the alleys, bug my flat and break down my door. What on earth do you think I owe you?"

"Your goddamned skinny neck, you! You are alive to-day because yesterday three gunmen were arrested."

"But how—?"

From my coat pocket I extracted a hard leather valise tag and flung it at Calvin. It slapped off his chest and landed at his feet.

"Had they not been caught, Lev Mikhailovich and his would have hunted down the fool who carelessly dropped *that*! Fiston!"

"*Oui, chef*!"

I gave the familiar nod and Fiston trudged his way heavily to his station behind Calvin.

"*You* were the fourth gunman, Mr. Stony! Were I you, I'd have selected my jobs far more prudently. And I'd have been damned well sure to pick up after myself before fleeing the scene. *Allez y*, Fiston!"

Fiston grabbed Calvin's arms and wrenched them behind the back of the chair. Calvin winced and let out a sharp cry, as Fiston applied cold metal handcuffs and made them bite deeply into his wrists.

"*A-a-aye!*" Calvin shrieked. "The fourth gunman! Are you mad? *A-a-aye!*"

Through shock and pain he eyed the valise tag on the floor before him. He recognised it—it bore his name and address.

"*E-e-ech!*" he hissed and spat like a trapped wildcat.

"Your valise tag, Mr. Stony, was found in the casino!"

He finally understood. His jaw bobbed erratically though he produced no sound.

"Such negligence," I said, hinting at a retraction, "is incongruous with intricate crimes that are otherwise flawlessly executed. It would seem the valise tag was left there intentionally, for the finding. Perhaps, after all, you were not involved in the hit, but only set up to take the fall. Perhaps there was no fourth gunman whatsoever."

The opening I presented Calvin afforded him rare breath. He sucked madly at the air and heaved, "It wasn't me! I lent the valise to a friend, months ago. Fitim wanted it. He must have used it for the job!"

"What's that I hear, Mr. Stony? Having only moments ago vehemently defended his honour, are you now contending that your good friend has set you up for a fall?"

"He wouldn't... He wouldn't!"

"No? But what do you know of this man, Mr. Stony? Tell me. Who do you trust now? Tell me. *Tell* me!"

"I don't know!" he howled. "I don't know!"

"Fiston!" I demanded.

"*Oui, chef!*"

"*Prêt-toi!*"

Fiston peaked like a jagged mountain behind our cuffed and snivelling subject.

"Now then, Mr. Stony, where is my goddamned knife! Tell me now! Save yourself! Where is the Omega!"

Calvin's eyes bugged with confusion at the unexpected shift in conversation. The truth is, I gave no damn for a lousy casino job.

"I don't know!" he cried. "Please! I have no idea!"

"The two lads gave it to your friend and she gave it to you."

"But I've already told you, it's only a cheap prop! See for yourself! It's in the bedroom, in the bottom drawer of the bureau!" he wailed.

From the bedroom, my man barked, "*N'est pas la, chef*!"

The knife was not there.

"*Fiston!*" I shouted.

For a fraction of a sickening second, somewhere beyond Calvin's field of vision, a speeding projectile was perceived to be ramming through humid late-summer air towards a target. The perception was clipped and erased as the knuckled projectile slammed bluntly, grotesquely into the side of Calvin's head. The second blow from Fiston sent him, and the wooden chair to which he was cuffed, to the floor. He lay motionless in a dark tunnel made wet with drool and heavy damage.

"Where is the Omega, Mr. Stony!"

Brass horns blared deafeningly in his head, causing my words to reach him muffled and dreamlike, as though he were somehow detached and protected against the imminence of his own devastation, by miles and miles of insane trumpeters.

Lying there in a wretched heap, Calvin served as a filthy reminder of all my worst failures—my failure to secure the Omega, my failure as a husband and a father and grandfather, my failure to protect fools like Calvin, the vulnerable, the decent. I shoved Fiston aside, fell on top of the boy and the chair and dropped a series of devastating bombs upon him. I drove my knee into his midsection several times, causing him to vomit.

In my anxiety and madness, I had identified an effigy of all my failures and an unseen demon demanded that I snuff it out altogether. With a forearm, I rammed his head into the hot, wet tile until I heard noises so unnatural they gave me chills. With my free hand, I twisted the chair until crimson rings swelled up and ran where the cuffs bit into his wrists.

"*Sale gosse!*" I wailed. "Deathwisher! You won't listen! You won't save yourself!"

I beat and berated him until I began to lose sight and sensed myself blacking out from outrage and exertion. Finally, I rolled off my latest mess.

Fiston ripped him up from the floor and into a seated position. His head hung down towards the floor. He was small and broken. Sticky streams from gaping sources of dark cardinal flowed down his face and hands. Red ran from his mouth and onto his lap. All life seemed to be escaping him.

Some time had passed. I can't say how long. My men had gathered round and helped me to my feet.

And then a startling, almost frightening thing happened. Calvin was alive. He lifted his head for all to behold his slashing green eyes, those that shone with emerald electricity through wet and swelling sockets. Still cuffed to the chair, he pulled himself up from his wretched slump so that he was sitting upright. And then, poised defiantly, with his chin held high, he chortled through red lips glistening like wet crushed rubies.

"Oh, protector! Oh, glorious protector! Glorious provider! Do me your best! Murder me that I might be spared death by the hands of your enemies. Free me, oh great liberator! Liberate me, my champion! Ha! What a grand farce!"

He spat freely onto the floor to clear his mouth and show his disgust.

"Your cover is blown!" he continued. "You have betrayed yourself! You liar! You swine! Your obsession has laid you to waste, stained you all the hideous shades that afflict the entities and philosophies you claim to abhor. You schemer! You crook! *Look at me*!" he demanded with wild eyes, spitting blood and teeth. "Regard the work of your murderous hands. Who is a man, sir? Ha! Who are *you*, sir! A fraud is who you are! A fraud! Kill me as you must and further murder the truth and dignity you profess to protect, as you have protected *me*! Slaughter me, your dewy lamb, and choke to death on the cancer of my sincerity and decency, those traits I could not abandon if I wanted to, those that surely perished within you a half-century ago, those infractions that you so thoroughly despise in me. You rabid wolf! You filthy tyrant!"

That cruel, clever lad! I beat him and beat him and in a blind fury brought him to the edge of death. But he did not falter. On the contrary, at death's door, broken down to nothingness, he found a long-lost and buried version of himself. He found his truth. He wrapped himself in it and grew larger. And in doing so, he overcame certain fears and adversaries. He deftly felled an aging monster without so much as a single blow, but rather a mere tongue tap to my only, albeit gaping, point of vulnerability.

And with that mere tongue tap, a flawed world construct came detached, broke free of the thin filament that had for so long fixed it precariously to a false heaven, and came crashing down, shattering all around me. Only one thought came to me, and it came with remorseless clarity—I had abandoned my family. I had abandoned my family.

"Well, Mr. Stony," I pushed forward, out of breath, heartbroken, dizzy with epiphany and downfall. "What should you like to hear from me? That I am sorry? That I deeply wish it had not come to all this? That I lost myself and rambled too far beyond the boundaries of decency and humanity?"

Fiston eyed me askance. "*Chef*," he said with a hint of disapproval.

"You want I should etch this into my long list of regrets? Enumerate my failures? You want I should beg your forgiveness? Bah, I dare believe you might actually forgive me, were I to ask. Very well, son—I apologise. I am profoundly sorry. I am in the wrong far more often than is acceptable—to a shocking extent, really. I can only hope you will find it within yourself to forgive me—"

"*Ca suffit, chef*!" boomed Fiston.

His disapproval was correct. I had long suffered a lack of inner command. My Fiston would come to make a very fine agent, far better than I had ever been.

But as I sat there thoroughly defeated, there at the depths of my demise, neither he nor any other could imagine the infinitesimal butterfly tickle that flapped joyously, if with invisible gossamer delicacy, at my heart's tattered edge.

"Look, Calvin," I said, allowing myself his Christian name, despite Fiston's ever-greater disfavour. "While you may know innocence in this ugly matter, the truth to which you cling for liberty is no fixed entity. It is, unfortunately, all too variable. To be sure, no man's morning truths have bearing on his evening fate, for his truths remain in constant flux, even after he has died. For even then, his truths will be hammered away at and sculpted to meet the needs of the living. This morning you may be innocent; this evening perhaps not. A fellow's nightly fate depends on the collective values of a million variables that align themselves precariously throughout the day. To-day I hold a valise tag, evidence that is unknown to all but me and my informant at the casino. To-morrow, who knows? Prosecutors, persecutors—who can say in whose hands the evidence may land? At best, the evidence ends up in the hands of the law, in which case you are embroiled in lengthy legal proceedings. At worst, it ends up in the hands of the underworld, in which case you will be hunted by mafia men."

"You rotten bastard."

"I know, I know. This is, at times, a deplorable racket and I've made an abominable mess of the responsibilities entrusted to me. I hope one day you will find a way to forgive me your role in this. But for now, there is much work to be done. However unfortunate, that fact remains. We need you. And my abject apologies notwithstanding, you wield very little leverage with which to refuse my solicitations. Make no mistake, you've stepped into a dark and dangerous wood, one in which there are very few clearings.

"Allow me to illustrate something," I said.

With my boot, I swiped an invisible line of demarcation on the floor. "Over here," I explained, drawing attention to one side of the line, "I am a minority, perhaps an occupied minority, a dominated minority, one without representation, as you have pointed out. Here I resist and I fight, and if I have to, I kill, and I am lauded as a freedom fighter. On the other side of the line, however, they slander my heroic name and call me a terrorist. Curious, no? The world is riddled with such invisible lines, all of them negotiated over, killed for, pushed and extended, drawn and redrawn and committed to the history of the day by so many cartographers. Here I am a freedom fighter, there I am a terrorist. Perspective presides over the courts of popular opinion.

"You are a good lad, Calvin. I like you. I think that is evident."

Calvin tongued gingerly about his closed gob, then opened up and spit out another tooth.

"Bah," I dismissed, "you'll have to take my word for it. Listen, you were not wrong to have befriended Fitim Kaleci. Your mistake was in befriending such a man without considering whether or not, by doing so, you were crossing over a divisional line between friends and enemies, and without considering the makeup of those friends and enemies. It would be an awful, awful shame to see you make an enemy of Lev Mikhailovich. Had our man not fortuned across your valise tag in the casino, you would not be with us to-day. *Basta.*"

"Fitim," murmured Calvin, hoarse for the damage, though submitting more, it seemed, to disappointment than pain. "He set me up for a fall."

"Who knows. And anyway, what does it matter?"

"It matters. I considered him a friend."

"Don't take it personally. Fire is fire, and on a cold and lonely night, fire can be life-preserving. But fire has no knowledge of its heat. It simply burns."

My men made a last pass through the flat. It had been rendered a dismal tip. Among the wreckage, croissants, Corsican fig jam of deep purple and black coffee littered and stained the old *tommette* tiles that must have been so beautiful a century ago. My men returned presently to the salon.

"No knife, lads?" I asked.

"*Rien, chef.*"

I looked to Calvin, no longer with malice, but with guilty commiseration, as though we had fought on the same side of the line and come up just short of victory. He shrugged without anger, without any emotion whatsoever. He didn't give a damn and I couldn't blame him.

"I don't know," he managed. "I put it in the drawer and haven't seen it since."

He would be OK, that Calvin. In time he would be just fine.

Blood and fatigue pulsed heavily in my head, hands and feet, rushing thickly with each heartbeat—a telltale sign of impending illness. And yet somehow there prevailed within my old leaden core the tiny diaphanous butterfly, flitting inexplicably about with drunken joy at my heart's edge.

"What now, sir?" asked my men.

The unbroken stares of eight eyes from four men trained to me, seeking direction. I ambled over to the windows, pulled them open and pushed back the shutters. The feeding rooftop gulls across the alley had sated themselves and flown off. A nimble jazz riff made its way up from the boutique down below, a light and airy melody in soprano, reaching my ears in stark contrast to the morning's savage score and carrying a surprise reminder of the more buoyant of life's offerings.

"What now?" I pondered aloud, leaning against the railing of the balcony. "What now?"

What an enormous, electrifying question, I thought! What now, indeed! I reached into my coat pocket and pulled out a pack of cigarettes. The pack was battered and smashed and unopened, the cellophane still intact. It was a foreign brand of cigarettes that was no longer made, brought back from Cambodia. I peeled the band away, removed the cellophane and let it go over the side of the balcony. It fluttered slowly down to the alley. I watched it fall with fond remembrances—the silent joy of a curious child when no adult is present, dropping little nothings and watching them fall from the heights of a quiet balcony. I tapped out one of the crooked cigarettes and smoothed it straight as it would go. It felt substantive between my fingers and smelt good.

"What now, what now?" I said.

I held an orange-blue flame to the tip of the cigarette and inhaled deeply. My men were struck dumb, none more so than Fiston, who seemed unable to stop blinking. Calvin's eyes were unflinching green gems. Parched beds of burgundy silt streaked his face and neck, still twinkling red and wet, the beds that ran deepest. But those eyes of his! So green with life, with uncertainty and wonder and perhaps fear. So very alive! What now? Why, the possibilities approached endlessness!

I inhaled again. It was the first cigarette I had smoked in more than six years. A vision of Maria, my wife, her long hair still startlingly black, my boy, my grandson. The butterfly flapped madly within, tickling my ribcage, fanning certain flames and extinguishing others. A possible birth, and a death, perhaps, too, of a significant thing, and a conjoined musing on the injustice of death's bad rap, for certain deaths – certainly that of one's albatross – can work open the locks of liberty.

"Well," I said, shelving for the moment my mounting excitement, "I would like a final word with Mr. Stony. Wait for me in the alley, lads, I'll be right down. Fiston, you stay."

From the balcony I ordered Fiston to remove the handcuffs from Calvin's wrists. He did so, and then went to the kitchen and rinsed them clean in the sink.

"You rest now, Mr. Stony, and attend to your injuries. You are still young and they will heal quickly. As for your door, it will be replaced presently," I assured him. "We have a man."

Fiston began to collect the various bugging devices we had been planted.

"For better or worse," I continued, "We still have work to do."

"*Allez*," said Calvin. "As you need. You couldn't possibly make this place any worse."

"I'm afraid you don't understand," I said. "Bah! Come now, don't look so sour. It won't be so bad."

"But how could I possibly be of use?" he asked sincerely.

"We are in a race for the Omega," I said. For the very first time, the name rang hollow. "If one speaks of the sum of men who know intimately the history of the Omega, and who have dedicated their lives to its pursuit, he speaks of three: Lev Mikhailovich, me, and the one called DeTorche."

"DeTorche," Calvin gasped, wincing in pain for his surprise.

"Easy, now. Easy," I soothed.

"But I don't know him. I swear to you."

"Shh. Easy, now. It's OK. It's OK."

I coaxed one more cigarette out from the crumpled pack, then tossed the pack over the railing and watched it fall from the height of the quiet balcony. There would, indeed, come a time for atonement.

Two figures appear, they shadows slide hard and flat along Addison. Streetlights approach and recede, make they shadows swing like flat gray beacons, keep them sliding forward over hard white terrain.

"Ladies and gentlemen of the jury, I instruct you to pay close attention to what you are about to witness."

"What are you thinking of doing, Kid," asks a boy shrouded in a dark winter coat. He pulls a red hat down over his head. "Why don't we just walk it off..."

"He going to pay."

Streetlights approach and recede. Snow blanket the streets, muffle the sound of wide black V8 on Randolph, it lumber by with low defiant headlights.

"This here is it."

They shadows stop swinging and sliding. Backlit, they shadows climb long and wide up the front window of a brick building.

"Why don't we just walk it off..."

A narrow cot among box units and galvanized steel.

Got to do something.

Dez lay sleepless and wonder after a cold so bold it got the audacity to push its way into a furnace shop. Make good money in a hard winter, boy, but what good does money do if the only woman he love *She once love me, she once kiss me with Christmas red lips* go to court to keep him away from her and the child *Still blinking, still blinking away brilliant red and green tears.* How many furnaces a man got to sell to buy back lost time with his baby girl *Got to do something, got to get that stump* Dez, he a world-beater in every joint of his body

There build an overflowing river But he ain't got his woman or his child. Dez, he drink too much *Carry me helplessly toward a breaking point* Can't protect them now, not even from a cold winter night *Body heavy and nauseas* Can't drink no more. Got to lick it *Gears hold and hold* Got to stay sober *And then slip. BANG!*

Lay sleepless on a narrow cot *Eyes fill with tears and the whole world go silent* He remember a broken furnace over on Franklin and remember the frustration in the eyes of a poor man who break his back to overcome and keep coming up just short *The disgust in they eyes* The way that man's hand wrench around his bicep, the pleading from his woman *And everything goes stark and bright white and crystalline* Same pleading Dez hear from his own wife *My love, my Laika* When she beg time and time again to put down the bottle. He remember the ragged confusion and pride in the boy's angry shoulders *The slander slide thick and leaden from my young lips and my mouth twist down low and ugly* Same wild emotions he himself had when he was coming up in Garfield *Laika Laika Laika!* He rise up and walk to the front of the shop to turn up the heat.

But James, it's freezing in here.

It ain't either, now!

"I'm a wolf," Dez convict himself. "See how cold it is up in here!" *Theys work to be done.* "I'm a sure enough wolf!"

Come on, now. Look at her hands! What can you do for us, brother?

He put his lamb on display before a wolf Got to do something *Got to do something* For that family *I be the one to lick it!*

I'm sick, I can't move He turn up the heat and notice out front two silhouettes backlit by street light, they shadows climb long and wide up the window.

We once lay on the long brown couch.

Kid pick up a broken brick from the gutter. Dez reach down slowly behind the front counter *The walls close in* Wrap his hand around cold metal *The long brown couch lay empty and beat* Dez going to be the one to lick it *I be the one to lick it* Sparks like shooting stars, his baby girl, his woman, his shop, his city, the poor family over on Franklin, his people *Oceans, deserts, an endless expanse of openness* Protection a front-line responsibility. Got to defend you and yours, got to defend your flowers. Dez grip that gun. Kid pick up a brick. They going to deliver theyself back to good. They be the ones to lick it.

22   A protector of bleating lambs

In which a Danish boy with
confetti eyes recites the poetry in
Gem's head.

The patient, emotional pain associated with the loss of a woman
had for a moment submitted to the more immediate, physical pain
associated with collisions and contusions. But in short order, as the
latter kind lost interest in Calvin and left him in search of a fresh
host, the patient lovesick pain peeked out through the blinds of his
fractured ribs; then curled up around his heart and snuggled against
it with great dedication and shine. Calvin gradually made it up from
the bed and down the stairs, venturing out into the sunlight, finally
setting foot to alley for the first time in more than a week. Despite
conditional promises to protect Calvin's identity in the wake of the
casino hit, it was only natural that he found his footing in the
alleyways – those that residents in the Vieux come to know as
something of a warren-like extension in pastel of one's own home –
newly insecure.

Gem prescribed a weekend in Laigueglia, a quaint seaside town
on the Ligurian coastal stretch running between Andora and Alassio,
to help Calvin get back on his feet. Calvin concurred, it was a fine
idea. Then, on the Thursday before the weekend in Laigueglia, just
like that, Klarysa rang.

"Calvin, it's me," she said pressingly. "How are you? Are you
healing OK? Is it all still so very painful?"

"Klarysa?" he said, shocked by the fact of her call.

The patient pain within smiled cattishly and sank its sharp, nasty little fangs deeply into his thumping heart.

"Why, hello," he managed.

"Oh, lover, how are you?" she begged. "Does it hurt so very badly? Tell me the truth."

"Boh. To be honest, yes, it does. Badly," he admitted. "I'm OK, though. Amazing, isn't it, how much pain can fill the void created by one's absence?"

"No, not that," she corrected him. "I mean... But aren't you hurt?"

"How do you mean?" he said defensively. He was intent on keeping secret the incident with Interpol, and how could she possibly know...

"How could I possibly know the details, Calvin? I only know I was overcome by the idea that you were somehow greatly damaged and that I needed to call you immediately."

"Where are you?"

"I'm home. In Barcelona," she said quizzically, as though she'd never left and where else did he expect her to be?

"Is Richard with you?"

"Richard! Of course not. What do you think?"

"Oh. What happened?"

"*Noth*ing happened," she said. "Even less than that. I bet you didn't know Richard is bankrupt."

"I did not."

"Oh, I know what you're thinking, but you're wrong—I've no need for money. You know that. But he hasn't any motivation. *That's* the problem. Why, he's content to sit and stare at his shoes for days on end. I need to move, you know. I made him take me dancing in San Tropez. What did he do? He sat on a barstool and watched, right leg draped over left, without so much as tapping his dusty toes. Not like *you*, my love. You are a fine dancer! One of the finest, really. There were entire numbers when I looked over at Richard and couldn't tell if he was still breathing."

"Is that all?"

"If only!"

"Go on then," he authorised, quietly overjoyed.

"Sometime before the lights came up, one of the creeps I'd been dancing with all night tried to steal me away, right out of the club!

And I tell you what, Calvin, he may have had his way even if I *had*n't agreed to go with him."

"You... You went with him?"

"Yes—to prove a point. Don't worry, I ran away as soon as we were outside. But what did Richard do about it? Nothing. He only smiled a horrible boozy smile and ordered another beer. Can you imagine? Besides, what kind of man drinks beer at a dance hall? A bankrupt one, that's what. And one without a trifle of motivation. There's the difference, my love—*you* have motivation. You do. You would have taught that creep a lesson about putting his hands on another man's woman. What did Richard do? Nothing! He only smiled contentedly and said I asked for it."

"He said that? Truly? Ha! Good old Richard!"

"How dare you, Calvin."

"How dare I? See here, little miss, you *do* ask for it. You've always asked for it."

"Be that as it may, you would have defended me—for good or ill, as you like to say. That's all I'm trying to point out. Don't you remember when I ran away from you after Manx's party? Why, you roamed the full length of Nice after me. And when you found me, my goodness, you looked worse than I did—far, *far* worse. Don't deny it; *you* would've knocked that creep's head off."

"You're probably right," he conceded. "Or I'd have had my own head knocked off in the attempt. But you know what, Klarysa? I never enjoyed that. In fact I hated it. I hated when you put me in a position to have to fight over you. And you hated it, too."

"I didn't hate it. You just don't know how to fight like a gentleman."

"You're impossible, Klarysa. You know that? Impossible. Just talking with you is exasperating."

"Oh, Calvin, it's true! It's so true!" she said, beginning to cry. "I can be a terribly wretched dish at times, can't I just! But you mustn't think for a second that I approve of it all. You mustn't! I positively de*test* it. Oh, the flame with which you must hate me, Calvin. You *do* hate me, don't you? You can tell me the truth. I couldn't possibly begin to handle it if you did hate me, though give it to me straight all the same."

He started to say something, but his words instantly gave way to affectionate laughter. At times he found her melodrama as adorable as it was ridiculous, mostly because hers was not an affectation, but an inescapable reaction to genuine fear. Klarysa had her fears, but above all, she was authentic. She was, indeed, her own woman. She was true to herself, and equally true to those around her. There were moments when she lacked the self-consciousness required of a girl to consider her standing in another's eyes; at other moments she was famished for flattery and recognition. Regardless of her state at any given moment, however, her behaviour was almost never calculated; she merely abided her instincts without consciousness or question. As it happened, her ways and actions most typically yielded favourable results, which is naturally reinforcing and can lead one to wrongly attribute credit where credit is not necessarily due, but there it is.

"Oh, you do!" she swooned. "You hate me! Oh, I just knew it. Don't question a girl's intuition, mister. And don't think I misunderstand your laughter, because I don't. You have every right to your satisfaction, after all. Only *do* breathe from time to time, my very cruellest love!"

"Stop!" begged Calvin in tears of laughter and pain, trying in vain to keep his fractured ribs from jiggling about. "Please, Klarysa, quiet! It hurts!" He finally calmed himself and sighed deeply, as one does upon finishing a stern vindaloo.

"Why, you *are* hurt," she gasped. "And badly at that."

"You are something else," he managed happily. "I'm just fine."

"Sadly, I am absolutely *not* something else. I am dead conventional, exceptional only in my wickedness. I am young, however, and hopeful for change."

He envisioned her on a divan; envisioned her perfect posture.

"My, but enough about me," she demanded. "My dear, you must tell me what happened to you."

But he would not. Given the horrific gravity of the recent stir and the delicacy of his safety and wellbeing going forward, Calvin wisely decided to keep the details concealed not only from Klarysa, but from the crew, as well. "Bah," he said flippantly, "just a random run-in with the wrong band of monkeys, that's all."

"I just knew you were hurt!" she said.

"Really? How?"

"It wasn't so long ago that I left you, Calvin—you should recall that I am very perceptive."

"I shouldn't, actually, because you're not."

"That's true. You're the perceptive one. You always bring me back down to earth and I love you for it. I'm liable to lose my head without you. Nevertheless, I *did* sense that you were hurt. All the way from Barcelona I sensed it. That must count for something."

"Maybe you really do love me."

"I love you madly. One day you may learn to stop doubting me."

Calvin woke the next morning feeling refreshed, feeling just a bit like a former, more optimistic, more inventive version of himself. Gem's idea of a weekend in Italy was a fine one, a familiar one, one that harkened back to the not-so-distant golden era of crew weekends. Calvin looked forward to channelling some of the coastal holiday excitement that had largely escaped him that summer. He stood bare-chested on the morning balcony and pondered the rising sun. So too, he pondered the density of the terracotta rooftops, the antique-green cupola of an old *église* glimmering above the rooflines, the constancy of generations to open shop in the alleyways down below and the constancy of those on their balconies to watch and wonder. There is a thick, gorgeous sense of timelessness to places that do not force a fellow over time to alter the vector of his life in order to remain relevant.

For the first time in months, Calvin looked up toward the ancient chateau, beyond the flap and call of crying gulls back-lit by the morning sun, beyond the thick pine mane of the chateau, and there he saw the vague free-form outlines of infinite opportunity. It may have only been a mirage—some places lend themselves to the careful cultivation of a man and his mirages.

Though he was most generally lithe of spirit, and though his soul was liable to fly on the lift of even the lightest breeze, so soon a metamorphosis for Calvin was highly unlikely. Klarysa's phone call the night before, however, was an adrenaline shot to the heart. Reflecting back on all the times he had been told by self-appointed authority figures that nothing good in life comes easily—forget the fact that most good things in life (e.g. sunrises, beaches and bonfires) *do* come easily—he admitted to himself that Klarysa wasn't truly impossible, as he had told her on the phone; she just wasn't easy. It is true that she could be sensitive and caring at times. He had long supposed that such were the times when fears and insecurities weren't needling her.

At any rate, none of it mattered greatly, for Klarysa embodied complex challenges at a time when Calvin was already up to his neck in complex challenges. All the same, no other person could have made him laugh that night, and it gave him hope – not that he might yet again be with her one day, but that he might yet regain the strength and optimism he had always known, that he might sit on the balcony as he'd done on countless days and nights, with a book and a glass, pinpointing the outlines of greatness and opportunity ever-twinkling somewhere high above the sea.

His strategy going forward, then, was to engage with Klarysa from a physical distance (that which ran between Nice and Barcelona) and an emotional distance (that which existed between platonic bodies, as opposed to amorous ones). By doing so, he might maintain his high without becoming dependent or further contributing to the madcap contraption of accords and expectations that neither of them, at the moment, had the wherewithal to meet and maintain, as it concerned couples in love. A cynic might contend that Calvin was engaging in a self-deluding game of hard-to-get, but hell, who could say what the future might bring for two friends, if they could, over time, show a common capacity for sober, steady love—a love that might extend beyond the bloody tips of antique knives and insatiate erogenous zones?

Calvin thought it was a brilliant plan, one that would engender brilliant results. And that, for what it is worth, was one of Calvin's more hopeful mirages. All the same, he was no longer insomniac and the mystery surrounding his spooks had been solved. The answers had come at a burdensome price, true, but he got them all the same. Those, at any rate, were the precursors of better days.

Calvin came in off the balcony, showered, dressed, and with an overnight bag slung over his shoulder, threw open the locks on the new door. They snapped open with the crisp, unanimous concurrence of a bank vault. Calvin sighed. We may have overestimated his appreciation for the security of a metal door. It is often difficult to strike a decent balance between aesthetics and utility, and armoured doors err precipitously on the side of utility. He rapped his knuckles on it to test its tone and winced in horror at the stiff, hollow *pong*, identifying what he considered the sound of a life trapped inside a heavy metal cistern. He looked longingly at the original wooden door, which leaned against the wall in the entryway at an angle that denoted retirement and obsolescence. He propped it up so that it stood a bit straighter, but it was no use. Staring regretfully at it for a count, he declared the death of an era.

Calvin rang the buzzer at Gem's, but there was no answer. They were to meet there and walk over to the train station in time to catch the twelve-o-seven to Imperia. From Imperia, it was a short bus ride into Laguéglia. They would arrive in time for a late lunch, a siesta, a dip in the sea, a walk about town and a few beers on a crowded terrace serviced by university girls from the Piemonte with baby fat and swivel-action hips.

Calvin rang again, but still there was no answer, so he installed himself at the café across the alley, where he ordered a coffee and a diplomat and snapped open the morning's *Nice Matin*. He flipped through the paper, looking for any lingering headlines concerning the casino hit, but it had been two weeks and to his relief there was nothing. He was finishing his coffee when he heard the unmistakable plaintive whine of Gem's scooter approaching. Calvin paid the coffee and the diplomat and met Gem as he killed the engine.

"Morning, Gemmo," Calvin hailed.

Gem wore a helmet that was two sizes too large and that hung down over his eyes. He wagged an index finger at Calvin, as though to help jog his memory.

"The name's Calvin," said Calvin, deadpan, though Gem had not forgotten his name, but rather the reason for his presence outside Gem's front door.

"Please don't tell me," said Calvin, "you forgot we're going to Italy today."

Gem had not forgotten the weekend in Italy, as much as his attention had been unexpectedly commandeered by the subject of a certain obsession, and like a cat before mice, Gem plainly did not have it in him to suppress the all-consuming urge to pounce.

"Forget? Of course I didn't forget. I simply didn't recognise you there, mate," said Gem, "wot wiv your eyes the colour of dodgy bananas. Who was it again did that to you?"

"You can't fool me, Gemmo. What are you hiding?"

"Asks the bloke wiv snapped ribs, a raspberry visage and banana eyes. Why, your face looks like a bowl of fruit salad. Tell me who did it. I can help you out, mate. We've got to set it straight wiv the wolves."

"You and your wolves. No, Arbuckle and Nadine helped out just fine," said Calvin. "One hell of a seamstress, that girl."

"I didn't mean help wiv the swabbing and stitching, mate. I meant wiv the payback, the retribution, the collection of an eye for your eye."

"Nonsense," Calvin replied. "Stop it with that."

"Give us a necktie, then, mate. I'll handle 'em on me own like."

"What now with you? Look, Gem, there won't be any *pay*back," Calvin said, shuddering at the thought. "No payback, no retribution. The words alone give me the shivers. I'm too old," he said, showcasing his face with open palms, "for *this*. Let's just get ourselves on that train, all right?"

Gem looked uncertain, but Calvin, throwing his arm winningly over Gem's shoulder, didn't notice.

"You know, Gemmo, I stood on the balcony early this morning and felt... Hell, I felt *ha*ppy. It's a trite word, I know, but it's the truth. Happy, for the first time in months. Hell if this summer hasn't had its teeth pointed straight at me."

Gem mumbled something indecipherable and then asked, "What time is our train, then?"

"Twelve-o-seven."

"Twelve-o-seven," Gem pondered. He mumbled some more, mentioned the need for a shower and admitted he hadn't yet packed a bag. Finally, he suggested that Calvin take the twelve-o-seven and he would follow him over on the next train."

"Nonsense!" Calvin rebutted. "Throw some shorts in a bag and let's get on that train. So what if you smell like a *sanglier*." Calvin smacked him enthusiastically on the shoulder. "Take a shower at the hotel after a nice swim in the sea. They have those lovely soaps at the hotel, remember? And the shower window that opens up over that terraced garden jammed with lemon trees and bougainvillea. That's the idea. Listen to your old mate."

Calvin led Gem over to the *portail*. "Let's go on up. Throw some shirts in a bag and we'll be off."

Once inside, Gem said quietly, lost in thought, "I'm going to shower."

"Fine, fine," said Calvin. "But make it quick. Mind if I have a beer?"

"In the frigo."

Calvin took a bottle of lager from the frigo and straddled the window sill. It was bright with warm sunlight. He took a pull from the bottle and turned his face to the sun. The beer was tepid, undrinkable. The English and their goddamned frigos, he thought— extra cupboard space is all.

He opened his eyes and shielded them from the sun with his free hand. Down below, the market on Cours Saleya was teeming. In the near distance, among the pine and palm leading up to the chateau, Calvin spotted a lone silver poplar flapping its shimmering leaves madly, dementedly, deliriously, for no reason at all, there on a scorching day with no breeze whatsoever. The spoon-like leaves, a million tiny airborne kites quavering hysterically without tails to keep them settled, would lay still for a count and then burst in shimmering silver-green violence at the slightest breath of hot air. The vision of those tormented leaves triggered within him a palpable sensation from somewhere in his past, of violated calm, of anxious states of unrest, of the destruction of peace and ease. An alarm clock could inspire a similar sickness within him, the crash and clatter of dishes being put away, the slamming of a door, evening news broadcasts, late afternoons in general, the sound of gunfire, the rush of wind through trees, especially through poplar, which crazily needed no goddamned wind whatsoever to flap with a fierce and rabid psychosis. Appetent nausea filled his belly and began climbing up his throat. He hurried off to the kitchen and vomited in the rubbish bin.

Calvin attributed the sensation to the creeping of cracks in the psychogenic shield that somehow protects a boy from all of the psychological toxins that are too noxious for him to process in his adolescence—toxins that are sufficiently, miraculously neutralised over time, so that a lad might not, in his adulthood, be poisoned and destroyed by them – whatever *they* may be exactly – though he may well remain tormented to the point of nausea and vomiting by the memory of their shape and colour alone.

He poured the rest of the beer down the drain, tied off the bin bag and put it out on the landing. He recognised the ridiculousness of such a nauseas reaction, though knew he was powerless to stop it. He retook his seat on the window sill, though he now faced the opposite direction, away from the poplar tree that flapped madly in the distance.

"Hey, what's the story in there?" he called to Gem, dismissing as best he could the sickening sensation.

Gem said nothing.

"We'll have to take a taxi to the station if we're going to make that twelve-o-seven."

"Go on, mate," said Gem, finally. "Go. I'll catch you up like. I'll be quick, I promise."

"Forget it. We're riding over together. Hell, anyway, it's already too late for the twelve-o-seven. We'll catch the next one. What's the hold up, anyway? You have any *cold* beer?"

"In the frigo," said Gem absently.

"Hey, in there!" Calvin snapped. "What the hell's wrong with you to-day?"

Just then, Gem entered the salon.

"What the—!" exclaimed Calvin.

Gem looked prepped for first communion. He was freshly showered, freshly shaven, sported a crisp white shirt, newish navy-blue trousers, matching blazer and an old black belt. Calvin had never once seen him dressed thus. He was only missing a tie. He sat himself on the arm of the couch and scented himself with cologne.

"Cologne!" Calvin blurted. "Hell if you're not cutting a damned queer figure to-day. What gives?"

Gem walked to the frigo, took two beers, uncapped them both and gave one to Calvin. Like the first, it was tepid, undrinkable. Gem took a seat on the couch and threw an ankle up onto his knee.

"Do you dream at night, dear Calvin?" he asked in earnest.

"Hell, I don't know, dear Gem. I promise you I only just learnt how to sleep. Why?"

"Mine are legendary, mate."

"Your dreams? I don't doubt it, you maniac."

"Noffing makes so much sense as when I'm asleep. Don't laugh."

"Who's laughing? Hell of a fine way to stay out of harm's way, as well, and there's something to be said for that."

"Up is down and down is up," Gem explained himself, "but no one gets his neck broken over it. Everyfing is what it is. No rules, no objections, somehow everyone knows how to live and how to behave wivvout finking about it. Everyfing is fluid like. The fing about the seas, right, is that they're always at equilibrium, anywhere in the world, guided only by gravity and shorelines. The seas settle in their rightful place, no questions, no complaints. They don't want for more. Fink of all the billions of people in the world. We could be like the seas, yeah? We could flow wivvout rules. How difficult would it be, really? Let a certain social gravity dictate a humane and decent course. The only problem is we blokes never do what we're supposed to do. We fight equilibrium like. We fight natural order. We fight gravity. We never fill our proper spaces. The way I see it, Calvin, we blokes harbour a certain death-wish, see."

Having just recently been accused of death-wishing, certain of Calvin's dark recollections came rushing back to him. On this side of the line, he recited to himself, they call me a hero. On that side of the line they call me a terrorist. There are very few universal truths.

"So what's to be done about it?" Gem asked. He ran the edge of his palm across his dripping forehead, and shot a resentful eye at his navy slacks for denying him a denimed leg on which to dry a wet palm. "I guess we elect men to make a million rules and laws, and employ a million more men to enforce them. A bloke can still manifest his death-wish, see, but it becomes a riskier proposition. A bloke, you see, needs freedom in order to destroy. So he walks a fine line, see, doing his best to destroy while maintaining his freedom. You don't have a necktie I could borrow," he asked, fumbling absently at his neck, "do you, Calvin?"

"Sorry, mate. Why the costume, anyway?"

"I could write a whole book," said Gem without a smile, putting aside Calvin's question for the moment. "A whole book on the lives and intrigues rambling through me head each night. Five-honrid-page books, I reckon. Much like Arbuckle does, but wivvout all the lunacy and speculation. Only, wiv the bed sheets pulled warm around me, I'm often too lazy to locate pen and paper. Or if I threaten to get up and commit it all to record, the fantastic angels, wiv their wings of heavy damask, thick as buttermilk, fly the coop and morning begins in earnest, like it or not. It is a delicate fing, dear Calvin.

"Two nights ago I ran into Sandoval, that Puerto Rican of ours who's always tickling a bloke's ear wiv one feather or another. He had a rare bit of news for me, he did, the baiting bastard. Later that night, lying flat on me bed and dead to the world, a sparkling dinner party appeared before me. During the *apero*, I was approached by a fair-headed Danish lad in a black tuxedo and leather shoes, black and shiny. He was the only bloke at the party wearing a tuxedo, and he was no more than ten-years-old, I swear it. This lad carried a gold pocket watch on a gold chain, wore his hair like they did in the 1920s and had confetti in his eyes.

"The boy and I were on the balcony overlooking the port, looking down over the yachts and dinghies. He spoke at great length of his father, who had quit him and the missus while on holiday in Hamburg in the summer of '36; quit them to go die on the side of the Republicans in the Spanish Civil War, he did. When the lad walked, fountains of colourful confetti spilt from his shiny black shoes. No lie, Calvin. I asked the boy; I said, 'Wot's wiv the tuxedo, mate?' It was an upscale affair and he was the host, but still, he was the only bloke in a tuxedo and he was just a small child. He looked at me, Calvin, as though he'd been waiting for this. He set his martini on the balcony railing, took a leather wallet from his coat and from the wallet a folder letter. 'Bah,' said the boy wiv a wink, 'we know it all by heart, don't we?' and he put the letter back in his wallet and the wallet back in his coat. He looked up at me; then turned and looked at his guests, acknowledged the tinkling of glasses, the merriment and the laughter. He looked down at the boats at port, the inky-blue water supporting them in their repose, silent in its respiration. From somewhere far down the quay, an Italian opera could be heard. 'My father,' said the lad very seriously, patting the chest pocket that held his wallet and the letter, 'wrote to me from the front line.' He took up his martini from the balcony railing and, looking out to sea, recited his father's poetry.

"'My dearest boy,' he began. 'Let me tell you how

I sat broken in the cradle of a golden eve, kissing the tail of summer, the nose of autumn
    with tight-thread valise and lacerated lips made rosy and new for the fortnight down
    and rode southerly; transitional light buttering the underbelly of a silver stretch vessel
    towards receding horizons en route to Huesca, Aragon, falling, your old man and the light
    to fight and face persecution at the hands of the Nationals, the church, the fascist Falange

On crepuscule, wave-like, rich with night's budding gestation, rides the sky-walker new
    with five hundred questions beyond Hamburg city, relations gathered and wondered
    and aimless barges, the duration of mere eyelashes, hatching cold-metal thoughts
    off cement coasts, where God's underworld lay reduced to major elements, all of them
    patient toys on the swell, unnoticed, so soon forgotten in the thick pitching Deutch Bucht

'Over all of Spain, the sky is clear', save for the lost generation of the Weimar Republic
    with chequered history hurtling underbelly, battle-scarred fields pocked and tagged
    the futile fighting, the countless bayonet charges against fortified positions, impaled
    we take our objectives and bury our dead and wait restlessly for to-morrow's orders
    strangers foreign, similar in our suffering, identical in our illness, born cooing, we are one

Shifting from vast mineral mass to vast mineral mass, gaping black chasms we roam
    with loves abandoned and eyes closed, to defend against a rebel coup, so many
    slices of tête pressée stacked cold and dead upon sacrificial altars built for fickle gods
    murderers conjoined in song to which no one can remember the sodden tune, lie in
    burnt earth, bombardier-lack, musky scent, pungent helmet sweat, enmity and rage

The dreams of your dear mother, Emma the Baffled, a girl invisible to friendly melodies
    with ears open wide, too sweet in her listening to endure the bitterest notes, and
    cursed for the worst of the Jutland Boys, I, with compound eyes and mad flapping wings

conceiver of nether-land projects, cacophonous scores to encourage the Thälmann Battalion
our Emma before such vulgar complications, so soft in her listening that we need not...

Shhh, quiet, they said.

And you, dear boy, my gurgling brook, my hopeful knight, our protector of bleating lambs
with mother's curls kissing your plum cheeks to help channel the whispers
on a stretch of Esrum Lake, dove-white for winter's firm grip, and keeping my fading heart
propped upright with your resolve, etched with torturous runic inscriptions of love lost
a clamouring heart pumping cold sadness and inglorious visions into wet candied boots.

Until a time when mephitic glaciers find motion, shake free of their malaise and fizz *animé*
and you, the anointed, glide forward and pluck nirvana from star-forested skies, and
hollow out the night with jagged spoons and freeze the moment where you touch, and
mark time by a new consciousness, a flowering of *l'esprit de luxe*, the Great Reclamation
and you, General, with bowtie and confetti eyes, vanquish the wolves in their relentless pursuit'

"Upon finishing his recital," continued Gem, "a wind picked up. The lad put his nose to the air and shook his head in resignation. He handed me the rest of his martini and told me to kill it, made sure his cufflinks were secure and tugged down on the sleeves of his coat. When he was done, he looked up to me and lowered his voice, as to not alarm his guests. 'The lambs,' he said, wiv a nod toward the dining room. 'The lambs will perish. The wolves will arrive and rape them one by one and eat them alive while they clutch in agony at their violated bellies.'

"You see, Calvin, they all come to me at the first signs of morning, wiv anecdotes, stories, from time to time wiv world-wisdom."

Gem said little to satisfy Calvin's curiosity concerning the trousers and blazer, and purposely withheld from him the remaining details of the dreamed dinner party. Instead, he encouraged Calvin to hurry along and catch the twelve-o-seven. "I'll catch you up directly, I promise," he said. "Move it. Go."

The dinner party had, nevertheless, ended thus:

"I've always believed," said the young Danish lad, his chin pointing portentously toward the horizon, "that a proper host will robe himself a fair cut better than his guests—just in case a battle should break out, of course, be it during the aperitif or the tiramisu, to aid the lambs in their identification of the general when the madness hatches and the ladies begin to weep. And they will surely weep."

During the dessert course, Gem leaned over to the lad, intrigued by what he had said earlier, and questioned, "Wot about the wolves?"

The question interrupted the boy as he was mouthing a spoon of tiramisu. He finished the bite, savouring it with closed eyes and then responded pleasantly, "Sure. The wolves."

Bringing a linen serviette up to his thin pink lips, he dabbed them delicately. "Take a look, mate," he said with a gentle, accommodating smile. 'Here they come now.'

And with that, all comfort and composure was instantly shattered. Through the front doors, the balcony and several of the fifth-floor windows came bursting a rabid pack of grey wolves. The women and many of the men wailed and wept and jumped up onto the dining table, kicking over their desserts and crunching wine glasses. It would have been a massacre were it not for the little general, who, having taken a brief moment to straighten his bowtie, unleashed a punishing, savage offensive on the encroaching pack and drove them off, one and all, out the windows and back into the *arrière pays*. That's where the dream ended.

Gem wiped his sweating brow.

Calvin said, "The twelve-o-seven is long gone, mate. It's OK. We'll take the afternoon train."

"Sure you don't have a necktie, Calvin? It needn't be a bowtie."

Before Calvin could respond, Gem had risen. "Forget it. It's not imperative, mate. Now excuse me, dear Calvin, I've a rendez-vous."

"A rendez-vous!" Calvin protested. "Where? At the boat? But we're one holiday!"

"Not at the boat. Don't worry, mate. Just a quick rendez-vous over at Les Idéales."

"Oh. OK. That's better," said Calvin, unable to show disfavour towards an obligation arranged to take place at a good bar. "I'll come with. We can go to the train station directly from there."

Gem studied Calvin, his best mate, the one he sought to protect like a brother, though he may have failed miserably from time to time. "You want to come with, do you?"

"Anything," said Calvin, "to get us closer to Italy."

"OK, mate," Gem conceded, killing Calvin's untouched beer "You know who the lieutenants are, Calvin? Those wiv noffing better to do. Come on, you can be my lieutenant—they require no fancy dress."

They left the flat. As they spiralled down the stairwell, Gem muttered regretfully to himself, "Should've caught the twelve-o-seven, lieutenant."

Gem and Calvin sat at a table on the terrace of the bar Les Idéales. The setting was undeniably holiday-like and the beer undeniably cold. The next train to Italy wasn't due for a couple hours yet and allowing Gem from one's sight was to lose him altogether, so Calvin sat patiently, thought of Italy and quit trying to squeeze Gem for information.

In the end, of course, there would be no weekend in Laigueglia. There would be no relaxation, no reflection, no ogling of university girls from the Piemonte, for as Sandoval had signalled and Gem had dreamt, the wolves did arrive. They arrived in the form Martin Hambone and company, five of them in the pack. Fangs were extended and women wept and Gem played the role of well-dressed general and pre-emptive protector of lambs, in a seaside town where the lambs were sorely outnumbered by the wolves. Calvin zipped about, clownish in a rodeo sense. He dodged fists and boots and tried his best to draw Gem away from the fray. The wolves fought a spirited fight and administered fair damages in return for those received.

In time, the mêlée was descended upon and diffused. Gem and Calvin were ushered brusquely away from the terrace and berated in searing French against any notions of returning to the bar in the future. They shuffled off, down the long-beaten path to Arbuckle's flat – Gem sated, wide-smiled and leaking fluids; Calvin cursing his every inch – where Nadine would be called on yet again to work her needled-tipped magic.

Stanley Arbuckle detested tisane. Arniche Van Brüsel, however, the star-crossed industrialist from Senegal via Willebroek, Belgium, and lead protagonist in Arbuckle's latest literary opus, *Dog Days in Dakar* (validation of which was cut drastically short by way of deportation), drank nothing but. And so Calvin sat with Arbuckle in the kitchen of the *maison de maître* just down the street from the Nice opera house and drank tisane, the latter making dour faces with each forced gulp. Meanwhile, Nadine put forth her best Florence Nightingale as Gem happily regaled her with the colourful musings of his ill-interpreted dreams, his latest victory over the wolves, his latest defence of the innocent lambs.

The weekend was intended to be one of relaxation, recovery and reflection—a weekend that might have allowed Calvin to square himself and establish a certain mental footing, that he might then step firmly in some decent new direction. But Gem couldn't help himself. Or maybe, thought Calvin, he just didn't give a damn. Hell if they weren't so close to being on that twelve-o-seven to Imperia, and from Imperia, a short bus ride to Laigueglia.

Just then, as though it weren't all quite bad enough, Calvin was touched by a tremendous aching for Klarysa. Rather thoroughly dominated and more than a little disgusted, Calvin stood and made for the door.

"Where you off to, mate?" asked Gem, as Nadine applied a final ointment to several of his lacerations.

"Bar des Oiseaux."

"Bah! Not that shite bar."

"The very one, in fact."

"Wait two minutes. We'll go to the Whales."

"I'm going to the Oiseaux."

"But I've been barred from the Oiseaux! You know that, Calvin!"

Calvin paused at the front door and turned to face Gem from across the room. "Yes, Gem," he said. "I do." And then he left.

Calvin installed himself at a table in the cramped space of the Bar des Oiseaux, dejected, misshapen, twisted around a pint of non-descript lager, provoked by determined demons and broad-reaching inquisitions. Sound experimentation requires that one hold constant all variables, and then tweak one variable and note the results. But what if, Calvin wondered, a fellow was at once the level-headed scientist and the anxious rat? How would the doses and placebos be administered? Who would sound the alarm, wheel in the gurney, tighten the straps, consign a flipped chap to the shock shop and notify the next of kin when it all went horribly awry? Sod it! Ring the bells, blow the whistles, let the attached catches collect psychic secretions.

He leaned back and tried to relax, but it was no good. He smiled feebly at the lovely waitress from Suriname as she passed by, and wondered what on earth might have become of the All-America surfer with the blue eyes and the golden-boy hands that once caressed a certain blonde girl's finest assets, so long ago, there in the back of a white van, in the levy of a burnt-up river delta.

He watched the collection of stuffed vultures and jackals, shaking and swinging, carnivorous piñatas in the humid bar of the birds, his heart tied to an old tangled cork-oak somewhere on the highest, greenest Peymeinade peak, long-arming dusty green apples into a late afternoon sky dense and combustible with corn-blue purity, clown-spotted cotton candy clouds, antique air sweetly stained with pine and pear and fig, reverberations in the lungs and ribcage, the rustle and hum of oak trees, young skin, puffing, calling, finistère tears welling up behind stones and cheekbones and in throbbing throats and roots, timeless remembrance of Friday afternoon love, Doberman, blurry and black as pitch, kicking up hot dust on fire roads, switchbacks gouged out of pine and oak, hills rising high above vibrant stillness of cool green valley and blue sea, of eager teens, of grandmothers foreign to the future, of dying histories and hand-painted towns, of Mougins and those without names, out where they cut loose, free of pain, a twin dog, Calvin on high after stretched limbs, lean and long on a green-apple rush attack, made new by the sun, stringered bolt-solid by girder and joist, ankles and knees and tapered calves, mandarin sunshine, laughter and clear-black nights, arms and legs, bed flops, gaping mouths, pained and painless, all and everything for the Spanish mare, blown glass and mercurial, a family, of which he, Calvin, for a moment, was the father and the son, the brother, the lover, the loved.

Having slipped under for a moment, Calvin was presently jarred to by a tubbing baritone: "Ho-ho-ho! Calvin, have you passed out in your beer?"

The Butcher!

"Why, we've not yet reached midnight," the Butcher noted.

"What of it, Butcher?" replied Calvin, pressing the heels of his hands to his brow. "Is the approach of midnight not my new greatest fear? What will midnight bring but another day of bracing against the fallout of one new storm or another, this one dropping black boots and bombs, that one raining sharpened knives, the other promoting who knows what—Russian slugs, Balkan entanglement, stone duck heads from atop black canes kissing ruddily against the temples of the blackmailed? Don't you know to leave a sleeping dog lie? Why, the gongs of midnight compose the death knell I specifically wish to avoid."

Eddie bought a bottle of champagne. When they had drunk the bottle dry, Calvin stood, bid them adieu and left. Having reached his building, he climbed the four flights of stairs, his shoes slurping a progressively heavier slide-step, up and across each tiny hurdle. Finally reaching the fourth-floor landing, he jammed his key in the armoured door, snapped open the locks, opened the door and fell headlong into a deep dark purple well...

> Snow stop falling. The night sky run slippery without end, slick and black *She can't feel her hands, she slice open a finger instead of the potato she holding. Learn to talk right, speak right, speak well simple no-account* Kid reach back and long-arm the brick toward the pane window *Could use a sea to pluck it from the night sky with a silent invisible kiss.*
>
> Biggest outcomes in life bloom web-like in fast running waves from a center point. A crack burst in the night and run in every direction through a pane of glass, like a firework exploding in silver dandelion, and only afterward hearing the gun-powder call that send it nightward *Stuck with what you got and what you ain't got* A body react instinctively, in silence, the brain note the sound of urgent motion sometime afterward *Laika stands shocked and numb at the jagged edge of the Pacific Ocean, without a pen and with no notes left to write* No time to ponder consequences, to dodge a bullet or catch it in the chest.
>
> A boy walk for the first time onto top court *Take him, Sugarbear!* and stand somewhere between what he is today and what he want to be

tomorrow *Stuck with what you got and what you ain't got. BANG!* A flat lightning bolt rip a gash in the hull of the night. Glass shatter and fly in all directions. A million midnight shards, silver stars gilded green, laugh and burn demonic, arch and fall to the earth *Theys burnt flowers, smell burnt stars* Streetlight cut its way into the ragged maw of a brick building and Kid catch a glimpse of a *Sure enough wolf* A sure enough wolf gripping a leveled pistol *A general without a tie.*

Kid spin away low and hard. *BANG!* Dodge a bullet or catch it in the chest. Willie Mays Rush, mouth hung open, the explosion still reflecting in his brandy eyes as death descend with fangs hinged on wide. Kid run off before the tinkling dreamsound die muffled on the snow-packed street *Could use a sea, a desert, a silent invisible kiss from Christmas red lips.*

Ears ring. Dez, he watch *I watch them walk away, Pop throw his arm over Ma shoulders* He try to watch for a way home *Throw back his head and laugh real loud. That great laugh from Pop shake and rattle the metal lockers.* Garfield, still and silent, and snow start to fall anew. Willie Mays Rush, my brother, in red Salford Ammies hat lay still, leaking purple liquid like oil from a cracked engine block. *They know about death. The long brown couch lay empty and beat.*

Bird, he lay in a motionless brown haze on the old leather couch in the back of the record store *Empty and beat* Rubber tubing run down to the floor from the underside of his strangled arm. On the wall, two whelps stand with arms locked at the shoulders and chins lifted above the horizon, looking down adolescent noses. A camera snap. Another needle obey its groove, this one slurping and crackling, gently breathing, floating on black vinyl, amplifying dust, an eerie woman *Oh, God, no! Oh, God, no! Viola cry out* Sing of a strange and bitter crop.

Kid cut through Garfield Park and stop running when he pass over top court. *Somebody need to repaint the lines. Theys too many fights. Can't nobody tell what's out of bounds and what ain't.*

Nicki stand before a mirror in a new pink dress.

"*I want to go home.*"

"Shhh, You're OK, mate."

"*I want to go home, Pug.*"

"You are home, mate. Take it easy."

"*Where am I?*"

"You're in bed. You're home, in France."

"*You sure talk funny, Pug. What's a Frans and a mate?*"

"Shhh. Take it easy."

"*That china cup sure look nice in your hands. I like to see you with nice things.*"

"Shhh. Get some rest, mate."

23   If it weren't all perfectly absurd

In which Klarysa turns down a
marriage proposal and Calvin
meets the mallard.

The afternoon would turn hot. But that morning on Avinguda Diagonal, just up from Camp Nou and the university buildings that found animation on September mornings, clung to a chill that signalled the death of another summer and the impending reign of relative seriousness. Later that morning, in the neighbouring barrio of Les Corts, a telephone rang.

"It's me. Did I wake you?"

"*No pasa nada.*"

"I've something to tell you."

"Tell me," said Hector from a cool white bed, awakened from the unbroken sleep of the carefree.

"It's about your friend."

"I'm listening."

"I mean to tell you he's a lousy murderer."

"What do you mean?" Hector said.

"I don't believe I minced my words."

"I see. Bah, very little surprises me anymore."

Hector eased his feet to the floor, sat on the edge of the bed and rubbed the sleep from his brow.

"Still, this is very troubling. I do not approve of murder and I make no practice of associating with murderers—least of all *lou*sy murderers."

"This is no joking matter."

"Very well. But just who is it we're talking about?"

"Calvin Stony, of course."

"Of course," repeated Hector. The very name he'd anticipated. *"Mierda. Esta es una mala noticia – muy mala noticia.* It is a pity; he has been marginally useful to me. I do not approve of murder, you understand. Still, gambling is worse." A sigh escaped him. "I suppose we have little choice but to dispose of Mr. Stony."

"Goddamn it, I said this is no joking matter!"

"Boh. Fine. My apologies. But you must agree it is very difficult to take seriously a fellow who speaks of himself in the third-person perspective."

"I suppose you're right," admitted Calvin. "In fact it's nothing short of farcical. Though that's precisely what it's come to, I'm afraid—one big farce!"

"Calme, calme," eased Hector, ever in possession of an effortless composure. "Let's meet and talk it over. I'm leaving to-night. I have a rendez-vous in Lausanne to-morrow morning—a delivery of Swiss clocks. I will come to Nice directly afterwards."

"Does nothing ruffle you?" asked Calvin. "How can you be so calm before a confessed murderer? What's the illicit gem where the Swiss clocks are concerned, anyway?"

"You are not a murderer, Calvin. Murderers don't speak of themselves in the third person; it is too queer, it draws looks, the wrong kind of attention. Each clock has had its mechanical cuckoo swapped out for a live Pine Flycatcher, though the colouring of the lower mandible leaves me suspicious."

"I thought you refused to deal with rare species. You just wait and see; your old pal Calvin *is* a murderer."

"You, Calvin, are the rare species. The Pine Flycatcher, on the other hand, is far from rare. It is, in fact, endemic in its native territory and a source of abject homesickness for an old Coahuilan codger living in Lausanne. Let's just hope the little buggers don't escape and take to the Swiss countryside in the manner they have Guatemala and Mexico. Shall we say to-morrow evening, then, at the Rive Bleue?"

"Oh, right, I forgot to tell you—I've quit Nice. Well, I've been granted short-term leave, at any rate."

"Granted leave?" Hector questioned suspiciously.

"Lest I go AWOL and a fellow doesn't want that on his record. Technically speaking, I'm on holiday. R&R, I think they call it. I'm renting a small flat in Barcelonetta."

"You are in Barcelona?"

"I never should've left, you know. Barcelona, I mean. It seems I am constantly fleeing the ghosts of my making. Bah, they always manage to catch up with a fellow no matter where he may go. One may wonder as to their opacity upon arrival. But arrive, they will."

"Come now, Calvin. Are you really so haunted?"

"Yes. Yes, I am. I thought that solving the mystery of my spooks would create a peaceful little void in my head that I might fill with daffodils, but no, weeds continue to dominate. Two nights ago it was the ghost of young Willie Rush. You remember mention of my friend Gem. Willie was Gem's older brother—until I got him killed."

Calvin recounted the details of Willie's death and how Gem's mother cried—loudly for a brief moment, then quietly and alone, which was so much harder to bear for the rest of the survivors, who would have preferred she kick and scream and get it all out. Viola loved Gem dearly, but Willie Mays Rush was her baby. Hell if that woman weren't a pushover for centerfielders. And how that child could play the position—extraordinary range, one hell of a hose. Funny, though; one of the things Calvin remembered most about Willie was how he could never come to grips with the constancy of broken glass in the dugouts. From a very young age, everyone knew the boy was in possession of an uncanny sense. Always the first to arrive at the ball diamond, he would sweep up the glass, then warm up by lining a hundred balls into the chain-link backstop, and finish by taking a dozen or so easy trips around the bases, tipping his cap every third or fourth tour towards the cheering fans in the centerfield bleachers, neither of which, the fans or the bleachers, in reality, existed.

By the time coach and the rest of the team would arrive, Willie would be sitting on the edge of the dugout with a chipmunk's cheek of sunflower seeds and his hat turned out in rally-cap fashion, to congress the intensity of a high-pressure situation, however simulated, as a backdrop against which to display a certain sagacity and fortitude. There he would meditate, philosophise, search for reason in a neighbourhood that all too often stumbled into madness. He did so purely for the sake of understanding, unlikely as it was for any young child to cure the ills that plague an inner-city society. Sometimes, when the rest of the team showed, he would abandon his meditation in favour of tarring a few bats, tightening a few cleats and fungoing a few flies out to the lads. Sometimes he would slip the coach a proposed line-up card, having leveraged inside neighbourhood info few adults were privy to, and stay mentally trained to the conundrum *du jour* until it was time to take the field, or until coach interrupted his introspection:

"Goddamn it, Willie Mays!" coach might say, eyeing the line-up card. "What's the meaning of this?"

Willie, ever-attentive, lipped sunflower husks. "Coach?"

"*Kim*ble in the *eight* hole!"

"Oh, that," offering a nonchalant shrug. "As you will, coach."

"Jesus, Willie, Kimble's the best stick we've got."

"Not to-day he's not."

"Why? What happened?"

"Trust me, coach, you don't want to know. Girl problems."

"Jesus," sighed coach. "What have I told you boys about keeping it in your pants!"

For all his sagacity and fortitude, Willie was not too old to blush at such words from an adult. "Hell," coach would say, "It can't be *that* bad, can it?"

"It can, coach. And it is. Possibly worse. We'll be lucky if he gets the bat off his shoulder."

"Goddamn it. Do I need to have a talk with his parents?"

Another nonchalant shrug. "Let me see what I can do first. Give me a couple days. I'll let you know."

"Well hurry up, we got the goddamned *Gi*ants on Friday!"

Meanwhile, his teammates would be loosening up, or running about and spitting bubble gum and pulling the hair of little girls who ventured too close. Willie was the only one who found it sad and unfortunate that the dugouts were always lined with broken glass. Those boys all grew up with broken glass, generations of broken glass. Everywhere they turned there was broken glass—bottles, windows, windshields, all of it. That gleaming shard of Garfield zeitgeist, which now twinkled like diamonds, now cut like blades, was a mystery to him. No one else gave it any thought. But Willie did.

"So you see—," said Calvin, but Hector had cut him off ahead of his self-conviction.

"What do I see? I see nothing. I know the conclusion you are running towards and it is preposterous. The revenge you sought was ill-conceived, but you did not lead that boy to his death. Next you will try to tell me you murdered…"

"Ah-ha!" said Calvin. "Go on, say it. Say her name."

"Ridiculous. *Eres loco.*"

"Victoria!"

Calvin had indeed been perseverating over her since the dream of Willie's death.

"You cannot save the world, Calvin."

"Don't be trite," said Calvin. "I should only like to stop facilitating the deaths of those I love. Had neither of them known me, they might both still breathe."

"*Egoista!*" cried Hector. "And should a mother condemn herself for her complicity in the life-pain and ever-approaching death of her own child, who would have avoided suffering and death altogether were it not for the matter of his own unsolicited birth?"

"Pah! Is it not a fair question? Do you contend that only an egoist could consider such a notion? Are we are so taken by the absurd notion of *life as a precious gift* that we have nothing left to offer the breathing, blinking, suffering individual? It appears to be true and that is a travesty! We promote and celebrate birth at every turn, but let a wayward youth commit the most minor transgression and the very same fanatics want him punished to the furthest extent of the law. Why, I believe we've got it perfectly backward—from any angle, life is a frivolous chance encounter. A fellow need only consider his utter lack of authorisation as it concerns his own birth, to understand that. And therefore, as it concerns any single life form – from the helpless kitten in the alleyway, to the beggar on the street, to the child with hungry eyes – the only decent approach to our vision and treatment of that individual is as though he, she, it were the true centre of the universe—God itself! By virtue of its unsolicited birth, it deserves, in all instances and at all times, the world's kindness, patience and acceptance. No, Hector, I cannot save the world. But may God damn us all for our embarrassing lack of effort in that regard!"

"You make a fine and noble point. Allow me, then, to add that freedom is perhaps the greatest bestowal of kindness and acceptance one can grant an individual. And in taking her own life, Victoria did in fact practice one of the few inalienable freedoms due every creature. As you say, she was given no authority in the decision of her birth, or the hell into which she was born, no less—a hell you may have known little about, not that it matters greatly, save that you might not otherwise feel quite so responsible for her decision. Let no man refuse another the right to say when enough is damn well enough."

Calvin swallowed back the profound sorrow brought forth by his remembrance of Victoria. No one, he thought, should suffer such feelings of futility and despair. "Of course," he said in agreement, "but you are skirting the point. I did know Victoria's hell. What I fail to understand is why that knowledge should absolve me of responsibility. Was she beyond saving? Bah, my actions on the winter night of Willie's death, and my *in*actions leading up to the day Victoria jumped, were born of recklessness and selfishness. My actions and inactions had a direct and tangible effect on those two children! I cannot simply be let off the hook for that, Hector."

"Look, Calvin, every chap must accept the fact that he puts his life in the jaws of a strange and fickle god each and every time he rolls from the bed. Willie supported you in your ill-conceived notion of levelling a score. You support Gem in the same manner. There is no difference. As I have told you countless times, I don't gamble. Yet every man gambles when he steps out into the world. Life is a risky proposition, and when fortunes turn, some will credit a god and some will blame a devil. I prefer to acknowledge the complex system of belts and wheels in each man's internal engine, the unconscionable mechanics that grind and turn – sometimes at a pace and rhythm beyond one's control and even beyond the limits of one's consciousness – and propel a fellow forward in a mad world that promotes and punishes at random, without reason, fairness or sense.

"Understand this, Calvin: despite the complexity of Man's inner mechanics, despite his desire, his will and his best efforts, he is, in the simplest terms, a frail and helpless leaf adrift on random, huffing winds. As no mother can protect her child, try as she may, you could not protect Victoria or Willie. And you cannot protect Gem. A fellow has but one life to live, and for better or worse, that one life can only be lived in accordance with that fellow's personal mechanics. The sooner we acknowledge that, the sooner we come to know the true space that is available for life and love, and we are shocked to find out that this space, which may have once seemed confined and restricted, is in fact endless and limited only by the walls of our fears. Bah, I will not agree that you are a demon or a failure. You are merely a man, and each of us is flawed. But let us not waste another breath on worthless debate. The wheel of life has turned and come full circle, and if you feel you must have your redemption, I am happy that you've been handed such an opportunity."

"Redemption? How do you mean?" asked Calvin.

"Bah, here you are, returned to Barcelona, once again in love with a girl that you cannot fully understand, and one that you cannot protect—neither from herself, nor any of life's myriad hazards."

Calvin was silent.

"That *is* why you have returned Barcelona, no?" Hector asked. "To make things right with Klarysa?"

Calvin was stunned by the assumption. He had returned to Barcelona neither for Klarysa nor a shot at redemption—not consciously, at any rate. It was as though, at that very moment, he acknowledged his whereabouts with full wakefulness for the first time since his arrival in the Catalan capital. Until that point, he had really only acknowledged where he was *not*, and given the recent unhinging of his life in Nice, his removal to any other location was the only certainty that mattered to him. In explaining his return Barcelona, he might reasonably have cited a needed holiday from Niçois hardships, or Barcelona as a beloved city in which he once prospered, or even an unconscious return to the cradle of newly revisited memories of Victoria. But now that Hector had voiced his assumption that Calvin had returned in pursuit of Klarysa, it would have been ludicrous of Calvin to deny the fact that a rendez-vous with her had been pounding and demanding celebrity somewhere in the backstage of his subconscious. The obviousness of Hector's assumption had not only given light to this realisation, but breathed life into it and lent the idea a certain credibility that can only come from an external source.

Hector interpreted Calvin's silence as an affirmation.

"The question then becomes," Hector ventured, "can you approach your love for Klarysa with the understanding that you cannot protect her from harm or steer her from the darker temptations of life, those that may take her away from you at any given moment? You need not worry yourself with the question of her safety in your keep, for there is no keep. Rather, use that energy to provide a safe and loving home for her head and heart, and encourage peace and healthy thought. And most importantly, perhaps, you must unlearn the illusions with which you torture yourself, that you might have the clarity and strength to accept Klarysa's vulnerabilities, insecurities and all her malignant propensities – whatever they may be – and enjoy with her the minute at hand, with conscious knowledge that it may be the last. Can you do that?"

Calvin might have stood there in silent reflection, through autumn and into winter, had a Spanish *señora* not interrupted his thoughts to inform him with the aloof and non-negotiable tenor of all pre-recorded voices that his credit was nearly depleted.

"Hell if I know," Calvin finally answered, thankful for the inability of another to witness the rapid blinking of humid eyes through a phone line. Though he really did not know, he had at that moment, regardless of the prospects of success or failure, found new focus.

Eyeing the impressive *modernisme* building just beyond the towering palms before him, Calvin said, "I'm out of credit. Mind if I pop up?"

"Pop-pop? What—? Where are you?"

"At the payphone outside your building. Can I come up?"

"Oh. I see. Sure. But first, very quickly—which crummy organisation was it granted you leave?"

"Bah, a little organisation we call Interpol."

"Yes. I see," said Hector, his voice dry and lean. "Come on up," he said, amid the subtle chuckle and clip of some perhaps metallic fitment finding its housing.

Calvin arrived at the landing and found the door to the flat ajar. He knocked, entered the cool foyer and announced himself, but there was no response. One eye of a cubist Picasso stared at him, the other hinted down a hall that led to the salon. He followed the regard of the second eye and after a cursory investigation of each room, declared the flat empty.

Suddenly the telephone rang. Under the influence of confusion, Calvin answered. "*Digame.*"

"Are you alone?"

"What the—? Where are you?" said Calvin.

"I'm at the payphone you just vacated," said Hector. "The receiver is still warm. Are you alone?"

"But of course I'm alone! Were you expecting an accompaniment?"

"Interpol, no doubt."

"Interpol? Bah, you needn't worry about those hacks. Oh sure, I've been committed to their books – I am officially an informant – but it has nothing to do with you. I've been charged with a very specific and ludicrous task."

"Very well. Mind if I pop-pop?"

"Pop *up*. Please do."

A half-minute later, Hector appeared from one of the rooms that flanked the salon.

"I see you've fitted this place," noted Calvin, "with multiple entries."

"More accurately," corrected Hector, "multiple exits. But yes. Café, café?"

"*Con leche. Gracias.*"

"If you don't mind," said Hector, heading towards the kitchen, "I'm rather bursting to hear anything you might be able to tell me of the task to which you've been assigned."

Hector stopped abruptly under an eave.

"Forgive me, Calvin," he said. "Have we quite sufficiently relieved you of your anxieties, before we begin to address some of my own?"

"Relieved me of my anxieties? Pah! All the same, you've helped immensely, my friend. You have given me something to think about, something to focus on—a goal, if you will. But now, honestly, you've no reason to be anxious."

Calvin sighed and threw himself on a rich sofa of chocolate leather.

"Interpol," he continued, "knows all about the running I've done for you, and believe me, they don't care in the least. Those fellows engage themselves with big dealings—international disputes of the highest order, murder, organised crime, the like. Ob*sess*ed is what they are. The swapping of Swiss cuckoos for Mexican Flycatchers? I wouldn't worry about it. They're gunning for that goddamned and cursed knife I told you about, by the way."

Hector reappeared with coffee and Spanish liqueur. "The knife Klarysa is after?"

"That's the one," Calvin confirmed. "One hell of a story behind that knife." He grinned a meek and sympathetic grin. "The poor girl has no idea who she's up against. Anyway, I'm sure she views it all with lottery odds. You can't blame a girl for dreaming."

"Are they blackmailing you?"

"Interpol? More or less." Calvin's smile turned sickly. "They want me to help them locate DeTorche."

"DeTorche."

"You recall the name."

"Of course. It was an interesting conversation we had that night. I believe you referred to him as a villain."

"And then we quibbled over the qualifications of a legend. It was a fun evening. Interpol believes he may be close to the knife. I'd be petrified if it weren't all perfectly absurd. It's inconceivable that I could be of any help in such an endeavour."

"How do you like the coffee?"

Hector's non sequiturs often had a calming effect on Calvin. "It's very good."

"Add a drop of liqueur, if you like."

Calvin complied.

"The world raves about Italian coffee," said Hector. "But I don't know. Listen, Calvin, I feel somehow responsible."

"For what?"

"Your predicament with Interpol."

"Bah, I'm telling you, they don't smash heads over marmot urine."

"Still, I would like to help you with your search. I make no guarantees, but who knows. There is just on thing, however," Hector added, diverting his eyes.

"What is it?"

Hector searched for the right words. Unable to find them, he said shamefully, as though he were favouring a business venture over protecting a son, "I'm afraid... Well, you see, I can't very well have an Interpol informant in my employ. I'm sorry. You understand."

For the second time that morning, Hector's words resonated with Calvin and woke him, as though from a long seasonal slumber.

"Why, that settles it then," said Calvin with vigour and shine. "No more running."

"I'm sorry."

Calvin leapt to his feet. "Hector, my friend, you need not apologise. In fact, I can't thank you enough. You've helped me more than you know. Now if you don't mind, I must be going. I must see Klarysa at once."

With great and unexpected intention, Calvin arrived at the familiar door on Carrer de la Providencia. His presence there surprised him as much as it did Klarysa, who, upon recognising his voice, made the *parlophone* crackle and squeal with delight.

He bounded up the stairs to the third-floor landing and found her waiting for him in the doorway. Her rump twitched like a cat's before the pounce; then she launched herself into his arms, wrapped her legs around his waist and kissed him passionately. They eventually retired into the flat and into her bedroom, where, though extremely few words were spoken, so very much was expressed.

Sometime later, at an unknown hour and with one thin line of cigarette smoke snaking its white silent way towards the ceiling from Klarysa's bedroom fingers, she said to that ceiling, "I hope autumn will arrive soon."

Calvin smiled lovingly next to her from within his haze and reckoned late September would likely continue to make a fine date for autumn's arrival.

"This summer was too hot," she said. "That kind of heat makes it hard to think straight. It was probably even hotter in France than it was here, no? It must have been; my thinking was not so good."

"When did you come back to Spain?" he asked because it seemed to be his turn to say something.

"A week ago. Ten days maybe."

"What have you been up to?"

"Not terribly much. I'm learning to cook, but it's too hot during the day for anything more than ceviche and gazpacho. No, I've not done terribly much at all."

Klarysa drew from her cigarette, disturbing the thin white line that rose from its tip, and which quickly corrected itself after she removed her lips. She held her breath for a count or two, in reflection; then exhaled a turbulent jet-stream that intercepted the line of rising white and frantically obliterated its thin white climb.

"A friend of mine," she said, "asked me to marry him last week."

"Fun. Fun," said Calvin, brought abruptly to some mental surface, now reaching for her pack of cigarettes. "Anyone I know?" he asked. The pack was empty.

"No. His name is Gerhard."

"Sounds German," he noted, as though there were no conceivable way she could be in love with a German fellow.

"Yes. But he lives in London. His English is excellent; maybe better than yours. That's saying something, don't you think?"

"How do you know old Gerhard?"

"We met in England—"

"When was that?" he interrupted.

"Almost a year ago, while I was on holiday. I was very much alone," she added, cutting into the yarn at a victim's angle.

"Around the time you and I met," he clarified.

"No, you and I met at the beginning of February. September minus February equals eight months. Gerhard and I met almost a year ago. We met under rainy skies. I was lost, you see—I don't care what anyone says, Trafalgar Square is perfectly hidden if you ask me. Gerhard was kind enough to help me find my way."

"In a world of swine, you have an uncanny nose for all the selfless gentlemen. Helped you back to your hotel after feeding the pigeons, did he?"

"Not at all. He had me stay with him at his flat. My hotel was clear on the other side of town and horribly appointed at that. What's more, he is very persuasive."

"Spare me the details. So he proposed. And what did you tell him?"

"I told him I couldn't possibly marry him—certainly not if it meant living in London. A girl can only spend so much time inside, regardless of how sweeping the flat, or how stunning the views. I need access to nature."

"You hate nature."

"That's not true at all. I love nature. I just can't stand being out in it. Anyway, the London weather is insufferable. Have you ever been?"

"Oh, fuck London! Honestly, Klarysa, did you tell him you wouldn't marry him because of the weather?"

"I said I wouldn't marry him because I'm not in love with him. Though that did nothing to keep him from coming here last week. Oh, Calvin, please don't be upset—not after all we've been through. There's really no reason for it, I swear. I told him over and over how much I love you."

Calvin, perched now upon his elbows, could only find it in himself to grumble.

"He didn't believe," she continued, "that I could love a no-account who—"

"A *no*-account!"

"That's what *he* said. But he doesn't know you like I do. I also informed him that he was rather fortunate you weren't about to hear such ideas. Why, my love, I don't care in the least that you haven't any money."

"*Grrrr*! Who was it took you to all those fancy restaurants in Nice, my little crumb cake?"

"Precisely! Why, that's exactly what I told Gerhard."

Klarysa found a long strand of hair on the duvet. She took it, studied it, wound it around the tip of her finger and said, "I guess he meant *real* money, for example."

"Where did he sleep while he was here?" Calvin demanded.

She hesitated. "Sorry?"

"I say where did he *sleep* at night when he was here, our boy Gerhard?"

Klarysa sat up straight and desperately accused, "Haven't you been listening?" Tears began to rim at her lower lids. "He is *very* persuasive!"

"Ah, Jesus," Calvin muttered, getting up from the bed. He was not angry, he simply felt a fool.

"Calvin!" she cried fearfully, clutching his wrist. "Please don't walk away. Please! I don't love him! I love you! I made him go away... eventually," she added, somewhat proud of the accomplishment, though she knew it would never impress the outside world, that slippery social sphere in which she could never quite win long-standing favour, try as she may.

Calvin sat on the edge of the bed, staring fixedly at her.

"I'm sorry," she stressed, with wet eyes. "I... I suppose I shouldn't tell you such things. I hate to hurt you. Oh, why do you *feel* so much? But isn't that a stupid thing to ask, for who can help such things? Besides, it's a beautiful quality. You are so beautiful, my love. But what am I to do? I need to tell you things. I can't lie. I don't know how to even if I wanted to."

Calvin's heart thumped before her honesty. He took her hand.

"I made him leave," she pleaded, "because I love *you*. Don't you see? I made him leave."

Smiling as best he could, Calvin said, "Please don't learn to lie. You are a beautiful woman in possession of a rare and beautiful gift, and I won't be one to muck it up. It's not easy, but I need to learn to trust your love, to be strong and patient in my listening. As for you, you might learn to say *no* once in a while, and we'll be fine."

"You're right. I will try. Part of the problem, too, is that I always say things the wrong way, unlike you. You always say the right words, the right way. I wish I could."

"Bah, if that is at all true, it's only because we always speak my language."

"No, I don't say things the right way in any language; not even in Ukrainian or Russian, or Castellano or Catalan. But you are my man and despite all my flaws – or perhaps because of them – I need to be able to tell you things. I have to get things out of my chest."

He smiled.

"Is that the right way to say it?" she asked, with her wet, uncertain eyes.

"It's perfect. *Off* your chest is good, too. But yes, perfect. You are perfect."

Lazing comfortably across the hazy plains that divided evening's sleep from morning's wakefulness, a prostrate Calvin instinctively pulled himself into the foetal position at the shriek and wail of a flock of bickering gulls, the eerie cry of which most recently coincided with the dropping of fists and forearms and heavy Interpol footwear upon the sum of his person. Having found the screams to be a false alarm, he spread himself liberally over the bed and wondered if the rabid pack of gulls had followed him over from Nice, to expressly remind him not only that he remained under surveillance, but of the hazardous consequences that would befall him were he to allow the celebration of his rekindled love affair to outshine the dim lights marking the unknown path to DeTorche.

But Calvin had his priorities straight; he needed no reminders. Why, Klarysa had in fact invited him to stay with her for the remainder of his stay in Barcelona, but he admirably fought off the temptation and declined, cleverly citing the virtues of restraint and patience, while keeping secret his ties to Interpol and the task to which he had been assigned. He was certain that any mention of the knife or Interpol would only unsettle her and jeopardise the delicate foundation of peace and tranquillity he was newly determined to build with her. How he wished the damned knife had never existed. In the race for the Omega, he and Klarysa had, in a sense, been pitted against one another.

The moon had long ceded the skies to the sun. Calvin lay on the bed, fatigued and disheartened to have not slept through the night. It was the first sleepless night he had suffered since coming face-to-face with those he considered his spooks. He lay on the bed and came close to wishing that he could pray.

He was early for his rendez-vous with Klarysa, so he sat on a bench in Plaça Rovira and checked to see that he had everything – a baguette, a few slices of *pata negra*, aged *manchego*, a baton of *fuet*, a mélange of olives, ripe melon, fresh juice, a chilled bottle of cava – all the necessities for a regal afternoon feast. At the agreed-upon hour, he rang at Klarysa's door. He rang a second time and then a third time and eventually the *parlophone* did crackle to life. Klarysa's voice sounded meekly through the speaker, as though from a world away. "*Digame.*"

"Klarysa? It's me, Calvin."

"Oh. *Hola, mi amor.*"

"Are you coming down?"

Something was clearly amiss.

"Is everything OK?" he asked. "I can run up if you need more time."

"No. I'm sorry, Calvin," she said.

He felt the familiar tip of a great blade touching his sternum.

"I can't to-day," she said. "It won't be possible."

"Are you OK?"

"*Si, si.* I…" she faltered. "Yes, I'm OK."

"Bah, Klarysa, what is it? Can we talk? Just for a minute? Then I'll leave you alone, if that's what you prefer."

"No, no. It's quite impossible," she began, but her voice fell away quickly, as though something had pulled her away from the *parlophone*. Then she was back. "I'm afraid it's not possible to-day, *mi amor.*"

"Klarysa, listen—are you OK?"

"*Si, si, si,*" she insisted. "Perfect, actually. Can we meet to-morrow instead? Same time?"

"Sure," he conceded. "No problem. But can I just…" but he stopped, sparing himself the ridiculousness of posing the same questions over and over.

"No, no," she replied all the same. "Thank you. I'm OK. To-morrow it will be perfect. I promise."

"You don't need to make promises," he said.

There was a bite to his words. Promises, after all, were issued to allay uncertainty and pending disappointment in another. Calvin had resolved to categorically deny himself his uncertainty and disappointment, and her promise reached him as a lack of faith in his ability to be durable and stout of heart. He corrected his tone and said, "Well. You know where I'm staying if you need—"

But she clipped him short. "No, no," she said, which caused him to curse heatedly, if silently and just once. "I'll see you to-morrow," she added in conclusion. "Same time."

She had rendered him speechless. In his frustration, he decided to hang up on her, but as it is not possible to call off from the street-end of a *parlophone* conversation, it was *she* who inevitably hung up on *him*, which caused him, yet again, to curse, this time rather audibly indeed and more than just once.

Calvin took the metro back down to Barceloneta, shoved the groceries into the frigo and hit the streets, frustrated and huffing. He didn't mind the grind, the work, the sacrifice, the compromise; he just didn't want to be made to feel a fool in doing so. A simple call to inform him that she needed to reschedule would have sufficed. No, no, he quickly censured himself for another disagreeable rise of pride and selfishness. Had he not, just the day before, bemoaned the notion that his foolish pride and selfishness were to blame for the deaths of Victoria and Willie Rush? He calmed himself for Klarysa's sake and for his own, focused his thoughts on the unexpected thrill of his reengagement with her and felt instantly better, if not exceedingly so.

It was a lovely September day. He resolved to spend it walking, walking and walking. It was a strategy as much as a pastime, really, intent as he was to leave his wangling mind no extra energy with which it might bait and needle him after dark and keep him from falling asleep when he finally lay down to bed. He walked Gran Via in the thick shade of trees made plump with overripe leaves and accessed Montjuic via Plaça d'Espanya. By seven o'clock that evening, he had not only walked Montjuic, but also the barrios of Sarrià, Pedralbes, Sants, Les Corts and Eixample Esquerra.

Every wanderer understands that intimate long-term relationships are a commodity that often go squandered in the pursuit of novelty and adventure, though even the wanderer will occasionally feel distress when there are no prospects of chancing upon an old friend in the streets and alleyways. Sometimes the price of chasing radiant fantasies is a long hike home through the marshes of seclusion and loneliness.

Having finally stopped for a cold beer on the terrace of a non-descript *cerveceria*, he reflected on just how badly he wished he were in the company of a few good mates. He thought of Arbuckle and Polish, Gem and the Butcher and the rest of the crew. How happy it would make him to stand them all a few drinks, to lounge about with them in sweet fatigue and lob back and forth memories and anecdotes from the voluminous crew annals. When one is tired, he finds comfort in known commodities, and for all the times Calvin had wished for a few brief moments of peace and solitude, there he was missing his beloved crack-pot crew and hoping all was agreeable back in Nice.

It was too early to be dozing off on the terrace of an unknown *cerveceria*, and too early to go back to the flat and call it a night. He decided to walk about a bit longer and eventually wind his way back to the flat. Crossing over Gran Via at Universitat, he made his way slowly towards La Rambla, the plagued centre attraction that had been a river in the days of ancient Barcino. One could not help but feel relatively healthy and justified in the midst of the low-rent spectacle and contagion that came to clog the once beautiful artery.

The city's guests and residents seemed to move about the streets only in pairs or better. Every fellow, it seemed, was coupled to another; millions of them, all hand-in-hand or arm-in-arm, all moving about as unfettered as the rising moon. Astounding, thought Calvin, feeling sorry for himself—everybody in the entire whoring city has somebody. The young and the old, the fat, the fit and the gaunt, the beauties and the hags, the queers and the straight, the kinky and the classy, the boring and the bored, the junkies, the delinquents and the suits, the cheaters and the just, the rich and the wretched and the abject and even the homeless, God bless them all.

Adrift in Barcelona during any season, at any time of the day or night, one had the impression that its citizens were carrying out tasks in preparation of a great fiesta, and most often, one could not help but feel drawn into its merriment. Other times, the festivity felt reserved for others and one was left feeling irrelevant, outside the periphery of some convivial secret. Calvin tried to deny his self-pity, but the joy and laughter seemed to congregate inaccessibly on the other side of any street, or in one small *plaça* or another, which he could only just make out at the end of a long alleyway. His head hung low. When he lifted his eyes, he saw only signs for peep shows, solicitations to drug deals and quick flops. Here a jolly whore, there a soiled fellow with a missing arm, now women with bandaged feet, then blokes with lacerated faces and bandages over their eyes. He felt the weight and hunger of their stares as he passed, as though they had been expecting him, as though he had finally arrived and what the hell had taken him so long.

But not one person walked alone. The only unaccompanied fellows were the mimes and jugglers and prostitutes, all of whom defended their square patches of La Rambla, and were unaccompanied only while they worked. One lifeless mime in an endless string of lifeless mimes, covered from tip to toe in bronze body paint and random accessories of faux armour, to affect the disturbing guise of some queer medieval automata, came whipping into a veritable frenzy of animation for exactly three seconds when the tentative hand of a very small child dropped a silver coin into its sauce pan-cum-helmet, and then fell back into a deep coma. The small child, refused of a second coin by his father, screamed his living lungs out.

Everywhere he looked, Calvin saw the snapping of photos before landmarks and statues and under stone archways and striped awnings, cooing and kissing, the reprimanding of over-exuberant children, the loss of patience, displays of disapproval and the voicing of sharp-edged words intended only to punish, the loss of direction, the navigation of winding alleyways, the cursing out of all blasted civilisations that chose to forego the irrefutable logic of rectilinear grid plans.

Pick-pockets, like most fellows with a job to do, pick first the low-hanging fruit—those they believe will offer little threat should the job go awry. To be sure, the metaphorical tree in question would have to be picked rather clean before one would have a go at picking Calvin. Nevertheless, there in the overripe pre-harvest orchard that is high-season Barcelona, Calvin was so picked. The execution of the pick, however, was bungling and crude and immediately detected. Spinning about, Calvin saw a powder-blue hood disappear among the tourist throng. His eyes widened and flashed green and a crafty smile spread evenly across his face. Finally, he thought, a bit of action to brighten the rising night!

Wasting no time, he licked his chops and gave chase. In the pursuit that ensued, no more than a few comatose mimes and several screaming brats were toppled. The hooded figure did not so much run, as call on a certain grace and lubricity in slipping deftly in and out of tight spaces in the crowd. Eventually, the thief shot off La Rambla and onto a quiet alleyway in the Barri Gòtic; an ostensibly foolish move, for there, free of obstacles and hindrances, Calvin quickly gained ground on the fleeing bunny, who advanced with the sleekness of shadows, and in doing so, cut an undeniably alluring figure.

In short order, somewhere between the Plaça del Teatre and the Passeig de Colom, in a small *plaça* whose perimeter was dominated by massive palms, the assailant halted, wheeled and faced Calvin, who in turn locked up and skidded to a stop before his quarry.

There, gathering a soft tropical light that seemed to emanate from the night sea, shimmered the big brown eyes of a girl with whom Calvin had wanted to remain strangers. She pulled back her hood and shook free a cascade of loose curls in Bulgarian rose.

"Blanche Neige!" Calvin gasped.

"Calvin Stony!" she replied, mockingly.

He held her at bay with his eyes and quickly patted himself down.

"I didn't take anything," she said. "I don't pick pockets."

"Ah! Such crimes are beneath Interpol, is that it?" he said scornfully.

"Of course," she condescended. "The aim of Interpol is to uphold the law, not break it."

"Ha!" burst Calvin. "Forgive my abused and blackmailed bones should they deign to disagree with you!"

"Anyway," she shrugged dismissively, "I'm not with Interpol."

"Oh, no? Well, *I am*!" he demanded, amazed and incredulous.

In the waning light, she admired her nails, freshly painted a soft and pretty heliotrope. "Not really, you're not," she said.

Her calm incensed him. "Who are you, and how the devil would you know one way or the other?"

"You might say I'm with the other side. Keep your friends close and your enemies closer. That's an adage, I think." She giggled charmingly. "I'm just kidding; you're not an enemy. Not mine, anyway."

"We sure as hell aren't friends," he slung at her.

Standing before her now, he remembered the effectiveness of her pout—quizzical, adorable.

An unseasonably cool breeze stirred the palm fronds overhead. Had Klarysa known something? Would autumn arrive early?

"I'm sorry," he apologised, as though for having shattered her faith. "But we're not."

"We danced together," she said, with dark glistening eyes. "You held me."

She frowned at the wind for having tussled her hair, and led an errant run of loose curls away from her lips and back behind her ear. "You were mean to me that night, too."

"Oh, I was not," he said, recalling the scent of her hair and that of her lips. "Not terribly, anyway. As for to-night, what do you expect? We met in Nice some months ago, and now you're in Barcelona trying to pick my pocket."

"It is no coincidence, that much is true—though I had no intention of picking your pocket. I only wanted to lure you away to a quiet place where we could talk."

"Start talking, then. If you're not with Interpol, who *are* you with? Give me that much. And hell, have the decency to tell me if I'm in for another beating. *I* may not deserve all the answers, but these poor bones of mine are innocent pawns in this whole wicked affair, and they're none too happy with the quality of care under my charge, I can tell you."

He allowed himself to be led over to one of the benches at the edge of the *plaça*, where she sat facing him and he sat facing the sea.

"I work for DeTorche," she said.

Calvin sat pensively, with his elbows on his knees, looking out to sea, out beyond the sea. At some point, Blanche had turned so that she, too, was facing the sea.

"He's here, in Barcelona," she said. "He wants to see you to-morrow."

Neither of them said anything further.

Calvin sat at a table for two at a café of wood and marble on La Rambla de Catalunya. He had awakened that morning nervous and anxious from a night of little sleep. But seated there now at the table with a tall, beaded *tubo* of gin and tonic, he was neither nervous nor anxious. He had nothing to fear after all; he was no threat to DeTorche and had done the man no wrong. And what if he had? What if DeTorche had designs, justified or otherwise, on teaching Calvin a thing or two? Why, if so, Calvin was prepared to step up and play his role, take his beating like a good lad. Why not, he thought. It would mean another winning anecdote to recount sometime in the future, after release from hospital. And should there be no release from hospital, then finally an end to the madness.

It was not this dark rationalisation that eased Calvin's nerves, however. And it sure as hell was not the gin. Rather, Calvin had the propensity, when spurned, to flirt with the edge, and the worse his luck in love, the more he was willing to risk in the pursuit of a thrill—or, more accurately, the less he felt there was to lose, should the thrill come armed and dangerous.

No, he had not nearly given up on Klarysa, but her peculiar lunch cancellation just hours prior – the second cancellation in as many days – left him greatly discouraged. Once again he had arrived at Klarysa's building with the picnic items, and once again he had rung the bell, but this time the *parlophone* never came to life. As he was standing in the street in a kind of stupor, the door suddenly opened and in its frame stood the *portera*, the Brezhnev of Catalunya. Having no desire to spar with the large mammal, he started off, when she called to him, "*Ella no esta aqui.*"

Calvin turned to face her, and said with defeat, "*Si. Yo sé.*"

The *portera* grumbled a bit, as she had during their initial encounter, those months prior, but missing from her former repertoire was the intense look of disapproval. On the contrary, there was a note of sympathy in her grumbling. She handed Calvin a small note. It was from Klarysa. He thanked her, took it and walked off.

The note offered very little information and brought very little relief. Klarysa was dreadfully sorry to have to cancel another lunch, she loved him very much, she hoped they would be able to meet that evening and would he mind calling back at nine o'clock.

Calvin took a draught of gin as a fine deliberate man in smart attire entered the café. The man carried a cane that boasted a polished blackthorn shaft, ringed at the top in gold and a handle of turquoise stone fashioned in the shape of a duck's head, its bill just visible beyond the man's elegant grip.

"Calvin," he voiced in a rich, easy tone.

Calvin smiled an indescribable smile. "DeTorche?" he asked.

The man nodded unapologetically.

Calvin looked not at him, but into him, by way of an unbroken stare.

How to describe the stare. What if, say, one fellow was approached by another, and this second fellow dropped upon the table at which the first was seated, a large box with some tens of thousands of sheets of paper, each covered recto-verso in small-font text. The seated fellow begins reading the first line of the first page and discovers that it describes his own birth. He continues reading and soon realises the text is an exhaustive record of his own life in impossibly painstaking detail. He reaches deep into the stack, selects a page and happens upon the details of that very moment in his life—the meal he is eating, the approach of the stranger, the lifting of the lid from the box containing the strange manuscript, so forth and so on, all impeccably committed to written record. He reaches deeper into the stack and reads accounts of his life that are yet to take place; every moment, great and mundane, in the same meticulous detail. Finally, thoroughly baffled, he looks up at the second fellow and demands an explanation, "Who did this?" he asks, however certain that it could only be the work of an omniscient and omnipresent god. The second fellow looks upon him agreeably and without fanfare and says simply, "I did."

As fantastic as such a scenario would be, if it were indeed to take place, the first fellow might well stare into the second by way of the same unbroken stare as that with which Calvin now stared into DeTorche.

After a moment, Calvin broke off his regard, puffed once or twice and took another hit of gin. In response to DeTorche's subtle gesture, Calvin said, "Yes, of course. Sit."

DeTorche pulled out the chair and sat. Finesse and finish reflected from even his slightest movements.

"Ah, yes," began Calvin with a whiff of false flattery, "the hands. They do not exaggerate—every bit as smooth as church mice."

DeTorche sat with one leg over the other, hands joined in his lap, the shaft of the cane in his effortless grip, its duck's head staring at Calvin.

"I bet you," challenged Calvin, "that under the unyielding flesh of that long blackthorn neck, your duck sports a double-edged spine of sharp tempered steel."

DeTorche smiled. "I would have to refuse that bet. It has never drawn blood, though."

"Fine. What will you drink?"

DeTorche called over a waiter, ordered a whisky and invited Calvin to order what he would. Without pause, Calvin asked for a bottle of champagne.

"Cava?" the waiter asked.

"No," barked Calvin. "Champagne."

The waiter politely informed him that they had no champagne, and tactfully assured him that their best bottle of cava would surpass Calvin's errant prejudices.

"It will have to do," said Calvin boorishly.

DeTorche's easy smile never broke, but his eyes betrayed a sense of embarrassment.

"You *did* call me here, after all," defended Calvin. "This was your idea."

"True," admitted DeTorche, nodding patiently. "If I understand correctly, however, you were looking for me. I am not entirely comfortable when I know a man is looking for me, you understand. I thought I would present myself to you, make your job a simple one, eliminate any of the unnecessary intrigue and false mystery that all too often clouds otherwise clear and rational minds."

Having temporarily lost his composure before DeTorch, Calvin suddenly regained his focus and realised the great value of this unexpected encounter.

"You're right," he said and jumped from his chair.

"DeTorche caught him by the arm before he could pass. "But where are you going?"

"To cancel the bottle of cava. That was extremely poor of me."

"Nonsense. Sit. Sit."

Calvin took his seat and sat in silence, sullenly staring out the window at a bulbous bronze sculpture of a great whiskered cat, and vacillated along a short, mystifying arc that divided the poles of gratitude and betrayal.

The drinks were served. As DeTorche filled a flute for Calvin, the latter said, "There is still the matter of the knife."

"The Omega," DeTorche confirmed.

"I understand you are one of its pursuers."

"One of many; yes."

"Lousy goddamned knife," mumbled Calvin.

"I understand your frustration."

"Like hell you do," said Calvin. "Do you know where it is? Personally, I don't give a damn, but Interpol is rather interested."

"Most believe it to be somewhere in the South of France. I am sorry you find yourself entangled in another man's obsession."

"It is queer of a fellow to speak of himself in the third-person," said Calvin bitterly. "Own up to your obsessions, sir."

"I was not speaking of myself. I was speaking of Jean-Louis Fauré."

Calvin shot him a look, the sick look of a short-sighted pawn falling forward, flailing, suddenly realising that the thin sticky line over which he had tripped was in fact the exterior thread of a complex interrelated web woven by the spinnerets of several competing factions.

"You know Jean-Louis Fauré?" Calvin asked tentatively.

"Of course. In a way, Jean-Louis and I are bound. We are brothers in a sense, which makes for unusual adversaries, though adversaries we are, to be sure. He and I worked together many years ago, for the Institut National des Appelations d'Origine. Jean-Louis was my superior; I was one of his many direct reports. Despite his flaws, Jean-Louis is a fine man, upstanding and principled. He would not say the same of me. I am an independent, a man of leisure. I always have been. My lack of what Jean-Louis considers a requisite degree of motivation was a source of gnawing agony for him. We quit the organisation at different times, and for different reasons. I left first, to pursue... shall we say *independent engagements*. Jean-Louis left some years later and became a man of the law, eventually joining Interpol. I had long come to accept from him a certain manner of kindred presence in my life, but I had not expected such a tangible, physical presence—a near constant shadowing, if you will. Jean-Louis is relentless in his pursuits. He is a true... *limier*."

"Bloodhound."

"Yes, a bloodhound. I left the INAO with many advantageous contacts in France and the former Soviet republics. One night I had arranged a rendez-vous at a *brasserie* in an unknown corner of Kiev. When I arrived, there was Jean-Louis, alone at a table for two, with a plate of *varenyky* and a bottle of Bourgogne, averting his knowing eyes from the bound exploits of Eugène François Vidocq only long enough to establish mutual recognition of one another's presence and thereby ruining the deal. It was maddening; no matter how clandestine my rendez-vous, there was Jean-Louis, waiting for me. How he was able to stay one step ahead of me I'll never know. The obsessed have their means. As I diversified my dealings and expanded the territorial boundaries of my business engagements, I came to realise that he only shadowed me on attempted dealings in France and the former Soviet republics. Naturally, I avoided those regions and the hounding ceased."

"He *is* obsessed and he does have ample means," said Calvin. "Why, then, is he using me to find you?"

"You have misinterpreted the true nature of your task. A couple years ago, rumours began to surface of the Omega's location in the South of France. Though only rumours, they were the first leads of any type in years and Jean-Louis gave them his full attention. He needs no help in finding me, but if he feels he is getting close to the Omega, he will assign all official resources to finding it, and use unofficial resources, like you, to keep an eye on me."

"What do you have on him?" Calvin asked directly.

"I'm sorry; I don't follow."

"In the way of dirt, I mean," he clarified. "You must have something on him—damaging evidence, proof of wrong-doing, recorded indiscretions, compromising photos. What keeps him from having you locked up?"

"Bah, he doesn't want me locked up. He can't afford it. He needs me. Beyond the resources afforded him through Interpol – all of which are leashed, so to speak, by the letter of the law – I am the best chance he has of finding the Omega."

"But how would your possession of the Omega benefit Jean-Louis? Surely, you won't risk your neck for the damned thing only to hand it over to him."

"Oh, I don't know," said DeTorche, with resignation. "There are considerations beyond oneself."

"Oh! Forgive my surprise over such a selfless admission. What sort of considerations?"

"Familial."

"But of course," said Calvin distastefully. "A wife? A child? How many, then? Two children? Three?"

DeTorche said nothing for a count; he only bestowed upon Calvin the same patient smile he had worn since his arrival at the café. "No, no," he said evenly. "No wife, no children. I am referring to an older sister, whom I love very much. She has a son – my nephew – and he has a boy who will be three-years-old in October. They are the family to which I refer."

"And do they know you?" asked Calvin pointedly.

"Of course—"

"I mean do they know the real you, the myth behind the man? Are they aware of your activities, your métier?"

The two men locked eyes, and for a moment DeTorche stowed his patient smile.

"Everyone I care about," he said, "knows the real me; or at least a very significant and genuine part of me."

"But do they know all of you?" Calvin pushed.

"*All* of me? Don't be absurd. Every fellow is due genuineness from his fellow man, even if the extent of their contact should fail to extend beyond a single random passing. But no one person, regardless of standing or relation, is due *all* of any other person— neither a husband his wife, nor a mother her daughter. Every fellow reserves at least some part of himself for himself alone, if only with the hope of clinging, however meekly, to some semblance of personal-truth and identity.

"Coming back to the knife," DeTorche concluded, his eyes still trained to Calvin's and pausing respectfully to obtain Calvin's permission to continue.

Calvin nodded the consent of the powerless and DeTorche continued. "Were I to secure the Omega, I would gladly hand it over to Jean-Louis. After all, what is the Omega to me if its possession means a life on the run from a band of rabid pursuers? What is it to me if its possession means my sister will forever lose her husband, her son his father, and the littlest his grandfather?"

Calvin's face went sour. "My god," he said, tamping down images of incest. "You're not married to your *sis*ter, are you?"

DeTorche's patient smile returned and held steady on his lips for a short moment. Then, against his will, the smile bloomed to fullness. He looked away, as his long, slender frame came to shake and rumble quietly in suppressed, near noiseless laughter. A tight fist pressed to his pursed lips helped him regain his composure.

"No, no," he said, straightening himself, his eyes still humid with laughter. "My beloved sister has been married for some twenty-five years to Jean-Louis Fauré. Jean-Louis is my brother-in-law. His son is my nephew. His grandson is my great nephew."

DeTorche allowed Calvin a moment of quiet reflection and then continued. "Jean-Louis and my sister met at an end-of-year holiday gala while he and I were both still with the INAO. Their meeting detonated the fireworks that accompany a genuine *coup de foudre* and by the following year's gala, they were married and expecting. Jean-Louis was a loving husband and a good father, but over the course of time, his obsession with the Omega rose like the waters of a flooding river, gained mass and momentum and overflowed all reasonable boundaries of acceptability, eventually eroding the roots of domestic bliss. He and my sister eventually separated. And though they have only ever had eyes for one another, they have lived as though divorced for more than a decade, both made miserable by the loss of the other and the disintegration of the family. And to-day my nephew is a young father, a young father who is estranged to his father by the curse of obsession.

"So while I know that Jean-Louis will never have me arrested, he knows equally well that I would never deal the Omega were I to get my hands on it. We are adversaries; there is no way around the fact. He does not approve of me. But we are, nevertheless, partners and family."

"Astounding!" exclaimed Calvin, inspired by such revelations. "*I* was given a knife, you know. Jean-Louis was convinced it was the Omega. He may well still believe, though he never saw it."

Calvin contemplated the impossible authenticity of the knife he once had.

"Hell," he continued, "the damned thing *has* gone mysteriously missing, which agrees with all I've heard about the Omega."

"The obsessed chase out onto weak branches even the most unlikely of leads—"

"That bastard brother-in-law of yours," Calvin interrupted, "brought me to the brink of the afterlife."

"—and then act fearfully, regrettably," concluded DeTorche, "when the branches break. The knife you were given was not the Omega."

"Impossible, right? All the same, it was quite a knife. Had you seen it, you may have—"

"I have seen it," said DeTorche. "I have seen it, I have held it, I have since discarded it as junk."

"But how..." Calvin began, and then fell silent. His face crumpled in anticipation of another verbal bombshell.

"Gem gave it to me," said DeTorche.

"Gem!" Calvin spat, displeased to find that his best mate had been one of the many spokes in a dangerous, spinning wheel, at the centre of which slowly spun Calvin the dumb hub.

DeTorche explained that he had known Gem through numerous dealings with the owner of the boat Gem captained. Gem had approached DeTorche some months prior, having learnt that Calvin had come into chance possession of an old ornate knife. As a port is the illegitimate brain-centre of any port-town, the place where inside information on illicit activities and dodgy goings-on is bought, sold and bartered, the right fellow could obtain such information on the cheap and easy. Gem was one such fellow, and had long known the rumoured details of the Russian collectibles heist, the curious crate that Aloysius had been asked to store at his shop and the recent prevalence of Russian artefacts and antiques in Vieux Nice.

Gem had never fully entertained the notion that Calvin was in possession of the Omega, but he would take no chances. One night at the Whales, Gem enlisted the aid of a girl Calvin had come to know only as Blanche Neige – a codename assigned to her by Interpol – Christian name Lucy. While Lucy distracted Calvin on the dance floor, Gem slipped over to Calvin's flat, broke in, removed the knife and delivered it to DeTorche. Gem, as is already known, returned to the Whales and proceeded to lose his wallet.

Calvin felt deceived upon learning of Gem's clandestine actions. Having passed thousands of hours on open waters, however, Gem knew, for example, not to tell a swimmer when a shark suddenly appeared in the vicinity. Instead, one enticed the swimmer quickly and calmly back onto the boat without any mention of the danger that eminently lurked. Calvin suffered a sound beating all the same, but Gem hedged and Calvin was still alive to tell about it, so there was that.

24   In the manner of toy dolls

In which Calvin finds a mirror
and Klarysa's lips freeze, as
though in mid-kiss.

"You're the best!" she said.

It was one hell of a consolation, he thought despondently.

Drained of their pent up tensions and frustrations, Calvin fell away from the mountain top, the summit, her precious alter, the lush antechamber to her power. He fell away, both of them exhausted of a mutual aching to be handled, groped, held, breathlessly and ruthlessly desired, fell away to face the long companionless descent into a cold valley, kept marginally warm by fading memories of the clear views from the peak on which they did their loving, fleeting, groaning best to convince one another of their relevance as young, able individuals on at least one arid square meter of Iberian earth.

Calvin soon discovered that he could not asleep. Long before he arrived at that conclusion, she had begun to snore like a lumberjack.

The lights in the flat were controlled by the twisting of knobs shaped like tiny water faucets. Calvin found one on the bathroom wall and gave it a quarter turn. A wan, fatigued light woke above the sink. The rest of the flat remained mercifully dark, lit only by a quarter-moon, and silent. On the wall above the sink, he found what he was looking for, that which he both needed and feared—a mirrored reflection of himself. It was not the quality of the image he would find staring back at him that caused him fear, but rather the visual proof of his presence there in the foreign, dishevelled flat. A fellow can hide out in the mind and forge truths from falsehoods, but mirrors tend to strip an honest man of his illusions and present him with hard facts. Mirrors do not withhold the truth from honest, seeking eyes. All the same, Calvin was desperate for signs of life, for proof of his existence, though not in any metaphysical or existential sense. On the contrary, the desperation that riddled him demanded tangible, physical proof of his flesh and bones, his blinking eyes, his beating heart. He needed a reflection of himself. He needed to poke and prod and study the reaction, as one does before purchasing the vehicle that is to be driven off the lot at top speed, to somewhere far away, never to return.

He leaned in close to the mirror, opened his mouth wide, blinked his wide eyes several times and tried out various grimaces and false smiles. He slapped himself across the face and beat his chest. He took mental note of himself, there in the flesh. Despite all, everything more or less checked out. The gash along his jaw-line had bled with the glistening viscosity he had come to count on – at once beautiful and frightening evidence of life – and had closed as it was supposed to after a half-hour of applied pressure. Never before had Calvin gone so absentminded while shaving. He hadn't noticed the cut until the bleed had traversed the creamy lather on his neck, trickled over the collar bone and started down his chest. Now studying himself in the mirror, the gash no longer twinkled. It laid still and ugly, sealed off by a dark thin shiv of dried blood.

He twisted open the hot-water tap and then tried the other, only to realise after several minutes that the water would remain icy, regardless. The tiles underfoot were cold; so then became his feet and soon the entirety of his naked body. He plugged the sink and let it fill, then splashed the cold water over his face and head, his arms and arm pits and chest, and patted himself dry with the grey hand-towel that hung over the shower curtain.

He had never before heard someone say that he was *the best*.

It had, indeed, been a singular day, unique not only for the accolade. The meeting with DeTorche had come to a clean and effortless close, with DeTorche offering to negotiate Calvin's release from duty as an Interpol informant. Calvin walked back to his flat from the rendez-vous a free man, high from the bottle of cava and his recent accomplishments.

He had even dispensed of his anger and tension over Klarysa's second lunch cancelation. By way of the note handed over to him by the *portera*, Klarysa promised they would meet that night, and he would have a wealth of exciting news to share.

He killed the wan light and watched out the bathroom window. Down below, under the Spanish night, street lights sparkled brilliantly. A neon sign in the distance glowed red, unblinking: HOTEL. He watched it all with the ease of the anonymous, in the comfort of darkness. He thought to return to the bed, but was suddenly held at the window by a familiar query—who, of anyone he knew, would he most like to find in the bed when he returned? The answer was always the same. He decided to stay upright a bit longer.

Though it seemed like days to Calvin, no more than eight or nine hours had passed since Klarysa had rung. He had been shaving. He pressed the receiver to his ear, with his neck and half his face still covered in shave cream. "Just you wait 'til you hear about my day," he said excitedly. "You won't believe it."

His newly won freedom had given him the hope and optimism he needed to shed his most recent insecurities and doubts concerning Klarysa and her agenda following the consecutive lunch cancellations. Aborted lunch plans or no, in the last twenty-four hours he had quit Hector and met with the phantom DeTorche. And just like that, Calvin was free. Free! It took guts and perseverance and he now looked forward to leveraging that same spirit and determination to make good with Klarysa.

"We have a lot to celebrate," he informed her. "I'll tell you all about it when I get to your place."

"Oh, love," she broke. "I'm afraid I won't be there when you arrive."

He flinched at her impossible disclosure, causing the razorblade to cut deeply along the length of his jaw.

"What on earth," he launched nastily, "makes you think I'm going to trudge all the way up to Gracia yet again if you have no intention of *being* there when I arrive?"

She was most often sincerely confused by the angles of his attack. "But I don't think you'll... I mean, why *would* you? I just said I won't be there."

He regretted the pettiness of his attacks. Nevertheless, the regret often mixed with his justified frustration and resulted in a maddening froth.

"But *why*, Klarysa?" he demanded, bereft of patience. "That's what I want to know. *Why*? *Why* won't you be there? *Why*?"

There was no immediate response. Somewhere in the background he heard several voluble male voices, possibly speaking French.

"Say something," he said, as blood ran unnoticed over his collar bone. "Where are you?"

He listened to the sound of her breathing. Beyond that there was only silence.

"I have to go," she said finally.

"We have to meet," he replied flatly, as though he hadn't heard her.

"Yes, of course."

"To-night. Nine o'clock."

"I can't to-night," she said.

"But you wrote nine o'clock. I have the note to prove it."

"I know perfectly well what I wrote, but I can't to-night after all."

"We can't go on like this, Klarysa. I need to see you. Give me five minutes, for crissake. That's it. Five lousy minutes. Can you give me that?"

"Of course," she said sharply. "I can give you that and much more, only not to-night."

"Why not?"

"Because I can't. I'm very sorry, Calvin."

"But you don't understand. Listen," he said desperately, "I'm done running. And I'm done with Interpol. It's all over."

"Interpol?" she questioned in a forceful whisper.

"Yes! Don't you see? I'm free!"

"Free from what?" she asked.

"Look," he said, "I need you right now. I need you to show me something, anything. Keep our rendez-vous, Klarysa. It's important to me. Give me something to believe in."

"Free from *what*?" she insisted.

"Interpol," he said impatiently. "I'll tell you all about it. Give me five minutes."

"I *am* giving you five minutes. Is this about the knife? Tell me."

"Not like this! Five minutes. Face-to-face."

"I'm sorry," she said. "I can't."

"But you refuse to tell me why."

"And you refuse to wait."

"*I have been waiting, goddamn it!*" he exploded. "Five minutes, Klarysa. To-night. Five fucking minutes!"

"Please, Calvin. Just a bit longer. I'm asking you to please understand."

"But what are you asking me to understand?"

"That I can't see you to-night! Christ, you—!" She quickly regained her composure. "Calvin, my love, come over to-morrow night. I have to go now. I'm sorry. Please understand."

He remained silent.

"Calvin, please. Tell me you understand."

Had it been success or failure that placed him there—a Garfield boy, semi-lost at four o'clock in the morning, cold, naked, in a moonlit ice-water bathroom watching neon glass glow tirelessly somewhere over a beat northern barrio? What did it matter? Either way, he felt it all, every twitch of life—he knew he was alive. Time is short and there are no miracles. Regardless of the existence of any god or gods, there never *were* any miracles. A fellow makes his way as best he can, knowing all the while that death pursues him with flawless execution, and until the bell tolls for him, he grinds and scrapes and digs and sometimes he gets lucky and sometimes he doesn't. HOTEL in red neon. Always watching, always wondering what was happening beyond the horizon, always eager for the next experience. At that moment, Calvin felt potent, tempered and dreadfully alone. He felt a vague urge to walk the night, to track the red neon.

He left the bathroom, nearly tripped over two bicycles in the hallway and came to stand in the eave of a large kitchen. Spanish kitchens of any size were sad rooms that would always remind him of Victoria. Lit only by what there was of the moon, dark silhouettes of dirty dishes climbed high towards the ceiling. No part of the countertops was free of dirty dishes or debris. The things we miss, he pondered, when chasing the night. Dirty dishes, dirty kitchen, dirty flat—what are the chances the body was clean?

No, he had never been called *the best*. Never once. He had never won any trophies, never scored a winning goal. Several hours prior, with the gash from the razorblade still winking red, he taped a wad of toilet paper to his jaw, stomped out into the narrow streets and headed for the Barri Gòtic. He entered a no-name bar, a stale dive, with the toilet paper still taped to his jaw, and let all the crooked stares wash over him. He slammed a few shots of a dirty liquid poured from an unlabeled bottle and felt somewhat improved, a couple inches taller. He muttered ravings under his breath to encourage more looks. Let them all watch. He left, entered the next bar and ordered something dark and reprimanding. It did the trick. He was that much taller, even better than the best.

Several hours later, soused and feeling like the devil's rag, he entered a sticky dive on a poorly lit alleyway in el Raval and threw himself onto a stool at the end of the bar, next to a great Swedish bear. He ordered a glass of bourbon. The Swede wondered aloud whether it wasn't still too warm out for bourbon. He assured her that bourbon knew no seasonal limitations; then ordered one for her and told her to judge for herself.

She was a big girl, the Swede, with astonishingly blue eyes, a beautiful round face, skin that demanded of a fellow far more discipline and restraint than Calvin had to keep from reaching out and touching it, and long waterslide curls of blonde hair. A big, solid, provincial girl; the kind of girl a fellow watches because it is pleasant to do so, though he may marvel: what if she shed a good few stone?

Like Calvin, the Swede had been stood up, so together they drank bourbon, cursed the dire ambiance of the bar, drank more bourbon, argued good-naturedly (the way one only can with a big girl), laughed and eventually left the bar in favour of the taxi stand at Plaça Catalunya. The queue at the taxi stand was long, but they joined the end of it despite their impatience and animal urgings. Taxis arrived frequently at Plaça Catalunya and almost immediately, one pulled up. Before it had come to a complete stop, however, three rambunctious punks approached from nowhere, ignoring the queue, and made for the car.

"Hey!" chimed Calvin anxiously, prodding those in front of him to look alive, but no one said a word, no one objected.

Without the slightest hesitation, he grabbed the big Swede by the wrist and pulled her after him, towards the taxi.

Calvin reached the open car door as the three lads were about to pile in. He grabbed the lad closest to the back bench seat, flung him aside and allowed the Swede to slide in.

"Back off!" Calvin threatened. "There's a lady here, for crissake!"

The three lads were perfectly stunned. Calvin closed the door and climbed in on the other side.

"*Donde vas?*" asked the driver.

Having regained their wits, the lads began to rap on the window with fists and profane gestures.

"Ignore them," said the Swede uncertainly when she saw Calvin scowling. "They're just kids."

"*Donde vas?*" the driver urged.

"*Kids!*" Calvin cracked, his teeth shining menacingly at them through the back window. "I know these kids! Damn if I wasn't one of them! We *will* learn," he promised, "but there is only one way to teach us!"

He jumped out of the taxi and trudged around the car towards them. They continued to berate him, as though unaware of the actions such words and gestures often induced. Without pause Calvin smacked the nearest lad in the mouth and watched him crumple to the ground. The other two froze for a beat, blank-faced, and then quickly moved away to a safer distance. Those in the taxi queue were rendered silent, aghast.

"What is wrong with you lot!" cried Calvin. "*Do* something! *Say* something! Or we're all doomed!"

He lifted the fallen punk to his feet. Blood coated the lad's mouth and chin. Calvin found a fresh wad of toilet paper in his pocket and shoved it into his hand; then pushed him in the direction of his mates.

"Won't anyone take a stand?" Calvin begged the silent bystanders. No one responded. He gave up and turned his attention back to the taxi, but the taxi was gone.

The kitchen was filthy. Dishes were piled high. Calvin went back to the bedroom and climbed into bed, but it wasn't Victoria who lay there asleep next to him. No, not for years. Not ever again.

It was warm under the duvet. He rolled over and turned his back on his sins and shortcomings. He needed sleep. But to-morrow! To-morrow he vowed to summon all of them – his sins, his demons, his skeletons and regrets – and together they would convene in a great hall over a long lunch for two or three hundred thousand, no expenses spared, and there he would negotiate his future through a bullhorn, to the best of his abilities.

"Please understand," Klarysa had urged. "Calvin, please. I have to go now. Tell me you understand."

The blood flowed through the shave cream, down his neck, as far as his chest.

"Sure," he said, lifelessly. "I understand."

"Good. I must go now. Meet me to-morrow night. I love you. You're the best!"

Calvin left the taxi stand mired in defeat, and had walked halfway to Barceloneta when a taxi pulled up in front of him. A window came down. Sitting in the back was the big Swede.

The Swede slept like a golden bear hibernating in a pillowed cave. Her warmth was heavenly, so cold was Calvin. He curled up against her. He longed to wake her, to kiss her, lick her, lap her up like warm honeyed milk, so very cold was he. Together they were mother sea lion with suckling pup. She was a big girl, young and firm, *museo de jamón*, walrus cow with pure satin skin.

In the early morning, with the Catalan sun ascending towards its throne, Calvin rose from the bed and dressed in the same smoky clothes from the night before. The big Swede did not budge. Calvin stood staring down at her for several minutes, wondering if it would not be too discourteous to simply leave. Finally, he bent down and kissed her not so lightly on the forehead. Nothing. Not even a twitch. He thought to check for a pulse, when all of a sudden, the sleeping beast started in with a tremendous snoring. Calvin cowered and eyed the ceiling, but the plaster appeared to be holding. He wondered after the nature of her Northern dreams—trapped mackerel, dominated tuna, captured sea turtle, so on and so forth, the fantasies carnivorous of the *ros marus* a-feed in the deep-blue sea of the subconscious. Well turned out for survival, that one there, thought Calvin. Not bad. Then he turned and left.

Calvin started back for Barceloneta and soon found himself in the small palm-lined *plaça* in which he had last sat with Blanche Neige. He sat on the same bench and tried to make sense of the previous days, but could find no traction. He had been staring mindlessly out to sea for the better part of an hour, when he heard the approach of soft-gravel footsteps at his back. He diverted no interest to it. Let the world march circles around me, he thought, until this bench sits bolted to a small island.

The steps came to a halt at his side, however, and a pleasantly surprised tenor called his name. Calvin raised his head and found Hector standing next to him.

"Calvin, what are you doing?" he asked. "Are you OK? You don't look well."

"It's not supposed to be this way," said Calvin without extending a greeting, giving voice instead to the principle thought to have dominated his thoughts for the last half-day. "I'm free," he said. "And yet, look at me."

Hector wore a dashing velour vest in grey-asparagus, a matching derby accentuated by an orange-tipped Lady Amherst quill, and a pince-nez.

"And there you are, like always," said Calvin, "annoyingly fresh and together."

"Just remember, Calvin," Hector advised, "it is all but a choice. I was just coming to see you, actually. I was worried about you. I see my intuition did not deceive me."

"I am rather obvious these days, I suppose. Good thing you didn't take the metro, you wouldn't have found me."

"Bah," puffed Hector. "Subterranean travel is for the beleaguered and disconnected. Last time I saw you," he continued, "you bounded away with rare élan. What on earth has befallen you?"

Calvin had begun recounting details from the previous evening, when I approached them from the far end of the *plaça*. It wasn't until I was standing directly before them that they fully recognised me.

"Gentlemen," I said, "put your eyes back in your heads and say something, for crissake. You're liable to make a fellow feel self-conscious."

Calvin was the first to speak; mollified, perhaps, by the rare refinement of my attire. "I wouldn't have guessed you the type to take holidays," he said.

"Bah, who says I am on holiday?"

"That suit of yours says."

"As far as I know," I began, opening the lapel of my jacket, to model the interior lining, "Isabelline linen has never precluded a man from working."

"*Is*abelline?"

"The colour of Isabella Archduchess of Austria's undergarments by the time Ostende was finally taken—a dubious three-year maturation process, granted."

Calvin made a face.

"Gorgeousness is occasionally born of hideousness," I said to him. "Keep that in mind, son."

"All the same, I wouldn't wear that suit during one of your interrogation sessions, if I were you."

Sunlight filtered through the leaves and palm fronds, making a beautiful dappling of light across the floor of the *plaça*.

I shrugged. "Not all interrogation need entail violence," I said. "Sometimes the spilling of blood only makes for a sticky mess."

"It is not the suit that astonishes," Hector interjected, speaking for the first time. "What astonishes are the qualities the suit connotes – relaxed elegance, prosperity, wellbeing – on a man of your history and repute."

"I've never been confused for a man of ease and leisure, that is true. Regardless of history and momentum, however, one extraordinary truth remains at the disposal of every man: *It is never too late*."

Surprised to hear such words from my mouth, Hector questioned, "It is never too late for what?"

"Why, let your imagination soar," I said. "A fellow may surprise you if given the opportunity. Take Calvin here. He surprised me. You, Calvin, feel the need to come face-to-face with the edge. And then sometimes you go too far and meet the fate that lies beyond the edge. I suppose I am like you in that regard. But it is never too late. For what? Let each man answer as he sees fit."

"You're wrong," Calvin objected. "Death robs of us time. When a loved one dies, for example, it is too late; there is no asking for forgiveness or atoning for one's failures."

"Don't misunderstand me. I said that *it is never too late*. I did not say that *there will always be time*. The former notion acknowledges the power possessed at present, to actively make changes for the better. The latter is a blind bet on the future, and the future is a mystery that will only ever be as agreeable as we make it through our actions in the present. But I say, what call have you, young man, to perseverate over the deceased?"

Why, when we began monitoring him, Calvin was eager, agile and full of heart. My god, he was a livewire!

"Look at you, child," I said sternly, "distinctly ravaged! Look about you. How can you give your energies to the deceased when life is shimmering all around you? Feel that autumn breeze! What does it say to you? This wild year is dying, son. What will you do, what will you create in its final months?"

Calvin had always been one to spot the glory in the sun's rays filtering through the leaves and branches, always one to rejoice in the active, flitting shadows thrown onto a patch of stone terrace. He made a feast of all the small wonders that presented themselves at any given minute. He slept little and dreamt actively and always found a way forward. His seasoned hands, did they not still long to explore and create and abide his every furious whim? Did his legs not still long to carry him victoriously through alleyways, across beaches and over mountains?

"What on earth is holding you back?" I challenged him. "Say a heartfelt prayer for the dead as you lay your head down to rest each night, and when you wake with the rising sun, commune with the living! Embrace the day!"

Had Fiston been present to hear me going on in such a manner, he would surely have renounced me.

"Forgive me, Calvin," I said in closing, "I've said too much. Each must live his life as he sees fit. Though I can't help but find it unfortunate—you were on such an admirable path before... Bah, forgive me."

Calvin lifted his head. "Go on. Before what?"

"No, no," I declined. "I've said too much as it is."

"Come," said Hector. "We have much to discuss. Let us leave Calvin to reflect in peace."

"Very well," I concurred. "Let's go."

We started off slowly in the direction of Drassanes.

"Have I ever told you," I said to Hector, "how much I admire your cane? The duck's head is exquisite. Is it a dabbling?"

"That's right; a mallard to be precise. The turquoise from which it was fashioned came from the mine in Serabit El-Khadim. I prefer a drake wood duck in a country pond; the longer bill of the mallard, however, is better suited for a cane's handle. Here; try."

Hector extended the cane towards me and I took grip of the duck's head. The turquoise was cool and heavy. It felt wonderful.

"It has a fine action," I complimented. "Does this one have a blade hidden in the shaft?"

"Yes," Hector confirmed. "It has never drawn blood, though."

We had almost reached the far edge of the *plaça*, when Hector excused himself to address Calvin. "Calvin," he said from across the *plaça*, "I don't know your plans, but I am leaving tomorrow morning in the direction of Nice, if you would be interested in a lift."

"I'm not sure I'm ready to return to Nice," he said. "And when I am, I know a perfectly good train, thank you."

Hector smiled and nodded. We disappeared around the corner.

Calvin slept away most of the day. It was late afternoon by the time he woke, and no gulls feasted on the neighbouring rooftops. Awake on his back in the Barceloneta flat, he heard only the sounds of children at play in the backstreets of the old fishing village.

He rose and showered and walked a long winding route from Barceloneta to Gracia and finally to the familiar door on Carrer de la Providencia. The barrio was quiet. Plaça Rovira was welcoming and gas-lit. Families gathered on the terraces under the plane trees to eat *calamar*, *merluza* and *bravas*.

Calvin rang, pushed open the heavy door and mounted the stairs to apartment 3A. Upon reaching the landing, he found the door to her flat cracked open. In the doorway, the first to greet him was Klarysa's grey cat. Though still very young, it had become a sturdy, dependable lioness that could no longer be leashed. It eyed him, mewed with indifference and slinked away with its tail held high.

He pushed open the door and called to Klarysa. She appeared from her bedroom down the hall, wearing ripped jeans and an amaranth cashmere top, and raced towards him excitedly on bare toes.

"My love!" she cried.

In a span of two brief seconds, he knew he had never seen her looking so at ease, so assured, so beautiful. She was a step away from launching herself into his arms when she saw his cold eyes and his uninviting posture. She stopped short. "Why, Calvin," she began, reaching out to him. "What has happened? What's wrong?"

Calvin had reconnected with Klarysa in Barcelona after she had left him for another man in Nice, only to have her immediately evade him for three days without explanation. He had quit running for Hector, and had, in fact, come to discover that the phantom DeTorche was Hector's anagram alter-ego. Subsequently, he was relieved of his obligation towards Interpol. He slept with another woman, broke the nose of an inconsiderate youth and painted himself a madman before a lengthy taxi queue—all of that in the span of four short days. What had happened? Where would she have him begin? There were no quick or easy answers.

He was hurt and angry and, moreover, confused. Under the influence of an emotional cocktail that was shaken and served cold by the girl he loved, he brooded and felt very little compunction to give of himself, either physically or verbally. He had no expectations of staying long, however. He fully expected her to denigrate him for his brooding. In return, he was prepared to tell her in no uncertain terms where to go and how to get there, and then off he would charge, lonely and despondent into the darkening night, never to see her again. To his great surprise, however, Klarysa did nothing of the kind. On the contrary, she allowed him his foul mood without consequence. She invited him in, pampered him and showed him great patience. She fairly doted on him—that was a first. Her apology was far from excessive: "I am very sorry for my absence of late," she said. "Though it was unavoidable, the timing was horribly unfortunate." But she did not press him to buck up. She did not attempt to force his tongue or his mood. She never once condescended.

He was tentative and suspicious and he held firm to a dark line. He felt he owed himself that much. But he concurrently sensed a wee shiver of excitement for this strange and generous version of Klarysa. At the drop of a pin, he could have broken down in her arms and let all the emotion run from him, but she was not the woman for that and no man can have everything. She made him a second drink and then led him to the bedroom, where she had been cleaning up or rearranging or perhaps only going through the motions. At any rate, the room was a perfect mess. She sat him on the edge of the bed and continued talking and flitting about with a remarkably pleasant demeanour.

"What do you think," she began, taking a skirt from the arm of a French giltwood fauteuil and tossing it onto the tummy of a black-leather Oscar Niemeyer lounge, "of spending tomorrow on the beach in Sitges? Wait until you see the new bikini I bought. You are sure to love it. Will you get it for me, please?" she asked, pointing towards the top shelf of the armoire. "It's a platinum number and there's precious little of it at that. Excuse me, love, while I run to the little girl's room."

"Admit it," Calvin suddenly accused, as though he was afraid she might yet again disappear for several days, "you only want me to help you get to that blasted knife."

"Calvin!" she said, genuinely affronted, "My love, please don't say such horrible, hurtful things. That is simply not true."

"You'll never get that knife, by the way," he pressed. "Let it go. You have no idea who you're up against. You are way out of your league."

She had stopped in the doorway to face his accusations. There she eyed him with a steely glint. "Darling," she said calmly, "I am never out of my league. Not ever."

There was nothing of the child in her eyes.

"Back in a jiff!" she added gaily and disappeared down the hall.

He sighed, stood and opened the doors to the armoire. The top shelf was stuffed with unfolded clothing, and was sufficiently high and deep to make it a blind reach for items crammed towards the back. A *tabouret* or wooden chair on which to stand would have kept him from having to root about blindly, but there was nothing appropriate in the bedroom on which to stand.

When Klarysa finally returned from the loo, she found the armoire doors thrown open, a *tabouret* positioned before it and the diminutive platinum two-piece strewn, with so many other pieces of clothing, on the floor. Calvin sat in silence on the edge of the bed, lost in thought, his lips drawn together around his middle finger.

She stood silently before him. "Well, Calvin," she said, finally, with an eerie purr he would never forget; a purr that was careful and curious, as though she were leaning in close and whispering a solemn oath into the gaping and trembling jaws of a precariously set bear trap. "Well," she said, "what do you think?"

He lifted his head and took his finger from his mouth in order to speak. "What do I think?" he asked. "What do I think?" he said again. "Of what—your new bikini?"

She folded her arms over her chest, took a step backward and leaned comfortably, patiently in the doorway. She shrugged her shoulders and with a proud smile, said nothing. They stared at each other in silence. Each had asked a question and each now waited for the other to respond.

Just five minutes prior, while she was in the loo and he was rooting about on tip-toe in the upper shelf of the armoire, he felt a sharp bite, the sharp and sickening sting of deeply splitting flesh.

Jerking his hand away, he found the tip of his middle finger gashed open to the bone. Wasting no time with a bandage, he sought out something on which to stand, found a *tabouret* in the kitchen and brought it into the bedroom for closer inspection.

"So, Klarysa," he began, breaking the silence. He stared into her eyes from the edge of the bed, as though for the very first time. His expression was a grim composite of sorrow, disbelief and disgust. He countered her shrug with one of his own and said with disarming seriousness, "Is that it?"

There before her, on the eve of an unenviable new millennium, blood, the ubiquitous sticky seepage of the summer of '99, coursed freely from Calvin's fingertip, down his hand and wrist and onto his pants and shoes and the hardwood floor. He paid it no mind. Nor did she.

Her lips puckered. She was about to say something, but a thought occurred to her and her lips froze, as though in mid-kiss. *Is that it?* The words caught her off guard. The three piddling words paralysed her. All colour and animation abandoned her.

In all her life, Klarysa Pavlichenko had never heard a question that made her balk. But with Calvin's arrival in Barcelona, things had changed. Her feelings for him had changed. Klarysa didn't just love Calvin in her coarse unorthodox manner, she had fallen in love with him. Now, after all they had been through together – the highs and the lows, the joys and sorrows, the love-making and the arguments – she had never seen him appear so certain, so resolute. No, that wasn't quite it, she retracted. His certainty was obvious, yes, but it was the look of distance and detachment that so calmly and snugly overlaid his extant features that unsettled her. Suddenly, her pose there in the doorway was one of discomfort. She would have liked to shift her weight to the other leg, or better yet, approach Calvin and tell him everything, but she found that she could not move or speak. She sensed herself poised at the precarious top step of a fragile and fracturing summit from which she could not move without plummeting to certain death. The sensation consumed her and robbed her of breath. She could not move, she could not think, and the fact that Calvin sat there staring at her, intently waiting, bleeding for an answer, only exacerbated her paralysis. At a loss for words or motion, time ticked away, raced away at dizzying speeds until anxiety took hold of her and the ground began to give way beneath her feet.

Klarysa had climbed for what seemed an eternity to one so young. She climbed and chased, unafraid of the adult challenges, undeterred by the corrupt and criminal competition, surviving all of the harrowing escapes and close calls, only to return home at the end of any given escapade, crawl into bed and cry her living eyes out—experiences that would petrify all but the most hardened of men. She was fire-tempered, but so, too, stunted in a way, denied as she was by all the premature mileage, all the gruelling wear and tear; denied of the natural slow-growth maturation that allows for the development of complex emotional intelligence and subtle nuances of character.

Klarysa had climbed and chased, had loved and had, perhaps, once or twice been loved. Mostly, she weathered storms of abuse from the seedy characters with whom she had forced herself to engage along the way. Though ultimately effective, her techniques were clumsy and amateurish and left bruises, both inside and out. She relied heavily on the same sleight-of-hand techniques used by magicians and conmen—first draw attention away from the point of action, and then execute the manoeuvre. For Klarysa, this meant giving herself over to the decadent bedroom spectacle defined by men weaned on power prospects, violence and smut, and then slinking about unnoticed under the cover of a post-orgasmic fog, to leverage the connections and proximal avails of those well-positioned and connected men, with a view to locating and recovering the Omega.

The last three days had not only been a frenetic blur for Calvin, but for Klarysa, as well. She loved Calvin, and had not fully realised just how much until he arrived at her door three days earlier. And then everything advanced with blinding quickness—a few revealing phone calls, a trip in the night, a rendez-vous of lunatic risk with a wretchedly depraved arch-bishop in the chapter house of a decrepit cathedral somewhere west of Carcassonne, a trap, a tipped bookshelf leading to a voluminous avalanche of religious and historical texts, shattered glass, two muffled gunshots and frantic flight. It were as though she had fallen asleep after making love with Calvin and had woken up three days later standing upon the summit towards which she had been climbing and clawing for as long as she could remember. She had, however, climbed with such singular focus that she ascended quite unaware of all she had broken en route. She now stood alone at the summit, while the man she loved lay battered and bruised by her kicking, digging heals somewhere far below and out of sight.

Calvin had been pushed to a limit—that, she knew. She had jerked him about, as she herself had been jerked about, in the manner all toy dolls are jerked about—by the arm or the leg, the hair or the heart; as an inanimate figure of marginal benefit, a source of diminishing comfort, an object to be heedlessly used, according to one's whims, until its button eyes came unstitched and fell away and the stuffing sprouted in white clouds from its split seams and it was finally consigned to the rubbish bin. There was a time when Klarysa took an amount of pride in her ability to manipulate men for profit, but she had come to realise that it was an illusion, that it was no form of self-glorification, but rather quite the opposite—a form of self-reproach and self-abuse, and that by engaging in such pursuits, she was in fact only living down to the low and vulgar expectations of her as a plaything, a toy, an object to be possessed and diddled, if also lavished with rare gifts and luxuries. And anyway, what need had she for a nineteenth-century mantel clock or a Louis XV cherry scriban, when the act of writing was, to her, a form of self-flagellation, and schedules and timetables picayune?

Calvin had been so gentle with her, so calm and so patient, even when she provoked him, even when she attacked him in hopes that he might lash out and provide her with the punishment she had convinced herself she deserved, that with which she was familiar, that which gave her sick comfort. He refused, though, to give her the negative reinforcement she sought. He had shown an ability to see beyond her fears and insecurities and stand with resolution before her blows. So too, he had allowed her spatial and emotional distance when she needed to run away, unlike those before him, who hunted her down only to catch her and teach her a thing or two about independence and insolence. He was consistently present for her, though until recently, she had considered his presence rather puppy-like. Only now did she recognise him for the protector he was, the fellow who had on many occasions rescued her before she even realised she needed rescuing. In truth, she needed only to look over her shoulder – all too often in the grips of some disreputable cad – and there would be Calvin, at the ready with his knotted shoulders and vice-like hands, to preserve what was left of her leaking honour.

Her recent, startling accomplishment had, however, changed everything, had opened her eyes and freed her mind to consider a new realm of possibilities. Suddenly, she had not only warmed to the notion of a peaceful, stable existence with a good and loving man, but had mentally added it to her shortlist of essential elements for survival.

There she stood, all at once bleary and lost, in the doorway of a unkempt bedroom that was chock-a-block with expensive furniture and collectibles, reminders of a seemingly endless era of errant decisions, which, at its frequent worst, prompted feelings of shabbiness and possession, so that she tried to hide it all as best she could under clothing and sundry junk. And there sat the man she loved, the one who loved her despite all her tawdry mistreatments of him, with blood coursing from his split finger, as though from a leaking hose, down his hand and wrist, onto his shoes and the hardwood floor and staining red what little there was of the platinum bikini. There sat the man she loved, the man who asked *is that it?*, the one who now sat in rapt attention, waiting for an answer.

My god, she thought, stricken by a hard-lined conviction that her very next word would likely determine her fate as it concerned Calvin, her first and only great love. She was desperate to find the right words, but that was not one of her strengths during the best of times, much less at that moment, when she was so thoroughly entangled in reflection and regret, that she no longer had an idea as to what he meant by his question. Her lips had softened slightly, but still maintained the shape of a kiss poised in mid-abandonment.

Is that it? he had asked. But was he referring to the knife hidden in the armoire? Was he asking if that was it, the Omega, the object-source of suffering and strife, the thing she had tenaciously ranked above him and all of mankind? She had not intended to fall in love with Calvin. Nevertheless, she did. And if his question was, in fact, pointed in another direction, and she were to address the knife at that critical and precarious moment, would such a response not confirm what he had come to suspect—that he was an ancillary other that would never know top classification in the province of her life and love; that his true value to her would forever be inferior to a sharpened length of cold blood-stained metal? Or, by his question, was he referring not to the knife, but to the suffering and strife, the debacle, her negligence, their relationship? Having achieved her goal, had their relationship run its course? *Is that it?* Is it over? Are we done?

She was overwhelmed. She very nearly said, "I love you," but stopped herself short, deciding with ever-mounting reprehension that she had, over the months, eroded the sentiment to the point of meaninglessness. With every subsequent second that slipped away in silence, she watched Calvin's eyes dimming, dimming; watched him detaching and slipping further and further away from her. She felt an urgency to speak, a suffocating urgency, the urgency of a free-diver with exhausted lungs charging to the surface for breath. Yet so thorough was her fear of voicing in a foreign tongue another maladroit line with skewed intonation, and thereby losing him forever, that she found herself perfectly gagged, voiceless and motionless, in the exquisite grip of an impossible paralysis.

Lost in the haunted forest of her new greatest fear, Klarysa felt something brush past her. She heard, as though from a million miles away, the door to the flat open and close. And there, standing perched in the doorway, numb and disabled, in her bare feet and ripped jeans and amaranth cashmere top, she watched the spilt blood, the rippled cloth of her bedspread, the rich silken wake of Calvin's quiet departure.

About the author

Kevin Panozzo was born and raised in the American Middlewest. He emigrated from San Francisco to Nice in 2000 and spent two years in Barcelona before moving to Brussels, where he resides as of the printing of this edition.